KU-131-328

THE MASK OF MIRRORS

Before she could think the better of it, Renata stepped forward. Her shoe came down on the blade of Mezzan's sword just as the Rook crouched to pick it up.

"As I understand it, Altan Mezzan gave the actor a chance to defend himself in an honorable duel," she said. "Surely you can do no less."

The Rook straightened slowly. Even close enough to touch, she could make out almost nothing through the darkness of his hood. The deeper shadows of his eyes, the line of his jaw; like the stars, she saw more when she didn't look directly. Then a glimmer of a smile came into view.

In two hundred years, no one had unmasked Nadežra's outlaw. Seeing him now, Ren was certain the hood was imbued to hide his face. The Rook could have been anyone: old or young, Liganti or Vraszenian or Nadežran. His voice sounded masculine, but who knew where the magic ended?

Though she couldn't see his eyes, she felt him assessing her, as surely as she was assessing him.

The Rook said, "I could do less . . . or a good deal more."

THE MASK OF MIRRORS

ROOK & ROSE:
BOOK ONE

M. A.
CARRICK

orbit

orbitbooks.net

ORBIT

First published in Great Britain in 2021 by Orbit

1 3 5 7 9 10 8 6 4 2

Copyright © 2021 by Bryn Neuenschwander and Alyc Helms

Map by Tim Paul

Excerpt from *The Obsidian Tower* by Melissa Caruso
Copyright © 2020 by Melissa Caruso

The moral right of the author has been asserted.

*All characters and events in this publication, other than those
clearly in the public domain, are fictitious and any resemblance
to real persons, living or dead, is purely coincidental.*

All rights reserved.
No part of this publication may be reproduced, stored in a
retrieval system, or transmitted, in any form or by any means, without
the prior permission in writing of the publisher, nor be otherwise circulated
in any form of binding or cover other than that in which it is published
and without a similar condition including this condition being
imposed on the subsequent purchaser.

A CIP catalogue record for this book
is available from the British Library.

ISBN 978–0–356–51517–5

Printed and bound in Great Britain by Clays Ltd, Elcograf S.p.A.

Papers used by Orbit are from well-managed forests
and other responsible sources.

Orbit
An imprint of
Little, Brown Book Group
Carmelite House
50 Victoria Embankment
London EC4Y 0DZ

An Hachette UK Company
www.hachette.co.uk

www.orbitbooks.net

For Adrienne, who left us unsupervised

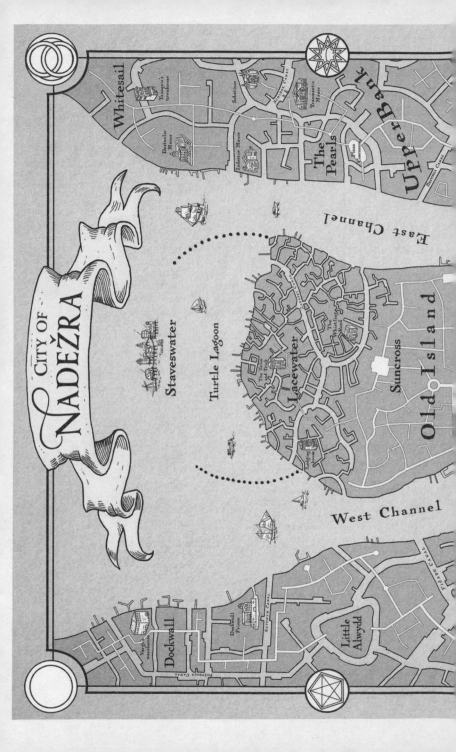

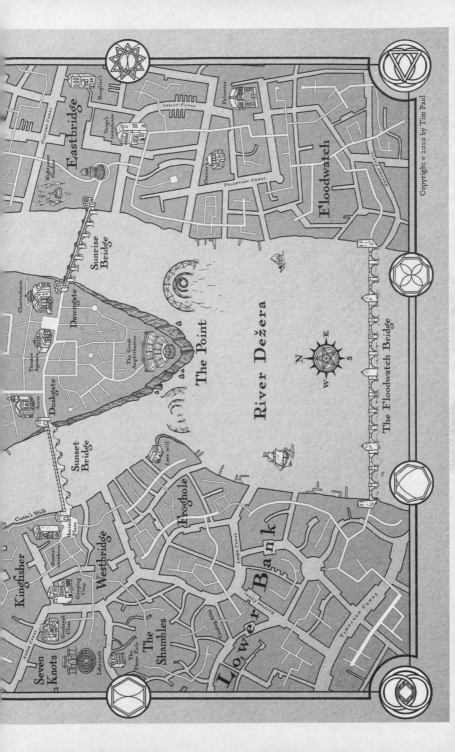

Copyright © 2020 by Tim Paul

Prologue

The lodging house had many kinds of quiet. There was the quiet of sleep, children packed shoulder to shoulder on the threadbare carpets of the various rooms, with only an occasional snore or rustle to break the silence. There was the quiet of daytime, when the house was all but deserted; then they were not children but Fingers, sent out to pluck as many birds as they could, not coming home until they had purses and fans and handkerchiefs and more to show for their efforts.

Then there was the quiet of fear.

Everyone knew what had happened. Ondrakja had made sure of that: In case they'd somehow missed the screams, she'd dragged Sedge's body past them all, bloody and broken, with Simlin forcing an empty-eyed Ren along in Ondrakja's wake. When they came back a little while later, Ondrakja's stained hands were empty, and she stood in the mildewed front hall of the lodging house, with the rest of the Fingers watching from the doorways and the splintered railings of the stairs.

"Next time," Ondrakja said to Ren in that low, pleasant voice they all knew to dread, "I'll hit you somewhere softer." And her gaze went, with unerring malice, to Tess.

Simlin let go of Ren, Ondrakja went upstairs, and after that the lodging house was silent. Even the floorboards didn't creak, because the Fingers found places to huddle and stayed there.

Sedge wasn't the first. They said Ondrakja picked someone at random every so often, just to keep the rest in line. She was the leader of their knot; it was her right to cut someone out of it.

But everyone knew this time wasn't random. Ren had fucked up, and Sedge had paid the price.

Because Ren was too valuable to waste.

Three days like that. Three days of terror-quiet, of no one being sure if Ondrakja's temper had settled, of Ren and Tess clinging to each other while the others stayed clear.

On the third day, Ren got told to bring Ondrakja her tea.

She carried it up the stairs with careful hands and a grace most of the Fingers couldn't touch. Her steps were so smooth that when she knelt and offered the cup to Ondrakja, its inner walls were still dry, the tea as calm and unrippled as a mirror.

Ondrakja didn't take the cup right away. Her hand slid over the charm of knotted cord around Ren's wrist, then along her head, lacquered nails combing through the thick, dark hair like she was petting a cat. "Little Renyi," she murmured. "You're a clever one... but not clever enough. That is why you need me."

"Yes, Ondrakja," Ren whispered.

The room was empty, except for the two of them. No Fingers crouching on the carpet to play audience to Ondrakja's performance. Just Ren, and the stained floorboards in the corner where Sedge had died.

"Haven't I tried to teach you?" Ondrakja said. "I see such promise in you, in your pretty face. You're better than the others; you could be as good as me, someday. But only if you listen and obey—and stop trying to *hide things from me.*"

Her fingernails dug in. Ren lifted her chin and met Ondrakja's gaze with dry eyes. "I understand. I will never try to hide anything from you again."

"Good girl." Ondrakja took the tea and drank.

The hours passed with excruciating slowness. Second earth. Third earth. Fourth. Most of the Fingers were asleep, except those out on night work.

Ren and Tess were not out, nor asleep. They sat tucked under the staircase, listening, Ren's hand clamped hard over the charm on her wrist. "Please," Tess begged, "we can just go—"

"No. Not yet."

Ren's voice didn't waver, but inside she shook like a pinkie on her first lift. *What if it didn't work?*

She knew they should run. If they didn't, they might miss their chance. When people found out what she'd done, there wouldn't be a street in Nadežra that would grant her refuge.

But she stayed for Sedge.

A creak in the hallway above made Tess squeak. Footsteps on the stairs became Simlin rounding the corner. He jerked to a halt when he saw them in the alcove. "There you are," he said, as if he'd been searching for an hour. "Upstairs. Ondrakja wants you."

Ren eased herself out, not taking her eyes from Simlin. At thirteen he wasn't as big as Sedge, but he was far more vicious. "Why?"

"Dunno. Didn't ask." Then, before Ren could start climbing the stairs: "She said both of you."

Next time, I'll hit you somewhere softer.

They should have run. But with Simlin standing just an arm's reach away, there wasn't any hope now. He dragged Tess out of the alcove, ignoring her whimper, and shoved them both up the stairs.

The fire in the parlour had burned low, and the shadows pressed in close from the ceiling and walls. Ondrakja's big chair was turned with its back to the door so they had to circle around to face her, Tess gripping Ren's hand so tight the bones ached.

Ondrakja was the picture of Lacewater elegance. Despite the late hour, she'd changed into a rich gown, a Liganti-style surcoat over a fine linen underdress—a dress Ren herself had stolen off a laundry line. Her hair was upswept and pinned, and with the high back of the chair rising behind her, she looked like one of the Cinquerat on their thrones.

A few hours ago she'd petted Ren and praised her skills. But Ren saw the murderous glitter in Ondrakja's eyes and knew that would never happen again.

"Treacherous little bitch," Ondrakja hissed. "Was this your revenge for that piece of trash I threw out? Putting something in my tea? It should have been a knife in my back—but you don't have the guts for that. The only thing worse than a traitor is a *spineless* one."

Ren stood paralyzed, Tess cowering behind her. She'd put in as much extract of meadow saffron as she could afford, paying the apothecary with the coin that was supposed to help her and Tess and Sedge escape Ondrakja forever. It should have worked.

"I am going to make you pay," Ondrakja promised, her voice cold with venom. "But this time it won't be as quick. Everyone will know you betrayed your knot. They'll hold you down while I go to work on your little sister there. I'll keep her alive for days, and you'll have to watch every—"

She was rising as she spoke, looming over Ren like some Primordial demon, but mid-threat she lurched. One hand went to her stomach—and then, without any more warning, she vomited onto the carpet.

As her head came up, Ren saw what the shadows of the chair had helped conceal. The glitter in Ondrakja's eyes wasn't just fury; it was fever. Her face was sickly sallow, her skin dewed with cold sweat.

The poison *had* taken effect. And its work wasn't done.

Ren danced back as Ondrakja reached for her. The woman who'd knotted the Fingers into her fist stumbled, going down onto one knee. Quick as a snake, Ren kicked her in the face, and Ondrakja fell backward.

"That's for Sedge," Ren spat, darting in to stomp on Ondrakja's tender stomach. The woman vomited again, but kept wit enough to grab at Ren's leg. Ren twisted clear, and Ondrakja clutched her own throat, gasping.

A yank at the charm on Ren's wrist broke the cord, and she hurled it into the woman's spew. Tess followed an instant later. That swiftly, they weren't Fingers anymore.

Ondrakja reached out again, and Ren stamped on her wrist, snapping bone. She would have kept going, but Tess seized Ren's arm, dragging her toward the door. "She's already dead. Come on, or we will be, too—"

"Come back here!" Ondrakja snarled, but her voice had withered to a hoarse gasp. "I will make you fucking *pay*..."

Her words dissolved into another fit of retching. Ren broke at last, tearing the door open and barreling into Simlin on the other side, knocking him down before he could react. Then down the stairs to the alcove, where a loose floorboard concealed two bags containing everything they owned in the world. Ren took one and threw the other at Tess, and they were out the door of the lodging house, into the narrow, stinking streets of Lacewater, leaving dying Ondrakja and the Fingers and the past behind them.

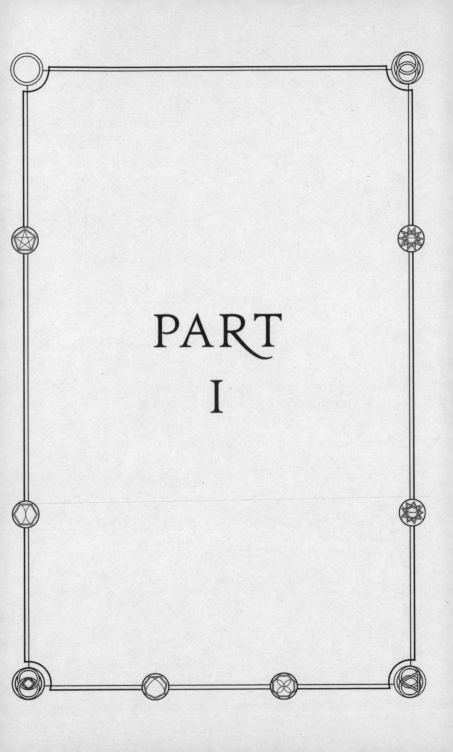

PART

I

The Mask of Mirrors

After fifteen years of handling the Traementis house charters, Donaia Traementis knew that a deal which looked too good to be true probably was. The proposal currently on her desk stretched the boundaries of belief.

"He could at least try to make it look legitimate," she muttered. Did Mettore Indestor think her an utter fool?

He thinks you desperate. And he's right.

She burrowed her stockinged toes under the great lump of a hound sleeping beneath her desk and pressed cold fingers to her brow. She'd removed her gloves to avoid ink stains and left the hearth in her study unlit to save the cost of fuel. Besides Meatball, the only warmth was from the beeswax candles—an expense she couldn't scrimp on unless she wanted to lose what eyesight she had left.

Adjusting her spectacles, she scanned the proposal again, scratching angry notes between the lines.

She remembered a time when House Traementis had been as powerful as the Indestor family. They had held a seat in the Cinquerat, the five-person council that ruled Nadežra, and charters that allowed them to conduct trade, contract mercenaries, control guilds. Every variety of wealth, power, and prestige in Nadežra had been theirs. Now, despite Donaia's best efforts and her late husband's before her, it had come to this: scrabbling at one Dusk Road trade charter as though she could milk enough blood from that stone to pay off all the Traementis debts.

Debts almost entirely owned by Mettore Indestor.

"And you expect me to trust my caravan to guards you provide?" she growled at the proposal, her pen nib digging in hard enough to tear the paper. "Ha! Who's going to protect it from them? Will they even wait for bandits, or just sack the wagons themselves?"

Leaving Donaia with the loss, a pack of angry investors, and debts she could no longer cover. Then Mettore would swoop in like one of his thrice-damned hawks to swallow whole what remained of House Traementis.

Try as she might, though, she couldn't see another option. She couldn't send the caravan out unguarded—Vraszenian bandits were a legitimate concern—but the Indestor family held the Caerulet seat in the Cinquerat, which gave Mettore authority over military and mercenary affairs. Nobody would risk working with a house Indestor had a grudge against—not when it would mean losing a charter, or worse.

Meatball's head rose with a sudden whine. A moment later a knock came at the study door, followed by Donaia's majordomo. Colbrin knew better than to interrupt her when she was wrestling with business, which meant he judged this interruption important.

He bowed and handed her a card. "Alta Renata Viraudax?" Donaia asked, shoving Meatball's wet snout out of her lap when he sniffed at the card. She flipped it as if the back would provide some clue to the visitor's purpose. Viraudax wasn't a local noble house. Some traveler to Nadežra?

"A young woman, Era Traementis," her majordomo said. "Well-mannered. Well-dressed. She said it concerned an important private matter."

The card fluttered to the floor. Donaia's duties as head of House Traementis kept her from having much of a social life, but the same could not be said for her son, and lately Leato had been behaving more and more like his father. Ninat take him—if her son had racked up some gambling debt with a foreign visitor...

Colbrin retrieved the card before the dog could eat it, and handed it back to her. "Should I tell her you are not at home?"

"No. Show her in." If her son's dive into the seedier side of Nadežra had resulted in trouble, she would at least rectify his errors before stringing him up.

Somehow. With money she didn't have.

She could start by not conducting the meeting in a freezing study. "Wait," she said before Colbrin could leave. "Show her to the salon. And bring tea."

Donaia cleaned the ink from her pen and made a futile attempt to brush away the brindled dog hairs matting her surcoat. Giving that up as a lost cause, she tugged on her gloves and straightened the papers on her desk, collecting herself by collecting her surroundings. Looking down at her clothing—the faded blue surcoat over trousers and house scuffs—she weighed the value of changing over the cost of making a potential problem wait.

Everything is a tallied cost these days, she thought grimly.

"Meatball. Stay," she commanded when the hound would have followed, and headed directly to the salon.

The young woman waiting there could not have fit the setting more perfectly if she had planned it. Her rose-gold underdress and cream surcoat harmonized beautifully with the gold-shot peach silk of the couch and chairs, and the thick curl trailing from her upswept hair echoed the rich wood of the wall paneling. The curl should have looked like an accident, an errant strand slipping loose—but everything else about the visitor was so elegant it was clearly a deliberate touch of style.

She was studying the row of books on their glass-fronted shelf. When Donaia closed the door, she turned and dipped low. "Era Traementis. Thank you for seeing me."

Her curtsy was as Seterin as her clipped accent, one hand sweeping elegantly up to the opposite shoulder. Donaia's misgivings deepened at the sight of her. Close to her son's age, and beautiful as a portrait by Creciasto, with fine-boned features and flawless skin. Easy to imagine Leato losing his head over a hand of cards with such a girl. And her ensemble did nothing to comfort Donaia's fears—the richly embroidered brocade, the sleeves an elegant fall of sheer silk. Here was someone who could afford to bet and lose a fortune.

That sort was more likely to forgive or forget a debt than come collecting...unless the debt was meant as leverage for something else.

"Alta Renata. I hope you will forgive my informality." She brushed a hand down her simple attire. "I did not expect visitors, but it sounded like your matter was of some urgency. Please, do be seated."

The young woman lowered herself into the chair as lightly as mist on the river. Seeing her, it was easy to understand why the people of Nadežra looked to Seteris as the source of all that was stylish and elegant. Fashion was born in Seteris. By the time it traveled south to Seteris's protectorate, Seste Ligante, then farther south still, across the sea to Nadežra, it was old and stale, and Seteris had moved on.

Most Seterin visitors behaved as though Nadežra was nothing more than Seste Ligante's backwater colonial foothold on the Vraszenian continent and merely setting foot on the streets would foul them with the mud of the River Dežera. But Renata's delicacy looked like hesitation, not condescension. She said, "Not urgent, no—I do apologize if I gave that impression. I confess, I'm not certain how to even begin this conversation."

She paused, hazel eyes searching Donaia's face. "You don't recognize my family name, do you?"

That had an ominous sound. Seteris might be on the other side of the sea, but the truly powerful families could influence trade anywhere in the known world. If House Traementis had somehow crossed one of them...

Donaia kept her fear from her face and her voice. "I am afraid I haven't had many dealings with the great houses of Seteris."

A soft breath flowed out of the girl. "As I suspected. I thought she might have written to you at least once, but apparently not. I...am Letilia's daughter."

She could have announced she was descended from the Vraszenian goddess Ažerais herself, and it wouldn't have taken Donaia more by surprise.

Disbelief clashed with relief and apprehension both: not a creditor, not an offended daughter of some foreign power. Family—after a fashion.

Lost for words, Donaia reassessed the young woman sitting across from her. Straight back, straight shoulders, straight neck, and the same fine, narrow nose that made everyone in Nadežra hail Letilia Traementis as the great beauty of her day.

Yes, she could be Letilia's daughter. Donaia's niece by marriage.

"Letilia never wrote after she left." It was the only consideration the spoiled brat had ever shown her family. The first several years, every day they'd expected a letter telling them she was stranded in Seteris, begging for funds. Instead they never heard from her again.

Dread sank into Donaia's bones. "Is Letilia here?"

The door swung open, and for one dreadful instant Donaia expected a familiar squall of petulance and privilege to sweep inside. But it was only Colbrin, bearing a tray. To her dismay, Donaia saw two pots on it, one short and rounded for tea, the other taller. Of course: He'd heard their guest's Seterin accent, and naturally assumed Donaia would also want to serve coffee.

We haven't yet fallen so far that I can't afford proper hospitality. But Donaia's voice was still sharp as he set the tray between the two of them. "Thank you, Colbrin. That will be all."

"No," Renata said as the majordomo bowed and departed. "No, Mother is happily ensconced in Seteris."

It seemed luck hadn't *entirely* abandoned House Traementis. "Tea?" Donaia said, a little too bright with relief. "Or would you prefer coffee?"

"Coffee, thank you." Renata accepted the cup and saucer with a graceful hand. Everything about her was graceful—but not the artificial, forced elegance Donaia remembered Letilia practicing so assiduously.

Renata sipped the coffee and made a small, appreciative noise. "I must admit, I was wondering if I would even be able to find coffee here."

Ah. *There* was the echo of Letilia, the little sneer that took what should be a compliment and transformed it into an insult.

We have wooden floors and chairs with backs, too. Donaia swallowed down the snappish response. But the bitter taste in her mouth nudged her into pouring coffee for herself, even though she disliked it. She wouldn't let this girl make her feel like a delta rustic simply because Donaia had lived all her life in Nadežra.

"So you are here, but Letilia is not. May I ask why?"

The girl's chin dropped, and she rotated her coffee cup as though its precise alignment against the saucer were vitally important. "I've spent days imagining how best to approach you, but—well." There was a ripple of nervousness in her laugh. "There's no way to say this without first admitting I'm Letilia's daughter...and yet by admitting that, I know I've already gotten off on the wrong foot. Still, there's nothing for it."

Renata inhaled like someone preparing for battle, then met Donaia's gaze. "I'm here to see if I can possibly reconcile my mother with her family."

It took all Donaia's self-control not to laugh. Reconcile? She would sooner reconcile with the drugs that had overtaken her husband Gianco's good sense in his final years. If Gianco's darker comments were to be believed, Letilia had done as much to destroy House Traementis as aža had.

Fortunately, custom and law offered her a more dispassionate response. "Letilia is no part of this family. My husband's father struck her name from our register after she left."

At least Renata was smart enough not to be surprised. "I can hardly blame my gra—your father-in-law," she said. "I've only my mother's version of the tale, but I also know *her*. I can guess the part she played in that estrangement."

Donaia could just imagine what poison Letilia's version had contained. "It is more than estrangement," she said brusquely, rising to her feet. "I am sorry you crossed the sea for nothing, but I'm afraid that what you're asking for is impossible. Even if I believed that your mother wanted to reconcile—which I do not—I have no interest in doing so."

A treacherous worm within her whispered, *Even if that might offer a new business opportunity? Some way out of Indestor's trap?*

Even then. Donaia would burn Traementis Manor to the ground before she accepted help from Letilia's hand.

The salon door opened again. But this time, the interruption wasn't her majordomo.

"Mother, Egliadas has invited me to go sailing on the river." Leato was tugging on his gloves, as if he couldn't be bothered to finish dressing before leaving his rooms. But he stopped, one hand still caught in the tight cuff, when he saw their visitor.

Renata rose like a flower bud unfurling, and Donaia cursed silently. Why, today of all days, had Leato chosen to wake early? Not that fourth sun was early by most people's standards, but for him midmorning might as well be dawn.

Reflex forced the courtesies out of her mouth, even though she wanted nothing more than to hurry the girl away. "Leato, you recall stories of your aunt Letilia? This is her daughter, Alta Renata Viraudax of Seteris. Alta Renata, my son and heir, Leato Traementis."

Leato captured Renata's hand before she could touch it to her shoulder again and kissed her gloved fingertips. When she saw them together, Donaia's heart sank like a stone. She was used to thinking of her son as an adolescent scamp, or an intermittent source of headaches. But he was a man grown, with beauty to match Renata's: his hair like antique gold, fashionably mussed on top; his ivory skin and finely carved features, the hallmark of House Traementis; the elegant cut of his waistcoat and fitted tailoring of the full-skirted coat over it in the platinum shimmer of delta grasses in autumn.

And the two of them were smiling at one another like the sun had just risen in the salon.

"Letilia's daughter?" Leato said, releasing Renata's hand before the touch could grow awkward. "I thought she hated us."

Donaia bit down the impulse to chide him. It would sound like she was defending Renata, which was the last thing she wanted to do.

The girl's smile was brief and rueful. "I may have inherited her nose, but I've tried not to inherit *everything* else."

"You mean, not her personality? I'll offer thanks to Katus." Leato winced. "I'm sorry, I shouldn't insult your mother—"

"No insult taken," Renata said dryly. "I'm sure the stories you know of her are dreadful, and with good cause."

They had the river's current beneath them and were flowing onward; Donaia had to stop it before they went too far. When Leato asked what brought Renata to the city, Donaia lunged in, social grace be damned. "She just—"

But Renata spoke over her, as smooth as silk. "I was hoping to meet your grandfather and father. Foolish of me, really; since Mother hasn't been in contact, I didn't know they'd both passed away until I arrived. And now I understand she's no longer in the register, so there's no bond between us—I'm just a stranger, intruding."

"Oh, not at all!" Leato turned to his mother for confirmation.

For the first time, Donaia felt a touch of gratitude toward Renata. Leato had never known Letilia; he hadn't even been born when she ran away. He'd heard the tales, but no doubt he marked at least some of them as exaggeration. If Renata had mentioned a reconciliation outright, he probably would have supported her.

"We're touched by your visit," Donaia said, offering the girl a courteous nod. "I'm only sorry the others never had a chance to meet you."

"Your visit?" Leato scoffed. "No, this can't be all. You're my cousin, after all—oh, not under the law, I know. But blood counts for a lot here."

"We're Nadežran, Leato, not Vraszenian," Donaia said reprovingly, lest Renata think they'd been completely swallowed by delta ways.

He went on as though he hadn't heard her. "My long-lost cousin shows up from across the sea, greets us for a few minutes, then vanishes? Unacceptable. Giuna hasn't even met you—she's my younger sister. Why don't you stay with us for a few days?"

Donaia couldn't stop a muffled sound from escaping her. However much he seemed determined to ignore them, Leato knew about House Traementis's financial troubles. A houseguest was the last thing they could afford.

But Renata demurred with a light shake of her head. "No, no—I couldn't impose like that. I'll be in Nadežra for some time, though. Perhaps you'll allow me the chance to show I'm not my mother."

Preparatory to pushing for reconciliation, no doubt. But although Renata was older and more self-possessed, something about her downcast gaze reminded Donaia of Giuna. She could all too easily imagine Giuna seeking Letilia out in Seteris with the same impossible dream.

If House Traementis could afford the sea passage, which they could not. And if Donaia would allow her to go, which she would not. But if that impossible situation happened…she bristled at the thought of Letilia rebuffing Giuna entirely, treating her with such cold hostility that she refused to see the girl at all.

So Donaia said, as warmly as she could, "Of course we know you aren't your mother. And you shouldn't be forced to carry the burden of her past." She let a smile crack her mask. "I'm certain from the caterpillars dancing on my son's brow that he'd like to know more about you, and I imagine Giuna would feel the same."

"Thank you," Renata said with a curtsy. "But not now, I think. My apologies, Altan Leato." Her words silenced his protest before he could voice it, and with faultless formality. "My maid intends to fit me for a new dress this afternoon, and she'll stick me with pins if I'm late."

That was as unlike Letilia as it was possible to be. Not the concern for her clothing—Letilia was the same, only with less tasteful results—but the graceful withdrawal, cooperating with Donaia's wish to get her out of the house.

Leato did manage to get one more question out, though. "Where can we reach you?"

"On the Isla Prišta, Via Brelkoja, number four," Renata said. Donaia's lips tightened. For a stay of a few weeks, even a month or two, a hotel would have sufficed. Renting a house suggested the girl intended to remain for quite some time.

But that was a matter for later. Donaia reached for the bell. "Colbrin will see you out."

"No need," Leato said, offering Renata his hand. When she glanced at Donaia instead of taking it, Leato said, "Mother, you won't begrudge me a few moments of gossip with my new cousin?"

That was Leato, always asking for forgiveness rather than permission. But Renata's minute smile silently promised not to encourage him. At Donaia's forbearing nod, she accepted his escort from the room.

Once they were gone, Donaia rang for Colbrin. "I'll be in my study. No more interruptions barring flood or fire, please."

Colbrin's acknowledgment trailed after her as she went upstairs. When she entered the room, Meatball roused with a whine-snap of a yawn and a hopeful look, but settled again once he realized no treats were forthcoming.

The space seemed chillier than when she'd left it, and darker. She thought of Alta Renata's fine manners and finer clothes. Of course Letilia's daughter would be dressed in designs so new they hadn't yet made their way from Seteris to Nadežra. Of course she would have enough wealth to rent a house in Westbridge for herself alone and think nothing of it. Hadn't Gianco always said that Letilia took House Traementis's luck with her when she left?

In a fit of pique, Donaia lit the hearthfire, and damn the cost. Once its warmth was blazing through the study, she returned to her desk. She buried her toes under the dog again, mentally composing her message as she sharpened her nib and filled her ink tray.

House Traementis might be neck-deep in debt and sinking, but they still had the rights granted by their ennoblement charter. And Donaia wasn't such a fool that she would bite a hook before examining it from all sides first.

Bending her head, Donaia began penning a letter to Commander Cercel of the Vigil.

Upper and Lower Bank: Suilun 1

Renata expected Leato Traementis to see her out the front door, but he escorted her all the way to the bottom of the steps, and kept her hand even when they stopped. "I hope you're not too offended by Mother's reserve," he said. A breeze ruffled his burnished hair and carried the scent of caramel and almonds to her nose. A rich scent, matching his clothes and his carriage, and the thin lines of gold paint limning his eyelashes. "A lot of dead branches have been pruned from the Traementis register since my father—and your mother—were children. Now there's only Mother, Giuna, and myself. She gets protective."

"I take no offense at all," Renata said, smiling up at him. "I'm not so much of a fool that I expect to be welcomed with open arms. And I'm willing to be patient."

The breeze sharpened, and she shivered. Leato stepped between her and the wind. "You'd think Nadežra would be warmer than Seteris, wouldn't you?" he said with a sympathetic grimace. "It's all the water. We almost never get snow here, but the winters are so damp, the cold cuts right to your bones."

"I should have thought to wear a cloak. But since I can't pluck one from thin air, I hope you won't take offense if I hurry home."

"Of course not. Let me get you a sedan chair." Leato raised a hand to catch the eye of some men idling on the far side of the square and paid the bearers before Renata could even reach for her purse. "To soothe any lingering sting," he said with a smile.

She thanked him with another curtsy. "I hope I'll see you soon."

"As do I." Leato helped her into the sedan chair and closed the door once her skirts were safely out of the way.

As the bearers headed for the narrow exit from the square,

Renata drew the curtains shut. Traementis Manor was in the Pearls, a cluster of islets strung along the Upper Bank of the River Dežera. The river here ran pure and clear thanks to the numinat that protected the East Channel, and the narrow streets and bridges were clean; whichever families held the charters to keep the streets clear of refuse wouldn't dream of letting it accumulate near the houses of the rich and powerful.

But the rocky wedge that broke the Dežera into east and west channels was a different matter. For all that it held two of Nadežra's major institutions—the Charterhouse in Dawngate, which was the seat of government, and the Aerie in Duskgate, home to the Vigil, which maintained order—the Old Island was also crowded with the poor and the shabby-genteel. Anyone riding in a sedan chair was just asking for beggars to crowd at their windows.

Which still made it better than half of the Lower Bank, where a sedan chair risked being knocked to the ground and the passenger robbed.

Luckily, her rented house was on Isla Prišta in Westbridge—technically on the Lower Bank, and far from a fashionable district, but it was a respectable neighborhood on the rise. In fact, the buildings on the Via Brelkoja were so newly renovated the mortar hadn't had time to moss over in the damp air. The freshly painted door to number four opened just as Renata's foot touched the first step.

Tess made a severe-looking sight in the crisp grey-and-white surcoat and underskirt of a Nadežran housemaid, but her copper Ganllechyn curls and freckles were a warm beacon welcoming Renata home. She bobbed a curtsy and murmured a lilting "alta" as Renata passed across the threshold, accepting the gloves and purse Renata held out.

"Downstairs," Ren murmured as the door snicked shut, sinking them into the dimness of the front hall.

Tess nodded, swallowing her question before she could speak it. Together they headed into the half-sunken chambers of the cellar, which held the service rooms. Only once they were safely in the kitchen did Tess say, "Well? How did it go?"

Ren let her posture drop and her voice relax into the throaty tones of her natural accent. "For me, as well as I could hope. Donaia refused reconciliation out of hand—"

"Thank the Mother," Tess breathed. If Donaia contacted Letilia, their entire plan would fall apart before it started.

Ren nodded. "Faced with the prospect of talking to her former sister-in-law, she barely even noticed me getting my foot in the door."

"That's a start, then. Here, off with this, and wrap up before you take a chill." Tess passed Ren a thick cloak of rough-spun wool lined with raw fleece, then turned her around like a dressmaker's doll so she could remove the beautifully embroidered surcoat.

"I saw the sedan chair," Tess said as she tugged at the side ties. "You didn't take that all the way from Isla Traementis, did you? If you're going to be riding about in chairs, I'll have to revise the budget. And here I'd had my eye on a lovely bit of lace at the remnants stall." Tess sighed mournfully, like she was saying farewell to a sweetheart. "I'll just have to tat some myself."

"In your endless spare time?" Ren said sardonically. The surcoat came loose, and she swung the cloak around her shoulders in its place. "Anyway, the son paid for the chair." She dropped onto the kitchen bench and eased her shoes off with a silent curse. Fashionable shoes were *not* comfortable. The hardest part of this con was going to be pretending her feet didn't hurt all day long.

Although choking down coffee ran a close second.

"Did he, now?" Tess settled on the bench next to Ren, close enough that they could share warmth beneath the cloak. Apart from the kitchen and the front salon, protective sheets still covered the furniture in every other room. The hearths were cold, their meals were simple, and they slept together on a kitchen floor pallet so they would only have to heat one room of the house.

Because she was not Alta Renata Viraudax, daughter of Letilia Traementis. She was Arenza Lenskaya, half-Vraszenian river rat, and even with a forged letter of credit to help, pretending to be a Seterin noblewoman wasn't cheap.

Pulling out a thumbnail blade, Tess began ripping the seams of Ren's beautiful surcoat, preparatory to alteration. "Was it just idle flirtation?"

The speculative uptick in Tess's question said she didn't believe any flirtation Ren encountered was idle. But whether Leato's flirtation had been idle or not, Ren had lines she would not cross, and whoring herself out was one of them.

It would have been the easier route. Dress herself up fine enough to catch the eye of some delta gentry son, or even a noble, and marry her way into money. She wouldn't be the first person in Nadežra to do it.

But she'd spent five years in Ganllech—five years as a maid under Letilia's thumb, listening to her complain about her dreadful family and how much she dreamed of life in Seteris, the promised land she'd never managed to reach. So when Ren and Tess found themselves back in Nadežra, Ren had been resolved. No whoring, and no killing. Instead she set her sights on a higher target: use what she'd learned to gain acceptance into House Traementis as their long-lost kin...with all the wealth and social benefit that brought.

"Leato is friendly," she allowed, picking up the far end of the dress and starting on the seam with her own knife. Tess didn't trust her to sew anything more complicated than a hem, but ripping stitches? That, she was qualified for. "And he helped shame Donaia into agreeing to see me again. But *she* is every bit as bad as Letilia claimed. You should have seen what she wore. Ratty old clothes, covered in dog hair. Like it's a moral flaw to let a single centira slip through her fingers."

"But the son isn't so bad?" Tess rocked on the bench, nudging Ren's hip with her own. "Maybe he's a bastard."

Ren snorted. "Not likely. Donaia would give him the moon if he asked, and he looks as Traementis as I." Only he didn't need makeup to achieve the effect.

Her hands trembled as she worked. Those five years in Ganllech were also five years out of practice. And all her previous cons had been short touches—never anything on this scale. When she got caught before, the hawks slung her in jail for a few days.

If she got caught now, impersonating a noblewoman...

Tess laid a hand over Ren's, stopping her before she could nick herself with the knife. "It's never too late to do something else."

Ren managed a smile. "Buy piles of fabric, then run away and set up as dressmakers? You, anyway. I would be your tailor's dummy."

"You'd model and sell them," Tess said stoutly. "If you want."

Tess would be happy in that life. But Ren wanted more.

This city *owed* her more. It had taken everything: her mother, her childhood, Sedge. The rich cuffs of Nadežra got whatever they wanted, then squabbled over what their rivals had, grinding everyone else underfoot. In all her days among the Fingers, Ren had never been able to take more than the smallest shreds from the hems of their cloaks.

But now, thanks to Letilia, she was in a position to take more.

The Traementis made the perfect target. Small enough these days that only Donaia stood any chance of spotting Renata as an imposter, and isolated enough that they would be grateful for any addition to their register. In the glory days of their power and graft, they'd been notorious for their insular ways, refusing to aid their fellow nobles in times of need. Since they lost their seat in the Cinquerat, everyone else had gladly returned the favor.

Ren put down the knife and squeezed Tess's hand. "No. It is nerves only, and they will pass. We go forward."

"Forward it is." Tess squeezed back, then returned to work. "Next we're to make a splash somewhere public, yes? I'll need to know where and when if I'm to outfit you proper." The sides of the surcoat parted, and she started on the bandeau at the top of the bodice. "The sleeves are the key, have you noticed? Everyone is so on about their sleeves. But I've a thought for that...if you're ready for Alta Renata to set fashion instead of following."

Ren glanced sideways, her wariness only half-feigned. "What have you in mind?"

"Hmm. Stand up, and off with the rest of it." Once she had Ren stripped to her chemise, Tess played with different gathers and drapes until Ren's arms started to ache from being held out for so long. But she didn't complain. Tess's eye for fashion, her knack for imbuing, and her ability to rework the pieces of three outfits into nine were as vital to this con as Ren's skill at manipulation.

She closed her eyes and cast her thoughts over what she knew about the city. Where could she go, what could she do, to attract the kind of admiration that would help her gain the foothold she needed?

A slow smile spread across her face.

"Tess," she said, "I have the perfect idea. And you will love it."

The Aerie and Isla Traementis: Suilun 1

"Serrado! Get in here. I have a job for you."

Commander Cercel's voice cut sharply through the din of the Aerie. Waving at his constables to take their prisoner to the stockade, Captain Grey Serrado turned and threaded his way through the chaos to his commander's office. He ignored the sidelong smirks and snide whispers of his fellow officers: Unlike them, he didn't have the luxury of lounging about drinking coffee, managing his constables from the comfort of the Aerie.

"Commander Cercel?" He snapped the heels of his boots together and gave her his crispest salute—a salute he'd perfected during hours of standing at attention in the sun, the rain, the wind, while other lieutenants were at mess or in the barracks. Cercel wasn't the stickler for discipline his previous superiors had been, but she was the reason he wore a captain's double-lined hexagram pin, and he didn't want to reflect badly on her.

She was studying a letter, but when she brought her head up to reply, her eyes widened. "What does the *other* guy look like?"

Taking the casual question as permission to drop into rest, Grey spared a glance for his uniform. His patrol slops were spattered with muck from heel to shoulder, and blood was drying on the knuckles of his leather gloves. Some of the canal mud on his boots had flaked off when he saluted, powdering Cercel's carpet with the filth of the Kingfisher slums.

"Dazed but breathing. Ranieri's taking him to the stockade now." Her question invited banter, but the door to her office was open, and it wouldn't do him any good to be marked as a smart-ass.

She responded to his businesslike answer with an equally brisk nod. "Well, get cleaned up. I've received a letter from one of the noble houses, requesting Vigil assistance. I'm sending you."

Grey's jaw tensed as he waited for several gut responses to subside. It was possible the request was a legitimate call for aid. "What crime has been committed?"

Cercel's level gaze said, *You know better than that.* "One of the noble houses has requested Vigil assistance," she repeated, enunciating each word with cut-glass clarity. "I'm sure they wouldn't do that without good cause."

No doubt whoever sent the letter thought the cause was good. People from the great houses always did.

But Grey had a desk full of real problems. "More children have gone missing. That's eleven verified this month."

They'd had this conversation several times over the past few weeks. Cercel sighed. "We haven't had any reports—"

"Because they're all river rats so far. Who's going to care enough to report that? But the man I just brought in might know something about it; he's been promising Kingfisher kids good pay for an unspecified job. I got him on defacing public property, but he'll be free again by tonight." Pissing in public wasn't an offense the Vigil usually cracked down on, unless it suited them. "Am I to assume this noble's 'good cause' takes precedence over finding out what's happening to those kids?"

Cercel breathed out hard through her nose, and he tensed. Had he pushed her patience too far?

No. "Your man is on his way to the stockade," she said. "Have Kaineto process him—you're always complaining he's as slow as river mud. By the time you get back, he'll be ready to talk. Meanwhile, send Ranieri to ask questions around Kingfisher, see if he can find any of the man's associates." She set the letter aside and drew another from her stack, a clear prelude to dismissing him. "You know the deal, Serrado."

The first few times, he'd played dense to make her spell it out in unambiguous terms. The last thing he could afford back then was to mistake a senior officer's meaning.

But they were past those games now. As long as he knuckled under and did whatever this noble wanted of him, Cercel wouldn't question him using Vigil time and resources for his own investigations.

"Yes, Commander." He saluted and heel-knocked another layer of delta silt onto her carpet. "Which house has called for aid?"

"Traementis."

If he'd been less careful of his manners, he would have thrown her a dirty look. *She would have* led *with that.* But Cercel wanted him to understand that answering these calls was part of his duty, and made him bend his neck before she revealed the silver lining. "Understood. I'll head to the Pearls at once."

Her final command followed him out of the office. "Don't you dare show up at Era Traementis's door looking like that!"

Groaning, Grey changed his path. He snagged a pitcher of water and a messenger, sending the latter to Ranieri with the new orders.

There was a bathing room in the Aerie, but he didn't want to waste time on that. A sniff test sent every piece of his patrol uniform into the laundry bag; aside from the coffee, that was one of the few perks of his rank he didn't mind taking shameless advantage of. If he was wading through canals for the job, the least the Vigil could do was ensure he didn't smell like one. A quick pitcher bath in his tiny office took care of the scents still clinging to his skin and hair before he shrugged into his dress vigils.

He had to admit the force's tailors were good. The tan breeches were Liganti-cut, snug as they could be around his thighs and hips without impeding movement. Both the brocade waistcoat and the coat of sapphire wool were tailored like a second skin, before the latter flared to full skirts that kissed the tops of his polished, knee-high boots. On his patrol slops, the diving hawk across the back of his shoulders was mere patchwork; here it was embroidered in golds and browns.

Grey didn't have much use for vanity, but he did love his dress vigils. They were an inarguable reminder that he'd climbed to a place few Vraszenians could even imagine reaching. His brother, Kolya, had been so proud the day Grey came home in them.

The sudden trembling of his hands stabbed his collar pin into his thumb. Grey swallowed a curse and sucked the blood from the puncture, using a tiny hand mirror to make sure he hadn't gotten any on his collar. Luckily, it was clean, and he managed to finish dressing himself without further injury.

Once outside, he set off east from Duskgate with long, ground-eating strides. He could have taken a sedan chair and told the bearers to bill the Vigil; other officers did, knowing all the while that no such bill would ever be paid. But along with stiffing the bearers, that meant they didn't see the city around them the way Grey did.

Not that most of them would. They were Liganti, or mixed enough in ancestry that they could claim the name; to them, Nadežra was an outpost of Seste Ligante, half tamed by the Liganti general Kaius Sifigno, who restyled himself Kaius Rex after conquering Vraszan two centuries past. Others called him the Tyrant, and when he died, the Vraszenian clans took back the rest of their conquered land. But every push to reclaim their holy city failed, until exhaustion on both sides led to the signing of the Accords. Those established Nadežra as an independent city-state—under the rule of its Liganti elite.

It was an uneasy balance at best, made less easy still by Vraszenian radical groups like the Stadnem Anduske, who wouldn't settle for anything less than the city back in Vraszenian hands. And every time they pushed, the Cinquerat pushed back even harder.

The busy markets of Suncross at the heart of the Old Island parted for Grey's bright blue coat and the tawny embroidered hawk, but not without glares. To the high and mighty, the Vigil was a tool; to the common Nadežran, the Vigil was the tool of the high and mighty. Not all of them—Grey wasn't the only hawk who cared about common folk—but enough that he couldn't blame people for their hostility. And some of the worst glares came from Vraszenians, who looked at him and saw a slip-knot: a man who had betrayed his people, siding with the invaders' descendants.

Grey was used to the glares. He kept an eye out for trouble as he passed market stalls on the stoops of decaying townhouses, and a bawdy puppet show where the only children in the crowd were the pickpockets. They trickled away like water before he could mark their faces. A few beggars eyed him warily, but Grey had no grudge against them; the more dangerous elements wouldn't come out until evening, when the feckless sons and daughters of the delta gentry prowled the streets in search of amusement. A pattern-reader had set up on a corner near the Charterhouse, ready to bilk people in exchange for a pretty lie. He gave her a wide berth, leather glove creaking into a fist as he resisted the urge to drag her back to the Aerie for graft.

Once he'd passed under the decaying bulk of the Dawngate and across the Sunrise Bridge, he turned north into the narrow islets of the Pearls, clogged with sedan chairs. Two elderly ladies impressed with their own importance blocked the Becchia Bridge entirely, squabbling like gulls over which one should yield. Grey marked the house sigil painted onto each chair's door in case complaints came to the Aerie later.

His shoulders itched as he crossed the lines of the complex mosaic in the center of Traementis Plaza. It was no mere tilework, but a numinat: geometric Liganti magic meant to keep the ground dry and solid, against the river's determination to sink everything into the mud. Useful...but the Tyrant had twisted numinatria into a weapon during his conquest, and mosaics like this one amounted to emblems of ongoing Liganti control.

On the steps of Traementis Manor, Grey gave his uniform a final smoothing and sounded the bell. Within moments, Colbrin opened the door and favored Grey with a rare smile.

"Young Master Serrado. How pleasant to see you; it's been far too long. I'm afraid Altan Leato is not here to receive you—"

"It's 'Captain' now," Grey said, touching the hexagram pin at his throat. The smile he dredged up felt tired from disuse. "And I'm not here for Leato. Era Traementis requested assistance from the Vigil."

"Ah, yes." Colbrin bowed him inside. "If you'll wait in the salon, I'll inform Era Traementis that you're here."

Grey wasn't surprised when Colbrin returned in a few moments and summoned him to the study. Whatever Donaia had written to the Vigil for, it was business, not a social call.

That room was much darker, with little in the way of bright silks to warm the space—but warmth came in many shapes. Donaia's grizzled wolfhound scrambled up from his place by her desk, claws ticking on wood as he trotted over for a greeting. "Hello, old man," Grey said, giving him a good tousling and a few barrel thumps on the side.

"Meatball. Heel." The dog returned to Donaia's side, looking up as she crossed the room to greet Grey.

"Era Traementis," Grey said, bowing over her hand. "I'm told you have need of assistance."

The silver threads lacing through her hair were gaining ground against the auburn, and she looked tired. "Yes. I need you to look into someone—a visitor to the city, recently arrived from Seteris. Renata Viraudax."

"Has she committed some crime against House Traementis?"

"No," Donaia said. "*She* hasn't."

Her words piqued his curiosity. "Era?"

A muscle tightened in Donaia's jaw. "My husband once had a sister named Letilia—Lecilla, really, but she was obsessed with Seteris and their high culture, so she badgered their father into changing it in the register. Twenty-three years ago, she decided she would rather be in Seteris than here . . . so she stole some money and jewelry and ran away."

Donaia gestured Grey to a chair in front of the hearth. The warmth of the fire enveloped him as he sat down. "Renata Viraudax is Letilia's daughter. She claims to be trying to mend bridges, but I have my doubts. I want you to find out what she's really doing in Nadežra."

As much as Grey loathed the right of the nobility to commandeer the Vigil for private use, he couldn't help feeling sympathy. When he was younger and less aware of the differences that made it impossible, he'd sometimes wished Donaia Traementis was his mother. She was stern, but fair. She loved her children, and was fiercely protective of her family. Unlike some, she never gave Leato and Giuna reason to doubt her love for them.

This Viraudax woman's mother had hurt her family, and the Traementis had a well-earned reputation for avenging their own.

"What can you tell me about her?" he asked. "Has she given you any reason to doubt her sincerity? Apart from being her mother's daughter."

Donaia's fingers drummed briefly against the arm of the chair, and her gaze settled on a corner of the fireplace and stayed there long enough that Grey knew she was struggling with some thought. He kept his silence.

Finally she said, "You and my son are friends, and moreover you aren't a fool. It can't have escaped your notice that House Traementis is not what it once was, in wealth, power, or numbers. We have many enemies eager to see us fall. Now this young woman shows up and tries to insinuate herself among us? Perhaps I'm jumping at shadows...but I must consider the possibility that this is a gambit intended to destroy us entirely." She gave a bitter laugh. "I can't even be certain this girl *is* Letilia's daughter."

She must be worried, if she was admitting so much. Yes, Grey had suspected—would have suspected even if Vigil gossip didn't sometimes speculate—that House Traementis was struggling more than they let on. But he never joined in the gossip, and he never asked Leato.

Leato...who was always in fashion, and according to that same gossip spent half his time frequenting aža parlours and gambling dens. *Does Leato know?* Grey swallowed the question. It wasn't his business, and it wasn't the business Donaia had called him for.

"That last shouldn't be too hard to determine," he said. "I assume you know where she's staying?" He paused when Donaia's lips flattened, but she only nodded. "Then talk to her. If she's truly Letilia's daughter, she should know details an imposter wouldn't easily be able to discover. If she gives you vague answers or takes offense, then you'll know something is wrong."

Grey paused again, wondering how much Donaia would let him pry. "You said you had enemies she might be working for. It would help me to know who they are and what they might want." At her sharply indrawn breath, he raised a hand in pledge. "I promise I'll say nothing of it—not even to Leato."

In a tone so dry it burned, Donaia began ticking possibilities off on her fingers. "Quientis took our seat in the Cinquerat. Kaineto are only delta gentry, but have made a point of blocking our attempts to contract out our charters. Essunta, likewise. Simendis, Destaelio, Novrus, Cleoter—Indestor—I'm afraid it's a crowded field."

That was the entire Cinquerat and others besides...but she'd only stumbled over one name.

"Indestor," Grey said. The house that held Caerulet, the military seat in the Cinquerat. The house in charge of the Vigil.

The house that would not look kindly upon being investigated by one of its own.

"Era Traementis...did you ask for any officer, or did you specifically request me?"

"You're Leato's friend," Donaia said, holding his gaze. "Far better to ask a friend for help than to confess our troubles to an enemy."

That startled a chuckle from Grey. At Donaia's furrowed brow, he said, "My brother was fond of a Vraszenian saying. 'A family covered in the same dirt washes in the same water.'"

And Kolya would have given Grey a good scolding for not jumping to help Donaia right away. She might not be kin, but she'd hired a young Vraszenian carpenter with a scrawny kid brother when nobody else would, and paid him the same as a Nadežran.

He stood and bowed with a fist to his shoulder. "I'll see what I can discover for you. Tell me where to find this Renata Viraudax."

2

The Face of Gold

Isla Prišta, Westbridge: Suilun 4

Some things were worth paying good money for. The materials for
Ren's clothing, for example: Tess was a genius at sewing, but even
she couldn't make cheap fabric hold up to close inspection.

The mirror Ren arranged next to an upstairs window was
another one of her investments, as were the cosmetics she set in
front of it. The one contribution her unknown father had made to
her life was hair and skin a few shades lighter than her Vraszenian
mother's—light enough to pass for Liganti or Seterin, with help. But
making herself look plausibly like Letilia Traementis's daughter took
extra effort and care.

Ren angled the silvered glass to take advantage of the natural
light, then brushed powder across her face, making sure she blended
it up into her hairline and down her throat. Years cooped up indoors
as Letilia's maid had done a fair bit to lighten her complexion, and
the oncoming winter wouldn't afford her many opportunities to
be in the sun, but she would have to be careful when the warmer
months came. Given half an excuse, her skin would eagerly tan.

But at least she didn't have to worry about the powder rubbing
off. All her cosmetics were imbued by artisans like Tess, people who
could infuse the things they made with their own spiritual force to

make them work better. Imbued cosmetics might be more expensive, but they would stay in place, blend until their effects looked natural, and not even irritate her skin. Imbuing didn't receive the respect given to numinatria, but compared to the pastes and powders Ren had used back when she was a Finger, these seemed like a miracle.

Switching to a darker shade, she thinned the apparent shape of her nose and made her eyes seem more closely set, adding a few years to her age by contouring out the remaining softness of youth. Her cheekbones, her mouth—nothing remained untouched, until the woman in the mirror was Renata Viraudax instead of Ren.

Tess bustled in with an armful of fabric. She hung the underdress and surcoat from the empty canopy bars of the bed before flopping onto the dusty ropes that should have held a mattress.

"Whoof. Well, I can't speak to the state of my fingers or my eyesight, but the embroidery's done." She held her reddened fingers up to the light. "Wish I could just leave the insides a tangle, but it'd be Quarat's own ill luck if a gust of wind flipped your skirts and flashed your messy backing for the world to see." She stifled a giggle. "I meant your embroidery, not what's under your knickers."

A masquerade was more than just its physical trappings. "Tess."

The mere pitch of that word was enough to remind her. Renata's voice wasn't as high as Letilia's—that woman had cultivated a tone she referred to as "bell-like," and Ren thought of as "shrill"—but she spoke in a higher register than Ren. Now she said Tess's name in Renata's tone, and Tess sat up.

"Yes, alta. Sorry, alta." Tess swallowed a final hiccup of laughter. Her part required less acting, but she struggled harder to get into it. With her round cheeks and moss-soft eyes, she'd been one of the best pity-rustlers in the Fingers, but not much good at lying. She stood and bobbed a curtsy behind Renata, addressing her reflection. "What would the alta like done with her hair?"

It felt uncomfortable, having Tess address her with such deference. But this wasn't a short-term con, talking some shopkeeper into believing she was a rich customer long enough for her to pocket something while his back was turned; she would need to be Renata for hours at a time, for weeks and months to come. And she needed to associate every habit of manner and speech and thought with Renata's costumes, so they wouldn't slip at an inopportune moment.

"I believe you had some ribbon left over," Renata said. "I think it would look lovely threaded through my hair."

"Oooh, excellent idea! The alta has such a refined sense of style."

Tess had never been an alta's maid. While Ren had run herself ragged satisfying Letilia's petty demands, Tess had been sewing herself half-blind in the windowless back room of a grey-market shop. Still, she insisted that obsequiousness was part of the role, and no amount of correction from either Ren or Alta Renata could stamp it out. Sighing, Renata put in her earrings—formerly Letilia's—while Tess retrieved ribbon, brushes, needle, and thread, and set to work.

Tess's skill at imbuing went toward clothing, not hair, but by some undefinable magic she twisted the strands into a complicated knot, turning and tucking them so the outermost parts were the ones bleached lighter by sun and wind, and the darker sections were hidden away.

Just as Ren herself was hidden away. She breathed slowly and evenly, nerves beginning to thrum with familiar excitement.

By the end of today, the nobles of the city would know Renata Viraudax's name.

The Rotunda, Eastbridge: Suilun 4

The Rotunda, situated on the Upper Bank side of the Sunrise Bridge, was a marvel of beauty and magic. Under a vaulted glass dome etched with colored numinata that kept the interior cool in the day and lit at night, a wide marble plaza allowed for casual strolling and diverting entertainments. In the center, a small garden offered benches where patrons could rest their weary feet. Around the perimeter, shops presented the finest imbued wares for the delight of those who could afford them.

Twice a year, in the spring and the fall, merchants from Seste Ligante arrived bearing the newest fabrics and fashions, setting up displays of their wares in the Rotunda. And all the nobles and delta gentry of Nadežra flocked to the seasonal Gloria, to spend, to see, and to be seen.

Despite her resolve to think only Renata's thoughts, Ren couldn't keep her pulse from quickening as she passed through the Rotunda's grand archway with Tess in tow. She'd often peered at the riches beyond, but she'd been inside only once before—with Ondrakja, not long before everything fell apart.

The scheme had been an audacious one. Ondrakja came in first, dressed as a rich merchant from one of the upriver cities, and examined some jewelry. While the jeweler's back was turned, a sapphire bracelet vanished. The Vigil constables guarding the Rotunda searched Ondrakja from head to foot, but found no sign of the gems, and the only people near her when the bracelet disappeared were nobility they dared not accuse. The hawks threw her in jail for the night on principle, but the next day they let her go.

Half an hour after Ondrakja was quietly force-marched out of the Rotunda, a beautiful girl who presumably belonged to one of the delta houses came up and browsed the jeweler's wares. It had been laughably easy for Ren to remove the bracelet from the putty Ondrakja had stuck to the underside of the counter, then walk out with no one the wiser.

Ondrakja had been so pleased with her for that one. She'd bought Ren a bag of honey stones to suck on, and let her wear the bracelet for a whole day before it was fenced.

"May I help you find someone, alta?" a man asked, stepping too close to her side. "You seem lost."

Djek. A hawk!

"Just taking in the view," she said reflexively. Long hours of practice paid off; despite the skin-shock of fear, her words came out in the clipped, fronted vowels of Seteris.

She got a second shock when she looked properly at the man who'd addressed her. *Since when are they making Vigil officers out of Vraszenians?* His accent was cleanly Nadežran, but there was no mistaking him for anything other than full-blooded Vraszenian, with his thick, dark hair—trimmed short though it was—and sun-bronzed skin.

Yet he wore the double-lined hexagram pin of a captain.

Maybe they just thought he looked too good in dress vigils to pass up. He was tall and broad-shouldered, with the lean build of a duelist rather than a soldier, his eyes a deeper shade of his coat's sapphire. Apart from his heritage, he was exactly the kind of man Nadežra's elite would prop up in a corner as decoration at an event like this.

But she'd used her own pretty face as a tool too often to let someone else do the same to her.

He stepped closer to avoid a passing couple, and Renata found herself expertly edged aside from the traffic. "Your accent—you're from Seteris? Welcome to Nadežra. Is this your first visit to the Rotunda?"

"It is indeed." She let her gaze drift across the tables and mannequins displaying wares for this season's Gloria. "I must say, it is… interesting, seeing what happens to Seterin fashion in its journey here."

Just a touch of condescension. To the Seterins and Liganti across the sea, Nadežra was a foreign backwater. Letilia had never hesitated to heap scorn on it, and her daughter wouldn't have shed those prejudices entirely.

The captain nodded amiably rather than taking offense. "The Rotunda can be distracting for those unused to it—and the pickpockets who manage to sneak in like to take advantage of that. Allow me to escort you until you get your bearings."

The worst thing she could do would be to hesitate. "I'd be grateful," she said, motioning for Tess to fall back a few steps. A Seterin woman who hadn't grown up among Nadežra's political tensions wouldn't turn her nose up at the escort of a handsome Vigil captain, even if he was Vraszenian. She laid gloved fingers on the sleeve of his coat. "Your uniform is that of this city's guard, I believe? No pickpocket will dare approach if I have you at my side."

"Captain Grey Serrado of the Vigil, yes. And I will make certain they do not, alta." He drew away from her touch, his smile betraying not a flicker of interest in her flirtation.

Serrado. She rolled the syllables around in her mind as she returned the introduction, comparing them against his appearance. *Szerado.* And "Grey" was hardly a Vraszenian name. So he was one of those types—the ones who tried to separate themselves from their origins, in hopes of currying favor with the Liganti.

Ren might play the role out of necessity. He was a slip-knot by choice.

She pushed the thought away. It wouldn't matter to Alta Renata. "This way looks more interesting," she said, glancing to the left when Serrado would have led her right—as though she didn't know the ebb and flow of the Gloria.

"The promenade progresses earthwise for the Autumn Gloria," Serrado explained, following the rest of the foot traffic that curved rightward from the entry. "In the spring, it circles sunwise. You'll find the newest and most expensive goods at the start, and the over-looked treasures near the end."

"Is that so." She stopped at a table of perfumes. The woman behind it sized her up in a blink and glided forward, inquiring whether the alta would like to sample any of the scents. Renata allowed her to unstopper a few bottles and wave their wands under her nose, then dab a touch of one to the inside of her wrist. It smelled of eucalyptus, mellowed by something earthier beneath, and the seller promised the scent was imbued to last all day. *Buy something now, to show that I don't care about cost?* she wondered. *Or demonstrate my taste and discretion by refraining?*

She was beginning to attract notice, and not just from the shop-keepers. Some of that was because she looked both noble and un-familiar, but mostly it was due to her clothing.

Even amid the splendor of the Gloria, she stood out like the blue of autumn skies. Her underdress of gold-shot amber silk was simple almost to the point of austerity, but the azure surcoat showed Tess's fine hand at work. The bandeau was stitched with clever tucks, lifting her bosom rather than crushing it flat. The surcoat's bodice lacked the rigid stays meant to give it a straight shape; instead it was tailored almost like a man's waistcoat, tight through her waist and flaring over her hips before falling into the apron-like panels of the fore and back skirts. On those Tess had exercised restraint; the beauty of the embroidered leaf motif came from quality rather than quantity—turning their tight finances into a virtue. Subtle imbuing made the gold threads shift with the colors of the season. Nobody could look at such a dress and doubt that Alta Renata had paid a small fortune for such work.

And then there were the sleeves. Attached at the shoulder and wrist, they parted and draped in between, leaving the entirety of her arm exposed. She caught one grey-haired old trout frowning in disapproval and hid a smile. *Good. I have their attention.*

That was the goal of today's excursion. If Renata Viraudax sat quietly in her townhouse waiting for Donaia to acknowledge her, she'd be easy to ignore. But if she made herself a public sensation, the Traementis would have to respond.

Besides, it was *fun*. Strolling the Rotunda in beautiful clothing, perusing the wares like she could afford to buy this whole place...if only it met her exacting standards. After a life on the streets, even a sip of this wine tasted sweet.

Renata made unimpressed noises at the perfume and wandered onward, attracting more eyes as she went. No one approached her, though—perhaps put off by the fact that she seemed to have her own personal escorting hawk.

She did her best to shed him. But no matter how long she perused wares and vocally dithered over whether they were the best the Gloria had to offer, Captain Serrado didn't oblige her with his boredom so she could send him on his way. She was halfway around the Rotunda, contemplating increasingly absurd schemes for getting rid of him, when she caught sight of the next display.

Velvet panels formed a backdrop for beautiful, empty faces of filigree and stiffened silk. While the masks that rich Nadežrans wore when slumming on the Old Island and the Lower Bank mostly marked them out as targets for plucking, Ren had always loved the masks brought out during the Festival of Veiled Waters. When she was five, her mother had bought her one—just a cheap paper thing, but she'd treasured it like it was made of solid gold.

But Renata Viraudax knew nothing of Nadežran mask traditions. "How odd," she said, drifting toward the display as if it held no particular allure. "I've never seen anything like this in Seteris."

"That's because Seteris doesn't have Nadežra's long and storied history with masks."

The reply didn't come from Captain Serrado. Behind Renata, Tess whimpered.

Tess liked a handsome man as much as the next person, but what really made her go faint was good tailoring. And the clothes of the man who had spoken were *exquisite*—even Ren could see that. Not innovative in the ways Tess could achieve, but the green wool of his coat was as soft as a carpet of stone moss, cut flawlessly so it didn't wrinkle as he moved. His waistcoat was much darker than Liganti fashion favored, appearing black until it caught the light and flashed emerald, and his coat and collar points rose to his jaw without threatening to wilt. Renata's gaze passed over an odd, iridescent spider pin clasped to his lapel, then snagged on the jagged scar ripping up the side of his neck, too high for even fine linens and high collars to entirely hide.

Ignoring Tess and Captain Serrado, the man stepped into the gap next to Renata. It would have felt invasive if he'd been looking at her, but his gaze was on the array of wares. "Masks are worn for many Nadežran festivals, and sometimes ordinary occasions, to sweeten the air and protect the skin. The Tyrant became quite attached to them in the latter stages of his...illness." He gave a delicate shudder. "Even our most infamous outlaw, the Rook, is known for hiding his face. One can't visit our fair delta and not acquire a mask."

He plucked down one of lapis caught in stiffened gold lace,

similar to the embroidery on Renata's surcoat, and offered it to her. "Derossi Vargo. Apologies for my presumption, but I had to make the acquaintance of the most stylish woman to grace this year's Gloria."

The flattery was unsubtle, but delivered smoothly enough to charm, and Renata was just grateful someone had finally broken the hawk-shaped wall at her back.

Derossi Vargo. The name seemed nigglingly familiar, and it annoyed her that she couldn't place it. It wasn't a noble name, but he might be from one of the delta houses, the gentry of Nadežra.

She accepted the mask and held it against her face. "How is a visitor to know which one to buy?"

"Why, whichever one pleases you best and costs the most."

Before Vargo could fetch down another, the shopkeeper hurried over. "There's more than just beauty to be had here, alta," she said, selecting a few other styles that complemented Renata's coloring and ensemble. "My husband does the finest imbuing in Nadežra. Take this one." She held up two circles of overlapping silver and gold. "It'll keep your complexion dry in our humid air. Or here." Up came a midnight-blue domino decked with shimmering onyx. "This will hide you from prying eyes on your way to an assignation. I've masks that'll clear up your spots—not that you've any need for that—or that'll protect you from the sick fogs that roll up from the Lower Bank."

"Really," Vargo murmured, reaching for that last one. "It fends off disease?"

Renata drifted away as the shopkeeper made improbable promises. The display was small—most of the focus in the Rotunda was on imported goods, not local products—and her wandering gaze alighted on a mask tucked into a bottom corner, as if the shopkeeper knew nobody was likely to want it.

Where her childhood mask had been clumsily painted with a rainbow of colors, this one was hammered prismatium, shimmering like the tail of a dreamweaver bird. The mask-maker had sculpted the metal into gentle waves, ebbing and flowing like the

River Dežera. It wasn't anything Renata Viraudax needed...but Ren wanted it so badly it took all her will not to let the yearning show.

"What's caught your attention?" Vargo's question was warm, amused, like they were old friends rather than acquaintances of mere moments. He drew close, peering over her shoulder. "Ah. That's a very...Nadežran mask."

"Vraszenian, you mean," Captain Serrado muttered. He looked away when Vargo glanced over.

"I suppose you would know, Captain." Vargo's tone rippled like the prismatium of the mask, full of colors hidden just under the surface. The smile he turned on Renata was equally pleasant and enigmatic. "Do you like it?"

Just be Renata. It had sounded so easy when she was getting dressed this morning. In practice, keeping unwanted thoughts from welling up was proving far harder than she'd anticipated. "What makes it so Nadežran? Or Vraszenian—whichever." She dismissed the quibble over terminology with a flutter of one hand.

If she'd wanted to persuade them she'd never been to Nadežra in her life, she couldn't have chosen a better method. Both men bristled, brothers in indignation. Serrado might be a slip-knot, but his ancestry was as Vraszenian as they came, while Vargo looked like a typical Nadežran, mixed Vraszenian and Liganti blood—and neither of them appreciated being lumped in with the other.

Vargo's indignation broke first, into rueful chuckles. He lifted the mask and turned it to admire the prismatium. Faint etching and the shape of the edges gave it the appearance of feathers. "Nadežran because the dreamweaver bird is a symbol of the city. They flock here every spring to mate, when we celebrate the Festival of Veiled Waters. Vraszenian because the Vraszenian people say they're descended from those same birds, so they flock here as well."

A muscle jumped in Serrado's jaw, but he said nothing to correct the inaccuracy or half-veiled insult in Vargo's description. Vraszenians did not consider dreamweavers their ancestors, but the symbol of one: Ižranyi, the youngest and most favored daughter of Ažerais, the goddess of their people. She and her siblings had founded the seven Vraszenian clans.

The Ižranyi clan was lost now, slaughtered centuries ago in a divine cataclysm that left their entire city a haunted ruin. But their emblem was still honored.

Taking the mask from Vargo, Renata held it up, comparing it against him. "It almost matches your spider pin! But not your coat, I fear."

Fighting a smile, Vargo absently touched the pin as Renata settled the mask on her face and checked the shopkeeper's mirror.

It was a mistake. Seeing the mask's sculpted curve cradling the line of her jaw like a caress, Ren found herself completely unable to care about Tess's budget and the limits of her forged letter of credit.

Her reflection assured that her yearning remained hidden, but nevertheless Vargo nodded. "I'll buy it for you—if the alta will allow." He lifted the mask from Renata's face, his gloved fingers brushing her cheek in passing, and handed it to the shopkeeper for wrapping, along with the mask that kept away disease. "Call it a welcoming gift."

Well, that solves the budget problem. "You don't even know my name," she said, smiling.

There was another scar through his brow, smaller than the one on his neck, that became visible when he arched it. Whoever Derossi Vargo was, he flung money around like a cuff and had the marks of a Lower Bank rat. He handed her the wrapped mask with a flourish. "There's an obvious solution to that."

In response, Renata swept him the most elegant curtsy she could in the confines of the stall, giving her name in a voice that carried to the onlookers. Vargo cocked his head and said, "Viraud—Oh! Number four, Via Brelkoja."

A chill washed over her skin. How did he know her address?

"I believe I'm your new landlord," he said, with a small bow. "I hope you're finding the house suitable to your needs."

That niggling sense of recognition flashed into clarity, and a sense of relief. She knew his name because she'd seen it on the papers she'd signed to lease her townhouse. "Ah, of course! Please forgive me—I should have known." Passing the mask to Tess, she curtsied again. "Thank you, Master Vargo, for the gift. It seems I could have no more fitting memento of this city."

Serrado was radiating disapproval like a blazing hearth. And it seemed Tess agreed with him, because she intervened. "Oh, alta, it's that cold in here. I've your wrap for you." She bundled Renata in an artful drape of silk, conveniently stepping in front of Vargo. "Do you wish to go back? I can ask the captain to call a chair."

Go back? At this point that would be disastrous. Renata was here to make an impression on the great and powerful, and her first conversation of substance was with someone of no social standing, rich and charming though Vargo might be.

But she'd seen Letilia make enemies by giving people her back when she decided they weren't important enough to merit her time. "Nonsense, Tess. Seterin winters are much colder than this." She let the wrap slip down enough to show her bare shoulders—which had, after all, been Tess's idea in the first place. "I've barely seen half the Gloria yet."

As if sensing the dismissal, Vargo swept the skirts of his coat back and bowed to Renata. "I've taken up too much of your time. I hope our paths may cross again. Perhaps an occasion that allows you to wear your new mask? Alta." After a brief hesitation, he nodded at Serrado as well. "Captain."

A sigh escaped Tess as Vargo sauntered off, giving an excellent view of his broad shoulders and striking bootheels and swinging green coat.

Serrado, unfortunately, did not follow suit. He'd gotten his disapproval under control, his face once again a bland mask, avoiding the eye contact that would let Renata gracefully release him.

Sighing inwardly, she turned to face the remaining half circle of the Rotunda. She saw people murmuring behind their fans and gloves, trying with varying degrees of success to pretend they weren't gossiping about her ... and among them, moving toward her, a recognizable golden head.

"Cousin!" Leato Traementis was upon her, taking both her hands. It was impossible not to answer his grin with one of her own, even as Leato's turned rueful. "Alta Renata, rather. But maybe someday soon—Grey! Lumen's light, man, I haven't seen you in forever. How do you know Alta Renata? Did Mother ask you to look after her?"

Renata kept her gaze on Leato, but in her peripheral vision she saw Captain Serrado stiffen.

Suddenly her oddly persistent shadow made a good deal more sense.

"Hello, Leato," Serrado said. "No, the alta and I aren't acquainted. I'm on duty and she seemed in need of an escort." His bronze skin didn't show blushes well, but Renata recognized the look he was giving Leato. She'd thrown just that sort of quelling glance at Tess when her sister said too much.

Her suspicions were confirmed when Serrado bowed, with military precision rather than Vargo's swagger or Leato's easy grace. "Alta Renata, I leave you in Altan Leato's care." Over the half-voiced protest from the Traementis heir, he said, "Enjoy the rest of the Gloria."

"Thank you for your assistance, Captain," she said, answering his precision with an excruciatingly correct curtsy. "It was most generous of you."

As Leato gaped at Grey's retreating back, Era Traementis came sweeping up behind her son. "Alta Renata," she said. Her expression was cordial, but her words were too melodious to be anything other than a performance. "I didn't expect to see you here."

"Your Gloria is the talk of the town," Renata replied. "And now that I'm here, I can see why. Such a display! We have nothing like this at home. The goods for sale, certainly—but not this kind of event, bringing everyone together to set the tone for the upcoming season."

"Yes, there are many things on display." Donaia's attention flicked briefly to Renata's bare arms. "I suppose I shouldn't be surprised to see you here. The Gloria was Letilia's favorite event as well."

"That's hardly a character flaw, Mother." Leato shifted to

Renata's side, forming a wall of solidarity against Donaia's disapproval. "Otherwise Giuna and I also bear the shame of enjoying it. Giuna, come meet Letilia's daughter that I was telling you about."

At Leato's wave, the girl who'd been standing in Donaia's shadow hesitantly stepped forward. She was dressed like her mother, in clothes more mature and restrained than someone her age should be wearing. Between that and her timidity, Renata had mistaken her for Donaia's maid.

There was no missing the resemblance to Leato, however. Or to Letilia, at least as far as features went. Not with all her artifice could Letilia have made that tremulous smile and coltish curtsy seem genuine. "Alta Renata. I hope you aren't finding Nadežra too strange."

"Not strange so much as . . . different from how Mother described it." She delivered her reply with a conspiratorial air, inviting Giuna to imagine the nature of the difference.

Giuna's laugh was a startling sound, like finches taking wing. Leato joined in, and even Donaia's lips curved in a reluctant smile. "Yes, I imagine she made most of it sound dreadful," Giuna said. To Renata's surprise, she nudged Leato out of the way so she could take Renata's arm. "Why don't we finish the Rotunda together and you can tell us how this is all hopelessly out of fashion already?"

She tilted her head close for an additional whisper as they began to stroll. "And maybe you can tell me what you were talking about with Master Vargo."

So he was well-known, even in noble circles. *I'm not the only one who leverages the appeal of good tailoring.* "He was explaining Nadežran mask traditions to me. Then we realized he owns the house I'm renting, so he bought me a mask as a welcoming gift."

"Yes, you'll need a mask if you want to do anything interesting while you're here. Mother won't let me wear them outside of festivals." Giuna sighed, more resigned than rebellious, and picked up a drape reminiscent of the one Renata wore. The wintergreen satin was embroidered with darting silver fish, and its fine weave slipped through her fingers. With another sigh, she carefully folded it and set it back on the display table. "Why did you come to Nadežra?"

Of course Donaia hadn't said anything to her daughter about Renata's hope for reconciliation. Donaia was close enough to overhear; should she press the issue? *No—if Leato has irritated her by approaching me, I'll gain more by playing her side.*

And besides, if half the point of coming to the Gloria was to be seen, the other half was to start making connections with people outside House Traementis. "I was hoping to see the city, of course. Not just the places, but the people. Mother claimed to know everyone in her day, but I have no idea which names to attach to which faces."

Sheltered she might be, but Giuna turned out to be a font of useful gossip, orienting Renata with the kinds of details Ren could never have picked up on her own. Donaia fell back, either satisfied that Renata wasn't trying to suborn her daughter or aware that hovering made her look suspicious. Leato sauntered along with his hands in his pockets, the picture of an indulgent older brother.

It was only when Giuna was pointing out the eldest son of Eret Mettore Indestor that Leato intervened. He took a delicate sculpture of blown blue glass from Giuna's hands and put it back on the table. "She doesn't need to know Mezzan Indestor, and you shouldn't know him, either. Not after what he did to that actor."

"Actor?" Renata said, turning so she could study the man in question without being obvious. "Do share."

Mezzan Indestor looked to be a few years older than Leato, with straw-blond hair and a slate-blue coat unsubtly brocaded with five-pointed stars. That was the emblem of the Cinquerat, where his father held the military Caerulet seat. But such stars were also associated with power and leadership . . . and therefore often worn by people who didn't understand either.

Leato glanced back at Donaia—now occupied with perusing the glassware—then at Giuna. Renata cocked her head, letting a dangling curl brush her bare shoulder, and Leato gave in. "There was a theatrical that premiered a few weeks ago at the Theatre Agnasce— had Her Elegance's stamp of approval and everything." He nodded toward a steel-haired woman and her circle of admirers. Giuna had identified her earlier as Era Sostira Novrus, holder of the Argentet seat in the Cinquerat, overseeing the city's cultural affairs. Among other things, that meant she ran the office that licensed theatrical performances—and now that Leato had drawn the connection, Renata noted Mezzan Indestor glaring at the older woman, face sour like he'd been force-fed an unripened plum.

Leato went on. "She must have wanted a chance to undercut Eret Indestor, because the show wasn't subtle in its mockery. There was a whole monologue about Caerulet encouraging graft in the Vigil. When he heard it, Mezzan jumped onto the stage and challenged the lead actor to a duel."

Renata said, "Perhaps I misunderstand Nadežran etiquette and law, but I thought civilian commoners weren't permitted to carry swords."

"You don't misunderstand," Leato said grimly. "The actor had a stage sword and no real knowledge of how to use it."

"That poor man," Giuna whispered. "Is he…"

Leato shook his head. "Even imbued medicines and a healing numinat weren't enough. He's alive, but they say his face is ruined."

Edging closer to her brother's side—and putting him between her and Mezzan Indestor—Giuna said, "Someone should *do* something."

"Who? What? Mezzan's father runs the Vigil and grants the charters for every mercenary company and private guard in Nadežra. You think Eret Indestor is going to let anything touch his son?"

"Leato, that's enough," Donaia cut in briskly. "You'll give Alta Renata the impression that the only law that rules here is power."

If it weren't for years of practice at forcing smiles at people like Era Traementis, Ren's anger might have caused her to lose character entirely. Power *was* the only law in Nadežra, and the Traementis knew it too well to pretend otherwise. The only saving grace was that all three were clearly united in loathing Mezzan—because that meant Ren didn't have to mouth words of approval just to continue ingratiating herself with them.

"How dreadful," she murmured, trying to achieve the disinterested condemnation of someone unfamiliar with the parties involved. "Is the theatrical still playing? I've half a mind to go see it."

"Sadly, no," Leato said. "They couldn't find another actor willing to take the role, so the backers pulled it to save face."

"Are we talking about *The Thief of the Old Island*? Dreadful production. Mezzan did Nadežra a favor, getting it shut down. I don't understand what Her Elegance was thinking, approving it."

The woman who spoke reminded Renata powerfully of Letilia. Not in appearance—her hair was pale gold instead of honey brown, her face all sharp features in a heart-shaped frame—but she shared the same air of ruthless social dominance, always alert for the scent of a competitor.

Letilia, however, wouldn't have shown nearly so much care to the elderly woman in the wheeled chair beside her. "You agree, don't you, Grandmama?" the young woman asked. "The play was dreadful, you said."

She'd pitched her voice to carry, and still a moment passed before the confusion cleared from the older woman's oddly unlined face. "Ah yes. That thing. Dreadful. Couldn't understand a word of it. Why are you bringing it up?"

"No reason." Smiling, the young woman transferred her attention. "Giuna, dearest! If I'd known you were coming to the Gloria, I would have included you in our party. Grandmama has arranged for coffee and cakes later. Grandmama, surely room can be made to include Alta Giuna and her family?"

It was hard to tell if the old woman didn't hear or was deliberately ignoring her granddaughter in favor of staring down Renata. Despite being in a chair, she managed to convey an impression of looking very much *down*.

Donaia stepped in before things grew more uncomfortable. "Alta Renata, may I present Alta Carinci and her granddaughter Sibiliat, heir of House Acrenix. Altas, this is Renata Viraudax, recently of Seteris."

Renata's smile as she curtsied was as much for Donaia's words as for the people in front of her. *Recently of Seteris*—not a visitor from Seteris. Whether she realized it or not, Donaia was beginning to resign herself to her "niece's" presence in the city.

And meeting the Acrenix women was a social coup. Their family had never held a seat in the Cinquerat, but their head, Eret Ghiscolo Acrenix, was the most influential noble in the city outside that council of five. "I'm delighted," Renata said, quite sincerely. "I understand from my mother that your house is one of the oldest in Nadežra."

"Mother?" Alta Carinci squinted at Renata, as much as a woman could squint when her skin seemed stretched taut over bone. "Ha! You said she couldn't possibly look familiar," she crowed, her bent finger pointing first at Sibiliat, then redirecting toward Renata. "She's the image of Lecilla, except better-mannered and with a nicer voice. No wonder you look sour in the puss, eh?" That last was directed at Donaia, accompanied by a smirk.

Donaia's expression grew even more brittle. "I don't know what you—"

"Clearly, you don't. Letting your poor niece wander alone. What were you thinking, allowing her to talk to that Vargo character?"

"Grandmama!" Sibiliat's expression of horror was a little too delighted to be earnest.

Carinci was clearly the sort of woman who reveled in the freedoms granted by power, wealth, and age. "I'm not saying he isn't pretty to look at, but you can't wash off that Lower Bank dirt, no matter how hard you scrub."

"Your pardon, alta," Renata said, breaking in. "I'm afraid you misunderstand. It's true my mother is Letilia—Lecilla—who was Gianco's sister, but she's no longer in the Traementis family register. So I am not Era Traementis's niece."

She let a touch of regret flavor the words. Carinci scoffed. "Registered or not, unless your mother is here with you—no? Of course she isn't—then Donaia should be looking after you and who you associate with. Gossip leaves dirt on everything around it."

"How fortunate, then, that Renata is joining us for dinner next week," Donaia snapped. "I don't need you, Alta Carinci, to remind me of my duty to my family—even those who aren't in the register."

Renata smothered a triumphant smile. Her flirtation with Vargo, though a misstep, had transformed into useful leverage. Where sweet words failed, public pressure succeeded. "Era Traementis has been very kind to me," she hastened to assure Carinci. "The fault lies with my mother, and with myself. I don't know my way around Nadežra and its people."

"Then let me be your guide." Sibiliat reached for her hands, and Renata controlled the urge to pull back. She'd seen Letilia engage in this kind of fight often enough to recognize it for what it was: claws sheathed in velvet. "We must make sure you have good stories to take back to Seteris."

Want me out of your city, do you? Better and better. Judging by Donaia's behavior, she didn't like the Acrenix women—which meant she *would* like watching Renata threaten Sibiliat's dominance of the social scene.

But Sibiliat was too clever to give Renata her back. As if an idea had just come to her, she made a small, delighted sound. "Leato! A few of us are going on a ramble tonight. You simply must join, and bring your cousin along." Leaning close to Renata—a shift that emphasized her advantage in height—she said, "There's a new card parlour on the Old Island that does pattern readings."

Giuna perked at Sibiliat's suggestion. "I've never had my pattern read!"

Sibiliat replied before Leato or Donaia could, stroking Giuna's sleeve. "Not this time, little bird. It's too rough."

"I'm willing if Alta Renata is," Leato said. "You don't have anything like Vraszenian pattern reading in Seteris, do you?"

"I've never even heard of it. Is it like astrology?"

Carinci's nose wrinkled as if she smelled something foul on the wheel of her chair. "Nothing nearly so sensible. A pack of cards, and some bent old Vraszenian crow claiming the random chance of their arrangement somehow reveals your fate. Utter nonsense. I can't believe you would waste your time with such things, Sibiliat."

"It's for fun, Grandmama. Didn't you do things for fun when you were our age?"

"I wish I got to do things for fun," Giuna grumbled, one finger running over the glass sculpture Leato had made her put down. Her voice was soft enough that Renata suspected nobody was meant to hear.

The crystal decorations, the scarf: It was painfully clear that Giuna craved something pretty for herself, and equally clear that her mother had tied the Traementis purse strings tight. It seemed that in all the years since Letilia ran away, Donaia hadn't changed a bit.

As Giuna reluctantly drew her hand back, Renata plucked the sculpture from the table and selected a green one to match, handing the pieces to the merchant. "Wrap them separately, please." To Giuna she said, "Those *are* lovely, aren't they? The green one is just what the mantel in my parlour needs, and I'm sure you can find a suitable place for the blue one."

Donaia caught the trailing end of her words and pivoted sharply, mouth open to protest. But it was too late; the merchant had placed the blue crystal in a protective case and wrapped that in an elegant fold of fabric, and Renata presented it to a dumbstruck Giuna. Donaia could hardly refuse the gift now—not without breaking her daughter's heart and creating a scene in front of the Acrenix women.

Renata felt a warm glow of triumph as the latter moved on a few minutes later, Carinci making no secret of her need to be seen speaking to other people. She'd attracted attention, made progress against Donaia, and now in place of a forbidding Vigil captain she had Giuna stuck to her side like a grateful burr.

Leato led them through the rest of the Gloria, even after Donaia quit the field, murmuring that she needed to rest her feet and have a warm drink. He introduced Renata to people along the way, then stayed with her as she backtracked to purchase perfume, gloves, a kitten-soft cloak. Tess accepted them all without complaint, though Ren could practically hear her crying, *The budget!*

The budget would survive. Some of these things would be useful in her masquerade, and the rest—like the glass bauble—she intended to pawn. The point was to be seen buying them, so that everyone would know Renata Viraudax had both money and good taste.

When Tess's arms were full, Renata mimed exaggerated exhaustion. "If I'm to be any use at all tonight, I should go home and rest. Where should I be and when?"

"The foot of the Lacewater Bridge in Suncross. Is second earth too early?"

Renata shook her head. Second earth gave her roughly two hours after sunset. Hopefully enough time for Tess to put together a suitable ensemble.

Leato's next instructions put that fear to rest. "Wear a mask, but don't dress too finely; Lacewater isn't the kind of place you want to draw attention to your wealth."

Lacewater. Unease roiled in her gut, like Ondrakja's hand curling languidly around her jaw before digging sharp nails into flesh.

After five years away, Ren was going home.

The Rotunda, Eastbridge: Suilun 4

Grey lost sight of Alta Renata and the Traementis family after they parted ways with the Acrenix. By then he could see the humor in the whole farce. Bad enough having to tolerate Derossi Vargo, when a year ago Grey would have had ample cause to arrest him. But then being caught out by Leato! In the space of a single minute, Grey had blown his cover to Renata *and* thrown away an opportunity to see his friend. Those had been too scarce, these past months.

He shifted his weight to relieve the ache in his back from standing too long on hard marble and tried not to track the passage of the sun across the ribs of the dome, waiting for this interminable day to end. He'd had to trade several favors to get his unit assigned to the Rotunda; soft duties like this were much in demand. But Donaia had assured Grey that if the daughter was like the mother, Alta Renata would be at the Autumn Gloria.

Perhaps she did resemble her mother in that respect, but Renata Viraudax hadn't been what he'd expected. Beautiful and elegant, yes—but she was also shrewder than she let on, plucking the strings of the Gloria like an expert harpist.

And he unnerved her. Not as a man or as a Vraszenian; it was the unease of someone being watched by a hawk. She'd hidden it well, even tried to divert him by flirting... but he'd once hidden that same unease, back when he and Kolya first arrived in Nadežra.

Were Donaia's suspicions correct? Or was something else going on?

The approach of Breccone Indestris pulled Grey from his musings. "Captain," the altan said, his voice round and polished with self-importance. "I've noticed Era Novrus's wife acting strangely. Someone suggested she may have taken aža before coming here. Please see that she's quietly escorted away before she causes an embarrassment. I'd hate for someone to have to bring her in for causing a public disturbance."

Djek. Could this day get any worse? Breccone had been born into House Simendis, but he'd married into Indestor. Clearly, he was doing his part to further Indestor's ongoing feud with Novrus, their rivals in the Cinquerat. Petty interference at the Gloria might be less destructive than burning each other's warehouses in Dockwall, but at least Grey could do something useful about the latter; here he had no way to avoid being used as a tool against House Novrus. "Yes, Altan Breccone. At once."

Breccone left without waiting to see his orders carried out. Grey nodded at four of his lieutenants who'd been idling nearby—delta gentry sons and daughters who might have a chance of convincing the wife of a Cinquerat seat to leave quietly.

When he'd finished dispatching them, he saw Era Traementis beckoning to him from the shelter of a pillar.

She obviously didn't want to be seen talking to him. Grey drifted over and took up his watchful stance again, close enough to speak quietly and be heard. "My apologies, era. I should have taken steps to avoid Leato."

Her sigh was heavy enough to carry over the Rotunda's noise. "No, I should have kept a better rein on him. He's missed you lately."

There was nothing Grey could say to that, and she saved him from needing to. "Have you learned anything about the Viraudax girl?"

"The house she's renting belongs to Vargo. I don't think they're colluding, though; she was surprised to meet him. He pretended the same, but he's much too well-informed not to recognize her as one of his tenants. I'm not sure why he feigned ignorance."

In his peripheral vision, he saw Donaia's lip curl. "Because he's too crooked to see straight. But Vargo isn't connected to—"

She stopped short of finishing the sentence. *To Indestor.* Grey left that part unspoken as well. "She can afford to rent from him, so clearly she isn't hurting for money."

"And yet she can't seem to afford enough fabric for sleeves."

Across the Rotunda, he watched as Renata pointed at something on a distant table, that drape of fabric curving gracefully beneath her bare arm. She was taking every opportunity to draw attention to her daring style—to great effect. "I imagine Vargo vetted her finances thoroughly before renting the house to her, but I can still check with the usual banking families and see where her money is coming from. In the meanwhile, I thought I might hire a few street children to watch the house. Keep an eye on where she goes, and who comes to visit her."

"After today? Half of Nadežra will."

"Yes, but there's still value in knowing who she sees, and who she turns away." He watched as Renata handed another package to her dowdy servant. With the coloring and accent of Ganllech making the girl nearly as foreign as Renata, she shouldn't have been so unremarkable. It was as though her dull uniform was a deliberate blind to turn focus toward her stylish mistress.

Well, Grey had noticed her. "I'll also have someone look into the maid and ask around Little Alwydd for any relations she might have." Ranieri would suit the task. He was Lower Bank born, which would raise fewer questions if he went nosing about. And it would make use of those looks of his, which were usually more hindrance than help. "She'll know things about her mistress that nobody else will."

Donaia sniffed. "If she's half as good as Colbrin, you'll get more from a stone."

"There are few servants in this world as good as Colbrin. And few women who can inspire loyalty like you."

He tipped his head at her startled look. "You . . . stop flattering me, you rapscallion," she sputtered, but a flush warmed her cheeks, and he'd managed to chase the frown away.

"Apologies for my presumption, era." A squabbling flock of nobles and hawks was approaching the gate. At their center was a dazed-looking Benvanna Novri and her furious wife. "And apologies for having to cut this conversation short. Duty calls."

Many duties. Between his assigned work for the Vigil, Donaia's commission, the problem of the missing children . . .

Grey sighed. It was going to be a long night.

The Hidden Eye

Suncross and Lacewater, Old Island: Suilun 4

Even at the Gloria, immersed in a world that had never been hers, little reminders of the past kept knocking Ren's mask askew. Now, disembarking from her sedan chair in the post-twilight bustle of Suncross, she didn't feel like Renata; she didn't even feel like an actress playing that role. She felt like a puppeteer, moving Renata around on long sticks, while behind the curtain hid Ren of the Fingers.

How often had she begged or tagged likely marks in this plaza? Or before that, coming here with one hand tangled in the drape of her mother's panel sash. The man who used to sell her sesame buns was gone—he lost a hand when she was eleven, supposedly for thieving, and died of infection afterward—and the flower sellers with the river-dark roses of Ažerais wouldn't be back until spring, but Ren still remembered Suncross as one of her favorite parts of the city.

Mama. What would you think of my life now?

Ren's jaw tightened. If she let thoughts like that start surfacing, she would never make it through the night.

She paid the chair bearers and scanned the plaza. Even after sunset, it was crowded with people selling broadside newssheets, secondhand clothing, toasted foxnuts, and more. Four competing ostrettas spilled customers onto the flagstones, drinking and eating in the fall-chilled air. A girl with a branched stick dangling knotted cords tried to push one into Renata's hands: a good-luck charm in the knot named for the roses of Ažerais. Renata waved it away and fought the urge to rise up on her toes, as if another few inches of height would make a difference. Sibiliat seemed the type to invite her to a rough part of town and then not show up.

But Leato had told her to come here. And while his family might have a reputation for obliterating their enemies, so far as he knew, she hadn't done anything to put herself among them.

Unless they hate Letilia that much.

Instinct sent Ren eeling to one side as a hand reached for her skirt. But the child it belonged to was a beggar, not a pickpocket, and not even the sort of pity-rustler who played up their injuries and malnutrition for sympathy. His appearance was too off-putting for that, with sunken eyes and hollow cheeks that wouldn't have looked out of place on a corpse.

"Help me," he said in a bloodless whisper, staring at Ren without blinking. "I can't sleep anymore."

For an instant she was a child again, begging for comfort after a nightmare. *Mama, I can't sleep.*

Hush, Renyi. It's all right. I will lay a thread around your bed to keep the zlyzen from you.

"Alta Renata!"

Ren recoiled from the boy. With a wrench that was almost physical, she dragged herself back into character and turned to face Sibiliat.

The sculpted paper mask Sibiliat wore clearly marked her as a noble out slumming, but she showed good sense, choosing a sedate aubergine half piece pierced with eight-pointed cutouts. Her voice was all bright edges as she said, "What a lovely mask. Is that the one Master Vargo gave you?"

"Alta Sibiliat," she said, forcing lightness into her words. "I'm so glad you like it. I didn't realize we would be such a large group tonight. But where's Altan Leato?" She couldn't see his golden head among the people clustered around Sibiliat.

"Traementis isn't here yet?" asked a slender man in shades of cream and coffee and a plain coppery domino. He draped himself languidly over Sibiliat, resting a pointed chin on her shoulder and making no effort to disguise his slow perusal of Renata. "So this is her. You didn't mention she was so pretty."

Sibiliat dropped her shoulder, leaving him to stumble. "Yes, I did. You just never listen when other people talk."

"Because other people are boring." He stepped in front of Sibiliat and bowed over Renata's hand. He'd painted his eyelids the same copper as his mask, gleaming bright in the shadows. "Bondiro Coscanum. That one's my sister Marvisal. Over there, Parma Extaquium and Egliadas Fintenus."

Noble sons and daughters all. None of their kin held seats in the Cinquerat, but the Acrenix family had a wide array of alliances, and Alta Faella Coscanum—the great-aunt of Bondiro and Marvisal, if Renata remembered correctly—ruled polite society with an iron fist. Befriending them would be *very* useful.

"Don't bother trying to get between Parma and Egliadas," Bondiro added, as Renata cast a smile of greeting at the whole group. "I've been failing at it since spring."

Marvisal was as slender as her brother, and almost as tall. She stood like a willow in a surcoat of gauzy green too thin for the night's chill, bending to whisper something to the short and round Parma. Waving Marvisal off, Parma stuck her tongue out at Bondiro. "That's because you're as lazy in bed as you are out of it, Coscanum."

"I like to take my time."

"Speaking of, are we waiting for Leato?" asked Marvisal, scanning the plaza.

"Can we not?" Bondiro groaned. "He makes *me* look punctual."

Sibiliat took Renata's arm. "He can meet us at the Talon and Trick. I'm *certain* he knows where it is."

Her dry comment caused the rest of the crew to snicker. Renata wondered how Leato got away with such a life, when his mother was so tightfisted that his sister couldn't have any luxuries at all. Maternal favoritism? Quite likely; Letilia always said the impending birth of Leato was what tipped Donaia from insufferable to unbearable.

"You wouldn't leave *me* behind, would you?" The voice was deeper than Leato's. And although Renata hadn't heard him speak over the noise of the Gloria, she recognized the straw-colored hair and the five-pointed stars, now decorating his mask as well as his coat.

"Mezzan!" Sibiliat released Renata to kiss both of his cheeks. "We would never go without you. We need you to keep us safe." One hand caressed the hilt of his sword as she stepped back.

Half of being a good con artist was the ability to read other people. Ren could have been the world's worst sharper and still read the meaning in how Marvisal stepped up to Mezzan's side, slipping her arm around his waist. "Alta Renata, let me introduce my betrothed, Mezzan Indestor."

The man who had maimed an actor over an insult in a play. Renata smiled at him and curtsied without any attempt to flirt. It should be easy to get Marvisal on her side; all she had to do was swallow her bile around Mezzan, and not behave as if she could have any man or woman she wanted with a snap of her fingers. "I'm glad for the protection, altan. This looks more dangerous than I expected."

"There's nothing to fear," Bondiro said. All the men wore swords, and Sibiliat as well; Marvisal and Parma had knives. "We won't go to any of the truly bad areas—they smell far too foul."

"And if anyone gives us trouble," said Egliadas, thumping his fist against Mezzan's shoulder, "we'll give them more than they can handle in return."

While the Vigil looked politely the other way. "Oh, that's a relief," Renata said.

"Shall we begin?" Sibiliat led them across the Lacewater Bridge without waiting for an answer.

The district was named for its countless tiny canals, too small even for splinter-boats to navigate; they served only to drain the marshy ground at the northern end of the Old Island, where the rocky heights of the Point descended to something scarcely higher than the flat mud of the delta. On the Upper Bank, numinata helped keep the ground stable, but not here; although the original land had long since been built up into the stone foundations of islets, their slow sinking made the houses lean drunkenly toward one another until they almost kissed.

Ren breathed more easily when Sibiliat angled right at the other end of the bridge. The streets she'd known best, both before her mother's death and after, were on the western side of Lacewater. Walking those as Renata might have been one challenge too many.

Still, every alley and bridge held as many memories as stray cats. On that stoop she'd found a drunk with three forri hidden inside his shoe; on that walkway, she'd gotten into an argument with Simlin and been pushed into the filthy water. The winding lane of the Uča Idvo had been her favorite hunting ground for cuffs just like the ones she traveled with now, so rich they didn't bother sewing their money into interior pockets no thief could easily reach.

The close confines meant Sibiliat's flock shifted like starlings in flight, changing partners to follow the banter. Renata doubted it was an accident that every single one of the nobles found occasion to walk alongside her and comment on her mask—and, by implication, the man she'd gotten it from. Their approach was more genteel than the river rats she'd known, but the behavior was the same: testing whether she was fit to run with their crew.

She deflected the comments with gentle flattery and self-deprecation, and meanwhile noticed they could have crossed the entirety of Lacewater in the time they'd been walking. Their path was taking them on a large, looping circuit around the edges of Lifost Square, where many businesses catered to slumming cuffs. Sibiliat was trying to get Renata lost.

Ren's lips curved in a secret smile. Even now, she could probably navigate Lacewater blind.

"You've found something here to amuse you?" Bondiro drawled from his position at her side. "Do share. Your presence is the only reason I'm not regretting accepting Sibiliat's invitation. But it was this or stay home and pare my toenails."

Renata laughed. "I'm glad I'm an improvement over toenails."

Before Bondiro could salvage the inadvertent insult, a Vraszenian man brushed past Sibiliat in the tight quarters of the street. Ren thought she was the only one who caught the swift dip of his hand, but Sibiliat yelped. "That man! He took my purse!"

In an eyeblink, the mood changed. Egliadas and Mezzan stalked after the Vraszenian, but he was no fool; the instant he saw them coming, he bolted, the two Liganti men instantly giving chase.

"Now we're running?" Bondiro whined, breaking into a jog. "Next time, I'll choose toenails!"

The Vraszenian hadn't made it very far, just to the tiny Dlimas Bridge. He was on the ground as the rest of the group caught up, and Mezzan had Sibiliat's purse in hand, but Egliadas's boot still slammed into the man's ribs.

"Tyrant's syphilitic nutsack. Not again," Parma grumbled, limping up alongside Renata and Bondiro. "Egliadas, let him go. The Vigil will take care of it."

"Dealing with this filth would be a waste of Aerie time and resources," Egliadas spat over his shoulder.

Mezzan bent to grab the Vraszenian. "We'll see if gnats can swim. Get his arms—"

His sentence ended in a flutter of black fabric. Mezzan went sprawling over the flagstones. Egliadas leapt back and snatched out his sword, but the dark figure slammed a hand into his wrist and Egliadas howled, dropping the blade. Parma said, "Bondiro, don't—" But it was too late; spitting a reluctant curse, Bondiro drew his own sword and advanced.

Ren stood, frozen and staring, at the whirling black coat, the boots that scuffed and stamped against the flagstones, the gloved hands dealing casual mayhem.

The hood that hid his face.

The Rook!

The Vraszenian had seized the opportunity to escape. Egliadas was scooting away on his ass, cradling a broken wrist. Bondiro took a knee to the gut and doubled over, retching for breath. Mezzan had his back to the bridge wall, his sword too far for him to retrieve it without exposing himself to the Rook. The shadows of Mezzan's mask hid his eyes, but the tight set of his jaw and the turn of his head said he was looking for allies. Unfortunately for him, Sibiliat showed no inclination to wade in, and Parma and Marvisal were keeping well back.

Leaving Ren.

Who could scarcely breathe for delight. A menace to the nobility, a wanted man to the hawks, a troublemaker to many law-abiding citizens...but to the people of the streets, the Rook was a hero. She'd never thought she would see him in the flesh.

"Mezzan Indestor." The Rook faced him with all the lazy assurance of a predator. "How convenient that we've met like this. I've come to repay a debt." His voice lowered to a mocking purr. "On behalf of Ivič Pilatsin."

Mezzan's scowl twisted into confusion. "Who?"

The Rook hooked his toe under Egliadas's fallen sword and kicked it up into his hand, examining the steel. With a disappointed sigh, he tossed it over the parapet into the canal. "The actor whose life and livelihood you ruined."

Bondiro's sword met with the same fate as Egliadas's. "Let's see how you fare when the field is leveled."

Sibiliat cursed in muffled disgust. Ren's hands curled. She wanted nothing more than to watch the Rook thrash Mezzan...but Renata Viraudax wouldn't cheer an outlaw on.

You wanted to give them something to talk about besides your flirtation with Vargo.

Before she could think the better of it, Renata stepped forward. Her shoe came down on the blade of Mezzan's sword just as the Rook crouched to pick it up.

"As I understand it, Altan Mezzan gave the actor a chance to defend himself in an honorable duel," she said. "Surely you can do no less."

The Rook straightened slowly. Even close enough to touch, she could make out almost nothing through the darkness of his hood. The deeper shadows of his eyes, the line of his jaw; like the stars, she saw more when she didn't look directly. Then a glimmer of a smile came into view.

In two hundred years, no one had unmasked Nadežra's outlaw. Seeing him now, Ren was certain the hood was imbued to hide his face. The Rook could have been anyone: old or young, Liganti or Vraszenian or Nadežran. His voice sounded masculine, but who knew where the magic ended?

Though she couldn't see his eyes, she felt him assessing her, as surely as she was assessing him.

The Rook said, "I could do less... or a good deal more." Their audience was growing as people crowded to watch the scene, but his murmur was for her alone. Then it lifted up with mockery, for everyone to hear. "But if I'm to play at noble games, shouldn't I get a noble's reward for my trouble?"

She bent to pick up the sword, letting it dangle from her gloved fingers. "What sort of reward could a man like you want?" It took every ounce of deceit she possessed to make the question sound dismissive. *What Mask have I offended, meeting the Rook as a noblewoman?*

"A man like me wants for little." The hood dipped to the sword in her hand, then rose once more. "But as they're such a treasure... I'll take the alta's gloves."

Her fingers tightened on the sword's hilt as the onlookers gasped. Most of those watching were common Nadežrans who cared little for Liganti ways; a few of them laughed. The nobles of Sibiliat's party didn't. People of quality were not properly dressed in public without their gloves. By their lights, the Rook might as well have demanded she strip.

"A fair duel," Renata said, wrapping her hand carefully around the blade so she could offer the sword hilt-first. "And *if* you win— then a single glove."

Her tone implied doubt. Inwardly she prayed, *I hope you're as good as the stories say.*

"Agreed." The Rook took the hilt, sliding the flat of the blade along her palm like he meant to cut his prize away early. "I trust you'll remind me of the rules if I stray. You nobles make simple things so complicated."

Flipping the blade, he tossed it to Mezzan and drew his own.

Mezzan caught it, his previous swagger returning. "I'm more than able to school muck-fucking scum like you. Don't worry, Alta Renata. I'll hand you his hood when I cut it off."

The Rook murmured, "She can make gloves out of it. Uniat." His blade swept down and up to a high stance as he spoke the opening challenge. Mezzan's grin slipped. The Rook might claim ignorance of noble rules, but he knew the proper terms and forms for dueling.

"Tuat," Mezzan spat in answer to the Rook's challenge, and barely finished cutting his own salute before he attacked.

Ren hastily retreated. Within two heartbeats she knew she hadn't gambled foolishly: The Rook dropped immediately from the straight-armed Liganti stance into the lower Vraszenian one and met Mezzan's charge without flinching, parrying the nobleman's thrusts with a few quick angles of his wrist. And he respected the rules of the game, passing up an opportunity to stomp on the arch of Mezzan's foot, the way Ren would have done in his place.

But she was a former river rat, and he was the Rook. He could be brutal when necessary—witness Egliadas's broken wrist—but it was his flair that won him the hearts of the common folk. He danced out of the path of Mezzan's thrusts with a little lace step, and when Mezzan made the mistake of rushing him, the Rook stepped in to meet it, locking them body-to-body in a brief, circling waltz. Only a swift tilt of his head prevented Mezzan's spit from flying into his hood, and he let go just in time to avoid an elbow to the jaw.

The hood turned toward Ren. "Remind me, alta—are elbows permitted?"

"They are not," she said, suppressing a laugh.

"I thought not." The tip of his blade rapped Mezzan's arm hard, right where the nerve ran between skin and bone. "Mind your manners, boy."

The blow and the words were both calculated to enrage. But the increasing wildness of Mezzan's attacks only left him vulnerable. Almost too fast for Ren to follow, the tip of the Rook's sword snaked through the looping guard of Mezzan's rapier and wrenched it from his hand. Metal grated as the hilt slid down the Rook's blade; he twirled the trapped weapon in a full circle like a child with a toy, then tilted his hand so Mezzan's sword flew clear.

It flashed through the open air and sank without a trace in the waters of the canal.

"I believe that's Ninat," the Rook said to Mezzan, who was gaping after his blade. "Do you submit?"

"I do not. Sibiliat, your sword!" Mezzan snarled, thrusting one hand out.

"But I thought being disarmed was a clear loss under the rules." The Rook stepped back, placing himself by the wall of the bridge. "Alta, you're the closest we have to an arbiter. Will you call Ninat?"

She pulled herself back into character, relaxing from the impassive posture she'd held during the duel. "Assuming the rules are like those of Seteris, then yes, to be disarmed is to be defeated. Ninat."

Sibiliat hadn't moved to help Mezzan. He took a step toward the Rook, hands curled into fists. "That rapier was imbued by the swordsmith Vicadrius herself. There isn't another like it in Nadežra!"

The Rook sheathed his blade. "Then by all means, go after it."

Renata saw the move coming. So did the Rook; she suspected he'd invited it. When Mezzan charged, the Rook faded out of the way and applied boot to ass. The kick provided the extra momentum needed to send Mezzan flying over the rail and into the canal.

"Though I believe it landed on the other side of the bridge. You might want to check there," the Rook called down over the laughter and cheers from the onlookers. He hopped onto the rail and bowed.

Then he turned to Renata. "Now we see whether you, like our local nobility, will break the rules when it suits you. I believe you owe me a glove."

The cheers around them turned to whistles and hoots. Bondiro had recovered enough to shelter Renata from the crowd's view with his height. "I'll give up my glove, alta," he said, reaching to strip it off. "You shouldn't be harassed by this kinless bastard."

She stopped him with a crisp shake of her head. "I gave my word. I shall keep it."

Stepping around Bondiro, she tugged on the fingertips of her left glove with clear, deliberate movements. Not flirtatious; cold. She needed the other nobles to sympathize with her, to see her as sharing in Mezzan's troubles rather than enjoying his humiliation. Her glove slipped free, and she folded it into a small, neat package. *Tess will kill me.* Gloves were a pain to sew.

Renata held the folded glove up in her bare hand, for all the crowd to see. "Since you enjoy putting things into canals so much," she said—and threw.

Perhaps he'd been expecting that, too. Or perhaps he was the Rook, and a two-hundred-year legacy of standing against the powers that ruled Nadežra was more than a match for a bit of pettiness. His hand shot out and caught the glove as neatly as if Renata meant for him to do it. Then he flipped it open and brought it to his lips as though it still covered her hand, breathing deeply.

"A shame to ruin a fine scent with canal water, don't you think?" He tucked the glove into his coat and looked down to the canal, where Mezzan was splashing and sputtering. "Indestor. Next time you think to beat anyone, remember this night—and know that any injury you give to someone, the Rook will repay in kind."

Three strides along the rail gave him enough momentum to catch the eaves of a roof and swing himself atop it. A heartbeat later, he was gone.

Lacewater and Suncross, Old Island: Suilun 4

The crowd had enough sense to scatter before the nobles could take note of who had been cheering Mezzan's downfall. Fishing him out of the canal cost Bondiro the cleanliness of his cream-colored breeches; the river was at low ebb, and the surface of the water some distance down from street level, leaving the canal walls slick with slime.

Renata sacrificed her hair ribbon to bind up Egliadas's broken wrist, while Parma held him steady and murmured dark things about what she would do to that hooded leech. "We have to report this to the Vigil," Marvisal insisted as Mezzan emerged from the filthy water, her voice rising toward hysteria.

Sibiliat rolled her eyes. "And after centuries of failing to catch the Rook, tonight they'll finally succeed? Mezzan has a better chance of retrieving his sword."

But Marvisal insisted on dragging them all in search of a hawk. Unlike the Upper Bank, the Island had no sentry boxes; they had to thread their way through the streets, with Marvisal declaring she would walk all the way to the Aerie if she had to.

Which might have been necessary if a familiar figure hadn't slipped out of a narrow alley just before they reached the Lacewater Bridge.

Renata was the only one who'd seen him. Leato cast a swift glance about as he emerged, sliding a simple white mask over his face. Orienting himself, he strode in the direction of Lifost Square—then stopped short at the sight of their group.

He started up again a moment later, calling out, "Leaving so soon? I can't be *that* late—" Then he recoiled from the stench coming off Mezzan. "Pfaugh! What happened—are you so drunk already you fell in a canal?"

Mezzan snarled, but Bondiro kept him from lunging at Leato. "We're going to the Aerie," Marvisal said shrilly. "We have a grave crime to report. Two!"

"Three. There's still that dirty gnat who assaulted Sibiliat," Egliadas said. "And we can't find a bloody hawk anywhere."

Leato's gold-lined eyes had gone wide behind the mask. "I saw Captain Serrado in Suncross just now. And if he's not there anymore, it isn't much farther to the Aerie. Come on."

Those last words were a formality; Mezzan was already stalking across the Lacewater Bridge. Instead of leading the way, Leato hung back to walk at Renata's side. "If I'd known Mezzan was invited, I'd have told you not to come. I'm sorry my tardiness left you to deal with him on your own."

"I would have met him sooner or later," Renata murmured.

The party straggled to a halt on the far side of the bridge, looking around as if expecting Captain Serrado to appear like a summoned servant. Leato waved for them to follow him, heading toward the Duskgate—only to pull up short as they passed the mouth of a narrow alley, so abruptly that Renata almost collided with him.

Looking past Leato's shoulder, she saw Captain Serrado kneeling on the paving stones, holding what seemed at first to be a lump of rags. But when he gently lowered the lump to the cobbles, a thin, grubby hand flopped free and struck hard enough to make her wince.

The child Serrado knelt over made no sound. The hand lay limp and still on the stone until he folded it back under the rags.

Without looking, Leato shot one arm out and stopped Mezzan's forward charge. Ignoring the other man's scowl, he advanced a few steps and called out softly, "Grey?"

Serrado stood slowly. Gone was the finery of the Gloria; he wore the loose broadcloth and dusty breeches of a common constable. Renata counted his breaths—one, two, three—before he turned his head just enough to answer Leato. "What."

"Is that boy..."

"I should have found him sooner."

The buoyant delight from having watched the Rook thrash Mezzan drained away like the tide as she caught sight of the dead child's face, leaving Ren feeling cold and dirty. "That boy," she whispered, her lips gone numb. "I—I saw him in Suncross Plaza earlier. He said he couldn't sleep."

"You spoke with him?" Whether he intended it or not, she heard recrimination under Serrado's words. *You left him.*

The last of Mezzan's patience evaporated, and he shoved his way in front of Leato. "You. Man. Fetch your captain."

Serrado's eyes were colder than a winter canal. With a slow hand that verged on insolence, he lifted his collar so his rank pin caught the light. "I am a captain."

Fortunately, the others chose that moment to intervene. The story poured out from several mouths at once, the Vraszenian man and the Rook and what happened to Mezzan and his sword.

Renata should have tried to insert herself, to make them think of her as one of them, but no words would come. She drifted back a half step, barely hearing what they said, until suddenly Leato was there, lifting her arm. She wore full sleeves now—the night was too chilly and the area too rough for stunts like the Gloria dress—and he held her by the forearm, courteously avoiding the bare skin of her hand. "That kinless bastard. Here, take mine." He pulled off his left glove and offered it to her.

She accepted, sliding her hand into the warmth of the leather. It was a little too large, but not so much that it looked absurd, and the gesture was comforting. "Thank you."

"Trust me, the Rook will regret his choices tonight," Serrado promised Mezzan. The icy steel of his words surprised Renata: noble or not, she didn't think Mezzan's humiliation would prompt such a fierce response.

"And the Vraszenian?" Mezzan demanded.

"I'll put Ludoghi Kaineto on it."

Mezzan nodded sharply. "A delta son—good. He'll take care of it properly."

Not a flicker of offense crossed Serrado's expression. "If we're able to find the sword, we'll have it delivered to Isla Indestor immediately."

"No. Have it delivered to Isla Coscanum. And leave it out of your reports. If my father hears of the loss, I'll have you stripped of your—"

Mezzan sneezed three times in quick succession, and Serrado's lips tightened, holding back what Renata suspected would have been a stony little smile.

"Understood. I won't keep you in the cold any longer, altan."

Serrado retreated with a bow, but beckoned Renata to draw a few paces apart. "Alta. Is there anything else you can tell me about your encounter with the child?"

"Grey!" Leato stepped close as if to shelter her from Serrado's question. "Must you do this now?"

"It's all right," Renata said. "I'm afraid I don't know anything useful, Captain. He tugged on my skirt and said he couldn't sleep—that's all." And he'd asked her to help him. But what could she have done?

"Couldn't sleep." Serrado's gaze drifted off into the middle distance, until a shuffling from the doorway snagged his attention back to the street. Two beggars were pulling at the rags the boy wore.

"Step away," he snapped at them. Then he nodded a curt apology to Leato and Renata. "I have to deal with this. Commander Cercel should know I found one of them—even if I was too late." Dismissing them, he stalked over to deal with the beggars and the body.

"I think we'd best leave as well," Leato said quietly, offering Renata his arm. Then he made a rueful face. "Will you think me entirely heartless if I suggest that you come with me to the Talon and Trick instead of returning home? Better to bed down with happy memories instead of upsetting ones, yes?"

She shivered. Happy memories wouldn't hold off the zlyzen, or so said the fire tales she heard as a child. If you couldn't sleep, it was because the zlyzen had been feeding on your dreams, good and bad.

The boy was just ill, she told herself. She knew as well as anyone that sickness and death stalked the streets all the time, without need of bogeymen.

She glanced over her shoulder. Sibiliat and the others were taking no notice of them; with Mezzan's immediate outrage pacified, he wanted nothing more than a bath, and Parma and Bondiro were already walking away with Egliadas, presumably to get his wrist treated.

Following her gaze, Leato said, "Don't worry about them."

It was the Traementis she needed to ingratiate herself with.

Everyone else was secondary. Renata mustered a smile for Leato and said, "Lead on."

Lacewater, Old Island: Suilun 4

The Talon and Trick wasn't a true gambling den of the Old Island. Though it stood in what had once been an elegant townhouse facing onto Lifost Square, the distressed floorboards didn't creak or squelch from water rot. The jasmine incense wasn't there to mask the smell of mold and vomit. Swags of draperies and lace partitioned the room, gaudy in pattern and color, but free from dust and mites.

Ren knew this kind of establishment well—deliberately made just seedy enough to give slumming cuffs a thrill, without any real danger. The clientele matched the decor: paper masks and gloved hands, upper-class accents sliding into common Nadežran.

"I hope Grey didn't offend you," Leato said, handing her a glass of yellow Vraszenian wine. The glass was cheap but clean, and when Renata took a small sip, she found the vintage palatable instead of aged into vinegar. "He takes everything much too seriously."

"The two of you seem to be friends," Renata said. "Isn't that... unusual?" Noble and hawk, Liganti and Vraszenian.

Leato laughed. "Very. His brother, Kolya, was a carpenter who used to work for us. But Grey and I became friends when Ryvček took us both on as students."

She kept her expression blandly curious. "Ryvček?"

"Oksana Ryvček. She's a swordswoman." Leato glanced away, leaving Renata to wonder why he might downplay the skill of Nadežra's most famous professional duelist. Most people thought imbuing only worked on physical objects, but that didn't stop the rumors that Ryvček could imbue her swordplay with supernatural speed and precision. "She's picky about who she teaches—says she doesn't have time for delta brats itching for a fight. And Grey had it hard because... well. He's Vraszenian. Kolya asked me to look after him, and... I don't know. We became friends."

He stared into his wineglass, running his ungloved finger around the rim until it sang. "Friends aren't enough, though, when you lose your family."

She'd assumed at the Gloria that Serrado was simply the Traementis family's pet hawk, but this sounded a good deal more personal. "His brother died?" she asked gently.

"A few months ago. In a warehouse fire." Unshed tears spiked Leato's lashes, glittering like diamonds in the shadows of his mask. His glance flickered over her mismatched gloves. "The Rook killed him."

She swallowed the answer that wanted to burst from her throat: *The Rook doesn't kill.*

She'd been out of Nadežra for five years, and the Rook had been around for much longer than one lifetime. Everyone assumed the role was handed from one person to the next, so who was to say the current Rook was the same one from her childhood? Was he someone who respected that limit? Or it could have been an accident. Either way— "Ah," she said. "That explains Captain Serrado's anger tonight. I expected any member of the Vigil would dislike such an outlaw... but it seemed rather more than that. I take it the fire was no accident?"

"The Rook does things like that—burns warehouses—to strike at the people who own them. Kolya... he was there the night it happened. So was the owner. Everyone assumes the owner was the Rook's target, but they both died. Grey's been hunting the Rook ever since."

Leato's tone was unexpectedly grim. Ren made a swift calculation—what Renata had seen; what she could plausibly guess at—and said, "I would expect you to cheer him on. From what the others said tonight, I gather this Rook fellow is a menace, one who should have been taken care of a long time ago."

"That's not the problem." Leato lifted the glass, hesitated, and set it down again. "The problem is what it will do to Grey. My grandfather—yours too, I suppose—he used to say, revenge will make you whole. The way Grey's been behaving... I'm afraid it will break him."

It didn't break me, she wanted to say. But that wasn't entirely true. Coming back to Lacewater made that all too clear.

Before she could think of a Renata way to pry further into Leato's concerns, he sighed and knocked back the rest of his wine. "I'm not in the mood for games yet. Are you interested in having your pattern read?"

She'd hoped he'd forgotten that part. The plan for this evening had always been risky; if the patterner had the true gift, Ren didn't want the woman's cards anywhere near her. But very few had the true gift, and she'd judged it worth the risk. Now she'd have to follow through.

She tucked her hand with its borrowed glove through the offered crook of Leato's arm, smiling as if she had nothing to fear. "It sounds fascinating."

"Most Liganti would tell you the future is only seen in the stars, not a stack of painted cards." He led her between the tables to a back alcove warded off from the rest of the room. "But Nadežra isn't Seste Ligante or Seteris. There's magic here that northerners don't understand."

Leato's eagerness sounded like more than a desire for distraction. He wasn't behaving like a man who'd come here to enjoy himself, or even to forget his cares; the patterner was his real goal.

Ren's step slowed when they approached a partition strung with thick wool threads. She recognized the shapes knotted into them; her mother's shop had a divider just like it. Ren would sit and pluck at them for hours while her mother worked, pretending to be a heroine from the stories—Tsvetsa the Weaver or Pračeny the Traveling Player. Everything else in the Talon and Trick might be false, but the szorsa reading in the back was real.

Hopefully not *too* real. "If it truly is strange magic, I volunteer you to go first," Renata said as Leato gestured her around the partition. "If your luck is good, then perhaps I'll try."

"Each person's luck is their own, alta." The Vraszenian woman at the table was of middling years, her black curls shot through with white and twisted into complicated braids. She passed a deck from hand to hand, shuffling smoothly without glancing down. Instead, her unblinking eyes studied Leato and Renata. "A szorsa neither gives nor takes it. We reveal the truth only."

It clearly wasn't the first time Leato had done this, because he knew not to hand payment to the patterner. Instead he went to the shrine at the side of the room, where there was an age-darkened statue of Ir Entrelke Nedje, the two-faced Vraszenian deity of luck. Removing his mask, he placed a decira in the shrine's central bowl. "May I see the Face and not the Mask."

Then he sat down in front of the szorsa. She began dealing, three lines of three cards each, the first closest to her, the last in front of Leato. Turning over the bottom row, she said, "This is your past, the good and the ill of it, and that which is neither."

Ren stood behind Leato, grateful for the prismatium mask concealing her expression. How many times had she heard her mother say those words?

The three cards thus revealed were The Face of Weaving, The Laughing Crow, and A Brother Lost. The szorsa smiled at Leato, touching the first one. "From a good family you come—a strong family, strong as the River Dežera, with connections throughout Nadežra. But no strength is without its weakness. Vulnerability. Someone has lied to you or your people." She tapped The Laughing Crow, then A Brother Lost. "This lie haunts you still, a worm at the heart of the peach. Until it is uncovered, it will continue to eat away."

On second thought, perhaps letting her skepticism show would be perfectly in character for Renata. The Laughing Crow veiled didn't indicate lies; that was the province of The Mask of Mirrors. It meant failures of communication: either people not talking, or someone not keeping their mouth shut when they should.

"Now I see my mistake," Leato said, nodding with exaggerated gravity. He broke to grin up at Renata. "You'll learn terrible things about our family and not want anything more to do with us."

"You forget who my mother is," Renata said dryly. "I sincerely doubt your registered kin are any worse than that." From what she could tell, Letilia and Donaia had deserved each other.

Leato gestured for the szorsa to continue. "This is your present," she said, "the good and the ill of it, and that which is neither."

Orin and Orasz, The Welcoming Bowl, and Sword in Hand. Ren kept her breathing steady, but her weight shifted, instinct preparing her to run if necessary. She could never interpret a pattern as clearly when someone else had laid it, but there was no mistaking those first two cards, the good and the ill of Leato's present.

They both indicated herself.

Orin and Orasz—the Vraszenian names for the twin moons, but here that duality meant two-faced behavior. The Welcoming Bowl meant a new arrival. Both described her...and the fact that Orin and Orasz was revealed, showing its good face, only partially made up for The Welcoming Bowl. That card, veiled, meant the new arrival brought danger.

Ren offered up a silent prayer of thanks to Ir Entrelke Nedje that this szorsa clearly lacked the gift. Instead she had only the mundane talent of any successful patterner: the ability to read the client in front of her and tell him pleasing things.

"Hospitality," the woman said, indicating The Welcoming Bowl. "To withhold it can be dangerous. Sword in Hand tells me the time has come for you deciding—will you take up another's cause? Will you stand, even if it brings you into conflict? From Orin and Orasz we know this will bring both reward and cost...but revealed it stands, and so in the end the reward will outweigh the cost."

I should pay her extra for that. The woman had clearly picked up that Renata was the newcomer in question. But instead of identifying the cuckoo in the nest, she'd all but told Leato to push his mother into accepting his new "cousin."

Leato responded like any hooked client: wary, but wanting to believe. He leaned forward, studying the upturned cards as if he could read their meaning. Then he met the szorsa's waiting gaze. "I think I've already decided—if I ever had a choice—but nothing here tells me what I need to..." Biting off the end of the question, he sagged back in his chair. "But I suppose it wouldn't. Apologies, szorsa. Perhaps my future has more answers."

His reaction took Ren by surprise. She'd been focused on the cards' significance for her—but it seemed Leato was thinking of something else entirely. She glanced back down. Sword in Hand. Did it have anything to do with why he was late tonight? And what he was doing in that alley?

The szorsa turned over the last three cards. "This is your future, the good and the ill of it, and that which is—neither."

Ren had been watching the szorsa closely and knew the shuffle had been honest. But the three cards she turned over were The Face of Stars, The Mask of Night, and The Face of Glass.

Not just three aspect cards, and not even just three all drawn from the same suit—the spinning thread—a commonality that indicated greater significance. The Face of Stars and The Mask of Night were the two aspects of Ir Entrelke Nedje, and they sat revealed and veiled, in direct opposition.

"Well, fuck." Leato slumped further. At the szorsa's glare, he rubbed the tired frown from his face and tried to appease her with a rueful grin. "Apologies, szorsa. And to you, cousin. You wouldn't know this, but those cards right there?" He pointed at The Face of Stars and The Mask of Night. "They mean I should stick to watching you play tonight rather than betting on any hands myself."

"I imagine they mean rather more than that," Renata said, keeping her voice steady.

"Yes." The patterner hesitated—probably debating between two finishing styles. Promise Leato glory and riches if he sought out Ir Entrelke's favor? Or warn him that his dire fate could only be averted by offering money to appease Ir Nedje, the aspect of the deity that brought bad luck? She might even be one of those who did a side trade in rose-knot charms and other methods of preventing doom.

"At a crossroads you stand," she said, her voice hushed. "This cause you have taken up—it may lead to great success, or to disaster. For you there is no middle road."

"There isn't *any* road," Leato muttered. "Not one I can see."

She lifted The Face of Glass. His future, neither good nor bad. "Revelations will come. Revelations, I think, having to do with that lie from the past. What then you learn will determine your path—what you learn, and how you use it."

If The Laughing Crow had indicated a lie, that might have been accurate. But the szorsa *was* right that The Face of Glass indicated truth and discovery, and Ren felt cold. *Does that mean me? Or whatever Leato is up to?*

"What I learn and how I use it," Leato murmured, twisting his head as if he could see the cards from the patterner's side of the table. She made a soft sound in the back of her throat, and Leato came back to himself with a shake. "Thank you, szorsa."

Rising, he once again approached the shrine. After a moment's frowning hesitation, he pulled out a thumb knife and pried two sparkling amethysts from the skirt of his coat. He placed one in each of the side bowls, for the Face and the Mask.

"Seemed fitting," he told Renata with a shrug, pocketing the knife. "Don't let my fate put you off, cousin. We'll hope there are happier cards for you."

She'd seen enough to pay her coin, remove her mask, and sit down with only a faint qualm. *If she turns up anything I don't want her to, I'll just lie my way out of it.*

The szorsa scooped up her cards and reshuffled them. Again it seemed honest, and when the first line emerged, it contained nothing to fear. The reader laughed at The Face of Gold, revealed. "You will think me a fraud, alta—anyone with eyes can see you come from great wealth. But there is loss also in your past, a sacrifice unwillingly made. Made for the protection of your family, perhaps."

Ren studied the other two cards, Hundred Lanterns Rise and Turtle in Her Shell, simultaneously trying to figure out their true significance for her, and what they might mean for Renata. The effort made her head hurt. "Are you suggesting my mother ran away for the benefit of her kin?" She dismissed the question with a wave of her hand. "Never mind; you don't know my mother, and it isn't her fate being read here."

"Our fates are often linked." The szorsa flipped the next line. All unaligned cards: A Brother Lost, A Spiraling Fire, and Drowning Breath. "That loss is healing. But just as someone injured must begin pushing herself, using the wounded limb, and yet not push too quickly, so it is with you. Favor not what has been hurt, but hurt yourself not in trying."

Leato had managed to hold his tongue during the first part of the spread, but now he blurted, "Perhaps that refers to Mother. She didn't care for Aunt Letilia, but anyone can see you're nothing like her. Be patient. She'll come around."

Renata gave him an uncertain smile, reaching up to take his bare left hand with the glove he'd loaned her. "Thank you."

Then the future. Ren was glad she had let go of Leato's hand before the cards turned; otherwise he would have felt her fingers tensing. But The Mask of Mirrors was revealed, not veiled; that meant lies told for a good reason, rather than to bring harm.

"More duality," the szorsa mused, looking at Orin and Orasz in the central position. "Though not as strongly as for the altan. The Mask of Fools, veiled, warns you not to ignore what is in front of you. A time will come when you must see both sides of the situation, the good and the bad. Exercise caution in which parts you reveal; it may be that you need more understanding than others."

She sounded dissatisfied, as well she might. There was neither true insight in what she said, nor a persuasive imitation of it. Ren wondered if her masquerade was somehow confusing the lines of pattern—if that was even possible. *More likely that the szorsa just isn't very good.*

At least it justified her not offering as large a gift as Leato had. Renata thanked the patterner and rose to deposit another decira in the bowl for the Face. Watching the money leave her hand, it crossed her mind that it would be easy to palm one of the coins already there . . . but that was one blasphemy she'd never committed. Stealing from a szorsa invited the curse of the deities themselves.

She'd blasphemed badly enough for one lifetime when she poisoned Ondrakja.

Out in the main room, Leato seemed preoccupied. Whatever he'd hoped to get from the szorsa, he hadn't received it—but he hadn't been disappointed, either. "Would you like to return home?" Renata asked. "This isn't the night either of us had planned."

"What? No." Leato dredged up a smile from somewhere, but he couldn't hide the heaviness that weighed his shoulders down. "I promised you good memories to sleep on."

Snagging two more glasses of wine, he scanned the open card tables in the main room. "I should have asked, do they play any pattern games in Seteris? Did Aunt Letilia ever teach you sixes? Probably not; Father once said she was hopeless. No patience and no restraint."

Renata had to swallow a laugh. Pretending to be ignorant of a game was the oldest trick in the book, and Leato was lying down in the path of it. "No, I've never heard of it. But I'd love to learn."

Setting a warm hand at her back to guide her through the maze of players, Leato said, "Then let's find a low-stakes table, and I'll teach you."

Isla Prišta, Westbridge: Suilun 4

Ren's purse dropped onto the kitchen table with a satisfying thunk.

Tess stared at it, then up at her. "What's this, then?"

"My winnings. Worry not; Leato saw nothing."

Tess set aside the Gloria underdress she was dismantling and reached eagerly for the purse, even as she frowned at Ren. "Cheating? Are you certain that's wise? You're the one who's always going on about breaking character. Or is Alta Renata the sort of woman who cheats?"

"We must pay for all of this somehow," Ren pointed out, stripping off her gloves.

The clink of coins being sorted into piles died when Tess saw the mismatched pair. "Where's your other glove?" Her narrow-eyed gaze flicked up. "What did you do, Ren?"

The beginning of the night seemed years in the past, but at Tess's question, memory came bubbling up like the Wellspring of Ažerais. Ren sank onto the bench, leaned in close, and whispered, "*I met the Rook.*"

Coins spilled as Tess's hip jostled the table. Clutching Ren's hands, she gasped, "You didn't!"

Through a grin so wide she could barely speak, Ren recounted the whole story. They'd both grown up on tales of the Rook: how he humiliated proud nobles, defended shopkeepers against corrupt hawks, stole and destroyed the evidence used to blackmail people.

There were darker stories, too. Judges who sentenced too harshly found themselves sailing away on their own penal ships. Inscriptors who sold ineffective numinata to the ill and dying got their hands shattered for it; clerks and hawks who took bribes and then failed to look the other way might land on the Charterhouse steps one morning missing an eye, or choking on blood from a cloven tongue. Common punishments by Nadežran law, but visited on people who were usually above it. Many found that frightening, but for kids on the street, the Rook might as well have been a god.

"And he has your glove? I made that glove!" Tess tilted her head with a wistful sigh, staring up into the dancing shadows of the cellar rafters. "Sedge would have been so jealous. Him always going on about that one time he saw the Rook on a rooftop."

Her words were gentle, as they always were when she mentioned their brother. She mourned him—they both did—but she knew full well that Ren's grief was mixed with guilt. It was Ren, not Tess, who got Sedge killed.

But Tess's role in their trio had always been as their conscience and their heart. Now she nudged Ren and said, "Things were a success with Leato, too? One Traementis down, two to go?"

"I wouldn't say that," Ren said, "but yes, it went... well."

Tess immediately caught her pause. "What else happened?"

She shivered when Ren told her about the dead child. Tess's earliest years had been in Ganllech, passed from relation to relation, but she'd spent enough time with the Fingers to have heard tales of the zlyzen. She'd been the one to put a red thread around Ren's pallet, even though Ren knew Ondrakja would mock them when she found out.

Rather than invite more nightmares by dwelling on it, Ren shared the patterner's readings for Leato. "Thank the Faces that he wasn't warned away from you," Tess said, scooping the counted coins back into the purse.

Ren picked up Leato's glove, smoothing out fingers curled from the shape of his hand. Leato's reaction to the reading wasn't the only strangeness of the evening. "He was late in meeting us. But I saw him coming out of the Uča Tromyet near the Lacewater Bridge—and acting like he wanted no one to see him."

Tess frowned. "Is that brothel still there? Maybe he was having a spot of fun before he joined."

It would fit with the stories she'd heard about Leato while preparing for this con—but he hadn't looked like a man fresh from some night-piece's bed. "I doubt it. On the other hand, I cannot imagine what other business he could have in that corner of Lacewater."

She folded the glove carefully. In Renata's accent, she said, "I think I should take a closer look at Cousin Leato."

The Kindly Spinner

As his chair swayed along the streets of the Upper Bank, Vargo reflected that Alta Renata Viraudax was the most interesting thing to come to Nadežra in a long time.

She'd piqued his interest when she first arranged to rent that house in Westbridge, simply because not many Seterins visited Nadežra if they didn't have business there. When he discovered her connection to House Traementis, he'd decided she merited a closer look. Her performance at the Gloria set Nadežra's elite afire with gossip—and then the encore that night, in Lacewater...

The sedan chair lurched to a crawl. A glance out the curtains revealed a plaza congested with traffic. Bearers did their best to nudge through the clusters of people on foot, and everyone parted around the occasional carriage trundling along like a sunning river turtle. Plaza Coscanum was always like this around sixth sun. That was why Vargo had chosen it when he invited the alta to a late lunch: the better to be seen entertaining Nadežra's newest curiosity.

He knocked on the roof of the chair with the head of his walking stick. "I'll get out here," he said, tucking a folder of papers under his arm and pulling on butter-soft leather gloves. Vargo didn't give a toss about the Liganti obsession with covering their hands, but it kept his own clean, and he only broke the mores when he had something to gain from it. He carried a cane for the same reason. The law forbade him a sword, and a visible knife might remind folk of a past he'd prefer they forgot.

That the solid blackwood cane was a sturdy weapon on its own didn't require comment. That it sheathed a blade as supple and strong as any nobleman's rapier, Vargo judged it best not to mention.

The cane's tip clicked on the plaza tiles as Vargo strolled to the ostretta on the far side. He'd considered well before suggesting the Heron of the South Wind for their meeting. Instead of Seterin, Liganti, or even the varied hybrid that was Nadežran cuisine, it served Vraszenian food—a high-end version of it, anyway. Vargo hoped a woman savvy enough to excite gossip by baring her arms at the Gloria and inciting the Rook to a duel in exchange for a glove would appreciate the furor such a choice would provoke.

The host led him to a semi-secluded table on the second-tier gallery ringing the main floor. Setting the folder on an empty chair, Vargo arranged himself in the seat that gave him the best view of the door, and waited.

And waited. No surprise that she made him cool his heels; he'd expected it. *Don't ask someone to dance unless you know the steps*, Alsius had once told him. After Vargo joined the dance of Nadežran power and politics, he made certain to learn every step. Forcing someone of inferior status to wait was one of the most basic maneuvers.

Fine. Let her think she was leading this dance—that the szorsa working at his card house hadn't reported everything she'd learned while patterning Renata and Leato Traementis. If he could convince her that doing business with him was a choice rather than her only option, all the better. People who felt trapped tended to struggle, snarling everything around them. He'd learned that from Alsius, too.

When she finally appeared, she mounted the stairs and approached him with as much speed as she could muster without endangering her dignity. "My apologies, Master Vargo—I didn't mean to keep you waiting. I asked some sedan bearers how long it would take to get here from Westbridge, but their estimate was *not* accurate."

"They never are." Vargo stood and bowed over her hand. "I consider myself fortunate that you agreed to make time for me at all. I imagine you've become quite popular since your debut at the Gloria—not to mention your encounter with the Rook."

"How could I turn down an invitation from the man who showed me such generosity and welcome?" She managed to sound sincere, with the apology and the flattery both. "And until I acquire more servants, I suspect I'll continue to dine out more often than not. My maid is a lovely girl, but her talents lie with dressmaking, not cooking."

Dressmaking, and finding fabrics on the cheap at grey-market stalls, Vargo suspected. Did she pocket the extra? "I think that talent owes more to her lovely mistress."

He swept a glance down her ensemble. No bare arms to be seen today; Renata's fitted sleeves carried past her wrist to end in a point over her gloved fingers. A second sleeve of heavy silk fresh from the Dawn Road draped like a capelet over her shoulders and upper arms. Northern fashion favored light colors, but a copper-shot lace over-lay darkened the rose silk of her bandeau and surcoat into autumnal shades. He knew that lace—a smuggled import only his people could supply. Curious that she'd come by it so quickly.

"I think you're insulting my maid in an attempt to flatter me," she replied archly.

"Or I'm flattering you in an attempt to poach your maid. But I see she's properly appreciated; I cry Ninat." Vargo held up his hands in surrender.

Her fleeting smile was a point tallied in his favor. If he accomplished nothing else here, Vargo wanted to make certain Renata Viraudax walked away feeling friendly toward him. Unlike the local cuffs, she wasn't predisposed to loathe him, and he intended to use that.

His opening move was flattery, and his second arrived a moment later, in the form of a server bearing a tiered rack of delicacies and a tray containing two small cups and an elegant silver pot. Vargo poured the first cup and offered it to Renata. "I hope you don't mind. I took the liberty of ordering before you arrived. Vraszenian spiced chocolate—I doubt it's made its way to Seteris."

She lifted the cup and inhaled the rich, decadent scent, redolent with cinnamon and vanilla. This met with an approving murmur; then she took an experimental sip.

The results were even better than he'd hoped. No sooner had it touched her tongue than her eyes fluttered shut in pleasure, a flush spreading across her cheeks and throat as the warmth of the drink and the spices flowed through her. Vargo watched in satisfaction, measuring his success by the length of time it took her to remember her surroundings.

"That is...astonishing." She half lowered the cup, then changed her mind and took another sip, closing her eyes once more like sight would be a distraction. "I've had chocolate before, but never like this."

"Neither of which assures me that it's to your taste," he murmured, enjoying the sight. Renata had the unscarred beauty of a woman who'd never known hardship, an elegant symmetry that called to mind the precision of numinatria. Her lashes made a dark curve against the fine skin of her cheek.

When she opened her eyes and caught him staring, he didn't look away. She must know her appearance was an effective tool; no harm in letting her see it work. "I'll take that lovely blush to mean that it is."

Her blush deepened, but she didn't simper and try to cover it up. "The only reason I'm not tipping the whole pot down my throat is because that would be gauche—and because if this is any indication, it would be a shame to leave myself with no appetite for lunch." She released the cup reluctantly.

"We can't have that," he said, even as he refreshed her cup. "Or else how will I satisfy my curiosity? Everyone with a tongue to wag is wondering why you've come to Nadežra. Most people think it's for some kind of trade deal, or because you're seeking a spouse."

She paid no heed to the cup, carefully folding her hands on the table. "Most. Not you?"

"You don't strike me as a woman who particularly wants a husband or wife. But you wouldn't have leased that house if your stay was temporary. Which suggests to me that you're trying to rebuild the bridge your mother burned—not for her sake, perhaps, but so *you* can get back into the Traementis family register."

Her gaze flicked away, chin raised. "If you've only invited me to sate your hunger for idle gossip, you'll find I have little appetite for it."

"I invited you here because we might be able to help each other."

"Oh?" Her tone remained aloof, but it was belied by the catch in her breath and the tightness of her interlaced fingers.

"By now I suspect you've realized that the Traementis reputation for insularity is well-earned. But it's possible I can give you something to sway them."

"Out of the goodness of your heart? Which is, no doubt, the same reason you gifted me that mask at the Gloria."

The mask had been a whim, but even Vargo's whims were calculated. He'd seen the sparkle in her eyes when she donned it. His real gift hadn't been the mask; it had been liberation from whatever made her hesitate to buy it.

Toying with his chocolate spoon, he said, "Call it enlightened self-interest. I have a proposal that might be of interest to House Traementis, if I can just get someone to hear it."

For anyone but him, it might not have been so difficult. But Donaia Traementis wouldn't let him through her door, and Altan Leato rejected Vargo's flirting before he even had a chance to move the conversation toward business.

As time ate away at their fortunes, though, they had less and less leeway to be so precious in their dealings. Vargo was gambling that Renata's desire to rejoin the Traementis was strong enough to encourage her to listen to him...and that she would be as good at getting them to play by her rules as she had the Rook.

Her expression betrayed a flicker of curiosity, but nothing more. "What sort of business proposition?"

The noise had risen as the crowd of diners grew. Vargo glanced down to the main floor, then twitched the gallery curtain closed. Let them speculate on what Derossi Vargo and Alta Renata were talking about in private. "How much do you know about the charter system in Nadežra?"

"Your seat of government is called the Charterhouse, is it not?" She showed more interest in the tiered tray of food than the direction of the conversation, selecting a marbled egg and a dumpling folded to look like a moonfish, shifting them to her plate. "Led by a five-member council, the Cinquerat. The way it's described in Seteris sounds very inefficient, but my impression is that everything—trade, defense, construction, and so forth—is handled through charters granted by the council to noble houses."

Compared to the aristocracy's hereditary rights in Seteris, it probably was inefficient. But since that also meant it offered opportunities to people like Vargo, he wasn't inclined to complain. "Granted to noble houses, but the delta gentry usually administer the charters on their behalf. It's the kind of system you cobble together at the end of a civil war after half the city has collapsed into rubble, and then never get around to fixing."

She might not be native to Nadežra and its convoluted politics, but her mind was quick enough to follow his meaning. "Correct me if I'm wrong, Master Vargo, but you aren't delta gentry."

"Would you be calling me *Master* Vargo if I were?" he drawled. "There's no law that restricts charter administration to delta houses. Only custom."

Renata tasted the dumpling, buying herself time to consider. "It's an interesting idea. However, I'm afraid I must disappoint you. As you noted, I'm not a member of House Traementis. I'm in no position to help you with a charter."

Vargo smiled. He imagined the frisson of excitement that washed over him was like the tremors a spider felt when something brushed the outer strands of his web. "That's another strange quirk of our charter system. You don't have to be a member of a noble house to advocate in the Charterhouse; some of the best advocates are delta gentry licensed to do so on a noble's behalf. I imagine House Traementis would be grateful to someone who could assist in repairing their fortunes."

"Repairing their fortunes?"

It was the first unguarded reaction she'd had since arriving—that, and the silent rapture when she tasted the chocolate.

"They're in decline, alta. Have been for quite some time now. Era Traementis does what she can to keep up appearances, but I know for a fact they don't hold nearly as many charters as they used to. If someone brought them a new one...that person might even find her name inscribed into their register."

Renata Viraudax had a good mask—good enough that he couldn't read what was going on behind her pleasant, curious expression. He could only guess, just as he could only guess what had caused her to leave Seteris. Scandal? A falling-out with her mother? Accusations of criminal activity? It might be worth paying some of his contacts to make inquiries across the sea.

But in the end, what mattered was that Alta Renata was clearly hoping to make her home here in Nadežra, in the bosom of her mother's former family.

And Vargo could help make that happen.

He leaned in closer, letting his voice drop like he was sharing an intimate secret. "Noble houses profit from all the charters they hold—even those administered by others. If you can get Era Traementis to license you as an advocate, I'm prepared to pay you for your services, and offer fair terms to them once the charter's awarded. We all get what we want."

Or at least take the first step toward what they wanted. Vargo suspected that admittance into the Traementis register was no more her end goal than a single charter administration was his.

She neither drew back from his closeness, nor showed any sign that it affected her. "You believe that I—a stranger to this city and its politics, whose main connection to House Traementis is an estrangement twenty-three years old—can...what's the Nadežran phrase? Navigate the shoals to get you what you want."

"I believe that in one day you managed to take the Gloria by storm, set the heir to House Acrenix scrambling to assert her dominance over you, and bested the heir of House Indestor *and* fair Nadežra's most famous criminal. All using only your sleeves and a glove." He laughed quietly. "Alta Renata, I'd far rather have a woman like you as an ally than a competitor."

That got her. She kept her expression serene, but this close, he could hear the slight intake of breath. Another noble might have sneered at the idea that someone like him could ever be a competitor. She didn't.

Retrieving the leather-bound folder from the empty chair, he set it next to her left hand. "House Quientis holds the Fulvet seat in the Cinquerat, which means they oversee the civil affairs of the city. Scaperto Quientis would be the one to approve the charter I'm proposing. All I ask is that you do me the favor of reviewing these documents."

She leaned back in her seat, looking at but not yet touching the folder. "You have an interesting way of doing business, Master Vargo."

He sipped cooling chocolate, as though it wasn't of great interest to him whether she took the folder or not. "I'd hate to have you think I—"

::You need to get to the Shambles right now.::

Vargo coughed at the sudden intrusion into his thoughts, thankful that he'd been taking a sip. Better to leave Renata thinking he was clumsy than mad.

Whatever it is, it can wait, he thought back. Hurrying Renata along at this juncture would do more harm than good.

::It's Hraček. Somebody drugged him and then cut him to ribbons.::

"Are you all right?" Renata asked, leaning forward in concern.

Half a bell, Vargo thought desperately.

::Ah, so you aren't concerned that one of your fists is dying for you. My mistake. Carry on with your seduction.::

Unleashing a stream of mental invective, Vargo set aside his cup and wiped chocolate from his lips. "I apologize, alta." The rasp breaking his words was only half-feigned. "Please excuse me..." He broke into more coughing, grabbed his cane, and was up and out before she could offer any sort of aid.

He caught the owner at the rear door. "Charge the meal to me, and send her home with more chocolate. Extend my apologies, not feeling well—you know what to say." It wasn't Vargo's first time at the Heron of the South Wind, nor was it the first time he'd had to leave abruptly.

Choking up on his sword cane, he headed for the river and a skiff to the Lower Bank. *I almost had her. If she slips the hook now...*

Whoever had gone after Hraček, he was going to make them bleed.

Isla Traementis, the Pearls: Suilun 8

Renata arrived too early at Traementis Manor. She was used to traveling the city on foot, not by sedan chair, and kept misestimating how long it would take her to get anywhere. After being late to lunch with Vargo, she'd erred too far in the other direction.

She wondered what could have sparked Vargo's sudden departure. Illness? He'd looked unwell, certainly. And she couldn't think of anything she might have said or done to drive him off.

The darkened skies were still echoing with the first bell of second earth as she climbed out of the chair. Two bells too early for her dinner appointment. Renata stood, trying not to fidget with tension, while Tess paid the bearers. What money she saved on food by accepting invitations to meals was instead going to transport, and then some—but what choice did she have? Someone of her status didn't walk everywhere.

But it might not matter soon. After lunch, she'd spent the afternoon reading through Vargo's proposal. He turned out to have a surprisingly meticulous mind; his documents laid out everything a Seterin visitor wouldn't know about the inner workings of the Charterhouse, from the responsibilities of the five seats to the legal terms of charters. The only thing it left out was why House Traementis was the perfect target for the idea—but that, Ren knew without being told.

Now all she had to do was sell his audacity to Donaia.

"If anyone can talk those two into striking palms, it's you," Tess assured her as she settled the drape of Renata's sleeves to the most pleasing effect. "But just in case dinner goes poorly, I'll send a messenger to tell Altan Bondiro you won't be joining him at the theatre later."

Before Renata could make up her mind to find an ostretta and spend the remaining two bells planning her attack, the door to Traementis Manor opened. Clearly the majordomo had been keeping watch. Renata had no choice but to mount the stairs and let him escort her to the same salon where she'd first met Donaia while Tess was sent downstairs to join the other servants. She didn't have Ren's knack for manipulating people, but she didn't need it; her natural sweet demeanor would work its own magic, and when the night was over, she might have some interesting gossip to share.

Nothing Renata saw supported Vargo's claim that House Traementis's fortunes were suffering. There were coffee and tea kept warm in imbued pots, and a mellow wine kept chilled in an imbued decanter. A fire crackled in the hearth, the numinat inlaid on the wall behind reflecting the heat outward into the room.

Compared to the days when the Fulvet seat had belonged to them, perhaps the Traementis had indeed declined. But Ren had seen real poverty; she knew how many of the furnishings around her could be sold, and for how much. *Their notion of hardship is probably having to buy Vraszenian rice wine instead of grape wine from Seste Ligante.*

"Era Traementis is dressing, and Altan Leato has not yet returned," Colbrin said, his tone mild but his words their own rebuke. "I will inform Alta Giuna of your arrival."

"No need, Colbrin." Giuna touched his arm and gave him a

smile of dismissal, then hurried in to take Renata's hands in greeting. "I shouldn't admit it, but I've been sitting in my window all afternoon. I'm so happy you came early. We'll have time to talk before Mother is done with her papers."

Unless Donaia intended to wear paper to dinner, one of the two explanations about how she was currently occupied was false. Renata let it pass without comment and followed Giuna's tug toward the hearth and mantel. "Look, see? I put it here because it catches the light so nicely." Giuna brushed her fingers over the glass sculpture Renata had gifted her. Its blue didn't match the peaches and golds of the rest of the room, but that hadn't deterred her from giving the bauble a place of honor.

Renata knew better than to swallow Letilia's stories whole, but the themes of her former mistress's complaints were clear enough: Donaia was a skinflint; Donaia was a prude; Donaia insisted that everything in the house be to her liking, and never mind what anyone else preferred. Even filtering for exaggeration, Renata was surprised Donaia had let the glass mar her lovely salon—especially when the less-favored child put it there.

Giuna's dress bore out Letilia's first two assertions. The dove-grey underdress and simple sleeves were pretty enough, if boring, but the murky plum and stiff, straight lines of her surcoat dragged on her like a rain-heavy cloud on a gloomy day. A ribbon of bright silver silk wove around and through her tresses, though, in a passable imitation of the style Renata had worn to the Gloria.

Catching Renata's glance, Giuna touched her hair and smiled shyly. "Our maid did the best she could with only my description to work from. I don't look silly, do I?"

"You look lovely," Renata said warmly. "And oh, what Tess could do with your coloring—she's my maid, and the one who makes my dresses. I've a mind to set her loose on you. I saw her looking at you during the Gloria, and I know that expression; it's the one she gets when she's busy sewing in her mind." It had the merit of being true.

Giggling, Giuna pressed fingers to her reddening cheeks. "Oh, I—"

"We couldn't possibly trouble you to lend us your maid's services, Alta Renata," Era Traementis interrupted from the doorway. *Colbrin must have run to warn her.* "I imagine she's kept very busy outfitting you."

An enormous hound with shaggy, brindled fur padded at her side as she glided to join them. Ren did her best to hold still. The only dogs she'd encountered before had been vicious strays, or attack dogs trained by some of the knots. The Vigil kept a pack for tearing apart rioters; Ren had been lucky enough to avoid those, but the stories were enough to send her pulse leaping double time.

Was Donaia looking for exactly that reaction? Renata forced herself to hold out one hand, palm up, as though her thin gloves were any sort of protection. "What a handsome..."

"Alwyddian wolfhound," Donaia said. She sounded surly, as if she'd been hoping for Renata to flinch. "He's called Lex Talionis."

At Giuna's laugh, the dog left off sniffing Renata's hand and looked up at her with liquid black eyes. His tail whapped Donaia's thigh hard enough to leave bruises. "That might be his name," Giuna said, "but I doubt he knows it. We call him Meatball. That was Leato's doing."

"Giuna, dear, have you offered our guest something to drink?"

"No, Mother." Creeping to the sideboard, Giuna hesitated over the offerings until Renata nodded toward the coffee. Foul it might be, but she didn't want to risk having too much wine.

"My apologies for not being ready to greet you, Alta Renata." The reprimand in Donaia's voice was less obvious than Colbrin's, but unmistakable all the same.

Any faint hope that Donaia's feelings toward her had mellowed drowned on the spot. But Ren had always loved a challenge. "The fault is entirely mine, Era Traementis. I was so worried I would insult you by arriving late, I quite overshot."

There were a variety of ways to ingratiate oneself, beyond being friendly to a person's pet. If she could have afforded it, Renata might have tried to buy the same sage-and-wisteria perfume Donaia wore—but other things cost no money at all. She subtly mirrored

Donaia's movements and posture as they all sat, leaning forward when the other woman did, straightening her gloves a moment after Donaia touched her own. Overdoing that risked the other person noticing and reading it as mockery, but small amounts of imitation would build a buried sense of rapport, whether Donaia wanted it to or not.

For a brief time she thought it was working, the conversation easing past stilted commentary on the weather. But as the topic drifted toward Letilia, Renata realized her hostess's seemingly casual chatter was nothing of the sort. "Whatever else she was," Donaia said, "your mother certainly was a beauty. Did she ever tell you about the time she lost her purse and had a dozen smitten altans and altas diving into the Becchia Canal to retrieve it?"

Renata wondered how long it had taken her to consider the possibility that her unwelcome visitor might not even be Letilia's daughter.

Fortunately, Donaia had chosen one of Letilia's favorite anecdotes—one she still told more than twenty years later. "I thought it was her fan. Which always seemed absurd to me, because of course the fan was ruined by the time it came out; at least with a purse, the contents might survive." Renata leaned in closer, as if sharing something not for Giuna's ears, even though the girl could hear her perfectly. "But then, I doubt the fan was the point. The way Mother tells the story, she was testing to see who was truly dedicated to winning her favor... and Ghiscolo Acrenix had his reward that night."

This was a fencing match, every bit as much as the duel between Mezzan Indestor and the Rook. If it went on long enough, Donaia would ask something Renata didn't know; that detail was a riposte, obscure enough to put a halt to the prying before it went too far.

The measuring look in Donaia's eyes said she'd come close to striking her target, but not quite. Renata had hoped to save the card up her sleeve for a later date, after Era Traementis had warmed to her... but she'd brought it just in case.

"Speaking of things that were lost," she said.

Reaching into her purse, she brought out a gold ring set with a baroque river pearl and laid it on the table between them. "Mother never gave me much of her jewelry, but I always loved this one, and pestered her until she let me have it," she said quietly. "The style is Nadežran, isn't it? Mother never used the word 'stole'; by her lights, she was only taking her due when she left. But I suspect that ring never belonged to her, and therefore it doesn't belong to me, either. I'd like to return it."

How many times had she picked someone's pocket only so she could return what they had "dropped" and thereby ingratiate herself with the mark? The catch in Donaia's breath and sheen in her eyes said Renata had played her card even better than she knew. Her hand trembled as she picked up the ring.

"This…" Only rapid blinking kept the tears at bay. Donaia swallowed and tried again. "This was my mother's. She gave it to me when Gianco and I…"

The dog had been sprawled quietly by Donaia's chair, but lifted his head at the waver in her voice. His bushy brows rose, a questioning whine at the back of his throat as he glanced between his mistress and the thing that made her sad.

Scratching his head in reassurance, Donaia curled her hand around the ring and tucked it under her surcoat apron. With a will even Renata had to admire, she reined herself in. "Thank you, Renata. I'm truly grateful to you for returning this."

Not "Alta Renata," but simply her name. Ren's surge of victory was tempered by an unexpected pang. She'd assumed the ring was simply a distinctive piece of jewelry. *If someone gave me back something of Mama's…*

She crushed that thought before it could get any further. All her mother's things were gone, save one. Hoping otherwise had only led Ren into Ondrakja's snare.

"You see, Mother? I told you she was nothing like Letilia." Leato stood in the doorway; how long he'd been there, Renata couldn't say. Long enough to lay a comforting hand on his mother's shoulder as he approached, and to give Renata a smile as warm as the fire in the hearth.

Donaia put her hand over his, then shook herself and rose. "Now that we're all here, let's go in to dinner. Meatball, stay."

It was still too early, but Renata wasn't surprised she wanted to escape the sensitive moment. Leato offered Renata his arm. Leaving Donaia's monster sprawled before the hearth like a hunter's trophy, the four of them went through to the dining room.

It was by far the grandest place she'd ever taken a meal. The table and chairs were fine wood, polished until they gleamed; the upholstery was plush amethyst velvet; the carpet was thick enough that Renata's shoes sank into it as she crossed to her seat. Even the molding around the edge of the ceiling and the chandelier chain was gilt, shining in the candlelight. It simultaneously made her feel small and grubby, and like she truly was an alta, born to dine in such lavish surroundings.

Dinner was as Liganti as her lunch had been Vraszenian. Not a single dumpling or grain of rice to be seen; instead it was duck sausage, mussels in cream, eels baked in pastry shells. Renata's intent was to wait and bring up Vargo's proposal toward the end of dinner, and while they were nibbling on the last pieces of fruit and cheese, Donaia unwittingly handed her an opening.

Leato mentioned that Fadrin, one of the Acrenix cousins, had heard of someone down in Dockwall selling exotic birds from Isarn. "I wouldn't want to keep one here, of course," Leato said. "Noisy things. But it would be amusing to see a bird that can talk like a human—"

"Absolutely not," Donaia said, her voice unexpectedly sharp. "There's pestilence in the Lower Bank right now, Leato."

He rolled his eyes. "When *isn't* there pestilence in the Lower Bank? I'll be careful—I'll wear a mask and everything."

"A woman at the Gloria said she had masks that protect against disease," Renata said. "Who knows how effective they are, of course, but Master Vargo bought one. Speaking of whom..."

She'd given it a great deal of thought that afternoon. Trying to obtain this charter through the Traementis was logical, but for all Vargo's flattery, she found it profoundly unlikely that the foreign-born daughter of an estranged former relative was his first choice. And while she couldn't guess at everyone he might have approached already, one candidate seemed obvious.

Renata caught Leato's gaze across the table. "Altan Leato, I imagine you've heard something about this? Derossi Vargo has a plan for replacing the numinat that used to cleanse the waters of the West Channel."

She left unsaid: *Before your grandfather destroyed it.*

Leato's soft snort sent ripples across the surface of his wine. "So Master Vargo gave up on me and decided to approach you." He savored the wine as he considered her. "Don't be taken in by him, cousin. He might have charm enough to summon dreamweaver birds out of season, but he only flirts to get what he wants. And you may be certain that the person who will benefit the most from his plan is Derossi Vargo."

"I'm not so green as to be taken in by a little flirtation," she said evenly. *Not even if he fed me chocolate.* There was no way the man could possibly have known how much she adored it, and how long it had been since she tasted it. "I read the documents he provided. Removing the filth that washes down from upstream would undoubtedly increase the value of the properties he owns along the Lower Bank—but that's hardly the only benefit. And I see no reason why others shouldn't reap their own share of the profits."

"I don't understand," Giuna said timidly. "Why would he approach you?"

Donaia arched a brow at Renata in an unspoken *why indeed*.

"Because it seems no one else will give his proposal a fair reading," Renata responded, not backing down from Donaia's silent challenge. "And he believes that House Traementis might stand to gain a great deal from this charter—if they gave it proper consideration."

Pushing back her chair as though she was about to declare the meal over and send Renata on her way, Donaia said, "And what did he tell you to make you believe we need—"

"Mother."

An entire conversation took place between Leato and Donaia,

without a word being uttered. Then Donaia's stiffness drained from her, and she waved one hand wearily in surrender. "Fine. Yes. House Traementis is not what it was when your mother was with us. You can blame it on my mismanagement if you like. But I would rather that not be common knowledge—though apparently it's known to common men like Master Vargo."

"I'd hardly call him common," Leato murmured, sharing an amused glance with Renata.

Donaia's wineglass struck the table slightly too hard. "And yes, we're the ones who broke the original numinat, so yes, it would certainly do our reputation some good to replace it. But not if it means entering into business with a man who made his fortune through criminal activities."

Giuna leaned over to whisper to Renata—a whisper that carried through the room. "She means he's a smuggler." Except she said it with a blush and a flutter instead of Donaia's disdain.

Her comment at least gave Renata cover for the unpleasant jolt that went through her. Not just lower class, but criminal. *That* was what she had been missing. It explained the elegant clothes and the scars they couldn't hide, the ambition to rise higher and the inability to get past the barriers in his path.

Associating with him didn't make it any more likely that someone would uncover her own past. But a tremor still went through her at the possibility; rather than hide it, she channeled it into a different kind of alarm. "You allow a criminal like that to wander about your Gloria?"

"It's amazing what regular bribes to the Vigil will achieve," Donaia muttered.

"What Mother means," Leato said with more patience, "is that Master Vargo has been expanding into legitimate business. And making key people more wealthy in the process."

Giuna cocked her head to one side. "So what's the harm in letting him make *us* more wealthy?"

Donaia almost choked on a bite of persimmon. Such things shouldn't be said in front of an outsider, and certainly not so baldly—but Renata was grateful for Giuna's backing. Leato said, "It isn't the money, minnow. What does somebody like Vargo know about numinatria? And even if he can do what he says, do we really want to help him gain even more power and influence over the Lower Bank? He's not acting out of charity, you can be sure of that—and probably not even out of greed. The man is rich enough already…which means he's getting something else out of this scheme."

For someone with such a frivolous reputation, Leato showed an excellent grasp of the situation. "I can understand your reluctance," Renata said, after considering for a moment. "Let me propose this, then. I won't refuse Master Vargo outright; instead I'll tell him that I'm working to persuade you, and in the meanwhile see what more I can learn. If I'm able to lay your concerns to rest, then you can pursue Master Vargo's proposal. If not, then House Traementis remains free of association with him."

Even Donaia couldn't stand firm against the combined weight of Renata's good sense and Leato and Giuna's restrained approval. She sighed and cut a slice of persimmon in half, toying with one of the pieces. "I suppose it does little harm to know more. Now may we speak of something else, before talk of business sours a pleasant meal?"

Giuna popped upright in her seat. "Yes! Cousin Renata—did you truly meet the Rook?"

"Giuna!" Donaia's voice cracked like a whip. "I don't want you taking an interest in that outlaw. He's despicable, and he's dangerous—or have you forgotten what he did to Kolya Serrado? Not to mention how he humiliated Renata."

An uncomfortable silence fell. Giuna shrank in on herself, her excitement wisping into smoke. "I'm sorry, Mother."

Leato rose. His face had settled into stony lines. "I hate to leave matters on such a note, but I promised I'd meet Bondiro at the Whistling Reed, and it's later than I realized."

This time it was Leato's name Donaia uttered in a scandalized tone. "We have a guest! You can't just wander off so soon—"

The chiming of the clock towers came through the windows, sounding fifth earth. "Oh, Lumen," Donaia said. "It *is* that late."

Renata dabbed her mouth clean with a napkin and also stood. "I should be going as well. I didn't mean to impose on your hospitality for so long, Era Traementis."

"Please think nothing of it, Alta Renata. It was quite...pleasant." Donaia looked surprised, as if the words were truth rather than mannered formalities. "And since my son is being so rude, the least he can do is see you out and call you a chair."

That held the weight of command. Leato did as he was told, summoning Tess from the servants' hall to wrap Renata in her cloak, and once again paying for the chair. Ren longed to ask Tess what she had learned below stairs...but before that, she had something else to take care of.

It was always possible Leato had been included in Bondiro's theatre invitation—but Ren doubted it. No, she suspected Cousin Leato was lying through his teeth.

And she wanted to find out why.

Lacewater, Old Island: Suilun 8

Renata followed Leato from the Pearls, instructing her bearers to wait until he left Traementis Manor, then disembarking when he got out of his own chair at the foot of the Lacewater Bridge and tugged his simple white mask over his face. No one took a sedan chair into that narrow tangle of streets.

Nor did they show up in the kind of fine fashion Renata had worn to dinner, masked or otherwise. She hastily stripped off her surcoat and yanked her hair down from its arrangement, throwing Tess's striped woolen across her shoulders. Even then she got odd looks as they tailed Leato at the closest range they dared.

When he went into the Whistling Reed, she was surprised. Maybe he was meeting Bondiro after all? She turned her surcoat inside out—the quickest way to make herself less flashy, and vindi-cation for Tess's insistence that the lining of her garments always be tidy—and drew her hair around her face, then eased through the door, half wondering if he'd just slipped out the back.

But no. He was waiting at a table along one wall, and two men were vacating a spot that gave her opportunity to watch Leato from behind. She slipped into one chair almost before the man's ass had left it and glared away the fellow who would have taken the other, until Tess arrived from the bar to claim it for herself.

"Zrel's still cheaper than canal water here," her sister said, setting down two mugs to make their presence look legitimate. She took a tentative sip and swallowed a coughing fit, eyes watering with the struggle. "And still as foul. Mother and Crone, did we really once fight for the dregs of this, and count ourselves lucky to get them?"

Only Tess could look around the seedy dance hall with bright eyes and a tapping toe, as though their adventures here were happy memories. Ren remembered it differently. There were full pockets to be plucked—gamblers tended to start and end their nights at the Whistling Reed, wherever they might have gone in between—but there were also guards at the doors, ready to collar any Finger too heavy or too slow. They'd only come when they were desperate for a good take to bring to Ondrakja, Ren aging herself with makeup and doing her best to keep her mark's hands from wandering until her knot-mates had lifted what they could.

Her knot-mates. She felt like she had a lump in her throat. *Con-ning the Traementis was supposed to get me away from all of this.*

Just then, a familiar figure shuffled into the room, scanning the place before heading for Leato's table.

Tess spotted him, too, if not his destination. She sat straighter. "Maiden's knickers, isn't that—Oof!"

In the steady noise of the dance hall, the odds of Stoček hearing her were low, but Ren didn't want to take the chance. Bad enough that Leato might spot her or Tess; now they had *two* pairs of eyes to worry about. "Sorry," she murmured, removing her elbow from Tess's ribs. "But I think I understand now."

Stoček was as close to an institution as Lacewater ever got, a middle-aged Vraszenian peddling little dreams off the Zatatsy Canal. He usually had a bag of honey stones in his pocket that he passed out to his favorites among the pity-rustlers and river rats— Ren included.

Five years hadn't changed him as much as they'd changed her. His long hair was still thick and black as river mud, gathered in braids woven through with colorful ribbons and bells. He was missing a few more finger segments than before, and he sported a fresh bandage around a joint too stubby to be a full thumb. That was the punishment for dealing aža if you couldn't afford the bribes. And Stoček had been dealing aža since before Ren was born.

So this was what Leato was up to. The same thing his father had done before him: finding refuge from life's hardships in a little echo of Ažerais's Dream.

But she'd seen countless people buy from Stoček, including any number of slumming cuffs in masks, and none of them had acted like Leato was now. He leaned across the table, as if he didn't want to be overheard, and talked while Stoček listened.

"That doesn't look like a deal to me," Tess murmured in Ren's ear.

Leato slipped some money across the table, but the expected trade didn't happen: Instead of handing over a vial of aža, Stoček began to talk.

Ren cursed the crowded dance hall. People kept moving into her line of view, interrupting her attempts to read the man's lips. She couldn't even try to drift closer and listen. If she'd had time to put together a proper disguise, she might have swiped a tray and some mugs and attempted to pass herself off as a server, but with her face painted like Renata and her underdress the same one she'd worn to dinner, she didn't dare risk it.

Whatever Leato had paid Stoček for, he'd paid well. One singer left the stage and another took it before the man stopped answering Leato's questions, crossing his arms and giving a curt shake of his head.

Leato was the first to leave. Ren couldn't follow, not with Stoček gazing after him with a pensive frown. His glance swept the room, and Ren ducked her head over her zrel to keep him from seeing her. Tess's head was already down, resting on the rim of her mug, her soft snores rising and falling with the dance hall music. She'd been up long hours altering and disguising Ren's clothing, when she wasn't trailing along in Renata's wake like a proper alta's maid.

If Ren came back to find Stoček later, as herself...

But no. Her gut twisted at the thought. There had to be rumors at least of what she'd done to Ondrakja; Stoček would never help her after that. She'd have to pretend to be someone else entirely, and she didn't have the coin to bribe him into spilling what he'd talked to Leato about.

She would have to work that out by other means.

Ren nudged Tess awake, and once Stoček was firmly occupied drinking his way through some of the money Leato had given him, the two of them slipped out, the cold late fall air hitting them like a slap after the overheated confines of the dance hall.

"Right. Was that worth me getting a new crease in my forehead?" Tess asked, touching the reddened groove where her head had rested on the mug.

Semi-disguised and away from anyone who would recognize Renata, Ren had no compunctions about slinging a sympathetic arm over her sister's shoulders. "I wasn't sure if you wanted me to wake you. For me, though, I would say it was worth it. We know Leato *is* up to something, even if not what."

Tess bumped Ren with her hip, making them both sway like drunkards. "Handsome one like that, a few secrets only add to his appeal. How did dinner go?"

They walked the rest of the way home, to save money on a chair or a skiff. Tess told Ren about the Traementis servants—friendly but uninclined to gossip about their masters; Donaia must pay them better than expected—and Ren told Tess about the ring and what the nobles had said regarding Vargo.

Tess's response was a *tch* and a shake of her curls. "Easy for them to judge. Don't forget that *I'm* a wanted criminal in Ganllech. Though you shouldn't trust my judgment; I'll forgive a lot from a man who appreciates fine tailoring."

When their chuckles faded, Tess gave Ren a comforting squeeze. "We've seen what the bad ones are like. If he's truly awful, then people will talk about it—our people, I mean, not the nobles. But you're smart to check the currents first."

Ren's hair couldn't be fixed in the dark, but Tess flipped her surcoat right side out again before they approached the house, then stripped it right back off once they got to the kitchen. While Ren laid their pallet in front of the banked coals of the fire, Tess went out the yard door to fetch water for washing.

She returned with a cheesecloth-covered basket and flaming cheeks. "Well, we won't have to worry about breakfast for the next few days," she said, setting the basket on the table and the bucket to warm by the coals.

Ren stiffened. "What is that?"

"Just bread." Tess pulled out a loaf still dusted in flour and waved it to show it was safe. "From the bakery down the way."

Turning, she started filling the empty breadbox. "I happened into the baker's boy the other day, and we got to talking. Well, not boy. Man. Son. And he was asking how their shop might get the alta's custom, and before I knew it he was promising to bring by samples. I told him it wasn't likely and about your delicate digestion and particular tastes and all, but..."

Tess was babbling. Tess only babbled when she was nervous, or when she was excited about a design. She seemed to realize it as well. She turned, leaning back against the table, lip buttoned by her teeth. "I didn't give anything away. It would have been odd if I hadn't talked to him. And rude."

Ren exhaled slowly. "No, it is all right. I am just cautious having people around here." The fastest way for her masquerade to fall apart would be if someone realized Alta Renata was sleeping on the kitchen floor.

Slumping dramatically, Tess placed a hand over her heart.

"There's a relief. Now I can be glad he's given our purses a bit of rest. Into the chair with you, and let's get that stuff off your face." Tess grabbed a cloth and dunked it into the still-cold water, then tossed it and a cake of soap to Ren. Perching on her stool, she took out a thumb knife and started picking the copper lace off the bandeau.

Someday I'll be able to afford hot water. Ren sighed and rubbed the soapy cloth over her face, wiping away the mask of Renata Viraudax.

Then she paused, looking at the residue on the fabric. "Tess...I need something tomorrow."

"Oh?"

So much for giving our purses a rest. "Go and buy more of the imbued face powder. But this time in a darker shade."

5

The Face of Ages

The Shambles, Lower Bank: Suilun 24

Grey's ambushers weren't as stealthy as they thought. He marked three trailing him and one running ahead as soon as he crossed the Uča Obrt into the Shambles. As he made his way through the warren of islets, he caught flickers of movement along the edges of roofs, and when he entered his destination—an alley strangled between two tenements—he spotted an elbow not quite tucked out of sight behind a pile of broken crates.

He continued on as though he'd seen nothing. If he spooked them now, he might never get another chance. And he could take care of himself.

Especially when some of his ambushers didn't even come up to his hip.

A shrill "Get him!" sounded the charge. Howling feral, the street children leapt down from rooftops and surged up from gutters, wielding sticks and cobbles and the occasional rusty knife. Grey leapt back, dodging a few desperate swings from a particularly ferocious boy before twisting the knife away and stabbing it into the mold-softened boards of the alley wall, too high for the kid to reach. Better hawks than him had wound up with lockjaw after failing to appreciate the dangers of a rusty knife.

At least they weren't trying to kill him. As the disarmed boy fell back, the rest pressed forward, herding him against the brothel wall that formed the back of the alley. Grey let himself be herded. He'd rather not have them on all sides of him, and if things got too dangerous, he had enough advantage in weight to just bull his way clear.

But escaping now would undo the work of the past two weeks. Hunting down clues about the boy who'd said he couldn't sleep, chasing rumors about other missing street children, hearing one name over and over again: Arkady Bones. Not a threat, but a protector. Arkady was organizing the child gangs. Arkady would keep them safe.

Arkady could be found in Splinter Alley, in the Shambles.

Grey had expected a challenge, not a nipper-cheeked ambush. Better to end this farce before someone got hurt. "I wish not to make trouble. I came only to see Arkady Bones." He dropped into his natural accent, easy as sinking bare feet into river mud. He'd donned his own clothes as well: loose trousers, wide sash binding his waist, high boots and collar, his black panel coat lightened by colorful, looping embroidery that bore little resemblance to the geometric shapes preferred by the Liganti. Only his cropped hair marked him as anything but river-born Vraszenian. He'd erased all signs of the hawk.

A hard-edged voice cut through the whispers of distrust. "What's an old uncle like you want with her?" One of the smaller kids shoved through the mob, spindle thin and brown from head to heel, her eyes snapping with scorn, like a sparrow with a grudge.

She had to be a favorite in Arkady's gang; the other kids made way with as much alacrity as a flight of hawks for their commander. Grey sized up her jutted chin and scab-knuckled fists, half hidden by the wide cuffs of a pilled woolen coat, and decided that straight talk might be the only virtue this girl appreciated.

"Kids are going missing. The ones who come back die from lack of sleep. I want to know why, so I can stop it."

The girl crossed her arms and flicked a disdainful glance over him. Not a sparrow, Grey decided. A rooster. One bred to fight.

"Right. I'm listening."

Grey blinked. She couldn't mean... "I would prefer directly with Arkady to deal."

"Yeah. And I said I'm listening. Who's talking?"

The girl facing off against him had all the tattered authority and bluster of a knot leader...but she couldn't be more than twelve years old.

"Grey Szerado." He fought the urge to hunker down to her level, suspecting that would only get him a fist in his face. "A few ideas I have about what might—"

"It's Gammer Lindworm." Arkady flicked her ear, as did the other children—an old gesture meant to keep the night haunts away. "She's taking them to feed to the zlyzen."

"Gammer Lindworm?" How many times had he heard such stories as a child, all the terrible things Gammer Lindworm would do to him for being such a wicked boy? As though he didn't have more to fear from his own kin. "If fire tales are all you can give me..."

So much for his lead. However world-worn she might act, Arkady Bones still saw the world through a child's eyes, finding in it a child's fears.

And lashing out with the strength of a child's frustration. Grey limped back as sudden pain shot up his shin. Arkady shifted on the cobbles, ready to kick him again. "Don't know why I wasted breath telling an old fart with shit between his ears. Go back to your people and leave my knot alone. We'll take care of our own."

You deserved that, Grey thought ruefully. If he'd been her age, he would have kicked himself, too. Anyone who organized the street children this well deserved more than his disbelief. Still... "And you are *my* gammer, that I should believe a night haunt has crept out of stories to hunt the children of Nadežra?"

"En't the *real* Gammer Lindworm," Arkady sneered above the snickers of her gang. "But what else you gonna call an old hag who takes children, eats 'em up, and spits 'em back hollow? Been around for years, but used to be she only took one of us every month or two. And the ones that came back were only shook and nightmarish."

Years? Guilt tightened around Grey's heart. He hadn't known. One every month or two—the Vigil wouldn't take notice of that. Street children went missing in Nadežra all the time. From disease, from drowning in the river, from running afoul of cuffs. "What changed?"

Her bony shoulder twitched. "Dunno. Ciessa went missing in late Colbrilun. Turned back up the first Meralny in Similun saying she couldn't sleep. And she couldn't. Went mad and died before Tsapekny that same week. Been over thirty since then that we know about. Most never turn up again. So what do we do?"

A ragged chorus answered her. "Don't go out alone; don't hit a mark alone; don't sleep rough alone; don't be a shit-wit hero alone. If you see something strange, tell Arkady."

Punctuating the recitation with an approving nod, Arkady set fists on hips and said to Grey, "Dunno what you think you can do that we can't, but I got tired of hearing reports about you."

"I can investigate it without the danger of being taken," Grey said, hoping her sense would overcome her distrust.

"Ha! Guess that's so. Better you than us." She flicked a hand at her gang, and they trickled away through gaps too narrow for him to follow. "You learn anything useful, drop a few centiras to the pity-rustlers in Horizon Plaza. They'll come find me."

And probably turn over at least part of that take. Grey didn't believe for a moment that Arkady was organizing the kids out of charity. Still, he had something to go on now.

"What if you need to find me?" he asked, before Arkady could slip away after her knot.

She thumbed her chin at him, a gesture he usually only received when he was in uniform. "We know where the hawks roost."

"So much for disguises," Grey muttered, tugging on the open collar of his panel coat as he left the alley.

When he reached Coster's Walk, he scanned the thoroughfare looking for Ranieri, finally spotting him next to a man selling secondhand shoes from a blanket, and not far from a patterner plying her cards. Grey passed the patterner without comment. He wasn't in uniform, and the woman had to eat; if he ran her off, she'd just set up again somewhere else. And compared with kidnapping, what harm was a little fraud?

Pavlin Ranieri was a sunwise man, born a daughter to his parents, but now a son. With his silky brown hair and delicately pointed chin, he could have had a lucrative career on the stage even if he couldn't act his way out of a puddle. Instead, for reasons surpassing Grey's understanding, he'd chosen to become a hawk.

Right now, he was slouched against a pillar, also out of uniform. "What have you learned?" Grey asked, leaning against the other side of the pillar. It shifted slightly, his weight counterbalancing Ranieri's.

"Not a lot," Ranieri said. "Tess is as loyal as they come, and she's Alta Renata's only servant, so there's no one else to talk to. Sir, I—I don't like doing this. Pretending to make friends, just so I can snoop."

If Ranieri had consulted him beforehand, Grey would have warned him not to use his real family and their bakery as a cover, no matter how convenient it was to Viraudax's townhouse. Hard to keep the professional and the personal separate when you let them overlap like Corillis and Paumillis during conjunction.

"Noted. Maybe I should put Kaineto on snooping and dump the Indestor business on you?"

Ranieri twisted to face him, horror and dread dueling in liquid dark eyes, until he caught the sardonic twist to Grey's brow. "Not necessary, sir. I wouldn't wish that on any of us."

"Good man. Did you find anything other than your conscience?"

Gaze shifting to the broad street, Ranieri said, "She's not from Little Alwydd—Tess, I mean. The alta hired her when her ship docked in Ganllech. Seemed grateful to be quit of the place— Tess, not the alta—but that's Ganllech for you. She's overworked, though." He frowned. "Which makes sense if she's the only servant, but if that's the case, then she's not overworked *enough*. Not for a house that size. They don't have day workers or accounts with any of the local grocers, either. Of course, Alta Renata takes most of her meals out—she's hardly ever home."

That supported what Grey had heard from the street children he'd hired—that the only people visiting Renata's townhouse were messengers. It might just be that Renata hadn't yet set up her household fully...but she'd been in Nadežra for several weeks. If she was planning to stay, he would have expected her to settle in more by now.

Or she was just feckless. She'd come home on foot two weeks ago, her hair all tumbled down, with her maid supporting her. It could mean a wild night, typical of a noble without a care for practical matters.

"What about other contacts among the nobles?" Grey asked. Any suspicious meetings would be happening outside Renata's house, but the maid might have dropped a hint.

"Lots, but none that seem like she's working with anyone." Then Ranieri laughed. "Oh, but you should have seen Tess go off like a firecracker when Indestor came up. You heard the story, sir, about Alta Renata losing her glove to the Rook? You've never seen a woman so frothed about a missing glove! Never would have guessed that girl had such a tongue on her—could have scorched the water from the West Channel and left a dry bed."

"It was an offensive demand," Grey said curtly. "And the Rook is a criminal."

"No, not the Rook! Mezzan Indestor, for being an ass. And his father for having such a useless son, and unto the seventh generation. No love there from maid or mistress." Ranieri grinned. Hawk he might be, but he'd picked up Grey's distaste for the house that oversaw the Vigil.

Grey was less amused. It sounded like his superiors weren't using Alta Renata to gain leverage over House Traementis—but that meant Donaia had wasted his time with this investigation. Time he could have spent helping those children...or pursuing Kolya's killer.

Still, he'd promised Cercel and Donaia both that he'd do his best. He would pull the street children off watching her house—that was coming out of the Vigil's coffers—but Renata's finances might bear a closer look before he gave up. And he didn't see much point in straining Ranieri's conscience any further by having him dig around Tess.

Grey was about to say so when a furtive movement caught his eye.

It was the patterner. Her latest client had given the deck its final shuffle and returned it to her. But she was facing Grey, and when she straightened her shawl to accept the deck, he was at just the right angle to see her swap it for another—one that was undoubtedly stacked.

He pushed off the post and wove quickly through traffic. She'd laid out the spread by the time he reached her. Grey caught her wrist as she reached for the cards of the past.

She wrenched free, but not before he twitched aside the edge of her skirt with his other hand and pulled out the swapped deck from under her knee. "I suggest you waste your money somewhere else," he told the mark, not breaking his gaze from the szorsa.

She twisted her face away. Sputtering indignation, the mark scooped up his offering from her bowl and huffed off. Grey dropped into Vraszenian to be sure the woman understood him. "And I suggest you cheat your marks with words alone. I see you cold-deck someone again, and every card you have I'll throw into the nearest canal."

She didn't even spit a curse at him. Just swept up both decks and ran.

Grey didn't bother giving chase. The momentary flash of righteous indignation passed, leaving him hollow. If Kolya had seen him treat a szorsa like that...

Passing clouds dampened the fading sunlight, heralding a spatter of rain. A shiver passed through Grey, leaving goose pricks in its wake. The szorsa had left her blanket and bowl. Fishing out two centiras from his pouch, he dropped them into the vessel to appease Ir Entrelke Nedje.

"Sir?" Ranieri said from behind him.

"Go home," Grey said heavily. "Don't worry about prying any more into the maid. I'll take care of it."

But after Ranieri left, Grey didn't return to the Viraudax nonsense, nor even go back to the problem of the sleepless children. Instead he headed to the nearest labyrinth to beg forgiveness from his brother's spirit.

Coster's Walk, Lower Bank: Suilun 24

Ren sagged against the crumbling plaster of a butcher's shop and pressed her hands to her mouth, trying not to hyperventilate.

Why did Grey Serrado have to pick that moment to visit Coster's Walk? Dressed like a proper Vraszenian, talking to some pretty youth she would have taken for a night-piece trawling for customers if he hadn't seemed so painfully shy. She'd been tempted to eavesdrop, but self-preservation took priority. The last thing she could afford was for Serrado to notice that the nearby szorsa looked oddly like Renata Viraudax.

But her nerves made her clumsy, so that he spotted her swapping decks. She shouldn't have taken the risk—but she'd been out there all day, hoping to snare one person in particular. Nikory, the leader of the Fog Spiders, who street rumors said operated under Derossi Vargo's command.

Renata couldn't look into Vargo's criminal activities, but Arenza Lenskaya could.

It was useful that a fine alta like Renata Viraudax wouldn't set foot outside her house before sixth sun, or receive guests before fifth. That left Ren the morning hours in which to put on a different mask and work her way through the Old Island and the Lower Bank. She didn't dare stray too close to the people she'd known from her days in the Fingers, but the city's Vraszenians were another matter.

She'd never really been one of them. Without makeup, her half-northern heritage showed. Ren was hardly the only Vraszenian to carry the blood of an outsider, but the kretse could be insular, and some of those traditional lineages didn't tolerate outsiders among them. Ivrina Lenskaya's family had been of that kind. As a result, she'd had to raise her daughter outside the networks of lineage and clan affiliation that still bound most Vraszenians—those from the free city-states of Vraszan—into a solid fabric.

In Nadežra, the warp and weft of that fabric was looser. By playing the role of Arenza Lenskaya, Ren could wheedle information out of the local-born Vraszenians, whose first question wasn't *Who are your people?* Some, like Ondrakja, were part of the criminal underworld; the rest just kept a finger on the pulse of the gangs for their own protection. They knew who held what territory and did what kind of work, and who was in charge—and they knew Vargo.

He ran a large confederation of knots across the Lower Bank, formed from the Blue Cobs, the Leek Street Cutters, the Roundabout Boys, and a variety of other gangs. Many were smugglers, as Donaia had said, slipping goods past the customs officials and selling them at a cut rate. A year ago Vargo had moved to Eastbridge on the Upper Bank and started buying up buildings and land in his knots' territories, putting his money into legitimate businesses.

But none of that told her whether his plan for the river charter was something House Traementis should back. If she couldn't answer that question, she couldn't suggest that Donaia make her an advocate. And she needed some kind of leverage to continue her progress—not to mention some kind of income, so she wouldn't run through her letter of credit before she got access to the house's accounts.

Working as a patterner gave her both. According to street gossip, three years ago a szorsa had warned Nikory not to trust his ladylove. He didn't listen, and got his tongue split when she reported him to the office of Argentet in the Cinquerat for seditious talk. Since then he'd consulted patterners on a regular basis. If Ren had hooked him, she could have used that to pry all manner of secrets out.

But the Masks had shown one mercy: Serrado hadn't recognized her. Dressed in full, kilted skirts with a sash belt and a shoulder-buttoned shirt, face made up to emphasize her Vraszenian features instead of the Liganti side, she'd been right in front of him and he hadn't realized it.

Ren's heart was finally slowing down. She cursed the money she'd left behind—undoubtedly gone by now. She'd been hoping to use it to get Tess a birthing-day gift without touching the budget, but now she'd have to nick something. And thanks to Serrado, the mark she'd spent half the day waiting for would never approach her again. Conning Nikory had been her best plan for getting information on Vargo's other business dealings. Now she'd have to risk something more dangerous.

Ren exhaled slowly. The sun was setting, but the life of the street continued: a ribbon seller with her stick full of colorful wares, a woman carrying a screaming child, a costermonger with a barrow of less-than-fresh mussels.

This used to be her world. Five years in Ganllech couldn't erase that, and neither could Renata Viraudax.

Out here, she knew exactly which risks to take.

Pushing off the wall, Ren straightened her disguise and set out through the growing gloom.

Froghole, Lower Bank: Suilun 24

All the rookeries clinging to the Lower Bank stank of waste and disease, but the bend that cradled Froghole captured that stink and fermented it into a fetid wine. The taste of it rolled thick over Vargo's tongue as he crossed a crumbling bridge into the bowels of the rookery. He tugged his cowl—imbued against smells—over his face and wished he'd brought his newest mask instead. The fists riding in his wake had to make do with kerchiefs and scarves.

A river mist had risen as night descended, the intermittent fish-oil lanterns painting it a dingy yellow. It hid the sight of their passage, but not the sound of their boots tromping. Only the rats failed to scurry into the shadows. The true masters of Froghole, they were.

When Vargo had been a boy, flea infested and rat bitten as any gutter-rutting cur, escaping the rookeries had seemed an impossible dream. Every return was a reminder that there was no waking up from reality.

Shaking off the weight of past memories, Vargo spoke over his shoulder. "Which depot got hit?"

Varuni, his Isarnah bodyguard, had the build of a pit bull and the determination to match. She took the task of keeping him informed as seriously as she took her job of protecting him—or rather, her people's investment in him. "The one on Glusky Lane. The old lace mill."

Vargo's step faltered. He'd mapped Froghole into his soul through days of hunger and nights of fear. But if he had a fondness for any squat from those days, it'd be the old lace mill. Hadn't it been his refuge when he'd no hope left but to die?

It didn't matter that Vargo had retired the mill to become just another link in his aža smuggling chain. It was his. And he was going to *end* whoever had poached it.

Nikory and Orostin stood outside, waiting for his arrival. Rot had overtaken the mill in the years since Vargo moved to less unsavory headquarters. Someone had tacked thin leather hides, checkered with mildew, over the places where the boards had rotted away.

"Who's on this patch?" Vargo asked softly. The decay was one thing, impossible to fight in sinking Froghole, but his people knew better than to let thieves slip through.

An uneasy look passed between Nikory and Orostin. "Hraček, before he died," Orostin said. "Been unstable round here since then."

Hraček, who'd been drugged by *someone* while Vargo plied Renata Viraudax with spiced chocolate. By the time Vargo had arrived, Hraček had been too far gone to talk. Not from the drug, but from the wounds covering him from scalp to heel, ragged slices shredding his flesh into strips. He'd struggled too much for anyone to treat them before he bled out.

The only thing that kept Vargo from punching the wall was the possibility that it might collapse under the blow and bring the roof down with it. Over two weeks since Hraček's death, and all he had was a corpse and questions. And now this. Had someone killed Hraček to take advantage of the confusion that would follow?

::You don't slice a man's skin to strips because he's inconvenient.:: Alsius's reminder froze Vargo's fury. Anger wouldn't get him answers or retribution.

"Get it stable," he snapped. "How long ago did they hit us?"

"Last night, but they didn't clear out 'til almost dawn," said Nikory, straightening. He shoved the creaking door open. "And the odd thing en't what they took—it's what they left behind."

Vargo followed the lure of Nikory's cryptic statement. Inside the old mill, the rot was worse. Clean circles edged with black mold decorated the floor where barrels had been left standing too long. Pigeons took advantage of gaps in the shingles to nest in the eaves; the walls wept tears of white shit. At Varuni's booted nudge, a tangle of fur broke apart into a half-rotted rat king, the corpses knotted together in death. Cold sweat broke across Vargo's forehead. Even his cowl wasn't enough to mask the stench.

::What's that in the center of the room?::

Blotting his brow, Vargo made for the markings that were neither mold nor shit. Gloves served a better purpose than just Liganti fashion; they also protected his hand as he brushed his fingers across a half-erased line of chalk that had once been a numinat. The power had broken with the lines; the taste of char lingered in the air. It had been active, and recently.

In Froghole, there was always someone who'd seen something and was willing to sell what they'd seen. "Check the eyes on the streets. Anyone saw so much as a rat out of place, I want to know it."

::Do you really expect anyone to say anything?:: Alsius asked.

Not without incentive, Vargo thought in reply. "Make it clear I'm the one asking. And stack those barrels. I need to get higher."

While his people sprang to obey, Vargo circled the room. Near the edge of the chalked perimeter, a splatter of dark liquid gleamed like an oily canal. Distilled aža had that surface, like trapped rainbows, but the splatter here was murky purple and stank of curdled milk.

::A sample might be—::

Not for nothing am I touching that, he shot back. *You think it's so necessary,* you *take the fucking sample.*

But Alsius had a point. "Nikory. Scrape up a sample of this."

"On it. Did you want me to climb up?" He gestured at the stacked barrels.

"Mastered inscription while I wasn't looking, did you?" Vargo drawled, shedding his coat. He snatched a roll of blank pages and a pencil from its pocket before handing the garment to Varuni and climbing the mountain of barrels. He could rely on his people for many things, but for some tasks there was only himself.

From his new vantage, Vargo weighted the paper flat and began sketching the remains of a numinat complicated enough to make his eyes cross.

Soon he had several pages of what amounted to chicken scratches. Varuni had brought in lamps, placing them around the perimeter of the numinat—a diameter that knocked up against opposite walls of the warehouse. With that size and the rough grain of the floorboards, no wonder the intruders hadn't managed to erase the whole thing.

Several sharp pops echoed in Vargo's head when he rolled it to relieve the ache in his shoulders.

::I do wish you wouldn't do that. Appalling sound.::

Setting out his sketches, Vargo traced lines with his finger, starting at the off-center point where the focus must have been, and spiraling out to the edges of the room. Along the spiral were the incomplete remnants of circles containing their own geometric figures, smaller numinata that refined the master numinat's purpose.

"It's an earthwise spiral," Vargo said, quietly enough that his people wouldn't overhear. Every numen had either an earthwise or a sunwise association, and the direction of the spiral determined whether the numinat was meant for good or ill.

::That doesn't help us unless we know which numen it was dedicated to.::

The problem with having a pedant in his head was that Alsius tended to repeat basic lessons Vargo had mastered years ago. "Really. I didn't know that."

"Sir?" Varuni took an abbreviated step toward Vargo's barrel tower. "Need something?"

He hadn't meant to call her attention, but... "Did anyone locate the remains of the focus?" The boards at the center of the spiral were scorched in a perfect ring no bigger than a plover's egg, marking Illi, the place where the divine focus was set, the starting point of every numinat. For more permanent numinata, the focus would be carefully drawn or inlaid in metal, but for temporary work, most inscriptors used wax blanks that could be stamped with a carved chop of whatever aspect of the Lumen they were drawing on. The discoloration at the numinat's center suggested such a seal had been used, the scorching another sign that the numinat had been hastily and sloppily dismantled. Whoever set it up had left someone less skilled to take it down. If they used a wax focus, the dismantler might have dumped the fragments.

"Nothing yet, sir."

Damn. Vargo waved Varuni back to her reports. "We do this the hard way," he said, soft enough that she wouldn't mistake his muttering for additional orders.

Without a focus at Illi to indicate the general purpose of the master numinat, the next best clues were the child numinata inscribed along the spira aurea's arc. The first of which, just to the left of Illi, was easy enough to discern despite the attempts to erase it—the overlapping circles of a vesica piscis.

::Tuat,:: Alsius mused. ::What were the phases of Corillis and Paumillis last night?::

Astrology and numinatria often went hand in hand, and the double moons were tied to Tuat, the self-in-other. But Vargo didn't think this had to do with astronomical timing. "First quarter and waxing gibbous."

::Neither matched nor in reflection. So much for that theory. It's probably some fool marrying their beloved in secret,:: Alsius grumbled.

"More like cursing them," Vargo mused, tracing the earthwise spiral again. Tuat was a sunwise numen. Charting it on the earthwise side of a spiral inverted its purpose.

He scowled at the floor and the chalky remains of the vesica piscis scraped across it. The lamplight caught that rainbow shimmer— the stuff that wasn't aža, staining the floor.

"Or...their dreams?" Like the dreamweaver birds, aža was sacred to Vraszenians. They even called aža the "little dream"—after the Great Dream that overtook Nadežra every seven years, when Ažerais's sacred wellspring appeared on the Point, full of glowing waters that offered true visions to anyone who drank them. Vraszenians believed that aža dreams were little echoes of those true visions, but most Nadežrans didn't use aža for such lofty purposes; they just wanted a brief, pleasant escape from their daily woes. Since the Cinquerat did their best to strangle the trade with their control, smugglers like Vargo made good money selling aža to Vraszenians and Nadežrans alike.

The inscriptor had chosen Vargo's aža depot to scribe their numinat, and stolen Vargo's aža stores. And Tuat was the numen of intuition and dreams.

::Still a fool's goal. Dreams are as ephemeral as love.::

Nobody who'd inscribed a numinat this complex would be so foolish. But there were dreams, and there were dreams. "Aža isn't."

Vargo scowled at the mental laughter that followed. "What? It isn't much different than using a numinat to improve the effects of medicine."

::Except that such effects fade quickly, and any power the numinat conveyed would break when it was erased.::

Alsius had a point. Barring jewelry and the little paper blessings exchanged on special occasions—weddings, christenings, the new year at the summer solstice—most numinata remained where they were inscribed, serving whatever purpose they'd been created for until time and geometric flaws cracked them beyond use.

"What about transmutation? Like using numinata to make prismatium?"

::The creation of prismatium is an arcane and lengthy process, one of the great master works of numinatria.:: Alsius's response came verbatim from the opening lines of Declasitus's *Principia Numinatriae*. ::It is not something that may be accomplished overnight in a slum.::

Arguing with Alsius when he took that tone was futile. Returning his attention to the sketches, Vargo traced farther along the spiral. Beyond Tuat, the other numina were too geometrically complex to easily discern from the remaining traces. That cluster of angles and crossed lines could easily be Tricat drawn for stability and harmony, or Ninat for death, endings, and apotheosis.

They could be at this puzzle for hours—days—without learning anything more. His eyes were getting bleary from squinting too long in the dim light of the lamps, and he could practically feel the walls breathing disease at him.

"Enough of this. We're not solving it tonight." Vargo climbed down, waving off Varuni when she held up his coat. "Don't bother. I'm having someone burn this entire outfit when we get home."

Pausing on the threshold, Vargo glared at the puzzle left for him. He had a plan to carry out, and the next step waited on a Seterin alta to prove her use; he didn't have time for new mysteries.

But someone had disturbed his web, and there'd be no sleeping until he knew who and why.

Froghole, Lower Bank: Suilun 24

The stench of Froghole was thick enough to gag on. Between that and the tension wiring her shoulders together, Ren was fairly certain that following Nikory here had been a mistake.

This wasn't her turf. Before she'd left Nadežra, this had all been

Blue Cob territory, and anyone else setting foot there risked bleeding for it. She didn't know the lookout points, the escape routes. Her sole defense was that she looked like a random Vraszenian woman out on her own business . . . but that defense weakened when Nikory stopped outside a dilapidated building and took up a guard position with the man at his side, leaving Ren to loiter suspiciously in the shadows.

And it got as fragile as blown glass when Vargo himself appeared, looking like he was ready to gut somebody with a dull knife.

A legitimate businessman didn't set foot in places like this. His presence alone was more than enough evidence for Ren to agree with Donaia that Vargo hadn't shed his criminal side.

But she couldn't flee, not without the lookouts seeing. Not until the sagging door opened again, revealing one of the men who'd gone inside with Vargo, and the guards turned to talk to him. She wouldn't have a better chance to leave unnoticed.

Ren eased backward, pressing herself against the wall for cover, even though it crawled with mold and river beetles. As soon as she rounded the corner, she started moving faster, trying to put distance between herself and whatever Vargo was doing.

She sacrificed caution for speed, and paid the price.

Hands shoved her shoulders from behind at the same moment a kick took her knee from under her. Ren fell hard, skidding in the mud, all the wind driven from her lungs. The man above her was nothing more than a silhouette, his weight dropping onto her before she could reach for a knife, pinning her wrists and trapping her legs. Ren would have screamed if she thought it would do any good.

The man snarled, "Right, then, what the fuck do you—"

She heaved with her whole body, trying to use the slime of the street to twist out from under him. Her shawl fell from her head, and the man's grip slackened.

It was an opening she couldn't waste. Her elbow slammed into his throat a half instant after he said, "*Ren?*"

He fell back, choking. Ren was on her feet and three steps away before the word sank in. Her name. He'd said her name.

Not Renata. Not Arenza. *Ren.*

Against every shred of common sense, she turned back.

He was on his ass in the muck, and although the alley was narrow, enough of Paumillis's copper-green moonlight filtered in to pick out his features. Dark hair, skin not quite Liganti-pale, a nose broken more than once, and scars cutting his cheeks, his lip.

But he knew her through the makeup, and she knew him through the scars.

Ren whispered, "Sedge?"

"Ren." Surprise scrubbed years from his features, making him young again—as young as they'd ever been. He'd been big for a boy in the rookeries, gangly limbed and rawboned. Whatever grace he'd gained growing into manhood abandoned him now. He lurched to his feet, never taking his gaze from hers. "How...I looked...They said you..."

Left. She and Tess had left—because Sedge was dead. Ren saw his body, broken and unmoving in the half-dry canal where Ondrakja threw him. She never would have abandoned him if—if she'd *known*—

Her throat closed up as if she were the one struck. Sedge took a half step toward her, then cast a glance over his shoulder.

"Fuck." Grabbing her shoulders, he force-turned her and pushed her along the path she'd been running. "Get out of here. Don't be seen. If Vargo hears..." Sedge left the implied threat hanging. His grip slid down to the inside of her wrist. The cuff of her sleeve covered the line there, faded but never quite gone—one of the few physical scars she had. His thumb brushed across the spot, and she wondered if she would even be able to find his matching scar amid the marks hashing his arms. "I'll find you at the hole as soon as—"

The echo of boots and voices just around the corner broke through that vestige of tenderness. His face hardened into a scowl. "Go."

Sedge. Alive. For years he'd been her brother, her friend, her shield, and when he said *Go*, she went.

Ren went.

Lacewater, Old Island: Suilun 24

She was fourteen years old again, wrapped in a filthy shawl and huddling in the meager shelter of a recessed cellar window on the south
side of the Tricatium in Lacewater. Never mind that five years in
Ganllech had made her taller, so that she didn't fit very well into her
old spot and there was no way Sedge would be able to cram in there
with her. The mist had chilled to freezing, she was losing feeling in
her fingers, and Sedge was *alive*. As if the last five years had never
happened.

He knew better than to sneak up on her again. She saw him
coming over the temple's retaining wall, dropping more quietly
than his size should allow. Ondrakja had been right to fear what
would happen when Sedge realized he was big enough to fight
back. But they had all been so used to shrinking from her rages,
groveling and scraping and taking their punishment, that rebelling
seemed unthinkable.

Ren had been able to dilute those rages, sometimes. Sedge protected her and Tess with his fists; she'd protected him and Tess with
her wits. And Tess took care of them both.

Sedge took one look at Ren squeezed into the space, sighed, and
held out a hand to help her up. "I need beer for this. Copper's should
be quiet at this hour, and Vargo don't got eyes there."

With his palm upturned and light coming from the lamps over
the temple's portico, she could see the scar on the inside of his wrist.
Sedge was showing it to her on purpose, because he knew how suspicious she was. It really was him: her blood brother, the other half
of her family.

Ren clasped his forearm, scar to scar, and let him haul her to her
feet.

Copper's was a seedy ostretta wedged into a five-way intersec-
tion. Entering was easy enough, but people coming out had to take

care or be plowed down by passing traffic. Sedge's attention was so fixed on Ren that he nearly knocked over an old woman emerging as they entered. The door shut on her curses.

Ren found an empty gallery alcove while Sedge commandeered spiced millet beer and cups. Closed curtains gave them privacy. Sedge poured for them both; then they sat in silence, staring at each other over steaming mugs, while Ren tried and failed to find a way to say *I'm sorry I got you killed.*

Almost killed.

Sedge's breathy chuckle broke the stalemate. "You must've changed. Never known you to run out of words."

Her muddy fingers shook on the cup. "It was my fault."

"Never marked you for the stupid one, neither," he said, prying the cup out of her hands and setting it aside before she could spill it. His hands engulfed hers, warming her icy fingers. "Getting knocked in the head was my job. Still is."

A sob caught in her throat at the reminder; her hands were corpse cold. Like he'd been. Like she'd thought he'd been.

Sedge chafed life back into them. "You been blaming yourself all these years?"

Now the words came spilling out—all the things she couldn't say to him before, because he was dead and it was too late for apologies. "I'm the one who got greedy, took that coffer because I thought nobody would notice and we could use it to escape. I'm the one who crossed the Cut Ears, got them pissed at Ondrakja. She hurt you to hurt me. I watched her beat you to death and I did nothing, I just *stood* there, because I was too afraid—"

Sedge's grip tightened, just short of pain. The thin veneer of tenderness peeled away, but instead of the molten anger she remembered from their childhood, what lay underneath was hardened steel. "Don't make it worse. That was our rule, remember?" His whisper shook like her hands. "If you'd done anything, said anything, you would have made it worse. And then I *would* be dead. You did the smart thing, trying to get us out before it got to that. Weren't your fault you got nicked. And you did the smart thing after, running. I'm glad at least——" The whisper broke. Releasing her, he drained his mug, then refilled it to overflowing. He scowled at the beer trickling over his fingers and pooling on the table. "I'm glad at least one of us did."

Ren's heart thudded painfully. *He knows not.* Of course. From his perspective, they'd vanished like the river fog. "Sedge—Tess is alive. She's with me."

More beer sloshed onto the table, its sour-spiced scent perfuming the alcove. The steel of Sedge's gaze turned brittle, the muscles of his jaw, his neck, his forearms corded with the effort not to shatter.

"You've been together. All this time. Safe. And together." No matter how he tried to disguise it, Ren could hear the hollowness at the core of his words. She'd had Tess. Sedge had been left to carry on alone.

Now it was her turn to grip his hands, sticky with spills. *If I'd realized—*

Before she could apologize again, Sedge shook himself. "Where? I looked everywhere. You weren't in Nadežra. Where did you go?"

"Ganllech. Though not on purpose." If he wanted to change the subject, she knew better than to push. Ren let go and took a healthy slug from her own cup. "After you...died...I fed Ondrakja meadow saffron, then conned a captain into believing Tess and I were experienced ship's monkeys. Got us out of the city, but he soon realized I lied, and at the next port of call put us off."

"Fed her..." A grin split Sedge's face, pulling at the scars crossing it. "So Simlin didn't lie. Heard Ondrakja got sick, but he said you'd poisoned her. And everybody believed him."

Then his grin faded, as the weight of it hit him. "Shit. You *poisoned* her."

"And I would again," Ren said violently. "I care not that it makes me a traitor. Ask me to choose my brother or my knot, and my brother I will choose, every time."

It was almost true. Ren wouldn't take her choice back...but killing the leader of her own knot was blasphemy. If she'd untied herself from the knot first, Ondrakja would have known, and then she never would have drunk the poisoned tea. So Ren had fallen back on the best weapon in her arsenal—her ability to lie.

But it meant no knot would ever take her again. Not unless she reinvented herself as another person. And if she was going to go to all that work, she might as well join the gang that held all the real power in Nadežra: the city's nobility.

Sedge saw through the bravado. His throat jumped as he swallowed. "Fuck. You did that for me. I . . . shit."

If she didn't say something, one or the other of them was going to wind up crying. "How could you *survive* that?"

He coughed, clearing his throat. "Somebody found me and dragged me to a leech—*after* they looted my boots." He'd loved those boots. So big they chafed and left blisters; he'd had to stuff them with rags. But they'd made wonderful clompy sounds that had all the Fingers feeling safer when Sedge was around. "Took about a month before I stopped sleeping and drooling on myself. A year before everything stopped hurting. I still get dizzy sometimes. But nobody raises a fist to me these days unless they're seriously stupid. And I got new boots." He propped a muddy heel on the empty stool at his side.

New boots. Ren choked on a half laugh. He'd never been as good with words as she was, but he was doing his best to distract her. The sight of him had torn the scab off a wound not nearly as healed as she thought, and she couldn't look at him without drowning in a flood of both guilt and joy. "Now you work for Vargo?"

His boot thunked to the floor. "Yeah. Guess we need to talk about that." Bracing himself with another gulp of beer, Sedge tugged his sleeve up, revealing a charm of knotted blue silk tied around his wrist. "I'm with the Fog Spiders now. They're kind of his main crew. So, uh, don't go asking me nothing you shouldn't."

The oaths for knots varied from gang to gang, but there were some things in common. Like sharing secrets with each other, but keeping them from outsiders. "I understand."

Nothing stopped him from asking *her* questions, though. "What the fuck were you doing, anyway, snooping near Vargo's warehouse?

Please tell me you en't involved in whatever went down there last night."

Her knee-jerk impulse was to ask what went down last night. Ren swallowed it and said, "I look into his business only. Not in a way you should worry about; just figuring out if, like he claims, he's gone legitimate. My impression is, not so much."

"Why do you care about his busi—Oh, fuck. Oh, Ren. Oh no." Sedge's head sank to the table. "Fuck, fuck, fuck." The pitcher and mugs rattled each time his brow hit the wood. "Please tell me you en't Vargo's Alta Renata who's gonna get him his fucking charter."

"Please tell me you won't give yourself a concussion if I say yes." She reached across the table and pushed him upright.

"I'll end up with a lot worse than that if Vargo finds out," he muttered darkly.

"Then he will not find out," Ren said, offering him a cocky grin. Some of her confidence was coming back, and bringing with it the things she used to say, when all three of them ran with the Fingers.

Sedge's mouth worked past several unspoken responses. Defeated, he sank back into his chair, face planted into one hand. "Just tell me what you need to get the job done."

Him ambushing her had been seven strokes of luck at once. "I need somebody who knows Vargo. I seek not to pry into his secrets—only that I never heard of him when we were with the Fingers."

"No, we wouldn't have. He took over the Spiders—used to be a Varadi gang—right around the time you left. There was a bunch of turf wars all along the Lower Bank then, but he mostly stayed out of them." Sedge grimaced. "Well. That's what it looked like. Turns out he was the one starting them. He'd let his rivals tire themselves out fighting each other, then wrap up the remnants, replace the leaders, and welcome them in like he was doing them a favor. That's how he works. Sets things up and waits for people to come to him."

He hadn't waited for Renata to come to him—or had he? Their chance encounter at the Gloria seemed much less like chance now.

"So with this charter business I walk into his web. Wonderful. Is he actually out to clean the river?"

"Near as I can tell, that's legit." Sedge blinked, as though he'd never thought to question his boss's intentions. "The man hates disease more than most cuffs. And he's smart enough to know if the people around him are healthy, he's less likely to get sick. He could just hide on the Upper Bank—but what he's built would fall apart without him there to keep it all running. Cleaning up the West Channel is good sense."

He exhaled slowly, shaking his head. "Look, Vargo's about as clean as you'd expect for a man from the rookeries, but he en't cruel like Ondrakja, or half the cuffs that run this place." Sedge snorted. "Name me one seat on the Cinquerat that wouldn't toss folks like us on penal ships to be sold in Ommainit. But Vargo? He pays fair, protects us from the Vigil's purges, and there en't been another turf war since he took over. This last year or so, when he started to go legit..."

Sedge trailed off. When Ren raised her eyebrow, he shrugged. "I dunno. He's different. More focused on the cheese-eaters at the top instead of the folks on the street. Don't try to cheat him or nothing...but an alta working with him should be safe. Just watch out that he don't wind up owning you when it's over."

"I have no intention of that. I'm out to join House Traementis, and bringing them this charter will help me worm my way inside. I need only to convince Donaia that Vargo seeks not to set himself up as Kaius Rex of the Lower Bank."

"Traementis. That's really your goal?" Sedge whistled. "At least you went for the house with the fewest pricks. If you'd gone Indestor or Novrus, I'd have to challenge you to one of them duels— *wait*." Sedge lunged forward, rattling the table. Ren caught the beer pitcher before it could topple. "Indestor. Duels. You met the Rook!"

And just like that they were children again, on one of the good days when Ondrakja was feeling generous and gave them wine and enough to eat. Ren opened her mouth to spill the whole story— then stopped.

"Not here," she said. Sedge cast an automatic glance at the curtains, but Ren shook her head. "No, I mean—come with me." She held out her hand to him, the same as he'd done before. Her sleeve pulled back just enough to show the scar. There were three of them with marks like that, and Tess needed to know their brother was alive.

What better gift to give her for her birthday?

"Come home," Ren said. "Hug Tess. And I will tell you everything."

Saffron and Salt

Isla Traementis, the Pearls: Equilun 7

Much had changed in the month and a half since Renata first climbed the steps of Traementis Manor. The days had grown colder, the sky more grey. She'd adjusted to her Seterin accent, no longer fearing that it might slip in an unguarded moment.

And she was now an invited guest to the manor.

The majordomo, Colbrin, hadn't yet gone so far as to smile at her, but his expression as he bowed her inside looked like it might at least inhabit the same neighborhood as such a thing. Renata gave him her cloak and chafed warmth into her hands. "If you would be so kind as to wait in the salon," Colbrin said, "Alta Giuna will be with you shortly."

Colbrin's "shortly" was measured in the time it took Renata to sit.

"Cousin!" To Donaia's dismay, both Giuna and Leato had taken to calling Renata that. House Traementis had lost enough cousins over the past twenty years that they hungered for familial connection. It was a hunger Renata carefully managed, not calling them cousin in turn—not yet.

"Alta Giuna." Rising, she took the girl's hands and pressed cheeks with her. "Thank you so much for inviting me."

"Must you always be so formal? You should visit whenever you wish. It's so cold these days that there's nothing to do but sit around the house in boredom. Speaking of which—" Giuna tugged Renata toward the salon door. "The solar is much warmer and more comfortable. Let's go there, and you can tell me whether you really did hit Illi five times in a row like Leato says."

Renata laughed and let herself be tugged. "Leato was so drunk I think he saw the entire dartboard as Illi." The whole group had been drunk. Her accuracy was good, but she'd also contrived to pour the majority of her mulled wine into a potted lily at Fintenus Manor.

Giuna could not have been more obviously starved for gossip. She might say it was too cold to do anything except sit around, but other noble scions—including her brother—found ways to entertain themselves, with darts or cards, the theatre or music. Only Giuna was mewed up at home.

But Renata walked a fine line between fostering Giuna's admiration and friendship, and alienating Donaia by encouraging the girl to ask for more than her mother gave.

The ringing of steel cut off Giuna's response. The sound was unmistakable: The younger nobles and delta gentry brawled often enough that Ren had learned to recognize it from streets away. She halted, head turning instinctively toward the noise coming through a half-open set of double doors on the far side of the hall.

From the other side of the door came a muffled whap and a yelp. Giuna stifled a giggle.

"Keep your focus, pup. If your attention wanders, so will your tip." The woman's words rolled like the smoke from a Vraszenian campfire. "Have I years of effort wasted only for you to forget everything I taught you?"

"No, duellante," Leato said. "You wasted years on me because I'm so pretty."

"You won't stay that way if your shoulder kisses your ear so often. Uniat."

"Tuat." The clashing resumed.

"The halls are too cold at the Palaestra, and the grounds are too muddy, so Leato's taking his weekly lesson here," Giuna said, voice low.

Leato had mentioned training under Oksana Ryvček. Was his teacher actually here?

Renata drifted a half step toward the door, as if the movement were unconscious. "Would you mind if...?"

Giuna had been grinning often these days, whenever Renata and Leato were together. "Well, he *is* fun to watch."

The room beyond the double doors turned out to be the manor's ballroom. It was an ideal place to practice swordplay: lots of open space, with light from the windows at the far end and relatively few things to break if the combatants got too energetic. The air inside was as chill as a cellar, but for those exerting themselves, that was likely a benefit.

The duelists took no notice of the interruption. They wore stiff protective jackets and used blunted practice swords, but apart from that they didn't seem to be holding back. Leato shifted to one side and thrust at the oblique; Ryvček blocked, blade sliding against blade, and diverted his tip past her shoulder. When Leato overbalanced, she rolled her wrist and came up under to tap his open arm.

"Better, but you overcommitted," she said, withdrawing. Then she winked at Giuna and saluted Renata with her blade.

Oksana Ryvček looked every inch the famous duelist: tall, thin as her rapier, her jacket of bone-pale brocade contrasting with her sleek black breeches and boots. Her coloring was as dark as Ren's without powders; faint lines creased the kohl around her eyes and framed a mouth made for smiling, and streams of silver swept through her dark curls.

"Well met, pretty Giuna. And who is this ravishing woman with you?" Ryvček caught Renata's hand and bent over it, the warmth of her lips penetrating the thin suede of Renata's gloves.

Even on the streets, Ren had heard of Ryvček. Nadežran born and raised, she bore her Vraszenian name proudly, rather than pulling on the Liganti threads of her ancestry the way many others did. Her father, a merchant, had trained all his children to fight in order to guard his business against the "protection" schemes of the Vigil. His youngest daughter had shown so much skill with knives and a staff that the delta house of Isorran had paid to train and license her as their duelist—a contract Ryvček had earned out in less than five years.

Ren had never seen her fight, though. The formal conflicts of the elite were almost never held where the common people could see, and she couldn't afford entry to the public tournaments the professional duelists sometimes held. But it was enough to know that someone like Ryvček was out there, trouncing rich cuffs, and wearing a Vraszenian name while she did it.

Now she was getting to meet the woman in person.

Leato approached, wiping sweat from his face with a towel. "This is my cousin Renata, from Seteris."

"Ah yes, Seteris. I hear they dislike sleeves there." Ryvček's gaze lingered on Renata's arms, fully covered today. "Alas, so soon you have our local customs adopted."

"Such things lose their effect if done too often," Renata said carelessly, as if the weather had nothing to do with it. She'd heard the rumors about Ryvček's many flirtations and affairs, too, but never expected to be on the receiving end of them. "I'll have to think of something else to make people gossip."

"Are you any good with a blade? A woman who knows her way around a sword always trails gossip." Ryvček stepped closer, curling Renata's hand against her chest. Her crooked smile wove innuendo into her words. "I could show you a few tricks."

"Yes, yes. Everyone knows the sort of tricks you prefer." Leato set a hand on Ryvček's shoulder, drawing her away. "Leave my cousin alone or I'll have to call you to the ring, and I don't think my pride can suffer the humiliation of losing in front of her."

Renata lifted her hands in preemptive surrender. "My knowledge of swordplay ends at 'you hold the end that isn't sharp, yes?' But I didn't mean to interrupt your practice. Please, continue—I'd be honored if you would let me watch."

Ryvček's smile deepened. "If watching is your preference..."

come along, Traementis. Let us give your lovely cousin a memory for warming her cold nights."

"You don't mind, do you?" Renata murmured to Giuna.

"No." Giuna settled in a chair against the wall and patted the one next to her. "Practices are boring, but it's fun when they show off."

There was no mistaking what ensued for sober practice. Ryvček's fame rested partly on her reputation for flamboyance, and whether it was to impress his cousin or just for his own pride, Leato was doing his best to keep up. The duelists circled each other like they were dancing—Ryvček even threw in a mocking lace step, humming under her breath—then Leato hurled himself into a ground-eating lunge, trying to catch her before she recovered her footing. But Ryvček had been baiting him, because she spun clear of his blade without even bothering to parry, and trailed her fingers across the back of his neck as she passed behind.

Ren was no swordswoman, but she knew fights. The playfulness of their exchanges spoke in every move they made, from the way Leato dipped under a high thrust to the elegant gestures of Ryvček's free hand. This was as unlike the grim and vicious struggles of her childhood as the Upper Bank to the Lower.

Their exchanges shifted like the shoals. Leato and Ryvček both started out in the high Liganti style, but when his tutor taunted him by dropping into a lower stance, Leato answered in the same fashion—she'd clearly also taught him Vraszenian swordsmanship.

The "lesson" came to an end when Ryvček managed to entwine her leg with Leato's and sweep him off-balance. She caught him with her other arm and dipped him, planting a kiss on his lips, then heaved him upright again and backed away, laughing.

Leato laughed as well, brushing the back of his glove across his mouth. "And that is why you're not allowed to duel my sister or my cousin." He bowed. "Thank you, duellante, for the lesson."

"If you fight like that, you might not embarrass me." Ryvček retrieved her sword belt and buckled it on, leaving the practice blade on the chairs in its place. "We will again meet here Epytny next?"

At Leato's nod, Ryvček crossed to where Renata and Giuna

sat. "Giuna, my light. Always a pleasure. Alta Renata, I hope you enjoyed playing voyeur. Perhaps next time we meet, you will with a dance favor me."

Leato joined them as the door closed behind his dueling master. "Duellante Ryvček jokes, but Nadežra isn't safe like Seteris." He gave Renata a sidelong glance. "It isn't a bad idea to know a little more of bladework than which end to hold; not every thief is going to stand still while you pelt darts at them." He stripped off his protective jacket and offered his hand, a courtly echo of Ryvček's bawdy flirtations. "I could show you."

"Oh, you definitely should," Giuna said. "I'll arrange refreshments for when you're done." Before Renata could decide whether to protest, she was out the door as swiftly as Ryvček.

I think someone is playing matchmaker. But there was no harm in cultivating Donaia's favored child. He'd already demonstrated his ability to influence his mother. Renata laid her hand in Leato's and said, "I'd be delighted."

He led her onto the floor. Rather than collecting Ryvček's practice blade, he handed Renata his own. "You're sun-handed, right? Good—we don't have any earth-handed swords here. Wrap your fingers like this..."

The leather of the grip, heated by Leato's exertions, warmed Renata's palm. He arranged her fingers around the hilt, looping one above the crossbar of the guard, and she brought the point up. "Keep your arm straight and high," he said. "That makes for the shortest distance to the target."

So that's why Liganti swordsmen keep their blades out like that. She'd always wondered.

But the last thing she wanted was to spar. She was used to fighting with knives, cobbles, elbows, and teeth, any solid object that came to hand—and some that weren't quite solid. If Leato came at her with a blade, all those instincts were going to surface, and he'd wind up wondering why his elegant cousin fought like a feral cat. So she deliberately stood badly, exposing her whole body to attack, making herself look as ignorant as possible.

"No, stand like this." Moving behind her, Leato aligned his limbs with hers. He gently turned her so they both stood at an oblique to the tip of the blade. "The idea is to present as small a target as you can."

"I see." He was so close that when Renata inhaled, her back brushed his chest. Leato was taller than her, but not by a great deal. He enveloped her like a blanket, warm against the chill of the room, and smelled not unpleasantly of sweat, with a lingering trace of caramel from what remained of his perfume.

"The positions and angles of attack are named for the numina," he said, resting one hand lightly on her wrist. "Your basic stance, like this, is called Uniat, because the parries form a sort of circle around it. Illi is when you lunge to strike center, like so." He guided her into the thrust, then brought her back. "Then it goes Tuat, Tricat, Quarat..."

Renata kept almost none of what he showed her. She was too distracted by Leato's presence behind her, attraction warring with the impulse to pull away. Tess and Sedge were the only people she trusted at her back.

He had just guided her into another lunge when the door opened.

"Leato, did Mistress Ryvček say when— Oh!" Donaia halted on the threshold, Meatball at her side and a pair of gloves hanging forgotten in her bare hand. "Renata. I didn't realize you were here. And you are receiving... lessons, I see?"

Leato cleared his throat and stepped away, grinning with only a little abashment. "I figured she was safer with me than with Ryvček."

"Is she?" Donaia's lips twitched, but she shook her head and allowed the moment to pass. Tugging on her gloves—with, Renata noted, the casual disregard of someone dressing to go out, not someone caught unprepared by a visitor—she said, "Am I correct in assuming you two have plans tonight? Giuna and I are bound for Isla Extaquium to sample Sureggio's newest pressing. I'd hoped for your escort, Leato, but I wouldn't wish you to abandon a prior commitment."

"I was going to teach Renata to play bocce," Leato said before Renata could respond.

He'd mentioned nothing of the sort, but she recognized the cue at once. "Yes, my apologies—I didn't realize you had need of Leato tonight. I can change my plans—"

Donaia refused, as she was meant to. "Not at all. I'm glad to see you enjoying a quiet night for once."

As soon as she was gone, Leato turned to Renata. "Thank you. I hope you don't mind, but Eret Extaquium's pride in his wine is...misplaced." He shuddered dramatically. "I'd rather not spend the evening drinking something that tastes like mold steeped in vinegar."

She wondered if he'd ever tasted anything that foul in reality. Her own memories supplied far too many comparisons. "Shall we do something more enjoyable, then? Bocce or otherwise."

"Perhaps another night? Orrucio Amananto's prize hunting dog whelped, and he's been after me for weeks to see the pups."

He looked sincerely regretful. Anyone but Ren would've likely believed it. "You owe me another lesson as compensation," she said lightly, and gave him back the practice sword with a bow. "I shall enjoy a rare quiet night at home."

Or maybe stop by the Amananto house, to see if you're really there.

Isla Extaquium, Eastbridge: Equilun 7

Giuna liked Parma Extaquium, but Extaquium Manor had never been one of her favorite places. It was as fine as any of the noble houses—and a good deal finer than Traementis Manor—but it lacked subtlety. Eret Extaquium favored overworked brocades, ostentatious marble, and gilt on every surface...including the lips and lashes of his house servants.

But it wasn't only the tasteless decor that was off-putting. The lush, heavy scents from incense and oils gave Giuna headaches.

The manor was always too warm, even in winter, and the illuminating numinata put out half the usual light, forcing her to squint. His servants made her uncomfortable, their voices too breathy or sultry, their movements too graceful and posed. Rumor said that at some parties—the kind Giuna wasn't invited to—they barely even wore clothing, just coats or surcoats, the flesh beneath painted and oiled.

She cleaved close to her mother's side, wishing her face weren't shining already with sweat. When someone handed her a glass of iced wine, she drank it, grateful for something to cool her, even if it was so cloyingly sweet the only note she could pick out was a hint of cork mold.

Donaia made a displeased face at her own glass. "We don't have to stay long, Giuna," she murmured. "Knowing Sureggio, all too soon this will stop being a civilized affair. But I need to talk to Mede Isorran about the possibility of caravan guards—can you survive for an hour?"

"I'll be fine, Mother." Donaia and Leato were always trying to shelter her, as though anyone gave her existence enough thought to threaten harm. "I'll just find a bench near a window, so I don't die from this heat."

Kissing her mother's cheek, Giuna separated before she became a burden. She drifted through the overwarm rooms, looking for Parma; where she went, Bondiro and Egliadas were usually paying court, and the three together could be entertaining. Better still, they didn't mind Giuna quietly playing audience to their antics.

Instead she found herself ensnared by Fadrin Acrenix and unable to escape his circle—mostly a gaggle of delta gentry sycophants. Fadrin was leading them in idle ribbing of Era Novrus's heir, Iascat.

"Now here's Leato's little sister all grown," Fadrin said, lifting Giuna's hand to Iascat as though introducing them for the first time. "Does she suit your tastes? She's too fresh for your aunt to have dirt on her."

"Stop it," Iascat said to Fadrin, and to Giuna, "Ignore him. I don't know how anyone could swallow enough of this wine to get drunk, but he's managed."

"It tastes better the more of it you drink," Fadrin said, and illustrated with a healthy swig.

Wine was at least a safe topic of conversation. "Hasn't anyone told Eret Extaquium that too much sugar slows the yeast?" Giuna asked. "You'd almost have to be doing it deliberately, to make wine this bad."

Iascat's full mouth curved into a sour line. "I wonder sometimes if it *is* deliberate. House Extaquium may not have a Cinquerat seat, but they're too important to ignore, so he makes people come and pretend to enjoy his terrible wine."

"Some people have a taste for sweetness," Fadrin said, leering at Giuna.

"Some people should lose their tongues," said a low, honey-smooth voice. Sibiliat edged into the circle, her arm around Giuna's waist.

"Hello, little bird," Sibiliat said with a sly smile only for Giuna. "Don't let a blue jay bully you, or he'll never stop."

Fadrin pushed his empty cup into a servant's hand. "Where's your cousin, little Traementis? She'd add some spice to this gathering— probably tell Extaquium what she thinks of his work. Whether she praises it, tells him the truth, or spews it into his face, it would be a good show."

"She had a prior engagement," Giuna said, wishing she'd been invited to play bocce with Leato and Renata.

Iascat chuckled. "Wise woman. Maybe she'll set a fashion for staying away."

Fadrin snagged another glass from a passing servant and raised it high. "Now there's reason enough to celebrate the Seterin beauty. To Alta Renata, who demonstrates her refinement by not catering to Extaquium's whims. May we all learn to emulate her."

Iascat and several others raised their glasses in agreement. Sibiliat did not. "You all are more cloying than this year's vintage. Come, Giuna. We can find better conversation than this."

With Sibiliat's hand at the small of her back, Giuna had little choice but to be swept away. "Is everything all right?" she asked as Sibiliat's scowl stopped Orrucio Amananto from approaching. "You don't look well. Has the wine put you off?"

"The whining has put me off more," Sibiliat snapped. Her voice rose in mockery. "'Oh, Alta Renata isn't here? I was so looking forward to seeing her latest ensemble' and 'What, no Alta Renata? No wonder the night seems so dull.' Even Eret Extaquium didn't take her absence as an insult. He assumed she was sick. He's sending her a case of tonight's wine to help her recover." She smirked into her fan. "That was my suggestion. He'll be dogging her for the next month to get her opinion."

"Don't be catty," Giuna said. "How many of these events have we all been to? Of course people are interested in anything new."

"Oh yes. And Alta Renata has been *very* careful to leverage that interest. You're not as innocent or naive as you pretend to be, little bird; you know this crowd. Half of them should be carving her to the bone with their tongues, especially when she's absent. But no, everyone *loves* her. It's obnoxious."

Then, softly and without as much vitriol, Sibiliat added, "And it worries me."

Giuna stroked her arm. Normally Sibiliat was the one reassuring *her*, but Giuna had never seen her friend so on edge. "You don't have to be jealous of Renata."

The crack of Sibiliat's laughter turned several heads their way, but her scowl warned them off. She tugged Giuna down a hallway to a small, empty parlour. The abundance of lushly padded couches made Giuna flush, thinking about the rumors concerning Extaquium's private parties, but Sibiliat sat down on one, and Giuna had no choice but to join her. The dim light and faint fragrance of gardenias drifting from Sibiliat's skin wrapped them in a blanket of intimacy.

"I'm not jealous," Sibiliat said. Then she sighed. "All right, I am—but that's not why I'm worried. I'm worried because I *know* her. I know what she's doing. I do it myself."

Giuna frowned. "What do you mean?"

Sibiliat glanced down at her gloves, tugging on the fingers of one until it slipped off. "Getting people to like you—our sort of people—it's not something you manage by being kind or good. It's a game. Part flattery, part disdain. You make them want you to want them."

This was why Giuna didn't like coming to these parties. Her mother had only brought her because people were starting to gossip about her being shut away in Traementis Manor—and with so few members in the family, everyone needed to do their part.

"Alta Renata is very good at that game." Sibiliat's bare finger crossed Giuna's lips when they parted in protest, warm, dry, and terribly distracting. "Just consider. Out of nowhere, a cousin you didn't even know existed pays your mother a visit. Then, while your mother is still deciding what to do about that, Renata attends the Gloria, creates a spectacle. She does something slightly daring—the sleeves, talking to Vargo—she makes herself *interesting*. And someone that interesting isn't a person your mother can just drown in the Depths."

Her words were a steady flood, as relentless as the Dežera. Giuna felt like she was in a skiff without a paddle. True, Renata had done those things—but they sounded so different when Sibiliat described them.

"And that's just the beginning. Now that the stage is set, it's time for her to make connections to influential people." Sibiliat's finger slipped from Giuna's lips. "I don't know what she had planned for the night the Rook attacked Mezzan, but she was oddly quick to step forward and confront an armed stranger. And—again—to make herself the focus of gossip and admiration." Her glove landed in Giuna's lap.

"But—" Giuna touched the glove, addressing it as if the embroidered silk, not Sibiliat, were the one she had to convince. "Yes, she did those things. That doesn't mean it was calculated, the way you make it sound. Or even if it was…people who want people to like them do likable things. What's wrong with that?"

"*Why* does she want people to like her?" Picking up Giuna's limp hand, Sibiliat began to strip her glove away as well. "People who are honest in their wanting—people like you—are honest about what they want. Renata said she wanted reconciliation, but she hasn't lifted a finger to make it happen. I thought perhaps she wanted to be added to your register, but if so, she hasn't admitted it. You think she might want Leato—but if so, where's the passion?"

Her bare fingers twined with Giuna's. It might be the most minimal flesh-to-flesh contact this room had ever seen, but the brush of Sibiliat's skin, warm against her own, stole Giuna's breath. She prayed no one would walk in and see them.

Sibiliat used their linked hands to tug her closer. "Alta Renata is very good at learning what other people want, and making use of that. And I worry because it isn't at all clear what *she* wants."

Giuna's voice came out a whisper. "Maybe this *is* what she wants. Just to be here—to live here. Away from her mother."

Caressing Giuna's lower lip with her thumb, Sibiliat said, "Oh, little bird. Listen to that from afar. A rich Seterin noblewoman with Renata's beauty and wit decides to settle in Nadežra, just to escape her mother? As though there aren't a hundred places such a woman would prefer, if freedom were her only aim?"

Places without any family. Giuna tried to shape an argument that would stand against the point Sibiliat was making. But her head felt like it was spinning, and every time she opened her mouth to speak, another touch against her lip sent the words whirling away again.

"I've heard stories of your aunt Letilia. How manipulative and selfish she was—how she could hide her cruelty long enough to make people love her." Sliding her cheek against Giuna's, Sibiliat delivered her closing thrust as a whisper in Giuna's ear. "Rather like I'm doing to you right now."

It hit like a splash of icy water. Giuna blinked at Sibiliat, not understanding—not *wanting* to understand. Then tears sprang to her eyes, pricking hot. "You—but—"

Sibiliat had always been kind to her. More than kind, sometimes...to the point where Giuna had wondered, without ever letting herself think about it directly, if there might be more to it. But now Sibiliat's words had torn that open, and humiliation spilled through Giuna's veins.

Sibiliat wouldn't meet her eyes. She disentangled their hands, gently pulling Giuna's glove back on. "I'm sorry, little bird," she said, her voice hoarse. She donned her own glove as well, fumbling her fingers into their proper places. "Your mother and brother protect you too much. You need to know the kind of person she is—the kind of person *I* am—so you can protect yourself."

Giuna refused to let her tears fall. "Everything you've done—not just right now, but the whole time I've known you—you're saying I shouldn't trust it."

Sibiliat finally looked up, and her expression crumpled into guilt. "May the gods drown me in the river. Giuna, you know me better than that. Come here, little bird." She looped an arm around Giuna and pulled her into a hug. "I'm only worried about you."

Giving in, Giuna let herself sag against Sibiliat. The acid of embarrassment began to fade. "Because of Renata. But I think you're wrong about her. Not that she isn't doing the things you said, and maybe even for those reasons, but...she gave Mother back a ring Letilia stole, and it made Mother so happy. Even if she did it to make us like her, if it works out well for everyone, what's wrong with that?"

Giuna wasn't accustomed to winning arguments with her brother's friends—all of them older and more experienced—but after a moment's stillness, Sibiliat relaxed and began stroking Giuna's hair. "Perhaps nothing. Perhaps I only think I'm looking in a mirror darkly. She returned a ring? I suppose it was expensive."

"I guess so. But the sentimental value is what mattered. It belonged to my grandmother."

"That was...very kind of her." The pause said what Sibiliat didn't: that kindness could also be calculated. "Did Letilia steal many things when she left? I wonder where they all went."

Giuna shrugged. "I doubt we'll ever get the rest of it back. Renata might have a few more pieces, but I don't think Mother will order her to turn out her jewelry box so we can search. The ring was the only one Mother truly missed."

"Yes, but those things belonged to your family. If Renata wants to do the same, she shouldn't hold back." Sibiliat groaned and shifted upright, easing out of the uncomfortable position they'd gradually slumped into. "And if I want to avoid Leato challenging me to a duel, we should return. Gossip won't care that we only held hands, and Leato will know that—" She bit her lip to stop the words.

"That?" Giuna prodded.

The bitten lip gave way to a faint smile. "That I wanted more."

"Oh." Then her mind echoed: *Oh*. Giuna's face heated. And it wasn't until she was back out in the rest of the house that she realized everyone else would see the blush, and gossip even more.

Isla Traementis, the Pearls: Equilun 11

"You were right to be suspicious of Alta Renata," Grey said to Era Traementis. "Just not for the reasons you thought."

The morning light streamed through the windows of Donaia's study, cold and bright. He'd come to her straight from the offices of House Pattumo and found her already at work. She hadn't lit the fire laid in the hearth, though, and the air lay like ice against his cheek.

"Not Indestor?" Her breath clouded the air. "Who then? Simendis? Destaelio? Who's paying her?"

"Nobody," Grey said. "She's not as wealthy as she pretends. She spends extravagantly but lives frugally. The house isn't staffed, apart from that one maid, and more often than not, she dines out—so long as others are buying."

Grey could almost see the ledger in Donaia's mind, figures crossed out and new ones scribbled in, recalculating what she knew of Renata Viraudax. She huddled in on herself, warding against the cold. As if she didn't have burdens enough, without this young woman adding to them. Leather creaked as his hands balled into fists.

"There's an issue with her letter of credit, too," he went on. "I just came from talking to Mede Pattumo."

Donaia's brow furrowed. "Odd. I would expect her to bank with someone who has better contacts in Seteris."

"I think she avoided that on purpose. Better contacts with Seteris means that confirmation comes through more quickly—or in her case, refusal." Grey put a hand up as Donaia's attention jerked to him. "They haven't shut her down yet. She's persuaded them it's some kind of clerical error; they've extended her credit and sent again to Seteris." He estimated she had maybe two months before there would be a reckoning with her bankers. Though it depended on how good she was at talking them in circles.

Which meant she might very well be able to buy more time. "She puts up a good front," he added. "Too good—which makes me think she's had to do this before."

Donaia rose as if to pace, and Meatball scrambled to his feet beside her. She rested a hand on the dog's shoulder—perhaps to hold him back, or to hold herself upright. "But...I questioned her about Letilia. She *knows* her."

"She may be Letilia's daughter, but...Leato's told me about his aunt. Is it possible she didn't land in the feathers after all? That Alta Renata learned from her mother how to put on a show? That she came here hoping House Traementis could provide the luxury she was raised to believe she deserved?"

Now Donaia moved with slow, unsteady steps. Grey held his silence, letting her think. House Traementis had suffered so many losses and setbacks—not just Gianco's death and Letilia's flight, but an array of mishaps and illnesses picking off their aunts, uncles, cousins—and through it all, Donaia had been the one to hold the dwindling house together, even before she was their official head. He wasn't surprised to see her back straighten, her balance grow steady. She didn't accept anything without a fight.

"What can the Vigil do?" she asked crisply, turning to face him. "This woman has lied to me and my family, and spent money she doesn't possess. Surely there must be some grounds upon which you can arrest her."

"At this point? Nothing." At least, nothing Grey was willing to do, not even for Donaia and Leato. Planted evidence and falsified charges might be the way of things in the Vigil—not to mention how House Traementis had brought down enemies in the past—but Grey had seen those tools used against too many of his people to ever reach for them himself. "She hasn't committed any offenses that we know of."

"But debt—" Donaia caught herself before finishing the sentence. "She isn't yet a debtor. Not until Mede Pattumo issues an ultimatum, and she's forced to admit she can't repay him." Her fingers drummed against her thigh.

"Yes, and that will take at least a month, likely more. I don't think you should wait that long. Leato and Giuna are already fond of her. After losing so many cousins..."

Grey had faced duels, riots, and attempts to knife him in the back. The sudden fury in Donaia's eyes unsettled him more than all of them.

"If she thinks she can come here and suck us dry," Donaia said grimly, "then she's about to find out how wrong she is."

Isla Traementis, the Pearls: Equilun 12

The moment Renata walked into Era Traementis's study, she knew something was wrong.

On the surface, nothing seemed amiss. Colbrin invited her to have a seat in one of the heavy, antique chairs, promising that Era Traementis would be with her shortly, and offering to bring her warmed wine. Renata accepted, grateful she wouldn't have to choke down more coffee, then realizing too late that it might be more of the vile mess Eret Extaquium had sent her. But by then Colbrin had shut the door, and she was alone.

Had Donaia discovered Leato's lie about the night of the

Extaquium party? But surely Leato would be the one taken to task for that. And why would Donaia summon Renata to the study instead of the salon?

Ondrakja had called it "feeling the currents," the instinct that guided Ren in knowing how to manipulate people, when to press and when to back off, what bait they would rise to and what would lay their fears to rest.

It told her now that something had gone awry.

She stood in the center of the carpet, eyes half-closed, mind racing over all the factors. Not Vargo; she'd been preparing to give Donaia her pitch for why the man's charter was worth backing, but hadn't done it yet. Not any kind of offense to Leato or Giuna. She hadn't spoken to anyone about Letilia in the last several days, so it couldn't be any error there; Donaia would have called her in sooner if so. Had the damned woman written to Seteris? Gotten a reply saying there was no Letilia there, that House Viraudax had never heard of anyone named Renata?

The bottom dropped out of Ren's stomach. *Writing to Seteris.*

House Pattumo. Her Mask-cursed bankers, who should have taken twice or three times as long to find out there was a problem with her letter of credit.

It wasn't a disaster yet. The advantage of claiming noble status was that no one leapt to accuse her of lying; they only politely informed her that there seemed to be some difficulty, and undoubtedly the alta would be able to clear it up. Renata had talked Mede Pattumo down and sent him away smiling, buying herself more time.

But not with Donaia. She must have been keeping watch—probably through her pet hawk—and heard there was a problem with Alta Renata's finances. For a clutch-fist like her, with a history of being annoyed by Letilia's profligate ways, that was the one misstep most likely to set her off.

And growing up in Nadežra, Ren had heard plenty of stories about the Traementis taste for vengeance.

Ren's eyes opened. She didn't move, but her pulse leapt as if she'd begun running. The study windows overlooked a small balcony;

from there she could easily get to the roof, climb down on a sheltered side of the manor, and escape through backstreets. Warn Tess, grab the two rucksacks that had been sitting ready by the kitchen door since they moved into the townhouse, and vanish.

Only as a last resort. She hadn't become Ondrakja's prized student by cutting and running at the first sign of trouble. If all Donaia knew was that Renata's wealth was in question, then the worst Ren currently faced was delay in her plans. She wasn't nicked. Not yet.

The best path was to distract Donaia. Give her something appealing enough that she would forget, or at least forgive, the money problem. Not the report on Vargo; that wouldn't be enough. Ren needed better leverage.

In three swift strides she was at the desk, riffling through the papers there, keeping an ear on the corridor outside. Everything went back exactly where it had come from, at the same angle. Letters, ledgers, scribbled calculations with no context. Nothing useful there. A quick glance at the hearth—cold, even in this season— showed her no wadded-up papers awaiting the flame.

She circled the desk and praised the Faces and Masks. It was ancient, dating back to the civil war at least—possibly before—and the locks on its drawers were no younger. Ren could practically have picked them with a fingernail. She slipped a pin from the ribbon in her hair, laid it over the edge of the desk, and used a stone paperweight to hammer its tip sideways. Then she knelt, not letting herself think about what would happen if Donaia walked in and found Alta Renata breaking into her desk. *You can't outrun the hawks if you're looking over your shoulder.* That was another thing Ondrakja used to say.

She slid the pin into the lock, closing her eyes so vision wouldn't distract her. Past the wards, fishing upward—there. Ren found the latch and flipped it. For House Traementis's sake, she hoped Donaia had a strongbox with a better lock where she kept truly sensitive documents. For her own sake, she hoped there was something moderately sensitive here.

In the first drawer, a ledger and numerous accounts related to various charters—mostly ones Donaia seemed to have sold off.

Given time, Ren could have made sense of them, but time was a luxury she didn't have. She shut the drawer, relocked it, and moved to the other end of the desk. Her breath came faster, but her hands were steady. Like the night she'd stolen Letilia's jewels and petty coin, with Tess keeping watch, ready to hiss an alarm if she saw the city militia coming. *I always did make a better thief than a maid.*

More letters, this lot important enough that Donaia had troubled to lock them away. One was creased as if someone had wadded it up, then smoothed it out again. Ren began to read.

Era Traementis,

You are a proud woman. I understand that, and I respect it. Never think that the current situation causes me to look down upon you. House Traementis is one of the oldest in the city, and it would grieve me terribly to see your name dragged in the river, your failures exposed to public view.

I therefore propose a compromise that will allow you to save face. In the register of House Indestor there are several minor cousins who would make acceptable matches for your son. Based on what I hear of his recent activities, I believe his tastes incline toward women, but if he would prefer to be contracted to a man then I have no objection; there are numerous Indestor children suitable to be adopted as his heir.

The contract is already drafted, only awaiting your approval. Betroth your son to someone of my house before the summer solstice, with his inheritance to pass down through the Indestor line, and I will forgive all your debts. Your family will stop sinking under its current burdens, and no one will think anything amiss. Taspernum, Persater, Adrexa . . . Nadežra's history is full of noble houses who had their day in the sun, then faded.

One way or another, House Traementis will join them. You have the power to decide whether it will do so gracefully, or with public shame.

Mettore
Eret Indestor
Caerulet of the Cinquerat

Ren started to flip to the next letter, but a door shutting in the distance told her she was out of time. She shoved the papers into the drawer, locked it, and flung herself back to the far side of the desk just as Donaia entered the study.

Isla Traementis, the Pearls: Equilun 12

For all her fury—or perhaps because of it—Donaia took her time preparing herself to confront Letilia's snake of a daughter. She powdered her cheeks so her tendency to flush wouldn't give away her emotions, and donned the surcoat and underdress she'd been married in—reworked several times over, but still her finest. Embroidered with a Tricat star pattern picked out in seed pearls, it felt to Donaia like a genteel sort of armor, the better to do battle in her house's name. The pebbled texture was comforting as she smoothed her hands down the garment a final time before entering her study.

"Alta Renata—"

"Era Traementis, thank you so much for being willing to see me." Renata's curtsy was hastier than usual, as if she could barely contain her excitement. "I've been looking into Derossi Vargo as you asked, and I recently uncovered something that might be of great interest to you."

Donaia didn't give a rat's tail about Vargo, but before she could reveal that she had also uncovered something of *great interest*, she found herself neatly strong-armed into a seat.

Renata perched at the edge of her own, cheeks flushed and eyes bright with her news. "His proposal to restore the cleansing numinat in the river. I've been investigating like I promised, and I'm very pleased to say that all the evidence I can find points to it being exactly what it appears to be. But that's not why I was so eager to meet with you."

Somehow Donaia had lost control of the conversation. Just like she did when Leato was excited about something and oblivious to the currents around him—including Donaia's disapproval.

And just like Leato, Renata failed to notice Donaia's frown. "*I* was the one who asked you here."

"Yes, of course. I was just so glad you wanted to see me, and privately, too. There's a matter I've been wanting to bring up, but I wasn't certain how...Am I right in guessing House Traementis has some sort of rivalry with House Indestor?"

Donaia's spine straightened another notch. "I see Leato has been gossiping," she said, cold as the Dežera in winter. That boy had been too welcoming by half. "I'll remind you that Traementis concerns are not yours, Alta Renata *Viraudax*."

Renata didn't even have the courtesy to look cowed. "I don't wish to get him in trouble, but I'm glad he did. If I hadn't found out, I might have abandoned any notion of working with Master Vargo. But if our enemies are his..."

Calm overtook Donaia, her anger hanging on a hope. "Derossi Vargo has something against Mettore?"

"How else could he have gained so much power over the Lower Bank, and in such a short time?"

Donaia toyed with a pearl that was coming loose on her surcoat. "I assumed he was Mettore's creature." Graft and corruption were the order of the day at the Aerie. Mettore saved his clout to strike at those he couldn't control: the Stretsko gangs, the Stadnem Anduske, the Vraszenians as a whole. Vargo's blood might be mixed, but in Mettore's eyes, he would be a useful tool against the alternative.

"Or Master Vargo has something on him," Renata said, leaning forward as though someone were around to hear her whisper. "Something damning enough to keep him at bay."

A useful tool against the alternative. That could be as true for the Traementis as for Indestor. But wasn't allying with someone like Vargo akin to asking the fox to guard your chickens from the wolves? "Why, pray tell, would someone like Vargo share such information with us?"

"He approached House Traementis for a reason," Renata said.

"He wants this charter, and you're his only means of getting it. If neither of you is a friend to House Indestor, perhaps he's using this to test whether you might be allies instead."

"Then the man's a fool. You think I haven't tried to improve our fortunes through new charters?" Compared to the flash over Renata's deception, this rage was an ever-burning ember. "Any proposal I take to the Cinquerat will be laughed out of the Charterhouse. Politely. With many apologies about what a grand old house Traementis is—or was. Mettore Indestor isn't the only one who wants to see us fall. He's just the most direct about it."

May the Lumen burn Gianco to dust. Donaia had loved her husband, but he was like a Vraszenian deity: equal parts smiling Face and scowling Mask. For members of his own family, he would do anything—often more than he should. But outsiders were another matter. The moment anyone crossed him, he didn't just revenge himself on that person; he took out their business, their family, anything he could destroy.

Nor was he the only one who behaved that way. It was a family trait, banding together against the world, and often treating that world as either an enemy or a pawn. It meant House Traementis had no allies outside their own ranks. And when those ranks began to dwindle, they had no allies at all.

Donaia squeezed her eyes shut and took several breaths, waiting for the heat to leave her cheeks and ears. When she'd calmed enough to keep her voice steady, Donaia said, "Even if Master Vargo can help us, we aren't in any position to help him."

"We *can* help him," Renata said, with quiet intensity. "I saw his frustration when he invited me to lunch. We have the legitimacy he lacks. He genuinely wants to cleanse the West Channel—for profit, yes, but that doesn't erase the good it will do—but he can't, because no one will hear him. As for getting it through the Charterhouse..." Her laugh was breathless, and a little self-mocking. "I believe that is the job of an advocate."

Renata's enthusiasm was tantalizing. Once upon a memory, Donaia had been that eager. Now she only sighed. "House

Traementis doesn't have an advocate." House Traementis couldn't afford an advocate. Not a good one.

"Then let me try."

Renata sat silently until Donaia met her gaze. What she saw there was more than mere enthusiasm; it was confidence as unshakable as the stone of the Point. And even as a part of Donaia whispered, *She's been lying to you. She isn't what she says she is . . .*

A drowning woman would snatch at any straw.

"And what happens when the rest of Nadežra learns of your financial situation, as I have?" she said, gentle now that her anger had been washed away. Wasn't Renata doing what Donaia had been these many years? Keeping up appearances so as not to sink into the mud. It seemed to be a Traementis trait. "I suggest you concern yourself with your own incoming debts."

If she'd expected Renata to flinch, she was disappointed. The girl looked annoyed, not guilty. "I should have chosen a more reputable house to bank with—someone who wouldn't make such errors."

Rather than asking if the bank story was truth or just a fiction she was clinging to, Donaia said, "You are certainly nothing like your mother." The idea of Letilia working—much less volunteering to do so—was as improbable as a hardened smuggler caring about the filth he swam in.

As improbable as the decision Donaia came to. She'd walked into her study expecting to shame Renata onto the next ship bound for Seteris. Now . . .

"Very well." She held out her hands for Renata to take. "Let us see if we can make use of Master Vargo, Advocate Viraudax."

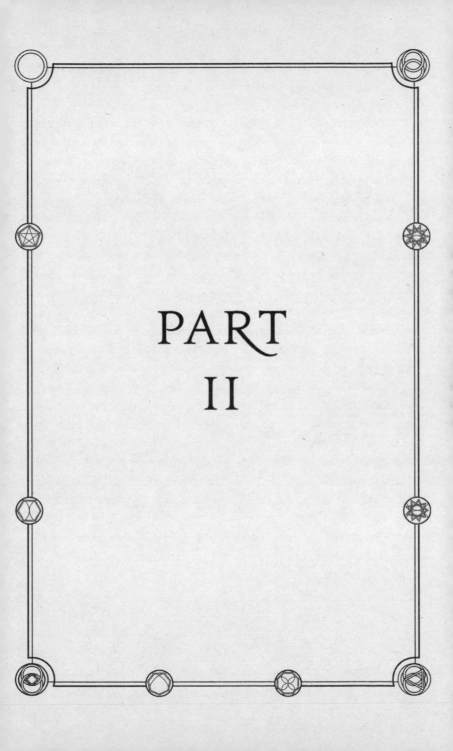

PART
II

Seven as One

Staring up at the spiraling red columns of the Charterhouse, Ren thought, *This was supposed to make things easier.*

All she wanted was money. Her share of Nadežra's wealth, which only ever seemed to rise to the top of the city, like cream, instead of filtering down to the people below. By now Ren was supposed to be enjoying the kinds of luxuries Ondrakja had promised her skills would bring. Instead she was still sleeping on the floor of the kitchen, taking the fees Vargo paid her as his advocate and immediately handing them over to House Pattumo as proof that she had money, so they could turn around and pay that money right back to Vargo for the rent on her patch of kitchen floor and the unused remainder of the townhouse.

She was beginning to think it would have been better to make her fortune as a thief. *I've got the Vigil looming over my shoulder either way.*

But if her resolve faltered, all she had to do was look at the common Nadežrans thronging the steps of the Charterhouse, one failed petition away from being thrown in jail for vagrancy, and from there to Caerulet's penal ships and a life of slavery. She'd been there with her mother. She wasn't going back.

Setting her jaw, she began to climb the steps.

The entrance hall of the Charterhouse was even more crowded, full of advocates and clerks, messengers and scribes touting for work. Over them towered five statues. A poet, a minister, a merchant, a soldier, and a priest, bearing five mottoes: *I speak for all; I counsel all; I support all; I defend all; I pray for all*. Below them stood desks for each of the Cinquerat's five seats: Argentet for cultural matters, Fulvet for civil, Prasinet for economic, Caerulet for military, Iridet for religious. Livery-clad secretaries for each member of the council sat at the desks, looking harassed.

Renata advanced with the confidence of someone who believed she deserved to be at the head of the line. That got her halfway there; she made it another quarter on river rat instincts, finding gaps to ooze through, feet to "accidentally" step on. After that she had to shuffle slowly forward with everyone else, until she finally made it to the secretary and presented her license and her request.

At that point, her expensive-looking clothing and the Traementis name carried enough weight to get her out of the press of public advocates crowding the entry hall and into the antechamber for Fulvet. A bribe—originating from Vargo's pocket, not Renata's—moved her name up the list there, but Donaia was right; no one at the Charterhouse was eager to do House Tracmentis any favors. Renata settled in for a long wait.

She knew a little about the history of the Fulvet office, from the days when it had been held by House Traementis. Letilia's father, prior holder of that seat, was the man notorious for polluting half the Dežera. Not on purpose; no, it was just Nadežra's usual graft and corruption, Crelitto Traementis pocketing so many of the funds for a bridge across the river at Floodwatch that the bridge later collapsed. Fifty-three people died, and the bulk of the wreckage washed into the West Channel, where it collided with the enormous prismatium framework of the cleansing numinat . . . and broke it.

If that had happened in the East Channel, Fulvet might have fixed it—and never mind that creating those numinata in the first place had required the inscriptors to imbue them, at the cost of their own lives. Channeling power on that scale carried a price. But the

West Channel ran between the Island and the Lower Bank, so the Charterhouse had merely shrugged. Let the gnats drink tainted water: There would be that many fewer of them to cause trouble.

Scaperto Quientis had taken the Fulvet seat shortly after Letilia fled Nadežra, marking the start of House Traementis's decline. Rumor said he was different. Less obvious about his graft, or else he'd found some lucrative source of additional income; under Scaperto, a startling percentage of the taxes raised by Prasinet, the economic seat, seemed to make their way to the public works they were intended for. It meant he was either honest . . . or far more clever than his predecessors.

Either one gave Renata cause to be wary.

She'd arrived not long after dawn. She finally stepped into Fulvet's office sometime after the clock towers rang fifth sun.

Scaperto Quientis seemed built of squares: square jaw, square frame, square posture. Grey dulled the gold of his hair, and the skin around his eyes sagged into faint lines, but that only added to the impression of solidity and power. Self-confidence wafted off him like the oak and amber of his perfume. Looking at him, Renata saw an old tomcat, sure of his right to his patch of sunlight.

He leaned forward, elbows on his desk and fingers latticed into a steeple, studying her over their tips. "Alta Renata. The newest curiosity from Seteris . . . House Traementis licensed *you* as an advocate?"

Everyone agreed that Eret Quientis's besetting sin was his bluntness. Looking at the cynical set of his mouth, Renata saw a man who might find it refreshing to be answered in kind. "House Traementis has many unpleasant memories of my mother, and I'd like to get out from under her shadow. If I can persuade you to see me as something other than her echo, Your Grace, that will carry a great deal of weight with them—especially as I believe you were once betrothed to her." Before Letilia broke the contract and fled.

"So I was. You favor her." The corner of his mouth twitched. "She must hate that."

Renata merely waited.

"And now you've come to pay your mother's debts?" Quientis

blinked slowly, the tomcat assessing whether a mouse was worth his time. "I think you're a bit young for me."

He was testing her. Unlike half the Cinquerat, Quientis had no reputation for letting seduction sway him. Renata said, "I've done my research, and I know what is more likely to attract your eye." She held up a leather folder. "I have a proposal for a new charter. A replacement for the West Channel numinat, to purify that half of the Dežera of mud and the filth that washes down from the rest of Vraszan."

She placed the proposal just out of his reach, enticing him to lean forward to take it. After a moment he did, skimming the overview Renata had drafted, the furrow in his brow deepening with every line. He didn't look surprised; political gossip must have carried word of this to him already. But the details were another matter.

Finally, he set the folder down—but didn't return it to her. "I imagine you're hoping this will redeem the Traementis reputation on the Lower Bank."

"I hope it will do some good," she admitted, "but that's hardly my only reason for backing it. I'm renting a house in Westbridge, Your Grace, and while my own water is protected, every day I pass by the evidence of the river's pollution. And every day I see its effects on the people around me."

She'd rehearsed this well before coming to him, polishing her words with the assistance of both Donaia and Vargo—separately. Renata didn't attempt to give him the pragmatic arguments; those were in the folder, Vargo's documents recopied in her own hand. If Quientis was the sort of man to be moved by dry facts, those would persuade him. This was her chance to sell him the grand vision: a Dežera running clear in both main channels.

He let her speak, only interrupting a few times with clarifying questions. After she finished, he leaned back in his chair, his fingers a triangle against his lips.

She resisted the urge to fill the silence with more arguments. Her passion had already bled through more than she intended. *If the river had been clean, would Mama have gotten sick?*

"It's a pretty idea, Alta Renata—but if it were easy to achieve, it would have happened years ago. Even if I grant Traementis the charter, you still need to execute it, and that takes cooperation from more than one seat in the Cinquerat. Religious matters like numinatria fall under Iridet's authority, and I'm not qualified to judge whether it's even possible to construct something like this on a permanent scale without asking the inscriptor to die for it. Prasinet will have concerns about the effect on taxation and anchorage fees in the West Channel. Argentet will find some cultural reason to intervene, because Era Novrus has to have a say in everything."

He left Caerulet unspoken. This had nothing to do with military matters, but Mettore Indestor would oppose anything that helped the Traementis escape his blade.

"I'm aware," Renata said. "But if I went to them now, they would say, you have no charter—why should we waste our time on this? Once I have the charter, I can begin negotiating with them."

"And you think you'll succeed?"

"Yes." She let the word sit there, unadorned. A con was a confidence game: not just the mark's confidence in the sharper, but the sharper's confidence in herself. Renata had sold Donaia on the belief that Vargo would help them against Indestor, with nothing more than a guess and a few vague comments from Sedge to back that up; she would sell Scaperto Quientis on this, too.

"Hmm." His fingers drummed across the folder, and Renata hid a smile.

But then he asked the question she'd been hoping he would overlook. "Who would administer this for you?"

There was no point in lying; he would find out eventually. "Derossi Vargo."

Quientis's expression went stony. Renata raised her eyebrows. "A moment ago you liked the idea, Your Grace. Surely it doesn't lose all merit because of one name."

"That depends on what influence the name has." Quientis looked out the window, while Renata tried not to fidget.

Finally he turned back. "You said you wanted to escape the

shadow of your mother's reputation. I want some demonstration that you have the skill and dedication to see this through—that you won't simply run away at the first obstacle. Era Destaelio has tied up a shipment of mine in the customs house, some saltpeter from the Dawn Road. Get her to release it and waive the fees—by some means *other* than crass bribery; I know Master Vargo has the pockets for that—and I'll give your proposal some consideration."

Consideration. Renata wanted to slap him. *Of course he promises nothing, and I have to work for free.*

But that was the way of things for those in power, and she had no choice but to play his game. "I'll need details on the shipment," she said crisply, as if this were no obstacle at all. Figuring out how to take care of it would come later.

He stood, a clear dismissal—but also more respect than he'd greeted her with. "Quarat's luck to you, Alta Renata. I look forward to seeing how different you are from your mother."

Kingfisher, Lower Bank: Equilun 27

The Gawping Carp wasn't the kind of tavern anyone sought out of their own volition. It was the sort of place you stumbled over and grew into, as Grey and Kolya had, that first day they arrived in Nadežra. Now Grey had to duck to avoid banging his head on the sagging lintel. Hardwood beams seasoned with smoke and unlikely stories kept the roof from sinking upon the patrons, like the giant of Brevyik holding up the sky. A circle of gnarled old men surrounded one of the back tables, playing a permanent game of nytsa. They'd been hunched there for longer than Grey had been coming to drink, like saplings rooted deep and grown into old oaks.

Grey hadn't been back since his promotion to captain, but Dvaran at the bar nodded as though he'd just stepped out for a piss. Grey's usual was already poured, with a sausage roll wrapped in a greasy broadsheet set next to it.

"Good to see you, son," Dvaran said, then glanced at the corner opposite the nytsa game. Leato waited there with his own mug and roll. "Both of you."

"It's been too long," Grey said, pulling out a few centiras.

"No charge." Dvaran waved off the coins with one hand. The other arm ended at the elbow, courtesy of a brawl years ago. "Sorry to hear about your brother."

Would he ever get used to it—feeling like he was being gutted from the inside? Would it ever go away? Grey swallowed down the misery and nodded. In a place like this, tears were only shed for the passing of heroes long dead. Kolya was a carpenter whose ashes hadn't been on the wind more than six months.

"Thank you," Grey managed, the words scraping his throat.

"How're his wife and nippers—"

"In mourning." It came out harder than he'd intended, but Dvaran only nodded and nudged the mug closer. Taking the sympathy offering, Grey joined Leato.

"I wasn't sure you'd come," Leato said.

Grey hadn't been certain, either, until he found his feet leading him here instead of home. "You asked me to." He searched for anything to look at besides the empty chair next to him, and settled on a knot in the grain of the table that, when he was drunk enough, resembled a raccoon poling a river skiff.

"Even so." Leato traced a triangle in a puddle of spilled beer.

"You'll ruin your gloves."

"You sound like my mother."

"Your mother appreciates the value of a good pair of gloves."

Leato snorted and pulled one off, flicking the spill from the table with his bare hand. "Better?"

"Yes." Only river-rooted Nadežrans frequented the Gawping Carp. Nobody here gave a frayed end about gloves.

But Leato seemed more interested in studying the table than explaining his invitation. It was possible he just wanted to meet without the worries of rank and blood, like they used to, but Grey didn't think that was the case. Something had changed in Leato—a change that predated Kolya's death. He might smile and play the wastrel for the rest of the world, but Grey knew better.

"Why did you ask me here?"

Leato stopped picking at the wrapping on his roll. "I need your help finding someone."

Grey stiffened. For the flash of an instant, he was tempted to cast his beer in Leato's face and cut all ties to anyone in the Traementis register.

"If you have a request for the Vigil, you should take it to the Aerie," he said evenly. Not here, the place where they were beyond Liganti and Vraszenian, master and servant. Not here, with Kolya's seat empty between them.

"Grey—"

"Why did your mother make Renata Viraudax her advocate?" He'd been fuming ever since he'd heard the news. It was the complete dismissal of his findings as much as the wasted time and effort that infuriated Grey—as though his honest assessment had less value than the flattering lies of a woman who happened to share Donaia's rank and blood.

Leato's blinking confusion said that neither his mother's previous fears nor Grey's conclusions about them had reached his ears. "Because she's more personable than Mother, more dependable than me, and more experienced than Giuna. Should she not have?"

The urge to tell clawed at Grey, but no. He'd promised Donaia. "It makes no difference to me," he muttered. "It just seemed sudden."

He pushed his chair back. He only needed some distance to collect himself, but Leato latched onto his sleeve as though he feared Grey would leave.

"Renata can't help me with this, and I don't want to go to the Vigil." He lowered his voice, leaning closer. "I don't want your help because someone ordered you. I'm asking you as a friend."

"And if I say no?"

Releasing Grey's sleeve, Leato slumped back in his chair. "Then I'll just keep looking for her on my own." From the resignation in his tone Grey suspected Leato had been at his search for some time already.

Grey sighed. "If this is on my own time, then I can't call on Vigil resources." Not true, but he'd already strained Cercel's tolerance enough with his hunt for the missing street kids. "What makes you think I can find this person when you can't?"

"Because she's a Vraszenian who used to work at the Aerie. Not that you all know each other...but you stand a better chance than I do. And that's also why I'm not involving the Vigil."

Grey's hands tightened around his mug. Vigil attention rarely ended well for his people. Neither did noble attention.

Friends or not, Grey was reluctant to help Leato disturb some poor Vraszenian's life. "What's her name?"

Leato's expression smoothed into unreadability. It was remarkable how much he resembled his mother in that moment. "Idusza, if the information I paid for is reliable. She worked as a laundress, quit a few months ago. She must have used a false family name—I've had no luck finding her."

His gaze flicked up to meet Grey's. "I think she's a member of the Stadnem Anduske."

That brought Grey up straight. The Stadnem Anduske were Vraszenian, all right. Vraszenian radicals who railed against the Cinquerat's rule and fought to take back Nadežra for the people, finishing what the Tyrant's death and the ensuing civil war had left incomplete. Sometimes they fought with words. Sometimes they used bloodier tools: Earlier that month they'd raided a prison hulk to free the people there, and killed a Vigil officer in the process.

Grey leaned over his mug, almost spilling it. "What possible interest could you have in the Anduske?"

"What possible...?" Leato jerked when Grey kicked him under the table, but he lowered his voice and leaned forward. The Nadežrans who frequented the Gawping Carp were no friends to the Cinquerat, but that didn't mean they had much love for their more violent Vraszenian neighbors.

"I want to know if they had anything to do with ... what happened. Don't you?"

Two rumors had flown around the city after the fire that killed Kolya. One said the Rook was responsible; the other blamed the Stadnem Anduske. The latter was the first lead Grey had chased—the first time he'd used Vigil resources for his own ends.

"Whatever crimes they're guilty of," Grey said, "I don't think the Anduske burned that warehouse."

"But if they knew there was black powder there—"

They *had* known. Kolya wasn't the only carpenter repairing the roof, and one of his fellows was an Anduske sympathizer. They'd both seen the barrels, hidden where they had no legal right to be.

But the Stadnem Anduske would have stolen the powder, not set it off. "I looked into it," Grey said harshly. "Do you think I wouldn't? I'm not defending them because they're Vraszenian; I'm defending them because they're innocent."

"What about the Vigil, though?" Leato persisted. "*Someone* tipped them off about the powder being there. And this woman, Idusza, quit the Aerie right after the fire."

Grey didn't want to have this conversation, any more than he wanted Dvaran's sympathy. He put his hand over the top of his mug and rested his head against it, wishing he could afford to give up and get ripped.

Then he made himself sit up again. "It probably wasn't a false name, just some other branch of her ancestry. It's something we do to make it harder for your people to find us."

"So ... you'll help me?"

The hope in Leato's eyes was as fragile as a dreamweaver's egg. "You're doing this to help *me*, aren't you? To find the bastard who killed Kolya," Grey said. Then he frowned. "How did you find out about this Idusza, anyway?"

"Hard work and luck," Leato said, far too breezily to be believed. Grey cursed inwardly. *I hope he hasn't sold himself to House Novrus for the information.* All too often, that was how Nadežran politics worked: The enemy of your enemy ate you alive.

Standing, he swept up his mug, and Leato's as well. "Very well. I'll help. But you're buying my drinks for the next month as payment."

Isla Traementis, the Pearls: Equilun 29

The worst part of being suspected of poverty was that Renata had to work even harder to give the impression of careless wealth.

The latest strain on her purse was Giuna. All of the girl's clothes were old, their colors muddied from re-dyeing; unlike Leato, she didn't get to prance around in new styles. *But why does the woman who can't even afford enough coal to heat her kitchen have to be the one who pays for Giuna's new dress?*

Because you're the genius who told Donaia you would.

And because Giuna would be a more useful asset at the engagement party for Marvisal Coscanum and Mezzan Indestor if she didn't blend into the paneling. So now the girl was standing on a round settee in the Traementis solar, squeaking every time she thought Tess might touch her with a pin.

With the patience of a river turtle, Tess finished marking the torso of one of Renata's underdresses—one they'd decided had been worn too often to be reworked—and turned to the sleeve. "Now if the alta will please stretch out her arms."

"Just don't poke me."

"I won't be poking you," Tess said through a mouthful of pins.

It was the sixth time she'd said it, and Renata was beginning to suspect that Giuna wore re-dyed castoffs because no dressmaker would put up with her twitching. "I take it absolutely everyone will be at this engagement party," she said, hoping to calm the girl. If even House Traementis was invited, Mettore Indestor must be casting a broad net.

"Of course. Alta Faella wouldn't accept anything less than the entire city turning out for her grandniece."

All the parts of it she cares to acknowledge, at least.

As Tess moved down to her hem, Giuna stuck one bare toe out from under the dress and said, "Do you know how to dance? Our local dances, I mean. We could teach you. I'm sure Sibiliat would help, and Leato."

Tess giggled. "I'm sure he would."

"Tess!" Renata's voice was reproving, as if they hadn't discussed in advance how to tease information out of Giuna. "Please forgive her, Alta Giuna. I'm afraid I've spoken too familiarly to her about your brother—the fault is mine."

Giuna laughed off Renata's apology. "No, she's right. Leato likes you."

"It isn't that. I shared with her some of the gossip about him, and I shouldn't have. I meant it to show that he wasn't like the rumors say, but—"

"He really isn't," Giuna said earnestly. "I don't know what he's doing when he goes out, but it isn't what people think."

"Oh?" Renata said, but her attempt at casual inquiry failed. Giuna hesitated, fiddling with the edge of her sleeve.

Despite her best efforts, Ren hadn't managed to figure out what was keeping Leato so busy, except that it regularly took him to parts of town she wouldn't expect any Liganti cuff to visit. He adored his sister; that was obvious. He might have shared with her whatever clandestine activities he'd been up to—but first Renata had to tip the girl over into speaking. "I promise, I won't share any secrets."

"Not even with Mother. Or Leato. She doesn't know, and he doesn't know I know," Giuna said rapidly. "I don't know why he wants her to think he's acting like a wastrel, but he's gone to a lot of trouble to make her think it, and *please*, you can't say anything—"

"Of course I won't, Giuna."

She'd been saving her first use of the girl's unadorned name for a key moment, and it did the trick. "People say he comes home drunk, but once his gloves are off, he's as sober as Sebat," Giuna said. "I've seen it. And you watched him fence Mistress Ryvček—is a drunkard's hand ever that steady? And...sometimes he comes and goes from his balcony window."

Now isn't that *interesting.*

Giuna hopped down from the settee and clasped Renata's hands. "I'm telling you because you *are* family. I'm Nadežran enough to say that, even though you aren't in the register."

"To you and Leato, at least." Renata let her smile dim as though Giuna's words were more troubling than encouraging; it wasn't far from true. "But that only makes me worry more. *Why* does he encourage that sort of gossip? Especially when he knows it bothers your mother so much?"

Tess stripped off the mock-up, giving Giuna a few moments to stew. When she looked up from her bare toes, her lips were pressed flat with determination.

"I'm not certain, but it's gotten worse since...You've heard about Kolya Serrado, yes? Mother mentioned him when you came to dinner."

Renata hadn't forgotten. "Yes—Captain Serrado's brother. He died, I believe. Or rather, the Rook killed him."

Giuna nodded. "Grey used to come by, to spend time with Leato. But the Gloria was the first time I'd seen him since right after Kolya died. And Leato used to go out, but not nearly as often as he has since then." Her voice dropped to a whisper, even though there was no one in the room to hear other than Renata and Tess. "I think Leato's trying to hunt down the Rook. For Grey's sake."

There were paper toys from Seteris that transformed when you tugged on them, collapsing into an entirely new shape. Ren's thoughts felt like one of those toys. *Hunting the Rook...*

Many people had tried. Leato didn't even have the resources of the Vigil to call on, like Captain Serrado did; for that matter, the entire combined might of the Aerie had failed for generations.

But that wouldn't necessarily stop Leato. Maybe he'd been following them in Lacewater, using Mezzan as a sacrificial offering, knowing the Rook was likely to go after the man for maiming Ivič

Pilatsin. Waiting in the shadows for a chance to pursue—and then, when that failed, going out again and again, seeking places where the Rook might strike.

Ren believed in Leato the dedicated friend more than Leato the wastrel. *I'm afraid revenge will break him*—that was what he'd said about Grey that night, in the Talon and Trick.

So Leato, in the grand tradition of his house, would get revenge on his behalf.

Giuna swept Renata's hands up in her own. "I'm sorry. I shouldn't burden you with troubles like this—not when you're doing so much for us." She paused and then brightened, as if an idea had just come to her. "We should do something for you in return. When is your natal day? We should celebrate it!"

The question pricked Ren's spine like the tip of a knife. Giuna's sudden change of subject was blatantly artificial, but her eyes showed no hint of suspicion.

It was just coincidence that she had asked on Ren's actual birthday.

"Colbrilun," she lied. "The twenty-ninth."

Giuna pouted. "Oh, bother—that's months away. But you'll be turning twenty-three, yes? What city did you say you were from in Seteris—Endacium? Is that where you were born?"

"Yes," Renata said, tension and suspicion curling through her like twin snakes.

"A-and what time were you born?"

Giuna was as transparent as The Face of Glass. The only reason to ask for Renata's time of birth was so an astrologer could calculate her natal chart.

Donaia put her up to this. The woman was ready to use Renata's services in the Charterhouse, but her suspicions still hadn't gone away. "Around sixth sun, I believe," Renata said, choosing the time at random. She didn't know the first thing about astrology. What answers would that false chart give?

"That's the mock-up done," Tess said, standing and drawing Giuna's attention. The little shake of her curls told Renata she had this in hand. "Now, would the altas like to talk fabrics and sleeve styles?"

Birthdays and brothers and fears of becoming a walking pincushion faded in the radiance of Giuna's smile. She gripped Renata's hand like she was trying to break bone. "Oh, yes!"

Isla Traementis, the Pearls: Apilun 2

"The sagnasse hold turns *earthwise*," Parma insisted, casting off Leato's hands and facing him with fists planted on her hips.

A muscle worked in Leato's jaw, but he managed to keep his tone amiable. "I thought the sagnasse always turned sunwise."

Parma's *tch* sounded all the more exasperated when echoed back by the high walls of the Traementis ballroom. "Yes. Except in the gratzet, where it's earthwise."

Leato mimed the turn as Parma had described it. "But then I'm on the wrong foot."

"That's why you kip-step—"

"Do you think they'll ever let us get around to dancing?" Giuna sighed to Renata and Sibiliat. They'd retreated to the chairs at the sidelines while the battle over technical details raged.

"If we don't die of boredom first." Sibiliat stretched, one arm coming down to rest lightly across Giuna's shoulder. To Renata's surprise, she'd claimed Giuna as her partner from the start of the practice session, leaving Parma partnering Leato, and Renata with Bondiro.

"Or stage a break like Bondiro did," Renata said dryly. She wasn't precisely sorry her partner had fled when this debate began; he'd been the opposite of helpful. The point of today was to teach her the dances popular in Nadežra—some of which originated in Seteris. Bondiro didn't seem to know any of them, and she couldn't fake her way through something her partner didn't know, either.

"Coward," Sibiliat muttered. "Abandoning us to Parma's mercy."

"She was harder on him than the rest of us," Giuna said.

Twining her finger around one of Giuna's curls, Sibiliat said, "Yes. But usually he likes that."

Giuna was innocent enough that Sibiliat's comment flew right past. Renata wondered what could possibly have drawn the Acrenix woman to her—unless Sibiliat simply enjoyed having an admirer she could dominate. Giuna's infatuation was obvious, as was Sibiliat's amused tolerance.

Having won the skirmish over the direction of the turn into hold, Parma clapped for their attention. "Shall we try again?"

Sibiliat stood, muttering under her breath, "Yes, Kaius Rex."

"We're odd numbers now, with Bondiro gone," Giuna said. "I'll sit out—"

"And abandon me? Nonsense, dearest." Catching her hand, Sibiliat pulled her from her chair, spinning her—earthwise—into hold. "You're made to sit out often enough."

"But the point of this was to teach Renata—"

A creak of boards at the door alerted them to Colbrin's entrance. The acoustics of the ballroom weren't good enough for Renata to hear what he whispered in Leato's ear, but Leato chuckled.

"Excellent. Send him in. Altas, our partnering problems are solved."

A moment later, Colbrin ushered Captain Serrado into the room.

The hawk's step faltered when he saw the group. "I...didn't realize you had company, Altan Leato. I can return—"

Leato caught him before he could flee as Bondiro had. "No. We're in dire need of you. Let's see—you know the gratzet, right? Well, Parma can remind you." Leato all but shoved Serrado into position in front of Parma, who eyed him with speculative appreciation despite him being Vraszenian, then took up his own post opposite Renata.

She caught the look Serrado fired at Leato. Mixed annoyance and impatience—the look of a man who had come on business and didn't want to delay it for frivolity. But what business?

Nothing to do with me, Renata thought, half in prayer. Serrado had to be wondering why Donaia hadn't given her the boot, but it was Leato he wanted to talk to, not Era Traementis. And if his information was some new dirt on her, he was hiding it well. She seemed to be of no more interest to him than Sibiliat—or one of the chairs.

Parma gave the count for the harpist in the corner. He set finger to string, and they swayed into motion.

Leato was a much better lead than Bondiro. He kept his frame strong, yet flexible enough for Renata to feel the shifts in his weight. In a way, dancing was like fighting; all her attention was on her body and his, responding to cues before her conscious mind could identify them. The challenge was exhilarating, and intimate—and left her absolutely no attention to spare for conversation.

A problem Leato didn't seem to share. "How goes the advocacy? I heard you've met with a number of people." They broke apart to cast to the bottom of the set, giving Renata a moment to string together her answer.

"I think I'm being run in circles," she said with a light laugh, aware of Sibiliat barely an arm's length away. So far her attempt to fulfill Quientis's request hadn't taken her to House Acrenix, but that might change. And even if it didn't, Sibiliat's father, Ghiscolo, might decide there was profit in getting involved.

"And here we're making you spend your Andusny doing more of the same," he said, just in time for the lot of them to clasp hands and circle the center in an inward Sessat. Then came the much-debated sagnasse turn. Passing back-to-back with Serrado, Renata was blessed with the singular joy of hearing him grunt when he started to turn the wrong way and was forcibly corrected by Parma.

Unfortunately, the following promenade realigned the dance, leaving her paired with Serrado. Renata fell silent, hoping his dislike would excuse her from having to talk—and that she could blame any mistakes she made on him.

No such luck.

"Alta Parma informs me that we're dancing for your instruction," Serrado said. His frame and lead were no worse than Leato's, but they lacked the distracting intimacy. "You didn't learn these in Seteris?"

"Some, yes. But there are differences, and I would hate to step on my partner's toes because I turned sunwise instead of earthwise."

Speaking was a mistake. She missed her cue and stepped forward when she was meant to retreat, colliding with Serrado's chest. She covered the mistake with a laugh. "As you see."

He steadied her and swept her along before her stumble left them in the path of Sibiliat and Parma. They escaped the collision, but not Parma's glare.

"The threat of Alta Parma's wrath does provide incentive, yes." His tone was so dry, Renata couldn't tell whether he was serious or joking. "Perhaps you could divert it by teaching us a Seterin dance."

Bastard. He knew about her letter of credit; was he also beginning to guess at more? The ring should have convinced Donaia beyond a shadow of a doubt that Renata was Letilia's daughter…but maybe he suspected Letilia had never made it to Seteris.

Her only defense against that question was to give him something else to think about. "Are you flirting with me, Captain Serrado?"

"An alta *and* Leato's cousin? I'd rather face Alta Parma's wrath." Serrado turned her—sunwise—so smoothly into the sagnasse hold that they were face-to-face over clasped hands before Renata realized they'd spun the wrong way. "*That* is how it's done."

Parma growled, but Renata had to admit it felt much smoother. "Perhaps I'll start a new trend for it."

Another promenade, another change of partners, brought her face-to-face with Sibiliat.

"A trend for what?" Sibiliat asked, gaze lingering on Serrado, now partnering Giuna. "Not your Gloria sleeves—not in this weather. Perhaps jewelry? I imagine you've brought some interesting pieces from Seteris."

"Not a great many," Renata said. After two repetitions of the set, it was easier to divide her attention. "Travel is such an uncertain thing—pirates and thieves, you understand. I didn't want to risk losing anything too valuable." Was everyone here out to uncover her vulnerabilities?

"Oh." Sibiliat's disappointment was as false as a snake pretending disinterest in a mouse. "But you didn't come completely empty-handed. Giuna told me you'd returned something to her mother."

Had Donaia originally come from House Acrenix? No, she was from a cadet branch of the Traementis—but Renata couldn't imagine why else Sibiliat might care. "A ring," she admitted cautiously. "An heirloom of her mother's."

"How kind of you." Sibiliat drawled the platitude, but her tone was brighter when the dance brought them together again. "If you're lacking in jewels, I can introduce you to a jeweler whose master came from Seteris. Nobody makes better numinatrian pieces."

Renata couldn't afford anything of the sort. Sibiliat's interest in her was clearly more than idle, though. She didn't know what the Acrenix alta wanted . . . but there might be merit in finding out.

So she smiled as they executed the sagnasse and entered the final promenade. "Thank you, Alta Sibiliat. Giuna has nothing but praise for your taste; I'd love to see what you consider worthy."

"Excellent." With a final squeeze, Sibiliat unwound herself from Renata and progressed back to Giuna. The harpist ended the tune with a coda of cascading notes, and Renata was left facing Leato again.

"Did you survive?" he asked, smiling over her wrist as he bowed.

Renata made a show of checking her feet and hands—for Leato's benefit only, as Sibiliat was wrapped around Giuna, whispering something in her ear, and Parma had caught Serrado mid-escape to impart her corrections. "I believe everything is intact. It helps when you have a good partner."

"Indeed it does," he said, holding her gaze, his blue eyes shining. Renata pressed her fingertips to her mouth, as if hiding a smile—a reaction that wasn't entirely feigned. She was used to thinking of all nobles as arrogant leeches; she hadn't expected, when she began her masquerade, that she would wind up liking any of them.

It was dangerous. She couldn't let herself forget that all of this was a lie.

Leato's glance at Grey reminded her of the danger. The hawk hadn't yet extracted himself from Parma, but he jerked his chin toward the door, reminding Leato that he hadn't come to dance. *One wrong step, and he'll have me pinned.*

Leato released her hand and stepped back. "I'd better rescue Grey before the ballroom becomes a dueling circle. Or a brawl."

"If it does, at least now I have some notion of how to defend myself." He'd taken her to an open practice at the Palaestra, a chance for athletic nobles and delta gentry to hone their skills alongside duelists like Ryvček, and had given her a handful of private lessons besides. She was still miserably bad at fencing, but she at least had learned to move like Renata, instead of Ren the river rat.

Leato bowed gallantly. "I have faith in your blade—but let's not put it to the test just yet."

I hope not. Caught between hawks and spiders, Indestor and Acrenix and Traementis...she might need her river rat instincts to get herself out of this mess.

Isla Prišta, Westbridge: Apilun 3

"—so I says to him, 'If those scratches came from a chicken, then you'd best be bringing eggs for me,' and sure if he didn't pull five lovely brown cackleberries from his pockets."

Laughter echoed through the kitchen cellar. Tess had missed this since leaving Ganllech a second time: tatting around a warm hearth, listening to the nans and mams trading gossip and bawdy tales. Half the reason she'd suggested this scheme to Ren was fear of going mad, talking to herself all the time.

"But did you ever find out if he was cheating on you?" she asked Old Mag.

"What did I care for that, if it kept me in eggs on the daily?"

Mag said. Parchment skin crinkled along the well-worn folds of a grin. "Finest man I ever had, that one. Lasses, I'll tell you. Marry a man what brings you good food, and you'll never starve for love."

The answering laughter was cut short by a rap at the door. Setting her bobbins aside, Tess hurried to open it.

It was the boy Tess had hired to keep watch. "Alta's coming back. Chair's stuck in traffic on Sunset Bridge."

"Good, my lad." Tatting with the oldsters sank Tess deeper into her native accents. "Here's a mill to keep watch again tomorrow."

A grin split the boy's grubby cheeks. "Yes'm," he said, taking the coin and dashing off.

Behind Tess, the women were swiftly packing up their work, laying the bobbins in careful fans for Tess to sort and finish later. "Same again tomorrow, then?" Old Mag asked as the others slipped away.

Tess followed her out to the narrow path and canal that ran along the back of the townhouse. "Yes. And please don't say aught to anyone about what we're doing here. If the alta found out, I'd be sacked for certain."

"Say aught about what?" Mag asked, patting fleece-white hair and glancing around with exaggerated confusion. "Have you seen my memory? I'm always leaving it in the oddest places." She winked. Pulling her striped woolen over her head, she shuffled off after the other women.

Tess turned back—and nearly stumbled into the canal when she spotted the baker's boy approaching.

"Careful," Pavlin said, catching her before she could complete the tumble. She gaped up at him, fingers clenched in his sleeves. He hadn't come around in weeks, and she assumed it was because he'd abandoned any hope of securing Alta Renata's custom.

"What are you doing here?" she blurted.

"Uh..." Pavlin glanced down at her hands, currently crumpling wrinkled stars into the loose broadcloth of his coat.

"Oh! Sorry!" Tess released him and did her best to pretend her cheeks weren't trying to match her freckles. "I only meant, you haven't been by in a while. I thought . . . maybe . . ."

"I had other work," he said. "I only help at the bakery when it's needed. You've found more servants, it seems."

Tess glanced over her shoulder. Mag and the others had already disappeared around the corner. "Ah. Yes." The idea was Tess's. Bring in a gaggle of Ganllechyn women from Little Alwydd under the guise of day servants, then set them to lacemaking and embroidery that Tess could use or sell. Swear them to secrecy on threat of Tess's position. Anyone looking would assume the house was properly staffed, and it gave Tess a respite and their budget another dribble of income.

Still, Tess wasn't the liar Ren was. She kept her eyes on the cobbles as she said, "The alta doesn't like the noise, so they only come while she's out."

"Oh. Well, it's good you have help now."

The lapping waters of the little-used canal battled with the chittering of a nearby finch in the awkward silence that followed. Tess managed to lift her gaze to Pavlin's cuff—too short by a handspan. That irritation carried her up a baggy sleeve to loose shoulders: a coat made for a shorter, rounder man. His father's castoff, she'd wager. Such a shame. Tess's fingers itched to drag the coat off him for a bit of nip-and-tuck.

"What brings you to—"

"I thought you might like—"

They both stopped, then spluttered into laughter.

"I brought you more bread," Pavlin said, presenting a muslin bundle with a grin.

She deflected it when he tried to hand it to her. "It's that sorry I am to say no, but the alta insists we don't need accounts. She's never had to run a household herself." At least that last part was true.

"No, this is just for you." Pavlin pushed the bundle on her again, and sure if it didn't smell like bliss, butter and yeast, spice and warmth. Tess latticed her fingers over her belly, hoping it wouldn't give her away with rumbling. "Call it an apology for . . . for my persistence before."

"Nothing wrong with a bit of persistence," Tess said, and promptly wished she could bite her tongue in twain. "But really, I can't. I've no coin to pay you."

"Are apologies bought with centiras?" His smile was like the bread, making her think of bliss... and hunger.

"N-no," she stammered, accepting the bundle while she tried to sort her thoughts. Thanks to Ren and Sedge, she'd come through Ondrakja's torments with fewer scars than either of them, but she knew not to trust anything offered for free.

So she grasped at the only thing within reach. "Give me your coat."

Supporting the bundle on her hip, she had Pavlin's coat half off him before he found his tongue.

"What are you—"

"Fixing an offense to every eye in Nadežra. Come back in two days and I'll have it done for you." Draping the coat over her shoulder, Tess gave him a firm nod of dismissal. "You can bring more bread then. I like the spice cakes especially. Now go on with you; the alta's returning, and I have work to do."

Leaving him bemused on the canal walk, Tess bustled back to the kitchen cellar with his coat, her bread, and a pleased little smirk.

With her secret sewing ring gone, there was no reason to waste more fuel on the hearth fire. Tess banked it so it would die down without going out entirely. Then she hurried to the front hall to keep watch for Alta Renata.

"We're near to finished with the insets for Giuna's underdress," Tess said once they were downstairs, clearing away the embroidery hoops and lace bobbins. "And I just need to put the finishing touches on her surcoat. There's fresh water for washing—should still be warm. And we have bread for our broth. How did it go in White-sail?" She rushed the question as though Ren would overlook the newly filled breadbox.

It must have been a hard day, dancing to meet Quientis's demands, because Ren just dropped onto the bench with an approving groan. "The only thing I can say for Mede Elpiscio's office is that it's warm.

But *he's* sent me to speak with Mede Attravi. I feel like a cat chasing a string, and it's being pulled too fast for me to catch."

Tess let Ren talk as she ladled broth into bowls and tore up a loaf of brown bread so fresh the center was still steaming warm. She'd learned long ago that listening and asking the occasional question helped Ren more than suggestions ever did.

"Here," she said when the food was ready. "Better eat now before it gets so cold in here we can't chew for our teeth chattering." Ren devoured the bread like it would vanish if she waited. Old habit for both of them, left over from when Fingers like Simlin would pinch anything not already in your mouth. She'd come home sick after a small banquet at Extaquium Manor, groaning that she'd taken too much of every dish they offered because she didn't realize how many more were coming.

Conversation died while they both sopped up their broth with the soft bread—and then a thumping came at the door, less a knock than someone banging it with their foot.

Cramming the last of the bread into her mouth, Ren bolted for what would have been the wine room, if they could afford any wine other than Eret Extaquium's swill. Alta Renata couldn't be caught in the kitchen. Tess moved for the door, calling out, "Spare your knuckles! More pounding won't make me move faster."

Hefting the cudgel she kept on hand and standing well back in case there was a knife on the other side, Tess cracked the door.

The cudgel clattered to the floor a heartbeat later so she could catch an armful of Sedge. Somehow she managed to prop him upright while she kicked the door shut.

"Ren!" She lowered Sedge onto a chair, fingers already weaving through his hair to look for bumps or bleeding. Ren was at her side an instant later, knife in hand, facing the door as if more trouble might come through it.

"I'm all right. Nobody's following, neither." He hissed when Tess hit a tangle tacky with blood. "'S my shoulder. Can't do it myself."

"Shoulder. Right. On the floor with you." Tess waited for Sedge to slump flat on his back and Ren to hold him in place. Bracing a

foot against his ribs, she straightened his arm and began to pull—
Slowly, firmly. Mother and Crone, does it have to make that sound?—until
she felt the joint pop back into place.

Sedge sighed, tension draining from his muscles. Tess blotted her
brow with her sleeve, then did the same for him.

"The fuck happened to you?" Ren might still be wearing Alta
Renata's dress, but everything from her posture to her voice was
pure river rat.

Sedge's laugh grated as he eased himself to sitting. "Just like
old times, eh? Got caught between some of them cuffs and their
brawling."

He said it like it was an accident, but Ren didn't seem to believe
him any more than Tess did. "And you failed to skin out of there
because..."

"Weren't there on my own business." Sedge's glance skittered
sideways like it always did when Vargo came up. This time it
returned on the back of a rueful grin. "Though I guess Vargo's business is your business now, Advocate Viraudax."

She sniffed primly. "So it seems, Master Sedge. What can you
tell me?"

Tess had witnessed the transformation from Ren to Renata often
enough: chin and nose coming up, posture straightening like she'd
been strapped to a board, accent smoothing like each word was a
pearl. It was new to Sedge, though.

"Now that's bloody unsettling," he muttered. "Nobody's been
told the whole of it, but Vargo's been digging around in Indestor's
business for a while now. I told you what he did with the other
knots, getting them to fight each other so he could sweep up what
was left—maybe it's the same here, stoking this feud with Novrus."
Sedge snorted. "Not that he'll end up running them. But he'll get
something out of the wreckage, sure."

Ren frowned, dropping the act. "The fight was Indestor and
Novrus?"

"Naw. Delta house business, between Essunta and Fiangiolli. But
everybody knows they're puppets for Indestor and Novrus; them

fighting lets His Mercy and Her Elegance smile at each other in the Charterhouse like they en't covered in the same shit."

Tess shook her head in disgust. At least on the streets knot bosses had usually been honest about hating each other.

"Been a lot of shit along the waterfront these last few months," Sedge added. "Aža stolen, warehouses burned, and the like—some of it's hit Vargo in passing. So he sent me to take a look, because en't like we can ask the Vigil."

"Because Indestor controls the Vigil," Tess murmured. With Ren's help, she levered Sedge to his feet. The kitchen bench wasn't much more comfortable than the floor, but leastwise he wasn't rump-down on the cold flagstones.

"Didn't mean to get caught in it," Sedge grunted as he settled onto the bench. "But—well, I got stupid. Essunta toughs ran into some Fiangiolli, got challenged, claimed they were chasing the Rook."

Ren smacked his good arm. "You got hurt trying to see him?"

"Can't let my own sister outdo me, can I?" He gave her a lopsided grin. "Din't see so much as a black glove, though. Kinless bastards probably made it up to cover why they were on Fiangiolli ground. I got bashed into a wall, and these days all it takes is somebody looking at it wrong for this thing to pop." He touched his shoulder gingerly and hissed.

"Don't be poking at it." Tess batted his hand away and started rooting around for what she'd need. Water, cloths, enough fabric to make a sling; a needle and some of her precious silk thread in case he needed stitching. "Fool boy doesn't have the sense the gods gave a goose," she muttered as she laid out her tools and got to work patching him up.

Ren ran the tip of her tongue across her lip, that look she got when the wheels were turning, handing items to Tess by reflex when she called for them. Tess filled the silence, scolding Sedge for all the scars he'd picked up while they were apart, but he shrugged them off like they were no matter.

By the time Tess had Sedge stitched and washed, Ren had reached a conclusion. "I told Donaia that Vargo would help us against Indestor. I said whatever came into my head, anything to keep her from throwing me out on my ear—but if Vargo truly digs into Indestor's business, maybe I can make it true. I need only to figure out a way for Alta Renata to have heard about this. And find out how Novrus is involved."

"And meet with Mede Attravi, and get Fulvet to give you that charter, and Donaia to scribe you into the register before we're out on the street," Tess said briskly. If she didn't take charge, these two would be at it all night and never get a wink of sleep between them. "Not one of those problems is being solved this evening. Better to face them fresh come morning."

Sedge's nails rasped through his stubble. "You en't far wrong," he said, the words opening into a jaw-cracking yawn.

Tess fixed him with her sternest eye. "You're staying here. We've broth and bread enough, you're warmer than any blanket, and I want to check that arm come morning."

"After twisting it so hard tonight?" Sedge traded an amused look with Ren.

"Aye," Tess said, pushing food on him and a second serving on Ren. "And if you don't annoy me past buzzing, I might even make you a harness to keep it from popping off the next time someone glares at it."

8

Pouncing Cat

Duskgate, Old Island: Apilun 6

"What about this one?" Leato held up a Luyaman-style torc with its wires bent into the shape of two Quarats interlocked as Noctat. "Quarat for wealth, Noctat for—"

"We *all* know what Noctat is for, Leato." Giuna giggled and made a face to match the one Leato directed at her.

Sibiliat poked through the display. "That's such a boring design, though. Now *these*..." Mouth compressed to mute a cheeky grin, she lifted a chain with octagon-engraved clamps at either end, each link etched with a variation on Tuat.

Giuna touched one of the clamps, frowning in puzzlement. "What's it used for?"

"Cloak clasps," Leato said, snatching them away and giving Sibiliat a quelling glare.

Pretending to ignore their antics, Renata let her attention drift across a tray of rings displaying the basic numinata. One fingertip brushed a heavy Sessat sized for a man's hand. This outing was pointless; she was too low on funds to purchase anything that couldn't be pawned, and most of the brokers she used didn't deal in numinatrian pieces. There were legitimate sellers for that.

But Sibiliat kept insisting, and Giuna wheedled, and by the time

Leato added his voice, Renata realized it would be more obvious if she kept refusing.

Sibiliat sidled up to her, too warm. Too close. "This must all seem so provincial to you. Perhaps we should try Eastbridge? You still haven't bought anything, and there's a jeweler near Nightpeace Gardens I recommend."

Renata edged away under the guise of examining a set of bronze seals, the sort inscriptors used to stamp foci into wax plugs, wrought with the names of gods in the Enthaxn script. "If I need something, I can always commission it."

"But the one in Eastbridge sells antiques," Sibiliat said. "Wouldn't you like to see those? I believe your mother owned a few like them."

She'd been pressing the point all day: Letilia's jewelry, her numinatrian pieces, whether Renata knew them or had them or cared about them. The same song she'd been singing since the day of the dance lessons. And Renata, it seemed, wasn't the only one who'd noticed—nor the only one irritated by it. "Why do you care so much about my cousin's jewelry?" Giuna snapped.

There was a dead silence. Leato was taken aback. And Renata...

"If you have a question for me, Alta Sibiliat," she said, with sharp-edged courtesy, "then ask it."

Sibiliat's rigid posture held a moment longer. Then she rubbed one weary hand across her face. "I'm sorry. I should have been honest from the beginning. But yes...there is something."

She squared her shoulders and faced Renata. "I don't suppose you ever saw among your mother's jewels a bronze medallion inscribed with three Tricats? A simple thing, not very elaborate. It's an Acrenix family heirloom, a gift to her from my father, Ghiscolo. A... promise between them, if you will. When I heard you'd returned a ring to Era Traementis, I found myself hoping you might have our medallion as well. Or at least be able to reassure me that Letilia still has it—that she didn't fling it into the river as she left."

So that's what you're after. Renata knew the piece; she'd swept it into her sack along with everything else in Letilia's jewelry box the day she and Tess fled Ganllech.

For an instant, she considered it. Return the heirloom, get Sibiliat's gratitude . . . but no. Why squander that leverage now? Better to keep her main rival hoping, and only satisfy her desire later.

"My apologies, Sibiliat, but I've seen nothing of the sort." She softened her denial with a sigh. "Though it's entirely like Mother to keep such a thing. I'll send a letter to inquire. Not to her, of course, but to our housekeeper. I'll let you know when I hear back."

Frustration flickered in Sibiliat's eyes, quickly suppressed. Giuna moved to her side, one hand touching Sibiliat's elbow; Renata gave them privacy, striding out of the store and across the embankment lane where the West Channel flowed. Winter's grip smothered the usual stink from the water; the breaths she took were cool and clean.

Along the quay below the boardwalk, a flotilla of skiffs—the sort that usually ferried passengers across the channels—had been roped together to form a temporary market. A variety of dories, dinghies, and scows painted in clan colors abutted the skiff walkways, their hulls filled with baskets of fruits and rice and river mollusks, or draped with coarse-woven silks and linens. Smoke rose from low-set grills piled with skewered crabs and delta fowl. The air rang with hawkers' cries in an amalgam of dialects too knotted to untangle.

Leato appeared at her side, leaning on the embankment wall without thought for his gloves or sleeves. "That was kind of you, cousin. Thank you."

"The kindness was for your sake. And Giuna's. Are they still inside?" Renata peered past Leato's shoulder to the closed door of the shop.

"Giuna took her for coffee. And either an apology or a scolding—I'm not sure which. Possibly both." His lips twitched in a battle between smile and frown. "I wish I could figure out if Sibiliat's just toying with her."

"What would you do if she was?" Sibiliat might have cast herself as Renata's rival, but she was the Acrenix heir. If her affection was real, and went as far as marriage, it would go a long way to recovering the Traementis fortunes—without the threat posed by House Indestor.

Leato's head dipped, but she doubted he was studying the bustling skiff market below. "I wish I could do something, but it's Giuna's choice." His golden hair half veiled his eyes as he glanced up at Renata. "Isn't it?"

His look begged for permission to interfere in Giuna's courtships—an interference Renata was half tempted to indulge in herself. But she couldn't afford to attract more of Sibiliat's attention, much less her ire.

Smoke from the skiff market, unctuous with the aroma of roasting fat, rose to tickle her nose. Her stomach answered with an audible gurgle, and she clasped hands over it in embarrassment. "My apologies. I ate very little before our outing." Only some porridge that was more water than rice, but she could hardly admit that to Leato. "My stomach is inconveniently delicate before fifth sun."

Laughing off his previous mood as though it had never been, Leato took her arm and led her down the nearest river stair. "Good thing it's almost seventh sun now. Enough of Seterin culture; let me introduce you to something uniquely Nadežran."

He supported her hand for balance as she made the small hop from stair landing to skiff, then kept his hold as they meandered along the gently rolling lanes of the impromptu flotilla, past knotted thread charms and pots of curly-headed mums, their bright blooms almost blinding in the gloom of the day. She waited while he haggled over a pair of roasted devil crabs with a Vraszenian man so dark he must have hailed from Pražmy, in the southernmost reaches of Vraszan.

Accepting her skewer, Renata pretended to watch Leato for how to eat it, only breaking the reed in half to crack the crab's shell after he demonstrated. They had to remove their gloves to pick out the steaming meat. Renata unaccountably felt her face warming at baring her hands to him, at seeing Leato's bare hands in turn. His skin was soft, pale bisque, his short nails buffed to a polish. "I've certainly never seen anything like this," she said, forcing her gaze away and ignoring a flutter in her stomach that had nothing to do with hunger. "But what makes it uniquely Nadežran?"

"It's a Charterhouse thing. You need a license to operate a shop on the Old Island or the Upper Bank, and most of those licenses go to people with Liganti ancestry. But a shop is defined as 'a commercial establishment with a fixed premise,' so that doesn't cover wandering sellers, or—" He waved his skewer at the weave of skiffs and boats, and the crowd of common Nadežrans picking through the river traders' wares. "I assume you've seen Staveswater, out past the Turtle Lagoon?"

She'd seen it every day of her childhood, from Lacewater's shore. The jumble of stilt-houses and houseboats was the largest Vraszenian-dominated enclave outside Seven Knots, and entirely controlled by the Stretsko gangs. Ren doubted even Vargo could get a foothold there.

"That collection of shacks? I saw it when my ship sailed in, but I assumed it was the remains of a flooded islet. You mean to say that people live there?"

Grimacing at the implied condemnation, Leato said, "It used to be bigger when I was a boy—spanned both sides of the lagoon. But Mettore throws the inhabitants in jail for any reason he can find, then gets Fulvet to tear the structures down as uninhabited. And the people there give him *lots* of reasons."

She turned away, pretending interest in the traders' wares before her true feelings escaped her grasp. The pretense became truth as she fingered cloth thick with colorful embroidery, hammered copper jewelry from the southern Toču Mountains, intricately carved flutes made of bored and fire-hardened reeds. Leato plied her with more food, most of it on sticks, but also steamed buns filled with sweet custard and a soup she had to drink quickly to keep it from leaking out of its oiled paper cup. The tang of lemongrass and pepper stayed on her lips long after the cup was tossed into the river.

The traders and skiffers were all Vraszenian, panel coats and braided hair, but most of the shoppers wandering the floating walkways had the stamp of Nadežrans born; even those clearly of mixed ancestry wore skirted coats and beaded surcoats, their hair loose or bound with ribbons. Renata and Leato stood out as the only nobility in the crowd, earning them some stares, but also the eager attention of every trader they passed. Cuffs not only meant money; they meant gullibility. Which was why Renata's hand instinctively moved to protect her surcoat pocket when a scowling youth with crimson Stretsko beads clacking in his braids shoved past her.

But he hadn't been going for her pocket, and Renata's defensive shift dislodged the stack of broadsheets tucked under his arm. They scattered across the skiffway, several of them blowing into the water.

"I'm sorry," she said, hot with shame. "I thought—" Despising herself a little for her reflexive suspicion, she stooped to help the young man gather the papers, but straightened again at the hatred in his glare.

"You're not wanted here, chalk-face. Take your bloodstained coin and go." Crumpling the stack of papers to his chest, he lost himself in the crowd.

Renata glanced down at the sheet clutched in her hand. It was tightly printed text, the ink so feathered on the cheap rag paper that it was difficult to read. But with the context of the boy's words and braids, the essence was clear enough. It was a screed against the Cinquerat, the noble and delta houses, and anyone else with "foreign" blood in Nadežra. The sort of thing that would get anyone caught with it arrested by the Vigil.

Crumpling the paper into a wad, Renata tossed it into the river just as Leato finished a purchase and turned back to her.

"Cousin, you must try this," he said, offering a hollowed-out section of reed.

She knew what was in the reed before she touched it, the scent curling around her like a blanket. She closed her eyes and breathed deeply, letting the aroma ease the self-disgust that shook her at the Stretsko's words. He didn't know her, didn't know what she was doing. If he did, he'd likely applaud her for pulling one over on the cheese-eaters. But when she opened her eyes and found Leato watching eagerly for her reaction, it was hard to recall why she should take pride in that.

Before Ren could bury those thoughts under one of Renata's smiles, a commotion from the riverbank sent a ripple through the unsteady ground of the flotilla. The trader who'd sold Leato the chocolate began swiftly untying the ropes that bound him to the skiff walkway.

"What's happening?" she asked, as other traders began doing the same. Shouts rose up from the wharf side of the market, and then something much stronger than a ripple rocked their skiff, sending the reed tumbling from her hands and into the river. Leato caught her with a strong arm around her waist before she could do the same.

Ren clutched him close, cold with sudden fright. There was a reason she'd never liked the river markets. She couldn't swim—and in a freezing river, wearing the heavy underdress and surcoat of a noblewoman...

"I have you," Leato said in a low murmur. She could taste chocolate on the breath warming her cheek. "It's the Vigil. Mettore throwing around his weight again."

He set her on her feet, but kept his arm tight around her as he turned to the woman casting lines off their section of walkway. "You, skiffer! I'll give you ten forri and the protection of my house if you get us away from this."

Most of the skiffers and river traders were doing just that, spreading out across the channel like ducks fleeing a barge. But Renata saw more than a few people, most of them fair-skinned Nadežrans, struggling to swim ashore after being unceremoniously knocked into the water by a skiffer's long pole.

The skiffer eyed Leato and Renata, pole raised as she weighed her options. Not far away, the hawks were dragging people off boats and out of the water. Only when Leato held out a fist of forri did she relent, swiping the coins from his hand and sinking her pole into the river to push them to safety.

Glancing back over her shoulder, Ren looked for the Stretsko, but all she saw of him was a school of sodden broadsheets floating downriver.

Froghole, Lower Bank: Apilun 8

Winter had its teeth deep in Nadežra's flesh, but that didn't stop Yurdan from sweating like the delta fens in summer. His eyes were too wide, pupils devouring the muddy blue, and he didn't blink enough—but he kept his wits enough to talk, and that was what mattered.

"I—I see things," he stammered, pointing one trembling finger at the walls of the old lace mill. "It. Them. Staring at me. The walls are watching. This whole fucking city is made of eyes. Everywhere I look, they're looking back at me. And they don't *blink*." He squeezed down on himself, eyes and fists clenched shut, arms wrapped tight around curled-up legs. "Masks have mercy—is that what happens? Places like this, all the bad shit that happens, all the shit we do . . . this is what we leave behind."

"He's starting to make less sense," Vargo murmured to Varuni, who was taking notes. To Sedge he said, "How long is it now?"

Sedge was kneeling by Yurdan, ready to act if something went wrong. He had Vargo's pocket watch in one hand, and took his eyes off Yurdan long enough to glance at it. "Not quite two bells."

Vargo slowly spun a half-filled glass vial between his fingers, watching the darkly iridescent powder inside slip from one end to the other like delta silt. He'd assumed Hraček's death was an attack on his organization, maybe by one of the Stretsko knots, his main rivals on the Lower Bank. But as autumn slipped into winter, he got reports from across the city—Froghole, Kingfisher, all down the Lower Bank, and even on the Old Island—of other people turning up bleeding like Hraček. Not Vargo's people; members of other knots, or even ordinary citizens. They all had one thing in common.

Ash. A drug nobody had heard of before this year. A drug Vargo didn't control, and didn't understand.

Not yet, anyway. One bell for the effects to set in. Another for

Yurdan's descriptions to unravel into babble. Vargo's stool creaked as he pocketed the vial and leaned forward, watching for changes in Yurdan's demeanor. Anything that might give him a clue.

"Yurdan. Do you remember why you're here?"

Glassy eyes rolled back and forth before fixing on Vargo. "You asked for a volunteer."

"Yes. For what?"

"I..." Something past Vargo's shoulder caught Yurdan's attention, and his answer died in a strangled moan.

"Yurdan, what day is today?"

Nothing but mumbles, then: "Fuck me. The curtain's gone."

"The curtain isn't the only thing," Vargo muttered. To Varuni he said, "Note that he's lost the ability to answer questions."

"Behind you—look—" Yurdan tried to lunge toward Vargo, but Sedge was ready for him, dropping the pocket watch to grab him by the shoulders.

::Nothing there,:: Alsius assured Vargo. ::He's jumping at shadows. This seems much like aža, only a good deal less pleasant.::

Agreed, Vargo thought in reply. *So what the fuck is the appeal?*

When Yurdan heard Vargo was looking for a volunteer to test ash's effects, he stepped forward. He and Hraček had been lovers since before Vargo's Spiders ensnared their knot. He wanted to know what killed his friend.

::See if he can feel other sensations. The descriptions of the violent ones make it sound like all their senses are dulled.::

Vargo nodded. "Sedge. Do something that will hurt, but don't injure him."

A quick shift of Sedge's grip bent Yurdan's arm up behind him in a way that made even Vargo wince. Yurdan didn't seem to notice, all his attention still fixed on the darkness beyond their circle of lights. Sedge grunted. "I don't think he—"

"Kinless bastards," Yurdan snarled, twisting. "You're the ones who got Hraček, en't you? Well, I see you now—you en't getting away this time!"

Sedge was one of Vargo's better fists. Nobody got away from

him that he didn't let go. His whole body tensed to hold Yurdan in place...and Yurdan threw him off like dandelion fluff. Only the wet, tearing sound of something giving way in Yurdan's shoulder hinted at the effort involved.

Vargo spun off his stool and out of Yurdan's path, but the drugged man wasn't going for him. Yurdan lurched to the edge of the lights, hands arching into rigid claws. "That's right, you fuckers. I'm gonna tear you apart!"

But as he swiped at the air, Yurdan was the one who got torn.

They all saw it happen. A bloody streak opened up across the back of his bare shoulders, like an invisible blade had cut him—or a claw. Yurdan paid that no more heed than his injured shoulder, howling incoherent threats at the empty darkness.

A darkness that answered with silent fury. Cut after cut shredded his skin, blood streaming from the wounds like rain; Sedge leapt to Yurdan's aid, but there was nothing for him to fight. Even when Yurdan seemed to seize hold of something, wrestling like a street performer with an imaginary foe, Sedge's hands passed through the space between his arms without pause.

Alsius, what's there?

::Nothing, my boy. I'm not seeing anything you aren't.::

Vargo had no fucking clue what was happening. But he couldn't stand by while one of his people got shredded.

"Drag him this way." Kicking his stool aside, Vargo drew his sword from his cane, muttering, "I have my compass, my edge, my chalk, myself. I need nothing more to know the cosmos."

::What in nine sigils are you doing?:: Alsius screeched in his head.

"What does it look like?" He set his sword tip to the wooden boards and walked a circle, carving a ragged, uneven arc that would make the most amateur inscriptor wince. Behind him, Yurdan's shouts had broken into wet, animal growls as he fought Varuni, Sedge, and whatever Primordial demons the ash was showing him.

::You can't just— You don't even have a focus!::

"I'll freehand one."

::No, you bloody well won't!:: Alsius said, even as Vargo tossed aside his sword and pulled out a knife. He knelt on the boards where he judged the spiral's center should be—more or less.

What would be best? Protection. Sessat. He ran through a mental list of the gods associated with Sessat. Avca? Teis? Which one had the easiest sigil to draw? Which one could he manage without fucking it up? "The alternative is to make myself the focus."

::Over my dead body.::

There was nothing funny in this moment, but Alsius's protest still spurred a grim chuckle from Vargo. "Yes, that's usually the result when an inscriptor becomes his own focus. Which is why I'm improvising." He dug the knife tip into the soft wood.

::Stop, Vargo. *Stop!*::

"Master Vargo," Varuni said softly. "You can stop. It's . . . too late."

The room fell silent, except for the unbroken stream of low curses from Sedge. Vargo made himself turn and look.

Yurdan was a bloody heap on the boards, his limp body lying just short of the ragged line Vargo had carved. Hraček had survived long enough for Vargo's people to find him, but Yurdan was gone in a mere instant—torn apart by absolutely nothing.

Vargo's knife clattered to the floor. It had all happened so fast, and he'd been too slow to react. No—he shouldn't have *had* to react. He should have planned for this. A simple protective circle; it seemed so fucking obvious now that Yurdan lay unmoving in a spreading pool of blood.

He'd seen dead bodies—he'd been responsible for more than a few—but he'd thought the days were gone when he'd be helpless to stop someone from dying. The lack of control burned in him like acid.

What. The fuck. Was that.

::I've not seen anything like it in all my years.::

Considerably more years than Vargo could lay claim to. He stood, dusting off his knees. Varuni hovered nearby. Sedge was still tense, his anger burning blue like flame, looking for something to kill. Both of them were waiting on Vargo's lead.

And Vargo needed to think.

"Take care of this," he told Varuni, and waved Sedge off when the fist would have followed him.

The streets of Froghole weren't pleasant, but after the stink of blood, sweat, and bowels, the air was positively fresh. The last quarter of silver-blue Corillis was hidden behind the rooftops, but copper-green Paumillis rode high and full, and the cold made everything so clear that the stars seemed cut into the blackness of the sky.

"What do we know, what do we suspect, and what do we need to know?" he asked, striking out at a pace brisk enough to battle the cold and outrun his impotent anger. He could keep this conversation to thoughts alone, but speaking aloud helped move things into place. And if people thought he was mad, walking around the islet and talking to himself . . . they quickly took their opinions elsewhere when they realized who he was.

Alsius answered him with sober precision. ::We know this so-called ash has hallucinatory effects like aža, but nightmarish. It allows the user to disregard cold and pain, and gives them tremendous strength. And it seems they can be hurt by their hallucinations.::

"That was no hallucination." Nothing imaginary could cause damage that real. Just thinking of those long, clawlike tears made Vargo's skin twitch. "Spirits of some kind?" Such things existed, as he and Alsius knew all too well.

But Alsius said, ::I doubt it. You would need a numinat to draw upon them, and there was no such thing here. Nor are they capable of affecting material things like flesh.::

Vargo kicked a loose cobble. "So what's invisible and intangible, yet has the power to slice a man to ribbons?"

::It has to be related to the ash. No one else was attacked tonight.::

Rounding a corner, Vargo followed the side of the lace mill. "Focus on the ash, then. It's new. Not an import, either, or we'd have rumors from the Dawn or Dusk Roads. Which suggests it's being made here." And where had they seen a questionable operation only a few months ago? "The break-in. That...substance...we found on the floor."

::It looked nothing like ash.::

True—ash was a powder. "It could be an interim stage. They used that numinat for *something* dream related."

::But this isn't numinatria,:: Alsius insisted. ::It's more akin to imbuing—if you could imbue aža to be nightmarish.::

They both fell silent. A pickpocket drifted close, saw Vargo's face, and drifted away like that was his plan all along.

Imbuing, which couldn't be integrated with numinatria in a stable fashion. An inscriptor who imbued a numinat fed it their own energy, burning them from the inside out. That was how the river numinata worked for nearly two centuries, and why the broken one was a fucking nightmare to replace. That was what Alsius had been terrified Vargo would do tonight. And when a crafter inscribed a numinat on their work, it might make the product incredibly potent, but only for a few moments. Not long enough to be useful for a street drug. And certainly not the sort of thing that could—

Vargo stopped dead in the street. Tyrant's syphilitic nutsack—he'd been right the first time. "Ash isn't imbued aža. It's *transmuted*. Like prismatium."

::...Impossible.:: The weakness of Alsius's response was nearly agreement.

Vargo began walking again, conviction instead of fury giving him speed. He was right. He didn't know *how* they were doing it, but he was right. Even though Alsius argued, ::The process required to transmute prismatium isn't something one can simply set up and dismantle in a night. And even if it were, why would they do it at the lace mill instead of taking the aža somewhere they controlled?::

"I don't know." There was too much they still didn't know. Hraček had died from ash before the lace mill break-in, and there was too much of it on the street for this to have been a one-time thing. It pointed to organization. Anyone that organized would have arranged for their own supply of aža, and a more permanent location to transmute it. Unless...

"Essunta has been buying a lot of aža from us since he hired us last year. And he's been dancing on Indestor sticks for a while now." They'd come full circle back to the lace mill door. Vargo rested his hand on the latch, letting the cold seep through his gloves. "Didn't Indestor lose a prison hulk in Floodwatch back in Suilun?" Roughly a week before the lace mill break-in.

::Yes. The Stadnem Anduske were rumored to be using it to print seditious literature. At least, that was the excuse Era Novrus gave when she shut it down.::

Novrus and Indestor were always at each other's throats these days. He'd assumed the prison ship was just another flimsy pretext— but what if there *had* been something there? Something that had to be relocated in a hurry afterward. Mettore Indestor had a good inscriptor to hand: Breccone Indestris, the grandnephew of Iridet's seat holder, Utrinzi Simendis, and married into Mettore's house through some cousin or another. He was capable of what Vargo had seen in the lace mill.

Vargo resisted the urge to kick the door. Wasn't this what he'd wanted? Dirt on Mettore Indestor, something he could use to cut the man off at the knees. But finding it on his own turf... Vargo couldn't help but wonder if Mettore had realized what Vargo was up to, and was preparing to strike back.

Fucking Indestor. Bringing their trash into *his* house.

Vargo threw open the door. Sedge and Varuni were too well-trained to flinch at the bang of it hitting the wall.

"We have a new priority," he said. "I want to know everything about this ash. Who's buying, who's selling, who's making. I want to know if Novrus's people found any remnants of numinatria during the anti-Anduske raid in Floodwatch. And get me a list of Indestor's holdings, official or otherwise. Any place they might be storing aža."

Coster's Walk, Lower Bank: Apilun 9

Sending Leato to talk to Vargo's contacts about shipping was good business sense for Renata Viraudax, but it also served a purpose for Ren: It put him on the Lower Bank at a known time and place.

She was tired of trying to pry indirectly into the man's affairs. As Leato emerged from the office into the clamor of Coster's Walk, Arenza Lenskaya stepped into his path.

A major gamble—but her disguise was more than just clothing and makeup. It was the pitch and accent of her voice; it was posture, body language, the deference to a handsome altan. It was the fact that no man in his right mind would look at a Vraszenian szorsa and think, *Is that Renata Viraudax?*

"Your fortune, altan?" Arenza fanned her pattern deck. "Let the threads guide you, showing the way to what you seek!"

Leato's step slowed, but his gaze slid sideways, the behavior of a man preparing to ignore the person accosting him on the street. Arenza edged back into his field of view and shuffled the cards, then drew one with a flourish, all but shoving it in his face. "In the cards there is much aid, altan."

It stopped him cold. The random-seeming shuffle was anything but; she'd jogged a card inward as she tossed them, letting her ensure The Face of Glass would be on top when she drew. The card of truth and revelations... and also the card from his reading at the Talon and Trick back in Suilun, the part of his future that was neither good nor ill. By the look on his face, he hadn't forgotten.

"All right," Leato muttered, half to himself. "Why not."

She led him out of the main flow of traffic, then whipped her shawl from her shoulders and laid it on the ground with a partitioned bowl on top. A surreptitious glance around as Leato dropped several centiras into the middle compartment showed her no hawks watching this time—and definitely no Grey Serrado.

Leato shifted from one foot to the other as she shuffled and laid out the cards. Most streetside patterners carried a stool for their clients to sit on. It kept them in one place and their faces at eye level for easier reading. But Leato had made his offering; he wasn't going to bolt over a bit of discomfort.

Arenza gave the cards an honest shuffle this time. She'd debated trying to stack them like she'd done with Nikory, but she didn't have a sure enough sense of what Leato was doing to know what cards would be best. Better to lay them true, and see if that did her any good.

She didn't attempt a full spread for him, though. That was usually reserved for card parlours and pattern shops, where it was easier to spend the necessary time interpreting everything—with less risk of the wind blowing something away. Instead she laid a three-card line, debating with herself. *All at once, or one at a time?* The former made lying easier, but the latter hooked the client more firmly.

One at a time. She flipped the first card and leaned forward slightly, forcing Leato to crane to see the image on it. Her cheap street deck was only woodblock-printed in black on white, so wavering lines across the eyeless face represented the warping effect of The Mask of Mirrors.

"Lies," Arenza mused, pitching her voice almost too quiet to be heard over the traffic. "The card I drew for you, it was The Face of Glass. Hlai Oslit Rvarin, the deity of truth and lies. This is their Mask. You seek the former, but in the latter you are mired."

He stopped shifting. "That's a strange way to begin a reading, szorsa. Are you calling me a liar?"

Crossed arms, direct eye contact, his feet angling to walk away—all signs of a liar. Giuna was right. "We lie for many reasons, altan," Arenza said gently. "Sometimes for good reason. Often to protect those we care about, because we know the truth would worry them."

His gaze dropped, and she went on. "But other people lie also. And not for such good reasons."

The leaning and the soft voice did their job. Leato gave in and crouched in front of her, balancing so he didn't have to touch his knee to the cobblestones. "I don't need a patterner to tell me that. You just described most of Nadežra."

He was nibbling at the hook, but not yet biting down. Fortunately, she had some bait ready to hand. "You have already gone to great effort, and spent much money—perhaps more than you can afford—to gain information," she said. "But it has not brought you what you seek. And so you ask yourself, in this city, can I trust anyone? Have those I've spoken to told me anything of use? Or have I for nothing emptied my purse?"

He cast a look at the bowl and the centiras he'd placed in it, mouth twisting into a sardonic smile. His world-weary sigh was nothing like the laughing, carefree man he pretended to be when others were looking. "You understand the people of this city well. For all the good *that* does me. Unless..."

She met his searching look as though she knew nothing of secrets and lies. "Unless?"

His gaze dropped to the cards. One finger idly traced a curl of embroidery on her shawl. "Not that all you people know each other, but—I don't suppose you know where I can find a Vraszenian laundress named Idusza."

He was going to all this effort for a Vraszenian laundress? She studied him through her eyelashes. Leato didn't show any of the signs of a man hunting for a former or future lover. Which meant Idusza had something to do with his actual goal: the Rook, if Giuna was right, or something else.

"For a Vraszenian woman, Idusza is a common name," she said, which was true enough. "But the second card is the path you must follow to find what you seek. Let us see what it has to say."

She almost cackled when she turned it over. The Mask of Hollows: not an amusing card normally, as the starving shape represented poverty and loss. But on the heels of what she'd said about Leato spending money, it was all too fitting.

And it gave her an excellent opening. Arenza held up one hand before Leato could make any comment; he clearly knew pattern well enough to recognize the card's general meaning. "In seeking your Vraszenian woman, altan, throw not good money after bad. When three cards are laid, there is no good and ill and that which is neither; each card may to any of those things speak. Your path is not bankrupting yourself."

"Bit late for that," he muttered, his knee touching down onto the dirty cobbles. She hid a smile of triumph. *Hooked.* "Well, go on. Where does my path lead, if not the poorhouse?"

"All cards contain their virtues as well as their pains. The Vraszenian woman you seek, Idusza—this card tells me she is a poor woman, one who works hard for what she has, in common jobs barely putting food on the table. A street-seller, or someone of that kind—a maid, perhaps, or a laundress."

She paced the flood of words carefully, keeping Leato in her peripheral vision. There was an art to this, feeding people information they'd already given so it felt to them like proof of her insight. By now Leato had forgotten that the word "laundress" came from his mouth first; she'd said "Vraszenian woman" often enough that he would think *that* was the phrase he'd used.

"Yes." Leato wrapped his hands over his bent knee, leaning in closer. "But for a laundress, she's got interesting friends."

"Her friends you know, yet you cannot find her?"

"That's not—" He shook his head. "A friend of mine found her family, but they've been no help. It's Idusza I need. And her...friends."

From the sound of it, "friends" was a euphemism. Arenza's interest sharpened even more. She laid one hand on The Mask of Hollows. "On the street you will your path find. And are you not on the street now?"

He settled fully on the ground opposite her. "So I am. How can the street help me?"

His gaze was direct. It seemed he was either desperate enough or convinced enough by her skills—or both—to at least consider trusting her guidance.

Arenza placed one hand over her heart. "Szorsas occupy a special place in Vraszenian society. To a Liganti man, her family may be closemouthed, but to one of their own...?"

He drew back, a shadow of caution dimming the openness of a moment before. "Who says it was a Liganti who spoke with them?"

Djek. She'd let herself fall into a wrong assumption. Serrado was probably the one helping him. "The offer stands, altan. But we have not yet finished the pattern; let us see what the final card holds."

She turned it over as she spoke, and found herself looking at the shattered, disarranged shape of The Mask of Chaos.

Three Masks. One from each thread: spinning, cut, woven. Her mother, Ivrina, had spoken disparagingly of szorsas who conned their clients, not just because they were frauds, but because she said their lies blinded them to what the cards showed. What might Ren have read from these three if she'd been thinking like a patterner, instead of a Finger?

Too late now. The eyeless faces were mute, and all she had to work with was what she could pull out of Leato and her knowledge of the cards.

Crime and disorder. Or, if read as revealed, working outside a corrupt system.

The way the Rook did.

Leato's breath hissed between his teeth. A quick glance at him showed that all his attention was on the card.

"It seems this has meaning already for you," Arenza said softly.

The leather of Leato's glove creaked as he absently clenched and unclenched his fist. "Yes. And no. It has too many meanings. Which one am I supposed to assume it's referring to? Idusza's friends? My enemy? Myself?"

"Perhaps all of them." The answer was reflexive, a way to sound wise while her attention was elsewhere. *Idusza's friends.* A Vraszenian woman, with criminal friends. Some Lower Bank knot, maybe— they would certainly keep their mouths shut. As for enemies...

It was a leap into the dark, but she had a candle. "Your enemy is free to act because he considers himself bound not by the law."

Leato scowled. "That's because he *is* the law."

Mettore Indestor. Digging around in the muck of the city, paying off men like Stoček and chasing someone in a Vraszenian knot... Leato wasn't hunting the Rook. He was seeking leverage over the man trying to swallow his family whole.

Standing, Leato brushed at his knees and the skirts of his coat, making a face when the dirt from the cobbles refused to yield. "Thank you for your wisdom, szorsa, but I think my problems are more than pattern can solve." He dug into his pocket and tossed a few more centiras into her bowl, murmuring low enough that the only words she made out of the closing prayer were "Face" and "Mask."

"Pattern solves no problems, altan," she said before he could step away. "It leads you to solutions. As it led you to me."

He gave her a curious look—as well he should. It was an odd thing, for a patterner to push after the closing donation had been made and the prayer spoken. "What can you do?"

"What I said I would: on your behalf speak to her family. Our people know the pattern holds wisdom. They listen when a patterner speaks."

"For another donation, I presume?" he said wryly. "Wasn't it your cards that warned me not to throw good money after bad?"

Ancestors knew she could use more of his coin. But it was in Ren's interests to help him against Indestor—and a concession now would put her in a position to learn more, too. She held up The Mask of Hollows. "Your path is not one of buying success, altan. It would go against the will of the Mask if I took payment for this."

After a moment's hesitation and another searching look, he nodded. "Polojny. Uča Avreno in Seven Knots. If you find anything..." He looked down at his finery. "Leave a message for a man named Serrado at the Gawping Carp in Kingfisher."

So it was Serrado who'd been helping him. "May you see the Face and not the Mask, altan."

Leato disappeared into the crowd as the clock towers chimed

ninth sun. Ren was supposed to have dinner with Mede Attravi at first earth. But if she hurried, two hours was enough time to visit Seven Knots before she had to change her face.

Dockwall, Lower Bank: Apilun 13

The warehouse was new, one of several behind a high enclosing wall, with a yard large enough for ten wagons at a time. A trade caravan was there now—one of the Vraszenian kretse responsible for carrying goods east and west along the Dawn and Dusk Roads—and an ant-line of people was busy unloading bolts of fabric from the wagons' beds.

Their shouts fell like familiar music on Ren's ears. She and her mother had never lived among Vraszenians, much less traveled with them, but she'd spoken the language growing up, and it still sounded like home.

Even if her tongue stumbled when she tried to use it. Visiting Idusza Polojny's family in Seven Knots had been a rude awakening on that front; all Ren's previous time as Arenza had been spent speaking accented Liganti. But a szorsa delivering fate's message had to speak Vraszenian, or no one would listen to her.

She hadn't found Idusza, but at least she got entertainment out of listening to Idusza's mother rant about the slip-knot who'd pestered her about her daughter. *Serrado should have worn a wig.* A traditional family like the Polojny didn't think much of a man who cut his braids off.

But Renata Viraudax didn't speak even five words of Vraszenian, and her business here had nothing to do with them. "I'm Master Vargo's advocate in the Cinquerat," she told the guards at the gate. "I need to speak with him."

She expected to be taken to an office, but instead the stable girl they flagged down led Renata through a winding maze of stock from half a dozen lands. Bales of wool and cured sheepskin from

Ganllech, a row of pungent casks stamped with the crimson markings of the Dubrakalčy, bags of salt from Nchere.

"Master Vargo has trading charters with so many places?" Renata asked. Vargo had led her to believe he didn't administer any charters yet. Certainly not enough to explain the variety of goods in his warehouse.

The girl shook her head. "We just hold the goods for the kretse and the delta gentry. Keep it from getting nicked or burned before it's sold. Oi, Master Vargo! Cuff come to see you."

Vargo was in the middle of a rapid exchange with a spare, angular person in a panel coat and the braids of a kureč leader. One of the lihoše, then: born a woman, but taking on a male identity so he could lead his people. Only sons were allowed to be kureč leaders, and if there were none—or if all the available ones were incompetent—then a daughter would become a son instead.

His rapid Vraszenian was so shot through with road cant that Ren had difficulty following it. Vargo answered in kind, a little more slowly, and only broke long enough to nod at Renata. Most of his attention was on the lihosz and the bolt of rose-patterned black lace half unrolled between them.

Either Vargo was already winning or he put Renata's presence above profit, conceding whatever they'd been arguing about. The lihosz spat into his hand and held it out for shaking. Vargo— gloveless—did the same, then gestured for a group of waiting haulers to follow the Vraszenian.

He approached Renata, grimacing and pulling out a kerchief to clean his hand. "My apologies, alta. If I'd known you were coming, I would have greeted you properly."

His knuckles weren't as marred as Sedge's, but Renata caught sight of multiple scars before he tugged his glove back on. "I apologize for troubling you here, Master Vargo. Though now that I've seen this place, I understand the complaints I've been hearing from Caerulet's office about 'off-book guards.'" She wondered how many of the people protecting the warehouses against thieves were thieves themselves—just on Vargo's payroll.

"I'd be more sympathetic to His Mercy's complaints if he weren't the main reason my clients need guards," Vargo muttered. "We live in a topsy-turvy world, Alta Renata, where the criminals are honest, and it's the upright folk you have to be wary of."

Trying to convince me you can be trusted? Sedge didn't spill Vargo's secrets, but he talked about the man readily enough. It left her no more certain what to think of him than she'd been before.

Vargo said, "I'm afraid you've caught me at a busy time. I have a caravan from Sefante and a ship from Ganllech, and no manager to deal with them. Care to talk while we walk?"

"Of course. And please don't take it the wrong way when I say I'm glad to hear you've had your share of problems with Eret Indestor. I've been trying to assist Era Traementis by arranging for some mercenaries to guard one of her trading charters, but he's made that nearly impossible. As for your own charter...you would think cleansing the river has nothing to do with military matters, and yet he's taking the strangest interest in it." She kept her words mild, but saturated them with bitterness.

Leading a winding path through stacked hardwood, Vargo said, "What sort of interest? Is Mettore aware of my involvement, or is this merely an extension of his siege against House Traementis?"

"Yes to both. Sadly, my attempt to help Altan Mezzan save face against the Rook sank under the weight of his petulance, so it hasn't done much to win me favor there. I tried to get a meeting with Eret Indestor, to see if I could strike some kind of bargain, but I appear to be utterly beneath his notice."

"Count yourself lucky." A runner came by with several cramped ledger sheets. Vargo skimmed them with a finger before nodding and sending the boy off again. After a moment of staring into space, lips moving silently, he shook himself and turned back to Renata. "Keep clear of Indestor. You're capable enough, but Mettore Indestor isn't the sort of enemy you're equipped to deal with. I'll take care of it— give him something else to occupy his attention."

Renata could imagine what he meant—she was learning the sort of man Vargo was—but he had no idea what sort of woman she was.

"I can hardly keep clear of him when I'm representing the Traementis in the Charterhouse. And I can't be a very effective advocate
when I'm fighting half-blind."

They'd passed into a tilted forest of silks and lace, the outermost
bolts leaning drunkenly against the inner layers. Dust hung heavy
in the air, mixing with camphor and cedar, and Vargo's particular
clove scent. He pulled Renata into a gap between the stacks, rendering them invisible unless someone passed directly alongside them.

"This is how the Cinquerat operates," he said, his voice quiet but
hard. "They make the rules, but they don't play by them. Indestor's
just the most obvious. And he's already shown he has no interest in
negotiating with your people, or Era Traementis would have found
a way to get her guards. So what's to keep him from shipping you
back to Seteris? Or wherever you'll fetch the highest price?"

"I'm guilty of no crime," Renata said, as if her heart hadn't staggered in its pace. Slavery was illegal within Nadežra itself...but it
was legal to sell certain types of convicts overseas as slaves. Impersonating a noble was on the list of offenses punishable in such a manner. "Are you suggesting Eret Indestor would falsely accuse me?"

"I'm suggesting that if you were to disappear off the street one day
and find yourself on a penal ship, there's not much anyone here could
do." Vargo's gaze was flinty. "If you were in the Traementis register it
would be one thing; the outrage of the noble houses and delta gentry
might protect you. But as things stand, you're not much safer than a
common Nadežran. You wouldn't be the first person framed and sent
into slavery without ever going before one of Fulvet's judges."

*Perhaps I wasn't weaving whole cloth when I told Donaia that Vargo
would work with us.* "A new Caerulet might prove more cooperative.
If that seat were to become vacant."

The space was close enough that when Vargo tilted his head in
acknowledgment of her point, his breath stirred the wisps of hair at
her brow. "Until then, your time and charms are better spent convincing those who don't have an immediate reason to stop you."

Before Renata could do more than draw breath to answer, a
voice interrupted. "Found him—Oh!" The runner stepped back

when he saw the two of them. "Er...sorry, Master Vargo, I din't mean to interrupt. Varuni was worried—"

"Tell her the alta has left me in one piece, and she can call back the corpse-seekers." Vargo stepped out of the alcove, watching the runner dash off. "Don't worry for your reputation, alta. My people won't talk."

It sounded like courtesy, but Sedge had told enough stories that she couldn't help reading a hint of leverage into it—which made her glad she'd brought her own. "Speaking of talk..."

Renata reached into her purse and brought out a small envelope of fine paper bearing the water lily seal of House Coscanum. "This is why I came."

Vargo opened the envelope with all the trepidation of a man asked to reach into an adder's nest. The scar running through his brow puckered, and his eyes flicked up to meet Renata's. "This is real? How the f—How did you manage it?"

She laughed. "Trade secrets. Would you tell me how you manage to obtain such splendid fabric, and at such prices?"

"No, but for this?" He raised the invitation. "I might let you have your pick of them."

I think that high-pitched sound I hear is Tess squeaking with joy. "The invitation is real. It's become apparent that people think I'm out to conceal my dealings with you. What better way to show we have nothing to hide than for you to attend the betrothal celebration of Mezzan and Marvisal?" She lowered her voice. "There might even be an opportunity to learn something useful."

He lowered his to match. "I'll be certain not to squander it." With a wave at the fabric forest around them, he set off to deal with business. "Tell your maid to at least *try* not to beggar me?"

The Shambles and the Aerie: Apilun 22

"Oi, hawk. You'd best get gone. En't doing Fiča any good nodding off like that."

Grey started awake at Arkady's words, catching her wrist before she could smack his head like he was one of her nippers. The girl he'd been sitting with, Fiča, paid neither of them any mind. She was tracking the progress of a spider up the wall, eyes rolling out of focus, head lolling to the tuneless accompaniment of her humming. Despite the ratty blankets piled on her, she was shivering. The bruise-purple skin around her eyes spoke to days of sleeplessness.

He didn't think he'd nodded off for long, but Arkady was right—it seemed beyond cruel to sleep in front of a child who couldn't. Fiča had stopped making any sense long before he arrived. He'd gotten a few things about what had happened to her—Gammer Lindworm, the darkness, monsters eating her dreams—but it sounded like something from a fire tale. Given her state, he couldn't be certain it wasn't all a product of sleepless hallucinations.

Using the wall to push himself up, Grey did his best to scrub exhaustion from his face. The rasp of stubble reminded him that sleep wasn't the only thing he'd gone too long without.

He'd already brought herbal tisanes, even one laced with aža, to see if those might coax Fiča into slumber. They hadn't. "I'll see if there's anything else I can do. Maybe imbued medicine—"

"Hawking pays better'n thieving if you can afford that."

It didn't, and most of Grey's money went to supporting the family Kolya had left behind—but the alternative was to sit by while another child died. "I know someone who will help."

Arkady had cleared her other kids out of the squat, but Grey felt eyes on him until he passed from the Shambles to Westbridge. Then different eyes as he made his way through the Aerie common hall wearing Vraszenian clothing. At least nobody stopped him on the pretense of not recognizing him, like when he first was promoted.

He shot a longing glance at the bedroll he kept in the corner for those nights he didn't manage to leave the Aerie, but shook off the urge to curl up and let the world pass for a few hours. He had duties to attend to.

Snagging his patrol slops from where they hung on the back of the door, Grey shrugged out of his panel coat. He'd just buttoned the flap of his breeches and was shaking the wrinkles from his shirt when the door to his office swung open.

Cercel coughed to hide a smile. "You're out of uniform, Serrado."

Grey yanked his shirt on, fumbling to close it. "Yes, Commander. Apologies. People usually knock."

"Do I hear a reprimand?" Cercel drawled, hipping up onto his desk so she could squeeze the door closed.

"No, Commander." He shoved his feet into his boots.

"I thought not." She leaned against the closed door, frown deepening as he set himself to rights. "You look like hell, Serrado. Are you sleeping?"

The anger he'd been swallowing flared. "Not recently, no," he snapped, yanking on a strap that refused to buckle.

Silence fell. She didn't dress him down for mouthing off to a senior officer; she just let the pause remind him whose side she was on.

Grey straightened and gripped the back of his chair, wishing he could slump into it. But Cercel was standing, which meant he stood. "My apologies. Another child turned up, unable to sleep. I spent the night at her side." He didn't mention that if Fiča didn't sleep, she was likely to die. Cercel knew about the boy in Suncross.

"Then this may help," she said quietly. "Balriat arrested an old woman today—not the one you're looking for. Brought her in for giving short weight. But he was laughing with Agnarsin about how ugly she is, and said, 'She's even uglier than that Gammer Lindworm hag Poltevis arrested back in Fellun.'"

The only thing that stopped Grey from barging out to speak to Poltevis right then was that Cercel was blocking the door. *Wait. Poltevis.* He slumped. "Didn't she take a knife in the Dockwall riots this summer?"

Cercel nodded. "But the arrest record should still be downstairs."

"Thank you, Commander," Grey said, meaning it. "Is there anything else?"

She didn't budge. "You need to sleep, Serrado. If you run your-self into the ground, you won't do those kids any good. And don't tell me you're fine; anyone with eyes can see you aren't." Her voice hardened, but not with anger. With sympathy. "I know you're still hunting the Rook."

"He's on the top of the Vigil's list of—"

"Don't give me that. First it was the Stadnem Anduske; now it's the Rook. You want someone to answer for your brother's death—and I understand that. But if the last two centuries are anything to go by, the Rook will still be here a month from now. Those kids might not be." She glanced pointedly at the bedroll in the corner. "You need to use that occasionally. Would it help if I got you a big-ger office? One at least as long as you are tall?"

The joke was a weak one, but it helped mute the sick fury that welled up every time he thought about Kolya's death. "Commander, if you can get me something larger than a channel raft, I promise to sleep at least four hours a night."

"I'll hold you to that, Serrado."

They parted ways at the stairwell, Cercel heading to the loft where the commanders and more senior captains had their offices, Grey descending into the half basement of the Aerie, where they kept the prisoners and the records locked up. Only captains and above were allowed access there—a preventative against black-mail.

The records archive was a long, low-ceilinged room sandwiched by a numinat above to provide light without threat of fire, and a numinat below to keep the room cool and dry. For all his many sins, Mettore Indestor followed in the footsteps of his predecessors when it came to good record-keeping. Great ledgers set out on tables by the door provided a brief catalog of arrests sorted by crime, and the shelves behind held the files themselves.

"It'd be nice to know what Poltevis brought the old woman in for," Grey muttered.

Cercel had said Fellun. He found the right shelves and began flipping through the records, scanning for the name "Gammer

Lindworm" and silently cursing his fellow hawks for their terrible handwriting.

He didn't have to search for long. Not because he found it—but because he didn't.

A page had been torn out of one of the arrest ledgers. If the person responsible had used a knife to cut it cleanly, Grey might have paged right past without noticing, but a trailing shred remained at the bottom, with a scrawl saying *held in the Dockw.* Which on its own was no evidence at all...except that he'd already run across other pages recording arrests by Poltevis, and the handwriting was the same angled scrawl.

"Djek." His curse echoed off the low ceiling. Grey worried the remaining scrap between thumb and forefinger, bare because in his rush to follow up on Cercel's information he'd forgotten his gloves. The back of his finger brushed the uneven surface of the following page.

Hardly daring to hope, he splayed his hand across it, feeling the faint ridges and bumps of writing that couldn't be seen even when raised to the light. There was no mistaking it; the pressure of a pencil on the thin paper had left a faint imprint.

He fetched a stick of charcoal from the shelf of supplies. Rubbing it carefully over the ridges revealed ghostly traces of the writing—incomplete and tangled with the next page's notes, but enough to confirm his suspicions. Although the line for the perpetrator's real name was blank, under aliases it said *amme* and *indw.* She'd been brought in for assaulting a young Nadežran woman...but try though he might, Grey couldn't make out the victim's name.

Maybe the victim was the reason someone had torn the page out. Someone of at least captain rank, to have access to this room.

With a brief apology to any future hawk searching for information on one Arvok Drazky, arrested for climbing the Rotunda naked, Grey pulled out a thumb knife and cleanly cut the page from the ledger. Then he stuffed it into his pocket and left, with new energy in his step.

Isla Prišta, Westbridge: Apilun 33

When Ren's mother died, Ren lost almost everything. Not that they had much by that point, not after two years on the streets...but Ivrina had clung to a few treasures, through every disaster Ir Nedje threw their way.

Now Ren had only one.

She kept it in a small hollow she'd dug out beneath a loose flagstone in the basement's wine cellar, with the crate of Sureggio Extaquium's terrible wine on top of it. Ren couldn't bear the thought of anything happening to this, the last remnant of her mother.

The oilcloth was stiff in her hands as she brought the small package into the marginal warmth of the kitchen. Tess was out laying waste to Vargo's fabric stores, leaving Ren alone with her memories.

She unwrapped her mother's pattern deck with care. These weren't the cheap, woodblock-printed things she'd been using on the street; cold-decking required two identical decks, and cards like Ivrina Lenskaya's were unique. Hand-painted, imbued not to wear down from use, with the symbols of the three threads forming a triangle on their backs, spindle and shuttle and shears.

A knot formed in Ren's throat as she brushed her thumb across the topmost card. *I still miss you.*

She had Tess and Sedge now, her sworn sister and brother, made so through Ren's best childish guess at the Vraszenian ritual of blood kinship. But Vraszenians were supposed to be defined by their lineages, their kretse. Ren only had her mother...and so in that sense, after Ivrina died, she had no one.

Drawing a ragged breath, she began shuffling and cutting the cards.

Ivrina had taught her daughter the art, giving her instructions and warnings both. The three threads, with their aspect and unaligned cards; veiled readings and revealed ones. Not to try to read for herself. Not to ask frivolous questions. Not to rely too heavily on the pattern, because sometimes the deities took the price of it out of the reader.

But if Mettore was falsifying convictions and sending innocent people into slavery, then House Traementis might have potential allies. Eret Quientis, if Fulvet's authority over the courts was being subverted; Era Novrus, given her feud. So even though it was harder to read for an absent subject, Ren laid out Eret Mettore Indestor's pattern.

Nine cards, three by three, and Ren murmured the ritual phrase under her breath, her words puffing from her lips like ghosts in the chill air. His past, the good and the ill of it, and that which was neither.

Hare and Hound, Jump at the Sun, and Hundred Lanterns Rise. Ren ran the tip of her tongue across her lip, thinking. All from the spinning thread; that meant the inner self, the mind and the spirit, and all three from the same thread meant they were probably linked. Jump at the Sun and Hundred Lanterns Rise—those two were clear enough, as far as it went. Mettore had taken some great risk and fallen short, losing something precious as a result. But what?

Ažerais didn't see fit to bless her with a flash of insight. But Ren was fairly sure that whatever event those two represented had led to the third card, Hare and Hound. Adaptability. Mettore had changed to meet his new situation, and from his perspective at least, it had turned out well. The card chilled Ren when she looked at it, though. The name was a reference to an old Vraszenian tale, Clever Natalya changing forms to outwit a pursuer. But the pursuer had changed, too—in hopes of killing Natalya.

Whatever Mettore had become, she doubted it was good.

Ren smiled in grim recognition at the next row. Sometimes the central card represented the client himself; here it was The Mask of Chaos, the same card she'd drawn for Leato when posing as Arenza. Eret Indestor, holding the Caerulet seat in the Cinquerat, should have been represented by the other half of that duality, The Face of

Balance. But with him, law and order were the Mask, and corruption was the Face beneath.

The good and ill cards were more intriguing. Again from the spinning thread, contrasting with The Mask of Chaos from the woven, which represented the outer self, the social world. The Mask of Fools, in veiled position, told her that Indestor was missing something—some vital piece of information, without which he couldn't proceed. And Lark Aloft, sitting opposite and revealed, spoke of messages and new information coming. He might not have it in his grasp, but it was out there, waiting for him.

His future was represented by Wings in Silk, Storm Against Stone, and Two Roads Cross. "*Djek*," Ren murmured, staring at them. Two more cards from the spinning thread, and one from the cut.

Whatever Mettore was doing...it wasn't some simple gambit for power or wealth. Not with seven of nine cards all from the same thread. It might have meant some internal struggle on his part, but Ren doubted it.

Which left matters of the spirit. In other words, magic.

But what did Caerulet have to do with magic? That came under the purview of Iridet, the Cinquerat's religious seat. *Well*, Ren amended, *numinatria does*. Imbuing mostly fell to Prasinet because the guilds controlled the crafters, and Prasinet controlled the guilds. And none of the Cinquerat gave a wet leech about pattern.

With Two Roads Cross at the center, it wasn't hard to see how the other two pivoted around it. That one meant decisive action, an opportunity to change the game.

Mettore wasn't content with his usual schemes. He was building toward something—and an opportunity for it was coming soon.

Unfortunately, pattern decks didn't come with a clock. "Soon" could mean anything from tomorrow to a year from now. Ren suspected the news represented by Lark Aloft, the information Mettore was currently missing, would send events rushing onward...so his plans depended on when he received it.

She shook her head in frustration. *If I knew for sure what it was, I could stop him from getting it.*

With most patterns, the left and right cards in the top row represented alternative outcomes, what would happen in the case of success or failure. That was the sense Ren had gotten from Leato's pattern, with The Face of Stars and The Mask of Night standing on either side of The Face of Glass. Here, though, she wasn't so sure. Storm Against Stone was raw, unstoppable force. Veiled, it ought to mean that Mettore risked being crushed by that force—and maybe that was true.

But Wings in Silk indicated a point of no return. Revealed—so from Mettore's perspective the change would be one he welcomed. Ren doubted she would like it half as much. And the force of Storm Against Stone... it might be unleashed either way. The only question was whether Mettore himself would suffer as a consequence.

Footsteps scraping on the flagstones outside jarred Ren from her musings. With quick hands she wrapped the cards and tucked them into her pocket, standing just as Tess bumped the door open with her hip, waddling backward under two bolts of velveteen. Sedge followed with four more of silk brocade.

"Are you that set on not marrying for money?" Tess asked, leaning the bolts against the wall with as much care as Ren had used in wrapping her mother's cards. "Because I'm fair certain I'd take Master Vargo for his warehouse alone, if he'd give me a second thought."

Ren and Sedge exchanged dubious looks. He shook his head minutely: *not marrying material*.

Tess pouted for all of two breaths before shaking it off. "No matter. You'll just have to advocate for him for the rest of our lives. Now light some candles. I want to show you what I've in mind for the engagement party."

9

Jump at the Sun

Isla Indestor, the Pearls: Pavnilun 5

Traementis Manor had seemed like unimaginable splendor when Renata first set foot in it. Since then she'd visited several others and seen what they looked like when the house wasn't in debt. But Indestor Manor, decorated for the wedding announcement of Mezzan Indestor and Marvisal Coscanum, put them all to shame.

Shimmering organza swags, imbued during their weaving to catch and reflect the light from the sconces, formed an archway from the entry hall to the ballroom. Renata and the Traementis party passed a card salon where Oksana Ryvček was collecting a pile of winnings from a rueful Ghiscolo Acrenix, then a parlour where early revelers sipped from flutes of aža-infused wine. The adjoining banquet room held cold tables of crimson fish roe and smoked mussels, ripe berries and Liganti cheeses, and hot tables of seared carp, turtle soup, and roasted partridges.

The ballroom fulfilled the promise of the organza hall. Numinata scribed for the occasion hung on heavy draperies of silver silk, the overlapping circles of Tuat's vesica piscis—two become one— prominent in all the figures, along with the sapphire hexagram of Sessat, a nod to House Indestor's hold on the Caerulet seat.

The floor was already crowded with couples treading figures

without any help of a dance caller; Renata sent a silent thanks to Giuna for the lessons. Music wove through the swish of skirts, as far removed from a single harpist plucking in an empty ballroom as one of Tess's muslin mock-ups was from the final ensemble.

"Oh, they've opened the gardens!" Giuna cried. She wended her way around the edge of the room, pulling Renata along with one hand. Trellises of creeping pearl roses blooming out of season decked the walls, spilling onto the terrace overlooking the adjacent garden. A canopy protected strolling couples from a steady drizzle, its patter a counterpoint to the music drifting from the open doors. The rose-woven trellises circling the garden formed a break against the winter rains, with braziers chasing away the chill. Treated with perfumed oils, the coals filled the air with scents of summer grass and honey. If Renata closed her eyes, she could almost believe she stood in a garden on a mild midsummer's night.

But she couldn't afford the luxury of immersing herself in the illusion. This was no different from casing a lace-maker's shop, checking sight lines and watching the flow of customers to identify the best moment to lift something and run. She wasn't here to steal—though the wealth strewn so carelessly about made her fingers itch—but the principles were the same.

Which was part of why she'd arranged a distraction. She was dressed in a surcoat of ice-blue velveteen, burned out in an intricate pattern to reveal the gold of her underdress—but these days, everyone expected elegance from Renata Viraudax. And it wasn't herself she wanted their eyes on; it was Giuna.

The Traementis daughter was radiant in her new gown. Her moss-green bandeau gave way to a sun-sparkling overlay of palest gold that floated about her pearl-pink underdress like clouds at sunrise—much more fitting for a girl on the edge of womanhood than the heavy, shapeless surcoats she'd been wearing. Tess had brushed gold into Giuna's hair and pinned the matching ribbon into place with a few brilliants, scenting it all with a perfume of apricot and mint that Ren pinched when their cash ran short. If the gardens held winter at bay, then Giuna danced through them like a herald of spring. Even her blush only enhanced the effect, shaming the trellis roses.

"Thank you," Donaia murmured in Renata's ear, gazing fondly at her daughter. "Giuna's needed something like this for quite some time."

"It was my pleasure—and Tess's," Renata said. Even though she'd done it out of calculation, it was hard not to smile at Giuna's delight.

"Ah, Alta Renata. You've discovered sleeves, I see." Carinci had Fadrin Acrenix pushing her chair this time. She paused him on her way to the terrace to give Renata a thorough once-over. Not even Tess reviewed her clothing with such a critical eye. "I suppose the cold defeats us all one day. Look forward to seeing what you dare for the Spring Gloria. I hear you're fond of doing away with gloves as well."

Donaia's sharp inhale warmed Renata more than sleeves. "We should all be willing to give up so much to stand against that criminal," Donaia said, snapping her fan open as though the red rising to her cheeks was the fault of the braziers.

"Yes, yes, noble cause and all that. I only meant that she's interesting. Don't get in a pother, girl."

Carinci waved Fadrin to push her onward before Donaia could take exception to being called "girl." With a shake of her head, Donaia went to support Giuna in a conversation with a delta son, leaving Renata to begin her own reconnaissance.

That was when she saw Derossi Vargo.

He stood on the threshold between the ballroom and the gardens, the light limning him from behind and hiding his face mostly in shadow. He hadn't yet spotted Renata; his attention was fixed on Carinci. So fixed that Fadrin almost rolled her chair right through him before he collected himself enough to step aside.

The light caught his expression then, stone hard and revealing nothing. But his body wasn't as well-masked: His hand stretched out as though he yearned to stop her, then clenched into a fist. He struck his thigh in . . . anger? Disgust? With Carinci? With himself? Renata couldn't tell.

After a moment's hesitation, she approached him. Halfway there, the light caught something else: a flash of color on his lapel that quickly scuttled into the shadows of his high, folded collar.

It startled her enough that she said exactly what she was thinking. "Did your lapel pin just run for cover?"

Tearing his gaze from Fadrin wheeling Carinci away, Vargo glanced at his collar, then at Renata. His stony expression relaxed into laughter. "No. That's Peabody."

She raised an eyebrow. Still chuckling, Vargo dipped his fingers into the shadows. When he drew his hand back, a large spider with symmetrical splashes of sapphire, indigo, emerald, and crimson across his abdomen was riding the back of Vargo's glove. "Alta Renata Viraudax, Master Peabody. Say hello, Peabody." Vargo raised two fingers, and the spider, to Renata's utter astonishment, raised its third set of legs and presented its colorful abdomen in response. Vargo stroked a finger over its fuzzy midsection. "Good boy."

It was unquestionably the same thing she'd noticed on Vargo's coat at the Gloria, riding quietly enough that she'd mistaken it for a pin. It was also the gaudiest spider she'd seen in her life: a king peacock, the emblem of the Vraszenian Varadi clan. She'd heard about them, but never seen one.

"That…is quite eccentric of you. Do you call him Peabody because of the peacock coloration?"

"No. It's because he was about the size of a pea when I got him." Vargo tried to coax Peabody back into the shadows of his collar, but the spider was having none of it. He turned about and continued to wave his legs at Renata in a complex pattern that was probably very appealing to lady spiders. "Stop flirting, you old reprobate, before someone sees you and decides you need to be smooshed."

His choice of word almost made her laugh. She'd seen the elegant man-about-town, the efficient businessman, and a fleeting glimpse of the crime lord Sedge worked for, but "smooshed" made him sound briefly boyish. He seemed genuinely fond of his pet.

A few more nudges got the spider to scuttle back to his hiding place, and with him went any softness in Vargo's expression.

Drawing Renata to one side, he said, "I would ask you to dance, but I think that would do my reputation more favors than yours. I don't suppose you've spoken with anyone from Indestor yet? Mettore and Mezzan might be unapproachable, but they've got more cousins than Mettore knows what to do with. It might be worth your time to charm one. Breccone Indestris, for example. He'll be the inscriptor for the register."

Renata wasn't about to admit that her plans for the evening went well beyond chatting up someone who'd married into the house. "Of course. Eret Indestor's activities must involve more than just himself; I have some ideas for where to hunt evidence of that."

"While I wander around being a model curiosity for Faella Coscanum to gossip about, in the hopes someone besides you might speak with me." Stepping back, he swept the skirts of his coat aside and favored her with a bow even an etiquette teacher couldn't fault. "I bid you good evening, alta. May you see the Face and not the Mask." Coat swinging and bootheels clicking, he sauntered back into the ballroom as though he had every right to be there.

Settling the mask of her persona in place, Renata went forth to do battle with high society . . . and plan a break-in.

Isla Indestor, the Pearls: Pavnilun 5

High society came first, and she made good use of the next four bells.

Mettore Indestor might have set himself against House Traementis, but all the delta gentry who administered charters on his behalf were present for the celebration, and they weren't as inflexible. While Renata didn't expect she could turn anyone directly against him, she didn't have to. Many people still wanted to hear about the fight with the Rook from someone who'd been there. She was in the middle of her third recounting of Mezzan's embarrassment when the servants invited all the visitors to gather in the ballroom for the announcement of the betrothal.

The two families stood in the gallery above, a long line of Indestor on the right, Coscanum on the left. Seeing them truly hammered home the dwindled size of House Traementis: There were older generations and younger, husbands and wives married in, cousins to every degree. Most Nadežran families didn't keep quite so many people on their register, allowing more distant kin to break off and form their own lineages, but the privileges granted by an ennoblement charter meant that some houses found it advantageous to band together in large numbers.

Renata stood with Donaia, Leato, and Giuna, not even the half step behind that an unregistered cousin might expect. The color in Giuna's cheeks hadn't faded—possibly because she hadn't left the dance floor since they'd arrived, floating from partner to partner. She was more intent on trading glances and shy smiles with a young Cleoter son than paying attention to the obligatory ceremonies that went with the union of two powerful houses.

First came the inscriptor Vargo had mentioned, Breccone Indestris. He was middle-aged and handsome enough, in a bland Liganti way, but the only thing he'd talked about when Renata arranged a dance with him was the state of numinatria in Seteris. She'd been forced to spin all manner of creative nonsense, and almost ruined it by laughing when he expounded on her lies as though he knew more about them than she did.

He made a great show of spreading out the betrothal numinat, offering a prayer to the deities Civrus and Pavlus, who blessed marriages, and then closing the circle with a swipe of his ink brush. His attempt at showmanship might even have been vaguely effective, if his performance weren't taking place up in the gallery where nobody but the family could see it.

Once he was done, a dark-haired woman who couldn't be more than a decade older than Renata moved into the gap between Mettore Indestor and Naldebris Coscanum, nodding solemnly to the heads of each family in turn. "Tanaquis Fienola," Leato murmured in Renata's ear. "She's the best astrologer in Nadežra. A friend of our family, too."

He was clearly proud of the connection. *Is she the one who drew my chart?* Renata wondered. She'd heard nothing after Giuna's clumsy questioning; her invented dates must have passed muster.

Mezzan and Marvisal stepped forward, taking a scroll from the astrologer and unrolling it between them. They held it up to show the crowd, though the writing was too small to read from the floor.

Resting a hand atop each of theirs, Fienola announced, "The charts have been drawn and the alignments read. With the blessings of Celnis, the year is set as 211. With the blessings of Esclus, the month is Colbrilun. With the blessings of Thrunium, the date is the third day of the third iteration. With the blessings of Sacretha, the day is Andusny. With the blessings of Civrus and Pavlus, the hour is second earth. Within this alignment, may all the glory of the cosmos be channeled to bless this union between Mettore Indestor and Marvisal Coscanum."

She brought Mezzan's and Marvisal's hands together, each still holding one end of the scroll. The idea was to close the circle, binding the dates much like a numinat was closed and bound.

And it would have gone beautifully, if Mezzan hadn't swayed and lost his balance. The scroll crumpled, and the tear of paper ripped across the silent ballroom as he fumbled for support. Fienola and Marvisal helped him recover, and they continued on as though nothing had taken place, but the mirrored scowls on Eret Indestor's and Eret Coscanum's faces marked the mistake.

Leato snorted. "Someone should have reminded him not to lock his knees," he whispered to Renata.

She made a vague sound in reply. *I wonder—if I follow up on that, can I spike the betrothal entirely?*

An ambitious thought, but worth considering, especially if she could gain some influence over the astrologer. Ren had never had any dealings with their kind; her mother had, in typical Vraszenian fashion, scoffed at their art. *They'd have you believe that two children born at the same time follow the same pattern*, Ivrina said. *But every person's pattern is their own.* Astrology was based on the same principles as numinatria, though, and the power of those principles was visible everywhere in Nadežra.

Half-formed notions of how to use it to break the betrothal vanished as a new thought came to her. Could this—astrology, not inscribed numinatria—be what Mettore's pattern referred to?

The ceremony concluded, Mettore thanking Tanaquis Fienola and then discreetly hauling his son off to singe his ears, leaving Tanaquis alone at the base of the steps.

"Would you like to meet her?" Donaia asked. Instead of waiting for an answer, she led Renata toward the bemused-looking astrologer.

"Your work is fascinating, Meda Fienola," Renata said after they'd been introduced. "Mother never paid much attention to it—she disliked the notion of anything governing her actions, even heavenly powers—but it seems Nadežra holds your skill in high regard."

"Interesting," Tanaquis said, her head tilting and grey eyes focusing as though it was Renata, and not her words, that evoked curiosity.

Before Ren could fear she'd given something away, the woman blinked and cast a sour look at the gallery, where the families were filing out so the musicians could retake their places. "If only Eret Indestor shared that regard. Instead, it's 'chart it again, chart it again,' as though the planets themselves change alignment on his whim. He—"

She bit down on whatever she'd been about to say, but Donaia nodded. "So the cosmos doesn't desire this union as much as the families do?"

Tanaquis's snort was answer enough. "Most of the families. The cosmos and Alta Faella are in alignment for once. Now I'm off to help Eret Coscanum explain to his sister that a ripped contract doesn't give her the right to annul her grandniece's betrothal." With a nod for Renata and a touch to Donaia's hand, Tanaquis excused herself to attend a glowering Faella Coscanum.

"It's a shame she's only delta gentry," Donaia told Renata, as though being born to such a lowly lot was a tragedy. "If she were noble, they wouldn't take her for granted the way they do."

"Such a pity," Renata agreed.

Isla Indestor, the Pearls: Pavnilun 5

"You must tell me where you obtained the brocade for Alta Marvisal's dress," Renata said to Faella Coscanum later on. "She outshines the moons."

Faella's mood had improved after her conversation with Tanaquis, possibly aided by the running stream of people laying flattery at her feet in the card salon. Renata had carefully orbited through several times, hoping to catch the old woman's eye without obviously angling for it. Though not the head of her house, Faella was the unquestioned arbiter of Nadežran society; the biggest obstacle in Ren's own climb was the fact that the woman had yet to take notice of her. But at last that had changed, with Faella beckoning her over.

She wasn't foolish enough to mistake this for a conversation. It was a test: a chance for Renata to prove she was worth taking notice of. If Faella approved of her, many more doors would open. If she didn't . . .

Her compliment lifted the bored sag of Faella's eyelids. The old woman shifted forward in her high-backed chair, actually looking at Renata instead of through her. "Why thank you, Alta Renata. Our Bondiro has dragged my ear into the soup, nattering on about your excellent taste, but I wasn't certain I believed him until this evening." A wave of her hand took in Renata's appearance. "Am I correct that you're responsible for the Traementis girl's transformation as well?"

"I couldn't bear seeing her in such appalling dresses any longer," Renata acknowledged. "I offered Era Traementis the services of my maid."

"I hope you reward her service well, or someone might steal her from you. And where do you come by *your* fabrics?" Faella hadn't, Renata noted, answered the original question. But her gaze flicked briefly to Vargo, who sat across the room stringing several Indestor and Coscanum cousins along in a game of sixes. "I haven't seen this velveteen on offer anywhere yet."

Renata smiled blandly. "I find it useful to have connections. Don't you?"

Faella could have soaked up the rains with the dryness of her response. "That depends on what use you put them to, I suppose."

"Why, for the benefits of one's friends, of course."

Nodding as though Renata had given the only possible correct answer, Faella said, "How happy I am to call a woman such as yourself friend, then. With so much to plan, I haven't been able to spare a moment to think of the wedding clothes for Marvisal and Mezzan."

Renata leaned in close, pressing one hand to her heart. *Victory.* "You must allow me to loan you my maid's services. She does such splendid work."

"If you think you can spare her." Faella's rheumy eyes twinkled, making Renata wonder how often she got to haggle for social favors like this. Many people wanted something from Alta Faella, but it must have been rare for Faella to want anything from someone else. "I trust your source for the latest materials will prove amenable as well? You must let me know if I can ever return your kindness."

Can I risk it? She'd only just met Faella, and the old woman had a reputation for burying people in the silt on a whim. But Renata had been searching for another solution for weeks, without luck. And she suspected Faella might admire a well-placed touch of audacity.

As if the thought had just come to her, Renata said, "I was intending to have tea with Nanso Bagacci tomorrow. I would be honored if you would join us—as a friend."

Then she tried not to hold her breath. Faella would know perfectly well that Bagacci had recently disgraced himself in a doomed love affair with a woman from House Simendis. Being seen in public with Alta Faella would amount to a social pardon.

Why Bagacci mattered to Renata, Faella might or might not

be able to guess. It depended on if her ear for gossip extended far enough into the political sphere. But that mystery might just be what tempted her.

Faella tapped her fan against her knee, transparently delaying to keep Renata in suspense. Then, as if it had required no thought at all, she said, "Who doesn't enjoy tea with friends? I'll tell them to reserve my usual table at the Eight Stars. Now stop wasting your best years on an old turtle like myself. Young women are meant to be dancing."

It took all of Renata's self-control not to skip with sheer triumph as she left the room. Faella Coscanum's public approval, a chance to widen the crack in Indestor's relations with Coscanum, and Nanso Bagacci taken care of—what more could she ask for?

Things could still fall apart. But with one victory so close, she couldn't resist veering past Scaperto Quientis in the ballroom. "Your Grace. Your shipment should be released by…the day after tomorrow?"

He blinked in surprise. After the long silence following his challenge, he must have written her off as a lost cause. "How—"

But before he could get the question out, a half-gloved hand closed around Renata's arm. "Alta Renata," a rich voice purred.

She turned to see Sostira Novrus, tall and severe in finely tailored grey. "Dance with me," Era Novrus said. It took the form of a command rather than a request, with no chance to disobey; she steered Renata bodily into the whirl.

Dancing with Sostira Novrus was a lesson in the difference between leading and dominating. Her spine was steel, her grip firm, and not once did she take her gaze off Renata's face. Being seen like this with a member of the Cinquerat should have been a positive thing. But Renata had no idea what the woman wanted with her, and that made her apprehensive. Her own movements were stiff, her pace a breath behind.

If Sostira noticed, she made no comment. "You're very beautiful, but I suspect you hear that often. Do you tire of it?"

Renata kept her smile in place, but inside, her gut twisted. *Your pretty face . . .*

Whether she appreciated such compliments or not seemed to be of little interest to Era Novrus. The woman had all the subtlety of the spring floods: One saw them coming and could only brace against their force. Then the whirl of the dance took them past Giuna, now in Sibiliat's arms. Giuna, who had mentioned at the Autumn Gloria that Sostira Novrus broke marriage contracts as soon as she got bored, and was always looking for her next wife...

I'm not a target, Renata realized. *I'm a horse at the fair, having my teeth and my gait examined.*

But just when she'd settled into thinking Sostira's interest in her was amorous, the woman changed tactics. "Gossip has you putting a bug up Mettore's nose with this charter of yours. You know the Traementis name isn't strong enough protection if a true falling-out with House Indestor should occur."

Renata only just managed to avoid stumbling. "I—what?"

Sostira pulled her closer, under the guise of steadying her. "If Novrus had reason to ally with Traementis, that might change. When the floods come, nobody wants to be stranded on a bridge between islets."

Idiot. Don't underestimate her. This was just the other side of the coin Mettore had "offered" Donaia: ensure the house's survival—at least for a time—by selling someone into marriage.

Renata couldn't afford to turn Sostira down cold. "You are most generous, Your Elegance. There might be a great deal our houses could offer each other."

The dance ended and Sostira released her, but not before running her bare thumb across Renata's lower lip. "I hope to learn more about what *you* have to offer," she murmured, and left Renata standing alone on the floor.

Her earlier triumph had faded away, leaving her cold. She cast her gaze around for Scaperto Quientis, hoping to retrieve her momentum, but saw no sign of him.

Instead she found herself looking at Mettore Indestor.

Who came at her as directly as Era Novrus had, though at least he offered his hand for the next dance rather than claiming Renata's without asking. *Unapproachable*, Renata thought with uneasy humor, remembering Vargo's earlier comment. *Didn't anyone notify Mettore?*

"You're an admirable woman, Alta Renata. Few come out of a conversation with Era Novrus looking so unrattled." He turned her in promenade, leading her right past where Sostira now stood with her current wife, Benvanna Novri. Both women could have carved ice with their glares—Benvanna's at Renata, and Sostira's for Mettore. His deep voice dripped satisfaction as he said, "She can be a bit much."

Renata made an innocuous answer while her mind whirled. It was inconceivable that Eret Indestor could be afraid of an alliance between Traementis and Novrus. But if not that, then why had he bothered to approach her? Two members of the Cinquerat in the space of a bell: It wasn't the kind of coincidence she liked.

"You're Lecilla's daughter, yes? Letilia, rather." The dance separated them briefly. When they came together again, Mettore seemed to have moved on to other topics. "I wonder how long you're planning to remain in Nadežra. Certainly until the Festival of Veiled Waters, I hope. You've heard of it?"

"Of course, Your Mercy." She left it ambiguous how many of his questions that was meant to answer.

"It isn't the proper year to see the Wellspring of Ažerais, of course, but in some ways that's better. You don't have to wade through a mob of Vraszenians lapping at it like parched dogs." Mettore was subtle compared to Sostira. His grip didn't tighten, nor did he yank Renata about or sneer with disdain—but the way his bootheels struck the floor, his tone going cold, echoed what she already knew. The man loathed Vraszenians and made no secret of it.

Did his plans have to do with the Festival of Veiled Waters, then? Ažerais's wellspring was undoubtedly magical; drinking its waters granted true dreams, glimpses of the pattern of the world. But the Great Dream only came once every seven years; the wellspring's appearance was more than a year away.

"I could hardly leave without seeing one of your famous Nadežran masquerades," she said lightly. "But as I understand it, the celebration of Kaius Rex's death comes before Veiled Waters."

"Yes. Though in Nadežra it's more politely referred to as the Night of Bells. Sadly, I've not been able to enjoy that since I inherited the Caerulet seat from my mother. I'm always busy that night with the commemoration of the Accords." Mettore's smile was more teeth than amusement. "More Vraszenians to wade through."

Did he expect her to empathize with his obvious distaste? "I wish you luck with that, Your Mercy," she said politely, at a loss for anything better.

By the time the dance ended, she'd achieved no enlightenment as to why Indestor had drawn her onto the floor. And his parting words provided no clarity for her reeling thoughts—only more worry. "Thank you for the dance, alta. I look forward to more dealings in the future."

Isla Indestor, the Pearls: Pavnilun 5

Renata spotted Leato and Donaia easily enough, standing near the mass of dancers. The ballroom was the wrong place to have a conversation about Mettore Indestor's intentions, but perhaps a stroll in the gardens—

Then Giuna came stumbling through the crowd, hands twisting into the delicate fabric of her underdress. Renata caught a glimpse of her face before her mother and brother closed around her, saw the bright streak of a tear down one cheek.

"Please don't f-uh-huss," Giuna said as Renata approached, her words catching on an unsteady breath. "It wasn't anything. I j-just need some air." Which was true enough from the way she was gulping it, but didn't satisfy Leato.

"Who was she dancing with?" he asked Donaia. When his mother shook her head, he stood taller to scan the ballroom.

That parted the family shield enough for Giuna to catch sight of Renata. "C-cousin," she sobbed, reaching out.

"What's wrong?" Renata asked, clasping Giuna's hand in both of hers and stepping into the Traementis circle. "You must tell me what happened, so I know who to shun."

A tiny laugh bubbled up between the hitched breaths. "Please don't on my account. You mustn't make it worse. It's only..." She ducked her head as though ashamed to look anyone in the eye. "I didn't want to, but I didn't know how to refuse, and then when we were all in the star, he said I'd never been much before, but now even he might consider taking me as...as a contract wife."

It was like a slap to the face. Being a contract spouse—lower in status than a primary husband or wife—might be a great honor for a commoner, or even delta gentry. But for someone of Giuna's upbringing and blood, such an offer was tantamount to calling her a night-piece.

"Who." Leato's steel-voiced question pierced Giuna's reticence.

"M-Mezzan."

Renata swallowed a curse. Donaia tucked her daughter under her arm, cheeks red and eyes flashing fury. How had Ren ever thought Giuna was the unloved child? "Where is Ryvček?" Donaia hissed through clenched teeth.

"We don't need a hired duelist to teach Mezzan a lesson," Leato said. "I can do it."

"I want more than a lesson. I want him *humiliated*."

"I can do it," Leato repeated calmly.

Without a single mention of the risks of offending House Indestor or jeopardizing the charter Renata had been working on, Donaia nodded.

Leato pivoted. The crowds in the ballroom parted like water around him as he headed for Mezzan Indestor. Caught between alarm and excitement, Renata followed.

Word must have already spread about Mezzan's insult and Giuna's flight. A flock of younger nobles surrounded the Indestor heir. Bondiro broke away to meet Leato's charge.

"Not here." Bondiro kept his voice low, catching Leato's shoulder to hold him back. "It's my sister's betrothal—"

"Your sister should think twice before marrying that mud-rutting swine," Leato said, raising his voice in counter. "That ripped chart should offer excuse enough to get her out of it."

A murmur and hush spread from their center, washing through the ballroom.

"What do you mean by that, Traementis?" The crowd fell back as Mezzan stepped forward, marking a dueling circle with their bodies. If he was still drunk, he showed little sign. His sneer and swagger said that whatever Leato's reputation with a blade, he didn't fear it.

Shrugging off Bondiro's hold, Leato joined Mezzan in the cleared space. "I mean that even a Seven Knots night-piece has better standards than to marry you."

The sneer dropped. Mezzan went white, then red with rage. "Get me a sword," he snarled at Bondiro.

"Two, if you don't mind?" Leato smiled at Mezzan. "Unless you mean to cheat like you did in your last duel."

Everyone had heard the humiliating story of Mezzan's Lacewater fight with the Rook—some this very night, from Renata's own lips. The murmurs broke into snickers at Leato's taunt, and the press grew tighter. Renata made surreptitious use of her elbows and heels to keep from being nudged out of place.

"What is going on here?" Mettore stormed through the edge of the ring. "Traementis. I showed courtesy to the noble history of your house by allowing your family to attend this gathering, and you repay me with insults?" His voice resounded through the now-silent ballroom. "Guards!"

"Uniat."

The crowd inhaled. In a context like this, the name of the first numen was more than just the precursor to swords crossing. It was a formal challenge. And Mezzan—not Leato—had just issued it.

Leato's answering smile was feral. "Tuat."

They were committed. Mettore couldn't stop the duel, not without disgracing his son completely. "Bondiro," Mezzan said, his voice velvet-soft, "get the swords."

Renata's heartbeat felt far too loud as she waited for Bondiro to return. For an instant, when she'd heard Giuna's tale, she'd wondered if that was the reason for her dance with Mettore—if he'd been drawing her away so Mezzan could deliver his insult. But the incandescent fury on his face said he'd intended none of this. And whatever the outcome of the duel, he would extract the price from Mezzan's hide.

Bondiro reappeared, bearing two swords. The rules of dueling said he had to offer the challenged man first pick, and Leato laughed quietly as he compared them. For a flashing moment, Leato's keen blue eyes caught Renata's down the shining edge of a blade, and she could swear he winked at her—but before she could be sure, his attention returned to Mezzan.

"No Vicadrius? Pity. But this will do." Shrugging out of his coat, Leato selected his blade.

Mezzan flung his coat aside and snatched up the other blade. "After learning with sticks, you should be grateful I'm allowing you a sword this fine."

If he'd meant to imply something about Traementis's low breeding or poverty, the insult fell flat. "Don't worry, Mezzan," Leato said, lifting the blade into guard. "There aren't any canals here."

Fury brought Mezzan straight toward Leato, and almost lost him the duel in that first pass. Leato's sword whispered past his ear, Mezzan only barely wrenching himself away, and the world suddenly went white around Ren.

The Rook.

The Rook hated the nobility. That was his entire reason for existing: to fight them and their corruption, the way they tried to leech Nadežra dry.

Surely—*surely*—the Rook would never *be* a nobleman.

But there was Leato, playing the part of a wastrel even to his own mother, and sneaking out at night on unknown errands. Coming out of a Lacewater alley like he'd been hiding from view—maybe so he could change out of a black coat and hood.

Hunting the Rook. That was Giuna's theory—but it was Indestor he was targeting. And maybe something else, too. Maybe he was trying to find who had really killed Kolya Serrado, so his old friend would stop hunting *him*.

A few private lessons and an open practice at the Palaestra weren't enough to teach Ren how to read someone else's swordsmanship. Facing Mezzan, Leato fought nothing like the Rook—but also nothing like the display she'd seen in the Traementis ballroom, playfully switching styles against Ryvček. His form was flawlessly Liganti, his stance high, his blade outstretched to present a constant threat. If anyone was looking for a comparison to the Rook, they wouldn't find it here. He was every inch the proud noble son, avenging his sister's wounded honor.

But that could be a mask.

Ryvček was watching from the far side of the circle, not bothering to hide her smile. She didn't seem worried at all. Nor, for that matter, did Leato. After that comment about the canals, he fell silent, his expression alive and watchful. It was Mezzan who snarled, spitting quiet curses when his attacks failed.

And it was Mezzan who lost.

The end wasn't dramatic. Mezzan thrust, and a subtle shift of Leato's wrist sent his blade out of line. Then it was a simple matter of realigning and extending, and Mezzan's left cheek bled.

"I believe that's Ninat." Leato stepped back, admiring the cut like an artist.

It echoed the Rook's words that night, and Mezzan tensed, preparing to throw himself at Leato despite the cut signaling the duel's end. Then a hand slapped his blade to the floor. The clatter of it falling was punctuated by the crack of Mettore's palm against his cut cheek.

"That. Is. Ninat." Shoving his son back, Mettore faced Leato, showing all the self-control Mezzan lacked. "House Indestor apologizes for the insult. I trust that satisfies. Now take your family and leave."

Renata tore her attention from the scene, breathing for the first time in what felt like a year, and looked at the Traementis women. Giuna had composed herself, blotting the tear marks from her cheeks, and faced the crowd with dignity. Donaia met Renata's gaze and turned her hand palm up—not drawing attention to it by holding her hand out, but the invitation was clear.

Renata might not be in the register, but when the Traementis made their exit, Donaia wanted her with them.

For all the good that does me. The night had turned from triumph into ruin, all in the space of a bell, and the wild idea burning in Ren's mind did nothing to make up for that. She couldn't even look at Leato as he retrieved his coat and joined his family.

The crowd parted to let them pass, a sea of faces pinched in judgment, alight with glee, or drawn with sympathy. Once they'd cleared the gauntlet, Donaia let out a soft breath. "Well. I suppose that leaves us truly fucked," she muttered, low enough for only the three of them to hear.

"Mother!" Leato and Giuna gasped, but she ignored them and glanced at Renata.

"I am so sorry, my dear. I believe we just sank any hope you had of—"

"Alta Renata. Leaving already?" Faella Coscanum called, stopping them at the threshold. "I wanted to confirm our appointment for tea tomorrow. Seventh sun?"

Reflex propelled the words out. "Of course, Alta Faella."

"Excellent. I look forward to it." Nodding at Donaia and the others, Faella breezed past them to return to her salon. The Traementis weren't the only ones left gaping in her wake. A second wave of murmurs rose up behind them.

Fire sparked through Renata's veins. If Faella was still acknowledging them—Faella, who was unhappy that her grandniece was Mezzan's betrothed... "Don't drown your hopes yet, Era Traementis."

Isla Indestor, the Pearls: Pavnilun 5

As the Traementis climbed into their carriage to escape the rain, Leato kept the leather strap of the door in his hand. "Colbrin can take you all home. I—" In the gloom, Renata could just see his jaw tighten. "I need a drink."

For once Donaia didn't chide him. "What if Mezzan comes after you?"

Leato laughed without humor. "I won't go anywhere he'll think to look for me. He has bigger things to worry about anyway."

Giuna caught his hand as he moved to climb out of the carriage. "Leato—"

"It's all right, minnow." He tipped his forehead against hers. "I'm only sorry that kinless bastard ruined your evening."

Then he was gone, out into the rain, jogging across the plaza to where some sedan bearers huddled in the marginal shelter of another building. Renata watched him go. *Follow him, or . . . ?*

Stick to the plan. "I should also take myself home. There's no point in going to Isla Traementis, then turning around and heading to Westbridge."

"You would be welcome to stay the night," Donaia said.

The offer warmed her, even if she had a dozen reasons not to accept—one of whom was almost invisible through the rain and darkness. "No, I wouldn't want to impose. Besides which, I have preparations to make for tomorrow's tea with Alta Faella. Good night to you both, and I hope I'll have good news for you soon."

Giuna's farewell trailed after her as she escaped. Tess held an umbrella over them both as they walked away from the carriage; it sheltered Renata's face, but did nothing to protect her skirts. Tess's were already waterlogged, and she muttered under her breath, "I hope the uniform is still dry. Getting it wasn't easy, you know."

"I know," Ren murmured. Behind her the carriage rattled away, Colbrin a dripping bulk of oilcloth in the driver's seat. When she looked across the plaza, Leato had also vanished. "Let's find somewhere sheltered."

The carriages clustered in the mews provided a changing place conveniently close to the kitchen door, with the drivers all staying dry and warm in the servants' dining room. Tess kept watch, and Renata tried to keep her balance in the well-sprung vehicle she'd chosen as she wrestled out of her finery. *If anyone sees it moving, they'll assume something else is going on.*

The betrothal party was a blessing, a big enough affair that Indestor's usual staff weren't sufficient; they'd had to hire additional hands. All it took was one stolen maid's uniform and some makeup, her hair reworked into simple braids and pinned up, to transform her into just another Vraszenian woman among the temporary servants.

"This is mad. You know that, right?" Tess whispered as they dashed from the mews to the kitchen. She grabbed a bucket she'd hidden out of the way and shoved it at Ren. "Ice. They're going through a passel of it, so you should be able to make your way in without anyone giving you a bother. But I still think this is a bad idea. I may be helping, but don't you go taking that for agreement."

"Use not common sense at me," Ren said, dropping into her Vraszenian accent. "I will never have a better chance. And I listened to the seasoned thieves talking; I know what to do." If Ondrakja hadn't tried to kill Sedge, by now Ren might *be* one of those older thieves, promoted from the Fingers to an adult knot. Assuming Ondrakja had let her go.

If she let herself stop to think, she'd be terrified. So she didn't stop. She just kissed Tess, settled the bucket on her arm, and strode into the house.

Inside, everything was chaos. There was supposed to be a grand meal in the dining room for select guests, but Eret Indestor was arguing with Eret Coscanum in the garden, and everyone was scrambling to keep the food warm until they saw fit to sit down. Ren dearly wanted to stay and listen to the gossip, but the Faces were giving her a gold-plated opportunity, and she knew better than to squander it.

Moving through the house was a process of trading one task for another. Ice to get through the door, then a pitcher of resinated wine to bring among the guests—but she took care to bump into another servant and spill a bit, giving her an excuse to hand the pitcher off and whip out a rag to clean up the mess. As much as she trusted her disguise, the last thing she wanted to do was walk straight through the mass of dignitaries. A vial of smelling salts from her pocket gave her a reason to hurry along the edges of the party to the rooms where the more delicate flowers were taking their ease. Then it was just a matter of waiting until she had a clear window to dash up the stairs.

She'd made good use of her earlier time. Ren knew Mettore's study lay off one of the three doors along the upstairs hall. She wasn't positive which one, but the odds of anyone being in any of the three rooms were low, and she had her apologies ready to hand.

When she listened at the first door, she heard nothing, and when she tried the handle, it opened into a trophy room, lined with heads from hunting trips outside the city. The second was a library.

The third was locked.

This time she'd brought proper tools. Kneeling, she took out a set of skeleton keys—a "welcome home" gift from Sedge. *Good thing, too; these locks are better than the one on Donaia's desk.* She kept watch to either side as she began trying the keys, but apart from the noise drifting up from downstairs, everything was quiet.

The second key worked. She disengaged the latch, stood, and slipped through the door—

And came face-to-face with the point of a sword.

The Rook said, "Be still, shut the door, and don't make a sound."

When she stayed frozen, the tip of his sword slid past her ear, nudging the door shut. After a breath, Ren reached behind herself and relocked it.

The Rook lowered his blade. "Now, this is unexpected. What could a Vraszenian maid possibly be doing in Mettore Indestor's locked study?"

Ren could practically taste her pulse. The impossible suspicion that had blinded her during the duel was back, and stronger. If Leato had changed as quickly as she had—circled back around—

Her breath caught with suppressed hilarity. Whether he had or not, it didn't matter. She couldn't ask. Not only because the Rook wasn't liable to confess his true identity...but because she was disguised as Arenza, not Renata, and he showed no sign of recognizing her.

So be Arenza.

She let the impulse to laugh spread into a smile. "You're the Rook," Arenza breathed.

"You've heard of me." An answering smile lurked in the shadow of his voice. With the blade swept to one side, he extended a leg, making the antiquated bow look elegant. "And you are...?"

"Arenza." It would have been better to give a different name, something with less echo of *Renata*—but her Vraszenian identity was as much a role as the other, a skin she felt comfortable in. "I must in the right place be snooping, if the Rook is here before me."

The room behind him was in darkness, brightened only by the lights from the garden outside, but that was enough to confirm it was a study, with a sturdy desk much like Donaia's and shelves of books lining the walls. A window opposite the door was cracked open, allowing the sounds of fading rain, music, and muted chatter to filter in. A few drops of water beaded on the Rook's hood and coat, giving up the secret of how he'd gained entrance.

"The right place, is it? That's a refreshing change. Usually the people I encounter feel they're in the *wrong* place. And what are you snooping for, Arenza?"

How much could she safely say? That depended on who was under the hood. Whether he was Leato or not, she couldn't tell him the whole story. But the possibility made her cautious. "Penal ship manifests. Or records of the sales made to slave traders," she admitted. Under normal circumstances, it would be absurd to expect someone to keep evidence of their illegal activity...but like all Caerulets before him, Mettore had a legendary reputation for organization and documentation. The shelves and cabinets that lined the walls of his study gave mute support to that reputation.

A sudden flare of cheekiness made her adopt the posture and tone of a shop girl. "Is there something I can help *you* find, Master Rook?"

To her delight, he played along. "Why yes, Mistress Arenza. I'm looking for anything that might shed light on the feud between Indestor and Novrus, the better to ruin both their days." He extended a hand, as though inviting her to dance. "Would you care to snoop together?"

"As long as we promise to share," she said giddily, laying her bare hand in his glove. *Please let him not recognize my hand* warred with *Faces and Masks, am I flirting with the Rook?*

He led her to one of the shelves, then opened a small thieves' lantern she hadn't noticed in the darkness. Unlike the candles the thieves of her acquaintance used, this one held a small numinatrian stone, its glow dim enough not to give away their presence. The lantern was turned so its light wouldn't be visible from the hallway, and made the room just bright enough to search.

"Happy hunting," the Rook said, and went to work.

The problem with Mettore's obsessive record-keeping was that it made for a daunting pile of material to search. She found the records of convict sales quickly enough, in a series of ledgers, and they helpfully noted the crime, age, sex, and physical condition of all those sold. But she had no way of telling if any of those details were falsified. She could only skim for family names in the hopes she came across a pattern, or a name she recognized.

The Rook, meanwhile, picked the locks on Mettore's desk drawers, made a faint noise of irritation at their contents, then moved through the various shelves more quickly. "This is all terribly interesting and terribly useless. He has to keep more private records somewhere." Hand flat and hood pressed to a bare stretch of wall, the Rook started moving along, knocking softly up and down.

There weren't any housebreakers in the Fingers, but half the kids there aspired to join their ranks, and devoured tales of the hidden doors and compartments rich cuffs used to hide their pearls. The best of those were imbued, making them almost impossible to find. Ren knew one old thief—"old" meaning he was nearly thirty— who swore the only way to defeat that kind of concealment was to decide there *was* a secret mechanism, and to work on triggering rather than finding it.

She began circling opposite the Rook, all too aware that they couldn't afford to spend the whole night searching. Tipping books in and out did nothing, no matter how confidently she did it, and tugging on the shelves produced no give that hinted at their potential to swing outward. She pressed every bit of decorative carving she could find, but nothing clicked.

Until she got to the pillars behind Mettore's desk. These were nearly flat to the wall—decorative rather than functional—but when she pulled at the edge of one, her fingers caught in an almost imperceptible seam.

"Here," she said softly, astonished that she'd found it. *Wait 'til I tell Tess and Sedge.*

The Rook came to her side, close enough that she could feel his warmth and smell the dampened lanolin from his coat. "What have you got there, Clever Natalya?"

After months of being Renata, the allusion to Vraszenian folklore made her feel like she'd come home—that, and the fact that she'd gone back to her criminal ways. "I'm not sure how to open it," she admitted.

"Hmm. Would you be so kind as to lend me a pin?"

The end of her braid slipped down over one shoulder as she pulled a pin free. The Rook slid it into the crack she'd found, moving it up as high as he could reach, then down. At knee height, the pin caught on something. A moment of poking and prodding later, he found the mechanism. The panel door swung open, revealing a narrow closet lined on both sides with shelves holding leather binders.

"Victory." The Rook straightened with a flourish. "As you're the one who discovered it, care to have first crack?"

The interior of the closet was even dimmer than the study. "I know not about you, but I cannot read in the dark. Bring that lamp closer."

Within short order, they had an efficient system of revolving documents. Arenza stood in the closet and handed things out to the Rook, who held them next to the lamp to read. Often after seeing just one or two pages, he could tell her to move on to the next folder. She twitched at trusting his judgment—would he really tell her if he found what *she* was looking for?—but the bits and pieces she was able to make out said his assessments looked correct.

Finally, the Rook broke the silence rather than handing her back the most recent paper. "What folder was this in?"

She glanced at the letter he was holding. "It wasn't. It was between folders."

The message was brief, and unsigned. *All is set at the Fiangiolli warehouse. Tell your men to look for the crates marked with a blue boar stamp.*

Before either of them could say anything more, voices sounded outside the study door. "Inside. Now," the Rook hissed, snatching up his lantern, squeezing into the hidden space, and pulling her after him.

The closet was barely large enough for the two of them. She rammed her hips into the Rook when she crouched to find and relatch the hook that held the door shut, but he didn't make so much as a muffled grunt.

The secret room went dark around her just as a key turned in the lock of the study door. The wood of the panel was thin enough that it only partially muffled the voices outside.

"Shut the door." That was Mettore Indestor. Ren stiffened, and felt the Rook behind her doing the same. One hand touched her waist, a silent message, and she pressed into him to keep from brushing against the panel and giving them away.

She could feel his heartbeat against her back. It was as fast as hers, but she didn't know whether to take consolation from that or not. If Mettore had come here to retrieve something from his hidden files...

"How may I serve, Your Mercy?" A woman. Too confident to be a servant, but clearly subservient to Mettore in his role as Caerulet.

"I need you to get me another dose." The wood-scrape of a drawer sliding open. *The desk*, Ren thought, and tried to breathe as silently as she could. "I need to test something."

"That...may be difficult. There's no knowing when those cre—"

"How long?" Mettore snapped.

"Sometimes a week or more..." The woman drifted into silence, and Ren wished there was a spyhole in the pillar. So much could be communicated without words.

"Then buy it off the street if you have to. In the meantime, take this." There was no mistaking the ringing clink of a bag of coins being tossed and caught. "Get Euscenal out of bed to come take care of my son's face."

"I'll see to it at once, Your Mercy."

The door opened and shut. Silence fell for long enough that Ren began to worry she'd spend half the night in the cramped closet, breathing in the silk-and-leather scent of the Rook's disguise and trying to tell whether he was the same height as Leato or not. But after a few endless moments, the door opened and closed again, the lock clicking back into place.

The Rook released her. Ren crouched—more cautiously this time—and listened at the panel, then unhooked it and pushed it outward.

The study was empty. After the warmth of the closet, the air felt as cold as ice.

"We shouldn't linger," the Rook said. "At the risk of insulting you, I don't care to do that again."

As much as she wanted to continue searching, Ren couldn't argue. The Rook folded the letter, and she wondered at its importance. Some kind of planted material, and apparently related to the feud between Indestor and Novrus. That would be of interest to Leato—which might be why the Rook was taking it.

But if he wasn't Leato, then she was letting a valuable piece of evidence slip away.

The Rook must have caught her frown, because he paused instead of tucking the document into his coat. "As this seems more pertinent to my business than yours, you don't mind if I take it, do you?"

She snorted. "What would I do—tell the Rook, 'no, gimme'?"

It was an edge of street cant she hadn't meant to let slip. His lantern was still closed, but the light from the gardens caught the barest curve of what might have been a grin. "Well, I was here first."

You also have a sword. He wouldn't hurt her without cause...but if she tried to lay claim to that letter, she might give him cause. Ren spread her hands, and he slid the paper into his coat.

Then he slipped the lightstone into a pocket and collapsed the small lantern. Boot on the window ledge and hand braced to haul himself up to the casement, the Rook said, "I suppose your presence here is enough to keep you from telling tales about where you saw me, so I won't insult you with a warning. It's certainly been a memorable evening. Sleep well, Arenza."

With a tug at his hood, he disappeared through the window.

10

Pearl's Promise

Eastbridge, Upper Bank: Pavnilun 9

In many ways Ossiter's resembled the Rotunda, where the Gloria was held. The ostretta's center atrium held a fountain, potted myrtle trees, and a collection of low tables and couches for casual patrons seeking only a glass of wine and a selection of fruits and cheeses. Galleries ringed the upper levels for those willing to spend the time and money on a full Seterin meal. Renata spotted several acquaintances among the diners, and tipped her head when they noticed her in turn.

As she ascended the stairs, the scent of roasted meats and spices overpowered the lighter dance of wine and myrtle blossoms. Renata placed a hand over her waist, grateful to Tess for shoving a bit of bread at her before she left. It would ruin the moment if Vargo heard her stomach rumbling.

"Alta Renata." Vargo stood, taking both her hands in greeting. Admiration lit his eyes, but as much, she suspected, for what she wore as for the body inside it. "Your maid has done amazing work with that wool."

"Yes, Tess is a treasure." She said it dismissively, as if she'd long since grown tired of praising her maid's work. As if she hadn't almost cried when Tess buttoned her into it. Halfway between a woman's surcoat and a man's full coat, the cranberry fitted bodice came with its own attached sleeves, and the foreskirt split in the center, closing down the front with a row of jet buttons. The double layer of skirts left Ren feeling like she was wading through the Depths at river's flood, but she would never complain. For the first time this entire winter, she felt _warm_.

Vargo cut an equally fine figure in sapphire wool that showcased the spider peeking out from under his collar. "Do you bring Master Peabody with you everywhere you go?" Renata asked.

"Only where he won't be a distraction." Vargo took his seat, frowning down at his pet, which sent Peabody scuttling back into the shadows of his collar. "Though even he would pale in comparison to you. I had difficulty telling which incited more gossip: your dance partners at the betrothal party, the duel, or your outing with Faella Coscanum the next day."

Renata accepted the wine he poured for her. "The duel, at least, I am not to blame for."

"I'd love to know the truth behind the gossip." He pretended to study the color of his wine, but his eyes were on her.

She could read between his words readily enough. Vargo hadn't pressed her, but he must be getting impatient. He'd hired her to arrange a charter and provided funds for bribes, but from what he could see, she'd spent the last two months on frivolities and unrelated conflicts. Renata took a small leather folder from a pocket inside her coat and presented it to him with both hands. "The truth is that I have the charter."

The glass paused halfway to Vargo's lips. Shadows moved under his collar, Peabody peeking out again. "I beg your pardon?"

"As you can see." She unwound the cord from the toggle holding the folder shut—a button bearing Fulvet's stacked triangle seal. Inside, a paper full of dense calligraphy outlined the terms of the charter and granted it to House Traementis for a period of nine years. "Era Traementis is prepared to sign the administration contract at your convenience."

Vargo took the charter and skimmed through it. Ossiter's hostess hovered nearby, and he didn't notice. Peabody scuttled all the way down to his wrist, and he didn't notice. Only once he'd gone through the entire document did he look up at Renata. "What Primordial powers did you call on to..."

He shook his head and chased Peabody back into hiding. Disbelief tucked away and urbane mask once more in place, Vargo laid the document down. "I'm impressed. Afraid to check the balance of your bribe account, but impressed."

She arranged her expression into grave lines. "Well...I know you told me not to bankrupt you...but you'll need to let Tess back into your fabric warehouse."

"Yes, of course. You can have whatever fabric you want." He dismissed that with a wave of his hand. "I meant, how much did you end up slipping to the Cinquerat to get this? Fulvet at the very least must have extracted a heavy price."

Now Renata let the gravity crack. She'd already enjoyed the pleasure of watching first Scaperto Quientis and then Donaia react to her tale, but it had yet to lose its savor. "You owe nothing, except material to make wedding clothes for Marvisal Coscanum and Mezzan Indestor."

"What do wedding clothes have to do with..." The rest of the question dangled from Vargo's incredulous expression. With a bemused shake of his head, he lounged back in his seat. "No hiding behind 'trade secrets.' I have to know. How did you manage to get a valuable nine-year inaugural charter from Fulvet in exchange for a set of wedding clothes?"

She counted the steps off on her fingers. "Well, in exchange for the loan of Tess's talents, Alta Faella was kind enough to take tea with myself and Nanso Bagacci last week. And Fluriat Bagacci was so pleased to have her brother restored to polite society that she revoked her bid to repair the bridge at Floodwatch. Which means Mede Attravi is certain to win that contract—so he can repay the debt he owes Mede Elpiscio for crashing his pleasure barge into the Elpiscio docking pier. With the pier repaired, Mede Elpiscio will no longer need to use the jetty in Whitesail, leaving it open for Era

Destaelio's use. After that..." She spread her hands, revealing the result of an invisible card trick. "Her Charity said she saw no reason to keep Eret Quientis's shipment of saltpeter impounded any longer. And *he* was so impressed with my methods that he granted Traementis the charter outright."

Vargo took a long pull from his glass to wash down his astonishment. "I knew from the moment I saw you bare-armed at the Gloria: You are a singular woman, Renata Viraudax."

Men had often looked at her the way Vargo was looking at her now, but always for her beauty—never her ingenuity. And Ren, who was used to treating that kind of admiration as nothing more than a useful lever, felt her breath catch.

The smile playing at one corner of Vargo's mouth said he noticed. But rather than lean on that lever, he lifted his glass in a toast. "I imagine congratulations will soon be in order? You're probably an inkwell away from being scribed into a great house register."

Frustration chilled her glow. Donaia had said nothing yet about any such thing. "Some deals are more easily struck than others," she said, keeping her voice light. "But if you have any more schemes tucked away in your pocket, I'd be glad to represent them in the Charterhouse."

"I'll review my pending schemes for how best to use your talents." Finally noticing the hostess hovering just out of earshot, Vargo waved for her to begin serving. "In the meantime, you've only explained the outing with Coscanum. I've yet to hear about the dancing and the duel."

Renata would have preferred the Vraszenian ostretta again—not least because she could have had spiced chocolate—but Vargo had clearly chosen this one to please her, as he kept asking how the food compared to Seterin expectations. Renata deflected his questions as best she could. In Ganllech the rich had their secret Seterin banquets, but as a mere maid, she'd never been allowed to do more than smell the food there. The rest of Ganllechyn cuisine kept a person alive, and that was about all one could say for it.

Fortunately, the gossip offered her plenty of material for

distraction. She told him about her peculiar conversation with Mettore Indestor, and the insult Mezzan had offered Giuna. "Either they're playing a deeper game than I can fathom," she said, "or father and son aren't communicating well about their plans." She strongly suspected the latter.

Then she paused and said thoughtfully, "I don't suppose you know anything about some difficulties around a warehouse belonging to House Fiangiolli?"

Vargo's fork slipped on the bit of roast duck he was attempting to skewer. He set it aside, then rinsed his fingers in a small bowl of lemon water. "There was a fire late last year. They say Mede Fiangiolli was storing illegal black powder there, and was killed when it detonated. Why?"

She had an excuse prepared, but it stuck on her tongue. "I think I heard about that, now that you mention the details. Didn't more than one person die?"

Vargo dried his hands with meticulous care. "A Vraszenian man, too. Some connection to the Traementis—I imagine that's why you know. Most people forget him. You haven't said why you're asking."

She cleared her throat. "I overheard something during the party that made me wonder if the fire might have been an early part of the conflict between Indestor and Novrus. Don't the Fiangiolli administer a number of charters for Novrus?"

That's why the Rook wanted that note, she realized. Because it had to do with the night Kolya Serrado died.

I have to tell Captain Serrado.

Except she couldn't. The last thing her masquerade needed was a hawk knowing she'd broken into Mettore's office. And how else could she justify having such information?

She could send him an anonymous message. He was too canny to give much credence to something like that...but it might do a little good.

"Rumor blames the Rook for the fire that detonated the powder," Vargo was saying, "but it could have been the Vigil. They were on their way to raid the place and arrived conveniently late."

His hands moved restlessly over the table, brushing away crumbs, rubbing at a small stain that had seeped into the cloth. "It's not as uncommon as you might think—the raiding, not the explosion. Novrus recently shut down one of Indestor's prison hulks, claiming it was being used to print seditious literature. It's a dance for them. They fight like other people flirt."

"I don't think Mettore is Sostira Novrus's type," Renata said dryly.

Vargo's bark of laughter made the patrons in several galleries look toward them. He smothered it with a sip of wine. "No, and I don't believe Mettore *has* a type."

"Certainly not me—and thank the Lumen for that. I wish I knew what he wanted from me...other than to make certain I'll remain in Nadežra for the time being." She wet her fingertips and wiped them clean, thinking.

"Of course you have to stay," he said. "And not only because leaving would ruin all your hard work. At the very least, you have to attend the Night of Bells masquerade; I want to see my gift put to use."

The mask he'd given her. She hadn't worn it since that night in Lacewater. Renata smiled and said, "I'm very curious to see what mask *you* will wear, Master Vargo."

Whitesail, Upper Bank: Pavnilun 12

The transition from winter to spring came as a string of daily downpours. Bored with months of indoor pursuits, nobles and gentry alike were on the hunt for novelty. So when Rimbon Beldipassi, merchant client of House Cleoter and most recent addition to the ranks of the delta gentry, opened an exhibition of curiosities and wonders, it quickly became the only subject worth discussing.

But Beldipassi apparently knew that exclusivity created value, because he only allowed a trickle of visitors instead of a deluge. Not even Vargo's money could buy access—though that might have been prejudice as much as canny business sense. Ren entertained the notion of a night break-in so she could drop knowing hints about the exhibit, but resigned herself to being on the outside of fashion.

Until Leato sent her an invitation. How he'd gotten it, she didn't know, but on a rainy afternoon in mid-Pavnilun, the two of them went to Whitesail.

Staring at a spread of wrinkled lumps of gold under glass, Renata was glad she hadn't bothered breaking in. She wouldn't have known how to describe half the things there. "What are these supposed to be?"

Leato tilted his head, as though a new perspective might illuminate the answer. "Numinatrian foci? Melted? Ah, no. See—" He pointed at a card tucked into the corner. "Painted walnut shells from the tomb of the Shadow Lily."

Renata bit down on her next question, not sure whether the Shadow Lily was something an educated noblewoman would know about, or the nonsense it sounded like. Instead she strolled to the next case, where she was confronted with the wide-eyed skull of a lemur—whatever that was—and a twisted scrap of metal purporting to be a broken link from the chain of office that once belonged to the Tyrant Kaius Rex. There seemed to be no rhyme or reason to Beldipassi's collection, nor anything beyond the cards to prove its authenticity. *Maybe he's as much of a con artist as I am.*

A smart con artist, if so. His exhibit mostly didn't bother with treasures from Seteris or Seste Ligante—things that might be expensive to acquire or easily exposed if faked. "I suppose many of these are from along Nadežra's trade routes. We get some southern goods in Seteris, of course, but I must confess I've never seen anything like half of what's here." She offered Leato a pert little curtsy. "Thank you for bringing me."

"Thank *you* for saving me from another afternoon chained to my mother's desk. She only let me escape because of you." He returned her curtsy with an overly elegant bow, reminding her of the moment with the Rook in Mettore Indestor's study. Ducking to peer at a filigreed pot that would never hold water, she took a moment to collect her thoughts. Leato's charm and eager friendliness already made detachment difficult to maintain. If she started thinking him a hero...

No, better to keep thinking of him as he was: the son and heir to one of Nadežra's oldest families. "As though your mother would begrudge you anything. You could run away to Arthaburi to become a bell-dancer and she would forgive you."

She thought her delivery light enough to be taken for teasing, but Leato's grin faded, and he looked away. "I'm not as free as you seem to think. I'd love to travel the Dawn and Dusk Roads, see all the places these things come from...but I can't. I have too many duties in Nadežra."

Duties that involve a hood? The idea was still absurd. The river rat in her kept stomping her foot and insisting the Rook couldn't possibly be a cuff. But it was undeniably true that there was more to Leato than she'd initially realized...and she couldn't just let her suspicion lie.

There was no one else in the room to overhear. She moved closer and gently rested a hand on his arm. "I know. And I'm sorry. I recognize that you aren't the frivolous layabout most people assume. Giuna's told me."

Leato's muscles tensed under her hand, and he shifted away. "Told you what?" He studied a case of strange metal implements labeled only *Ritual artifacts from Xake* as though he'd developed a sudden interest in joining the Xakin priesthood.

"That you don't spend nearly as much time with Orrucio Amananto as you claim. That you play up being more drunk than you are. That you go out at night sometimes, in secret." She nudged him around to face her. "What are you after, cousin? I'd like to assist...but I can't if I don't know what you're trying to do."

"You know what I'm trying to do," Leato said. "Help my family. Is that Ganllechyn embroidery behind you? I thought frivolous decoration was declared a sin there thirty years ago."

His attempt to change the subject was as transparent as fine glass, but instead of continuing to push, Renata turned to look at the white fabric thickly stitched with strange, twisted animals in red, green, and gold silk thread. "A crime, actually," she said, before she could think the better of it. *Why would Renata Viraudax know that?*

Because of Tess. And it gave her a more subtle angle of approach. "Believe it or not," she said, with a conspiratorial tilt of her head, "my maid is a wanted woman in Ganllech."

"Tess?" Leato threw a startled glance at the door to the entry hall, where Tess had settled with Renata's cloak and a lap full of tatting. "For *sewing*?"

"Ganllech," Renata said dryly, "is a land where one can utter the phrase 'illegal embroidery ring' with a straight face. They still have luxuries there, in clothing and otherwise; they merely keep them hidden, with reversible garments and secret panels easily tucked away when in public. All in violation of the law, of course—but it's the seamstresses, not the nobles, who catch the worst of it when such things are exposed. When I met Tess, she was desperate to escape Ganllech before she could be sent to a work camp."

"So Ganllech has its share of hypocrites, too." He glanced sidelong at her, the fine lines of his features softened by the lamplight. "That was when you were coming here from Seteris, I assume. On your mission of reconciliation."

Detachment, she reminded herself. *Don't let him play you—whether he means to or not.* "Do you find that funny?" she asked, drawing back.

She only meant to feign joking offense, but Leato touched his heart in silent apology. "More like unexpected. House Traementis isn't exactly renowned for *mending* bridges. Are you sure you're related to us?"

"Knowing Mother, could anyone doubt?" Her laughter sounded a trifle forced; she shifted over to study a dress form wearing a gown covered in iridescent beetle wings. "She's quite proud of the time she got Callia Fintenus branded on the cheek for implying she had Vraszenian blood."

"You only got a fraction of the stories, I suspect. Our grandfather once had an entire delta family sentenced to drown in the spring floods because they embezzled from the charter they administered for us." He stood at her side, close enough that she could feel his warmth, but not quite touching her. "House Traementis has a long history to answer for."

That quiet, grim certainty wouldn't have been out of place for the Rook. But surely the outlaw would have directed his justice at the Traementis, rather than at their enemies?

Unless the point was not justice, but atonement. "Well," Renata sighed, "I'm doing my part on my mother's behalf."

Leato's brow creased in curiosity. "Do you really think you can get our mothers to reconcile? You haven't said much about that lately—at least not in my hearing."

"Because I fear it's a lost cause." Renata trailed one hand along the edge of a display case. "I was foolish to try."

"The world would be better if everyone suffered such foolishness." He captured her hand and squeezed it. "Would you still want that? Not for your mother . . . but for yourself?"

Her breath caught, for an entirely different reason than Leato would assume. Was he offering to speak on her behalf to Donaia? For a fraction of a heartbeat, Ren wished she really *were* Letilia's daughter—because then she truly could be returning to the embrace of the family her mother had lost.

But Ivrina hadn't run away from her kureč; they'd cast her out. Because of her daughter. The only reconciliation Ren could get was a lie.

It was still better than having nothing.

Stifling the urge to draw away from Leato's grip, she ran her thumb across his knuckles. "When I came here I feared you would see me only as her daughter. Getting out from under the weight of her errors . . . yes. I want that very much indeed."

Isla Traementis, the Pearls: Pavnilun 14

"Meda Fienola is here with the chart you requested, era."

Donaia blinked at Colbrin. She and Leato had been eyelash-deep in calculations for Derossi Vargo's charter, trying to work out how much they could safely skim off the allocated funds to pay other debts, how rapidly House Traementis might see profits from the numinat, and how many deals they could make on the strength of those future profits. It took her a moment to realize what her major-domo meant.

Then she remembered, and swore softly. *I forgot to tell her not to bother.*

All that scrimping and saving to pay for Tanaquis's services, asking Giuna to fish for information, all so Donaia could pry into Renata's background and fate...but against all odds, and on the heels of Leato's public humiliation of Mezzan Indestor, Letilia's daughter had managed to secure a new charter. It hardly seemed to matter now whether she was as poor as Grey Serrado claimed. And she hadn't spoken of reconciling Donaia to Letilia in months; she seemed content to make a place for herself in Nadežra, far from her insufferable mother.

But it was too late for Donaia to take back her request.

"Chart?" Leato uncurled from his hunch over the ledger, wincing as his shoulders cracked. "What did we need charted? And since when can we afford Tanaquis's services?"

Quelling Leato's questions with a glare, Donaia said, "Thank you, Colbrin. Please show her in."

Leato stayed silent only for as long as it took the door to close. "Please tell me this isn't to do with Renata."

"It's only sensible to find out what the stars have fated for her."

"You still don't trust that she means us no harm? This isn't the old days, Mother. Not everyone outside of the family is our enemy. And even if they were, do you still number Renata among them?" He thumped the ledger to illustrate. "After all she's done for us?"

Donaia was saved from answering by the door opening. Oblivious to the tension she'd walked in on, Tanaquis crouched to scratch behind Meatball's ears. Her dove-pale underdress and surcoat of lavender broadcloth were as simple as the bun that held her dark hair; the tendrils snaking free were a product of absentmindedness rather than artifice. And her gloves, as always, were spotted with ink stains.

"Donaia, Leato, I'm sorry I wasn't able to visit sooner. Indestor and Coscanum each want a different date for the wedding, they can't agree on which one, and none of them believe me when I tell them the date isn't the problem." Rising, she set down her satchel and clasped hands with Donaia, eyes sparkling.

"You don't need to apologize for being busy. And really, there was no rush." Donaia's friendship with Tanaquis was proof that Leato was wrong: She didn't treat outsiders only as enemies or tools. The woman was more than ten years her junior, from an insignificant delta family that had largely died out. They didn't share any interests; Tanaquis was practically made of paper and ink, whereas the only books Donaia had time for were ledgers. Any one of those differences would have been barrier enough—but Donaia counted Tanaquis as a friend.

"But you were so concerned when you—" Tanaquis's glance faltered toward Leato. Donaia supposed she should be grateful that her friend realized this might be a sensitive topic, even if it was too late to stop her from speaking.

"I shouldn't have imposed on your time in the first place," Donaia said. As a sop to Leato's frown, she added, "It was just my fears talking. Foolish of me to listen to them."

"Caution is never foolish. You told me that." Sitting, Tanaquis studied Donaia and Leato with eyes trained to gaze into the cosmos and find truth. It was a struggle to meet such perusal without blinking. "But it sounds like your concerns have been allayed."

"They have," Leato said at once.

"Oh?" A sly grin curved Tanaquis's lips. "Should I draft a chart for an auspicious date?"

Leato twitched in his chair, cheeks going red. "What? No!"

Such an emphatic denial, it was almost a confession. Amused that her son could still be flustered so easily, Donaia joined in the teasing. "Leato is very fond of his cousin, but it's far too soon to consider anything of the sort."

"Mother!"

"Oh, you've nothing to worry about." She patted his flushed cheek. "Renata has too much sense to be turned by a pretty face."

But would it be a bad thing if she were? A month ago, Donaia would have said Renata would bring nothing into the marriage. But Donaia had been refusing all opportunities to sell Leato off for a profitable alliance, and if he liked the girl, who was to say Renata's acumen wasn't dowry all its own?

"Does she? Interesting. Speaking of which..." Tanaquis pulled a scroll out of her satchel. "I should thank you for asking me to do this. It was the most puzzling chart I've drawn up in some time. Quite unusual."

The word brought Donaia's suspicions lurching back to half-life. "Unusual? How so?"

Unrolling the chart, Tanaquis walked them through the maze of intercrossing lines that laid out Renata's personality and fate. "A daytime birth in Colbrilun means she was born sunwise under Eshl, making her Prime Illi direct, with no influence from Uniat. That indicates a powerfully spiritual person, a conduit that ever strives to open herself further for cosmic energy to cycle through her— though that energy can turn inward, making her oblivious to the world and people around her." Tanaquis pushed a stray wisp off her brow and cocked her head. "To illustrate, my Prime is also Illi direct."

"Renata's the opposite of oblivious," Leato said, finger tracing the lines spanning from planet to planet. He'd always had more interest in such things than Donaia. The chart might as well have been a Vraszenian pattern deck for all the sense it made to her.

"I thought as much. So I went to my almanacs to see if there was any unusual celestial activity that might alter it, but found nothing. No eclipses or comets. Corillis was waning gibbous and Paumillis was full, which might indicate *some* influence from Tuat, but not enough to explain this. It's honestly baffling."

Then Tanaquis flipped the chart. "Her birth date makes more sense. Second day of the fourth iteration, so her Alter is Tuat influenced by Quarat. The path she walks through life is a long one of duality and intuition, with many stops along the way. Alliances and exchanges during her journey will lead her to wealth and luck—both good and ill. However, in walking this path she may encounter difficulty finding a home. More likely her home is found in the people she meets on her path."

That was plausible. The girl certainly enjoyed luck, and as for wealth...those difficulties with her letter of credit didn't seem to be hampering her much. And it might explain her wandering.

Tanaquis said, "I won't get into the yearly details. Those are always rather general and boring. She's the same year as you, Leato, so I'm certain you know it all."

"Yes, but what does it *mean*?" Donaia asked, wondering if she might have been wiser to seek the astrologer's help from the start.

Tanaquis rolled up the chart and handed it to Donaia. "I'm not sure, but it does make me wonder...is it possible she lied? From the little I know of her, I would have put her birth month in Suilun or possibly Equilun, but..." Pressing her lips together, Tanaquis leaned closer. "Is it possible she was conceived before Letilia left? That her father isn't who Letilia says?"

Letilia hadn't said anything about who Renata's father was, because Donaia still hadn't written to her. Come to that, Renata herself talked only rarely of her father. Could that be because—

Donaia's eyes widened. If Renata was conceived before Letilia left...then her father might be here in the city. And perhaps *that*—not some naive hope for reconciliation—was her real reason for coming to Nadežra.

"Who would it be, if not Eret Viraudax?" Leato demanded, quick to defend his cousin as though she were already in the register. "And why would Renata lie?"

Tanaquis studied her hands, interlacing her fingers with mathematical precision. "I apologize. It's probably a mistake in my charting, and nothing to do with a false date. I shouldn't have said anything."

"A mistake in your charting? Next you'll tell me the Dežera is flowing backward." Donaia passed a weary hand over her face. "No, I'm grateful. Your suggestion makes a great deal of sense—it would explain why Letilia fled, and why Renata gave the date she did. Perhaps she didn't lie," Donaia said to Leato before he could take offense, then softened her words with a hand on his knee. "It's possible she doesn't know—that Letilia lied to her."

Possible, but Donaia had her doubts.

But who might the unknown father be? Scaperto Quientis? That might explain how Renata got the charter, if he realized...but no. Letilia had been engaged to the man. If she'd gotten pregnant by him, there would have been no reason to run away.

But it would be just like Letilia to somehow lose her contraceptive numinat. Though the father would need to have done the same thing—unless he was too poor to afford one. Donaia groaned silently.

Tanaquis said, "Whatever the case, I can't possibly accept this. Not that I felt right taking it in the first place." She drew another package from her satchel, this one a pouch shifting with the dull clink of forri. Donaia pulled her hands away, but Tanaquis caught her wrist and set the heavy bag in her palm. "I insist. We're friends, Donaia. You don't charge me when I eat dinner here, and I don't charge you for my advice."

Donaia knew she should insist right back. The comparison wasn't valid; Traementis Manor wasn't an ostretta, while Tanaquis was a professional astrologer. But Traementis luck had been bad for so long that pragmatism snarled at her to swallow her pride. Those forri could be put to a dozen other uses, and Tanaquis wouldn't miss them.

Tanaquis leaned into her view, catching her gaze. "Please. Let me do this for you."

Reluctantly, Donaia curled her fingers around the purse. "Thank you."

She set it on the table at her side, and Tanaquis relaxed. "If you'd like me to look into this, I wouldn't mind at all. Perhaps you could arrange an informal meeting? I have some experience with clients lying about dates in hopes of a better chart. And you know I can't leave a mystery unexamined."

That was true enough. If the cosmos was a clock, Tanaquis wanted to take it apart and study all the gears under a magnifying lens. "Very well."

"But discreetly," Leato said. "I don't want Renata's reputation dragged into the mud."

Hers or ours, Donaia thought. Surely Letilia wouldn't have stooped to bedding some nameless commoner. Surely?

With the compassionate smile of someone much older and wiser than her years, Tanaquis said, "Of course. I won't mention these suspicions to Alta Renata, either. It doesn't take astrology to know she's had enough family troubles in her life. She doesn't need to know we suspect anything until we're certain there's something to it."

Regardless of what that something might be. If Renata's father was some muck-grubbing commoner, no need to burden the girl with that knowledge. And if he was a noble scion . . . Donaia thought back to her earlier musings and sighed. As much as the girl might be an asset to the Traementis, Renata should have a chance to see her name in her father's register, rather than shackling her life to the cursed fortunes of a failing house.

Kingfisher and Seven Knots, Lower Bank: Pavnilun 18

"Serrado! You been keeping secrets," Dvaran said the moment Grey ducked under the lintel of the Gawping Carp. Since his meeting with Leato, he'd found himself dropping by the establishment more frequently. He'd even managed to enjoy a drink and a hand of nytsa with the elders now and then—as he'd done when Kolya was alive.

Grey's step faltered. "Secrets?"

"That you got a sweetheart. She came by looking for you." Dvaran leaned his truncated arm on the bar, giving Grey a friendly leer.

"Pretty thing, too. I think you found a keeper. Time to burn the love charm and braid one of them bridal tokens into her hair."

"I'm not looking for a wife, and I don't have time for a sweetheart." Especially one he hadn't even known existed. "What the hell are you on about?"

Dvaran sighed at Grey's refusal to rise to his bait. "Vraszenian girl named Idusza came by. Said you was looking for her. Ha!" He crowed and pointed a finger at Grey's dumbfounded look. "Seems you do know her."

"I do." And was more likely to arrest her than marry her. How had she known to find him here? When he'd spoken with the Polojny family, they'd been predictably tight-lipped. He'd tried more than once, but finally quit before the gammer glaring at him from her fireside stool used him as a pincushion for her embroidery needles.

"Did she say anything else?" Grey asked.

"Said to come find her in Grednyek Close in Seven Knots, above the chandler's. You want my advice, stop by Sweet Mlačin's and buy some fried honey cakes. Nobody likes a suitor who shows up empty-handed."

"I'll keep that in mind." Grey slapped a mill on the counter for the message and stepped out to find a runner.

By the time Leato arrived, it was almost ninth sun, and Grey had nursed his beer to the dregs. Leato came in breathless, like he'd hurried there as fast as he could. "You found her?"

"Read this." He'd been folding and unfolding a note, and now he passed it to Leato. "It showed up at the Aerie the day before yesterday. Nobody can tell me who brought it."

Leato's eyebrows climbed toward his hairline as he read. "Who— no, it isn't signed. But..."

He fell silent, mouth pressing into a hard line. When he finally spoke, his voice was flat. "So Indestor was trying to frame the Fiangiolli. Who placed the black powder for him? House Essunta, do you think?"

"Or someone working for them." That was always the way of it.

The cuffs gave orders to the delta gentry, and they contracted the actual work out to others. The sick anger that had nearly drowned Grey in the wake of Kolya's death was back. It came in waves, and every time it found a new target, it surged higher. "But that doesn't explain who set it off."

"You still believe it was the Rook."

"You don't know what I believe."

"I know he's an easy scapegoat compared to—"

"You're a cuff," Grey snapped. "Why are *you* defending him?"

Leato shook his head, gaze sliding to one side. They hadn't argued about the differences between them in years. Carefully, Grey refolded the anonymous note. "Perhaps you're right that Idusza knows something."

Leato studied him for several moments before responding. "And if she's Anduske, then she's got no reason to be loyal to Indestor." He said the name tentatively, as if afraid Grey himself was black powder, primed to go off. "But Idusza didn't send this—that wouldn't make any sense, sending an anonymous note, then contacting you herself."

"No, but the person who did might be Anduske, too. I say we find out." Grey drained the last of his beer and stood, waving for Leato to follow him into a back room. When Leato glanced at Dvaran, Grey said, "Don't worry. We have permission."

Dvaran kept a sack of the clothes that had been abandoned in the taproom on rowdier nights, bits and pieces that never found their way back to their owners. Grey rooted through it and found a few that would work. He tossed them at Leato. "Strip. Put these on."

Leato made a face at the musty smell. "Do I have to?"

"Unless you want to get knifed. The stink of the West Channel is more welcome in Seven Knots than the perfumes of the Pearls." Grey let the accent he'd worked so hard to scrub away drag his voice down into his throat. "And there is no putting you in a panel coat. Not even a horse-brained Meszaros would mistake you for one of the people." He might be Kiraly, but his mother's clan was Meszaros; he was allowed to mock them.

Sighing, Leato stripped off his coat, waistcoat, and shirt. "It's odd hearing you talk like that. Not bad odd or anything, just—it reminds me of when we met."

Grey swung one leg over a chair so he could rest his elbows on the back. "Funny. I recall not our first meeting. To me, all you cuffs looked and sounded the same." He smiled to take the sting out of the teasing.

Leato's snort turned into a sneeze when he made the mistake of beating dust from the patched trousers. "Yeah, yeah. We're all rich and blond and arrogant. I'm actually Orrucio Amananto, but I didn't want to embarrass you by correcting the mistake."

The chair legs scraped across the floor as Grey stood and gave him an exaggerated bow, knife proffered across his forearm like he was presenting a duelist's blade. Where they were going, anyone bearing a sword would raise questions. "And I am secretly Prince Ivan from the tales. But then, so is every Vraszenian man. Ready?"

Grimacing, Leato took the knife and tugged a cap over his forro-bright hair. "Lead on, Prince Ivan."

The Gawping Carp was on the edge of Kingfisher where it butted up against Westbridge and Seven Knots. The streets took an abrupt turn for the worse when they entered the Vraszenian rook-ery, halving in width, formed into tunnels by lines of hanging laun-dry and sun-faded shade-breaks. The scent of garlic, steaming rice, and strong spices battled with the stink of bodies and slightly turned meat. To others—to Leato—it might be unpleasant. To Grey, it smelled like home.

He led the way through streets that had formed according to convenience rather than planning, until the tangle opened up into the wider lanes and courtyard houses owned by the more successful trading kretse.

Even Leato could tell the nice parts of the Lower Bank from the rest. "I thought you said her family wasn't very rich."

"We go not to where they live. Perhaps this is the house of one of her friends."

They passed through a small plaza where every porch was peo-pled with gammers and naunties nattering over embroidery, or gaffers and nuncles arguing over family rivalries a century old. An archway up ahead marked the entrance to Grednyek Close, but Grey stopped Leato before he could walk through. "Aren't we both going in?" Leato said. "I thought that was why you called me here."

"It is—but I want to be careful." Something about this wasn't sitting right with him. The nice neighborhood, the anonymous note, Idusza coming out of hiding at last. "Let me first ask around. See what the people who live here say."

Leato grimaced. "I...didn't bring much money with me. Sorry—I didn't think we'd need it."

Grey stared at him, uncomprehending. Then a laugh bubbled up. "You think I will bribe them to talk?"

"That's how I've had to do it," Leato said defensively.

Clapping him on the shoulder, Grey said, "That's because you are not Vraszenian. Give me a bell or two."

The gammers and gaffers would have liked him better if his hair was braided, but Grey had better success than he expected—because even a short-haired Vraszenian met with more approval than the "cheese-eater" who kept visiting Idusza in the rooms above the chandler's shop.

Leato frowned when Grey shared that with him. "I thought these Stadnem Anduske types would never take up with one of us."

"It is odd. But stranger things have happened."

The air around the chandler's shop was heavy with the scents of oil and beeswax, the door at the top freshly painted the red of the Stretsko clan, just like the door at the Polojny apartment. Grey knocked, leaning in to speak through the panels.

"Is Ča Idusza Polojny at home?"

"Who are you?" The voice was muffled and wary, but female, and not elderly.

"Grey Szerado. Of the Kiraly."

After a moment, the door cracked slightly, and a suspicious eye showed in the gap. "And your friend?"

"Orrucio," Grey said, suppressing a smile as Leato coughed. "I would not disturb the household. Is there somewhere we can speak?"

A pause. Then she said, "You won't disturb anyone." The door swung wider, and she gestured them in.

Idusza Polojny was young and pretty, with big dark eyes and her hair braided in a gentle curve over her left shoulder. She could have been any street-seller or housemaid. But the wariness in her eyes suggested to Grey that she had a knife on her somewhere to protect her from the strangers she was letting into her house.

Had he seen her at the Aerie, working in the laundry? Probably. But he didn't remember her—and *that*, more than anything, made him believe she was Stadnem Anduske.

That, and the way her gaze fixed sharply on him. "You're the hawk asking after me."

No offer of a seat, nor tea. Not even the grudging hospitality her family had shown. The parlour she led them into felt nothing like that warm house; it was clean and well-furnished, but looked like a painting rather than a home. "Yes. Though I am curious why you let yourself be found." She hardly seemed eager to talk.

She gave him a sour look. "My mother believes every word from a szorsa's mouth. I am not so credulous, but she would not stop insisting I contact you, and in the end..." Idusza shrugged. "This is easier."

"A szorsa?" Grey asked, even as Leato breathed an astonished "Oh." Grey shot him a dirty look. What had Leato done?

Idusza stared at Grey, then at Leato. "So you are not the one who paid her. *This* one did?"

"He...doesn't like patterners very much." Leato gave an embarrassed laugh. "Look, I—I asked the szorsa for advice, and she offered to help. What did she tell your mother that made you come forward at last?"

Idusza seemed willing to answer him, so Grey kept his mouth shut and tried not to seethe. "She said I might some great injustice set right. And my mother swore my womb would run dry, my looks fade, and my hair never in a wife's braids be bound if I ignored a szorsa's advice. As though I care for such things." Her expression straddled the divide between indignation and petulance. "What I care for is knowing why you have gone to such effort."

Grey knew only too well the look Leato cast his way. It said the man was about to hang permission and ask for forgiveness later.

"You know about the Fiangiolli fire? My friend's brother died in it—"

"I know nothing of that," Idusza snapped, too quickly for it to be anything but a lie.

"Of course," Leato soothed. "But you were working for the Vigil at the time. Maybe you know something about who planted the black powder in the warehouse, or who set it off. Or who sent my friend a note about it, recently?"

Her arms crossed, warding herself. The silence stretched like a thread on the verge of snapping, until finally she said, "There's no point dancing around this. You know I am Stadnem Anduske, and you think we set the fire. We did not. That was Novrus and Indestor, fighting through their lapdogs."

Leato winced, but gamely tried again. "We don't think you or your...friends...were involved. We only want—"

"Enough," Grey said roughly. She might look soft, but Idusza was too hardened to give anything away.

Unless he did something to throw her off. "Strange that one of the Stadnem Anduske should play house with a chalk-faced Lig," he said, one arm sweeping at the lovely, unused sitting room. "A flush one, by the looks of it. Perhaps we should wait and ask him what he knows about you."

Even without the neighborhood gossip, he might have guessed. There were no heirlooms, no baubles picked up at a dozen stops along the Dawn and Dusk Roads. No weavings handed down from her gammer, the colorful silk threads faded to precious silver by time. This was no residence, nor a Stadnem Anduske safe house. Grey knew a love nest when he saw one.

The crossed arms came loose. Grey saw it coming, and let it happen; she shoved him back two good steps. Nobody worked as a laundress without building muscle. "Righting some great injustice," she spat. "What know you of that, slip-knot? You work for those who beat us into the mud, while my man turns his back on his own f—"

She bit off her words, but not fast enough. Leato's sudden intake of breath broke the silence that followed.

"Mezzan," he whispered. "You're the lover he's been hiding away."

It sounded insane. Mezzan Indestor, taking up with a Vraszenian lover? The moons would set in the northern sea first.

But Idusza wasn't denying it.

"Get out," she said, her voice trembling. With rage, with fear—maybe both. "Whatever you want, you will not find it. Get out!"

Leato started to speak, but Grey seized his arm and dragged him toward the door, fumbling it open with his free hand and steering them both onto the landing. "We are very sorry for having—"

The door slammed shut.

"—troubled you." Sighing, Grey slumped against the wall. "That was...enlightening. But not in the way I expected."

"Do you think it was Mezzan?" Leato whispered, cheeks pale and bloodless as he stared at the red door.

"Her lover? She admitted it."

"No. Who set off the powder."

Grey was glad for the wall's support. "Why would he..."

"Because he's with the Anduske? Or framing them? Or it was on his father's orders, or *against* those orders, out of rebellion? Maybe just because he's an asshole. I should have skewered him on my blade."

When Grey couldn't dredge up a response, Leato headed down the stairs, each step jolting the whole structure. "It doesn't matter. I know enough. She's Stadnem Anduske and Mezzan's having an affair with her; once that comes out, Indestor will be humiliated."

Grey took the steps rapidly, edging ahead enough to block his friend's way. "What do you mean, 'once that comes out'? I thought we were..." He jerked to a halt just outside Grednyek Close, betrayal hitting him like a punch to the gut. "This isn't about finding Kolya's murderer. This is about your fucking feud with Indestor."

"It isn't just a feud!" Leato slammed his hand against the wall. "It's the safety of my family! Do you think he'd stop short of selling us onto the penal ships? You work for the man; you know what he's like. And I wasn't lying to you, Grey. Even before I saw the note about the black powder, I wondered if Indestor was behind it all somehow. It was just too bloody convenient, Novrus's client taking a hit like that."

He was talking too rapidly for Grey to get a word in edgewise, his hand coming off the wall to bury itself in his golden hair, knocking his cap askew. "I've been digging for the last year—ever since I found out how badly off we really are. Trying to find something I can use against somebody in that house to get Mettore's boot off our necks. I was hoping I could get justice for your brother at the same time. But if I can't have both, I can at least have this."

Grey wanted to hold on to his hurt, his feeling of being used— but he understood too well Leato's hollow desperation.

He forced himself to soften his voice. They'd already attracted too much attention. "But you can't. You cannot use this. You know what will happen, what Mettore will do if he finds out his son has taken up with a Vraszenian. And she isn't the only one in danger. He'll go after her family—sell *them* into slavery. Them, and any other scapegoat he can catch."

"Then let's get *rid* of him!" Leato's hands balled into fists. "Instead of being fucking puppets for that kinless bastard to play with, let's get him out of power! Don't you want to drag him down?"

"I want to drag them all down, from the man who lit the spark to the puppeteer behind the screen." Grey clamped both hands on Leato's shoulders and gave him a shake as though sense would follow. "Tell me how we get to Indestor without destroying those we love. Force him into the street and condemn him? You take his arms; I'll take his legs? You're Traementis. You know better than any how vengeance ends."

He felt the moment Leato deflated. "Fuck."

Grey forced his own rage down, back into the box where he kept everything he couldn't let himself think about—everything that would drown him if he let it. When his breathing was steady at last, he draped one arm across Leato's slumped back and steered him toward Westbridge. "We'll find some other way of getting Indestor and protecting your family."

"How?" Leato's voice was devoid of all emotion. "I've been trying. Mother's been trying. Renata's been trying. But Indestor has everything we don't: people, money, power. How do you win against that?"

Grey's heart ached for his friend's despair, even as he wanted to rail at the irony of a noble son of a Liganti house bemoaning such things in the narrow, dirty streets of Seven Knots. "You take a lesson from my people," he said, nodding at the wall of tenements draped in a shawl of laundry lines, the elders gossiping on their stoops, the children playing skip-hop in the street. "You give up on winning. You learn to survive."

Seven Knots, Lower Bank: Pavnilun 18

Ren didn't follow the two men out of Seven Knots. She'd risked enough by tailing them—and heard enough to make her skull overflow.

Mezzan had a Vraszenian lover? And not just any lover, but a seditionist? One who had something to do with Kolya Serrado's death—no, it sounded like that lead hadn't come to anything. But Captain Serrado had gotten her message, and gave it enough credence to show it to Leato.

Leato's rage against Mettore Indestor . . . was that just the anger of a man trying to protect his family, or the fury of the Rook, blamed for a cuff's crimes? Would the Rook come back tonight and pay Idusza Polojny a visit?

No, not tonight. Any Rook stupid enough to show such coincidental timing would soon be caught. And Serrado was right; exposing Mezzan's relationship with Idusza might hurt House Indestor, but at terrible cost for the Vraszenians caught up in it. She hoped Leato understood that, Rook or not.

Even so . . .

Ren cast a speculative glance at the entrance to Grednyek Close. A young, pretty woman emerged, tugging her shawl over her hair, and hurried away. Good odds that was Idusza.

Not for one heartbeat did Ren believe that Mezzan Indestor had taken up with her out of love, or even lust. The latter might explain a random Vraszenian woman, but not a member of the Stadnem Anduske.

Which meant he was up to something else. Something she *could* use against his house. And if the Rook did pay Idusza a visit later . . . that would be very interesting to know.

But how to get Idusza to talk to her?

The Kindly Hawk. Grinning, Ren tugged her own shawl straight and turned toward home. She needed to speak to Sedge and Tess.

Westbridge, Lower Bank: Pavnilun 26

The following Epytny, Arenza set herself up at the border of Westbridge, laying her shawl on the ground near the ostretta where Idusza worked. She got a few customers—enough to pay for the scrap of heavy wool Tess had bought for the plan—and then, at the last bell of sixth sun, Tess appeared and loitered nearby, waiting for Arenza's current client to be done.

They nearly failed right then, because the young man seemed more intent on flirting with Arenza than heeding what his pattern said. It finally took A Spiraling Fire and warnings of impending impotence if he didn't propitiate the Masks at the nearest labyrinth to drive him off. Tess hurried up and settled in front of Arenza before anyone else could claim the space.

Just in time, too. She'd barely rattled off her story about her sweetheart and would his parents ever accept her when Idusza emerged onto the stoop barely a wagon's length away, with a zrel bottle in one hand and a pipe in the other. She lit the pipe, and sweet-scented smoke drifted up to curl around the eaves. Taking a swig of what was probably her lunch, Idusza leaned against the wall, head back and eyes closed.

"Your sweetheart, what is he named?" Arenza asked, shuffling the cards—Sedge's signal.

Tess had always been better at improvised truths than practiced lies. It seemed she'd taken Ren's advice not to overprepare to heart. "P-Pavlin?"

So—there's more there than I realized. Arenza didn't try to hide her smile. "A good name. Pavnilun is the dreamweaver's month, after all."

The swing of Sedge's balding velvet coat and the strike of his cane on the cobbles did as much to scatter people out of his path as his scowl. Even Idusza raised her head as he clomped up and stopped at the edge of Arenza's blanket, where she'd only just turned over The Face of Roses.

"I was wondering where you'd got off to. Found a nice new patch for yourself, did you? But it en't getting you out of what's owed me."

It took Arenza a moment to pinpoint why his condescending drawl and his affected swagger seemed familiar. And when she did, she almost broke character.

Vargo. He was imitating *Vargo*.

She'd deliberately chosen a bad spot, tucked into the space where the front of a tinsmith's jutted out past the neighboring apothecary. It let Sedge trap both her and Tess in the corner, and half the pass-ersby didn't have a clear line of sight—but Idusza, lounging on the stoop with her pipe and bottle, had a perfect view.

"I—I am sorry," she stammered, in the thickest Vraszenian accent she could manage. As if she'd come to Nadežra from the furthest depths of Vraszan. "I knew not—but you own not that shop—"

He kicked her bowl, clattering it against Idusza's stoop in a spray of centiras.

"Own this corner, don't I? And I don't need no mouthy card-juggler stinking up the place staked out for my night-pieces." He leered, and she wondered uneasily how much of this came from years on the street, and how much was lifted from watching Vargo. "Unless you're looking for better things to do with that mouth, sweetheart."

Tess scrambled to her feet, but Sedge grabbed her arm as she tried to dodge past and threw her against Arenza.

"No you don't, sow. No running for the hawks. We can finish up here easy if the gnat gives me what I want, and then you can—"

"Why don't *you* fuck off and stop stinking up this corner, you Liganti leech," Idusza snarled. She knocked the embers from her pipe and ground them into the cobbles with her foot. "Before I find better uses for *your* mouth. Like breaking my bottle on it." The remains of her zrel sloshed as she raised the heavy glass.

Sedge pivoted to face her. The way the three of them used to run this scam, some hawk or virtuous passerby would intervene, and he'd keep the mark busy long enough for either Tess or Ren to pick their pocket—or if that didn't work, he'd let himself be run off, and then they'd swipe things while clinging to their savior in gratitude.

But money wasn't Ren's target this time.

"She's a stranger. Hurt her not," Arenza cried, stepping forward. Without looking, Sedge smashed one elbow backward. He'd insisted on practicing before they came out here, because both of them had grown; she was glad of it now, as he came within a sneeze of genuinely hitting her in the teeth. She hurled herself into the wall and bit down on the packet she'd slipped into her cheek, spitting out blood.

"You stay out of this," he snarled at Idusza, reaching for the bottle and wrenching it out of her hand—but leaving himself open for the fist that cracked him in the jaw.

It sent him reeling back a step. Cuffing the blood from his split lip, Sedge snarled, "You're gonna pay for that, just as soon as this one pays what she owes me."

Arenza rose to her feet. "I owe you nothing except the curses of fate," she spat, bending to snatch up her deck. "You have a szorsa struck. Let us draw three cards and see what your doom will be."

A twitch of her finger sent the bottom card into her waiting hand. "The Mask of Night," she said. "May Ir Nedje curse your eyes with the blindness of your heart."

Sedge lifted his cane to strike her. "I'll show you where you can shove your cards, you damned—" The insult died as he swung and missed by two handspans, stumbling off-balance and smashing shoulder-first into the wall. He hunched against it, blinking and staring at nothing.

"You . . . what did you do? What did you fucking *do to my eyes*?!"

He charged again, waving his arms wildly as though uncertain of his target's position. Arenza easily stepped out of the way. As did Idusza, whose furious scowl was fading into surprise.

Arenza dealt another card. "The Mask of Worms. May Šen Kryzet curse your mouth with the foulness you spew."

Sedge lurched "blindly" into a man who shoved him away, dropping him to one knee. That gave him cover to palm something into his own mouth. Then he staggered upright again, coughing and gagging—and a mass of bloody, writhing worms spattered to the cobblestones.

They had an audience now, not just Idusza. Arenza brandished the third card high. "The Mask of Ashes. May Ezal Sviren curse your hand, which you use only for bringing pain and destruction."

Sedge's arm burst into flame.

Gasps and screams rose from the crowd, and they all backed away from the flailing man and his blazing arm. He fell to his knees, beating at the flames with the opposite glove until they went out, leaving a smoking, well-singed sleeve behind. Then he began to crawl, burned arm blindly outstretched, seeking aid. "Help! Someone help me! That witch cursed me!"

Arenza didn't see what happened next, because she sagged backward into the corner between the tinsmith's and the apothecary, then slid gently to the ground. From the sound of it, someone was helping Sedge away. But mostly what she heard was Tess doing her pity-rustler best to keep Idusza's attention off the cursed thug, and on the patterner who'd cursed him.

Against Tess's hand-wringing and helplessness, Idusza had little choice but to take charge. Arenza stayed limp as Idusza browbeat the apothecary into letting them into his storeroom and even giving them a restorative for the price of the centiras Sedge's kick had scattered.

"Here, szorsa. You must wake up so you can drink." The apothecary's back room smelled of dust and dried herbs and sharp pine resin. They'd set Arenza on a worktable with her patterner's shawl as a pillow. The table creaked as Idusza jostled her.

Tess's voice sounded from nearby while Arenza fluttered her eyelids in a daze. "I really should be going now. My nan—"

"Go," Idusza commanded with a weary sigh. "She is my people, not yours. I will see to her."

The door snicked open and shut, leaving Ren alone with her hooked mark.

She groaned and tried to sit up, then spoke in Vraszenian. "What happened?"

"Drink this." A cup pressed into Arenza's hands, and Idusza helped prop her up. "That man... Caused you those ills, szorsa? Or was it the Faces and the Masks working their will through you?"

She drank, coughing a little. "I—I'm not certain. I was so angry, and then..."

Ren hadn't quite planned this part. The usual form of the Kindly Hawk only required brief contact with the mark. She needed to win Idusza's trust in the long term.

Hence building the scam into something more dramatic. Idusza's mother had complained that her daughter didn't respect patterners— but that was because she didn't believe most of them had any gift. A display of the sorts of powers szorsas were reputed to have in legend stood a chance of breaking through her skepticism, turning Arenza into someone Idusza might confide in.

"That man." Arenza widened her eyes in horror. "I— He *caught fire.*"

"He did. He—" Idusza's frown collapsed into something between a hiccup and a cough. She clapped her hands over her lips, but the giggles refused to be contained. "He flapped like the chicken

I butchered last week. All that was missing was the clucking. Oh, what I would give to be able to set my enemies on fire."

Should I look proud, or—Arenza dropped the cup. "No. No, that cannot have been me. Something else—he wandered too close to someone's pipe—"

"And too close to someone's worms?" Idusza pointed out ironically. "He coughed those up also. No, my friend; you were the vessel of the Masks in cursing him as he deserved." She retrieved the cup from the floor. "Who are your people?"

Sooner or later Idusza would talk to her family, and then she might find out Arenza was the same patterner who'd spoken with her mother about Grey Serrado. But Ren would leap that canal when she got to it. "The Dvornik. I am Arenza Lenskaya Tsverin. I know not how I can thank you—"

Idusza quieted her with a pat on her hand. "Ah, Dvornik. Always making complicated what is simple." She wrinkled her nose, but it was the usual teasing between Ažerais's children. "Idusza Nadjulskaya Polojny of the Stretsko. And I would never turn my back on someone who keeps to our ways. Arrived you recently to Nadežra?"

When Arenza nodded, Idusza patted her hand again. "Then I will help you find your feet."

She returned to work not long after that, but not before making Arenza promise to meet her the next day. Her performance ended, Ren went looking for Tess and Sedge.

The latter was rinsing his mouth out with zrel and spitting into the nearest canal, then scraping his tongue with the heavy woolen undersleeve that had protected him from the flames. "Oh, come now," Ren said, grinning and clapping him on the shoulder. "Like you have never eaten worms before." They all had, when food got really scarce.

Sedge glared sidelong. "I take money to beat people up so I won't *have* to eat worms anymore." He touched his jaw and hissed at the tenderness. "Too bad she's Stadnem Anduske. With a hook like that, she could make good money working for Vargo."

He hissed again when Tess flicked his hands away so she could apply a salve, but his gaze was merry. "Now, Tess, why don't you tell us about this Pavlin fellow..."

Charterhouse, Dawngate, Old Island: Cyprilun 4

Vargo had been in and out of the Aerie a dozen times, sometimes as a prisoner, sometimes to spring one of his own from lockup. But the Charterhouse, scarcely a mile to the east, was less familiar territory—the domain of legitimate bureaucracy.

Now he had an invitation to walk its halls...from the very man he'd been targeting for months.

It hardly seemed like coincidence.

::Stop stalling, my boy. We won't learn what Mettore wants from out here,:: Alsius said impatiently.

If what Mettore wanted was to arrest Vargo, he could just send his hawks to Eastbridge. Knowing the man, Vargo doubted he'd bother with anything so legitimate; more likely that they'd ambush him somewhere on the Lower Bank and leave his body in a canal.

Vargo's fingers tightened on the head of his sword cane. *They'd try.*

No, this wasn't an ambush. An invitation to the Charterhouse meant Indestor intended something more civilized.

A clerk was waiting just inside the threshold, catching Vargo before he could do more than eye the line of people waiting at the desk. "Good morning, Master Vargo. If you'll follow me?"

Keep the commentary to a minimum, he told Alsius as the clerk led him upstairs, along a hallway, and to a set of double doors. *I need to be able to think.*

Silence was his only answer.

The doors opened, and Mettore Indestor stood to greet him. "Master Vargo. Have a seat."

No coming around the desk to offer his hand, no courtesies or small talk. Either Indestor was getting right down to business, or he didn't think Vargo was worth the effort. *Probably both.*

"Your Mercy," he said, tasting the irony of the title. "You wanted to see me?"

The office of Caerulet was made to be imposing, with heavy furniture, dark wood, and the banners of the Vigil and Nadežra's military companies passing as decoration. Indestor even sat with his back to a window, putting his face in shadow while leaving his visitors well-lit. Recognizing the techniques blunted their effectiveness, but didn't negate it entirely.

Mettore said, "I understand you're interested in getting a contract for your . . . people. To legitimize them as a mercenary force."

Now that *I wasn't expecting.* Vargo kept his posture relaxed, but allowed some of his puzzlement to show. "Interested, yes. But such contracts are rarely granted to delta gentry—much less to a simple businessman like myself."

"If I say it should be granted, it will happen," Mettore said bluntly. "In exchange, you will do something for me."

Vargo blinked. *Is this actually happening? Alsius?*

::. . . You told me to be quiet.::

Then Vargo's sense caught up with his astonishment. Mettore wasn't presenting this as a favor, then working his way around to casually mentioning some favor in return. *He's giving a dog a command and offering a treat if the dog obeys.*

::That's his way.::

Vargo smiled, sharp as a rookery knife. He wouldn't be here if Mettore had any other option. "That's very generous, Your Mercy. But what could I possibly do for you that you can't do yourself?"

If Mettore heard the implicit resistance, he didn't bother to acknowledge it. "The Night of Bells is in two weeks. I'd like Alta Renata to attend the Ceremony of the Accords at the Charterhouse. You can make certain she does."

The allure of a mercenary contract glittered less with every passing moment. No surprise that Mettore couldn't approach Renata— or any of the Traementis—himself, not after the debacle at the betrothal party. Nor was it a surprise that he might come to Vargo, as the person with the most to gain and the fewest scruples.

But "few" wasn't the same as "none." "Alta Renata has shown herself to be an extremely competent advocate, but I didn't think House Indestor lacked for such people. Why do you need her to attend the Accords?"

Mettore's gaze slid off to the right. He might as well have raised a banner saying, *I'm lying.*

"The Accords are a time for peace and reconciliation, are they not?" Mettore asked. "It's time this silly feud ended. But after that nonsense with Mezzan and the Traementis girl—well, they'd hardly accept an invitation from my hand."

Vargo's finger tapped twice before he stilled it. *Every hook needs a lure . . .*

::You can't actually be considering—::

Why not? He won't kidnap her or kill her at the Accords. It's too public. And the information we have on his ash dealings isn't nearly enough to sink him—not to the degree our plans require.

"House Indestor's dedication to keeping the peace in Nadežra is well-known, and Your Mercy's willingness to bridge this channel is admirable," Vargo said, painting a conflicted expression onto his face. "But I can't help worrying that someone might wish to curry your favor by avenging the insults to House Indestor." He shrugged. "Or perhaps I've seen too many theatricals."

The thinning of Mettore's lips said he was wearing on the man's patience. "Anyone who offers her harm will answer to me," he said. "Does that put your conscience to rest?" His tone questioned whether Vargo had a conscience at all.

Years of smiling charmingly when he wanted to murder someone were all that kept Vargo's pleasant expression in place. He believed Mettore was being honest . . . but in that moment, he didn't care.

As he was tensing to rise, though, Mettore added, with no subtlety at all, "You might gain the right to administer a military charter, rather than being merely contracted to one."

Vargo sank into his chair again. Now *that* was the sort of honey that could only come from Caerulet's hive. With administration rights, Vargo could offer Era Traementis the caravan protection she so desperately needed, and Indestor couldn't do anything to stop it. At least, not anything overt.

Fuck if he could tell what Mettore was really after, though. *Maybe he really does want reconciliation?* he thought at Alsius, not believing it for a moment.

::And I want a pony. But maybe you're right, and we can turn this to our advantage.::

Every night-piece has a price. "Full administration rights?" Vargo asked. "Standard charter?"

"Of course. On behalf of House Coscanum—I wouldn't want you to alienate your advocate. My secretary will draw up the details. He also has the invitation for Alta Renata." Mettore stood again, and Vargo bit down on the desire to make any snide parting comments about what a pleasure it was doing business.

But Mettore's voice caught him as his hand fell on the doorknob. "Naturally this arrangement stays between the two of us. I'm sure you can come up with some story as to how you obtained the invitation."

As though Vargo had any intention of telling Renata he'd just cast her onto the shoals to further his own interests. "I'm certain I'll think of something," he said, and let the door slam behind him as he left.

11

A Spiraling Fire

Isla Prišta, Westbridge: Cyprilun 17

Ren's jewelry box wasn't nearly as full as it used to be. Over the months she'd sold off many of the pieces she stole from Letilia before fleeing Ganllech, to extend her grace period with House Pattumo and her forged letter of credit. Lately she'd been doing her best to start a trend for minimalism, in the hopes that Renata's limited supply of jewelry could be read as elegant restraint rather than poverty, but her income from advocacy and the nascent river charter weren't enough to replace the missing items.

The only unworn piece she had left was a numinatrian medallion—the one Sibiliat was looking for. Almost as big across as her thumb, the many-sided bronze pendant was etched with Tricats: three overlapping triangles that stood for stability, community, and justice.

Which one the numinat was supposed to foster depended on the sigil etched at the center of the design, naming the god whose power it channeled. But Ren couldn't read Enthaxn, the archaic script from the empire that birthed Seteris, which inscriptors used to scribe the names of their gods. Nor was it one of the Seterin gods worshipped widely enough in the south for her to recognize its sigil.

She still wasn't sure why she'd pretended not to have it. Winning

Sibiliat over by returning an Acrenix family heirloom could've proven useful. But it might have looked suspicious—not to mention that Tricat also signified home, family, and the completion of plans. It was possible its power could help her complete her plan to get into the House Traementis register.

She traced one Tricat with the tip of her finger. The bronze wouldn't harmonize with the costume Tess was currently swearing at on the other side of the kitchen—as usual, Tess's vision threatened to outstrip her ability to finish the work in time—but numinata didn't have to be visible to work. Ren could hide it under her clothing, and Sibiliat would never know it was there.

The sound of a bell cut off Tess's stream of invective. Her head came up, body tensing to stillness. "Tell me I didn't just hear that," she whispered.

The bell rang again. The one at the front door.

"Get you upstairs! I'll stall as long as I'm able." Tess's needle-reddened fingers twisted her curls in a vain attempt to smooth away a sleepless night's worth of frizzing. The scowl on her face as she headed for the entry hall promised cheerful murder to the person tugging on the bell.

Ren darted up the stairs to the second floor before Tess answered the door. This wasn't the first time she'd had an unexpected visitor; cultivating a reputation for privacy didn't entirely prevent people from stopping by. She habitually wore a suitable house robe even while down in the kitchen and didn't remove her makeup until it was time to sleep, so she wouldn't be caught out if someone showed up without warning. But she hated having to shift modes so suddenly.

Voices drifted up from below. Ren couldn't quite make out the words, but Tess's brief comments were answered by a familiar baritone. *What the fuck is Vargo doing here?*

That wasn't a Renata thought, and she smoothed it away. Only when she was secure in her persona did she enter the salon they kept furnished for inconvenient visitors, one hand holding the robe shut over her underdress, as if she hadn't been up for hours already.

"Here's the alta now," Tess said. "Alta Renata, Master Vargo come to see you. I'll get tea."

Vargo craned his head to watch Tess's retreating back. "Did I do something to offend your maid? Perhaps she found some fault with the spoils from her most recent warehouse raid?"

"She's putting the finishing touches on my costume for this evening. Even I tread carefully at such times." Renata seated herself, wishing she had dressed properly. A house robe wasn't inappropriate attire for receiving a guest before noon, but Vargo's impeccable courtesy somehow made her even more self-conscious than if he'd acknowledged her informal state. "What brings you here at such an early hour?"

"The expected answer on a day like this is that I came for a peek at the alta's costume, but I already have an idea of what to look for tonight." He tapped his cheek, doing his best to look all-knowing, then dug into his coat pocket. "I'm a dull, business-minded fellow. I only came with an opportunity for you."

With a flourish that belied his claim to dullness, he presented her with an envelope of silk-smooth paper.

The seal displayed the five-pointed star of the Cinquerat. Curious, Renata broke the wax and unfolded the paper to reveal a card inside, inviting the bearer and one guest to attend the ceremony at the Charterhouse commemorating the signing of the Accords.

She couldn't prevent her startlement from showing. "How did you get this?"

"Trade secrets," he said, his voice rich with restrained laughter. "I'd go myself, but even the Vraszenians in attendance will be too important to speak with the likes of me. Besides, I already know Nadežra's history. You should have to sit through the official pageant at least once."

She'd seen many versions of it, staged in a variety of ways, ranging from blood-spattered horror to sex farce. The Charterhouse rendition, she imagined, would be more sedate. "Surely you have more in mind than my historical education."

"The entire Cinquerat will be there, with the usual crowd of hangers-on." Vargo leaned back in his chair, grinning. "Including Mettore Indestor, who will be in a particularly foul mood since he has to share a cup with a Vraszenian—Kiraly this year, I believe. Who knows what he might let slip?"

Renata's fingers tightened on the card. *Another dose.* That was what Mettore had told his hireling to get, the night Ren broke into his office. Poison? Could he be planning to assassinate the Kiraly clan leader? No, because they would be sharing the cup...but someone else at the event, perhaps.

She ran her thumb across the calligraphed letters and said, "If nothing else, I imagine there's benefit to being seen at such an event. Thank you."

"Anything for my favorite advocate." Vargo rose and bowed. "Don't bother Tess—I'll see myself out."

Dawngate, Old Island: Cyprilun 17

The streets of Nadežra were filled with noise and color and movement, from the Upper Bank to the Lower. Performers and vendors clogged the narrow lanes and bridges, and even on the wider spans of the two Island bridges, sedan chairs moved more slowly than snails, forcing their way through the crowds one hard-won step at a time. The skiffers would have no rest tonight, ferrying passengers back and forth across the river's two channels—but tomorrow they'd have their own celebration, spending the coin that had flooded into their pockets.

On a night like this, Renata could get away with forgoing the expense of a chair and simply heading north on foot. Tess followed close behind, guarding her hem as much as her back as they crossed the Sunset Bridge and slipped through the masses of people crowding the Old Island. Renata kept her hood up and her cloak held close, not wanting to risk damage to her costume before they reached the more exclusive precincts surrounding the Charterhouse.

Constables from the Vigil controlled the lanes leading to that area, keeping the riffraff at bay so the wealthy could enjoy the Night of Bells in greater safety and comfort. Renata passed them without difficulty and found herself in the marginally freer air of the plaza—where she stopped short, gazing in delight at the wonders all around her.

An enormous white curtain hung across the facade of the Theatre Agnasce, across which the dark silhouettes of shadow puppets danced, acting out a comedic scene. Just past them a troupe of acrobats built themselves into an impossibly tall tower, their throwers hurling a tiny woman through the air to balance atop the rest. Music echoed from the temporary shell facing the Charterhouse steps, and dancers whirled in dizzying glory across the pavement there, punctuated by a roar when a fire-breather spouted a great gout of flame into the air. The mix of scents was dizzying: roasting meats, spilled wine, perfumes of every variety masking the sweat of bodies underneath. Above it all, strings of colorful numinatrian lights bathed the entire area in a warm glow.

The river rat in Ren's heart spat at the sight of so many cuffs pissing their wealth away behind a protective cordon of hawks. But now she was one of them—pretending to be, anyway—and river rat or not, she couldn't stop her heart from lifting with delight at the beauty around her.

She paused to let a massive dreamweaver puppet by, with seven puppeteers for the trailing plumes of the bird's tail. As it passed, she found herself facing a familiar figure in tan-and-sapphire dress vigils.

Captain Serrado's eyes narrowed in recognition of her prismatium mask. Boots striking on the flagstones, he moved to her side. "Alta Renata. You arrived alone?"

"As you see." She unfastened the neck of her cloak and let Tess take the heavy fabric, revealing her costume.

The azure surcoat she'd worn to the Autumn Gloria had given its life for this night, Tess shredding the fabric of the foreskirt and backskirt into strips that fluttered with her every movement, while the bodice flowed over her figure like water. More strips dangled from her sleeves, those on the right in a dozen shades of blue and green, those on the left fading into grey. The fabric would reappear in future garments, but Tess had glowed with smug pride when she realized she could use her scraps to suggest streams of water without spending another centira.

"The Dežera?" Serrado asked, even as Tess replaced the cloak with a drape of mist-silver organza that settled around Renata's shoulders like fog. "I would have expected something more Seterin."

"On the night when Nadežra celebrates its freedom from a foreign tyrant? It seemed more appropriate to honor the city—and House Traementis's new charter." Renata swept her arms outward, so the ribbons of fabric displayed to full effect. "But unless you're so lacking in imagination that you couldn't think of any costume other than 'Vigil captain,' I take it you're on duty."

"I wouldn't claim to have the alta's gift for creativity." His tone was mild, but she couldn't help wondering if there was a rebuke hidden in those words. "On festival days, all officers of the Vigil are expected to be a visible presence, whether we're on duty or not." He shifted as a passing crowd following a pair of stilt-walkers threatened to wash over them, protecting Renata from being swept along.

Sudden murmurs erupted from the crowd. Renata, hoping for some way to escape Serrado, glanced in that direction—and gasped involuntarily.

A real dreamweaver soared through the air above the plaza, swooping low to investigate his puppet cousin. In the colorful numinatrian light, his iridescence rippled through the full spectrum of the rainbow, the usual blues and greens and violets shading over to the warmer tones of fire.

"What is it?" Serrado turned in the direction of her gaze, right hand going instinctively for his sword. It dropped when he spotted the bird alighting on the puppet's head. The dreamweaver pecked a few times at the colorful paper feathers before twisting a clump free and flying off again.

Ren turned with the crowd to follow her flight, and was

astonished to see a slow, unguarded smile spread across Grey Serrado's face.

It dimmed only a little when he caught her looking. "The first dreamweaver of the season," he said. "You know what that means?"

Ren had to swallow down the answer her Vraszenian heart wanted to make. *Of course I do.*

Already musicians were striking up a tune as old as the Dežera, and the people around them were pairing off, forming a large circle of a sort never seen in Seterin or Liganti dances. Serrado took her silence for uncertainty, and held out one hand. "Tradition says we dance now, to welcome the season of the river's flooding. Don't worry—I'll show you how." One brow quirked in challenge, waiting to see if the Seterin alta would turn her nose up at Vraszenian customs.

That wasn't the problem. The problem was that, having pretended to know dances she'd never performed before, now she had to pretend *not* to know one she'd loved since she was old enough to toddle alongside her mother.

One of the acrobats had already swept up Tess, leaving Ren and Serrado the only ones unpartnered. She laid her hand in his. "How could the river not join in at such a time?"

It was a dance meant for everyone, from children to the old to the infirm, so the steps weren't complicated: a circle round that turned to laughter when it shifted direction, causing everyone to knock shoulders with their neighbors, and then again when the circling stopped. Serrado held firm in place as Ren was crushed against him by several neighboring dancers who apparently didn't know how to count to eight. But it was all in good fun, and after he'd righted her, she skipped into the middle with the other women, before spinning back out to her partner in a tangle of blue ribbons.

Like many Vraszenian dances, it sped up as it went, until the final figure called for them to spin in pairs around locked hands, so fast the rest of the world blurred. Ren came out breathless, dizzy, and laughing, as did everyone else—including Serrado. He tried to steady her, but given that he was swaying like a man who'd drunk too much aža-laced wine, he wasn't much help. Which only made them both laugh more.

"Thank you," she said when she'd gulped enough air to form words. "That was..."

She trailed off, utterly unable to think of what comment a Seterin alta should make. Serrado rescued her by saying, "A pleasure. Which is what dancing should be. But tell Alta Parma not that I said such things."

He might as well have been a different man: smiling, laughing, forgetting himself enough that he dropped into the throaty tones of his native accent. He still wore the uniform of a hawk, but now it *looked* like a costume—and underneath it she could see Leato's friend, the man welcomed into Traementis Manor despite the differences of ancestry and rank.

Him and his brother. She watched the shadow of guilt settle over his expression, like a cloud masking the sun. Ren remembered the first time she'd laughed after her mother died...something Tess had said, though she no longer remembered the specifics. Only the guilt stayed with her, that she could be so careless as to laugh when Ivrina Lenskaya was gone from the world.

She was so used to seeing Serrado as a threat to her masquerade that sympathy caught her like a blow under the ribs. Of course he was grim. His brother was dead, and even a captain's hexagram pin couldn't bring him the justice he sought. His family was broken; no amount of wanting could make it whole again.

As though realizing he'd shown too much, Serrado shuttered away the sadness. "I'll leave you to your evening, alta," he said, his voice and demeanor blandly Nadežran once more. One bow later, he was gone.

"Whoof! That was a bit of fun, wasn't it?" Tess stumbled up, fanning herself with her mask. Then, remembering where they were, she lowered her eyes and tamped down on her smile. "I hope the alta wasn't offered any insult. I understand this is a local custom."

"A very energetic one," Renata said, using her own breathlessness to cover for anything out of place. "You may enjoy yourself,

Tess, as long as you keep near the musicians. I will find you if I need anything."

With Tess freed to her own entertainments, Renata soon lost herself in the swirl of celebration. The costumes in the Charterhouse plaza tended toward Liganti and Seterin themes—the various numina and their associated planets, figures from history and legend—but to her surprise, she counted no less than six Rooks in the space of an hour, four male and two female, most of them young delta blades who thought it very daring to take on the guise of an outlaw who despised their kind. Four of them danced with her, the last of whom was Oksana Ryvček.

"What luck to find the river so nearby," she said, pressing closer to Renata to avoid the elbows of a passing Ghusai sultan. Close enough that her intimate murmur was easy to hear even over the din. "After all this dancing, I crave a sip of cool water."

Renata offered her right hand to kiss—the one representing the pure East Channel, rather than the polluted West. "Mistress Ryvček. I commend your originality; the three Rooks before you tried to get me to surrender a glove."

"Ah, but have I not one already?" Ryvček's words were warm against the net that covered Renata's fingers. "It only seems sporting to leave an alta her modesty."

Ryvček danced with the same confidence as Leato or Captain Serrado, and a good deal more panache. After a breathless series of turns ending on a sedate promenade, she said, "Speaking of sporting, I have watched you at the Palaestra. Leato goes easy on you. The next time you're there, I'll give you a real lesson with the blade."

"Thank you, Mistress Ryvček," Renata said—hoping she wouldn't regret accepting the offer. Judging by the wink Ryvček gave her just before vanishing into the crowd, the ambiguity was intentional.

She does it on purpose. But that didn't make it any less effective.

Renata glanced around, wondering if she should climb the Charterhouse steps to scan the plaza. She had a half-formed notion to look for Mezzan Indestor and see if she could provoke him into revealing anything. She'd met with Idusza twice since the Kindly Hawk, but it hadn't yielded anything useful, even though Ren had cold-decked her in order to strongly hint that Idusza's lover was keeping dangerous secrets. Instead Idusza wanted to recruit Arenza into the Stadnem Anduske, saying that her talents would be greatly valued there. At their last meeting the woman had admitted point-blank that they wanted to steal something—the saltpeter Renata had worked so hard to secure for Quientis—and wanted the guidance of pattern before they moved.

It wasn't that Ren minded assisting them. The saltpeter had already served its purpose for Renata; if it could help Arenza, too, so much the better. But she was reluctant to involve herself with them without any surety that it would shed slight on Mezzan's activities.

It did make her wonder if Mettore planned to frame the Anduske for whatever scheme he had devised. Their leader, Koszar Andrejek, had published a broadsheet last year condemning the ziemetse, the leaders of the six surviving clans, for bending the knee to the Cinquerat. It wouldn't be hard for Mettore to persuade everyone that Andrejek had abandoned words in favor of more drastic measures.

She didn't have any leverage to make Mezzan talk, though, unless she threatened to reveal his secret relationship. And Ren wasn't nearly desperate enough for that yet.

Deciding that she might as well look for Leato and Giuna instead, and enjoy herself for a time, Ren turned toward the steps—and this time came face-to-face with Derossi Vargo.

She nearly swallowed her tongue. Vargo's open, ground-length coat of whisper-thin indigo silk was weighted with tiny jet beads that ticked against each other with every breath. Its cobweb embroidery carried over to his bare chest, gold-dusted skin shimmering with traceries of black, and blue brilliants caught in the web like dew in shadow. Those same brilliants wove through his loose, dark hair and sparkled at the corners of his kohl-rimmed eyes. A sheer veil that barely qualified as a mask draped across his lower face, doing nothing to hide the smirk of a man who knew exactly how provocative he looked.

With a hand bare of anything but gold dust, he lifted Renata's glove to his lips. "Blessing of the Tyrant's downfall," he said. "May the waters of the Dežera renew us all."

If invited to wager on Vargo's costume for the night, Renata would have bet on Kaius Rex himself. She assumed Vargo would want to associate himself with someone powerful, and knew he was cynical enough to dress as someone both powerful and despised. Instead, he had chosen the guise of one of the three courtesans who—according to legend—had brought down the unkillable Tyrant with venereal disease.

It was an audacious gesture of contempt toward the city's elite . . . but laid against that was the open invitation of his body, provocative and mocking at once.

Vargo's smirk deepened. He kept hold of her hand, curling it into the warmth of his bare chest as he stepped closer. "I hear a dreamweaver was spotted earlier. Doesn't that mean it's too late in the winter for the river to stand frozen? Much better to hear her rushing breathless. Care to dance?"

Renata scrambled to find words. The best she managed to come up with was "Lead the way."

Out among the dancers, she resolved not to let his attire distract her into clumsiness. But the intensity she'd seen in his eyes the day she delivered the charter echoed in his every movement, heating the air between them, making her pulse race.

Unlike the Dreamweaver's Welcome or the dances she'd learned in the Traementis ballroom, the dance Vargo drew her into was meant for pairs alone. She wound up snared in a loose embrace, his hand warm against her shoulder. Searching for some safer resting place than his kohl-lined eyes, her gaze alighted on the scar torn through the side of his throat; he'd made no attempt to hide it, letting his dangerous past speak for itself. When her eyes skittered away, she found herself staring at the painted skin of his chest, which held its own danger.

This close, she could see some kind of mark, not quite fully hidden by the paint. Its circular shape suggested some kind of numinatrian tattoo, but she couldn't make out the details without obviously staring.

If she didn't find something else to focus on, she was going to embarrass herself. She dragged her gaze up to meet his. "People say I've been setting Nadežra on its ear, but you seem determined to spin it around until no one knows which way is up."

"Given this costume, I think whichever Kaius I choose tonight will be up, and I will be down." Vargo's chuckle said it was more than a metaphor. And yet the jet-glitter of disdain in his eyes could have belonged to the original courtesan whose guise he wore. "Isn't that always the way of it for Nadežrans?"

"You would know better than I."

So his pragmatism extended to himself. She wondered what he intended to gain tonight, and who he intended to gain it from. Derossi Vargo wasn't just out to scrape whatever wealth and status he could from the edges of the city's current power structure; he wanted to break the structures that blocked him from his goals. And he would use whatever tools he had—including his own body—to make that happen.

Ren had limits. Vargo, it seemed, did not. It chilled her a little, but also made for an odd sense of camaraderie; they were not so different, the two of them.

Vargo was silent until the tempo and time of the music changed, signaling the beginning of the next dance. Then he led her out, stopping near a young and very muscular Kaius she recognized as Fadrin Acrenix. Acrenix, however, wasn't looking at her at all; his attention was entirely on Vargo.

"I believe this is where we part for the evening," Vargo said with a faint smile.

The ease with which he dropped her hand to take up Fadrin's sent a shiver down Renata's spine, one that stayed with her as she retreated, no longer in the mood to dance.

Long tables laid at the edges of the plaza served drinks and food, and at one of them she caught sight of a familiar copper surcoat picked out in Tricat patterns of pearls. Renata pressed one hand to her chest, where the Acrenix medallion lay hidden under her dress. Tricat to Tricat: Surely it would do some good.

Certainly Donaia seemed pleased to see her as Renata approached. "Are you enjoying the festival, my dear?" she asked with a smile.

"The masks add a fascinating touch. As do the puppets," Renata said. All the Vraszenian clan animals were represented tonight: the Anoškin ghost owl soaring overhead; the Meszaros horse circling the plaza in stately procession; the Varadi spider, the Stretsko rat, the Dvornik fox, and the Kiraly raccoon; and of course, the dream-weaver, emblem of the dead Ižranyi. Displays of that kind were common throughout the city, but she was surprised to find them here, at the heart of Liganti power.

She groaned inwardly as another Rook approached them, but it turned into a coughing fit when she realized the man under the hood was none other than Leato.

"I hoped to leave you lost for words, but not like that." Leato's drawl scraped the bottom of his usual tenor. The tailoring of his costume was similar enough to the Rook's to be instantly recognizable, but scattered brilliants caught the light of the numinatrian lamps, like stars on a field of velvet black. The shadows cast by his hood were unremarkable; the line of his jaw and curve of his smile were clearly his and not some magically obscured stranger's.

Still, she found herself comparing him to the man she'd stood beside in Mettore's office. Was Leato the right height? His shoulders the right breadth? It would suit the Rook's reputation to pull a stunt like this, showing up to the Night of Bells in a theatrical version of his own disguise.

Leato handed her a flute of cider. "Though I realize the irony of offering a drink to the river herself. Let me know if you'd rather I gave you a good thump on the back—you seem to need one."

"Leato!" Donaia knocked the hood from his head, revealing his golden, artfully mussed hair. "What are you thinking, dressing like this? Do you want to pick another fight with Mezzan Indestor?"

He pressed a hand to his chest as though deeply affronted. "Mother, give me some credit. Of course I don't want to pick a fight with him." He tipped Renata a wink. "I'm hoping he'll pick a fight with me."

"Oh, you impossible boy." Throwing up her hands, Donaia turned away.

"Quitting the field so soon, Mother?" Leato called after her.

Donaia paused, favoring them both with the cool look Renata was coming to recognize as a mask to hide her affection. "No. Leaving you under the command of a more cunning general than myself. Do try to keep him out of trouble, my dear?"

Renata didn't even try to hide her smile. Letilia was wrong; that had become too clear to deny. Donaia, far from being the controlling harridan she'd expected, only wanted to protect her family—much like her son. That desire united them, and since Renata had gotten them the charter, it swept her into their circle rather than closing her out.

Now if only it would sweep me into their damned register.

She offered Donaia her best curtsy. "One can only do one's mortal best."

"Good. Then I'm off to find something stronger than this fizzing fruit juice."

"I've driven my mother to drink," Leato mused fondly as she departed. Then he shook himself and glanced down at Renata. "Are you intending to keep me in line? I'd rather hoped I could lure you off into less wholesome amusement."

He did a good job of playing the careless man-about-town, but Renata knew it was a facade. Stepping in close, she said, "Actually...I thought I might lure *you* off somewhere unwholesome."

Leato's gaze fell to her mouth, and his own lips parted on a response that never came. With visible effort, he drew himself up and leaned even closer, murmuring, "That's hardly fair. You're supposed to be the responsible one. If you keep offering invitations like that, I'm liable to lose another glove to you."

Every other Rook save Ryvček had asked for one of her gloves;

none had offered one in return. Renata searched Leato's eyes, wondering if he was rendering a coded apology for that confrontation in Lacewater. But she saw only temptation there, a softer, less confrontational version of what Vargo had offered.

She hadn't expected this—any of it—when she set out to infiltrate House Traementis. Not that she would find the family charming, not that she would suspect the son of being the Rook, not that she would wind up genuinely liking Leato. She might be like Vargo in some ways... but maybe she didn't have to be as cold.

No killing, no whoring. Her two rules. But was it whoring if she chose it for herself, out of attraction instead of profit? Was it using Leato if her interest was one of the few truths she could give him?

His hand rose to cup her chin. She could easily have pulled away, but there was warmth in his touch, in his eyes, and she was tired of being cold.

Leato tasted of apples and cinnamon, the cider lingering on his lips and tongue. And like a sip of cider, the heat of his kiss slid down her throat and blossomed through her. His thumb brushed the hard line of feathers curving along her cheek, and she would have pressed up, hungry for another taste, but he was already pulling away.

"You see?" he said softly, a light touch still slipping along her jaw. "You don't need to lure me anywhere. I'm quite content to follow."

Renata licked the last traces of the kiss from her lips. He had utterly distracted her from what she meant to say. "I, ah—oh, Lumen, now I'm going to disappoint you." Reaching into the fluttering layers of her costume, she drew out the Accords invitation. "When I said somewhere unwholesome, I meant the Charterhouse."

Leato reared back, blinking at the invitation, at her. Then he laughed and ruffled his hair ruefully. "Surprise, yes. Disappoint, never. Wherever did you get that? You realize my family hasn't been invited to the Accords since we lost the Fulvet seat to House Quientis. Their way of reminding us we don't matter anymore." The touch of bitterness sobered him, but then it softened into a smile. "I'd love to accompany you."

He shifted back a half step. "But if I'm to do that, I need to go disappoint some people myself first. I'll meet you at the steps when the bells sound?"

At Renata's mute nod, he bowed, pulled up his hood, and slipped away into the crowd.

"Well. I suppose if you can't be adopted in, that's the next best route," Sibiliat drawled, sauntering up to Renata with Giuna tucked against her side. Their costumes were a coordinated pair: Sibiliat in moon-blue and silver as bright Corillis, and Giuna in green and copper as shy Paumillis.

"Don't be mean," Giuna said, but not even Sibiliat's barb could dim the radiant smile she turned on Renata. "You don't know how hard I worked to keep her from interrupting you two."

Renata was glad of her mask, which helped to hide her blush. She almost retaliated with a comment about Sibiliat's own pursuit of Giuna, but swallowed it for Giuna's sake—and because she still didn't know why Sibiliat was playing with the girl. Giuna was easy enough to read; she wanted to be seen as an adult instead of a child, to move out from under Donaia's sheltering wings and Leato's shadow. But Sibiliat...

The world spun in a dizzying arc, making her stagger. Giuna caught her elbow, her face etched with worry. "Are you all right?"

"Too warm," Renata managed, not sure if it was an excuse or the truth. The curl of Sibiliat's lip said she blamed the unsteadiness on too much drink. "If you'll pardon me, I think I should find somewhere to sit for a few minutes."

"Let us help you." Giuna started to lead Renata away, but Sibiliat caught her trailing shawl like it was a leash, tugging her back.

"Don't be silly, little bird. Weren't you just saying that sometimes people appreciate being left alone? Besides, your cousin's a grown woman. *She* can take care of herself." The edge that crept into Sibiliat's voice wasn't for Renata's benefit. And judging from Giuna's blush, it cut just as intended.

Renata would have tried to do something for Giuna, but she wasn't lying about wanting to sit down. The world kept echoing around her, like a ringing in her bones instead of her ears, and every time she looked at Sibiliat she felt even shakier.

With a nod at Giuna, she moved toward the edge of the crowd, away from the lights and the noise, closer to the shadowed corners of the plaza, and the feeling slowly faded. The corners too were occupied, and the sounds coming from them made it clear why, but she found a wall she could lean against and catch her breath. For once she was glad of the chill air.

She never used to have trouble keeping attraction from influencing her behavior . . . but tonight there'd been Vargo, then Leato. She brushed her lips with her fingertips. *I'm losing track of my real purpose.* Which was dangerous.

The minutes slipped by and she stayed where she was, leaning against the wall, ignoring the curious looks from passersby. And because she was at the edge of the plaza, she saw when a blot of darkness appeared from behind the enormous light that illuminated the puppet theatre's canvas screen: a man slipping up the front stairs of the theatre, unnoticed amid the lights and noise of the masquerade.

Another Rook. One who'd concealed his approach to the theatre—and whose costume didn't glitter like every other Rook she'd danced with.

It's him. Ren pushed away from the wall. How much time had passed? Enough for Leato to change from one Rook costume to another—or to somehow transform the festival version into the real thing?

Before she could think twice, she slipped up the stairs and through the doors behind him.

The theatre had been transformed by painted papier-mâché columns and arches to resemble a cleaner version of the Depths, the catacombs that riddled the foundations of the Old Island. The flickering light of candles cast the arches and shadows into even more confusion. Instead of sewage, mold, and rot, the air carried the faded scents of beeswax, wet paper, woodsmoke, and sweat.

Out of the corner of her eye, Renata saw a figure pacing her in the next row of columns. She spun, heart thudding...and realized it was her own reflection, staring back at her with wide eyes and a hand halfway to the knife strapped to her calf.

All around her, other reflections wearing the same shimmering prismatium mask cast rainbows from the glass.

A mirror maze. She'd heard of them; the glassworkers' guild sometimes set them up during festivals as a way of advertising their wares.

How was she supposed to follow the Rook in this?

A playful shriek and echo of laughter from ahead told her that was an unlikely direction to explore. Setting a hand to the mirror that had frightened her, she veered left into the maze.

The countless moving reflections kept confounding her, and the columns made it seem like she wandered endless hallways. More than once she thought she'd found an opening, only to discover the hard way that it was a cleverly angled mirror. But after a time, she started looking at the ground rather than what lay ahead of her, and then it became easier. There was a logic to the maze, a pattern to where it branched and turned; she began following the rhythm of that, only glancing up periodically to look for a telltale shadow moving between the reflected lights.

Not often enough. She almost missed him—in fact she would have, except he stepped back to hide, only to bump into a mirror where there seemed to be empty space.

A breath of stillness passed. Two. Then another hoot of laughter broke from the next passage over, jarring them both into motion.

He caught her before she could decide what to do, grabbing her wrist and pulling her into what turned out to be a dead end. The finger he raised to the shadows of his hood was an unnecessary warning. The laughter increased in volume as the other group exploring the maze approached. Ren recognized Fadrin Acrenix's voice, boasting in graphic detail what he'd done with "that jumped-up Lower Bank night-piece," and then an unsettled reprimand from Iascat Novrus, Sostira's adopted heir. The words echoed and then faded as they moved on.

Once the party of chattering nobles had taken themselves off to another part of the maze, the Rook released her wrist. "If you've come to demand the return of your glove, I'm afraid you'll be disappointed. It's gone the way of Mezzan Indestor's sword."

"I don't give a damn about the glove," she said, keeping her voice low. "I want to know if you killed Kolya Serrado."

It wasn't what she'd meant to ask. She'd followed with the intent of asking him point-blank whether he was Leato or not. But the pain she'd seen in Serrado tonight, the distance between two men who had once been close . . . she had to heal that if she could.

For her own sake, too. For the child who'd once adored stories of the Rook and had to know whether he'd crossed that line.

The papier-mâché column he'd braced himself against crunched under his grip.

"Yes." The admission was like jagged glass, shredding one of her last remaining childhood illusions.

"But you *don't kill*." It burst out before she could stop it, the protest of Ren instead of Renata Viraudax. The Rook's head came up, and she rushed onward to cover. "I've heard the stories. The Rook—you—you aren't a murderer."

"Tell that to Kolya Serrado," he hissed. He turned away, but came up against his reflection boxing them in, black glove pressing against the glass.

Ren prided herself on her ability to read people, and tonight that ability had been preternaturally sharp. But she couldn't read the Rook. With his body shrouded in leather and silk, his face hidden in shadow, his back to her, the entire thing could have been an act put on for her benefit.

But she didn't think so.

"The fire killed him," he said into the mirror, so softly that she had to strain to hear it. "I didn't start it. But it's my fault he was caught in it."

Relief gutted her. *Not a murderer.* The guilt he carried was of a different sort.

He twisted, addressing her over his shoulder. "What interest does a Seterin alta have in the Rook? Or in a dead Vraszenian, for that matter?"

What answer could she give? Ren opened her mouth, not sure what she would say—and outside, the bells began to ring. Legend said the same bells had miraculously rung the night the Tyrant died, rippling outward from the Charterhouse tower and across the city to announce the passing of the man who'd held the land of Vraszan in his grip for decades.

The Rook looked up as though he could see the bells through the roof. The faint light showed his jaw tightening, but his voice was deceptively light. "A puzzle for another time, it seems."

Opening his coat to shield Renata, he shattered the mirror at her side with a slam of his elbow.

"I trust you can find your own way out?" he said, as shards rained down from the top of the frame. On the other side of the broken mirror hung a heavy canvas drape. Glass crunched under his boots as he pulled it aside to reveal a door set into a paneled wall.

"Blessings of the Tyrant's downfall upon you, Alta Renata," the Rook said. With that, he escaped through the door.

Charterhouse, Dawngate, Old Island: Cyprilun 17

Renata was out of breath and full of questions by the time she made it to the Charterhouse steps, none of which were answered by seeing Leato waiting there. She already knew the Rook's disguise was imbued; it might transform from practical garb to gaudy costume with almost no effort at all.

The curious look he turned on her was no evidence, either. He didn't act like a man she'd just accused of murder . . . but Ren lied too well herself to trust anyone else's mask of innocence.

Among the dignitaries assembled on the steps, the five members of the Cinquerat stood out. Clothed in the colors of their seats—grey, brown, green, blue, and the many-hued silks of Iridet—they looked bored and ready for the night to be over with. Mettore was scowling at Leato, the hard set of his jaw visible beneath his sapphire-studded mask.

Then he looked at her, and the bottom dropped out of Ren's stomach.

It's me.

She knew it with the instinct that had guided her mother in reading patterns, the same instinct that had translated the pattern she'd laid on the kitchen floor. The missing information signaled by The Mask of Fools, the message Lark Aloft promised was coming— it was *her*.

And she'd handed herself to him.

The peal of the bells was fading into the distance. Everyone began climbing the steps, passing through the great double doors. Renata's only choices were to follow, or to publicly flee.

A choice made more difficult as Leato took her arm. "Renata?" he asked when she didn't move with the others. "Don't waver on me now. Mother was positively gleeful when I told her you'd landed an invitation."

Her hands tensed. *I need this*, she thought. To get into House Traementis. And she'd put herself in front of Mettore at the engagement party; the damage was done. She didn't know what information he'd gotten from her, what she'd supplied that he'd been lacking... but he already had it.

What would he *do* with it?

The only way to find out was to keep an eye on him. Renata allowed Leato to escort her through the great archway and the public atrium, the five stern statues of the Cinquerat glaring disapproval at her. Beyond them lay the audience hall where the council issued public pronouncements. Renata and the other observers filtered through the rising arcs of benches that overlooked the floor, while Mettore and the others took their seats on the dais, facing the door.

When they were ready, a single bell tolled.

The show of power wasn't subtle: the Cinquerat entering first, with their people, into their own halls of power, then ringing for the

Vraszenian delegation like they were servants. But the Vraszenians knew the ceremony, and had a century and a half of practice at subverting it.

First to appear was a team of four bays pulling a beautifully joined and painted wagon filled with the traditional gifts the clans brought in offering. It was for show only; they must have carried both wagon and gifts up the steps and harnessed the team at the top. The driver was another show of false humility. His raccoon mask and the rich silver and grey embroidery of his panel coat marked him as the Kiralič, the head of the Kiraly clan. Renata wasn't certain how he managed it, but as he circled his team around the audience hall, the lead horse let tumble a cascade of droppings right in front of the Cinquerat seats. They broke on the five-pointed star laid into the floor, and the wagon's wheels ground them into the grout between the tiles.

Mettore Indestor's stony facade twisted into fury, and only Era Destaelio's hand clamping down on his arm kept him in his seat.

After the first pass, the driver stopped the wagon in the middle of the room, and the rest of the ziemetse who led the clans filed in, followed by their retinues. A young woman in Kiraly colors hurried forward to take charge of the team so their clan leader could join the line of ziemetse, but nobody moved to do anything about the horse droppings, scattered between the standing Vraszenians and the seated Cinquerat like a gauntlet thrown.

The Vraszenians made a splendid display, easily as grand as the Cinquerat, but in a wildly different style. The men's panel coats were sumptuously embroidered, the back panels so thick with silk thread the fabric underneath could barely be seen. The women's sash belts were the same, and fine lace dyed crimson and saffron edged the slightly belled ends of their sleeves. Men and women alike had pinned their hair into elaborate constructs of braids, with charms of knotted silk cord dangling from the ends of the pins: the triple clover for family, the rose of Ažerais for good luck, and the great flat-woven knots symbolizing their role as the representatives of their lineages, their clans, and the Vraszenian people as a whole.

"Ryzorn Evmeleski Kupalt of Clan Dvornik gives greetings to

the Cinquerat of Nadežra," said a dapper old gentleman on the far end of the line, doffing a cap from his bald pate and bowing with a grandiose flourish. Even without the name, his mask and green embroidery marked him as leading the clan of the fox.

The next of the ziemetse was one of the lihoše, like the person Renata had seen bargaining with Vargo at the warehouses. "Sedlien Hrišaske Njersto of Clan Meszaros gives greetings to the Cinquerat of Nadežra," he said. He was the only Vraszenian looking at the horse apples with disapproval.

On down the line it went, from oldest to youngest of the clan elders: the Kiralič struggling to look stern in the aftermath of his trick and the grey-haired Varadič with his eyes narrowed in calculation; the Anoškinič with his ghost owl mask hiding his expression, and the Stretskojič watching the rest of the crowd as though he expected an attack.

Until they came to the seventh, standing slightly apart. Her black braids were silver-shot, and her dreamweaver mask was made from the feathers of the birds themselves. "I am Szorsa Mevieny Plemaskaya Straveši. I stand for Clan Ižranyi, in memory of the kin who died when the city of Fiavla fell. May we never forget their names; may we never forget their spirits, lost even to Ažerais. May we never again face the Primordial horror that turned sister against brother, husband against wife, until the ground of Fiavla itself wept blood."

Her words produced a chill in the room, and in Ren's bones. Even growing up in Nadežra, she'd heard the stories; everyone knew why there were only six Vraszenian clans, where once there had been seven. The slaughter was centuries in the past, but the memory lived on: a whole city overwhelmed by the madness of the ancient forces imprisoned outside reality by the gods. Something had slipped free of those chains and infected Fiavla. One day it was a prosperous city, the heart of the Ižranyi. Eleven days later, every person bearing that clan's name—whether in Fiavla or not—was dead.

Sostira Novrus broke the silence. Dressed in the pearl-grey robes of Argentet, she stood with a false smile and began a speech about Nadežra's great history.

Ren's teeth worried her lip. Was there any way Mettore could have figured out the truth—that she was kin to these Vraszenians in their animal masks? But if so, it made more sense that he would wait for Renata to be scribed into House Traementis before he revealed her true identity. For the Liganti, connections were built out of contracts, not blood; there was nothing preventing a family from adopting a Vraszenian woman. For a noble house, though, the scandal would be devastating.

Right now, he just looked bored. This ceremony happened every year; he must have sat through it a dozen times, with each Cinquerat seat in turn making a speech and being answered by the clan leaders. Ren herself would have been bored if her mind weren't racing, mapping out different ways this could all go wrong. She kept coming back to *another dose* again and again, then running aground on the fact that the council and the clans would drink from shared cups, and that poisoning someone here would be deeply unsubtle.

Besides, the cards had spoken of magic, not murder.

The Nadežran and Vraszenian leaders seated themselves for the pageant, while a servant finally scurried out to clean away the droppings. Then the actors took the floor: a Kaius Rex in splendid armor, against six people representing the scattered might of Vraszan and its conquered city-states.

Ren knew the story the way any Vraszenian child did. How Kaius Sifigno had sailed an army across the sea from Seste Ligante to conquer the broad, rich valley of the River Dežera; how he made his stronghold in their holy city, the site of Ažerais's wellspring, banishing the Vraszenians and forbidding them her blessing for nearly forty years. When he died, the clans drove his forces from most of Vraszan, but failed to retake the city. After eleven years of war, they finally settled for a truce: the right to visit the wellspring and hold their conclave around the Great Dream every seven years, in exchange for leaving the city in foreign-born hands.

She wasn't surprised to see the Charterhouse pageant tell a different story. This version showed no particular interest in Vraszenian traditions; instead it focused on the Tyrant himself, how he could have conquered not just Vraszan but half the world had he not become lost in the indulgence of his own desires. The actor playing Kaius—an Extaquium cousin she vaguely recognized—didn't hold back in depicting the Tyrant's cruelty, his greed, his gluttony and lust. Legend said he could not be killed. Many people tried—with blades, with arrows, with poisons, with black powder—but he seemed to lead a charmed life, always evading even the most well-laid attempts. Only when word leaked out from his palace that he'd caught a simple flu did the courtesans of Nadežra realize he had a vulnerability: disease.

According to the stories, one of the three courtesans to bring the Tyrant down had been a Vraszenian man, and all the clans claimed that man as their own. This year, somebody in the Charterhouse must have wanted to curry favor with the Varadi, because that courtesan was depicted in blue and spiderweb embroidery. Ren wondered if Vargo had caught wind of the pageant preparations before choosing his own costume.

All three were executed for their treachery, of course. The Tyrant went on a rampage when he realized he was ill. But nothing could cure him—not imbued medicine, not numinatria, not prayers and sacrifices to the gods—and so he rotted away, the victim of his own excesses.

When everyone lay silent on the floor, the female courtesan rose. Their names were all lost to history, assuming any such trio had ever existed; by tradition, she was simply referred to as Nadežra. In a simple, clear voice, she described the war that followed, and the peace struck between the first Cinquerat and the clan leaders of the time. "And so, in honor of that accord," she said, "we gather on this night of miracles, at the hour when the bells tolled with no hand to ring them, and we share a cup as we once shared sorrows."

Along the tiers of benches, servants were passing with trays of goblets, distributing one per two people. At the head of the room, the members of the Cinquerat descended from their seats, each one pairing with a Vraszenian counterpart. Mettore, she saw, stood as far as courtesy allowed from the Kiralič. His expression of restrained distaste mirrored the one worn by the Meszarič, paired with the courtesan playing Nadežra—a tradition born of necessity, in order to match five Cinquerat seats with six clan leaders. Only Scaperto Quientis seemed to be enjoying himself, chuckling at something the Dvornič murmured into his ear.

Leato took the glass the servant passed to him and held it up so Renata could fold her fingers around his.

"To Nadežra, and to the peace that benefits us all," the actress said, and drained half her glass. The Meszaros clan leader finished it.

"To Nadežra," every voice in the hall echoed. Leato tugged the glass toward him, careful to drink only half.

Then it was Renata's turn. A rainbow shimmered across the surface and along the inner sides of the glass. Aža was supposed to be sacred; in the years when Ažerais's wellspring didn't flow, people customarily added a bit of the drug to their wine to simulate the water's effects, a little dream in echo of the great one. Ren had been a child when she first tasted it, and she'd giggled through the rest of the night, batting at things that weren't there. It wasn't meant for mockeries like this masquerade of peace.

"Cousin?" Leato whispered. "You have to drink."

Everyone else had done so. *He wouldn't poison us*, Ren thought wildly. *It's too public. He didn't even know we would be here tonight.*

She tipped the cup to her lips and drank.

The wine slid across her tongue and down her throat, like an oil slick instead of shimmering light. Leato grimaced in sympathy. "I think it's gone off."

It wasn't off. It was *wrong*. It burned in her throat, seared through her until her necklace and mask and gown burned her skin. The light around her fractured into sickly rainbows, forming a web of threads connecting her to Leato, to Mettore, threads everywhere she looked. She heard murmurs from the crowd, people turning to one another with worried expressions, and she tried to speak, to warn them that they should run.

But it was too late. The world was unraveling around her, the warp and weft sliding apart, and she fell through the gaps between.

12

Drowning Breath

The Charterhouse was empty.

No Leato. No Cinquerat. No clan leaders with their wagon.

Ren was alone.

"What the..."

Her whisper echoed through the silence, and a shiver ran down her back. When she shifted her foot, even the brief scuff of her shoe resounded. The audience chamber was impressively large when filled with people; when it held only one, it was cavernous. The weight of the empty air beat down on Ren, making her pulse speed up, her mouth turn dry, even though there was nothing to fear. She was tiny. Insignificant. A fleeting spark that would soon be snuffed out.

She was moving before she knew it, down the risers, the echoes of her footsteps building and multiplying and chasing her toward the door, back toward the light and the life of the plaza—

"Stir the pot," Ivrina said, "then come sit with me."

Ren blinked. *I...know this house.*

The stove with its pot, the small table, the knotted curtain that separated the kitchen from the front parlour where her mother laid out patterns for her clients. Upstairs was the bedroom, and outside was Lacewater, with its narrow lanes and smelly canals. Everything was warm and cozy and familiar, down to the deep scratch at one end of the table and the chipped flagstone by the back door.

I'm home. The realization wove through her bones, restoring a fabric she'd thought torn beyond repair.

"Dinner will burn," Ivrina said with a laugh. "Stir the pot, Renyi, then come here. I want to show you something."

Rich aromas rose from the pot as Ren stirred it. Nothing fancy; they couldn't afford fancy. But good, solid rice porridge, with mushrooms and cabbage and peppercorns. There were buns, too, waiting to be toasted above the embers. Her stomach growled as if she hadn't eaten in months.

She caught her shawl when it tried to slip off her shoulder. For an instant it was glittering silver fabric, delicate as a breath; then it was sturdy wool. Beneath it she wore a shoulder-buttoned blouse, wide belt, and full Vraszenian skirt. Clothes that fit this place, just as Ren herself fit. This place was hers, theirs, and they were happy.

Ivrina was shuffling her pattern deck, not the overhand shuffle used with cheap street decks, but the cards arching up beneath her hands and then falling flat in a rain. She shifted so Ren could nestle against her. "Remember you the prayers I taught you?" Ivrina asked.

Ren nodded and recited as her mother shuffled.

"Kiraly, bless my hands with grace to lay the pattern true.

"Anoškin, bless my mind with light to know the Faces and the Masks.

"Varadi, bless my eyes to see the pattern as it truly lies.

"Dvornik, bless my tongue with words to speak of what I know.

"Meszaros, bless my heart with warmth to guide all those who seek my aid.

"Stretsko, bless my soul with strength to bear the burden of this task.

"Ižranyi, favored daughter of Ažerais, bless me with your insight, that I may honor my ancestors and the wisdom of those who have gone before."

Ivrina laid the cards out, three by three, from the bottom row to the top, right and left and center. "This is the past, the good and the ill of it, and that which is neither."

Whose past? Ren wanted to ask, as her mother turned over The Mask of Hollows, Sword in Hand, and Four Petals Fall.

But Ivrina didn't stop to interpret. Her hand moved up to the next row without pausing. "This is the present, the good and the ill of it, and that which is neither."

The Face of Glass, The Mask of Chaos, Storm Against Stone.

"This is the future, the good and the ill of it, and that which is neither."

The Face of Gold, Drowning Breath, Three Hands Join.

Ivrina's arms curled around her, holding her close. "Can you read them, Renyi? Understand you what they mean?"

Ren tensed as she studied the cards. She knew their images like her own hands, but now they looked wrong. The cards in the right-hand column—they were supposed to represent the positive forces in a situation, the things the client could look to for happiness or aid. But they seemed twisted, as if even the good had gone bad.

"Build up the fire, Renyi," Ivrina whispered. "I'm cold."

But her mother wasn't cold. She was hot, burning hot, her skin as dry as paper. Ren climbed to her feet, staring. "Mama—"

The fire beneath the stove roared up. Too high—the flames licked the wall above, the rug below. Smoke filled the air. Ren gagged on it.

"Renyi," her mother whispered, choking.

And Ivrina burst into flame.

Ren screamed, hands outstretched. No, no—this wasn't how it had gone! They weren't at home when the house caught fire; Ivrina hadn't died in the blaze. That came later, in the streets. But Ren was just as helpless now as she'd been when she was six, watching everything she loved be destroyed before her eyes.

The pain ripped her heart in two. Ivrina was shrieking as she burned, her screams piercing Ren like knives. "Read the cards, Renyi. Read them!"

But the cards had turned to ash. And though Ren tried to force her way toward her mother, to beat out the flames with her shawl, her traitor body refused. Instead, she turned her back and fled, out of the house and into the cold streets beyond.

Ren ran, breath sobbing in her lungs, while the smoke snarled behind her, clawing at her heels. Around a corner and into a shadow where she could hide. The smoke passed by, but it was still seeking, still hunting.

She would never be safe again.

The stink of the narrow lanes rose up in her throat. The shops around her were faceless, their signs taken from their hooks, but she knew where she was.

Seven Knots. The Vraszenian rookery.

Soft nickers and stamping came from one side. A stable; she could take shelter there. But when she dodged through the archway, a stallion reared up, hooves lashing out, and Ren fell backward into the filth of the lane. He struck sparks from the cobbles when he came down.

She scrabbled on her hands and knees, away from the stable, deeper into the shadows.

But others had already staked out the darkness. Rats swarmed her in a horde, sharp teeth gnawing a thousand cuts, claws scratching at her cheeks. She fled the shadows just as she'd fled the light.

A ghost-pale form, depthless black eyes in a heart-shaped mask of white, swooped down on silent wings. Ren ducked just in time, ran through Seven Knots under lines of low-hanging laundry, all paths leading her closer, closer...

To the center of the web.

The threads pulled tight around her. Not a welcome; a trap. The peacock spider descended on his line of silk, enormous fangs reaching and flexing, anticipating food. Ren tore at the web, desperate, gasping, writhing away just before the spider reached her, and fled once more through the wilds of the city.

A shriek stopped her cold. It sounded like a woman—no, like a *child* being murdered. One of the alley shadows disconnected; she saw rust-red fur, a white tail tip, and yellowed teeth. The curl of a black lip and blood rosettes staining the white ruff of a gentleman fox. He stepped out of the alley, black gloves hiding bloodstained paws, his charming smile a trap more honeyed than the spider's web.

She backed away, shuddering. Then hands began touching her, little clever hands, picking her pockets and stripping away her shawl, tugging and plucking and taking what shreds she had left. Like the streets had taken everything Ivrina had, leaving her body cold and naked in the gutter.

Ren snarled and lashed out. The small body of the raccoon went flying into the wall. She fought them off, the fox and the spider and the owl and the rat and the horse, instinct taking over, the need to survive. They didn't want her—none of them wanted her. Vraszenians were supposed to help their kin, but Ren didn't have any; whoever her mother's people were, they'd cast Ivrina out. Because of Ren. Because Ivrina had a bastard child, the daughter of an outsider.

And so they abandoned her to the savagery of the streets.

> *"Find them in your pockets,*
> *Find them in your coat;*
> *If you aren't careful,*
> *You'll find them on your throat . . ."*

The song echoed down the alley, down the street, down the hall-way of the lodging house. Ren tiptoed past sleeping Fingers, clutching a small purse to her chest. It wasn't much, but she'd tried all day. Better to come home with something than with nothing.

She didn't want to disappoint Ondrakja. Disappointing Ondrakja meant more than the pain of punishment. It meant she would never help Ren get back what someone had stolen the day Ivrina died.

"What have you found, little Renyi? Come forward. You know

I don't like you skulking in the shadows." Ondrakja's smile was as brittle as the spun sugar on fancy cakes as she beckoned Ren into her parlour, where several Fingers crouched around her chair, a miniature court for their queen. She caught Ren's chin, but her long nails didn't dig in. "You must show the world your face if you want to shine. This pretty face is your gift."

She tilted Ren's head back and forth, like Ren was a mirror for Ondrakja to see her own beauty in. "What gifts has my pretty face brought me today?"

Tension eased out of Ren's spine. Ondrakja was in a good mood. "I was in Suncross," she said, "and saw a cuff there..." She spun it into a story, because Ondrakja liked stories, liked to see how clever Ren was—how clever she'd taught Ren to be. At the climax of the tale, Ren presented the purse.

Ondrakja emptied it into her hand, spilling out a forro, a few decciras, and a ring. She held the ring up to the dim firelight, making Ren hope hope *hope*—

"Are you playing a game, little Renyi?" The syrup-sweetness of her voice held Ren fast. "Are you holding something back? What have I told you about lying to me?"

Panic welled in Ren's throat, but she fought it down. She could still save this—keep Ondrakja from flipping from Face to Mask. She just had to figure out which answer Ondrakja wanted.

But she'd taught Ren too many lies, too many lines. Which one did she expect to hear parroted back now?

"N-not to lie to you?"

"No!" Ondrakja's hand came up, and Ren flinched. But no. Not Ren's face, her pretty face. Not even rage would make Ondrakja damage something so valuable.

The ring flew across the room, striking the wood paneling with a sharp *ting*. "I said you *can't* lie to me. I will know. I will *always* know..."

Another day. Another try. Another failure. And when Ren came through the door, Sedge was already there—he must have taken a shorter path back after the job went sour.

He looked at her with mute, pleading eyes, trying to send some kind of message, but she couldn't read it. She only knew the smile on Ondrakja's face spelled pain for them both if they didn't step exactly right.

"Here she is now. Tell me, Renyi—what happened?" Ondrakja held up a long-nailed hand when Sedge tried to speak. "No, I've heard from you. I want to hear it from her."

Djek. Ren's mind raced. What had Sedge said? The truth? No. A lie—but which one? They hadn't had a chance to match their stories before they split. One of the older Fingers must have dragged him to Ondrakja; otherwise he would have waited for her.

She couldn't delay to think about it. That was as good as announcing her dishonesty.

Ren drew a deep breath and started talking. Making up the words an instant before they left her mouth, remembering the times she and Sedge had done this before, so she'd give something like the story he'd be most likely to tell.

But it wasn't enough. His wide eyes and flattened lips signaled every misstep. Ren tried to correct course, but Sedge's wince told her she'd only burrowed further from his lie.

"What an interesting tale. Thank you, Renyi, for being so... *honest*. As for you, Sedge?" Ondrakja rose, drawing a reed cane from the tall Isarnah vase she kept near the door—one of the many spoils brought by her Fingers over the years. "You know how I feel about liars. Against the wall."

Ren's ragged fingernails cut into her palms, but she kept her eyes open, because Ondrakja might turn around to make sure she was watching. The swish of the cane sounded like the rush of water, the floods rising in the Depths, and Sedge's muffled grunts echoed off stone.

Tears stung Ren's eyes, though she refused to let them fall. *Always wrong. Never good enough*. Always praising the Face and propitiating the Mask. She tried—she did better than the others—but she would never live up to Ondrakja. Not in skill, not in cleverness, not in beauty.

She wasn't even smart enough to realize that was the point. That Ondrakja kept her starving on purpose—always hungry for crumbs of approval, scrabbling after them through the muck.

The muck of the Depths. She wasn't in the lodging house at all. Sedge's hands were braced against the slimy edge of a crumbling niche, and Ondrakja stood ankle-deep in water, and the flood was rising—

Higher and higher, up to her ankles, her knees, her hips. Things brushed past her in the water, some blessedly unseen, others floating on the rushing current—a bloated corpse, a fisherman's net tangled into a solid mass, rats swimming frantically for dry ground that wasn't there. All of it painted a ghastly green in the dim light coming off the slime-coated walls.

But a moment ago she'd been in the lodging house. The streets. Home.

It's a dream, Ren realized.

Not a dream—a nightmare. And now she was in the Depths, the old burial niches where they used to put the ashes of the dead, and she didn't know how to get out.

Her only warning was the rush of water behind her. A surge swept her off her feet, slamming her into the walls, spinning heels over head—she didn't know which way was up, and she *couldn't swim*—

Then there weren't even walls or rats to grasp at, just water everywhere.

Until she collided with something soft and grabbed it, crawling up, clawing desperately for the air above.

"Let *go*, you stupid—" The thing—the person—she'd latched on to kicked, trying to free himself from her grip, but she clung to him like the drowning rats had tried to cling to her. For her to rise, he had to sink. It was the way of the world.

"Help! Somebody help us! Hel—" His shout ended on a gurgle

as Ren got a knee on his shoulder. They were in the West Channel, people passing along the river walk and the Sunset Bridge, as remote and uncaring as the moons above. She shoved harder, reaching for the stones, sinking her fingertips into a crack. When she risked a glance back, she saw Scaperto Quientis flailing for the surface once more, mouth open in a drowning plea.

Only for an instant. As she hauled herself above the edge, the steady flow of the city transformed into chaos.

Not erupted into chaos. *Transformed.* One moment, people were idly strolling past, ignoring the splashes from the channel; the next, she was surrounded by bodies that hadn't been there a blink before, all jostling elbows and knees and screams. They forced her along, little different from the rushing waters of the Depths. A bottle shattered against the wall beside her, raining glass and sour-smelling millet beer.

She'd hoped the tide would lead her away from trouble, but instead it spilled into the plaza in front of the Aerie. Bodies littered the steps, some in Vraszenian panel coats and embroidered sashes and skirts, many more in Vigil uniforms. A bare dozen hawks held the steps. The rioting Vraszenian crowd battered against them, hurling objects and a few recognizable obscenities, though most of what they shouted was garbled and unintelligible—the howling of beasts, rather than the speech of human beings.

Mettore Indestor stood at the top of the Aerie steps, behind his line of hawks. His face was scarlet with rage, his voice booming out over the plaza, louder than it should have been. "—order, if I have to kill every one of you to get it!"

But his men were the ones dying. The mob surged upward, sweeping Ren along, and then she was inside the Aerie.

Not the front rooms, full of hawks and paperwork. The cells. An impossibly long hallway lined with iron-barred doors, and they slammed shut on the Vraszenians, cutting them off in ones and twos, while the rest tried to outrun the trap.

Ren wasn't quick enough. A faceless hawk shoved her into a cell with a young woman who looked distantly familiar. She shoved past Ren and grabbed the bars. "Where is my grandfather?" she shouted in Vraszenian. The hawks walked past, callous and unhearing. "Please, his health is not good! Put me in with him!"

The shadow of the crossbar painted a mask across the woman's eyes, large, dark, and wet with tears, and Ren recognized her: the Kiraly girl who'd taken the horses at the start of the Accords.

She sank to her knees, sobbing. "Please! Let him not die alone!" Twisting to look at Ren, she begged, "Please help me. Make them listen."

"This is a dream," Ren said, backing up. She retreated farther and farther, not hitting the wall of the cell. "All we need do is wake up."

"But we cannot," said another voice.

Ren turned and saw a woman sitting in the corner, crying blood tears from the empty sockets where her eyes had been. Ren recognized her: the szorsa from the Vraszenian delegation.

"We've been poisoned." Ren's voice shook. "All of us. The aža in the wine—something was wrong with it."

"That was not aža. This dream is not a gift from Ažerais...but we are in her dream."

Ren's breath caught. Ažerais's Dream: the otherworldly reflection of the waking world, the many-layered place glimpsed by those who took aža. But this was no mere glimpse; they were *in* it, trapped like flies in honey.

She'd never heard of anyone entering it bodily. And she had no idea how to get out.

The szorsa lifted her chin, nostrils flaring as if she was scenting the air. "You are not a dream, though you are by Ažerais touched. Help me to my feet."

Hesitantly, Ren took the szorsa's hand in hers. It was bird-light. "You must be my eyes," the szorsa told her. "You carry the gift. Use it to see—to find our path through this storm."

Ren bit her lip. What path? What gift?

She means reading pattern.

The Mask of Hollows. Four Petals Fall. Sword in Hand. The Mask of Chaos. And at the center of the pattern, Storm Against Stone.

Leading the szorsa, Ren walked into the darkness.

The statues of the Charterhouse loomed above them, impossibly tall.

For a moment Ren thought this was the answer—that they had to get back to the Charterhouse, where it began, and then they could escape. But the five lifeless gazes fixed on her, and the nightmare didn't end, and outside she heard the wind howling.

Ren lifted her chin, made her voice as strong as she could, and said, "What is going on?"

She expected her voice to echo like before, a tiny thing lost in the vastness of space. Instead it rang out, clear and pure.

Her answer came like the crashing of bells, announcing the death of the Tyrant.

"I deceive all."

"I manipulate all."

"I bribe all."

"I kill all."

"I damn all."

Those weren't the right mottoes. The statues were supposed to represent the servants of Nadežra, the ways they aided the people. Instead they answered her as the city's masters, gloating in their power.

At Ren's side, the szorsa shook her head. Blinded though she was, she said, "No. There were seven when the city was ours. Where is the crafter? Where is the szorsa?"

Seven? Ren had never heard of there being seven on the council.

When she looked more closely, she saw shadows within the statues, ghosts carved of wood instead of marble, clothed in Vraszenian style instead of Liganti. A poet, a kureč leader, a trader, a guard, a mystic.

And at their sides, two more. A weaver with a shuttle of thread, and a szorsa with her cards.

Storm Against Stone signified uncontrolled and uncontrollable force. Outside the wind might roar, but the true power was here, at the eye of the storm; Ren felt it in the air, felt it resonate along the threads of pattern. Felt it connect to *her.*

She was the reason this nightmare had begun. When she drank the drug-laced wine, she fell through into the dream—and pulled everyone else with her.

But that was only part of it. By coming to the Charterhouse, she'd given Mettore something he needed—but whatever that was, it had gone wrong. Storm Against Stone wasn't just this moment; it was also his ill future, in the pattern she had laid.

When the nightmare began, the Charterhouse had tried to crush her with her own insignificance. Now she felt the opposite—the scale of her significance—and it was more horrifying still.

"Only those born of Ažerais can save the children of Ažerais," the older woman whispered. She faced the statue of the szorsa unerringly, as if listening to it speak. "And only those born of Ažerais can destroy the children of Ažerais."

Those born of Ažerais. Children conceived on the night of the Great Dream—as Ivrina had always claimed Ren was. They were said to carry a connection to pattern, and to the goddess of the Vraszenian people.

But the power whose storm was raging outside—that wasn't the goddess of her people. It was something else.

Like looking through glass, Ren refocused her eyes from the old Vraszenian statues to the newer Liganti ones. They might gloat over their power—but power could be lost, traded, broken...and stolen.

When she'd found herself in Nadežra again, she'd decided to claim what the city owed her. There was so much more for the taking, though. Leato. The Traementis. Her original plan had been to siphon off enough money to start a new life elsewhere, but why let go of a good thing? With the Traementis bound to her, she could make the city *pay* for taking her original family from her.

Ren's certainty burned like a coal on her chest, the desire for vengeance, for control, for *power.* Around her, the wind began to stir.

The szorsa's hand clamped down on her arm. "No—reach not for that thread. Your dreams will devour you if you let them!"

But the winds were rising, every door in the atrium slamming open, and the tempest was upon them. It lifted Ren from her feet, tearing her from the szorsa's grip and flinging her through the air.

She skidded across polished wood and slammed to a halt against a wall.

From above came a cynical snort. "Another of Mezzan's lovers, I take it?"

Ren climbed to her feet. She was in Traementis Manor...but not. They were in Donaia's study, but all the hangings and decorations were Caerulet blue, the Vigil hexagram, the Indestor seal of two overlapping wheels.

And Leato—

Ren froze, caught between relief and fear. It was the real him, not a dream version, because he was still dressed in his Rook costume. When he saw her face, his brow furrowed. "Wait...I know you. You're the patterner from Coster's Walk—the one who helped me find Idusza." A beat passed, and the furrow deepened. "Aren't you?"

She was in Vraszenian clothing still, but not made up. Ren hid behind the curtain of her wet and tangled hair and answered in her natural accent. "Altan Leato. We are in a nightmare." But was it his or hers?

"You think I don't know that?" Leato said bitterly. "Mother's lost to aža, Giuna is Mezzan's contract wife, Renata's given up on us and gone back to Seteris—Indestor took everything but our ennoblement charter. We're fucked."

He didn't understand what was happening. Ren bit her lip, wondering how to get through to him. Lean on being a szorsa? But she didn't have any cards.

The Face of Glass.

The good present, in the pattern Ivrina had laid. The turning point of Leato's future, when that szorsa patterned him in Lacewater.

Truth and revelations.

Fear clawed at her chest. *I can't tell him.* Impersonating a noble was a capital crime. If word got out, she would be sold as a slave, or hanged. And this nightmare warped everything, turning even the good to bad.

But staying in it would be worse.

"Why is some Vraszenian szorsa coming to..." Leato's breath caught, face blanching. Grabbing her shoulders, he shook her once. "It's not Grey, is it? Ninat spare us—did something happen to him, too?"

She looked up at him reflexively, even though instinct screamed at her to hide. "No, it—"

Renata's given up on us. That was part of his nightmare. And now she was going to make it worse.

Her hands curled over his. "Leato. Look at me."

His eyes focused on her. Saw her properly—not through the filter of the nightmare. And understanding began to dawn.

Just not the understanding Ren expected.

"Lumen burn him—*Renata.* Not you, too. Is Mezzan playing house again? Did he force you into this?" He touched the bell of her sleeve. "That mud-rutting swine. I'll stop him from— I'll make him pay for—"

"No! Leato, I..." She choked on the truth. It would be so easy to play along, to let Leato think she was shackled as a contract wife or concubine to Mezzan Indestor, dressing up in Vraszenian clothing at his command. But the cards were clear.

The Face of Glass. To escape, she had to remove her mask, and make him see the truth.

"I am Renata," she said, her accent Vraszenian, her lips numb with fear. "But I've lied to your family. You have no cousin."

"No cousin?" Leato's grip loosened. "Then...Letilia's daughter..."

"There is no such person." Telling the truth was so much harder than lying. But having begun, she couldn't stop. "I am a con artist."

"No." Leato stumbled back, shoving one hand into his hair as though trying to root out his confusion. "This is some new part of the nightmare, isn't it?" The look he gave her was so lost she nearly crumbled. "Isn't it? Why would anyone bother to con us? We've got nothing but our pride, and you can see the value of that."

His gesture took in the ancestral manor, now claimed by House Indestor. But even with the nightmare warping matters to their worst, it fell like salt on the open wounds of Ren's own past. "You think you are poor?" she said. "My mother died in the streets because we could not afford *food*. I found her body naked in a gutter—people as poor as us had stolen everything, even her clothing. I was *eight*."

"Then con them!" he snarled back at her. "That gives you some right to lie to us, to make us *hope*? My grandparents died when I was too young to remember. My father lost himself in aža and was killed in a duel over his debts when I was ten. Great-Uncle Corfetto's entire family went that same year, in the grain riots *they* started. The next year it was Sogniat's household, burned to the ground by a spurned lover. Her husband drank himself to death from guilt, and then everyone else, one by one... Do you even know how much it meant to us, *gaining* family for once instead of losing it?"

He wrapped his hands around the back of his head, curling in on himself as though that would protect him from the truth. "Please let this be part of the nightmare. Please let me wake up."

His helpless plea cut like shards of glass. As if she'd found Sedge alive... only to realize he wasn't Sedge at all.

That's not the same, Ren thought desperately. *Sedge is my brother. Renata was no one to Leato.*

But she had become someone to him, these last few months.

She made herself breathe, even though her throat felt strangled tight. "Leato. We can shout at each other all we like—*after* we get out. I think that to escape I must keep moving. I can bring you with me." *I hope.* "Will you trust me at least this much?"

"Trust you?" he spat. "I don't even know your name."

She almost said *Arenza*. But that, in its own way, was still a lie. "Ren."

He swept aside the skirts of his coat and gave her a bow that was all mockery. "So very nice to make your acquaintance, Mistress Ren."

It was the bow that did it. Furious and hurt as he was, the odds that he would answer were nonexistent, but the question burst out of her anyway. "Are you truly the Rook?"

"Am I what?" He gaped at her, then down at his costume. The laughter that followed held a trace of hysteria. "Sure. Why not. Let's both be liars and thieves. Why would I be the Rook? He *despises* the nobility. What sort of nightmares have you been having, that you would think that?"

"Lacewater! You said at the Gloria how angry you were, and then the Rook came out of nowhere to thrash Mezzan—"

"Giuna was the one who said he deserved a thrashing! Maybe *she's* the Rook."

"Giuna was not late joining us and was not conveniently nearby afterward. And you always run off, but not to where you say you'll be—and at Indestor Manor—" Ren cut herself off, breathing hard. She'd known some excellent liars in her time, but she didn't think she was looking at one now.

Leato wasn't the Rook. And he was laughing at her for suggesting he might be.

Her face heated. The nightmare had taken many forms so far, but humiliation was a new one.

"Never mind," she muttered, shoving her damp hair back. "That's not the point. Give me your hand, and I will see if I can get us out of here."

After the faintest pause, he offered her a gloved hand. She took it in her bare one and closed her eyes, thinking. "Next was The Face of Gold. That is wealth, and it was the good future." It would wind up twisted, but it still gave her guidance. "Were it not for this, my future would have been right here. So perhaps we need not go anywhere."

She opened her eyes, and the study transformed around her.

The blues warmed to rich amber and brown, the wheels of the Indestor seal shifting to form the crossed triple feathers of the Traementis.

And there was a second Ren in the chair.

No, not Ren—*Renata*. Dressed in all the splendor Tess's needle could achieve, without any need for scrimping or trickery. The bronze wool of her underdress was so finely woven that it shimmered like brushed silk, and her surcoat was encrusted with rubies. A fire blazed in the hearth, a crystal wineglass stood at her hand, and she smiled with the satiety of a woman who wanted for nothing.

Donaia hunched over a small table in the corner. Her dress was thin cotton, mended and stained, and her hands were knobbled claws from clutching a pen. She was scribbling in a ledger, and even from where she stood, Ren could see the numbers there were enormous.

She didn't spot Giuna at first. The girl knelt near the desk, in a cheap imitation of the dress Renata had worn to the Gloria—sleeveless and daring, but on Giuna it draped like a banner of sale.

Giuna kept her eyes low as she spoke. "Sibiliat said she wasn't in the mood for my games. I failed—I'm sorry—but I'll do better next time, cousin, I swear it."

Renata studied the wine in her glass. "You're calling me cousin again. Need I remind you that you lost that privilege the last time you failed?"

The hand crushing hers brought Ren back to herself. "What have you done to my sister?" Leato hissed.

"I—" Ren stared, unblinking. "I know not what this is. I only wanted money, I swear—not to make your family my servants!"

The study door opened, and Leato—another version of him—entered. Gone was the bright-haired, laughing, gallant young man who'd offered Ren his glove and kissed her so softly only a few hours past. This Leato had more in common with Vargo: hard-faced, scarred, and ruthless.

He tossed a cloth bag onto Renata's desk. The blood soaking through it smeared the shining wood. "That's the Rook taken care of." His voice grated, no more a light tenor. Something had broken inside.

"You took his head?" Renata eyed the bag with a moue of distaste.

"His hands. This city will think twice before challenging you again, cousin."

Casting a poisonous smile at Giuna, Renata said, "You see? Your brother knows how to please me."

Leato—the one standing beside Ren—went slack in her grip. "What did you do to *me*?"

The answer drifted out of Ren, a hollow whisper. "I turned you into my Fingers."

And turned herself into Ondrakja.

She'd been in the imaginary Giuna's place too recently to hide from the truth. Now the other half of the coin was right there in front of her. The satisfaction in her tools, the way she'd molded them to serve her purpose. Her approval was the music they danced to, because she had manipulated her way not just into House Traementis, but all the way to the top of the city. She'd felt the seed of it when she faced the statues in the Charterhouse. Here was the fruit.

After all... didn't she deserve this? Didn't Nadežra owe her for all she'd suffered? If she had everything now, it was simply the prize for finally winning: She'd outplayed even Ondrakja, proving herself better and smarter and—

Renata rose and caressed the other Leato's scarred cheek with one hand. Her long red nails dug into the ridged flesh, and Leato's eyes flashed with a dull hatred Ren knew all too well. "If only you'd been good enough to keep him from ruining this pretty face."

Ren clamped her hands over her mouth, as if that would keep the bile down. She backed away, shaking her head, but this time the wall stayed behind her; there was no escaping as she watched the twisted future version of herself reign over what remained of the Traementis.

And then Leato, the real Leato, was standing between her and the awfulness of what she'd become, taking her hands and drawing them down from her mouth. "Cousin—Renata—*Ren.*" He tugged harder, forcing her attention to him. His blue eyes were wide, fierce . . . and understanding?

"This is your nightmare," he said urgently. "Everything here is nightmares. Don't let it pull you in. Whatever you did before, you need to do it again, and get us out of here."

Out. There was no out but through. If this was a pattern, they had to finish it. And the next card was Three Hands Join—allies.

She knew exactly where to go.

"And don't come looking for me, neither," Tess said, shoving her sewing basket into the half-filled rucksack on the kitchen table. Her breath frosted the air, with no fire in the hearth to give the room warmth. The breadbox was open and empty. Tugging at the little embroidery sampler she'd hung on the wall—their only decoration—Tess threw that into the bag, too. "I know you're smarter than me, can find me if you set your mind to it, but don't. Let that door stay shut. I don't want to end up another victim of this mad scheme of yours."

She paused in her packing, looking around, but they had so little, half a rucksack was all she needed. Planting her hands on her hips, she turned to face Ren. "We could have lived simple and honest—a dressmaker's shop and you sweet-talking the clients. But that wasn't smart enough for you, and now see where it's led us. I don't want to have anything to do with you anymore. I can't."

This time there was no other Ren—not even that tiny shred of distance to protect her. It felt like someone had torn the ground from under her feet, and she was falling into the abyss. She reached out, hands shaking. "You cannot—"

Tess struck Ren's hands away. "I have to, before the Traementis sell you off as an imposter. Before someone does to me what

Vargo did to Sedge. He *told you* Vargo was dangerous. He told you he shouldn't share secrets. And now Vargo finished what Ondrakja couldn't. I'm cutting before the same happens to me."

Reaching into her rucksack, she pulled out a pair of shears and slashed them across the scar on her wrist—a shallow cut, just enough to bleed. Just enough to scar when it healed. She held her arm out and let the blood drip to the floor. "There. It's done. You're no sister of mine."

Tess could have slashed Ren's wrists open wide and it would have felt less like she was bleeding to death. They'd been together through everything. Ondrakja. Ganllech. Coming back to Nadežra.

And now Tess was leaving.

Ren searched desperately for words, but Tess laid a soft finger on her lips. "Now you'll say something to make me stay. Don't. I know you can talk the birds from the trees, but I deserve better than that. If you ever loved me, don't go making me another one of your marks."

Tess turned and picked up the bag. And Ren had to stand, swaying, the world fading to black at the edges, as Tess walked out the door.

Leato caught Ren as she collapsed. "Renata—Ren. Breathe. It's just another nightmare. Tess isn't really leaving. She wouldn't, would she?"

Ren turned over her own wrist, revealing the scar there. "She is my sister. For her I would do anything—but if I blinded myself with my own schemes, if I forgot that she is not just a resource..."

"A resource," Leato said softly. "Like Mother, Giuna, and myself?"

It startled her into looking up. "You—"

His blue eyes caught and held her. The first time she met him, she'd only seen a wealthy cuff, lazy and sure of his own worth. But her attempts to worm her way into the Traementis family had changed things. They were people to her now, not marks: Donaia's hardworking devotion, Giuna's good-hearted kindness, and Leato...

Leato, who had kissed her outside the Charterhouse.

And she'd kissed him back because she wanted to, not because it would sink her claws in deeper.

"No," Ren said softly. "Not anymore."

His frown softened. Not a smile—there were no smiles in this hell—but the anger had abated. "Good. Because whatever lies you've told, what you've done for my family is real. And we may not shed blood to add people to our register, but that doesn't mean someone can't earn a place among us—if they try."

It stole her breath again, but this time not in pain. He knew the truth...and he wasn't turning away.

He wasn't forgiving her, either. Not that easily. But he was offering her a chance to earn it.

The emptiness of the kitchen still closed around her, trying to insist that she had no one, that she was alone. But it wasn't true.

The last card was Drowning Breath, the card of fear—and the ill future.

"Whatever comes next will not be pretty," she warned him.

"Because everything until now has been roses?" He snorted and helped her stand.

Roses. They were a symbol of Ažerais, blooming during Veiled Waters every year.

"The wellspring," Ren said. "I've been to the Charterhouse, where this began, and that helped not. But this is Ažerais's Dream, twisted. And her wellspring is a source of dreams."

Leato frowned. "I don't want to correct a Vraszenian, but I thought the wellspring only appeared on the night of the Great Dream."

Ren shook her head. "It is always present, here in this realm. The Tyrant paved over it with his amphitheatre, but it is still there, beneath the stone. We should—"

The door splintered inward with a crash.

She expected a jump, to find herself and Leato suddenly up in the

Great Amphitheatre. But they were still in the kitchen, and hawks with bared blades were streaming through the door, with Grey Serrado at their head.

His steel-cold eyes fixed on her. "There she is. Arrest the imposter."

"Grey?" Leato said in disbelief, his sword half drawn to defend them. "Grey is part of your nightmare?"

Ren didn't stop to explain. She grabbed him by the arm and ran.

Up to the ground floor, but the hawks were flooding in the front as well—no, not hawks; it was Vargo's people, all the knots of the Lower Bank. Ren cursed and flung herself sideways, into one of the unused rooms. A quick jab of her elbow broke the window glass, the shards gouging her arm as she writhed through. "Come on!"

Leato followed, not asking questions anymore. Ren tried desperately to control the dream as she'd done before, to jump them from Westbridge to the top of the Point without covering the ground in between, but it wouldn't let her; this was the terror, to be hunted through the streets by every enemy she had. Hawks, Spiders, soldiers from Ganllech—she heard Mettore Indestor bellowing commands, and even Donaia's voice raised in strident demand, promising rewards to anyone who would bring the imposter "Renata" to her in chains.

They made it across the Sunset Bridge and onto the Old Island. Ren's breath burned in her chest as they began their climb, and she knew with the certain dread of a nightmare that their pursuers wouldn't be similarly slowed.

"What will we do if it's there?" Leato asked between gasps. "I can't imagine drinking for true dreams is going to fix this."

"I don't know," Ren admitted. "But I think if that were not the right place to go, something would have chased us back down by now."

They'd left the buildings of the city behind. The stone of the Point rose above them, and atop it the shadow of the Great Amphitheatre, the Tyrant's failed attempt to obliterate the wellspring.

The sounds of pursuit vanished as they entered the amphitheatre. But they were not alone.

Figures flowed along the stones of the stage, their joints bent and angular, but their movement sickeningly smooth. Their skin was charred and pitted, like the ribs of burned buildings, and they were skeletally thin: emaciated as starved corpses, but still, somehow, alive.

Ren had seen them in her nightmares. Not tonight, but all through childhood, when her mother put a red string around her bed to keep her safe.

"*Zlyzen*," she whispered, her stomach twisting.

Someone was moving among them, a bent and tattered woman, the flesh of her face stretched paper-thin over her cheekbones, sagging at the jowls. Hair dry and brittle as winter grass covered her head in tufts, leaving other patches bare and spotted liver-dark. One of the zlyzen nibbled at the edge of her sleeve, and she caressed its head like a pet's.

Something about that gesture struck a memory in Ren, the grace of it at odds with the woman's diseased appearance.

The zlyzen chittered at the woman and she glanced up, rheumy eyes fixing on Ren and Leato.

"Aren't you a pretty couple," she croaked, slinking forward. The zlyzen fell into a pack on either side of her, creeping belly-low to the ground. "Out for a nice stroll, are you?"

Leato took Ren's hand in his own. "She's just another nightmare."

"No," Ren whispered, staring. Her skin was trying to crawl right off her body at the sight of the zlyzen...but that was nothing compared to the woman. Old and decayed, her teeth sharpened to points, she was still recognizable—by the ruins of her voice, by the way she caressed the zlyzen, by *aren't you a pretty couple*.

"*Ondrakja*."

The old woman cringed back. The zlyzen clustering around her hissed and growled. "How do you know that name?" she snarled. Then yellowed eyes widened, catching the light of the moons. "You! You ungrateful little bitch. You poisoned me!"

The amphitheatre echoed with the sound of Ondrakja's delirious screams the night Ren killed her. Or tried to kill her?

No—it's a nightmare. Don't be drawn in.

Breaking into giggles, Ondrakja leveled a clawed finger at Ren. "But look at this. I poisoned you right back!" Her laughter crawled over Ren's bones like maggots.

Leato looked as sickened as Ren felt. "You're the one who caused this?"

"This? Yes, this. Though I never expected it to blossom so beautifully." She bared her sharpened teeth. "Is that your doing, my pretty girl? You may be a traitorous little rat, but you always were my best."

It called up the feeling Ren had in the Charterhouse—that her connection to Ažerais was the reason this had all been unleashed.

But she was fucked if she'd let Ondrakja—even some horrible nightmare vision of Ondrakja—know that. Ren might be a traitor who bound herself to a knot and then turned against it; she might be responsible for all the horrors tonight... but she wasn't going to give Ondrakja the satisfaction of the truth.

She fought down her nausea, closed out the oil-slick movements of the zlyzen. Made herself focus. "Me? I was only ever a Finger. You were the hand moving us." She eased a half step closer, mimicking the body language of years before. Sinking once more into that familiar habit, trying to figure out what to say or do to escape the nightmare around her. "But I cannot have been your target. You didn't know I was here."

"You?" Ondrakja edged closer, feigning friendliness, but it was as clear as glass that she only wanted to dig her claws into Ren. Her sweetness had always been nothing but a mask... and now the mask was rotting. "No, *him*. Indestor. He's going to pay me like he promised, or I'll make him swallow all the chaos I can shove at him."

Ren was only half listening. "The wellspring," she murmured to Leato. "It might be our way out." The edge of it was visible, the ring of ancient stones rising above the amphitheatre's stage the way it never did in the waking world.

But getting there would mean getting past the zlyzen.

"Might be?" Leato muttered, but his hand tightened on hers. "Right. Too bad you don't have a sword—and another year of lessons. Stay close."

Releasing her hand, he drew his blade and charged the zlyzen.

Ren snatched the knife from Leato's belt and slashed right and left as she followed in his wake, screaming as if that would keep the zlyzen back. Instead it drew them in, feinting at her legs, snarling and snapping with their inhumanly sharp teeth. Then something seized her by the collar, and she choked.

It was Ondrakja, moving faster than any crone should. Her grip was like iron, twisting Ren's collar tight, and the medallion she'd put on for the masquerade was strangling her, the chain pulling taut across her throat. Ren stabbed backward with the knife and hit something, but Ondrakja didn't falter.

Then Leato was there. He slammed into them both and the pressure broke, the chain snapping. Ren stumbled forward, seeking the waters of the wellspring like a lodestone, praying to Ažerais—

The ring of stones yawned in front of her, an empty, dry pit.

She tried to halt her momentum, but it was too late. For an instant she teetered on the edge of the pit...and then, screaming, she fell.

Something caught her arm, stopping her momentum and swinging her body into the wall. Leato, leaning halfway over the edge and clutching with both hands. His fingers caught and tangled in the open, belled cuff of her shirt, and he grunted with the strain of holding her weight. "I've got you. Take my hand. Can you find a foothold—"

He convulsed, howling in pain, and his grip slipped. A zlyzen had pounced on his back, its twisted, blackened limbs raking. Then a second joined it, and a third.

"Leato!" She tried to grab hold of his sleeve with her other hand, but her palm was slick with blood from her cut arm. He dragged her upward anyway, but the zlyzen were tearing into him, their maws red and wet, and there were more and more of them until they blotted out the stars—

His grip went slack, and she fell.

Fell, into darkness, into the dry and echoing void of the vanished wellspring, into nothingness—

—and then her desperate hands caught a shimmering, iridescent thread.

Slender as a thought, it should never have supported her weight. But Ren wrapped her fingers around it, and it held. She climbed, staining its brightness with blood, and the thread grew thicker as she went, from thread to cord to rope, and around her were both the nightmare of the empty pit, and the luminescent waters of the true Wellspring of Ažerais.

Above her, a circle of grey broke the blackness. Something was there, reaching out to catch her: a black-gloved hand that caught her by the wrist, and for an instant she thought it was Leato, whole and unharmed.

"I've got you," he said, pulling her upward. "You're safe."

The Rook. As real as the waking world he stood in. Which meant Leato—

Ren twisted, looking down. Below her, impossibly far below, she saw a writhing mass of zlyzen, still tearing, still feeding.

Her fingers dug into the leather of his glove. "No! Leato—we have to go back for him—"

"You first. Then him."

The Rook drew her up and out of the pit. She felt the threads around her again, the world weaving itself from dream back into reality—and then she realized what that would mean.

"Wait!"

But it was too late. Ren had dragged everyone into the nightmare with her; when she left, it ended. The paved floor of the amphitheatre was smooth and flat.

And Leato was gone.

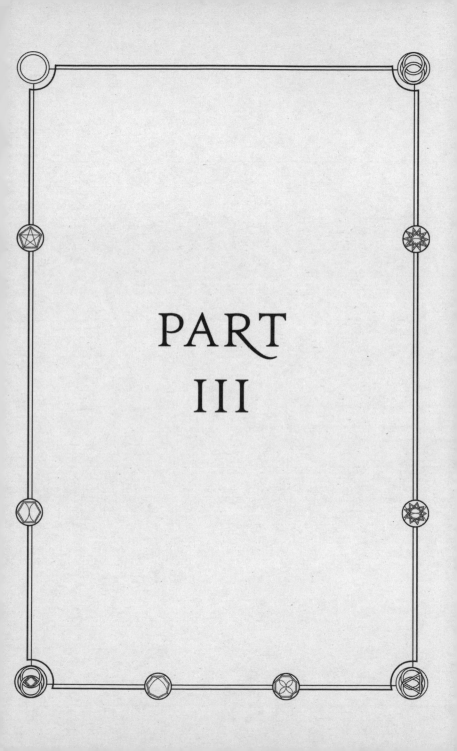

PART

III

PART

III

13

A Brother Lost

Vargo didn't often live in his body. He'd grown up thinking bodies were for pain—inflicting, receiving—a belief that lingered even though pain was rarely a concern for him anymore. These days, he mostly thought of his body as a tool. He spent the majority of his time in his head, where he was unassailable, calculating how everything around him could be used.

But he recognized the appeal of the physical. And sometimes he wanted the slap of flesh against flesh, the grind of hips and the slickness of sweat, the *fuck* and *yes* and *almost there* of it all.

Like now, with Iascat Novrus pinned between Vargo and the side wall of the Theatre Agnasce, only the columns and the shadows shielding them from discovery. Calculation still played a part; most cuffs were too terrified of Iascat's aunt Sostira and her uncanny ability to ferret out secrets to get close to her heir. Which left Iascat starved for affection...and for touch. Only someone who didn't fear blackmail—someone without shame—could give him what he wanted. And that, in turn, was leverage.

But they were past calculation now. Vargo was well and truly in his body—his and Iascat's, with his hand wrapped around Iascat and their ragged breathing lost under the noise of the plaza.

The Novrus heir bit down on his own fist to keep from crying out as he peaked. And Vargo was excruciatingly close to the edge when the voice in his head broke in.

::Something's happened at the Charterhouse.::

Not. Bloody. Fucking. Now.

::Yes, now,:: Alsius snapped. There was no amusement in his voice, no sardonic commentary on Vargo's current activities. ::The people here—they've *vanished*. The Cinquerat, the clan leaders, all of them.::

It jolted him back into his head. His body still chased release, but cold shock washed through him, dulling the sharp edge of pleasure to mere friction. *What do you mean, vanished?*

::I mean they disappeared before my eyes.::

"Is . . . is something wrong?"

Vargo had stopped moving. Iascat twisted to look at him with pupil-blown eyes made larger by the paint that lined them. The man's lips were soft and his ash-pale hair mussed; bits of grit stuck to his cheek where it had been pressed into the wall. He should have looked irresistible. But Vargo had bigger concerns now.

"Too much aža," Vargo said, snatching for the first lie that came to hand. "I'm finished for the night."

"But you . . . didn't. Did you?"

::Vargo!::

I'm coming. The irony of that reply didn't escape him. But Vargo hadn't spent two bells on his knees convincing Fadrin Acrenix to make this introduction to let his chance go to waste.

He brushed the grit from Iascat's cheek with deliberate tenderness, giving him a languid, open-mouthed kiss, as if he had all the time in the world. "Some other night?"

His question was met with a shy smile and an enthusiastic nod. "Yes. Next time. D–Derossi."

Something in Vargo's chest twinged at the name. He fastened his loose trousers and settled his bead-heavy robe back in place with a shrug. The paints on his chest were smeared, their mirror printed onto Iascat's back. "Call me Vargo," he said, and slipped out from the columns into the crowded plaza.

Tell me what happened.

::The usual, at first. Speeches, pageants, wine. Should have been tedious mingling after that. But everyone who drank the wine just…faded away. People don't do that, Vargo!::

No, they didn't. Not by any magic Vargo knew of. And Alsius sounded more panicked than he'd heard in years.

He'd sent Renata in there.

What the *fuck* had he let Indestor manipulate him into doing?

Vargo wove toward the Charterhouse, the oblivious crowd offering little resistance. But as he neared the steps, a functionary in Fulvet livery flung himself through the door and shrieked, "They're gone! The Cinquerat have all vanished!"

Only a few people heard him over the noise of the masquerade, but those whispered to their neighbors, and like the ringing of the bells, word began to ripple outward. *Something's wrong. Something happened at the Charterhouse.* By the time it crossed the plaza, rumor would have built it into a dozen different stories, none of them accurate, and all of them dangerous.

Vargo had been in riots before, and while he wasn't sure a crowd of cuffs could rouse themselves to the lethal panic of a Lower Bank brawl, he didn't want to find out.

He diverted sideways without stopping, down an alley whose previous occupants were hurrying to see what the problem was. Pulling off his beaded robe, he thought at Alsius, *I need to change into something more practical. Meanwhile—find me a sample of that wine.*

Old Island: Cyprilun 17

The sound swept toward Tess, a rising tide of murmurs and alarm.

She'd found a place near the dancing to watch the costumes go by, wistfully curious whether the girls at the Westbridge revels were giving Pavlin a moment to rest. Now she tugged on someone's sleeve—a man in an outrageous costume that took up twice as much space as his body, with hasty seams that offended her professional pride. "Begging your pardon, but can you tell me what's happening?"

"It's the Charterhouse ceremony," he said, too full of his news to realize he was gossiping with a mere servant in a plain two-color mask. "Everyone there has been murdered!"

"What?" She tore a badly stitched ribbon loose when she clutched at his sleeve. "They can't have—"

A little distance away, a woman shrieked. This one, Tess recognized: It was Benvanna Novri, the current wife of Era Novrus. She had her hands pressed to her mouth and her gaze fixed on the backs of a cluster of delta gentry.

"They're attacking her!" she wailed, shrinking back. "Oh, Sostira—all her wives—Lumen have mercy, *I'm* attacking her! Please, someone help her!"

But there was no Sostira Novrus to be helped. Benvanna lurched forward, hands waving, and moaned in dismay when she realized she couldn't touch whatever she was seeing.

Tess knew enough about aža to recognize Benvanna's dilated pupils and distant look, like she was gazing right through this world into the next one. And she wasn't the only one: All around the plaza, shouts and cries rose from the aža-spun. One said he saw some old Vraszenian man weeping amid the bodies of murdered children; another babbled that the Tyrant still reigned, that the blood-soaked city was celebrating the 242nd year of his rule.

Unlike Ren and Sedge, Tess had never been one of Ondrakja's favorite Fingers, but she shared their river rat instincts for moving through a crowd. Ren had done it with charm and a smile, Sedge with fists and elbows. Tess just found the spaces between bodies and slipped through them like a needle. Only this time, she wasn't looking for an easy mark or a dangling purse; she was looking for the sister of her heart.

"Alta Renata! Has anyone seen my alta? Alta Renata!" *Ren! Ren!* The name rode the fear crawling up her throat, a fraying net of caution holding it back. But Ren had a cat's knack for landing on her feet, and see if she wouldn't give Tess a scolding for giving away the game when she'd been perfectly safe the whole time.

Tess pushed her way across the plaza to the Charterhouse steps, where Ren ought to have been. But there, a wall of bodies too solid for her to pierce blocked the way: sober nobles and delta gentry demanding to know what was going on.

A stern-faced woman with a Vigil commander's gold pin did her best to respond, shouting replies as if she'd been doing it for a while and expected to be doing it for bells more. "There has been no murder! People have vanished! We do not know how or why, but we are looking into it! Please keep order so that we can concentrate on our search!"

Someone bellowed back up to her, "But the people out here can *see* the ones who have gone missing, and they're in danger! Why aren't you doing anything to help them?"

Tess faded back, breathing through the fear. Missing, not dead. The people on aža could see them—sometimes, some of them—and it might be a badly spun thread, but it was all Tess had to cling to.

She started moving with new purpose, seeking out people staring at things not there, asking them if they'd seen her alta. There was no rhyme or reason to it she could find; everyone she talked to described something different. Riots or plagues. The city in flames or the city flooded. A cowering man insisted he'd seen one of Era Destaelio's assistants being chased by rats the size of hunting hounds. Another swore he'd seen Scaperto Quientis drowning in the West Channel alongside a pretty Vraszenian woman.

Tess pressed a hand to her belly to quiet the flutter of hope. "What did she look like? What was she wearing?" Had Ren swapped to her Arenza disguise? How could she have? Tess had dressed her. Nothing in the Dežera costume would look Vraszenian.

But the woman the man described sounded like Arenza. No—she sounded like *Ren*. "Mother and Crone, let her not be discovered," Tess prayed as she struck off for the opposite riverbank. "I mean, excepting by me."

Only she saw nothing of Ren at the river. Tess pounded her thigh in frustration. "Of course not, you fool. You aren't seeing anything but what's really here."

If she wanted to find Ren... she needed to find aža.

Tess was about ready to cosh the nearest corner dealer over the head, when she heard a name that pierced her worry. Propriety be damned, she grabbed a delta gentlewoman by the arm and yanked her around. "Say that again?"

This one wasn't so caught up in the chaos that she didn't notice Tess's lowly status. She pulled free and answered haughtily, "I said I saw the Rook climbing the Point, toward the amphitheatre. And the Vigil will hear of it."

As if they would give a drop of tainted river water for the Rook right now. But the woman was as sober as Sebat—which meant what she'd seen was real.

If the Rook thought there was something worth doing up on the Point, when the Cinquerat had gone missing and the entire Old Island was erupting into madness, then Tess had a mind to see what he was about... and to ask him for help.

She set off for the Point at a run.

A run that all too soon slowed to a desperate plod as the path steepened upward from the low-lying mass of the Old Island. Tess pulled off her mask and gulped for air. Her calves and thighs burned as she pushed on to the amphitheatre; she would have prayed if she'd had wind to spare. When a black shape flitted past at the periphery of sight, she almost ignored it, thinking it a product of her breathlessness.

Except how often did fainting spots resemble famous outlaws, or carry women over their shoulders? "Ren!"

Tess realized her mistake a moment after the shout burst from her. As the Rook pivoted in her direction, Ren's voice, with just an echo of Ondrakja behind it, prodded her to action: *If you think you're about to be caught in a lie, better to push through than to retreat.*

"Run!" She jerked her mask back over her face and lurched toward the Rook, waving her arms. *Try not to sound Ganllechyn.* "The

Vigil got wind of a fuss up at the amphitheatre. They're headed this way!"

"I'm sorry, what?"

Someday, Tess hoped to tell her grandchildren about the time she threw the Rook off-kilter. But first she had to get Ren away from here. "What's wrong with that woman? Is she—"

He lowered Ren to the ground, and the last of Tess's breath left her. It was Ren, sure enough—looking exactly like *herself*, under the blood and dirt. The River Dežera costume was gone like it had never been; she was in Vraszenian clothes.

But she was alive. Staring and wordless, she huddled in on herself when the Rook let go. She showed no sign that she realized Tess was even there—but she was *alive*.

Rough stone cracked against Tess's knees as she fell at Ren's side. "Oh, Mother and—What happened to you?"

"You know this woman?" the Rook asked.

Tess wasn't Ren, didn't have the knack of weaving lies together into a good strong fabric that resembled truth. So she just kept her head down, hoping her own simple costume was disguise enough and that the Rook hadn't realized he held Alta Renata. Especially if he was really Leato, like Ren thought.

His hand fell on her shoulder. "I said, do you know her?"

"Yes," Tess replied. Ren still hadn't moved. If she hadn't been breathing, in shallow, erratic gasps, Tess would have thought her dead.

"Then I'll leave her with you." The Rook's voice was bleak as winter ice. "If the Vigil's coming, she shouldn't be caught with me."

Tess nodded. Her sight was blurred from tears, but she didn't dare wipe them away until the Rook was gone and she could take her mask off again. "Get you gone. I'll take care of her—get her back to her people."

He set off before she finished speaking, down the path and then leaping from it to a rooftop, out of sight in moments. Tess curled herself around Ren, using her own generous padding as a cushion against the stone. Shaking, she pressed her brow to Ren's and allowed herself a moment of relief. *Thank you, Mother and Crone.* Whatever else had happened, Ren was alive.

She brushed her sister's hair back from her brow, then lifted her head. Their troubles weren't over yet. Ren didn't look like Renata anymore, which meant they had to get out of sight.

Home, Tess decided. But she wasn't the Rook, and couldn't carry Ren all the way to Westbridge.

"Right, then," she said, her voice strengthening. "I need you to help me, Ren. Up with you—"

They lurched upright, Tess bearing more of Ren's weight than Ren did, but at least her sister was on her feet, and something like moving. One careful step at a time, they made their way down, headed for home and for safety.

Aerie, Duskgate, Old Island: Cyprilun 17

"Serrado! Where in Ninat's hell have you b—"

Cercel's frustrated shout withered to nothing as the crowd in the main room of the Aerie parted to let Grey and his constables through, with their bloodstained burden.

When his patrol found the body, Grey had tried to carry Leato himself. He couldn't do it for Kolya—there'd been little left to carry—but at least he could do this for the man who'd been almost like a brother to him. It didn't make up for not being there when Leato needed him, but he'd tried.

After two stumbling steps, Ranieri had quietly taken command, wrapping the body in his coat and ordering the other constables to take Grey's burden. Now he faded back, ceding control to his captain once more, as Cercel shoved through the crowd to meet them.

Grey owed Ranieri thanks for the respite, even if it hadn't been enough. Not to recover from everything he'd seen that night. The walls of the waking world blurred around him, the front room of the Aerie briefly awash in blood—a dream of the building as a place of violence. Grey pressed the heel of his hand into his brow, willing himself to see only what was real.

"Commander. We found him in the amphitheatre. Where—" Grey's voice broke. He cleared his throat and tried again. "Where are we placing the bodies? We need to inform Era Traementis that her son…"

This time the blurring was entirely due to tears. Grey drew in a shaking breath. Then a second. Then a third. He just had to get through these last steps; then he could sink into the grief that was waiting to tear him apart.

Cercel's jaw tightened so hard she risked cracking a tooth. "Downstairs," she said. "Ranieri, see to it."

She stepped in close as Ranieri and the others took Leato away. What was left of Leato. Dropping her voice so no one else could hear, she said, "I need you to tell me right now, Serrado. Are you on aža?"

"I needed to see what was happening," he said. "I gathered my unit as quickly as I could."

"I know you did." The compassion in her voice almost broke him. Her initial anger was easier to deal with than this. Cercel's hand twitched as if she wanted to lay it on his arm, and he was unspeakably grateful that she held back. "With everything that's going on, I can't afford to let you go home, but I'll—"

"Where is he? Someone said they found him. Leato?" Donaia Traementis appeared at the top of the stairs leading to the commanders' offices, where people of rank would be sent to wait. Her hair was in wild disarray, and a streak of mud darkened her surcoat at the knee. Giuna hovered behind, looking more composed than her mother, but only just.

Grey stumbled back a step. He wasn't ready for this. Donaia spotted him and rushed down the stairs. Cercel, damn her, cleared a path.

"Grey!" Donaia clutched his hands. "Was it you? You found him? Where is he?"

He couldn't. He opened his mouth to speak…but he saw the

desperate hope in her brown eyes, and he couldn't be the one to destroy her world. He shook his head.

Behind her mother, Giuna pressed a fist to her lips, holding in a sob of understanding.

"I'm sorry." The words cut him open. "He's not... I'm so sorry. We found his body."

"No." Donaia's weight dropped, dragging Grey down with her. "No, you must be mistaken. It must be someone else. Not Leato. *Not my boy.*"

She kept repeating it, over and over, and Grey felt the threads of the Traementis family fraying around him, the last remaining strands.

And the last strands of himself, too.

Donaia's denials became fists beating against his shoulders. Grey let her strike him, because he deserved it. The aža shifted his vision again; now he saw the Aerie as a place of chains, of strangling order that did more harm than good. He squeezed his eyes shut and tried to rub comfort into Donaia's curved back, his hand brushing Giuna's as she did the same.

It was Giuna who finally brought him back to his surroundings. She drew in a sharp breath, and Grey opened his eyes.

"What about Renata? She was with Leato in the Charterhouse. Did you find..." Giuna swallowed hard. "Anything?"

"Nothing." Grey glanced up at Cercel, who was doing her best to move traffic around them. "You've had no reports?"

Cercel shook her head. "We're still locating people. I don't know how they got scattered across the Island, but—some of them might not even be *on* the Island."

"Then expand your search beyond it!" Giuna snapped, rising to her feet to square off against Cercel. Even with her eyes reddened from tears and her body trembling, she had never looked so much like her mother. "Renata doesn't know Nadežra. She might be lost. She might be hurt!"

She might be dead.

Giuna didn't have to say it. The more time passed, the more likely that became.

Grey rose, swaying as the aža tried to show him another dream of the Aerie. Alone on the floor, Donaia wrapped her arms around her own body, rocking back and forth. He didn't want to leave her with only Giuna for support, but he could do more for her grief out in the city than he could by staying here. "She lives in Westbridge—might have gone there. I can take my unit and—"

The door to the Aerie shrieked clean off its hinges, the heavy panels slamming into three hawks and knocking them to the ground. Mettore Indestor thundered through the gaping threshold, wrapped in the spangled robe from someone else's costume and streaked with dried blood from his wounds. A Caerulet secretary scurried in his wake, braying for his master to stop and let himself be tended, but Indestor showed no sign that he even noticed the pain.

"I want to know who did this to me!" he roared.

Grey had seen the man in a fury plenty of times before, but this was pure, elemental rage—and something more besides. Indestor gripped the edge of a desk, and the people behind it scattered on instinct, a heartbeat before the desk splintered against the wall.

Ash. They'd seen its effects enough on the streets lately for Grey to recognize them on sight.

The hilt of his sword was cold against his palm. Drawing steel against Caerulet would get him killed, but that strength, combined with Mettore's rage...

Indestor's dilated eyes fixed on him, and for one paralyzing instant Grey felt like the man could see what he'd almost done. "It was *your* people," Indestor snarled. "Fucking gnats. They did this to me. I want to know who. Bring me answers or I'll spit you on that pin you wear, and everyone who vouched for you."

It was all too clear what methods Mettore expected Grey to use. Cercel interposed herself between the two of them, not quite putting her back to Indestor, but blocking Grey's view enough to force his attention onto her. "Go," she told him. "I'll send someone else to Westbridge."

"My people didn't do this." Grey wanted to shout his fury at Indestor, but he'd been a hawk and a Nadežran too long for that sort of pointless idiocy. Even with the aža showing him glimpses of Ažerais's Dream, even with Leato's death bleeding him dry inside, he had enough sense to keep his voice low so only Cercel could hear. "Our ziemetse were poisoned, too. We would *never* do something like that."

"But they might know something, and you're the only person they're likely to talk to."

It twisted another knife in his gut. Most Vraszenians saw him as a slip-knot. The clan elders were from the upriver city-states, but they knew perfectly well what a Vigil uniform meant.

Indestor shoved his secretary back when the man tried to dab at his cuts with a damp cloth. The man went reeling, and would have fallen if there weren't so many people behind him. "Do you want him sending somebody else?" Cercel growled at Grey. "If we're going to get justice for this, Serrado, I need you to do your job."

Grey looked down at Donaia. Giuna was crouched next to her, setting her own grief aside to comfort her mother. Finding Renata wouldn't do much to make things better, but finding her dead could only make things worse. How could he leave that responsibility in someone else's hands?

But Cercel was right. As bad as he was for talking to the clan leaders, any other hawk would be disastrous.

Indestor had already stormed upstairs, bellowing for the high commander. Grey clenched his jaw, wishing anyone had the authority to subdue the drugged-up cuff before he threw another desk at someone. "Fine. I'm taking Ranieri with me." Pavlin had only traces of Vraszenian blood, but he wouldn't use this as a chance to jockey for Caerulet's favor, the way Grey's other constables would.

"Take whoever you think will be useful. Just go, before this gets worse."

With all the noise in the Aerie, he couldn't possibly hear Donaia's broken sobs as he left. But the aža seemed to sense her grief, and all he could see as he headed for Seven Knots were people weeping all around him.

Isla Prišta, Westbridge: Cyprilun 17

The sound of the doorbell made Ren flinch.

Tess's arms wrapped more tightly around her. "Ignore it. You don't have to be facing anybody right now."

Even Tess's embrace couldn't chase the cold away. The fire was built high, flooding the kitchen with warmth, but Ren shivered uncontrollably. Whether her eyes were open or shut, all she saw was Ondrakja.

And the zlyzen tearing into Leato as she left him behind.

The doorbell rang again.

Tess cursed and sprang to her feet. "I'll deal with that. Just you stay here and drink your tea." She hurried out.

At first all Ren could make out were indistinct murmurs. Then Tess's voice rang down like one of the well-washers from Ganllechyn fireside tales. "No, you may *not* come in to confirm, and the alta won't be coming down so you can poke at her, neither!" she shrieked. "I told you she'd returned with only some scratches. Are you calling me a liar?"

The following murmur didn't seem to satisfy Tess. "I don't care if you were sent by Mettore Indestor himself; I'm not letting you—what's your name?—right then, Lieutenant Kaineto. You're not setting one foot through this doorway."

She's screeching like that to let me know what's happening, Ren realized.

"You do that. And while you're at it, you tell this Commander Cercel of yours that we don't much appreciate being hassled at this hour. After what my alta's been through . . ." The door thudded shut.

Moments later, Tess slumped down the stairs, hand to her heart and face pale as a pearl ghost. "That's taken care of for now. We should have at least until morning. Later, if the hawks are as scattered as they seem to be." She laid a hand against Ren's brow and her own cheek, as though testing for a fever. "Do you want to talk at all? Or would you rather rest?"

Ren's heart was racing as if she'd run up the Point again. As if the Vigil really had kicked in the kitchen door, Grey Serrado at their head, to arrest her for her crimes.

That was the first of it to come out, in broken fragments. Then, like floodgates opening, the rest: Her turning the Traementis into pawns, Tess leaving, Sedge dead at Vargo's hands, Ivrina in the flames. Crawling to Ondrakja again and again, and the blind szorsa going with her to the Charterhouse statues.

Leato. Over and over, trying to say what had happened to him, how she'd abandoned him, but the words caught in her throat like barbed fishhooks. Tess must have known he was dead, long before Ren managed to give it voice, but she just sat and stroked Ren's hair and murmured comforting nonsense until the last of it was done.

Enough silence passed that Ren wondered if Tess had fallen into a doze, but then her breath stirred Ren's hair. "I can't speak for the rest of it, but I would never leave you." She caught Ren's hand and turned it over, laying her arm beside it so their scars formed the line that bound them in sisterhood. "This means as much to me as it does to you. I'd sooner cut off all my fingers and never sew again."

Ren's eyes had been dry and burning since the Rook dragged her away from the vanished wellspring, but now the tears came, blinding her.

"Oh dear. Now see what I've gone and done." Tess wrapped her arms around Ren, rocking her gently.

The knock that came on the door seemed almost like pattern at work. Sedge's knock, so they would know it was him. Tess let him in, and at the sight of Ren, Sedge swore and dropped to his knees in front of her.

"She's only scraped and bruised a bit, but she's in a bad way. She saw Ondrakja," Tess said as she locked the door.

Sedge took Ren's hands and looked up into her face. "Shoulda been here earlier. We was all out looking for Vargo—guess I hoped you'd be with him. Fuck. Ondrakja? But it wasn't really her, right?" He glanced over his shoulder at Tess. "Way we was hearing it, it was all in people's heads."

Ren gripped his hands hard enough to bruise. "Not in my head, but not—not real. Masks have mercy, *not real.*" Sedge was alive. And she wasn't going to pry into Vargo's secrets ever again, not if it would get him killed.

Sedge got up on the bench with her, and Ren leaned into his strength. He didn't have Tess's knack for soothing words, but he was solid and real, and she could see their scar on his wrist, half buried among the others he'd picked up along the way.

Without these two . . .

It didn't matter. She had them. And she wasn't going to lose that.

Cold dawn light streaming through the high windows of the half-sunken kitchen took her by surprise. She hadn't slept, but somewhere along the line the animal panic had faded. Not gone; just far enough beneath the surface that she could think.

Until morning, Tess had said. People would want to know what happened, to make sure Alta Renata was all right.

Either I run, Ren thought, *or I put my mask back on.*

It made her skin crawl, calling to mind the version of herself she'd seen ruling over the Traementis. But simply vanishing, grabbing the bags she and Tess kept ready and fleeing Nadežra, would leave Donaia and Giuna to face Leato's death alone.

Leato, who'd died to save Ren. She owed them whatever she could do now—however pitiful and inadequate it might be.

"Tess," she said, her voice creaking as if she hadn't used it in a year. "I need my makeup. And my mirror. And a dress."

Sebatium, the Pearls: Cyprilun 18

The Liganti temple where Renata was called to give her testimony was one of the most beautiful buildings she'd ever seen. It was dedicated to Sebat, the numen of perfection in imperfection, of purity, of beauty and art and craftsmanship—and of inscription, the highest of all arts.

Spring sunlight shone through the window at the end of a nave built of imported marble and gold-hued wood. In Seteris and Seste Ligante, that window would have depicted a peacock in full spread, but over the decades, local custom had adopted the dreamweaver birds of Vraszan in its place. Rainbows scattered across the walls and splashed across the mosaics embedded into the floor. The path of numinata started at the door with a simple Noctat, passed through Illi, and worked up the chain to end in the center of the nave at an intricate figure of Sebat.

Renata followed that path like any good Seterin would, feeling as if she were walking the path of a dream. She was several steps along before she realized the dreamweaver hues weren't only coming from the window above; they were embedded into the stone. Some master inscriptor had laid out the numinata in pure prismatium.

I lost my mask, she thought irrationally. Where had her costume gone, and the mask Vargo had given her? Where had the Vraszenian clothes come from that she was wearing when she left the nightmare? Tess had puzzled over them as she packed them away, but neither of them could find an explanation.

An acolyte met her as she finished walking the path. "Alta Renata? Please wait in the meditation hall. Meda Fienola will see you as soon as she can."

Fienola. It took her much too long to place the name. Tanaquis: the astrologer who was friends with the Traementis. She worked for Iridet, the Cinquerat's religious seat.

Renata wasn't the only one waiting. Several other people were there, faces she recognized from the Charterhouse: clerks, dignitaries, the courtesan who had depicted Nadežra in the pageant. None of the Vraszenians, though.

She knelt on the floor inside one of the Sebat numinata and tried to look like she was meditating, so no one would try to talk to her. Before the warm rainbow air could put her to sleep, the acolyte approached again and bowed deferentially. "Please come with me, Alta Renata."

Scaperto Quientis was emerging from a side door that clearly led to some back chambers. He looked haggard, and his expression settled into even grimmer lines when he saw Renata. *Does he blame me?* she wondered as he passed without more than a nod. Not for the incident as a whole—she prayed to any deity listening that no one knew her role in that—but for Leato's death. He'd only been in the Charterhouse at Renata's invitation.

The hallway beyond was cool and lit by numinata. The acolyte led Renata into a small library where Tanaquis sat at a table, scribbling rapidly in a notebook in some of the worst handwriting she'd ever seen.

Dragging her attention from her notes, Tanaquis blinked owlishly at Renata. Her eyes widened and lips parted in a flash of surprise before battening down into concern. "You look like you're about to fall over. Why didn't you send word that you needed to rest? I could have delayed until later this afternoon."

Renata had expected her interrogator to launch right into questioning, and faltered at the unexpected kindness. "I didn't know the summons was from you."

"I confess, I'd hoped to meet you again—but not under such circumstances. Please, sit down. And have some coffee." Tanaquis poured before Renata could decline. "Have . . . have you seen Donaia at all?"

Renata's breath caught. "No. I—I'm the one who invited Leato to the Charterhouse." Her hand shook as she accepted the coffee, and the next words came out raw. "How can I show my face to her, after . . ."

"Oh dear. Now I've broken my chalk on it. I didn't mean . . ." Tanaquis bent to catch her eyes. "None of this is your fault. Certainly not what happened to Leato. Donaia would never blame you, and you're not under suspicion. I wish I could give you time to grieve with her, but Eret Simendis has asked me to lead the investigation, so I need to interview everyone as quickly as possible, to get a true sense of what happened. Can you tell me what you saw? It might help me find who *is* to blame."

The hideous face of poisoned Ondrakja rose up in Ren's mind.

It wasn't real, she thought. It couldn't be. Ondrakja was dead. It was like Ivrina burning alive, Ren's worst nightmares made manifest. Out loud she said, "I'll do anything I can."

"Thank you." Tanaquis marshaled her pencil. "Why don't we start with your arrival at the Charterhouse. Did you notice anything unusual?"

Mettore Indestor, looking at her as if he had the final piece he needed.

"No," Renata said.

She kept to the simple truth, describing what she'd seen in the Charterhouse. "I've not had aža before, but I'd heard it was supposed to taste pleasant. What we drank—" She reached reflexively for her cup, to clear her palate of the memory, but put it down again when she smelled the coffee.

"And then?" Tanaquis prompted.

At least she didn't have to hide her shudder. "I was in Seteris. With my mother."

"Ah." Tanaquis's nod said she didn't need further explanation: Letilia was nightmare enough. Then she paused. "You were there immediately?"

Ren's heart was beating too fast. It was like trying to match Sedge's lie to please Ondrakja. What had other people experienced? "Not immediately," she said, hoping that was the right answer. "I was in the Charterhouse, but alone. When I walked outside, I was in Seteris."

The little furrow wrinkling Tanaquis's brow suggested that wasn't what others had experienced. "Interesting. You changed location?"

Djek. "Yes," she said, because she could hardly take it back.

Chewing on the end of her pencil, Tanaquis nodded, then scribbled something illegible in the margin of her notes. "We may come back to that. What happened next?"

The best lies were built from truth. "I was my mother's servant," Renata said, and began describing her life in Ganllech under Letilia. Her real experiences there paled into insignificance next to what she'd gone through the previous night, but it didn't take much effort to infuse them with horror.

"Was that your only nightmare," Tanaquis asked when she was done, "or were there others?"

Had other people had more than one? Probably—but her brain, fogged with lack of sleep, failed to come up with anything else Renata Viraudax might plausibly fear. "No, that was the only one."

More marginal notes, making Ren nervous. She wished she *had* pled exhaustion; then she might have been able to gather information before coming here, and give the right answers instead of fumbling through.

"Did you happen to see a Vraszenian woman at any point?" Tanaquis asked. "She would have been young—about your age—and pretty. But plainly dressed, not like the clan leaders and their retinues."

"A Vraszenian woman? There aren't any of those in Seteris. Not that I'm aware of, at least." She wished she'd worn a scarf; that might cover the rapid beating of her pulse. She was too tired and too mudheaded to keep it under control. "Why do you ask?"

Tanaquis waved the question aside. "It isn't important. A few people have reported seeing the same woman, despite being in different nightmares. She tried to drown Eret Quientis. And she was seen leaving the amphitheatre with the Rook." She tapped her notes with her pencil, thinking. "What about the Rook? Did you see him?"

"Lumen, no. You think this was his doing?" Renata shuddered.

"The initial attack was on the Cinquerat. That's exactly the sort of thing the Rook would attempt." Tanaquis's frown showed her dissatisfaction with that answer. "But I'm here to learn the truth, not leap to conclusions."

Setting her pencil down, she studied Renata with eyes as shrewd as any szorsa's. "If there's anything you're keeping back, for whatever reason, I need to know. Otherwise, the wrong people might be blamed."

Hoping Tanaquis would take the unsteadiness of her voice for trauma, Renata said, "Do you think I don't want answers? I can barely recall what I went through without wanting to curl up in a ball and never move again. Not knowing how or why it happened only makes it worse."

"I can imagine," Tanaquis said, softening to frank sympathy. "I have to keep details of the investigation confidential, but since several people have guessed this already, I can tell you that the aža intended for the wine in the Charterhouse was replaced with a drug called ash. It causes hallucinations, along with increased strength and resistance to pain and cold. I'm not certain what was different last night, that people were drawn into those hallucinations as though they were real."

"They weren't real?" Renata let out an unsteady breath. "Then why...?"

"I've learned that the cup you and Altan Leato drank from contained a double dose," Tanaquis said. "So your reaction may have been different—more extreme than the others. I've been asking everyone to write out an account of their experiences, in as much detail as possible. I know it isn't pleasant, reliving what happened...and of course when it comes to nightmares, everyone has things they'd rather hide. But yours may be particularly important. I promise you that all the written accounts will be kept private; only I will read them."

The patient compassion of her gaze was seductive. A double dose: Could Ren use that to explain away what really happened to her? It would mean backing down on her earlier claims, but Tanaquis was clearly no stranger to this kind of inquiry, and would know how often people—even innocent people—tried to hide behind lies at first.

But Ren knew that once she admitted to part of the truth, she'd have a harder time keeping the rest back, and the next thing she knew, Tanaquis might realize she was the Vraszenian woman people had seen.

And whatever Tanaquis said about not leaping to conclusions, others were already looking for an excuse to blame her. Her and the Rook.

"Thank you," Renata said. "I know you're a friend of Donaia's, and it's such a relief to have you leading this inquiry. I promise, I'll be as detailed as I can." Out from under her shrewd gaze, it would be easier to come up with some additional material—things Renata Viraudax might have experienced, but been ashamed to admit.

Her stomach twisted with unease as Tanaquis went through what sounded like well-rehearsed comments about avoiding aža and alcohol until they were sure the ash was purged from her body. Then the acolyte returned and guided her to another room, where she was given pen and paper to write out her account.

It took far too long. The world felt distant, like it was on the other side of a pane of glass—like the nightmare was still holding her trapped. The truth of the situation was lowering onto her with crushing, inexorable force: The investigation wasn't going to discover what had happened, because Ren was doing her damnedest to hide it.

It is not *my fault*, she thought fiercely, staring at the page until her careful handwriting blurred. *It's Mettore Indestor, and whoever else did this to us.*

And I will make them pay.

Isla Traementis and Isla Prišta: Cyprilun 18

After Renata left the temple, she didn't go home. Instead she forced herself to tell the sedan bearers, "Isla Traementis."

Colbrin was wearing black when he answered the door. Renata wasn't; she didn't own anything black, and as neither a member nor a servant of House Traementis, nothing required her to change to Ninat's color. But when Giuna came out to greet her in full mourning, all Ren could hear was Leato's voice, reciting the litany of family he'd lost.

Of course the Traementis owned mourning clothes. They had constant need of them.

The worst part was that Giuna didn't blame her. If she had, Ren might have fallen back into her usual defensive habits of thought, and it would have hurt less. But when Renata tried to say she was the one who'd brought Leato to the Charterhouse, Giuna only hugged her tight and sobbed thanks to the Lumen that at least one of them had come out safely.

Donaia will blame me. She fought the urge to pull free from Giuna's embrace. *And she should.*

But Giuna had convinced her mother to drink a sedative, and Donaia was asleep upstairs. Renata wouldn't see her until the funeral the next day.

"You have to come," Giuna said fiercely, swiping at her tears. "I don't care about the register. We need you there." And Renata had no choice but to agree.

She didn't escape until nightfall, by which point her steps were weaving with exhaustion. Tess welcomed her home with another hug and bundled her in a blanket on top of the cranberry wool coat, because Ren was shivering again.

"Master Vargo called while you were out. He left some pastries and makings for spiced chocolate, and the address of his physician." Tess's hands twisted in her apron. "I . . . I asked if he could send some imbued medicines and creams against scarring. The way I see it, we might as well let him help."

Ren touched the bandage over her elbow. She wasn't the only one to come out of the nightmare with injuries, so she'd been able to explain away the cut the broken window had left on her arm. "Yes, that is . . . good." She went to scrub one hand over her face and stopped when she felt the scabs there. "I will have to talk to him tomorrow." Him, and Donaia, and the rest of the world.

The evening was still early, but neither of them had gotten any rest the night before. They devoured the pastries, washing them down with a weak tea of thrice-boiled leaves, then laid their pallet out in front of the hearth. Tess put Ren closest to the fire and curled against her back, enveloping her in warmth. Within moments, Tess was snoring gently.

But sleep wouldn't come for Ren.

She felt as if someone had cored her like a pear. She wanted nothing more than to sink down into oblivion; she was so tired, she doubted she would even dream. But she closed her eyes, and time passed, and she was still awake.

After a while she got up, easing out carefully so she wouldn't disturb Tess, and wrapped herself up again to pace and think. Then she lay down once more.

Still nothing.

She knew the truth long before dawn came. But she let Tess go on sleeping, even as fear wound itself around her spine like a snake, unease slowly growing into terror.

When Tess finally woke, she sat up and faced Ren, a worried question forming on her lips. Ren answered it before she could ask, in a bloodless, horrified whisper.

"I can't sleep."

14

The Mask of Bones

Isla Prišta, Westbridge: Cyprilun 19

Ren was staring blankly into the mirror when the doorbell rang.

This time she didn't flinch. She was too tired for the instinctive fear that had possessed her after the Night of Bells—what Tess said people were calling the Night of Hells, now. She just listened while Tess let the visitor in, and pressed her lips together when she realized it was Vargo.

A moment later Tess's voice came from the doorway. "Do you want him to go away?"

He'd sent her into the Charterhouse.

He thought he was doing me a favor.

"I'll have to face him sooner or later," Ren said dully. "Just...tell him I'll be down as soon as I can." Once she was done putting her mask on.

It took longer than it should have, and Ren doubted she could have given herself a plausible semblance of Renata's face if she hadn't done it so many times before. But finally the mirror told her she passed muster, and so she strapped a knife to her thigh, gathered her robe about her, and went downstairs.

Anticipating a rush of callers in the wake of the Night of Hells, Tess had taken extra care to set the stage of their one usable room. Even with the river-green drapes open to the street, the parlour was warm, thanks to a cheerful fire burning in the hearth. The fresh-polished wood mantel and wall paneling caught the light from the beeswax candles, the scents of almond oil and honey lying thick in the air.

Vargo stood with his back to the door, watching the late-morning street traffic go by. The peacock blue of his coat complemented the green-and-gold striped couches and amber gleam of the wood, but for a moment all Ren saw was the king peacock spider, the Varadi clan animal, that had tried to snare her in its web.

He turned when she entered, the sunlight cutting shadows across his face that obscured his reaction. She must not have done as well as she thought in hiding her exhaustion; Vargo hurried to her side and ushered her to a chair as round and inviting as a mushroom cap.

Then he took the seat across from her. "You look like you've been dragged through the river. I should have let you rest longer, but with Tess unbending enough to ask for something other than fabric, I was worried." His glance passed over the scrapes not even good makeup could entirely hide. "I brought an entire apothecary's worth of remedies. Also more chocolate. She's making it now. Am I being too heavy-handed?"

It wasn't his fault that tension wound her shoulders tight. But her own behavior was so often a performance, she couldn't help looking at him and wondering how much of what she saw was a mask. Would he really kill Sedge if Ren asked her brother to pry too far into Vargo's secrets? Or had he left those ways behind?

She hadn't answered him, and the silence had stretched too long. "My apologies. I—haven't slept well," she said, shaking herself to alertness and casting about for what else to say. Normally she could do this in her sleep; now she had to do it without.

Her gaze settled on the trim of his collar. "Master Peabody isn't with you today?"

Vargo glanced at his shoulder. "No. I know better than to bring a spider when visiting people troubled with nightmares."

"Oh. Yes. That makes sense." She pinched the bridge of her nose. "I'm not at my best."

"I could send something to help with that, although..." Vargo sat back, studying his folded fingers. "That might not be wise. I've heard they used ash. I've also heard that ash . . . doesn't play well with other drugs."

Right now, she wasn't sure she cared. She was so tired she wanted to cry. It took an effort of will to channel that into something useful instead. "You know about ash?"

Vargo grimaced. "As much as anyone does. It's a derivative of aža. First came to my attention back in Suilun—I looked into it because I hadn't heard about it before. Because I didn't control it. And because . . ." He looked away. "Because I *am* the aža trade in this city, which means they've been using my supply to make it."

Not so honest a businessman, are you? She only barely managed to keep that reply behind her teeth. Aža was harmless. If the Tyrant hadn't outlawed it, and the Cinquerat hadn't maintained nominal control, it wouldn't even have to be smuggled in.

She sorted carefully through her mind, trying to figure out what she could safely tell him. "Meda Fienola thinks Leato and I got a double dose."

"That's fast work. Did she say how—" Vargo's question tumbled into a self-deprecating huff. "Sorry. I expect the last thing you want right now is another interrogation."

"As long as you don't ask about the nightmares, it's fine." Those were dangerous territory; the moments leading up to them, less so. "I have no idea how the ash got into the cups."

The scar cutting through Vargo's furrowed brow gave it a permanently cynical look. "I can't imagine a reason he'd dose himself, not even to ruin relations with the Vraszenians, but I have to ask . . . did anything strange happen with Mettore Indestor?"

The whole conversation felt like balancing on a rope while drunk. "We didn't speak, but when he saw me . . ."

She shouldn't have let herself continue that sentence. Vargo's gaze flicked up, sharpening with curiosity.

Then inspiration came. "You must promise you won't mock me for this," she said.

Vargo's lips twitched. "Well, certainly not to your face."

Annoyance twanged along her nerves, but that was exhaustion

talking and she knew it. He was trying to lighten the mood. "I...
consulted a patterner. About Indestor."

"I didn't realize pattern had much of a following in Seteris." *Or
any*, the lift of his scarred brow added.

"It doesn't. But I was having abysmal luck finding anything we
could use against him, so I—well, I figured, what was the harm in
trying? And the woman I spoke to..." She let her fingers curl open
and closed, as if grasping for words. It wasn't much of a pretense
anyway. "At the time I dismissed what she said, but now I find that a
great deal harder."

"You should have a care with which ones you talk to," Vargo
warned her. "Most of them are harmless frauds, but others sell their
information. Era Novrus owns more than a few."

I bet you do, too. Masks have mercy—if she didn't sleep, she was
going to wind up letting one of those thoughts escape her mouth.
"If anyone paid to find out that I'm concerned about House Indestor,
I'm not the one who got fleeced."

Vargo frowned. "What did she say, to turn a rational Seterin
noblewoman into a believer?"

"She warned me that Mettore was planning something that
involved magic—she didn't know what kind, or why. That he
was—or is—building toward some decisive action, some turning
point, and that he would unleash a power he couldn't control. That
whatever he was doing would change things forever. And—"

Even with a lie to cover her source of information, it was difficult to make herself say the words. "That I was part of it somehow.
That Mettore...needed me for something."

"Needed you," Vargo murmured, his gaze growing distant.
"Interesting. I'd give a great deal to know what made her so sure of
that." He clearly didn't believe the answer was "pattern."

He fiddled with the edge of his collar. "Magic. Inscription? If he
wanted to do something that used you as a focus, that would prove
very bad for you—you aren't a god, endlessly channeling energy
from the Lumen. But there are easier and more subtle ways to kill a
person, if that was his goal."

"I don't think this was what he planned—I think it was some kind of accident. Whatever he's doing, it isn't finished yet." She couldn't suppress her shudder.

Vargo reached for her. She jerked away without thinking, leaving him with a hand suspended between them. He let it drop to his lap, his expression shuttering before she could read it.

But he spoke as though the rebuff hadn't happened. "What's her name? The patterner."

"Lenskaya." Then, too late: *Djek. I should have said I didn't know.*

"And where did you meet her? I'd like to speak with her myself. If only to make certain she doesn't have some other agenda."

"I, ah—" *I didn't think this through.* "Coster's Walk. Leato sent me there; he went to her before." At least Vargo's lieutenant Nikory hadn't gotten far enough into her snare to learn her name before Serrado drove him off. "But she isn't always there."

"Lenskaya on Coster's Walk." His fingers tapped a rapid beat against his knee. "That should be enough for my people to find her."

Not if I'm not there to be found. But would that make things worse? Some mysterious patterner gave Renata information, then vanished? She couldn't make that calculation—not right now, with Vargo right there. It was a problem for later.

She had a funeral to get through first.

When was the last time the bells had chimed? "I should get dressed," she said. "You'll be there today? At the Ninatium?"

Vargo took his cue, standing and giving her a slight bow. "I will. If you need a moment of peace, tug on your left earlobe. I have some skill at being a distraction."

It was the same signal she used with Tess, from their time in the Fingers. *I'll have to tell Tess to look for something else, or they'll both come stampeding in.* And it meant Vargo would be watching her closely throughout.

But the way she was feeling, she might need that assistance. "I would be grateful," she said—and for once, it was the unvarnished truth.

Seven Knots, Lower Bank: Cyprilun 19

Time was running short as Grey approached the Polojny family apartment. He'd spent the past two days tangled in Seven Knots, trying to persuade the Vraszenian clan leaders that dealing with him was preferable to dealing with anybody else the Cinquerat might send, and if he didn't leave soon, he wouldn't have time to clean up before Leato's funeral.

But he didn't dare leave this last stone unturned.

His knuckles struck the door of the Polojny family apartment with the weight of fatigue. The rooms above the chandler's shop in Grednyek Close were empty; the local gammers and gaffers told him Idusza hadn't been there in days. Grey hoped she was here, with her kin. The alternatives were all a good deal worse.

"Open the door for Vigil business," he said in Vraszenian, knocking again. As much as his people resented him for being a hawk, they resented it even more if he tried to hide it. "I must speak with Idusza Polojny about the attack on the ziemetse at the Charterhouse."

The door opened a crack, wide enough to reveal the apple-round face of Idusza's mother and not much else.

"Take your business elsewhere, slip-knot. Our Idusza was home that night. She did nothing and she knows nothing."

Grey resisted the urge to shove the door wider and force his way in. "I'm certain she was," he said, though he was nothing of the sort. Nobody stayed in on the Night of Bells unless they were ill or infirm. "The one I seek isn't her, but someone she might know. I just need to talk with her, and I'll be on my way."

He didn't have to try hard to look weary and uninterested. He let his exhaustion do it for him. The woman's expression didn't flicker, but from behind her came a familiar voice. "If you seek your Liganti friend, I haven't seen him."

"My Liganti friend is dead," Grey said harshly. "Same as the Kiralič and half a dozen more."

The door swung wider. Idusza shouldered in front of her mother and said, "I know nothing about that."

"No, but you..." Grey bit down on his antagonism before it could take control of his tongue. He'd passed all the other tests against his temper today. He could weather one more. "Please, is there somewhere not a doorstep that we can talk? I have only a few questions. And if I ask them not, someone else will."

Idusza's jaw tightened, and he saw her gaze flicker sideways, as if she could look through the back of her own head at her mother. "Follow me," she said abruptly, and came outside.

She led him though the crowded plaza to one of the canals, and a broken-down landing fronted by the blank face of a building. As long as they were quiet, people on the nearby bridge wouldn't hear their conversation. "Speak."

"The ziemetse think you and your friends were behind the attack on the Charterhouse," Grey said bluntly.

Idusza stiffened. "You think *we* did this? That we would give our own elders poison, and cause such suffering?"

"The Stadnem Anduske want Nadežra back in Vraszenian hands," Grey pointed out. "Killing the entire Cinquerat might help with that." What it would really do was start a new war—but radicals weren't known for their moderate thinking.

"At the cost of betraying our own people," Idusza snapped.

Grey forced himself to spread his hands in a mollifying gesture. "That *you* would not do this, I believe. But any large group has differences of opinion. And..."

She folded her arms tight against her ribs. "And?"

If she tried to shove him again, this time he would dodge; he didn't want to wind up in the canal. "There is another possibility. Which is that you are not behind it...but someone else uses you as a convenient scapegoat."

Idusza's jaw sagged. "You think...no. *No.*"

"He wouldn't be the first cuff wanting his inheritance sooner rather than later. Has he done anything—encouraged your lot to make plans or take steps that at least look—"

Grey got no further. Idusza's arms swung free and he retreated a step, but she held back from striking him. "You know nothing about him. Mezzan despises his father, yes, but he supports our cause. Already he has done things—" She cut herself off, spitting a curse. "I owe you no explanations. But he is not simply my lover. He is our ally, and he has risked much for our sake. He would never betray us."

Not for one second did Grey believe that Mezzan truly supported the Stadnem Anduske and their cause. Whatever he was doing with Idusza, it must serve some deeper plan. But pressing her further right now would get him nothing except a fight.

Which left him with one final lead. "Many people that night in the dream saw a young woman. Vraszenian, but not anyone they recognized. In several people's nightmares she appeared, and even spoke to a few of them—including the szorsa Mevieny Straveši, and Dalisva Mladoskaya Korzetsu, the Kiralič's granddaughter."

Idusza spat before he could ask the question. "Even if I knew anything about that, think you that I would turn her over to *you*?"

Grey's temper finally frayed out of his control. "Yes. Because I'm the only Mask-cursed hawk in this city who will make sure the clan elders talk to her first, instead of hauling her straight to the Aerie."

It rocked her back on her heels. The clans had no official authority in Nadežra, not since the conquest; one of the persistent complaints among Vraszenians was that their people were always handed over to Liganti judges. But their Accords delegation had been hurt every bit as badly as the Cinquerat—worse, since one of their leaders had died—and Grey giving them the chance to handle the problem first would go a long way toward placating them.

Once Caerulet found out, Grey would be dead. But he'd long since resigned himself to the likelihood of dying for the sake of this city.

The clock towers chimed, calling him back to the present. "Think on it. I must go," Grey said heavily. "My friend's funeral..."

He wasn't able to finish that sentence. Idusza's expression softened from its usual fierce lines. "Go. And—may your friend's spirit find peace in heaven, kin in the dream, and a new life down the road."

Ninatium, Owl's Fields, Upper Bank: Cyprilun 19

After the multicolored glory of the Sebatium the previous day, the Ninatium in Owl's Fields on the edge of the city was as stark as the space between the stars. Walls draped with black velveteen dampened all sound to a reverent hush. They were supposed to bring a sense of peace, closing out the bustle and distraction of the world, but to Ren they felt more like a shroud.

It wasn't a place for ordinary worship. People who wished to remember loved ones who had passed on, or to focus their minds in contemplation of the boundary between death and life, went to one of the smaller Ninatia elsewhere in the city. This one served only a single purpose, which was to reduce the bodies of the deceased to ash.

Even thinking that word made Ren flinch. Leato had been poisoned with ash; now he would become it.

She and Tess joined the slow parade of mourners down the path of numinata laid into the floor. Bitterness flooded her mouth. The Traementis had so few friends, and even fewer kin; in the normal way of things, she doubted many would have attended Leato's funeral. But he'd died on the Night of Hells—one of eight to perish, and the only one the city's nobles cared about. The rest were Vraszenian, or minor Cinquerat functionaries. So if the cuffs wanted to be seen showing their outrage at what had happened, this was their best chance to do it.

If it weren't for the oppressive silence of the temple, broken only by shuffling feet, she might have raged at their hypocrisy. The leash on her tongue was unraveling with exhaustion; sooner or later she was going to say something she shouldn't. Or take the knife from under her skirt and use it.

The mourners filed into the chamber and arranged themselves on the curved benches. Most were nobility—even Mettore Indestor was there—but she saw Vargo among them, and Tanaquis, and Grey Serrado, bleak-faced in dress vigils, with a black armband. Renata took her own seat and looked down into the half-sunken chamber at the center of the floor.

At its bottom, contained in a circle broken by a single missing tile, was a numinat: a nine-sided figure cast in liquid silver, as wide as the Sunset Bridge. Figures within spirals within spirals swirled around the nonagram with dizzying geometric precision: the channels along which the power of the cosmos would flow once the focus was set in place and the circuit closed.

Donaia and Giuna stood alongside a black-robed priest, three small figures in an area that should have held a dozen close kin. Dressed in black, they waited, not looking up at the crowd filling the room, until a gong sounded to mark the beginning of the ceremony.

Eight bearers carried out the bier, led by Bondiro Coscanum and Oksana Ryvček. Behind them came a woman singing a funeral chant, praying to Anaxnus: the Liganti name for the Mask of the deity Ren knew as Čel Kariš Tmekra, the bringer of life and death. Leato's body had been washed clean and wrapped in black cloth, hiding the wounds that killed him. Only his head was visible, antique gold hair shining painfully bright against the starkness of the scene.

Donaia's sobs echoed through the quiet.

They set the bier at the terminus of the numinat's main spiral, and together Leato's mother and sister approached to bid him a final farewell before laying a veil over his face. Ren squeezed her eyes shut to close out the sight, knowing people would be watching her, too, and not caring. With the ritual area set down below like that, she felt as if she were in the amphitheatre again, looking down the endless pit of the empty wellspring where she'd left Leato to die.

If Leato had been Vraszenian, she could at least take comfort that he'd died so close to Ažerais's heart. The three parts of his soul would find their roads easily from there: the dlakani ascending to heaven, the szekani lingering in Ažerais's Dream as an honored ancestor, and the čekani moving on to be reborn. But Leato had not been Vraszenian, and who could say if his soul would find its way free of the dream to pass through the spheres of the numina, as the Liganti believed. Perhaps his imperfections would not be burned away by the pure fire of the Lumen until he came to rebirth.

Shuddering away the thought, Ren opened her eyes in time to see the priest accept a sigil-marked disc from an attendant: the focus for the numinat, calling on the deity of destruction to bring cleansing fire. He raised it above his head and recited a series of prayers, then stepped forward and placed it at the center of the numinat.

Retreating outside the circle that would protect the onlookers from the forces within, he knelt and set the missing tile into the floor, closing the line.

Flames leapt up within the ring of tiles, blazing high. The heat of them beat at Ren's face. She remembered again the heat of her burning childhood home, and then she couldn't hold herself together any longer; she broke down crying. The weight around her shoulders was Tess's arm, trying to comfort without publicly overstepping a servant's bounds, and Ren held on to that sensation like it was a rope.

Only when Tess nudged her did Ren recall she had one more part of the rite to endure. Others had already risen from their seats, passing by a priest who stood ready with a tray of black tapers. She followed and took a candle. The wax already felt warm and soft from being so near the heat of the active numinat. All she had to do was touch the wick to the border for it to catch flame. As the mourners returned to their benches, their lights became stars in a sea of black—a reflection of the cosmos to which Leato's spark returned.

Or so the Liganti believed. Despite the heat of the crematory blaze and the warmth of candle wax dripping onto her gloves, it seemed like cold comfort to Ren.

When the ceremony ended, she wanted nothing more than to flee. But the crowd flowed out of the cremation chamber to a room laid with simple food. "I'll get you a bite to eat," Tess said, and hurried off. Unable to replenish her energy through sleep, Ren was making up for it by eating more than they could afford.

Unfortunately, that gave Scaperto Quientis a chance to drift up alongside her. So far she'd avoided talking to anyone who'd been in the Charterhouse when they drank the ash-laced wine, but she could hardly dodge him now.

"Alta Renata," he said, his voice a low rumble. "I apologize for not greeting you yesterday at the Sebatium. I don't imagine you were in the mood for niceties any more than I was."

She kept her mouth shut while she tried to remember. Yesterday? Yes—he was leaving when Tanaquis summoned her in. She cast about for something to say. "I'm glad you weren't drowned, Your Grace." *Shit. I hope people have gossiped about that.* Yes—Tanaquis had told her. She was safe.

"You heard about that?" Quientis asked. His eyes narrowed as he searched her face. She fought the urge to touch her skin, as if that would ensure her makeup was still in place. "Did you see her, too? The Vraszenian woman?"

"No, I—I only heard." What would Alta Renata say? "She sounds dangerous."

"Dangerous? No." His scowl was for the room in general, but she felt the weight of it all the same. "Only as dangerous as anyone who's afraid—which I suppose is enough. But I don't think she was trying to harm me. I suspect she couldn't swim." His scowl turned to Mettore Indestor. "But some seem more inclined to pin blame rather than seek truth. Probably best that Simendis handed the investigation to Meda Fienola."

Was he trying to send her some kind of coded message? She couldn't tell, and Tess hadn't come back yet; she was still gathering a plate of food. Ren caught her eye and tugged on her left earlobe.

Much too late, she remembered that she'd meant to arrange a different signal.

"Your Grace," Vargo said, sliding in next to Renata like he belonged there. "Alta Renata. Here, let me dispose of that for you." He tucked his walking stick under his arm and took the burned-out candle from her limp grip.

"No, I can take it," Tess said, breathless from hurrying across the room with a plate and a cup. Somehow, in the juggling act that followed, Scaperto ended up with the candle, Vargo with Renata's food and drink, and Tess with Vargo's cane.

Which left Renata empty-handed, and empty-stomached as well. She didn't realize she was staring at the food and drink Vargo held until Quientis said, "I'll go put this candle where it belongs. Good day to you all."

At Tess's pointed glare, Vargo cleared his throat. "It appears you don't need me anymore," he murmured, handing the food to Renata and accepting the cane from Tess. He leaned closer in what she briefly mistook for a bow, before she realized he was taking a better look at her in the dim light of the temple. "At the risk of being rude, you look ragged about the edges. Go home. Get some sleep. There's nothing more you need to do here."

She wished she could take his advice. But before she could escape, Donaia found her.

Tess took the plate back again so Renata could accept Donaia's hands in greeting. "You've ruined your gloves," Donaia said, thumb pressing into a spot of soft wax curving over the back of Renata's hand.

After so much time spent worrying she would say the wrong thing, Ren found herself utterly void of words.

Donaia supplied enough for both of them. "Thank you for being here. Have you eaten? Oh, I see you have. The food isn't much, but you should eat. I know it must be hard after... after the past few days, but don't think your youth will protect you from ill health. You have to take care of yourself. There's more than—"

"Mother." Giuna's hand on Donaia's arm stopped the flood of concern. "Don't badger her."

Donaia released Renata to wrap her arms around herself. "Yes. Of course. I apologize. It is only... you don't look well, and..." She released an unsteady breath.

"You should hate me."

For one terrifying instant, Ren wasn't certain which accent she'd said that in. But Giuna's confused reply of "Hate you?" and Donaia's terse "Don't be ridiculous" gave no sign that she'd spoken like a Vraszenian.

"I—if I hadn't taken him with me—" *If I'd made the Rook save him first. If I hadn't been who I am.*

"If, if, if. I thought you had more sense than Letilia—"

"Mother." Giuna touched Donaia's arm again, but her mother shrugged it off.

"No. I've flogged myself with 'if' since that night, and I am tired of it. This wasn't my doing, and it certainly wasn't Renata's." Donaia dashed away tears as though she was as impatient with them as she was with the rest of it.

"I only mean . . . it's hardly fair for you to be harsh with Renata for *not* being to blame."

"She knows I don't mean it like that. Don't you?"

Ren wished Donaia *would* mean it like that. This lack of resistance, this unwillingness to hurt her back, gave her nothing to brace against. And without that, she found tears slipping down her face again. "I'm sorry," she said, breath hitching as she fought for control.

But there was no control to be had, especially when Donaia's tears started to flow again, and then Giuna's breathing became unsteady, too.

"Oh dear, there's the lot of you done for," Tess murmured. She nodded at Giuna. "You've brought a carriage, yes? Why don't you let me call it and send you home."

"Yes. Th-thank you." Giuna had an arm around her mother. She slid the other around Renata. "You'll come home with us."

Donaia's grip on Renata's hands tightened, preventing her from pulling away. "Of course she will."

Isla Traementis, the Pearls: Cyprilun 19

Just when Donaia thought she was emptied out and couldn't possibly shed one more tear, a new wave of grief would pass over her. It started as a tightening in her throat before settling in her gut. Her head filled with the rushing sound of her own blood, like the spring flooding of the Dežera, and all she could do was curl up and clamp down and wait for the anguish to pass.

She remembered when she'd gone into labor with Leato. At the time, she'd thought she would die from the pain. It had been a wretched, grueling experience, only made tolerable because in the end, she had her precious boy.

That pain was nothing compared to the anguish of his death. And there would be no end to it, no Leato to hold and make it all worthwhile. Not until she died.

But she had to try to be strong. Renata was here and drowning in undeserved guilt. And Giuna deserved a chance to mourn. She'd loved her brother as much as any sister could. More, because they'd seen each other through the loss of so many others.

The cheerful peach upholstery of the salon's furniture seemed to mock her with all those losses now: her parents, her husband, their family, their wealth and power, and now, worse than the rest combined, her son.

"This family truly is cursed," she whispered, while Renata hunched on the settee and Giuna moved to pour them all wine. Donaia's hands tightened on the back of her favorite chair. In a surge of rage, she twisted and threw it to the ground. It didn't fall far; she wasn't strong enough for that. Just as she hadn't been strong enough to protect her children. She kicked the fallen chair again and again, ignoring Meatball's anxious whine and Giuna's attempts to hold her back, relishing the pain shooting from toe to hip.

"We're cursed! And it won't pass until every one of us is dead." She spun to face Renata, stumbling on her aching foot like a drunken woman. She didn't care what a sight she must be, with her face red and streaked and her hair falling in witch-locks out of its pins. "You should leave. Go back to Seteris. The curse didn't follow Letilia there. Maybe you can escape it as well."

Renata's pale face looked like a mask, her hazel eyes sunken deep. "Cursed? Leato told me..." The words died off. She cleared her throat and forced herself to continue. "That you've lost so many. But surely you don't mean...cursed?"

"How else do you explain this?" Donaia's gesture encompassed more than just their mourning clothes, the unheated salon, the faded Traementis glory. "You're the only luck to have come to this house in twenty years. Gianco always said Letilia took our luck when she left." Her throat was so raw that laughing was painful. "I'd actually started thinking you might have brought it back with you. More fool I."

As quickly as it had risen, the anger receded, leaving her hollow once more. Her chair was overturned, and she didn't have the heart to right it. She sank to the floor, crouching there like a street beggar, while Meatball crept close to press at her side. She wrapped her arms around him and buried her face in his ruff. "Leato is gone. What else can I call that but a curse?"

"Malice." The word burst out sharp enough to bring Donaia's head up. Renata crouched in front of her, speaking urgently. "Somebody *did* this to us. On purpose. Mettore Indestor, or—or—I don't know who. Or why. What they want. But this isn't the hand of the gods at work; it's...something else."

Taking the glass Giuna pushed into her hands, Donaia stared into the red depths of the wine. "Gods or men or monsters, the results are the same. Ill fortune haunts us, and there's nothing I can do to stop it."

She raised her gaze to meet Renata's. There was so much of Letilia in the girl, at least as far as looks went. But her kindness and intelligence and fire must come from her anonymous father. Perhaps her luck did as well. "You should protect yourself."

Renata went very still. She seemed to be looking straight through Donaia at something else—or at nothing at all.

Her voice sank low and rough, the cultured elegance of her accent cracking. "If you want me to leave, I will. I—don't want to be a burden, at a time like this, when you can't afford more weight on your shoulders. But if you're saying that only for my sake..." She shook her head. "I will not abandon you."

A soft sound from Giuna broke through Donaia's self-pity. Of course losing Renata would be another blow for Giuna. As it would be for Donaia, if she was being honest.

She grasped Renata's hand as though the girl meant to hie off that very moment. "For your sake, I should urge you to go. You have better, safer options—more than you might know—" She shook her head. She couldn't talk of parents now, not when she'd just sent her own son to the Lumen. "But now's not the time for that. You've been the opposite of a burden. Forgive me. I'm just a pathetic old woman who—"

More tears threatened. Donaia looked away, gaze fixing on the smudges of dirt she'd kicked into her chair's upholstery. Her foot throbbed, hot in her boot. She swallowed past the tightness and lost her breath in something between a hiccup and a giggle. "Who possibly just broke her toe. Bad judgment still beats out bad luck, it seems."

That pulled Renata from her reverie. She got Donaia up into a chair and her boot eased off; after a moment's painful but efficient examination, she pronounced the toe only sprained, not broken.

With that done, she sat back on her heels, looking much younger and more vulnerable than Donaia was used to. "Then if you do not want me gone . . . I will stay. And I will find some way to turn your luck around."

Isla Prišta, Westbridge: Cyprilun 19

Sedge must have been waiting for Tess and Ren to come home, because his knock came only moments after they reached the kitchen. *Knew better than to wait for us inside,* Ren thought. *Though, the way I am right now, I would probably have just blinked at him.*

No sooner had the door closed behind him than he demanded, "Why the fuck is Vargo telling his people to look for a patterner named Lenskaya?"

"What?" Ren stared at him, gape-mouthed. Then memory

came crashing back. "Oh, *fuck*." She collapsed onto the bench. "I completely forgot."

"Forgot what? What did you do, Ren?"

Ren buried her head in her hands. Through the fog of her thoughts she heard Tess explaining to Sedge, and his answering curse. Ren knew she should speak, but her exhaustion was overwhelming her mind. She sat, in a daze, until something Tess said broke through. "But she can't go. He'll know for sure."

"Might be worse not to go," Sedge said. "Vargo don't believe in pattern. Not as any kind of magic, anyway. Just women who are good at reading people and trading information. So now he thinks this Lenskaya is part of that. She vanishes into the river, he'll start dredging it to find her."

Ren began laughing. It wasn't funny—it wasn't even within spitting distance of funny—but her choices were laugh, or break down crying. "What is the worst that can happen? He finds out who I really am? Let him. Who gives a shit if the con ends; I've tried already to hook myself to a cursed house. Can't do much fucking worse than that."

"Cursed?!" Sedge and Tess echoed, both of them staring at her.

Shivering, Ren got up and grabbed a blanket, then moved toward the empty wine cellar, talking as she went. "Donaia said it. The Traementis are cursed—and I think she meant it literally. She blames Letilia." Ren retrieved her mother's pattern deck and stumbled back out into the main kitchen, pushing past Tess and Sedge, who were trying to follow her wanderings.

She sat down as close to the fire as she could get without risking the flame. *Don't want to end up like Mama.* Except Ivrina had burned to death from fever, not fire.

Ren stared at the cards. She would need them when she went to face Vargo as Arenza…but no, that wasn't why she'd gone to get them. She began to shuffle and cut.

"What do you think you're doing?" Tess asked.

House Traementis wasn't a person. Was it possible to pattern a group, an institution? Ren didn't know. But it was more of a question than an overall pattern, anyway, and no reason she couldn't try the three-card path, like she'd done for Leato.

Tess knelt and put her hand out to stop Ren before she could start dealing. "Are you certain this is a good idea? What with not having slept and all—who knows what you're like to find because of that?"

"Vargo said ash is derived from aža," Ren said. "Aža is supposed to help patterners." Sometimes. Maybe. It certainly made them *feel* like they understood the pattern better, but Ivrina had always been skeptical. Then again, Ivrina hadn't needed any help making the cards speak to her.

Sedge growled. "Ash is *nightmare poison*. Who's to say it en't going to make you see things as worse than they are?"

Another bitter laugh. "I'm not sure that's possible." She batted Tess's hand aside and dealt three cards.

An instant later she was on her feet and halfway across the kitchen, Sedge catching her mid-flight. Ren lashed out at him instinctively, twisting out of his grip. "No. No. I refuse—I *will not* do that to them."

"Do what?" Sedge asked, hands spread flat to show no threat. "Pattern them?"

"Turn into Ondrakja," Ren snarled. "In the nightmare, Mama laid a pattern—The Face of Gold was me with the Traementis. Ruling over them like Ondrakja, turning them into my Fingers. Donaia was right; they are cursed. All this destruction they've suffered, it isn't coincidence. All the people who have died, Leato, Gianco, their other kin, even Letilia leaving...it is all the same thing. And still the curse plays out. Donaia is next." She felt it in the marrow of her bones.

Tess and Sedge were exchanging worried glances. "Ren," Tess said hesitantly. "I don't doubt your skill with the cards...but you haven't even looked at them yet."

That stopped her dead. Tess shifted out of the way, showing Ren the cards she'd dealt—still lying facedown on the flagstones.

Ren trembled from head to foot. She hadn't turned them over. But she could see them in her mind's eye anyway: The Mask of Ashes for the current point, The Mask of Night for the path, and The Face of Gold for the end. Destruction, ill fortune, and doom.

She flipped the cards. All three were exactly as she'd seen.

"That's fucking unsettling, that is," Sedge muttered. Then he shook his shoulders, like a dog throwing off water. "You know those cards, though. Must have recognized them by their backs." It wasn't impossible. Ivrina's deck was imbued, and withstood the wear and tear of use better than most—but not perfectly.

Ren's eyes burned; she was forgetting to blink. Tess said hesitantly, "Does it have to mean bad things, though? The Face of Gold is wealth, isn't it? I know it was bad in your nightmare, but it might mean something else here. Maybe them getting rich again."

Ren swallowed the automatic scoff that rose to her lips. Three cards; two possible interpretations for each. The Mask of Ashes was destruction, no question about that. Hadn't she watched Leato's body burn just hours before? But the other two...did they mean disaster and greed, or calamity averted and a return to wealth?

There had to be a way to make sure it would be the latter. To help the Traementis, instead of letting their bad fortune tear them apart. But when Ren went to collect her cards and ask the question, Tess intercepted her with a cup. "Oh, no. You aren't touching those again until you've had some sleep. Drink this, and we'll see what it does for you."

Ren recoiled from the cup like it was a viper. "What is that? What are you trying to do to me?"

"Help you sleep," Tess said with patient determination. "I got it from Vargo's physician—told him you were up all night with bad dreams. And I've some nice chamomile tea for you, and lavender sachets tucked into the bedding. We'll have you sawing logs in no time, and see if you don't feel better in the morning."

Not poison. Why would Tess try to poison her? Ren drank the medicine down, grimacing at the taste, and accepted everything else Tess handed her after that.

But she knew, even before she lay down, that it wasn't going to work. The zlyzen had gotten her. They'd killed Leato, but they'd torn some part of her away, too, and she was never going to sleep again.

15

The Face of Glass

Ren had much less practice being Arenza, compared to Renata. The next morning she had to redo her makeup three times, swearing throughout, before Sedge pronounced it good enough to pass. "You sure you want to do this?" he said when she was finally done.

"You're the one saying he will be more suspicious if I don't come," she said grimly. "Tell me what other option I have."

Running away. But she'd told Donaia she wouldn't, and Sedge didn't suggest it. He only dug in one pocket and produced a battered little tin. "Swiped this from Orostin. Should help keep you alert for a bit."

She opened it to find snuff tobacco inside. Ren had never used it before, but she knew how; she placed a pinch on the back of her hand, sniffed hard—then promptly sneezed several times in quick succession.

Sedge managed a weak smile. "Try not to sneeze all over Vargo."

He took her to a seedy nytsa parlour in Froghole—exactly the sort of place where the leader of half the rookery knots in Nadežra might conduct the illegal side of his business. At fourth sun, even hardened gamblers tended to bury their faces in pillows rather than card hands, but the parlour was far from empty. A half dozen men and women cast in the same mold as Sedge loitered around a front table. The way they didn't glance over when the door opened said their presence was anything but casual.

Soot blackened the windows, leaving the room in a perpetual gloaming. Vargo sat near the far wall, his finery a jarring counterpoint to the cheap, wine-stained baize covering the tables and the bare, gnarled wood of the flooring. Even here, it seemed he preferred to dress elegantly. But he'd forgone gloves, scarred knuckles on display as his bare fingers drummed the table in boredom.

He wasn't merely waiting. Across from him, a man in a much cheaper coat droned on in a voice too low for Arenza to make out. Behind Vargo's left shoulder, a stocky, stern-faced woman with the dark skin of an Isarnah was as alert as her boss was bored. When she noticed Sedge's entrance, she nudged Vargo, and he interrupted his companion.

"I've heard enough. Take Varuni around to remind Udelmo that I expect him to report *all* income from the dice games, not just the income he thinks I should know about. Thank you for bringing this to my attention, Nikory."

Arenza's pulse thudded like a drum. *Nikory.* She ducked her chin and tried to look like her nervousness was at meeting Vargo rather than fear his lieutenant would remember the patterner who'd tried to cold-deck him.

Either way, she was waving a flag of weakness, with no chance Vargo wouldn't notice—and use it to his advantage. "On second thought, Varuni, you stay. Sedge can deal with Udelmo."

Sedge had the benefit of sleep to help him disguise his hesitation. Half of what made Ren willing to walk in here was knowing Sedge would be around if something went wrong. But if he balked now, something *would* go wrong.

He touched the inside of his wrist. An old gesture, from back when Ondrakja used to split them up: It was his way of reassuring Ren. "Limping or bedridden?" he asked Vargo.

"Limping—for now. It's only a first offense."

The casual tone belied the harshness of Vargo's answer. Sedge nodded and left with Nikory, and Vargo leaned back in his chair, studying Arenza. The twist to his smile was all the clue she needed to tell her this theatre was for her benefit. "You're Lenskaya?"

She nodded, concentrating on her mouth, her throat, so her accent would come out right. The more Vraszenian she could make her speech, the better for her disguise. "What is this about? Why has your man brought me here?"

"I understand you recently laid a pattern on behalf of an acquaintance of mine. A most *interesting* pattern." He leaned his elbows on the table, steepled fingers pressed to his lips. "Alta Renata Viraudax. Do you remember?"

Of course she did; she'd spent most of her sleepless night reviewing it. "I remember."

Vargo tilted his head. "Care to be more forthcoming?"

The soft words of his invitation held a sharp, threatening edge. She said, "What a szorsa tells her client should remain private, but—I will show you. If you wish."

"I wish. Sit. Please." He waved at the chair Nikory had vacated. Holding out his hand to Varuni, he accepted the forro she placed in his palm and set it on the table where a szorsa's bowl should be. "It seems only fair, even if the reading isn't precisely for me."

She left the coin where it was for the time being. Vargo might mean it as a bribe, but to her it was a gift to Ir Entrelke Nedje, and to snatch it up right away would look greedy. Then she began to lay out the cards, with no attempt at showmanship or artifice whatsoever. She'd even placed them all at the top of the deck, to reduce the chances that she would forget what she was doing halfway through. *Faces and Masks, just let me get through this.*

The past row she went through quickly. It hadn't been entirely clear when she laid the pattern before, and she didn't gain any new insights now. When she came to the present row, she slowed. "Here the alta's fate runs afoul of another's—Lark Aloft, and The Mask of Fools. They fit together, you see; they say Eret Indestor lacks some knowledge, some information. And I warned the alta this somehow involved her. But more I could not say."

"So she knew going in that he wanted something from her," Vargo murmured, studying Arenza rather than the cards.

"No!" The denial burst from her, unbidden. "She had no idea. Had I seen that, think you that I wouldn't have warned people? Tried to stop it?"

She regretted the protest, but it was too late to take it back. Vargo's eyes narrowed. "I don't know you. Maybe you would have." He might have a touch of Varadi in him, but his skepticism was that of any Liganti-leaning Nadežran. "Too bad your patroness isn't more direct with her warnings."

Patroness? She didn't think he was referring to Ažerais or the deity of fate, but if not them, then she didn't know who.

"What does the alta's future hold?" he asked, tapping next to the final row.

"Not hers. Indestor's." Her fingers trembled as she turned over the top row. "You see that seven of the nine cards come from the spinning thread. That means magic. Two Roads Cross means he plans some decisive action—but I doubt the Night of Hells was it. He wants to change something." She tapped Wings in Silk, then Storm Against Stone. "To do that...he will unleash a terrible power."

"Power usually implies numinatria," Vargo said, his gaze fixed on something past her shoulder. "But numinatria is rational, contained..."

A flicker of movement caught Arenza's attention. She glanced down and found a jewel-toned shape the size of a child's hand scuttling over the arm of the chair toward her lap.

One part of her mind said, *That's Master Peabody.* The rest of her shrieked and overturned her chair.

It was staged. She *knew* it was staged. But in that moment, she felt spider legs all over her skin, remembered the sticky strands of the web wrapping her in the nightmare. The only thing that brought her back to reality was the sound of Vargo's people snickering. If he hadn't kept his own face straight, the rage flooding her would have made her throw a knife at him.

"Ah, that's where he got to. Come here, Peabody." Vargo ducked

under the table. When he emerged, he had the spider on his sleeve—
and one of her cards caught between two fingers. "I believe you
dropped this."

Because she'd laid the original pattern using her mother's cards,
she'd brought that deck with her. Seeing the card in Vargo's hand
now added to her fury. She snatched it back from him with shaking
hands—then froze.

"The Laughing Crow," she whispered. "Communication—
Argentet. Era Novrus knows something."

"Does she, now." Vargo turned to the silent, watchful Varuni.
"And you thought this was a waste of time. It seems I'll need to follow up with someone from House Novrus."

Varuni snorted, stony face cracking into something that was
almost an expression. "I'll arrange somewhere safe from prying
eyes."

Vargo tucked the spider under his collar, then turned his attention back to Arenza. "Thank you for sharing this information. Is
there anything else I should know?" He obviously thought she'd
dropped the card on purpose, that the whole thing was a ruse to pass
along a hint.

*At least I did one good thing. If he had any suspicion that I looked like
Renata, screaming at the sight of Peabody probably convinced him otherwise.*

She hoped.

Vargo cleared his throat, bringing her back to her surroundings.
He'd asked her a question, and she couldn't remember what it was.
The fabric of her mind was thinning to gauze. "No," she said, hop-
ing it was the right answer.

"Then I won't waste any more of your time." Vargo took another
forro from his bodyguard and set it next to the first one. "Thank you
for coming, szorsa . . . What's your given name?"

"Arenza." Then, too late: *Fuck. I should have lied.*

"Arenza? Arenza Lenskaya." He said her name like he was tasting it. His gaze dropped with casual menace from her face to her
hands. "You must be new to the city. The punishment for graft
here is so harsh, I've hardly ever seen a Nadežran-born szorsa with

all her fingers intact. You have lovely hands. Don't you agree, Varuni?"

The Isarnah woman didn't even glance at Arenza's hands. "Yes."

Fingers drumming again, Vargo studied Arenza for long enough that the beat began to sink into her head, becoming the rhythm of booted feet coming to arrest her. To pull her fingernails, break her bones, brand the backs of her hands so clients would know she was a liar.

Then Vargo smiled. "But I wouldn't allow anything like that to happen to a friend. You can relax, Szorsa Arenza. So long as you don't disappear again, I'll keep your secrets."

Because she might be useful to him. Whatever he thought of Alta Renata, Arenza Lenskaya was nothing more than a tool.

"I understand," she said, answering the spoken and unspoken messages alike.

Seven Knots, Lower Bank: Cyprilun 20

If Vargo had half the brains he'd shown in his dealings with Renata, he would send somebody to follow Arenza after she left the nytsa parlour. So instead of turning her steps toward Westbridge and home, Ren wandered the streets aimlessly, trying to think of where a real Vraszenian patterner would go.

Someplace I could lie down. But that was out of the question.

Seven Knots. Not every Vraszenian in Nadežra lived there, but plenty did, and in its warrens she would have a better chance of losing a tail.

She kept an eye out as she walked, but her tired and twitchy mind insisted every fourth person was following her. Some of them stared when she flinched away, and that only made her flinch more. The narrow streets of Seven Knots seemed to tighten around her, reminding her of the clan animals hunting her through the darkness, the spider tangling her in his web. She'd thought of it as male—because of Vargo? Was that pattern instinct warning her, or just her own fears talking?

Tension hummed in the air as Ren roamed the lanes. Between the close-packed eaves she could see dreamweavers flocking, their feathers bright in the sun. The rising waters of the Dežera were bringing shoals of tiny moonfish; the dreamweavers fed on them, then wove grasses and river weed into the teardrop-shaped nests from which they got their name. Their presence was a sign that Veiled Waters was fast approaching. But the office of Iridet had closed the Great Amphitheatre so Tanaquis could investigate whether the wellspring had played some role in the Night of Hells. The city's Vraszenians might not be allowed to hold their customary celebrations there.

What had Mettore intended? To somehow poison the Vraszenians, but not those who shared their cups? Or had it all been someone else's plan?

In Ren's dream, Ondrakja had taken credit. But Ondrakja was dead.

The tightly packed buildings gave way without warning to an open plaza, surprisingly large for Seven Knots. It was filled with people in grey and silver—Kiraly colors—many with an embroidered koszenie lineage shawl knotted around their shoulders or hips. The sharp pain she felt at the sight nearly buckled her knees: She had no koszenie of her own. That was proof that she wasn't really Vraszenian. And her mother's shawl had been stolen along with everything else when she died.

The hope of getting it back was what had led Ren into Ondrakja's snare.

But of course the Kiraly were gathering. Their ziemič had died; every clan member in the city would come to mourn him on Tsapekny, the day named for their clan animal.

Beyond the crowd stood a columned building. Ren had never gone inside, but she recognized the place; it was the labyrinth of Seven Knots. All her own childhood devotions had been done in the labyrinth on the Old Island, a tiny, cramped place that seemed to huddle under a disapproving Liganti gaze. When she was a child, she hadn't minded. But if she went there now, it would only dredge up memories she couldn't endure.

Here, she might find comfort.

Ren threaded her way through the crowd before she could change her mind and passed through the labyrinth's open gates. The building was a large, square colonnade, each column hung with two images: a Face and its matching Mask, the two aspects of a given deity. Their mouths were open, receiving the offerings of worshippers who begged the favor of the Face, the mercy of the Mask. Ren circled the colonnade, sidestepping other worshippers, trying to decide who best to make her prayers to. There were too many to choose from—too many curses weighing on her, the Traementis, the whole city.

In a sudden fit of desperation, she began emptying her purse. Ir Entrelke for good luck and Ir Nedje to avert bad, Hlai Oslit for revelations and Gria Dmivro to avert madness. An Lagrek to be not alone, Nem Idalič for justice, Šen Asarn to make her well, and Šen Kryzet to purge the taint of ash from her body. Čel Tmekra to guide Leato's soul, even though he wasn't Vraszenian. She put coin after coin into mouth after mouth until she had no more to give, and some people in the colonnade were staring at her.

Ren ignored them and faced the labyrinth.

It filled the inner part of the building, a broad courtyard open to the sky, laid out with ankle-high stones set in a thick carpet of grass. The builders must have imbued the labyrinth to keep the grass green and lush, or the path would have been trodden to dirt by countless passing feet.

She found the opening of the path and drew a deep breath, closing her eyes. Dizziness washed briefly over her, but when it passed, she opened her eyes and began to walk.

It wasn't a maze like the mirrors she'd chased the Rook through, designed to confuse. A labyrinth was a single path, winding back and forth, inward and then out again, bringing the worshipper close to the center only to swoop away again at the next turn. Walking it was meditative—not the sitting meditation of a Liganti temple, but the calming, steady movement of the road. Of the river.

When Ren was a child, her mother had hung a small thread labyrinth above her bed to trap bad dreams. Walking the path here was supposed to trap misfortune, giving one a chance to leave it behind. What misfortune it trapped depended on which deity one had made offerings to. Ren was trying to leave everything behind.

She walked with slow steps, timing her breathing to them. How long had it been since she'd done this? Years, but she wasn't sure how many. There were no labyrinths in Ganllech, and Ondrakja had mocked any Finger who went to one. *Not since Mama died*, Ren thought. She'd done it for Ivrina because she could do nothing else: not afford a cremation in anything other than a mass bonfire, not dance the kanina for her to let the ancestors know she'd passed, the way the Kiraly in the plaza had gathered to do. A Vraszenian could make offerings alone, could walk a labyrinth alone—but some parts of their faith required a community, and she'd had none.

She didn't lift her head until she came to the circular space at the heart of the labyrinth. She was nearly alone; most of the people in the building had crowded at the doorway, music drifting in from the plaza beyond. The dance had begun. Every Vraszenian in Nadežra who belonged to the clan leader's kureč was joining in, stamping and clapping, while the other members of their clan watched, mourning.

Ren drew an unsteady breath. The point of walking the labyrinth was to find peace, not to upset herself more. But it took nothing now to bring her to the edge of tears, just as it took nothing to make her angry. Her foundation was washing away more with every sleepless hour.

There was a bowl of water at the center of the circle, in echo of Ažerais's wellspring. Ren knelt, dipped her fingers, and touched them to her brow, murmuring a soft prayer. Then she stood and walked a straight line out of the labyrinth, leaving her misfortunes behind.

At least in theory.

She didn't try to leave yet, though. The temple was teeming with people watching the kanina, and she didn't want to join them—to see whether the dancers had succeeded in calling the spirits of the ziemič's ancestors. Instead she wandered into the sheltered depths to one side of the labyrinth, where some toothless old Vraszenians were selling knotted charms: roses for good luck, stars for fertility, double wheels for wealth. She stared blindly at their wares while she waited for the crowd outside to disperse.

There was a red-threaded labyrinth laid out on one of the blankets, the sort one hung over a bed. Like the charm she'd had as a child. She didn't have a proper bed anymore, just a pallet in front of the hearth that she shared with Tess, but she could still buy it and see if it did any good.

Except she couldn't. When Ren reached into her purse, she remembered she'd given all her money to the Faces and the Masks.

Someone next to her reached out and picked up the labyrinth, handing a centira to the seller. Seeing it go made Ren want to burst into tears. Biting down so hard her jaw ached, she turned to leave.

The young woman next to her pressed the labyrinth into her hands. "Here."

Ren stared at it, not understanding. Then at the young woman, who met her gaze with steady eyes. After a moment of mute silence, the young woman said, "You remember me not?"

Where is my grandfather? Please, his health is not good! Put me in with him!

The Kiraly ziemič had died during the Night of Hells. The young woman in front of her was wearing Kiraly grey. That was his funeral kanina Ren had just heard, and this woman—

"You were with me in the cell," she said quietly. "And then you vanished."

Panic seized Ren by the throat and shook her like a terrier with a rat. This woman remembered her. Tanaquis had said the investigators were looking for the Vraszenian woman people had seen—the woman who might be responsible for the Night of Hells. Ren.

"Wait!" The Kiraly reached for her. "Wait, I—"

Ren didn't stay to hear the rest. She bolted, slamming through the people returning to their devotions in the colonnade, through the horde of Kiraly outside mourning their dead elder, through Seven Knots and out of it, running for Westbridge, running for a home that had vanished years ago.

Crookleg Alley, the Shambles, Lower Bank: Cyprilun 20

There were a few places in Nadežra safe from prying eyes. Vargo had made a point of acquiring several, houses and warehouses and other locations not associated with his name and used so infrequently that anyone keeping watch would waste enough of their time to give up. And to his satisfaction, the letter he sent at fifth sun was answered before seventh.

It seemed he'd left Iascat Novrus hungry for more.

With a clean room and a luxurious bed instead of a grimy alleyway and the wall of the Theatre Agnasce—and no crisis to interrupt—Vargo had all the time he needed to break Iascat in a variety of ways, all pleasurable to them both. He made full use of it, and afterward they lay in a tangle of sheets and cooling sweat, Iascat half draped over Vargo in boneless lassitude.

His forefinger toyed with the pair of tiny, etched discs dangling from Vargo's navel piercing. One was a standard contraceptive numinat; the other at least theoretically fortified his body against disease. Whether it worked or not, he had his doubts—but certainly it didn't do him any harm.

Then Iascat's hand drifted upward and began tracing the lines above Vargo's heart.

"That tickles," Vargo murmured. He didn't exactly mind, but it bordered on an intimacy he wasn't inclined to share.

"I've never seen a numinat inscribed on skin before." Iascat's breath ghosted over the tattoo. "Isn't it dangerous?"

Plucking up Iascat's hand to keep it from straying more over forbidden territory, Vargo brought his fingers to his lips. "It might be, if it was more than a bunch of nonsense scribbles I got because I thought it would be intimidating." At Iascat's startled look, he shrugged his free shoulder. "I was young. And stupid."

That part, at least, was true.

Iascat's fingers brushed Vargo's lower lip. "It's hard to imagine you like that."

A snort escaped Vargo. "I've changed. Grew up." Nothing remained of the boy he'd been. Not even his name.

"I suppose we all do." Iascat sighed and turned onto his back, his hand slipping from Vargo's grip, his gaze fixed on the canopy overhead, amethyst silk imported from Arthaburi. "Are you going to ask me? Or are you going to keep playing this out?"

The question roused Vargo from his own languor. "Ask you?"

"Whatever it was you wanted on the Night of Bells. When you sent Fadrin to tell me how talented—and interested—you were." Rolling his head to the side, Iascat fixed clear blue eyes on Vargo. "I'm not my aunt, but I am her heir, and I wasn't scribed into the register yesterday."

"Ah." It *had* seemed like a remarkably easy seduction. Vargo should have realized that wasn't entirely due to his charms and Iascat's hunger.

"It's fine." Iascat waved away an apology Vargo hadn't intended to give. "It was nice to pretend for a while."

He was too flip, too studied in his casualness. Iascat might know the game, but the flush in his cheeks and flutter beneath the love-bites down his throat suggested that he was holding out for a denial.

The only kindness Vargo could offer now was honesty. He might gain more by pretending ignorance and reeling Iascat along, but... "Caerulet."

Iascat failed to hide his flinch. Vargo sat up and pulled the sheets over his lap, annoyed more at himself for being soft than at Iascat for inciting that moment of sentimentality. "I know House Novrus has no love for Mettore Indestor. I hoped to convince you that it would be mutually beneficial to share some of the secrets you keep."

Iascat pushed himself upright and sat on the edge of the bed. Tiny moles speckled the ivory skin of his back, like Vargo had spattered him with Froghole mud. "If you think my aunt isn't already using all the information she has to fight him, you're not as cunning as gossip suggests." He rose, collecting the clothing strewn across the floor.

"I think there are avenues available to me that your aunt can't use."

"Like fucking someone's heir?" Iascat yanked his breeches up. "Good luck with that. You're not Mezzan's type."

There was a hint of something useful there, underneath the acrimony. "Oh? And what is Mezzan's type?"

When Iascat's fingers fumbled with the fastenings of his waistcoat, Vargo rose up to his knees and touched the man's hip. After a moment of hesitation, Iascat turned back to face him and let Vargo handle the buttons. "Until recently, I would have said bitchy society girls."

He could be referring to Marvisal, but Vargo didn't think so. "Sibiliat Acrenix," he said, grateful Alsius was pointedly absent from his thoughts. House Coscanum might rule Nadežran society, but Acrenix was everyone's friend. A solid alliance between that house and Indestor would be devastating. "What changed?"

"He met a girl. A Vraszenian girl. A seditionist. With friends in the Stadnem Anduske."

Vargo had enjoyed himself a bit too much; it softened his self-control, and he scoffed in disbelief. Iascat reacted with sudden anger, tangling his fingers in Vargo's hair and gripping hard. "I'm not making that up. He's been sneaking off to meet her since before the new year. Leato Traementis found out. Convenient, don't you think, that he can't share that information with anyone now?"

Vargo studied Iascat's face, but his skin was too fair, his eyes too clear, to easily hide deception. "And your aunt hasn't used this because..."

"Because it's not terribly useful as leverage if Mezzan's doing it on his father's orders." Iascat released him and sat in a nearby armchair to tug on his boots. "Which I think he is. Mezzan likes a good armful, but he isn't enough of a rebel to go against his father by playing house with a Vraszenian radical. It only makes sense if he's deliberately stirring them up. But until we know to what end, it's just idle gossip."

Vargo ran through the other strands of knowledge he'd gathered, trying to connect them. Ash production in the Froghole lace mill. The Night of Hells. The lengths Caerulet had gone to so that Renata would be at the Charterhouse, and the chaos that had followed there. The warning from that morning—that Indestor was planning to unleash some sort of magic. Something catastrophic.

"Does your aunt have a patterner named Lenskaya working for her?"

"Not that I know of. Why?"

Vargo shook his head. No surprise that Iascat didn't know all the secrets his aunt kept, but it bothered him all the same. Why would Lenskaya point him at Novrus if she wasn't working for them?

He should have sent more than a single fist to follow the szorsa. But hopefully Dneče would have some useful information for him, once Vargo finished up here.

Iascat swept up his coat and shoved his arms into it. "I trust that information is adequate payment for services," he said, struggling to pull on his gloves.

Vargo hid a smile. Iascat was too hurt and angry for the insult to hold any sting. He slid from the bed, trailing one hand down his chest so those wide, earnest eyes couldn't help but follow. "Didn't you listen before? 'Mutually beneficial' means ongoing."

Iascat offered no resistance when Vargo took his hand and helped him work his fingers into his gloves. "The longer this goes on, the more likely it is my aunt will decide to put an end to...it."

You. Vargo knew what Iascat's warning meant. It had always been a calculated risk, going this route. His protection lay in the fact that everyone already expected the worst of him. There was a certain freedom in being scum.

He placed a chaste kiss on Iascat Novrus's gloved palm. "Then we should make the most of the time we have."

Isla Prišta, Westbridge: Cyprilun 20

Tess carefully hung up the labyrinth Ren had forgotten to drop as she fled Seven Knots—for all the good it would do.

"That's it," she said briskly, clapping her hands as though Ren's sleeplessness was a particularly dusty shelf that only wanted some effort to fix. "I'm for Vargo's physician, and don't you dare complain that it's the middle of the night. The whole point is that you should be abed, and you're not, so why should we let *him* sleep?"

As she spoke, she wrapped herself in the length of striped wool every Ganllechyn woman from child to crone wore to keep out the cold and damp. Ren knew it was too late to protest, but she said, "We tried already. And we cannot afford—"

"Vargo can. And he said he'd pay." Brushing back Ren's hair, Tess pressed a kiss to her temple. "I won't be but a moment. Just rest your eyes while I'm gone. Chances are you'll fall asleep the moment I step outside. Isn't that always the way of it?"

Ren mustered a wan smile, but Tess's forced optimism rang hollow. Exhaustion had taken her through fear to resignation: She was going to die from this.

But she couldn't say that to Tess.

With her gone, the emptiness of the kitchen haunted Ren. Sedge was busy on Vargo's business; he'd slipped away long enough to make sure she'd survived the meeting, but he didn't dare stay. Once she was alone, her gaze kept drifting to the door, waiting for the pounding, for someone to kick it in. Which would be preferable: hanging for her crimes, or dying by inches?

Shuddering, she touched the hilt of her knife. Then she wrapped herself in a blanket and drifted through the rest of the house.

The unused rooms weren't any better. Dustcloths shrouded the furniture, and the moonlight was scant, leaving Ren to navigate by locating the darker shadows amid the lighter. She couldn't stop shivering. The river was rising in flood, the dreamweavers building their nests, the weather warming with spring, but inside her, everything was ice.

The house was new construction, but without decorations to give it life, it reminded Ren of the ancient and moldering building on the Old Island that Ondrakja had passed off as a lodging house, calling the children her "tenants" whenever a hawk asked, and passing him a purse to make sure that answer sufficed. A vaguely plausible lie and bribes supplied on a steady basis: That was all it took for the hawks to leave her to her business.

Ren remembered tiptoeing her way along the floor at night, trying not to step on her fellow Fingers, learning which boards creaked and which ones were bent enough to catch an unwary toe. Down the hallway was Ondrakja's parlour, and Ren didn't have anything to give her. Ondrakja would be so angry…

Ondrakja's dead. And I'm hallucinating.

Leaving the kitchen had been stupid. She wasn't any safer in the rest of the house, and she was a lot colder. She should go back and wait for Tess to return. Somehow she'd wound up on the top floor; she inched her way down the steps, wondering the whole time why she bothered being careful. Did it really matter if she pitched head-first down them?

Back in the kitchen, the embers glowing below the grate pulsed red with threat. Or with a warning. The door closed, and Ren knew she wasn't alone.

She threw off the blanket and snatched out her knife, stabbing on instinct. Hard fingers grabbed her wrist, and a sudden burst of pain forced her to drop the blade. Ren broke free and grabbed Tess's cudgel, but the dark figure blocked her panicked strike and wrenched her around, tearing the club from her hand. She groped for another weapon, half-blind with desperation; a stale heel of bread came to hand, and she followed that throw by brandishing the bread knife, knowing it wasn't any use: The nightmare had come true.

He took the bread knife away and advanced, and Ren, retreating, caught her heel against the floor and fell onto the pallet in front of the hearth. She scrabbled for anything else to defend herself with, but there was nothing.

Her attacker knelt over her, gripping her jaw in one gloved hand. Ren's scream died in her throat, choked by terror. But instead of striking, he forced her face toward the fire—toward the light.

The explosion of brightness burned out her sight. When he wrenched her back toward him, all she saw was shadow. "You're not Arenza," he growled. "Or...you are. But you're also— Who the fuck *are you?*"

She had no answer. No words. She was fear, inside and out, and couldn't speak. The silhouette was familiar: the hooded shape of the Rook.

He released her chin, hauling her to her feet. "Here I thought you were just a victim. Wrong place, wrong time. But maybe what they're saying is true—that you caused the Night of Hells."

"No!" She tried to wrench away, but in her weakened state, she didn't stand a chance. "I swear it—"

His grip tightened painfully, printing bruises into her arms. "Then why did it end when I dragged you out of it?"

Now his hands were the only thing keeping her upright. Because she couldn't deny it: She was the reason the nightmares began, and she was the reason they ended. She didn't fully understand why, but she knew that much to be true.

"Nothing to say?" he snarled. "Should we try another? Where did 'Alta Renata' disappear to? Nobody on aža reported seeing her. How did she make it out safely while the Traementis heir died? Why were *you* with him instead?" A gloved thumb smudged her cheek, but for once, she had no makeup to protect her. "Except the answer's clear now—isn't it. The real questions are, what game are you playing at, and who are you playing it for?"

"I'm not! I—I—" Her words caught. She was breathing too fast, fighting back tears, because the Rook wouldn't give a damn if she cried; he would only think she was playing for sympathy. "If you think I would put myself through that—put *Leato* through it— I tried to get him out, I swear, but the zlyzen..."

She could see them again, writhing and tearing. She was in the kitchen with the Rook, but at the same time she was in the amphitheatre, in the wellspring, with Leato above her and far below, screaming, dying. And she couldn't save him. If she'd been smarter, quicker, not gone up to the Point, not drunk the wine, not gone to the Charterhouse at all.

If she hadn't been herself.

The Rook let go of her and she collapsed to the flagstones, huddling inward as if that would protect her. She felt like she was drowning. From a great distance she thought she heard the Rook talking—not the hard, angry voice of a moment before, but something softer, the same words over and over again. She couldn't answer. She could only shake from head to foot, caught fast in the grip of memory and fear, until the flood receded and left her stranded on the shore.

Her face and body were soaked with sweat. Her damp clothes caught the chill in the room, and her hair was plastered to her brow. The Rook knelt on the far side of the kitchen, far enough that she had room to flee—if she was ever able to stand again.

But he hadn't left. And he hadn't hurt her. She'd been utterly vulnerable, but he just waited for her to recover.

Waited... and set a cup of water within easy distance of her knee.

She picked it up with both hands, trembling hard enough that she risked dropping it. Sipped, swallowing past the swollen tightness in her throat. Set it down again.

"Better?" he asked softly. "Better enough to tell me the truth? Maybe you weren't the one who fed ash to everyone—but can you tell me honestly you had no part in it?"

"No." She was too tired to lie anymore. "I— The szorsa I met, and the statues in the Charterhouse—they talked. Mettore Indestor wanted me for something... but not that disaster, I think." He'd been dragged in along with everyone else. "I was conceived on the Great Dream. So when I drank the wine—the ash—I fell through. Into the dream. And I took everyone with me."

She thought every tear in her had already escaped, but a few more slipped down her face all the same. "I meant no harm. But it's my fault."

"Your fault," the Rook repeated. He stood abruptly and she flinched, almost knocking over the water, but he only began pacing the far end of the kitchen. His hands twitched in abbreviated gestures, as though he was arguing with himself, but he kept his distance, and he didn't touch the sword at his side.

"Why?" he said at last. "Why are you doing this—Renata, Arenza, whoever you are? What do you want out of it?"

Money. But the answer she would have given a week ago seemed hollow now. And besides, it wasn't the truth anymore.

Her laugh sounded more like a sob, even to her own ears. "I wanted to feel safe."

Everything that had gone wrong in her life, from the fire that destroyed her childhood to the desperate flight from Ganllech, could have been better if she'd only had the money to fix it. That, more than anything, was what she longed for: the assurance that when trouble came, she'd be able to survive it.

Something obscured her vision, and for a moment she thought she'd gone half-blind. It was only a blanket, though—the one she'd dropped during the scuffle. She looked up, confused, and saw the Rook holding it out.

"You're shivering. I'd build up the fire, but..."

But the kitchen was as close to sweltering as it could get. Tess was burning more fuel than they could afford, because no matter how many cloaks and blankets she piled on, Ren couldn't stay warm. She accepted the blanket anyway and wrapped it around herself. "It wouldn't do any good."

"Why? Are you ill?"

"I have not slept. Not since that night."

He took a step back, as though her sleeplessness was catching. "It's been three days."

Her mouth twisted. "Four, if you count the day before. And I have counted every bell. I am beyond exhausted; I have taken medicine..." A twitch of her hand beneath the blanket was meant to be a gesture at the labyrinth charm, hanging from its nail. "Nothing works. I cannot sleep."

"Have you tried *telling* someone?" He glanced at the thread labyrinth. "Someone who might have a better cure than a tangle of string?"

It sounded so simple when he said it. She couldn't explain the tangle within, the way it felt like admitting one thing would lead to admitting everything—the way terror stitched her mouth shut.

But the alternative was to go on as she was, until it killed her. And despite all her morbid thoughts, when the moment had come, she'd fought with everything she had to stay alive.

In a whisper, she said, "I'll try."

"Good." He moved toward the kitchen door. "Once you're feeling better, we'll continue this discussion. Because we aren't done."

A chilly gust washed over Ren as he slipped out of the kitchen. Then another, what felt like only a breath later—Tess, coming in and beating the mist from her shawl.

"Oof! What a rude man. As though folk only take ill when it's convenient to him. I had to screech half the street awake before he'd give me what I asked for." She held up a clinking basket in victory.

Then she set it down in a hurry. "What is it? What's amiss? Mother and Crone, what did you do to the kitchen?"

Ren blinked, looking around. Tess's sewing basket was overturned, the breadbox gaping open and its contents scattered, the table shoved askew.

Tess knelt before Ren. Her hands, cold from her trip to wake the physician, still felt warm against Ren's skin as she pressed them to her brow and brushed away the tears streaking Ren's cheeks. "What happened? What do you need?"

"The Rook." Ren coughed and tried to get out from under the blanket. "He was here. I...attacked him. We talked. He left."

"He came *here*?" Tess glanced about as though one of the shadows might be a hooded outlaw in disguise. "How did he know to come here? What did he..." She went rigid, eyes fixing on the rucksacks that waited by the door. "Is it time to go?"

Ren couldn't have run even if the Vigil really were on their way to arrest her. She'd burned out the last of her fire fighting the Rook. "No. I'll take the medicine you brought, but..." She took Tess's hands in her own, all too aware of how feeble her grip had become. "Tomorrow, we tell someone. Donaia. Tanaquis. Whoever. We cannot fix this on our own."

Tess sagged, her brow coming to rest against Ren's. "Oh, thank the Mother. Coming back here, I was thinking the same thing, but..."

But they were used to doing for themselves. Trusting anyone else with an admission of weakness was hard—and there was usually no point, because who would help?

Only now it might be different.

"First thing in the morning," Tess said, tucking the blanket back around Ren, "we'll go to Traementis Manor."

16

Three Hands Join

Isla Traementis, the Pearls: Cyprilun 21

Donaia's foot ached. Even bandaged and propped up on a stool, it pulsed with a dull pain that sharpened whenever she put weight on it. But she was grateful for that pain, because it provided an ongoing distraction from the howling grief of losing her only son.

She was also indescribably grateful for her only daughter. Giuna didn't know her way around politics and business, not nearly as much as she would need to...but when Donaia tried to retake the reins of management from her daughter, Giuna had said firmly that she'd rather help Donaia than hide in her room.

They'd both had a good cry after that. The next morning, dry-eyed, they settled in Donaia's study and dug into the charter work that wouldn't wait for their convenience.

Giuna's golden head bent over a lapdesk as she reviewed a complaint from Era Destaelio that alterations to the West Channel would shift trade away from Whitesail in the east. Donaia had a query from the offices of Iridet, demanding to know what inscriptor she intended to hire for the replacement numinat—but she found it hard to concentrate. Every few breaths, her gaze fell on Giuna, and she fought the urge to cling tightly to her only remaining child.

Colbrin's knock on the door startled her. It couldn't be time for lunch already, could it? "Alta Renata is here," the majordomo said. "With her maid."

That should have been good news. Of course Renata would visit them, even during the nine days of strict mourning; she was close enough to family to count. But something in Colbrin's expression made Donaia's gut clench with foreboding.

She saw why the moment he escorted Renata into the study. She'd eschewed fashion in favor of warmth, but still she shivered. Her maid had done the best she could with cosmetics, but they weren't enough to hide the dullness of Renata's skin and hair, the bruise-purple hollows around her bloodshot eyes. The maid had to assist her through the room as though she might lose her way between door and sofa.

Giuna made a stifled noise. "Cousin—"

"Apologies, Era Traementis," Renata said as her maid lowered her to the cushions. She made no attempt to carry out the usual greetings. "I took the liberty of asking someone else to meet us here today."

With the study door open, Donaia could hear the front bell ring again. Colbrin gave his mistress a mystified look; at her nod, he disappeared to let the new visitor in.

"Renata, you look..." Giuna barely managed to bite back the hurtful truth. "Do you need anything?"

Her maid jumped in to answer. "A lap blanket, if you have it. And would the era mind if I stoked up the fire? It's that cold in here."

Not nearly as cold now that spring had arrived, but Donaia nodded. She nudged Meatball over to Renata; the hound curled up like a comforting foot warmer while the maid tended the fire and Giuna fetched a blanket from the pile Donaia kept hidden in a cabinet.

By the time that was done, Colbrin had brought the second visitor. "Tanaquis?" By reflex, Donaia held out her hands in greeting. "What is this about?"

Renata roused herself with visible effort. "Since the Night of Bells, I've been completely unable to sleep."

Like a sea wind worsening to storm, the foreboding grew to

full-blown dread. Donaia caught her balance on the edge of her desk. *Not again. Not her, too!*

Thank the Lumen, Tanaquis retained a level head. She perched across from Renata, journal flipping open to a fresh page, eyes bright with an inquisitiveness that felt wildly out of place in response to calamity—but also, in its way, comforting. "When you say unable to sleep, what do you mean? Since when? How does it feel? What steps have you taken to remedy it?"

Renata began answering in a faltering voice, but she repeated herself and often lost the thread of her thought. After a while her maid took over, rendering the account in a brisk tone that couldn't quite hide her fear. Donaia had thought her simply a talented dressmaker, but the strength of her loyalty and concern reminded Donaia of Colbrin.

"We thought it was just the alta's nerves—that it would pass," the maid said at the end. "But it hasn't, and I'm that worried for her."

"Yes, going too long without sleep can cause irreparable harm," Tanaquis said absently, still scratching away with her pencil.

"Tanaquis!" Donaia snapped. The woman was a dear friend, but sometimes she forgot that others didn't see the world as a puzzle to be solved.

Jerking out of wherever her thoughts had gone, Tanaquis blinked at Donaia's scowl. "Oh. I apologize," she said, though Donaia would bet what little money she had that Tanaquis didn't know what she was apologizing for. "Our first task should be to relieve Alta Renata's sleeplessness."

"Yes. It should be." Donaia sat at Renata's other side, taking her hand. "What do you suggest?"

"In the usual course of things, I'd calculate the subject's birth chart and compare it to the day the sleeplessness set in, but . . ."

"I see," Donaia said, before Tanaquis could go on. "Giuna, why don't you take Renata's maid to the kitchen? Have the cook put together a basket to take back with her. At the very least, we can make certain she's comfortable."

"But—" At Donaia's quelling glance, Giuna nodded meekly. "Yes, Mother. Come along, Tess."

Renata clutched briefly at her maid's hand, as if her one security was leaving. Tess brushed her thumb across the inside of Renata's wrist, then left with Giuna.

Donaia could see Renata marshaling what remained of her strength. "You asked something. I'm sorry; my mind is like a sieve. What was it?"

This time Tanaquis waited for Donaia's nod before proceeding. "I've already calculated your birth chart at Donaia's request. And it was... odd. Do you have it to hand, Donaia?"

"Of course." Releasing Renata's hand, Donaia fetched it from the locked drawer of her desk. Tanaquis rolled it out and walked through the calculations briefly, but by the glazed look in Renata's eyes, she might as well have been speaking Enthaxn.

Finishing up, Tanaquis said, "So it seems... I don't know how to phrase this delicately. It seems highly unlikely to me that you were born in Colbrilun. Is there any chance you might be mistaken?"

"Colbrilun?" Renata frowned. "No—I was born in Equilun."

"Does that mean you were conceived in Nadežra? Before Letilia left? Perhaps during Veiled Waters?"

The rapid volley of questions disoriented Renata. "Conceived in— I— What? Yes, of course I was."

Donaia's grip on her hand tightened. *Tanaquis was right.*

But she knew that look in Tanaquis's eye. At moments like this, she reminded Donaia of an osprey, swooping for the kill. She was going to ask who Renata's real father was, at a moment when the girl was too weak to dissemble. And Renata, by her sudden shallow breathing, realized she'd given something away.

It was clear she'd lied to Giuna about her birth date. Donaia didn't know why—and right now, it didn't matter. Protective instincts roared to life. "Tanaquis," she said sharply.

She could see the question poised on Tanaquis's tongue, but after a heartbeat the astrologer reluctantly swallowed it. "On the twenty-ninth? During the day?" At Renata's unsteady nod, Tanaquis scrawled several more notes in her book. "I'll recalculate the chart immediately."

She was halfway to the door before she seemed to recall the problem at hand. "Oh, and I'll send some remedies for you to try. No one else has yet mentioned these symptoms, but I've been learning as much as I can about ash. Can your maid read and write? Good. I'll include instructions on when and how much to take. Tell her to keep notes on your reactions. I'll be in touch again this evening."

She left, neglecting to close the door.

"I'm sorry," Donaia said, stroking Renata's arm. "She can be very...focused. Which is usually a good thing."

"Thank you." It was nearly inaudible, and not a response to what Donaia had said. "I—I should have told you sooner, but—" One hand scrubbed across her cheek. "I'm not used to having...help."

Donaia had long hated Letilia for her own sake, and for Gianco's. Easy enough to hate her for Renata's sake as well. How anyone could have a child and not treasure them was beyond Donaia's understanding.

Wrapping her arms around Renata, she pulled the girl close. "Of course you should come to us. We'll take care of you." Leato had been so welcoming, so happy at Renata's arrival in their lives. Donaia was ashamed it had taken her so long to agree with him.

She stroked Renata's hair, biting down on tears. "I'm not going to lose you, too."

Isla Prišta, Westbridge: Cyprilun 21

The world was growing more and more unreal, more and more distant, like she had to reach across miles to touch the nearest object. When Tess appeared in Ren's field of vision, her voice seemed to come from the far end of a tunnel. "Captain Serrado's at the door. I told him you're sick, but he says it's urgent."

Serrado. Terror choked like a noose around her throat—he'd come to take her to the Aerie. But Tess talked her down, the lilt of her Ganllechyn accent buoying Ren up. She pushed herself upright with one trembling arm, dragging herself closer to the world by force of will. "I'll see him. Where's that snuff Sedge stole?"

Tess had to half carry her to the front parlour, because Ren kept lurching sideways into walls. When Tess let the patient captain in from the front step, the crispness of his dress vigils felt like a threat. Not even his frown of concern could assuage it.

"Donaia warned me you were ill, but I . . ." He cleared his throat. "I'll keep this brief, I promise."

Standing at attention as though giving a report, the captain said, "Era Traementis told me you aren't able to sleep, and I've confirmed the details with Meda Fienola. For the past several months, I've been looking into something similar. People—children—unable to sleep."

Like the one she'd seen on the Old Island. Hope stirred in her heart. "Do you know how to fix it?" She'd spent months speaking in Renata's voice more often than her own; it stood her in good stead now, making the words come out in Seterin accents without any effort.

The lowering of his eyes answered before his mouth did. "I . . . don't."

She sagged back into the sofa. *No one does.* "So I'm just fucked."

Serrado didn't flinch at the profanity. "You're much healthier than the other victims. That has to be good."

Other victims. A hand snagging on her gown, bruised eyes in a hollow face. An equally hollow voice saying, *I can't sleep.*

Serrado, cradling the dead child on a Lacewater stoop.

For a moment that child was Tess, or Sedge, or one of the other Fingers, and Ren was thirteen, or ten, or eight, looking at death coming for her. She couldn't sleep because she was a child of the streets, and she'd betrayed her knot. This was the doom that should have fallen on her for that, striking home at last.

Serrado's voice broke through the hallucination before it could really take hold, cursing in Vraszenian. She came back to awareness to find him hesitating a short distance away; then Tess was there, with a blanket and soothing words, holding her steady against the uncontrollable shaking.

Soothing words for Ren, at least. Serrado was lucky he didn't get his ears blistered. "If you've nothing useful to share, you can leave," Tess spat when she'd run out of colorful invective.

He knelt so he wasn't looming over them and spoke urgently. "Whatever happened to these kids, it isn't caused by taking ash, and it isn't a physical ailment. That's important to know for helping you. And maybe now that an alta's affected, I'll be able to get more support in hunting down the person responsible. The children say an old woman is kidnapping them—they call her Gammer Lindworm. Have you seen anyone like that?"

It jolted her, like falling once more into the empty wellspring. *An old woman.* She didn't realize until Serrado replied that she must have echoed him out loud. "You know about her?" he asked.

Since the Night of Hells, the world had been on the other side of a pane of glass. That glass was Renata, and it cracked more with every incautious move she made. "There was an old woman—" she stammered. "I–in my nightmares. She said she had done this, poisoned us all, but..."

"She said she poisoned you? What else?" he asked, softer but no less insistent. "Did you tell Meda Fienola?"

What had she written in her report? She couldn't remember. "She... There were these...creatures." No effort could suppress her shudder. "Skeletal, but not bones. Blackened, like burned wood. But she didn't call herself Gammer Lindworm. She said her name was Ondrakja."

"Zlyzen," he whispered, his accent flavored with Vraszenian smoke. "They are called zlyzen."

The word made her shudder again, but it saved her from showing that she knew it already. "What are they?"

"Monsters. From the old stories. They feed on..." Serrado faltered. When he continued, his voice was pure Nadežran. "Dreams. So they say, at least. And there was a child gang in Lacewater run by a woman named Ondrakja. But she wasn't old, and she's been dead five years."

He stood, filled with sudden energy. "It's still more than I had before. I'll tell Meda Fienola. For now, do what you can to rest."

In the silence following his departure, a single question echoed through Ren's bones, until Tess finally gave it voice. "Could she have...survived?"

Recent events might be evaporating from Ren's mind like mist, but not old ones. "The apothecary warned me not to give more than three drops. I gave her nine. She *must* have died." But even to her own ears, it sounded more like a prayer than certainty.

A prayer that seemed even more flimsy when Tess repeated it. "She must have. And didn't the captain just say it? Ondrakja wasn't old. She might have been a horrid old hag on the inside, but you wouldn't know it from looking at her."

Two years on the streets had aged Ivrina visibly, and Ren had seen what happened to people who survived serious illness. The poison alone couldn't account for the way Ondrakja had appeared in the nightmare—but that was in Ažerais's Dream, where outward appearance might reflect inner reality. "It could be her," she whispered. "And if it is..."

"Then there's nothing to do about it until you're well," Tess said, as though that was an end to it. Wrapping an arm around Ren's waist, she helped her to her feet. "Downstairs with you, and let's pray Meda Fienola has a good head for more than astrology."

Isla Prišta, Westbridge: Cyprilun 21–24

Over the next few days, Tess's world shrank until she measured it one bell at a time.

That evening a courier showed up with medicine from Tanaquis and instructions on how to apply a numinat to it. *I fear this won't be pleasant,* her message said, *but I hope that purging the remaining ash from your body will resolve the problem.*

The possibility of cocking up the activation of a numinat terrified Tess. She reviewed the instructions several times, knowing that she'd only have a short while before the amplifying power of the numinat burned out the efficacy of the imbued purgative. Then she had to chase Ren across the kitchen to make her take it, because for a while Ren saw her as Ondrakja, come to poison her in revenge. In a twisted way, it was good that Ren was weaker than a sick kitten. Tess wound up pinning her and pouring the tonic down her throat by force, before its power could fade.

Any doubt as to whether it was still effective vanished not long after, as Ren was mercilessly sick. Thank the Mother and Crone—and Giuna's good sense—that the basket Tess had brought home from Traementis Manor contained several jars of salty bone broth. Getting that and water into Ren proved even more difficult than getting her to drink the purgative, though. Tess resorted to waiting until her sister was lost in delirium, then singing a Vraszenian lullaby, one of the ones Ren had learned from her mother. After that, she coaxed her "little Renyi" to drink as much of the broth as she could manage.

"It's for your own good," Tess whispered past the tightness in her throat. Ren curled on her side, limp as river weed, and gazed glass-eyed into the fire. Sometimes she closed her eyes, but never for long. The darkness behind her lids only served to make her more restless.

The purgative didn't work, and Tess duly reported this fact via messenger; she didn't dare leave Ren's side. The next day a second batch arrived. Tess wrote a reply telling Meda Fienola exactly where she could shove her remedies—then promptly burned the paper. Instead, she sent the medicines back with a terse note: *She won't be here to cure if you kill her first.*

Tess was quite proud of her restraint.

After that things only got harder. Giuna showed up, wanting to help Tess nurse Renata, and it was all Tess could do to find a reason to turn her away. She'd barely closed the doors on the girl's heels when someone else rang the bell—another courier, this one not bearing any tonics, just a message from Meda Fienola saying that she'd spoken again with Captain Serrado and conceded, based on his experience, that medicine wouldn't solve the problem.

The problem with Ren not sleeping was that Tess couldn't sleep, either. She didn't dare nod off, not with the hallucinations and paranoia making Ren so unpredictable. But sooner or later weakness would drag her down, and what would she do then?

It came as a crying relief when she heard Sedge's knock on the door. "Vargo's orders, if you can believe it," he said when he came in.

A flash of panic raced through Tess. "How did he find out?"

"That she's sick? Probably from that physician you terrorized. But Fienola talked to him, too, because you told her he was sending remedies."

"But why send *you*?"

"I know a bit about people dosed with ash," Sedge replied grimly, and refused to say aught more.

His presence meant she could sleep through the night, though she had to take the pallet to the parlour to do it. The next morning Sedge helped her carry Ren to the Tuatium in the Pearls, where Fienola had prepared some kind of numinat she thought would help the alta sleep. The only thing Tess could say for it was that it didn't cause the mess and fuss of the purgative.

Another night without sleep. Another day without answers. Sedge was summoned to talk to Vargo, because Vargo was talking to the Traementis and Serrado was talking to Fienola and Tess tried not to fret her fingernails off over what everyone was saying where she couldn't hear. Where *Ren* couldn't hear: Ren was the one who knew how to steer such things. But Ren was in no state to steer anything.

Tess couldn't leave her sister alone in the kitchen anymore, not even for a moment—not after Ren, in her growing delirium, tried to escape while Tess was busy relieving herself. That left the wine cellar, and Ren fought like a feral cat every inch of the way.

"You dare lock me up, you kinless bitch? I'll send you to the Vigil for this treatment!" The words were Renata's, but growled in Ren's throaty accent.

Catching a flailing hand before Ren could add to Tess's collection of scratches, Tess said, "You'll do no such thing."

"No? Maybe I'll just ship you off to become someone else's problem. Seemed to work for your family."

A shove sent Ren stumbling into the wine cellar so that Tess could slam the door shut and lock it. "You don't mean that," she whispered, too softly for Ren to hear through the heavy wood. But then, the words weren't meant for Ren. "She doesn't mean that."

Normally the kitchen was a comforting place for Tess. It was the center of every Ganllechyn home; some of the places Tess had lived as a child were little more than a kitchen and a few sleeping alcoves built into the walls. But the townhouse's kitchen was too fine, and with Ren locked up, too empty. The sampler Tess had hung proudly on the wall seemed now to mock her. How many kitchens had she passed through, handed from aunts to uncles, from cousins to kin only by marriage? Until the last of them packed her aboard a ship to Nadežra, only for her to learn on arriving in Little Alwydd that her great-uncle had died of mud fever months before, and her with no way to get home—and no family who'd take her if she could.

A sampler on the kitchen wall meant home: something Tess had never had, until now. But it was a stolen home, built on lies...and thanks to a single night of misfortune, it was crumbling away.

"You're being a maudlin ninny. Stop it." She dashed away tears. Perhaps a moment's respite and a bit of air would help. Scraping crumbs from the empty breadbox, she stepped out to the back walk to feed the finches.

Her heart thumped when she saw someone approaching along the canal's rim. *Pavlin.* And her a tearful wreck and too tired to care.

Tess did her best to wipe away the evidence of her self-pity, but he saw her attempt, and his step quickened. "Did something happen?" he asked, setting his muslin bundle on the canal wall and tentatively touching her cheek. His fingers were cool, and it was all she could do not to turn her face into that comfort.

Marry a man what brings you food, and you'll never starve for love. Tess shivered at the stray memory. And now her cheeks were warm for a different reason, though it didn't make her any less of a ninny. The ruse with Ren made such hopes impossible. It wasn't like she could tell him the truth.

"You're cold," he said, and made to take off the coat she'd re-tailored for him. The first of several over the past weeks—coats, waistcoats, a binder imbued for comfort—in trade for the bread he kept bringing.

"No, keep your coat. I'm tired, is all. The alta's taken ill, and there's only me to see to her needs."

"I heard. That's why I brought this. One less thing for you to worry about—and I included the spice cakes you like."

Tess took the bundle, tears pricking again. Pavlin came by so rarely. She hadn't seen him since before the Night of Bells. "Thank you," she whispered. She couldn't say why it meant so much that he'd come now, amid all this chaos. Perhaps it was like the kitchen sampler and the spice cakes: a moment of comfort that was only for her.

Before she could second-guess herself, she rose on tiptoe and pressed a kiss to his cheek. The softness of his skin lingered on her lips, even as she backed away. "I...I should get back to the alta," she stammered, and rushed inside before she committed any more foolishness.

And perhaps the Faces were smiling at last, because the next knock on the door brought word from Tanaquis that she might have a solution.

Tuatium, the Pearls: Cyprilun 25

Sedge and Vargo arrived at the Tuatium just as Ren's sedan chair did, with Tess at a panting jog behind it. Sedge forced himself to wait for Vargo's nod before he hurried to help.

"Vargo thinks I'm sweet on you, so if I'm giving you odd looks, that's why," he whispered to Tess while Ren cowered in the shadows and Tess reassured her that it was safe, that she'd be sleeping fine soon. "Was it bad, getting her here?"

"Three escape attempts on the way, and now she's afeared of daylight." Tess caught one wrist and Sedge the other, and together they managed to coax Ren out of the chair.

Convincing Vargo to bring him instead of Varuni had taken some doing, but the hours Sedge had spent at Alta Renata's manor gave him reason enough to argue for it. Vargo's assumption that Tess had caught Sedge's eye just helped the lie along. It was a rare bit of fortune, because Sedge was fucked if he was going to let Ren and Tess go through this without him.

So he tolerated the bath and the shave and the haircut and the nail-trimming that were the price of entry, and he did his best not to squirm too much in the layers of restrictive clothing a servant was expected to wear—clothes that would rip in the first hard scuffle. He tried not to cringe as he helped carry Ren through the sanctuary. He'd never much liked Liganti temples. There was nothing to steal and no fighting allowed, and the precise lines and carefully wrought mosaics left him feeling grubby and unkempt. Even now, cleaned up as he was, he felt like a man bound in a very fancy sack.

They led Ren to a library already full of elegantly dressed cuffs: Meda Fienola, Era Traementis, and Alta Giuna. Poised behind them was that hawk who kept showing up in and out of Ren's nightmares—Captain Serrado. Who sent a brief glance his way, and Sedge felt the miasma of distrust that stewed between the Vigil's hawks and Vargo's Spiders sour into mutual dislike.

Fienola didn't even wait for everyone to be seated before bringing the meeting to order. "What Alta Renata is suffering from seems to be an affliction of the spirit rather than the body. My tests and calculations indicate that when she came out of the realm of mind—what Vraszenians call Ažerais's Dream—she didn't emerge whole. Some part of her spirit was left behind."

She addressed her next words to Ren, even though whether Ren heard them was debatable. "It isn't quite true that you aren't sleeping, Alta Renata. Right now, there *is* no difference between sleeping and waking for you."

Sounded like dogshit to Sedge, who'd spent the better part of eight days watching Ren not sleep. But a glance at the cuffs showed that they believed.

Serrado cleared his throat. "Meda Fienola and I disagree on terms, but it's in keeping with how my people understand such things. Our souls have three parts, and one of those parts—Renata's szekani—has become lost in Ažerais's Dream."

"Therefore, the most obvious solution," Fienola cut in, "would be to sever her dreaming mind from the rest of her. She wouldn't ever dream again, but she'd be capable of restorative rest—"

"No!" Ren shrieked, jumping to her feet. Her hand swiped under her surcoat where she usually kept a knife. Sedge whispered a prayer of thanks that Tess had taken his advice and locked away everything sharp; then he moved forward and got Ren's arms behind her, and only Tess was in a position to see him touch the inside of her wrist. *We're here. We'll keep you safe.* Ren went limp, sobbing.

"Don't you worry, Alta Renata," Tess murmured into her ear, trying to sound soothing. "I'll send for your mother in Seteris if they dare try. Alta Letilia will put a stop to any such nonsense, see if she doesn't." Sedge guessed what she was about. *Remember Letilia. Remember the con. Remember who you're supposed to be.*

Once Ren had subsided, Alta Giuna raised a timid hand. "Could she go back to this realm of mind and recover the missing piece? Perhaps if she were given another dose of ash—"

"No!" The refusal burst from every throat in the room save Ren's. Vargo's chuckle broke the startled silence that followed. "Who would have guessed this crowd would agree on anything?"

"Ash is unknown," Fienola explained. "That makes it unpredictable and dangerous. It seems to allow people to interact physically across the boundary between here and the realm of mind, but even when they aren't drawn in bodily, the experience is often negative. I suggest experimental numinatria. It's dangerous in its own way... but it may be our only answer."

"I was under the impression numinatria was for channeling energy, not traveling between cosmic realms," Vargo drawled—

like he wasn't a better inscriptor than half the priests working for Iridet.

"The art is far more versatile than most believe, Master Vargo. 'I have my compass, my edge, my chalk, myself. I need nothing more to know the cosmos.' Those words aren't mere ritual to start a numinat. At the point where Illi becomes Illi, the purpose of numinatria is to seek enlightenment through the Lumen." Fienola's smile was condescending, making Sedge tense on instinct. If this were Froghole, he'd have punched that smile off her face at a lift of Vargo's finger.

But there was a reason Vargo was boss. He didn't take insult unless there was something to be gained from it. "Really," he murmured. "Interesting."

Sedge stifled his laugh with a cough. How did Varuni keep a straight face when she had to back Vargo playing cuffs at their own game?

Oblivious, Fienola nodded. "And in this case, possibly useful. There are meditative numinata that allow an inscriptor to separate their spirit from their body and walk the many realms of the cosmos. I've read the accounts of Mirscellis's experiments, which suggest this technique can be used for the realm of mind, too—the place where part of Renata's spirit is trapped."

She glanced around the room. "Giuna wasn't entirely wrong. Someone needs to retrieve it . . . but not Renata."

"I'll go," Tess blurted. "I've been with the alta the longest. I know her better than anyone."

"Your loyalty is commendable," Fienola said, "but an understanding of meditative practices would make success much more likely—"

"I'm a fair hand at imbuing—"

Era Traementis broke in, not unkindly. "If we were sewing a dress, you would be the first we'd ask for help. But I believe—I hope—that Tanaquis was suggesting *she* be the one to do it." She gave Fienola a pleading look. "You were, weren't you?"

"It would be fascinating," Fienola said slowly, gaze wandering as she became lost in the possibility. Then she shook herself back to the present. "But no. What I'm proposing involves changing the numinat after the seeker's soul has separated, in order to call it back. I wouldn't trust another inscriptor to do it correctly."

Sedge knew why Tess had volunteered. In Ažerais's Dream, who could say what Ren would look like? Tess and him were the only ones safe to go. But before he could find a good argument for it, Captain Serrado leaned over and whispered something to Era Traementis.

She pulled back, brows rising. "You?"

Serrado spoke for them all to hear. "I've had enough aža to be familiar with Ažerais's Dream. And I was spun during the Night of Bells, so I have some notion of what to expect—not just for myself, but for what the ash may have done to Alta Renata. Besides, sending me wouldn't put Tess or your family at risk."

Fuck that. Half of Ren's hallucinations featured Captain Serrado bursting through their door with a flight of hawks at his back. But Sedge couldn't very well say so.

Then inspiration struck. "If we're deciding who's expendable and knows aža, might as well be me who goes after her. Wager I got twice the experience of a hawk." His lip curled as he looked Serrado over. "Even a Vraszenian one."

Sedge pretended not to notice the suspicious shift from Vargo. Sedge had taken aža all of twice in his life: once to tie himself in with the Fingers, and once to do the same when he joined the Fog Spiders. Part of the reason he'd climbed so high in Vargo's knot was that he never touched aža again, and everyone knew it. He gave Tess his most sappy, lovelorn look, and hoped it didn't look like indigestion.

"I'm certain Alta Renata would be flattered that even strangers are concerned for her well-being," Vargo said, his voice dry. He folded his hands and studied Fienola. "But there might be a simpler way to decide. You've performed calculations; would it be possible to calculate our birth trines to see who's most likely to find Renata's spirit and return safely?"

"I could," Fienola said thoughtfully.

"Then let the cosmos determine who's best. Captain Serrado, what's your birthday?"

The hawk arched a skeptical brow, but said, "The fourteenth of Lepilun. At night."

"Sedge?"

Fucking Vargo. Sedge wished he understood enough of astrology to give a date that would meet Fienola's needs, but Vargo would know it for a lie anyway. "Will the year do?" Sedge asked grudgingly. "Think I can guess at that."

"Let's not leave it to guesswork. Tess?"

"We don't measure dates the same in Ganllech, but I once worked it out to be the twenty-fourth of Suilun. Daytime."

After Era Traementis and Alta Giuna gave their dates, Vargo said, "And I'm the twentieth of Colbrilun, during the day. Will any of us do?"

Sedge stared down at his boss, who was deceptively relaxed in his chair. Vargo, who *did* understand astrology. Vargo, who didn't do anything without a plan.

Fucking Vargo, a motherless river rat who didn't know the date of his birth no more than Sedge did. What the fuck was he up to?

Fienola had scribbled down each date and was now muttering to herself and making notes. The room fell silent save for the scratching of her pencil and an unearthly hum from Ren.

"Prime in Illi, influenced by Uniat. Alter in Tuat, influenced by Tricat," Fienola said at last. "Congratulations, Master Vargo. It seems the cosmos favors you."

He gave a seated bow. "I'm honored by its trust."

"I still don't like it." Fienola frowned at her calculations as though they'd betrayed her, then at Captain Serrado. "If there's anything to this business of Ažerais's Dream, a Vraszenian might be better."

Sedge's hands curled into helpless fists. He hated problems he couldn't punch his way out of. Serrado would be even worse than Vargo—but he couldn't think of a way to stop either one.

"I understand your hesitation," Vargo said. "Could we speak alone for a moment?"

A wave of his hand stopped Sedge from following as Vargo and Fienola slipped out of the room. All Sedge could do was stand there and trade worried looks with Tess—until he caught Serrado watching, and then he was forced to spread his glowers about equally.

When the other two returned, one look at Fienola's face told Sedge all he needed to know. The boss spider had wrapped up this one but good.

"After further consideration, I believe my calculations were correct," she said, cheeks flushed and eyes bright. "Master Vargo will be assisting me with the ritual."

With everyone else agreeing to it, there was nothing but for Sedge to carry Ren down to a large chamber lit with normal lamps—not imbued, not numinata. A platinum circle was permanently embedded in the smooth slate floor, with the spiral Vargo called a spira aurea looping inside. Fienola had been at work with her chalks; clean white lines and circles cut across the slate in confident sweeps. Mostly circles, the overlapping kind that Vargo chalked out at the start of every numinat Sedge had ever seen him draw.

At Fienola's instruction, Sedge crossed the lines without stepping on them and set Ren in one half of the largest set of overlapping circles. Vargo removed his coat and sat in the other half.

"How're you going to make certain she don't run off halfway through?" Sedge asked. "Maybe I should stay in it with her."

"That won't be necessary, nor advisable," Fienola said absently, checking her lines against a smaller version of the numinat in her notebook. "A Tuat working needs two people, not three, and I've strengthened the containment circle. Nothing will get in or out."

Sedge liked that even less, but Vargo sat unconcerned. And Sedge was out of ideas.

"All right, then. Guess you're the boss," he muttered. With a final brush of fingers across their shared scar, he left Ren in her circle and settled at the edge of the numinat with arms crossed and jaw tense.

"Then we begin," Fienola said, and closed the circle.

The Realm of Mind

For the first time in years, Vargo was alone.

No Alsius. No body, even. And maybe there was some truth to what Serrado said about different pieces of the soul, because he felt like he'd shed everything Alsius had given him, and what was left was a thin strand spinning out into infinite nothingness.

But he hadn't spent years observing spiders without learning a few tricks. He let that strand balloon him along until it caught and tangled with something denser than nothingness. Something thick as thought. The realm of mind. The dream of Ažerais.

He slipped inside and found himself bathed in cool silver light, standing on the steps of the Tuatium, at the overlapping edge of a vesica piscis so large it seemed to encompass the entire world.

The light came from the other half of the figure, sealed behind glass thin as a soap bubble. Vargo pressed a hand to it, but it was cool, slick, and unyielding. That was Alsius's world, not Vargo's... and without Alsius, he had no way to cross over.

"This just got harder." The glass echoed Vargo's words back to him. However closely bound the two of them were, Alsius would always know things Vargo didn't. He could feel them like missing teeth, pieces of himself he hadn't even realized weren't his until they were gone. In the few hours they'd spent planning this madness, neither of them had considered what it would mean for Vargo to be on his own, without Alsius's years of knowledge and wisdom.

Vargo wasn't even certain what he *was* without the old man's guidance.

"Guess we're going to find out," he muttered, and turned his back on the Tuatium and Alsius's world.

Vargo's world wasn't made of light. The streets of Nadežra spread before him in a murky web, full of shifting shadows and eyes flashing like knives in the dark. Everything here was waiting for a moment of weakness—for the right time to strike. The weight of those gazes was a physical thing, part hunger and part hate. He shivered and pulled his robe closer in a futile attempt to ward them off.

A robe that was nothing like the amber velvet coat he'd worn to Fienola's meeting. It wasn't even the beaded decadence he'd worn on the Night of Bells. Instead of sheer, the fabric was dull and threadbare. A garment easily lifted or opened, depending on which part of his body had been bought. Cheap tin bells clacked dully, advertising the wares for sale, and his fingernails were dirty and broken, as if he'd scraped them against countless stone walls.

Vargo shuddered. Without Alsius, this might have been his fate: not the master of the Lower Bank, bending Nadežra to his will, but a night-piece selling the only thing he had in order to survive. The thought made his skin crawl, and he stripped the robe off with angry movements, tearing the flimsy fabric and throwing it aside.

It vanished as soon as it left his hand—and reappeared on his body.

"Fuck you," Vargo snarled, addressing the darkness around him. "Dress me in what you like; it isn't who I am."

But a treacherous part of his mind whispered, *Isn't it?* He'd thought it himself, when he sat across from Mettore and sold Renata Viraudax out for a charter. Because it would get him closer to his real goals. Just because he wasn't paid in coin and didn't hand over his body in trade didn't change the truth.

In the real world, he could present whatever facade he liked. But here, all his facades were stripped away, locked behind the glass bubble that contained everything Alsius had made him.

The cold of that thought made him shiver. "I en't got time for this shit," he muttered. His urgency wasn't only because the realm of mind was determined to dress him like a cheap night-piece. He'd recognized that name Fienola used, Mirscellis: a Seterin inscriptor who'd lived in Nadežra before the Tyrant's conquest. Vargo couldn't remember most of the details—Alsius probably had them—but he knew the man's experiments with the realm of mind had ended with his spirit being lost there. Forever.

He had no intention of staying long enough to risk that. But how the hell was he supposed to locate Renata?

Fienola had said Renata's nightmare took her to Seteris, but his surroundings looked like Nadežra, more or less. Everyone had been dosed in the Charterhouse; if she'd lost some piece of herself, maybe it was still there.

As Vargo struck out across the Upper Bank, heading for the Sunrise Bridge, the city shifted around him. One moment the islets of the Pearls were carved out of literal pearls; then they turned into green, muddy fields, as if all of this were still ancient farmland. As he crossed into Eastbridge the houses curved around him, edging the Isla Čaprila like an embrace, with the center of the islet an open plaza. Surrounding him were the ghostly, half-there figures of Vraszenians, waving farewell to a caravan rolling out onto the nearest bridge. *A kureč*, Vargo thought, noting the similarity of faces. In the early days of Nadežra, Vraszenian lineages had built the foundations of the islets for their own people, different branches living in the various houses.

He stepped carefully on the bridge, walking a little faster every time it shifted from stone to wooden planks and back. That turned into an undignified leap when the sun rose just as he reached the Old Island and the bridge transformed into a beam of dawn's light.

Light that snuffed out like it had never been the moment he touched down, leaving him in the Tyrant's Nadežra. Vargo hurried along, head down, hoping none of the phantom soldiers around him would notice a lowly night-piece—or take him for the Tyrant's use.

Except he was headed to the Charterhouse, which had been the Tyrant's stronghold. *Please change before I get there*, Vargo thought, half in prayer.

He doubted any gods were listening, but the Charterhouse was its familiar bureaucratic bustle when he arrived. Vargo slipped through the crowds toward the audience chamber—and found it as echoingly empty as the antechamber had been full.

Given how things shifted, though, he wasn't going to take that for granted. "Renata?" he called out.

The name seemed to vanish as soon as it left his lips. Still, Vargo tried again. "Renata? Are you here? Ren—"

A shimmer caught his eye. Her prismatium dreamweaver mask— the one he'd bought her at the Autumn Gloria—lying on a bench.

Vargo climbed up to it. Was it his imagination, or was the metal warm against his fingertips, as if she'd just taken it off?

It felt solid, in a way nothing else here did. But unless the realm of mind had turned the missing piece of her spirit into a mask, he was no closer to finding her.

"Are you in there?" he muttered to the mask, feeling foolish. No response. Sighing, Vargo lifted it to his face, wondering if that would summon her.

It didn't. But it changed the dream around him.

He was still in the Charterhouse. Only now everything he saw had the faintest iridescence, like aža, like the feathers of a dream-weaver bird...everything except a trail across the floor. That was iridescent, too—but with a murky, rancid cast. Like ash.

Didn't szorsas say it in their readings? *The good and the ill of it, and that which is neither.* Aža was the good. Ash was the ill. This place was that which was neither—or both.

Vargo tied the mask on and pursued that trail. It led him out of the Charterhouse, into the Old Island. Then, as if he'd stopped paying attention while he walked—a thing he never did—he was suddenly in Lacewater, standing before the smoking wreckage of a small row of houses on the Uča Mašno.

For one mouth-drying instant, he thought it meant she had burned there. But the thing sticking up out of the ashes wasn't a bone; it was the corner of a pattern card. Vargo knelt and tugged it free.

The starved shape of The Mask of Hollows stared blindly up at him.

He frowned, looking at it. The Mask of Hollows represented poverty and loss—he knew that much—but it wasn't among the cards Lenskaya had shown him. So why did he feel like he ought to know what it meant?

No answers here. But the sickly trail led onward, and he followed it.

This time he knew the dream was acting oddly. He had no memory of crossing the Sunset Bridge, but suddenly the streets around him were as Vraszenian as if Kaius Rex had never conquered them. He was in Seven Knots, and from the shadows he could hear the calls of the Vraszenian clan animals, the hoot of an owl and the yip of a fox and the threatening stamp of a horse's hoof, warning him away.

No sound from the Varadi spider, of course. But the ash trail led him to a web, and caught in its strands, he found another card. A wolf slept beneath a flowering bush, or seemed to; one eye was a watchful slit, and its muzzle was stained with blood.

He couldn't remember what Four Petals Fall signified. Yet that feeling nagged at him again, that there was meaning here, and he was too stupid to see it.

The trail jumped him to the inside of a moldering townhouse, the kind of building Vargo knew all too well. Facedown on the carpet in front of a high-backed chair he found Sword in Hand. Then to the cells of the Aerie, where The Mask of Chaos was caught between iron bars. Then back to the Charterhouse—

For a moment he thought he was chasing his own tail. But a single statue stood where the five of the Cinquerat ought to be: an old one, wooden and Vraszenian, depicting a szorsa. In her hand she held Storm Against Stone.

Vargo scowled up at the carved, enigmatic visage. He remembered what it was like, listening to people have conversations with meanings he couldn't quite follow. He'd built up an information network to rival Argentet's just so he wouldn't have to put up with that feeling anymore. He didn't much appreciate the realm of mind inflicting it on him again.

So he kept moving: to a study that wasn't Mettore Indestor's, but had his colors and emblems all over it, where The Face of Glass seemed to be trying to hide in a corner; then he turned around and it was the same room, only with Traementis markings, and The

Face of Gold sitting in what he suspected was Donaia Traementis's own chair.

Onward to Westbridge, and the townhouse he'd rented out. The fire blazing in the kitchen hearth showed him Three Hands Join, gummed to the floor by a smear of blood. Not hers, he hoped. He had eight cards now; nine was Ninat, and death, and endings. There were nine cards in a pattern reading—one of the few places where numinatria and pattern overlapped.

The ash trail led upstairs. Her home—could it be that easy? But the house had the air of a place abandoned a hundred years... or one that hadn't yet welcomed a tenant. Everything was covered in dust-cloths and mist, as though rarely seen and even more rarely used. Only the front parlour had any life to it, and that was all gilt and hard edges, a place for show. Beauty whose only purpose was to be useful.

Was this how she saw herself? A facade, and emptiness beneath?

He found no ninth card there. Instead the twisted, desecrating touch of ash led him back to the Old Island, and the Point. To the heart of the City of Dreams: the Great Amphitheatre, and the Well-spring of Ažerais.

Except there was no wellspring. Just a ring of stones around an empty pit, and caught between two of the stones, Drowning Breath.

The final card. The trail ended there. And Vargo was alone.

He took off the prismatium mask, but that didn't summon her. If he had chalk and compass in this fucking place, he'd turn to them, but he only had the cards in his hands.

Pattern was the magic of Vraszenians. Pattern was the magic of Ažerais. Pattern was the key here.

Pattern was something he knew fuck all about.

Sighing, Vargo slung the mask over his wrist, then turned his back on the empty wellspring and knelt, laying the cards out, three by three, in the order he'd found them. Too late, he realized he'd done it the wrong way: szorsas laid the right-hand card in each row first, then the left, then the center, following their words. *The good and the ill of it, and that which is neither.* He'd gone straight across the rows.

But apparently that was correct, or else the dream decided he'd thrown his dart close enough to count. Because as Vargo set down the final card, a mist rose around him, and a gentle glow suffused it, coming from behind him.

Vargo was fully Nadežran. He scoffed at suggestions that his peculiar fascination with spiders spoke to some distant Varadi connection. And yet he couldn't quite bring himself to turn around and look at Ažerais's wellspring, outside the night of the Great Dream. He wasn't meant to be here, and he didn't want to offend whatever power might be present.

He cleared his throat and stood, mist swirling at his movement. "Are you here?" No answer. "If you are, let's not play a game of seek-me-out?"

"Seek me out."

A repetition of his own words, but not in his voice. Her whisper threaded through the air, barely more substantial than the fog. An instruction? Or just an echo?

Sighing, Vargo closed his eyes. "Uniat."

He was thinking of the children's game, but before he could continue his count, her whisper answered him. "Tuat."

As if they were about to fight a duel. "Tricat," he said before the dream realm could make that happen.

"Quarat," she answered, and his shoulders sagged in relief.

"Quinat."

"Sessat."

"Sebat." Was he drawing her to him? Or just wasting precious time?

"Noctat."

"Ninat." He opened his eyes and took a careful step, then another. The mist slid around him like silk.

"Illi," they said in unison, and the mist coalesced into the shape of a woman.

A shape even more indistinct than the phantoms of the dream.

She faced him, but showed no sign of seeing or recognizing him—a small mercy, he supposed, given how he was dressed. When he tried to reach for her, his hand passed through her like fog.

"Wonderful. How do I drag you out of here?" Vargo muttered. He and Tanaquis had assumed it would be enough to find her, which seemed foolish now.

The mist softened the ghostly form's beauty, making her look younger, more vulnerable. Or was that just how she felt, lost here? At least it didn't resemble her current state in the real world, bloodshot eyes and bloodless lips. That image haunted him: She'd looked like The Mask of Hollows.

The Mask of Hollows. When he looked down, the nine cards had vanished. But they'd gotten him this far.

What else did he know about pattern? Not much. Mostly that it was a bunch of metaphors about textiles: shuttles and spindles, weaving—

And threads.

Vargo exhaled and shifted his focus. Instead of a bowl of mist, he imagined the amphitheatre as a Varadi might see it: a circle spanned by a great silver web, with him at the center.

The mist coalesced into a cobweb, its filaments as fine as lace. Vargo looked for the thread that connected him to Renata's ghostly form, untangling it from all the others.

It was broken. All the threads around her were broken.

No wonder she couldn't come back.

Vargo gritted his teeth. Fine. People called him a spider, didn't they? Spiders made their own damn threads.

He held out his left hand, concentrating. He had no idea what the threads were made from, and had a definite suspicion he might regret this later... but he needed Renata, and the alternative was to sit here until his soul came permanently untethered and Tanaquis sent the fucking hawk in to retrieve them both. A silver thread unspooled from his palm, floating in the air, reaching out toward her.

She saw it. Her left hand rose, mirroring his gesture, and the thread touched her palm—

Tuatium, the Pearls: Cyprilun 25

::You're back! How was it? Fascinating, I imagine. Rather quiet here.
Though I do like this Fienola girl—very precise in her chalking.::

Waking felt like surfacing from very deep water. Vargo could
feel his body: stiff from sitting too long, one leg numb from being
bent under the other, head aching, mouth dry. But this was more
than his usual distance from his flesh. He eased himself back into it,
like putting on unfamiliar clothes, and opened his eyes just in time
to see Tanaquis remove the focus from the deactivated numinat.

The moment she did, Tess, Giuna, and Donaia all shot toward
Renata like bullets from slings, while Sedge and Serrado both hung
back trying to pretend they weren't craning their necks to look. But
Vargo, still seated, could see between the women's skirts to where
Renata lay in the other crescent of the vesica piscis that connected
them, curled up like a kitten . . . and snoring like a dockworker.

::Well done,:: Alsius said softly.

"Master Vargo." It was Tanaquis, pencil and notebook in hand.
"When you're ready, I'd love to collect your report."

17

The Peacock's Web

The Pearls and Eastbridge: Cyprilun 27–28

Ren drifted upward, unsure of where dreams ended and reality began. She felt as if she were wrapped in a cloud, and even once she surfaced enough to feel bodily discomfort, the cloud feeling didn't go away.

When she finally cracked an eye open, she realized why. She was lying on a thick mattress, with a heavy blanket over her, and a down pillow beneath her head.

Her first attempt to sit up produced only a twitch of her limbs. But that was enough to bring Tess into her field of vision—Tess, with an imprint of chair upholstery on her cheek, like she'd been sleeping upright. Relief and uncertainty warred in her eyes. "Ren?" she whispered. "How are you feeling?"

Understanding came as slowly as waking. Ren's memories smeared together, a mass of exhausted days and nights. The Charterhouse. The horrors that followed. And then the horror that didn't end: her inability to sleep.

Until now.

Her second attempt to sit up got farther, but Tess pressed her back down. "If you're up for it," she said, still in that whisper, "I've your cosmetics with me. I've done what I can, but you should fix it. We're in Traementis Manor."

An urgent need to use the closestool gave her good motivation to get up and away from the door. While Ren scrubbed away the previous makeup and reapplied her mask, Tess explained matters: the days of delirium and weakness, and the numinatrian ritual that healed her at last.

"*Vargo?*" Ren said, pausing with her eyes half-done to stare at Tess.

"He was that concerned. We all were."

She would have to think about that later. She'd been asleep for an entire day, and still felt like Sedge had stomped all over her in his boots—especially around the ribs, which Tess explained was from the purgative she didn't remember taking. But no worse than that, which alone was a miracle.

Ren was in Traementis Manor because it was that or the Tuatium, and Donaia had won that fight. "They wouldn't let me take you home," Tess said. "Tanaquis wanted to keep an eye on you."

Not surprising. And Ren honestly couldn't disagree. Tess had already done the work of twenty women, caring for her this past week; blurred and absent as most of her memories were, she remembered that much. It was dangerous, spending this much time in someone else's house, but Tess had managed to keep Renata's face on her well enough to pass scrutiny—and drooling into her pillow, it wasn't like Ren could do much else to ruin her own con.

Once Tess allowed the rest of the world in, things became a blur of a different sort. Donaia and Giuna cried over her in relief; then Renata inhaled an enormous meal while someone went to fetch Tanaquis. Donaia hovered through the whole examination that followed, as if guarding Renata from something, which was puzzling. Not until Tanaquis was gone did Tess get the chance to tell her that she'd apparently given away the real month of her birth at some point during her sleeplessness.

The suppressed question in Tanaquis's eyes made sense then, and Ren swore inwardly. How was she going to explain that away?

More problems for later. She slept again—more fitfully this time, in the too-soft bed with its smothering pillow—and woke to eat again, then more sleep, blessing every forro she'd spent on imbued cosmetics, which didn't rub off all over the sheets.

The second day, over the protests of everyone else, she rose, got dressed, and ventured out to visit the man who'd saved her life.

Her memory of the last week insisted Nadežra had been locked in the depths of murderous winter, but the streets were filled with brilliant morning sunlight and the trills of dreamweavers migrating northward for the spring. The canals were beginning to rise, the river's flood bringing them toward Veiled Waters. Renata threw back the curtains of the sedan chair and breathed in the sweet Upper Bank air, feeling alive for the first time since she had drunk the ash-spiked wine.

Though possibly not for long. Tanaquis had complained that Vargo's report was woefully short on details; Tess said that Sedge had heard even less. Whatever Vargo had seen in Ažerais's Dream, he was keeping it to himself.

Blackmail material lost its value, after all, if one shared it with too many people.

Vargo's townhouse was almost a mirror of Renata's, on the other side of the river in Eastbridge. When she knocked on the door, it opened to reveal the dark-skinned woman she'd seen around Vargo before, though her name slipped through the holes in Ren's mind. She'd been there when Vargo met with Arenza, but showed no flicker of recognition—or anything else—as she said, "Yes?"

"Alta Renata Viraudax. I'm here to see Master Vargo."

The woman's expression didn't alter. "He's not at home."

Truth, or a servant's well-practiced lie? "Can you tell me where he is? Or when he'll be at home?"

"No."

"It's all right, Varuni." Vargo's familiar baritone preceded his appearance in the doorway. His hair was mussed, and he wore a river-blue dressing gown only slightly less decadent—though considerably more opaque—than his courtesan costume from the Night of Bells, with Vraszenian-style trousers beneath. "I'm always at home for Alta Renata."

Renata half expected to be on the receiving end of a surly look, but the woman merely said, "Understood," and stepped aside.

As Varuni strode away, Vargo shoved his hands into the pockets of his robe—possibly to avoid taking hers bare-handed. "Are you certain you should be out? You look realms better than the last time we met, but it was a hard week even before you fell ill."

His expression was unreadable, but he didn't act like a man gloating over his leverage, nor one who'd recently found out that a river rat had conned him. The tension winding her shoulders tight eased a notch, and she managed something resembling a lighthearted smile. "I'm certain that as much as I appreciate my pillow, I'd prefer to resume my life."

"Then I shouldn't make you stand around." Tilting his head in invitation, he led her to a small salon at the back of the house. The south-facing bay window caught the morning light and channeled it through a warming numinat etched into the glass, and a teapot sat on a low table between two plum velvet couches. "Please, sit. Would you care for tea? It should be warm."

Of course it should, because the tile underneath the pot was also inscribed. She hadn't seen such widespread use of numinatria anywhere but the finest of the great houses.

The plush cushions cradled her as she sat. Renata accepted a cup of tea and curled her fingers around it, searching for words. She could count her life-debts on one hand: Tess, Sedge, Leato, and the Rook. And now, Vargo.

Her attempt to put that degree of gratitude into words came out awkwardly formal. "I understand that I have you to thank for my life."

"You don't need to thank me." Vargo cleared his throat. "It's the least I owe you, after..."

He kept his head bent, stirring honey into his tea, but the stiffness of his shoulders spoke for him. She blamed herself for Leato's death. Did Vargo blame himself for what happened to her?

Hesitantly, she said, "You didn't know there would be any danger."

When he straightened up, his expression was unreadable. "Do you remember anything? I mean about the past week, not...*that* night."

The Night of Hells. "Very little," she admitted. "Or rather, I'm not certain how much of what I remember is real, and how much is hallucination. After Leato's funeral, things get increasingly muddled."

"What about the realm of mind?"

There was a thread of tension in his words. She almost fumbled her own cup, setting it down. She'd been so worried about what he might have seen that she'd never considered—but he'd been nearly as exposed as she'd been. Was he worried about what *she'd* seen? "If you're asking whether I remember what you did, I'm afraid not. I only know that you took a risk for my sake."

The morning sun caught his profile as he glanced away. He hadn't shaved yet, and the light picked unexpected hints of red out of the stubble. "Don't mistake me for a hero. I'm just loath to lose the best advocate in Nadežra."

If she had to ask outright, there was no point in attempting subtlety. "I'm glad you still think of me as such. I shudder to think what you saw of me while I was ill—or in the realm of mind."

That brought his gaze back to her, with a faint quirk of his mouth. "You needn't worry, Alta Renata. I know the value of a secret kept." The half smile faded. "I went after you because I didn't trust the others to keep yours."

Before she could decide what to make of that, he stood. "Have you eaten yet? Would you care to?" He cocked his head toward a small table in the bay window and held out his hand in invitation.

She hadn't lied when she said she didn't remember Ažerais's Dream. But in that instant, a flash of memory overwhelmed her: Vargo, standing in a sea of mist, holding out his hand as a silver thread unspooled from his palm.

And another man, holding the rope that drew her from the pit.

Reflex laid her gloved hand in his bare one, even as her mind reeled. Vargo escorted her to the table, then departed to fetch the food, leaving her alone in the salon, hand hovering in midair. *A secret kept.* Her whisper was the barest ghost in the silent air of the salon. "The Rook..."

The idea was absurd. Vargo was a Lower Bank crime lord. Sedge himself had warned her about his ruthlessness.

But Sedge also said Vargo had changed recently.

Legitimate business. Replacing the river numinat. And hunting evidence against Indestor—that was the kind of thing the Rook might do. She'd seen for herself the disdain he had for cuffs and their fine society, while simultaneously playing their game. He could have broken into Mettore's office after the Traementis left the engagement party. He could have been in Lacewater the night Mezzan lost his duel. He could even have been in the mirror maze; if the Rook's hood was imbued, it stood to reason that the rest of the disguise was likewise more than ordinary, facilitating the kind of swift changes the outlaw must engage in.

He could have been in her kitchen the night after she was idiot enough to present herself in front of him as Arenza.

His voice from behind made her jump. "I wasn't expecting a guest, so it's only tolatsy—rice porridge with mushrooms, onions, and smoked pork. More or less a staple of every Vraszenian breakfast. But it's good. And filling."

The dish in his hands smelled of warmth and home. Did he mean the food as some kind of taunt—a nod to Ren's true ancestry? No; whoever the Rook was, he must be diligent about hiding his identity. He wouldn't give it away in a moment of pettiness.

Vargo set the dish on the breakfast table in the bay window, then scooped Peabody off the back of one of the couches and placed the spider on his shoulder. "I have something else for you. Meda Fienola wanted to confiscate it—she was fascinated that I'd managed to bring it out of the realm of mind—but I told her no lady should be without her mask."

The lump in the side pocket of Vargo's dressing gown caught in the fabric as he tugged it free, but the moment she saw its edge, she knew what it must be.

The prismatium mask.

Her breath caught, and her hands trembled again as she accepted it. "I thought I'd never see this again."

"It led me to you," Vargo said. "That, and a series of pattern cards. The realm of mind is . . . an interesting place."

She made herself stop running her thumb over the feathery edge of the mask and set it aside. Vargo had given her an excellent opening, and she meant to use it. While he collected two bowls and spoons from the sideboard, she eased herself into a chair and said, "Did you ever find that patterner I told you about?"

"I did." Vargo handed her one bowl and sat across from her with the other. His expression was as bland as if they were discussing the weather. "Sedge found her. One of my men; I don't know if you remember him. I sent him to help after I found out you were unwell. But let me know if he's bothering Tess, and I'll find other ways to occupy him."

She blinked in confusion. *Bothering?* Tess had mentioned nothing of the sort. "I'm sure he's no problem. Did the patterner give you anything of use?" She remembered a card had fallen when Peabody surprised Arenza, but not which card, nor if Vargo had followed up with Renata about it. The problem with forgetting things was she didn't know how *much* she'd forgotten.

Vargo spooned a helping of tolatsy into his bowl. "That remains to be seen. She put me on Era Novrus's scent, though it's unclear whether she works for Novrus herself. And when I went looking into that, I turned up some interesting gossip—that Mezzan Indestor has a Vraszenian lover, possibly on his father's orders."

He knew about Idusza? "Rumor has it there was a Vraszenian woman involved in the Night of Hells. Could that be this secret lover?" Before Vargo could respond, she continued, "But no, people said she was with the Rook. I can imagine Mezzan poisoning the Cinquerat out of spite for his father, and I can imagine the Rook poisoning them out of dislike for the nobility, but I can't imagine the two of them being connected through some Vraszenian." She served herself some tolatsy and stirred it thoughtfully.

The scar through Vargo's brow appeared briefly, then vanished. "You can imagine the Rook doing that? True, he hates the nobility—but he usually ignores Vraszenians. Or at least doesn't go after them."

"What about the story that he killed a Vraszenian?"

He stilled. "You mean the Fiangiolli fire? Accidents happen—even to the Rook."

"So you think it was an accident," she said. "Perhaps not the fire itself, but the man dying."

His face might as well have been a mask: mildly curious, but no more than anyone might be at an unexpected conversation. "Why so much interest? You've asked about this before."

And you've acted oddly when I did before. As if it were a sensitive point with him.

Ren drew a deep breath and met his gaze, keeping hers as clear as she could. If he was the Rook, he'd been in her kitchen that night, and he would understand her now; otherwise, let him think her entranced with the legendary outlaw who'd claimed her glove. "Because I want to know what sort of man the Rook is."

He didn't look away. It was a game: who could read more, who could hide better. Vargo ended it with another quirk of his scarred brow. "I see I've lost my place as your hero. Probably for the best. He's better suited to it." Picking up his spoon, he lifted it like a toast. "Eat your tolatsy. It's getting cold."

Isla Traementis, the Pearls: Cyprilun 28

Ren found out the hard way that she'd pushed herself too soon. She returned to Traementis Manor with the intention of thanking Donaia for her hospitality and then relocating back to her own townhouse; instead she put her head down for just a moment and woke four hours later, at which point she remembered to ask Tess what on earth Vargo had meant about Sedge bothering her.

"Didn't you know? Sedge has succumbed to my womanly charms." Tess simpered and draped herself over the edge of the bed like she was posing for a painting. Then she spoiled it by giggling. "The looks he was giving me ... You should show him a few tricks in case he *does* take a liking to someone, so he won't scare them off."

It finally made sense once Tess explained the situation as a cover for Sedge being around more. Given their sworn bond, Tess and Sedge sleeping together would be incest, and would break Ren's mind to boot. "But what about Pavlin?" Ren asked teasingly.

Tess blushed to match her freckles in response. "I see somebody is feeling better. Now hold still or I'll send you down with your hair half-done."

When she was coiffed to Tess's satisfaction, she went downstairs to be examined one last time by Tanaquis, who was taking extensive notes on her recovery. When that was done, Renata said, "Meda Fienola, if you wouldn't mind staying a moment longer, I'd like to speak with you and Era Traementis."

Tanaquis settled back into her seat, gaze sharpening. "Of course."

She'd been restrained in questioning Renata on matters unrelated to her sleeplessness, but her curiosity was clearly bubbling not far beneath the surface. The three women settled themselves into Donaia's study, and once the door was securely closed, Renata took a deep breath and began.

"Era Traementis, I must apologize. A few months ago, when Giuna asked when I was born, I—I lied. I didn't mean to, but my whole life I've been accustomed to saying I was born in Colbrilun ... and then after I said it, explaining the truth seemed unthinkably awkward."

Donaia exchanged a glance with Tanaquis. "We thought perhaps ... It doesn't matter. But why?"

When Tess brought Ren to the Tuatium to be cured, she'd brought something else along as well, as a good-luck charm. It was in her pocket now, and with a silent prayer to steel herself, she drew it out.

Her mother's pattern deck.

"Two years ago, I found this at an agora in Seteris. I didn't know what it was—it merely looked interesting, and though it sounds strange to say, I felt as though I should have it." She smiled in self-deprecation. "After I bought it, I learned it was a Vraszenian pattern deck. A silly superstition, and a diversion for myself and my friends; I performed a few readings for them.

"But then...Mother found out."

Renata raised her eyes to meet Donaia's. "I've never seen her so angry in my life. She almost threw the cards into the fire, until I stopped her. I demanded to know why she was so upset, and she told me that before she left Nadežra, she and some friends visited a szorsa."

It was the kind of thing bored young nobles did—witness her own abortive outing with Sibiliat and the others. "I don't know what the woman said to her, but Mother admitted she went back several times more, on her own, in secret. Whatever they talked about, when Veiled Waters came, Mother was persuaded to take aža and go up to the amphitheatre...where she met a man."

She let her lips twist into another ironic smile. "Mother claims he was beautiful beyond words and must have been a god, but I think that was the aža talking. She lay with him, and soon afterward, realized she was with child."

Given that she'd already admitted to a different month of birth, they must have suspected she was working toward a revelation of that kind. But the look they exchanged was even less surprised than that—as if they'd anticipated it long before she began talking.

What do they know? Neither of them said anything; she had no choice but to go on. "Which should have been impossible, of course. Mother insists she still had her contraceptive numinat, that she hadn't lost it in her revels; at this point we'll never know. But that day, when she caught me with the pattern deck, she swore it was the fault of the szorsa that she found herself pregnant. That the woman had done something to alter her fate—as if Vraszenian superstition could overpower numinatria!"

"It most certainly can't," Tanaquis said. "But numinata can be poorly inscribed, and if the man wasn't wearing one himself..."

Renata sighed. "Whatever the cause, it put Mother into a panic. From what I've seen of Eret Quientis, I imagine he would have duly registered me once they were married...but it would have broken the story Mother liked to tell herself. Not a celebrated beauty with the hearts of everyone laid at her feet, but a prosaic bore's fiancée who got spun on aža and had sex with a stranger in the Great Amphitheatre. Mother couldn't endure the thought. She decided the only thing to do was to run away to Seteris and find her beautiful lover there."

"So the man she met was Eret Viraudax?" Donaia asked, brow furrowing.

"Hardly," Renata said with a bitter snort. "The man I've always known as my father has never left Seteris. He was merely a rich altan who liked the look of my mother and was willing to indulge her fantasies. His wealth, laid against a man who might not even be in Seteris, or have any fortune or position even if Mother succeeded in finding him...It was no choice at all. She persuaded Father to adopt me as his own, and ever since has told the world—myself included—that I was born in Colbrilun, to hide the fact that I'm not his natural daughter. That I was conceived in Nadežra."

Renata sagged in her chair, as if admitting the truth had lifted a great weight from her shoulders. "After that I decided I must come here and see—well, see what I could discover. Only I'm not certain what I'm looking for." She made herself meet Donaia's gaze again. "I'm sorry, Era Traementis. What I said to you when I first arrived, about wanting to reconcile you with my mother—that was utter nonsense. Both moons will sink into the northern sea before that happens. But I couldn't bring myself to explain the truth to a stranger, and having started in that fashion...I didn't know how to stop."

"You're hardly to blame for your mother's foolishness," Donaia said. Then she passed a weary hand over her face. "Though I'm relieved *you* weren't foolish enough to expect reconciliation."

Tanaquis looked like she wanted to be taking notes. "You were hoping to find your father? Or some news of him? There are some

Seterins here besides yourself, but you don't seem to have been seeking them out."

"And say what?" Renata asked ironically. " 'Do you remember impregnating a spoiled young alta more than twenty years ago?' No, I realized when I got here that it was beyond impossible."

She needed to turn the conversation before they prodded any more closely at the fabric of her lie. Fortunately—if it merited that word—she had something guaranteed to drive the subject from their minds. It was the reason she'd involved the pattern deck at all.

"But there's something else I should tell you, though I apologize for bringing this up when you already have so many other things to grieve you. The other day, Era Traementis, after the funeral... you said House Traementis was cursed. And I—I was delirious at the time, and perhaps what I saw was only my sleeplessness talking, but..." Placing one hand atop the cards, she said, "I laid a pattern for your family. And I believe you *are* cursed."

She hurried onward before either woman could respond. "I know it sounds absurd. Ever since I bought this deck, though... Maybe there *is* something to what Mother said, about that patterner manipulating her fate and mine. I've always felt like the cards speak to me. But they've never spoken as clearly as they did that night, when I asked them if House Traementis was under some dark fate."

It was a risk, revealing her connection to pattern at all, when that was firmly a Vraszenian tradition. But it was the only way she could think of to give Tanaquis some hint of the role she'd played in the Night of Hells, and the only way to warn Donaia—short of blaming it all on a szorsa named Arenza Lenskaya again.

Donaia's fingers were digging divots into the edge of her couch. "Gianco always said his sister took our luck with her, but... could this patterner have cursed us?" Her gaze shot to Tanaquis. "Is that even possible?"

Tanaquis's gaze reminded Renata of an owl's—astute and detached. "Anything in the cosmos is possible. One only needs to know the right numen, and the right power to call on." She shook herself and picked up her journal, flipping to a new page. "Vraszenians believe that children conceived on the night of their Great Dream have a special connection to pattern. You were conceived three years too early for that, but the wellspring is said to be present in the realm of mind at all times. Given all that's happened recently with aža and ash, it's possible a connection is there. Have you ever—"

"How do we find out if this is true?" Donaia broke in. "How do we remove the curse, before it takes anyone else?" She turned to Renata, eyes wide. "Did these cards of yours give any indication?"

Renata shook her head. "I can try again, but...this is well beyond me." And that was entirely true.

"That shouldn't be necessary," Tanaquis said briskly. "We need to verify your claim first—not that I question your words, Alta Renata, but pattern is notoriously unreliable at best. I'll have to calculate some charts, too. Donaia, I'll need dates—not just birth, but registration, death, any other event of significance—for the entire Traementis line going back to the Veiled Waters when Alta Renata was conceived."

She closed her journal with a decisive snap, then took Donaia's and Renata's hands in hers. "I've never lifted a curse, but I can hardly pass this challenge up. If it's possible to save you, I will."

The Shambles and the Aerie: Cyprilun 28

"I swear on Ninat," Kaineto complained to Ecchino, "if this bite festers, I'm going to go down to the cells and knock every tooth out of that girl's mouth. Fucking river rat's tongue was so foul, I'm sure it's got diseases."

Grey was used to tuning out his lieutenant's complaints. He did what he could to curb the actual abuses, but when it came to teaching Kaineto basic human decency, the man was a lost cause. As Grey passed on his way to his office, though, Ecchino pitched his voice to a mocking falsetto and said, "I'm Arkady Bones, boss of the biggest knot in the Shambles!"

Grey spun, grabbing Kaineto's arm, cutting off their laughter. His lieutenant's hand bore a few scabbed-over marks where teeth had done more than just bruise. "You arrested Arkady Bones?"

"Caught her defacing the steps of the Charterhouse this morning. She was chalking a picture of His Mercy, naked, being stoned by the crowd." Kaineto pulled his arm free with an insolent shrug. "We ought to put a stop to that sort of thing, right, *sir*?"

They should—if only because Mettore had exerted his considerable power to make sure that part of his own personal nightmare didn't become widely known. But children weren't supposed to be kept in those cells.

Two bells later he had Arkady out, spitting mad and glaring retribution at every hawk they passed on the way to the main doors. When she spotted Kaineto, she tensed to launch herself at him, but Grey tightened his grip on her shoulder. "Try not to get arrested again before we get outside," he hissed.

"That one's a pisspot shitglob," Arkady hissed back, loudly enough that a cluster of guild carpenters preparing to hang the new front doors gave her startled looks.

Commander Cercel came up behind the two of them. "Problem, Serrado?"

"That one said if I cursed like a Dockwall thug, then he'd lock me up with them," Arkady said, baring her teeth at Kaineto, before Grey could explain the situation. "Fucker was trying to get me raped."

"Is that so." Cercel's tone cooled to iced-over steel. "Thank you for bringing that to my attention. Captain Serrado will deal with it."

As if Grey could. Lud Kaineto came from an influential delta family and threw his weight around like he was noble instead of mere gentry. Cercel had put him under Grey's command in a bid to prevent him from abusing his Vigil authority—but in the end, Grey was a Vraszenian. If he disciplined Kaineto the way the man deserved, he'd be lucky if the only thing he lost was his hexagram pin.

"But that doesn't answer my question," Cercel said. "Where are you taking her, Captain?"

"Back to Seven Knots. She's with the Kiraly delegation."

Cercel hesitated. Had she noticed the complete lack of braids in Arkady's filthy hair? He quickly added, "I thought a bit of leniency was in order, given their losses. And the cooperation they've given us so far." Hard-won cooperation. They usually stayed in the city until Veiled Waters was over, but more than half the clans had been in favor of leaving immediately.

"Yeah," Arkady said. "I was Grandpa's favorite. Was right broken up when he kicked it. But hey, at least I got to spend two days in the hole where he died—What?!" she snarled at Grey when his grip tightened again.

"Don't. Help."

Coughing, Cercel stepped aside. "Tell her people to keep her out of trouble."

Grey nodded and steered Arkady through the doorway. *Almost free*, he thought—too soon. Mettore Indestor was stomping up the steps toward them, the vanguard of a wedge of secretaries and lackeys.

Djek. Shoving Arkady behind him, Grey did his best to melt into the shadows of the door the carpenters were hanging.

And it might have worked, Indestor passing them without so much as a glance, if Arkady's belligerence hadn't outstripped her sense. "Huh. He en't nearly as funny looking with clothes on."

For an instant Grey thought she was about to die, and him with her. But Indestor must not have heard the words over the workmen's cursing—only her tone of voice—because he glanced their way with annoyance, not outright fury. That was enough to make him divert his course, though, and Grey's heart began to hammer.

"Who is this?" Indestor asked, his frown directed at Arkady instead of Grey.

Cercel did her best to draw his attention. "Child from the Vraszenian delegation. Got lost. The captain's returning her to her people."

Indestor grunted, examining Arkady with a suspicious eye. "Filthy little gnat, isn't she? Not surprising."

The look he turned on Grey wasn't much friendlier. "What

about you? It's been over a week. Iridet's woman hasn't turned up answers, which means the Vraszenians are probably responsible. If you don't have anything useful for me, maybe I should put someone else in charge." His scowl flicked down to Arkady. "Or hold on to one of their own—see if that convinces them to talk."

"Sir!" Cercel interposed herself before Grey could respond. "The delegation has cooperated so far. If we start imprisoning their children, most of them will leave, and that will badly damage our ability to find the one responsible. Give us a little longer; I promise we'll have answers for you soon."

Grey held his breath, and Arkady. Thank the Faces, she had enough sense to keep her mouth shut now. One insolent look from her, and Indestor would have her right back in that cell.

"Fine," Indestor said, through his teeth. "But none of them leave this city until we have answers. No matter how small."

The workmen had finished hanging the first door and were standing about uncertainly, because Indestor was in the way of the other one. He transferred his fury to them. "Why hasn't this been taken care of? Can't my people even fix a damned door?"

Grey recognized an escape when he saw one. With Cercel guarding their retreat, he got both hands on Arkady's shoulders and hauled her down the steps of the Aerie.

"Now I know why hawks are brown," she said as they fled back toward the Shambles. "It's 'cause you all take turns diving up that mudlicker's ass."

Lower Bank and Old Island: Cyprilun 29

Sedge was surprised to find Ren lurking at the foot of the Sunset Bridge dressed and painted as Arenza. For what they had in mind, she couldn't be Renata, but— "En't that dangerous?" he asked, waving off the girl trying to sell him new-blooming roses of Ažerais. "Thought you said people was looking for you."

"They are," Ren admitted. She'd bought a rose and was twiddling the violet bud nervously between her fingers. "But I had to meet with Idusza."

"Hope you got something useful from her."

"Gave more than got." Ren grinned. "Did I tell you they want to steal Eret Quientis's saltpeter?"

Sedge rubbed his eyes. Ren's schemes made his head ache sometimes. "The saltpeter you chased all over Nadežra to get for him? Now you're helping somebody else take it?"

"Idusza told me before the Night of Hells that she wanted advice from the pattern. I finally laid that out today. When the things I told her prove uncannily accurate, her faith in my abilities will be complete—and then perhaps she'll trust me enough to talk about Mezzan." The wicked bent to Ren's grin told Sedge that "uncanny accuracy" would be no coincidence. He sometimes thought his sister couldn't look at a piece of string without calculating what useful knots she could tie in it.

Since his own life had enough knots in it already, he changed the subject. "You look better."

It fell short of what he really meant, but there was no good way to say, *You looked like a walking corpse last time I saw you; glad you en't dead.* Ren only nodded—she of all people understood—and led the way into the crowd thronging the bridge, shuffling slowly toward the Old Island.

"Is it my imagination," she said as she dodged around the clanging bulk of a pot-seller, "or does your boss know more about numinatria than he lets on?"

"Let on to that Fienola woman quick enough." It all worked out in the end, but it had been a harrowing few hours waiting in that chamber. Worrying that Vargo couldn't bring Ren back. Worrying that he could, and then Sedge would have to kill his boss for learning the truth about Ren. Worrying that *Vargo* wouldn't come back, and then Varuni would kill Sedge and wear his scalp as a wig.

"Just be glad he does," Sedge added. "Most people in the gangs don't know Illi from Uniat, but Vargo . . . you know he took Ertzan Scrub's crew without breaking a single bone? Just chalked one of them figures in an empty warehouse and starved 'em 'til they agreed he was boss."

The reason for the slowness on the bridge became apparent: two wagons up ahead had come nose-to-nose, and neither was giving way. Ren eyed it for a moment, then cocked a questioning brow at Sedge; when he nodded, she hopped up onto the bridge's railing and began skirting the crowd, with him close at her heels. "Have you noticed ever a mark on his chest? A numinat, I think, but I couldn't make out the details."

Sedge waited until they'd cleared the crowd and jumped down onto the berm on the Duskgate side of the river's channel before he asked, "When did you see that?" Ren was usually much too wary to go taking up with somebody like Vargo, no matter how pretty the man dressed.

"The Night of Bells," she said dryly. "Or did you not see his costume?"

Sedge snorted. "Weren't much of it to see. But yeah, some of us have seen that tattoo. There was a riot in Froghole two years back; Vargo took a bottle to the neck. Varuni used his shirt to sop the blood. We all thought he was dead as Ninat, but he's up and walking the next day like he's fucking Kaius Rex. Dunno if the tattoo had anything to do with it, though. He says it's just scribbles." Then again, Vargo was like Ren. He lied as easily as he breathed.

Ren fell silent as they skulked along the berm, stinking mud sucking at their boots with every step. Another week and the flood would cover it, the river licking at the edges of the Island and seeping into the streets and houses of Lacewater.

Though maybe not this year. Fulvet's office had work gangs going all along the canals there, piling up bags of sand to keep the water out. Almost like Eret Quientis gave a shit what happened west of the Sunrise Bridge.

Bags of sand didn't do much good down here at the river's edge, but at low tide it was safe enough to risk—even with the shadow of the Aerie looming over them. "We couldn't go in through the Dawngate hole? Smells better, and we en't right on the Vigil's doorstep."

"I came out into Quientis's dream near here," Ren said, distracted. "Sedge...after the nightmare, when you came to the house, you said all night you'd looked for Vargo. Where was he?"

Sedge frowned. "Why all the questions about Vargo?" he asked. Not Vargo's business. Not his reputation. Questions about the man himself.

They weren't the only ones on the shore. Barefoot kids were rooting through the mud for anything of value dropped from above or swept downstream. Ren waited until they'd passed the kids and were nearly at the dripping mouth of one of the tunnels before she turned to face Sedge.

"I would say 'mock me not,' but you will anyway. I..." She grimaced, then spat the words out in a hurry. "I need to figure out if he could be the Rook."

Back when they were Fingers, they'd played a game, Tell the Lie, in which one kid would tell a story, and the others tried to guess which part wasn't true. Ren had been the best. Even so, Sedge had sometimes been able to tell—not because he knew when she was lying, but because he knew when she was telling the unvarnished truth.

"You're fucking serious."

Then the laughter dragged him down. He laughed until he was bent over. He laughed until it felt like his ribs were stabbing his lungs. He tried to climb out, caught sight of her increasingly annoyed frown, and fell back in.

"I'm no street fool, pulling this from my ear," she said when she got tired of waiting. "I know it's unlikely. But—"

Sedge managed to mute his guffaws to wheezing as she laid out her reasons. They weren't bad; if she'd been talking about anybody other than Vargo, he would have thought she was onto something. But—*Vargo.*

When he pointed that out, Ren said, "You yourself told me he recently has changed. Perhaps this is why. And it might explain why he was so determined to be the one who helped me...because he knows my secret and wanted to protect it."

This was Ren's real talent. She made implausible things sound completely reasonable, to the point where you started looking for other details to support it. Vargo *had* been cagey about what happened in Ažerais's Dream. And he'd come in there prepared, with that oh-so-innocent question about astrology and a fake birth date ready to hand.

Sedge squeezed his eyes shut and shook his head. The Rook was a hero, standing against the cuffs. The Rook had been *Sedge's* hero, when he was a kid. How could he make her understand? "Vargo controls half this island and most of the Lower Bank. He don't *need* to be the Rook."

And yet...Ren's arguments wormed their way into Sedge's mind. Like the Night of Hells. Vargo had slipped Varuni's guard when he went off with Fadrin Acrenix. Sure, there'd been something with the Novrus cuff afterward, but that didn't cover more than a few bells at most. Where had Vargo been for the rest of the night?

"Mask take it, Ren." Sedge kicked a broken pot half buried in the silt. "Why'd you have to go muddling my thoughts?"

She made an exasperated noise. "I hoped you could unmuddle mine. I realize it seems unlikely, but we know the Rook has been around for centuries. It cannot all this time have been one person; even the Tyrant aged. But maybe what passes on is more than a hood and a name—maybe it's some kind of spirit or ghost."

He'd seen Vraszenians call up their dead ancestors with a dance, and Fienola had said part of Ren's soul was lost in Ažerais's Dream. Anything was possible. And—

A chill chased across Sedge's skin, one that had nothing to do with the river wind. "Vargo talks to himself sometimes. Not just muttering—half a conversation, like."

Ren went very still. "Does he."

Sedge could see the questions coming, piling up in Ren's mind like a flood behind a dam. But to his surprise, she dismissed them with a slice of her hand. "I want to ask you what he says...but you are sworn to Vargo. I'll stop."

That put a rock in the pit of Sedge's stomach. "I...yeah. About that."

Ren grimaced. "Already you have told me more than you should. I'm sorry—"

"No, it en't that. It—" Sedge wrestled with himself. This wasn't a violation of the knot bond...not exactly. And that was the whole problem.

She was his sister. She'd betrayed Ondrakja for him.

"Vargo en't sworn to us."

Ren lurched on the uncertain footing of the shore. "What?"

"He en't sworn. Not to anybody. All the knots he controls are, but not him." Sedge tugged back his sleeve enough to show the blue silk charm on its braided cord around his wrist, the emblem of his membership in the Fog Spiders. He wasn't required to wear it openly, but Sedge's kind of work didn't call for subtlety. "Way most people assume it works—even in his knots—we tie in with his lieutenants, and they tie in with him. Except that en't true."

Because while the vows for knots varied from gang to gang, they tended to have a few things in common. Like doing favors for your knot-mates, no questions asked and no debts owed—and Vargo wouldn't tell somebody the time of day without tallying up the favor.

Like protecting the knot's secrets from outsiders...and sharing your own secrets inside it.

Ren's mouth shaped a silent oath. It was a good five years since Vargo had started taking over the Lower Bank—but if he was the Rook back then, or knew he was in line for it, there was no way he could share that with others.

Well, he could. Just because people swore vows didn't mean they always lived by them. The Fingers had kept secrets from each other plenty. But little things, mostly, not big stuff like *I'm the fucking Rook.*

A splash sounded down the bank. Two of the scavenger kids were fighting, and one had just gotten knocked into the water. The tide was still low, but it wouldn't stay that way for long. "'Less you want to drown, we should get in there," Sedge said.

Ren kilted her skirts up, then fished in her pocket and unwrapped a small, glowing stone. "'Borrowed' from Traementis Manor," she said as Sedge's eyebrows went up. "I'll put it back."

It would be a lot better than a torch or a lamp. But since when had Ren cared about putting back the things she stole?

He didn't ask. He just squared his shoulders, faced the tunnel, and led her into the Depths.

The Depths, Old Island: Cyprilun 29

Ren hated the Depths.

That was the name given to the tunnels that honeycombed Nadežra, the Old Island in particular. Originally dug as part of the drainage system for the wetlands, they'd been roofed over and turned into sewers for the buildings above, until—in the poorer districts, at least—they'd fallen too much into disrepair to serve that purpose any longer. Then they just became catacombs: hiding places for the desperate, and underground roads for those whose business shouldn't be seen.

That was during the fall and winter. Every year come spring, people drowned down here as the river rose, staying too long and getting trapped in pockets they couldn't escape. If Ren and Sedge weren't careful, the tide might do the same to them.

But she'd been down here in the dream, when she broke out of the lodging house and started walking through other people's nightmares.

If Ondrakja was alive, maybe she was in the Depths.

The numinatrian lightstone she'd taken from Traementis Manor cast a steady glow over crumbling walls slick with slime. The water was up to their ankles, hiding just enough that Ren and Sedge had to hold on to the walls for balance whether they wanted to or not. She cringed at the soft wetness against her fingers, then mocked herself silently. *Too much the fine alta for this now, are you?*

"Which way?" Sedge asked softly, not turning to face her. He was in front to look menacing or hit anybody who didn't take the hint, and he didn't want the brightness of the stone to dim his vision.

"I know not," she admitted. "I couldn't exactly draw a map."

He grumbled a half-audible curse and resumed his slog.

Time, distance, reality—all grew muddled in the splashing darkness. Sedge waved a hand in front of him to break any spiderwebs, and Ren used a piece of chalk to mark their passage, so they could know where they'd been and how to get back.

"Do you remember anything about what it looked like?" Sedge asked. Ren could mostly stand upright, but he was hunched over, one hand raised to prevent knocking his head on an archway keystone.

"Niches. The ones they say Nadežrans used to put ashes in, so the floods would carry them away. And the rats...they *really* did not like being near there."

"Niches are mostly in the natural sections, en't they?" They came to a crossing. Sedge hesitated, then shrugged and took the tunnel that would lead to the oldest parts of the Depths, chipped into the stone of the Point itself. "Maybe people keep clear of it same as rats. Gotta be some reason I en't heard no talk about it."

The farther they went, the more the blackness pressed in on Ren, until it felt like the feeble light of the stone shrank to a mere flicker. No amount of telling herself that the Dežera wouldn't flood so soon erased the memory of being swept through these tunnels. How long had they been down here? Even the normal rise of the tide would be enough to trap them for hours. The corridors twisted the echoes of their breathing and footsteps, until Ren couldn't be certain they were alone. Every bend they came around, she half expected to come face-to-face with a knife...or something worse.

They reached the first of the niches, and Sedge stopped. "I en't seen nothing," he said, his voice hoarse. "Dead end, I think. We should go back. Tide's gotta be rising."

Agreement was on the tip of Ren's tongue when she stopped. "Nothing," she agreed in a whisper. "No rats. No spiders."

She lifted the lightstone to the wall, studying it. A faint hint of putrid violet shimmered back at her, and she touched it with one hesitant fingertip.

An instant later she doubled over, retching, flailing her hand in the shallow, filthy water as if that would cleanse it and her mind both. "Fucking hell," she gasped. "On the walls—*don't touch them!*"

Sedge crouched next to her. "What is it?"

"Zlyzen blood," she said. "Making us afraid. Keeping people away—rats and spiders, too." She forced her head upward, looking deeper into the blackness. "We're headed in the right direction."

"Zlyzen? I thought those were just part of the hallucination." Sedge scrubbed his hands on his thighs, even though he hadn't come into contact with the blood. When he spoke, his voice was as high as it'd been when he was still a boy. "*Fuck.* I bet it was zlyzen. Vargo's gonna lose his shit."

His words didn't help dilute her fear. "What was zlyzen?"

"Huh?" Sedge's darting gaze settled on her. "Fuck. Forget you heard any of this. We . . . we lost somebody to ash. All clawed up—by something in the dream, I guess. The one it happened to, he broke out of my hold like it was nothing, dislocating his own shoulder. Died before anyone could do anything." He scrubbed his hands over his face. "Leave it to fucking Ondrakja to make friends with zlyzen—like she weren't nightmare enough on her own. C'mon. Stay close." He sloshed past, his slower pace having nothing to do with the water that had risen to their calves.

They were well under the Point now, the stone above their heads natural rather than blocks held together with crumbling mortar. The niches continued at regular intervals—and then Ren's wavering light caught a change.

Iron bars across their mouths.

Sedge swore. "That lunatic's been keeping zlyzen caged?"

Ren edged past him, lifting the stone to light each niche in turn. The gates were open and the holes all empty now—*thank the*

Faces—but in one she found a small lump of rags. Sedge's breath hissed between his teeth when she reached between the bars to pick it up.

The rags were tied in the vague shape of a human. A doll, not much different from the one Ren had made when Tess first joined the Fingers.

"No," Ren whispered dully. "This is where she kept the children."

And in the silence that followed she heard a voice, rising in a croaking parody of song.

> *"Find them in your pockets,*
> *Find them in your coat;*
> *If you aren't careful,*
> *You'll find them on your throat . . ."*

In the deepest shadows, something stirred. The paltry gleam of Ren's lightstone caught the edges and angles of limbs as withered and bent as dried branches, the sag of torn and filthy clothes not even fit for a rag heap, the brittle swampgrass hair and skin-draped skull of an old woman who might have stepped out of the darkest fire tale.

Gammer Lindworm. No wonder the street kids called her that.

And yet in the bones of her face, in the long red nails that clacked along the wall and the smear of purple across her lips like paint, Ren could see the ruined shreds of Ondrakja.

Sedge made a choking, terrified noise.

"What have you found, my little friends?" Ondrakja creaked. Her eyes seemed too large for her face, as though they might fall out of their sockets. When the light from Ren's stone caught them, they gleamed like a cat's at night. "Come closer, come closer, where I can see."

Ren couldn't have moved even if she'd wanted to. It was a nightmare come to life, and not because of the zlyzen blood on the walls. "You're supposed to be dead. I killed you."

Pointed teeth flashed in reply. "You didn't kill me enough, little

Renyi. And it seems I didn't kill Sedge enough. We're all failed murderers here." Her voice might be broken, but the words sounded just like Ondrakja. Her creaking shivered into a ghastly laugh. "Or maybe not. I killed your friend, after all. You shouldn't have run. It's always better to stay and take your punishment, rather than let other people get hurt."

Leato. Ren's gorge rose.

Ondrakja crept closer, easing into the light as though testing to make sure she wouldn't burn. She kept talking—she'd always loved the sound of her own voice. "I could have saved him, if I wanted. Like I saved myself. Fed him the blood." Her nails came away from the wall dripping viscous purple, and Ondrakja licked them clean. "Or fed him little dreams and let my friends feast. They grow fat on it, fat with nightmares, then bleed those nightmares out to feed others."

She was only a few arm's lengths away now, close enough for Ren to smell her stink, even over the rot and mildew of the catacombs.

"Then there's you. Little Renyi." Ondrakja's voice hardened. "Little traitorous bitch, turning against your own knot. Do you still dream of that night? Is that a sweet dream for you? They prefer the sweeter dreams. Food and family and warmth. The sweeter the dream, the more bitter the nightmare that follows."

Ren felt Sedge tense behind her. It was the confrontation they'd never had five years ago: Sedge against Ondrakja, pitting his growing size and strength against her viciousness and experience, and the years of habitual obedience. By the time she stopped to cut his charm, casting him out of the knot—by the time he realized she meant to kill him—he'd been too broken to fight back.

He wasn't broken now.

"But where's the other one?" Ondrakja said, her ruined voice suddenly warming to a parody of friendliness. She pressed her clawed hands to her breast. "There were always three of you. Where's little Tess?" From under her rags she drew the Acrenix medallion she'd torn from Ren's neck in the nightmare, inscribed with three Tricats. "We must do things in threes. Isn't that why you gave me this? I can't punish you properly without all three."

In the cellar of the old lodging house there was a small room where Ondrakja used to lock misbehaving Fingers, alone in the dark and the damp, saying the zlyzen would come for them soon. But Ren and Sedge weren't the children they'd been, cowering in fear of Ondrakja's rage.

"You don't fucking touch my sisters," Sedge growled—and lunged.

He was bigger now, and stronger, and she was a withered husk of her former self. He drew two knives as he hurled himself forward—

—and with one negligent hand, Ondrakja slammed him against the iron bars of a cage.

"Now, now," she said, in a singsong tone. "Doesn't matter if you're a pinkie or a fist—you don't threaten your knot's boss. There's only room for one traitor here."

"You en't my boss no more." Sedge lurched to his feet, one dagger still in his left hand, but Ondrakja caught his arm and twisted it. Even through his cry of pain, Ren could hear the snap as his wrist broke.

She couldn't stand frozen while Ondrakja killed him again.

Drawing her own knife, she ran at Ondrakja. Rather than matching herself against the woman's unholy strength, she ducked under the swipe of Ondrakja's free hand and stabbed upward, trying to catch her in the soft pit between ribs and arm. But the hag twitched back, fast as a snake, and the only good thing was that she let go of Sedge. He pulled out another knife with his good hand and threw it, but Ondrakja avoided the blade with ease, retreating a step.

"Such rebellious little children," she sighed. "Don't you want your mother back?"

"You are *not* our mother," Ren spat. That was one mask Ondrakja had never tried to wear: She was their knot leader, but never tried to call herself family. *I would have poisoned her years earlier if she had.*

Ondrakja pouted. "Is it because I look like this?" She plucked at her robes, at the spotted parchment skin of her arms. "Don't worry. I'll be better soon—he promised. Then we can be a family at last.

You don't want it now, but that's no trouble." Her teeth gleamed in the faint light. "I can *make* you want it."

Her certainty was even more unnerving than her words. "Like hell you fucking will," Sedge hissed through his pain, but Ondrakja just clicked her tongue.

"You'll see. I'll come for you. All three of you, and then I'll punish you like you deserve. Like a good mother should."

At first Ren thought the light from the stone she carried was fading. But no, it held steady; Ondrakja was the one fading, wisping into nothingness like she was made of smoke.

Ren made one last, desperate lunge, but her knife passed through the empty air where Ondrakja had been. As though the woman had been nothing more than another nightmare.

18

Aža's Call

Eastbridge, Whitesail, and Duskgate: Cyprilun 29

Vargo's repertoire of curses would have impressed even Tess. "Just the two of you. Alone in the Depths. With the floods already starting. You have an excuse for not understanding how dangerous that is, but Sedge..." His glower promised retribution.

She'd told him almost all of it, after stopping at the townhouse long enough to change disguises and hand Sedge over to Tess for bonesetting. The zlyzen blood, the children's cages, the unnatural strength, even Ondrakja vanishing into thin air—everything but Ondrakja swearing to punish Ren for her betrayal.

"Blame me, not your man," she hurried to say. "I told him that if he didn't guide me, I'd go on my own. A rashness I heartily regret now. We're lucky he suffered nothing worse than a broken wrist."

"And he's lucky you came to no harm. Forget the floods; you're still recovering. Don't you know how much filth is down there? You could have gotten sick." Vargo shifted back as though to protect himself with distance.

"I scrubbed thoroughly afterward."

That didn't seem to reassure him. "I suspected Indestor was behind the ash production, but it's some madwoman in the Depths using stolen children and...monsters? How?"

"The zlyzen were feasting, she said. Growing fat."

His fingers drummed on the arm of his chair, which Master Peabody seemed to take as a cue to peek out from his collar. A row of four bead-bright eyes fixed on Renata. Vargo said, "The walls—they were covered in zlyzen blood?" Setting Peabody on the table, he rose and retrieved a sheaf of loosely bound papers and spread them in front of her. "The blood on the walls...could some of it have been numinata? Anything that looked like this?"

Vargo's "this" wasn't much. Sketches of unconnected lines; notes in a much neater hand than Tanaquis's saying things like *vesica piscis* and *acute enough to be Ninat?* and *who the fuck uses Ekhrd to estimate regression???* Even when he set them in a grid to show the whole figure, there was more missing than present.

The pulsing dread had made it difficult to even look at the blood, but she'd seen enough to be confident in shaking her head. "It was just splashes—nothing precise. As I understand it, numinatria requires concentration and a steady hand; I doubt that madwoman is capable of anything of the sort." Renata looked up from the papers. "Why? What is this?"

Sighing, Vargo gathered up the sheets and tapped them against the table to straighten them. "Found the remains of an operation in Froghole. This was what was left." He cocked his head. "Was it iridescent, the blood? Like dreamweaver feathers, but putrefied?"

"More violet than a dreamweaver's feathers. But yes, it had something of a shimmer." She rubbed her thumb against the tip of her finger, as if the residue were still there.

"We found something like that, too. Disgusting, but it didn't have any unusual effect. So she's dosing the children with aža, letting the zlyzen feed on their dreams, then taking the zlyzen blood and transmuting it into ash with a numinat. You said she disappeared—could she have gone into the realm of mind?"

"I think she must have. We know it's possible; that's what happened to all of us at the Accords. But it looked like she could control it at will. We don't know where she is...or when she'll appear."

Vargo gave her a sour look. "Thank you for tonight's nightmares,

Alta Renata. *You* didn't grow up with tales of zlyzen eating your brain while you slept."

If he was the Rook, he knew she *had* grown up with such tales. But in his shoes, she would have said the same thing, to throw her off the scent. *I'm going to go mad, trying to guess whether he knows.*

Vargo's thoughts had moved on. "Indestor's got an inscriptor capable of doing what this Gammer Lindworm hag can't. And you say she made it sound like they're working together." He absently riffled the edge of his notes. "But why?"

Renata leaned back in her chair. That night in Mettore's office, when he'd asked for another dose, saying he needed to test something—had he meant ash, intending it solely for her? If Ondrakja had then poisoned *all* the wine, that explained the double dose she had received.

"Someone's selling it on the streets," she said slowly. "Gammer Lindworm? Or that inscriptor of his. But Indestor must want it for some other purpose." Something magical, if that pattern spoke true. "What would happen if you drew a numinat with ash?"

Vargo fell silent, contemplating her question. She watched the minute twitches of his jaw and lips. *He talks to himself sometimes*, Sedge had said.

"Nothing, I think," he finally replied. "The powder form is inert unless ingested. I could try...but I'd rather not."

"*Don't.*" It came out more vehemently than she intended.

Vargo scooped Peabody up and tucked him under his collar. "Don't worry, Renata. I'm not the sort to take unnecessary risks."

That fleeting touch of familiarity, Vargo using her unadorned name, stayed with Ren as she left his townhouse and went to share what she'd learned with Tanaquis. She couldn't tell whether it was deliberate, or so accidental he hadn't even noticed the slip.

It's Vargo. I don't think he blinks *accidentally.*

But that didn't stop her from thinking about it all the way to Whitesail.

Tanaquis's frown was enough to drive such thoughts from her mind. "You said nothing about seeing the Depths in your nightmare."

"I know, and I can't apologize enough." Renata twisted her fingers around each other. "That portion . . . I was searching for my true father. But I didn't feel I could say that, even in a private report. I should have, I know—but all I can do now is share what I held back. I assure you, that *is* everything." Another lie, but if she needed to tell Tanaquis anything else—like what she'd felt in the Charterhouse with the statues—she could always claim she'd learned it from the pattern cards.

The astrologer had her write down her account, which Renata dutifully did, making sure to work Ondrakja into it. Then she gritted her teeth, squared her shoulders, and went to the Aerie.

She didn't expect Captain Serrado to be standing quite so close when he opened the door to his office. Nor did he, in only shirtsleeves and a waistcoat, seem to be expecting visitors. "Alta Renata," he said, surprised. "Can I help you?"

"I need to report something," she said. "Concerning your investigation with the sleepless children."

His head jerked back, surprise deepening. "And you came here? You could have summoned me to your house."

The thought hadn't even crossed her mind, and she cursed inwardly.

Serrado backed up a half step. "Please, come in. I apologize for the cramped conditions."

She soon realized why he'd been pressed so close. If it weren't for the window, she would have suspected his "office" was a repurposed broom closet. A stack of ledgers behind the door prevented it from opening all the way, and more occupied the seat of the one visitor's chair. When Serrado made an abortive move toward them, she said, "Don't trouble yourself; I can stand. I went looking for that old woman—the one we spoke of before."

He stilled. "You went wandering around the Lower Bank?"

At this rate Alta Renata was going to get a reputation for being mad, but . . . "No, I went wandering around the place you call the Depths."

A pile of papers cascaded to the floor.

Save for that one twitch, he stood utterly still as she gave her account for a third time. When she was done, he planted his fists on his desk and struggled against what she suspected was language inappropriate for an alta to hear. *He should have heard Vargo earlier.* "You said Vargo's man knows the way?"

"Yes, although his wrist is broken." Not that it would stop Sedge.

"I'll assemble my people." Yanking his patrol coat off a hook, Serrado shrugged it on. "If he's well enough—and Vargo allows it— he can show us the way. If not..." He eyed her surcoat, fern green in honor of the spring and embroidered with a motif of silver reeds and herons. "Perhaps you could draw me a map."

"We left chalk marks on the walls, and if all else fails, just go directly toward your sense of dread," she said darkly. "But, Captain...if the old woman truly can slip into what you call Ažerais's Dream, how can you possibly catch her?"

That stopped him short. Deflated, he leaned against his desk and rubbed his eyes. He looked like he'd barely slept more than she had after the Night of Hells.

"That's an annoyingly logical point. The elders might know a way. Or Szorsa Mevieny." He shook his head, sighing. "With the floods coming, the main thing is to ensure she can't use that place to trap any more victims, rather than wait and hope we can catch her."

He shifted, and Renata realized he couldn't leave with her blocking the way. As she started to open the door, though, he caught its edge and eased it shut again. "Alta," he said, his voice too soft to be heard in the corridor. "You should know...back when I was first investigating Gammer Lindworm—Ondrakja—I found that someone had torn her arrest record out of the ledger. Like they wanted to hide that she'd ever been here. Not many people have access to our archives. It could have been one of my fellow officers..."

"But you don't think it was," she murmured.

His eyes were bleak. "I reported what you told me about the old woman you saw, and her claim that she'd poisoned everyone. Eret Indestor accepted the theory a little too readily for a man who shouldn't have had any idea who she was."

Her heart thumped so loudly, Serrado could probably hear it.

She'd told neither Serrado nor Tanaquis what Ondrakja said in the nightmare about making Indestor pay. That was the kind of accusation that could end with her in a hangman's noose if she didn't have evidence to back it up. But now she had a hawk—someone under Caerulet's authority—all but accusing his superior.

A Vraszenian hawk. Who couldn't possibly have failed to notice Indestor's hatred for his people.

She almost let slip a wildly inappropriate giggle. For a brief instant, an impossible image danced through her mind: Derossi Vargo, master of the Spiders, and Grey Serrado, Vigil captain, allying to bring down Mettore Indestor.

It was already miracle enough that they'd made it out of the gathering to cure her sleeplessness without stabbing each other. But...if they were both willing to work with *her*...she could make use of that.

"Captain," she said quietly. "I'm trusting you not to spread this where it shouldn't be heard—but I believe Eret Indestor is behind a great deal of this affair. I think he's the reason Leato and I received an extra dose of ash, and I think he's the one behind the ash production, though I don't yet know why. If I can find out, and find proof...will you help me?"

He was standing close enough that she had to tilt her head to look him in the eye. His expression was carefully neutral as he said, "I can't bring an accusation against a nobleman. That would have to be done by another noble. But as you're probably not familiar with our local laws, I'd be happy to deliver copies of the relevant statutes to your house."

Her heart thumped again. "Thank you, Captain Serrado," she said, and opened the door.

Isla Prišta, Westbridge: Cyprilun 29

The parlour of Renata's townhouse was a study in refinement, from the Dusk Road carpet thick beneath Giuna's slippers to each vase, box, and figurine on the mantel and shelves. Giuna examined a few as she waited: a lithe, deerlike creature carved from black stone, polished enough that she could see her inverted reflection in the creature's rump; a fan painted with purple irises, the flowers shimmering from the pearl dust mixed into the paints; a polished box that tinkled a delicate tune until the key wound to a stop. All statements on the owner's refined sense of taste.

All gifts Renata had received from her admirers.

After days of being her mother's bulwark, Giuna had finally unloaded her own grief in Sibiliat's arms. It left her hollow, scraped clean of everything inside. A fragile shell that couldn't weather another blow. But the more she examined the parlour, the more she flinched in anticipation of just that.

By the time Renata entered, wrapped in a periwinkle dressing gown, Giuna had half twisted her gloves off with fretting. Renata clasped her hands anyway, with the same sincere-seeming warmth she'd shown ever since she came to Nadežra. "Giuna, dear. What's wrong?"

That "dear" clanged like an off-tune chord—the word people used when they were condescending to her. Not that Renata had ever done so. She wouldn't.

Would she?

"It's nothing," Giuna said. "I only noticed that the glass figurine is gone. The one you bought at the Gloria that matched the one you gave me."

Real tears pricked through the false cheer. Leato had teased her that day. Leato always teased her, but that day he'd put forth his most brotherly effort, showing off for Renata.

Renata said, "Oh—it's in my bedroom."

A perfectly reasonable response. There was no cause for suspicion.

Except that Sibiliat had given Giuna plenty of cause.

"Might I see it?" Now *that* was a peculiar request. Giuna cast about for some excuse. "I was thinking about that day at the Gloria, and how happy we were then, and Leato . . ." She choked on the rest.

She couldn't force herself to use her brother's name to lie. She was a terrible person for even trying. *I'm so sorry, Leato. But I have to know.*

Renata winced. "Giuna, while I was sick, my bedroom became...It isn't really fit to be seen."

She'd only meant the figurine, not the room, but Renata's refusal—before she'd even asked!—tipped her over the edge of the cliff.

"The dining room, then?" Giuna suggested, dropping all pretense. "The study? Library? Or maybe the kitchen, since apparently that's where you really sleep."

Renata's body went rigid. Only that: Her face was too well-disciplined to show her shock. Two heartbeats passed, then a third—

—and then the rigidity broke. Renata's throat worked silently for a moment before words came out. "Oh, Lumen. Giuna—I—"

"It's true," Giuna whispered. Some naive part of her had hoped that Sibiliat was lying out of jealousy. That the person Sibiliat sent to search Renata's townhouse while Renata lay unconscious in Traementis Manor had found nothing out of the ordinary.

But Renata's own reaction confirmed it. "We trusted you, and..." Swallowing a sob, Giuna turned to leave.

Then she stopped. There was nobody else. Leato was gone, and her mother didn't need more grief. Handling this was Giuna's responsibility. She faced Renata again, grasping at composure. "Who were you working with? Master Vargo? What did you hope to gain from us?"

"No, I—" Renata groped behind her, found a chair, and sank into it. "I'm not working with Vargo. I'm not working with anyone. I only..."

She buried her head in her hands. The silence stretched out like a chasm between them. Then Renata lifted her face. "Please, will you sit down? And I'll try to explain."

Everyone said Giuna was too soft. Naive. Minnow, Leato had called her. And Sibiliat, little bird. Her mother had allowed Leato to shoulder some of the family misfortune, but they both thought it best to leave Giuna in the dark.

Maybe they were right before, but not now. Giuna sat, crossed her arms, and tried to harden herself. "Very well. Explain."

"Some of this your mother knows already—though I lied to her as well initially, and even she doesn't know about..." A helpless twitch of Renata's hand took in the house. Not just the elegant parlour, but the rooms beyond, which according to Sibiliat were covered in cloths and dust. All except the kitchen, where the fine Alta Renata Viraudax slept on the floor.

Giuna listened, jaw tight, as Renata related her tale. The half-unknown truth of her conception, and her real reason for coming to Nadežra. "I had very little money when I arrived," Renata said. "My father isn't as well-off as he was when my mother married him, but that's beside the point; they forbade me to come here, so I had to run away. And yes—I admit it. I came here hoping to rejoin the Traementis. Because what I knew of you was what Mother had described: a wealthy and powerful family, who surely wouldn't feel the burden of an extra cousin."

"You must have been so disappointed." As disappointed as Giuna was now. She didn't even try to hide her bitterness. "And now that Leato's gone, you've lost your easiest path into the register."

"*No*," Renata said urgently. "I was *not* trying to marry my way in. Lumen burn me, Giuna—if I were that coldhearted, don't you think I would have turned around and left after he died? When Vargo approached me, I took on his proposal because I thought it would help House Traementis. Yes, I came to Nadežra thinking I could simply live off your wealth. I'm not proud of that. But even before the nightmare, that was changing, and since then..."

She trailed off, eyes lost. Was her grief feigned? Sibiliat had pointed it out months ago, how Renata excelled at playing the people around her. Making them *like* her, while hiding the truth of herself.

"I'm sorry." The words were almost too quiet for Giuna to hear. "I know I've hurt you, at a time when that's the *last* thing you need. All I can do now is try to make up for it."

The urge to comfort was strong. *Soft. Naive.* Giuna tightened her fists, clenched her teeth, and resisted. "How."

Renata met Giuna's eyes for the first time since she began her explanation. "What your mother said the other day. After L—After your brother's funeral. She was more right than she knew: Your family is cursed. I don't know why, but I'm sure your constant ill fortune isn't mere chance, and I've told her so. I'm working with Meda Fienola to lift that curse. Once that's done..." The will seemed to drain out of her. "Then I'll go back to advocating for you in the Charterhouse, if you wish it. If not... then I'll simply go."

A curse. All Giuna's bitterness compressed into a knife-point prick of fear. Why hadn't her mother told her?

That was a question for Donaia, not Renata. In fact, Giuna had many questions for her mother, and until they were answered, she wouldn't be able to decide what to do.

She stood, back straight enough to make Sibiliat proud. "Thank you for your honesty. I'll see myself out."

She heard the intake of breath and braced herself. Renata was going to ask how she'd found out, and Giuna was going to refuse to say, because she wouldn't betray Sibiliat like that.

But all that came was a soft exhale. "I truly am sorry, Alta Giuna."

The apology dogged Giuna's steps all the way back to Isla Traementis. Or perhaps it was the title. She'd been so happy when Renata had started using her name without it. Had that also been calculation?

Did Leato know? She'd forgotten to ask. She hoped he hadn't.

Giuna's father had died when she was too young to remember him clearly, but she knew the stories about her family in generations past. The Traementis had been legendary for their vendettas, for the ferocity with which they destroyed those who crossed them.

She couldn't imagine what they would have done to Renata—and she didn't want to.

Soft. Naive.

Giuna refused to call that a bad thing.

"Colbrin," she said as the majordomo took her wrap. "I noticed Renata's rooms had a chill. Send over a few scuttles of coal." She began to head for her mother's study, then stopped. "Oh. And a mattress."

Isla Prišta, Westbridge: Cyprilun 30

The following morning brought an odd assortment of deliveries. The first came from Traementis Manor, and Ren had to fight back an absurd urge to cry at the sight, because she didn't want the footman wondering why she'd teared up over coal and a mattress.

There was no note, but the message was clear. Whatever Giuna's feelings were toward her now, they hadn't turned entirely hostile. And that was more than Ren could have hoped for.

On the heels of that came a whole series of baskets from Vargo, containing a variety of foods with helpful notes on how they would fortify her against any diseases she might have contracted in the Depths. Sedge laughed when Ren asked him about those. "The man en't afraid of much, but he loathes sick people. Hey, it saves you larder money, right?"

It did indeed. Then came the last and most startling item—a plain-wrapped package left by the servants' door. "Something from Pavlin?" Ren asked when Tess brought it in.

"If this is bread, somebody forgot to bake it," Tess said, dropping the package on the table. "It's heavy."

Ren unwrapped it with wary hands, and then gasped at what she found inside. It was a beautifully embroidered Vraszenian shawl—the sort of thing a respectable szorsa might wear. A *heavy* shawl, and she had to search carefully to figure out why: The fabric's edge was weighted down with seven cunningly hidden throwing knives.

"Isn't that a fine piece of work." Tess rubbed the fabric between her fingers, admiring the imbued concealment of the knife pockets. When she unfolded the shawl, a slip of white fluttered to the floor.

Its slanted script was brief and to the point. *So you aren't disarmed again. Meet me outside the Three Eels in the Shambles. Fifth earth. We need to finish our discussion.*

Ren's pulse thundered in her ears. No signature, no identifying mark of any kind . . . but the source was clear.

Even rapture over excellent craftsmanship couldn't make Tess miss Ren sinking onto the bench. "What is it?"

Wordlessly, Ren showed her the note. Tess bit her lip. "What are you going to do?"

"Go," Ren said, resigned. "What choice have I?"

A sudden thought made her reach for the instructions from Vargo. The handwriting on the two notes didn't match at all—she would have been disappointed if it had—but she still had to check.

Before she could face the Rook, though, she had another appointment to keep.

Grednyek Close, Seven Knots: Cyprilun 30

Idusza laughed in delight as she poured a liberal splash of zrel into tea as black as river mud. "Your cards have painted the faces of the skeptics with shame, szorsa. Never has a theft gone so easily. It was as though the dogs were helping the fox enter the coop."

They were sitting together in the apartment above the chandler's shop, with Arenza listening to Idusza recount the theft of the saltpeter. Waving off the offered zrel, she made suitably pleased and amused noises as Idusza told her about a guard distracted by a jilted lover, a service door with a broken latch, and the saltpeter waiting exactly where Arenza had predicted it would be.

Sipping her tea, Arenza said, "Pattern guided you well. I was only the messenger."

More like the architect. Ren already knew where the saltpeter was and how it was guarded, thanks to Renata's earlier work with Quientis; a little delicate interference and a stacked deck for Idusza let her pass along the vulnerabilities as divine inspiration.

"In these times, our people have need of such messengers." Idusza pressed the rim of her cup to her lips, eyes narrowing as she studied Arenza. "Andrejek said the same. He wants to meet you."

Idusza had been feeling her out for recruitment to the Anduske since they first met, but this was something more. Arenza let her startlement show. "But—I am a stranger. He is a wanted man, by the ziemetse as well as the Cinquerat; surely he meets only with those he trusts." Which apparently included Idusza. Had Mezzan managed to target someone that high in the Stadnem Anduske's leadership?

"He trusts me, and I trust you." Idusza drained her cup and set it to one side. She leaned forward, curved braid swinging in the air. Not even her soft, rounded cheeks could dull the hard edge to her words. "For decades we've fought to take back what is ours. So long that we have forgotten it belongs also to Ažerais. The ziemetse are useless; they accept a stalemate with Nadežra's captors. We treat not with our enemies as they do. But you've reminded me—your assistance has reminded us all—that this is our goddess's *blessed* city. How can we take it back without her blessing?"

"You treat not with your enemies. And yet—" Arenza cut the words off, ducking her head. "Forgive me. You've heard that song already from me."

Idusza bypassed the tea and poured a straight shot of zrel into her empty cup. "Mezzan has had many chances for betraying me, and taken none. He supports us. And...he is useful."

Useful. Was Mezzan how the Stadnem Anduske had learned about the saltpeter? Maybe not; Quientis had held that trade charter for years.

Arenza held her tongue, waiting. The whole point of conning Idusza had been to find out what Mezzan was up to, but so far, the woman had resisted all her efforts to pry into that relationship. At last there was an uncertain note in her voice, and she stared at the zrel in her cup rather than drinking it.

Finally, Idusza said, "My relationship with Mezzan is...complicated. My mother says always I go against her wisdom to do things she likes not. I think it's the same for him with his father. I hoped..." The words trailed off, and Idusza shook her head. "It matters not. Your cards give true guidance—I doubt that no longer—and they say he is a problem. But we need him only a short while longer."

Arenza's pulse quickened. Idusza wasn't turning on her lover, not yet...but·that was more than she'd ever let slip before. "Need him for what? If he supported you publicly, I would understand why it is worth holding Caerulet's son so close. But he keeps his silence."

"You think it chance that the Vigil has this past year accomplished nothing against us? Mezzan turns their eyes aside when we need it most. I will tell the others to be cautious—I will myself be cautious—but that is too valuable to throw away."

A short while longer, Idusza had said. What were they planning? And more to the point, how much did it matter to Indestor?

But Idusza looked like she had already said too much. Arenza poured her more tea and said, "Then I hope Ažerais watches over you, and blesses what you do next."

The Shambles, Lower Bank: Cyprilun 30

Like all of Nadežra's rookeries, the Shambles never slept, only rested its eyes. As Ren passed one stoop, a bundle of rags stirred, the haggard man under them watching her with hunger and speculation. A pair of night-pieces working a corner watched with similar speculation, but no hunger; they could judge customers, and knew they'd get no coin or interest from her.

She wore the same nondescript dark breeches and Liganti-style coat she'd used when scouting prior to starting her con, with a kerchief in her pocket in case she needed to cover her face. If the Rook expected her to wear the shawl he'd sent, he wouldn't have invited her to the Shambles; such fine fabric would only get ruined or stolen here.

She was, however, armed with as many knives as she could reasonably conceal.

The Three Eels stood at the end of a blind alley, across from a wainwright's abandoned workshop, where boards were nailed over the mouth of a yawning entry large enough to drive a cart through. It was exactly the sort of setup the Fingers might have used to ambush drunken patrons emerging from the ostretta. The sort of place an outlaw might lie in wait? Ren hesitated in the shadows, watching for any suspicious movement.

Not even a rat.

Which left the Three Eels, looking only slightly less abandoned than the wainwright's shop. A sign hung from the eaves; if Ren squinted, she could just make out three loops spotted with flaking grey paint chipped into wood eaten away by black mold.

The Shambles was a long way from her old turf on the Island. She didn't know the streets here, the best places to hide and the fastest routes to escape. She didn't know the people, either, except what Sedge had told her; Vargo controlled parts of it, but not all.

The distant sound of bells told her she still had an hour and a half before her appointment. That was enough to buy the drunk on the stoop a cup of unwatered zrel from the Three Eels and get a gutter's-eye view of the area. Then she scouted around, making sure she had several good routes by which to bolt if she had to run. From the Vigil, from Vargo's people, from the Rook himself... The ash was well and truly out of her body, but the fear it had created remained, like a stain in her bones.

She needed a place to watch and wait. Old habit made her look up: The close-packed roofs of Nadežra's slums offered lots of vantage points and shadows to hide in. A narrow gap between two dormers on the tenement at the alley's entrance was her best bet; it would let her watch the whole length of the alley, and a good portion of the rooftops besides.

The only difficulty was getting up to it. Old habit might die hard, but it didn't do a lot for atrophied climbing skills.

Fortunately, a shouting match inside the tenement covered the noise she made as she scaled the building. Ren settled into the sheltered space between the dormers, tucked her bare hands under her arms for warmth, and tried not to think about curses.

"You took my spot."

Only the fact that she'd half expected him to sneak up on her from behind kept her from twitching reflexively for a knife. "Then I chose a good one."

She turned to see the Rook leaning against the sloped roof of one dormer, distant enough that she could flee if she wanted. The hood tilted—in acknowledgment? In greeting? Ren might be good at feeling the currents, but not even she could read shadows. "You're early," he said.

As though he hadn't arrived three bells before the appointed hour. *Or earlier still.* How long had he been watching? "Call it curiosity," she said, aware that her voice sounded tight. "When you said we would continue our discussion, I expected something other than a summons to the Shambles in the middle of the night."

"I considered tea at Ossiter's, but they wouldn't give me a reservation."

"You could have knocked on my door and had a conversation like a civilized person."

It carried a bit of Renata's sharp edge. Not wise, given the circumstances, but what she could see of his mouth twitched in a faint smile. "You have an odd impression of me if you think I knock."

He crouched between the dormers, gripping the edge to avoid sliding into Ren, as the entrance of the Three Eels creaked open and slammed shut. A Vraszenian man ambled around the stoop, swinging his arms, leaning to one side and the other until his back cracked and he sighed with relief.

A passerby might have mistaken him for a patron just out to stretch his legs, but he was too interested in the empty street—including the rooftops.

"Civilized conversations can wait," the Rook murmured. "There's the reason I invited you tonight."

She frowned down at the man. "What do you mean?"

"I need to get into the old wainwright's shop, but it's always watched. That fellow down there is tonight's sentry. Do you think you could make friends with him long enough for me to slip inside?"

At least with the Rook, she could be sure that "make friends with him" didn't mean "kill him." But he'd summoned her out here with reference to their unfinished confrontation—and now he wanted her to do something for him instead?

He had leverage over her and knew it. And she had little choice but to bend. "How long of a distraction do you need?"

"Long enough for me to get in without being seen. Half a bell?"

Her jaw tightened. "Why? What's in there?"

While they whispered, the sentry returned to the ostretta. When he was gone, the Rook said, "A printing press."

"And?"

"And, I hope, the seditious literature the Stadnem Anduske have been using it to print."

"Vraszenian radicals. Not your usual target." Ren knew she should keep her mouth shut and do what he said, but some reckless instinct rebelled against knuckling under. "Or is it because one of them has taken up with Mezzan Indestor?"

The Rook's hood swiveled toward her. "Now that's an interesting bit of gossip. Wherever did you pick it up?"

How long would it be before guilt and grief stopped strangling her? "From Leato," Ren whispered, trying to take comfort in the fact that the Rook hadn't known she knew about Idusza. *At least I still have a few secrets.* "He investigated her—looking for something to use against Indestor."

"More likely it's Indestor who's doing the using," the Rook said. He stood, extending a hand in invitation. "So, are you up for it? Or do I need to give the fellow down there a very bad evening?"

She looked past his hand to the shadows of his hood. In Mettore's office, she'd gotten around the imbued concealment on the hidden door by acting as if she knew it was there. But that trick didn't work on the Rook's disguise. Even with her saying to herself, *That's Vargo*, the face in the darkness could have belonged to anyone, from Colbrin to that Kiraly granddaughter.

She stood without accepting his hand. "All right."

Embarrassingly, she did need his help climbing down from the roof. Nine days without sleep had cut badly into her strength and endurance. But when her foot touched the alley's broken cobbles, he held on to her hand instead of letting go. "There's a window at the back of the shop. It's too small for me, but you might fit. I'll leave it unlatched."

He couldn't have missed the surprised twitch of her fingers. "I thought you needed me for distraction only."

"If all I wanted was a distraction, I wouldn't have invited you," he said, and slipped away.

Ren's exhale was unsteadier than it should have been. Fair enough: He was the Rook. If he couldn't distract a guard himself, he should hang up his hood. But why play these games with her?

She wouldn't get any answers with him gone. Ren straightened her coat and considered her options. She wasn't dressed for conventional distraction, and if the guard was worth a salted herring, he'd ignore anything like that anyway. She could start a brawl in the Three Eels, but—

The wind gusted, swinging the sign on its rusted hinges. She thought back to what the drunk had told her about the ostretta and its history, and for the first time since she read the Rook's note, a genuine smile rose to her lips.

Ren soon had cause to be glad she'd scouted some escape routes, and by the time she circled back around to the wainwright's, she was seriously out of breath. The window the Rook had mentioned wasn't too inaccessible, but he was an optimist if he thought she could fit through it. She wasn't about to quit, though, so she scaled the wall and wormed her way through at the cost of only a few bruises and one snagged button.

As she landed, she heard him say, "I'm impressed. On a second look, I honestly wasn't sure a cat could squeeze through." The Rook leaned against the far wall of the workshop, past a graveyard of joiner's tools, wheel spokes, and axles.

"You could've helped," Ren muttered, dusting herself off.

"And miss observing a master in action?" The hood shook from side to side, and he skirted a stack of rotted boxboards to join her. "I saw the furor outside. Well done, if a little noisier than I expected."

He took out a small glowing stone on a short chain, which he latched around his wrist. The same one he'd had at Indestor Manor? Or did he have Vargo's kind of money, to buy numinatrian pieces whenever he needed them?

"Help me with this," the Rook said, and reached for the stack of boards.

They concealed a small printing press and, stacked beside it, a bound sheaf of broadsheets smelling of pulp and fresh ink. He worried one free, holding it so they could both skim the Vraszenian text.

" 'The Liganti are the cuckoo invading our nest. We must starve them out,' " he read. " 'Novrus has turned the Wellspring of Ažerais into her pocket. We must not fill it . . . Let's see how the vulture fares when there are no bones to pick clean . . .' Someone needs to choose a metaphor and stick to it."

"They want people staying away during Veiled Waters?" Ren said, frowning. In a normal year, it would have made sense. Argentet's control over the city's cultural affairs included the amphitheatre, and therefore access to the wellspring, and they charged for the privilege of going near it. Even during off years, when the wellspring didn't manifest for the Great Dream, Vraszenians paid to hold their celebrations in what remained of their sacred site. The money was supposed to fund the city's cultural institutions and events, but in practice, most of it went into the pocket of whoever held the Argentet seat—a long-standing point of grievance.

But people were furious when Iridet closed the amphitheatre for investigation after the Night of Hells. Only two days had passed since Tanaquis had persuaded him to reopen it—and now the Stadnem Anduske were telling people to stay away? "Sostira will be furious."

The broadsheet crinkled in the Rook's tightened grip. "Friend of yours, Alta Renata?" For all the softness of his words, they held an edge of threat that hadn't been present before, and Ren's breath caught. She'd spoken without thinking—and spoken like a noble.

Carefully folding the broadsheet, the Rook tucked it into his coat and scanned the rest of the workshop. His voice eased. "But Novrus is no friend of Indestor's. Still, seems unlikely he'd use the Stadnem Anduske just for this. Unless he's hoping Novrus will crack down on Vraszenians for *not* going to the amphitheatre."

"Hard to punish people for that—though she could find ways

to hurt them if she wanted." Ren twitched aside a filthy canvas to reveal a stack of blank paper underneath, ready for printing. "He could just want to hamstring Novrus. But he has other ways of doing that—safer ones than his son cozying up to a Vraszenian."

A box of type blocks rattled as the Rook shifted it. "So what's his play here?" he muttered, quietly enough that Ren suspected he was talking to himself.

"He might provoke the Stadnem Anduske to do something he can punish them for. But it doesn't fit. I patterned Met—Eret Indestor. Whatever his plan, it involves magic." She found a jug of ink, opened it, and sniffed, trying to detect any trace of ash. "This isn't magic."

"Unless they've figured out how to imbue bad rhetoric, I agree." He glanced toward the door and the board he'd pried away to gain entry. It was propped back in place, but wouldn't fool a close inspection. "How long is the sentry likely to be occupied?"

She snorted, a touch of humor slipping through despite her tension. "Depends on whether I accidentally started a gang war. They are apparently *very* proud of that sign."

According to her gutter informant, the Three Eels used to be the Three Wheels, after the wainwright's, before the rise of a knot called the Eels led the ostretta's owner to declare his allegiance and crudely modify the sign. At the moment, he was under the impression that the sentry, working for the rival Mudslingers, had stolen it.

"*Accidentally*." The Rook chuckled and searched the press, running a gloved hand over the paper frame as though he could read the sheets it had once held. "Maybe these people should hire you to write for them."

He sounded like he might mean it as a compliment. She found a few more broadsides on a table—and then a drawer set into the side of the table, whose handle wasn't dusty. She tugged it open to reveal another printing frame, already set with text.

"We should go before—You found something?"

"Another plate." She rubbed her thumb across the letters; it came away clean. "Not used yet, or they wiped it down very well."

The Rook approached, but not close enough for her to make out the reversed type by the light of his stone. "Now that's a reading I'd be interested in hearing. What offering should I make, Szorsa Arenza?" A soft huff of air might have been a laugh, and he lifted one hand. "I understand gloves are a common currency, but I'm afraid these are an heirloom."

Ren tried not to stare. Was he offering her some kind of bargain, in exchange for the plate?

Several responses tried to leap free. *I want to know if you're Vargo and playing with me like a cat with a three-legged mouse. I want to know something that will give me power over you, the way you have power over me.*

But neither of those things were what she wanted most.

Her lips had gone dry. She wet them and said, "I want to know what you will do with me. With what you know."

The Rook's hand disappeared into the shadows of his hood, rubbing at his jaw. "You mean, am I going to expose you. No. Bit hypocritical of me to go revealing other people's secret identities, don't you think? If nobles are fool enough to welcome you, that's their problem."

It sent a tremor through her, not of fear, but of surprise. "You— But—"

Every street-sharpened instinct said, *But what you know is a weapon.* He could use it to control her.

Yet it sounded like he wouldn't.

He sighed. "Look... what should I call you?"

The question cut deeper than it should have. Whether she was painted and dressed as Renata or Arenza, she wore a mask to face the world; only Tess and Sedge saw *her.* But the Rook had broken through all the masks when he ambushed her in the kitchen, uncovering the real person beneath the lies.

Which left only one answer. "Ren."

"Ren. Your business is your own. I don't think you caused the Night of Hells, and you're working against Indestor. So you can stop pressing back into that table like you want to crawl under it for safety. I'm not going to turn you in or use this against you. Deal?" He spat into his glove and reached out.

She held on to the table while the world danced around her, details shifting into new positions. The shawl full of knives. The message summoning her to the Shambles. The window left unlatched. *If all I wanted was a distraction, I wouldn't have invited you.*

The Rook wasn't blackmailing her. He was making amends for that night in the kitchen.

Ren spat in her own palm and took his hand. The leather of his glove curled around her palm; she felt the strength of his grip, and returned it in kind. "Deal."

"Good." The light at his wrist revealed the curve of a smile as he craned his neck to peer at the plate half-hidden behind her. "Now, are you going to share?"

She wiped her hand dry and picked up the plate, holding it carefully so the trembling in her hands wouldn't make her drop it. Reading the reversed text would have been difficult enough on its own, given how rusty her Vraszenian was; her head spinning in relief didn't help, nor did the Rook leaning in at her side. She'd only puzzled through a few lines when he spoke.

"It's not just avoiding the amphitheatre. They're calling for a gathering at the Charterhouse." His exhalation ruffled the hair near her ear. "That's a lot of Vraszenians in a Vigil-heavy space."

Ren found the date, sitting on a line by itself. "The thirty-fifth of Cyprilun. Five days from now. If they tell people too far ahead of time, the Vigil will try to stop them; they must be saving this for closer to the actual day."

The Rook's finger traced down the lines of backward text. "What better way to arrange a massacre than by first arranging a protest?"

And what better way to make a protest seem legitimate than to have it organized by those who hated the Cinquerat?

"But—"

The strike of boots on the cobbles outside cut her off before she could tell him what Idusza had said about Mezzan. The Rook spoke rapidly. "Put it back. Out the window." He set himself between Ren and the doorway. "I'll draw him off."

She moved without hesitation, returning the frame to the drawer and shutting it to the exact depth where she'd found it. Then she ran for the window, planting one foot against the wall to give her the extra lift she needed to catch the frame. Two more buttons tore free as she squirmed through; speed mattered more than caution now, and she took bruises when she tumbled to the ground outside.

From inside the abandoned shop, she heard a shout of discovery, a laugh, a scuffle, and the crash of wood breaking; then she was too far away to hear anything more.

Isla Prišta, Westbridge: Cyprilun 30

Tess had sworn up and down that she'd stay awake until Ren came home from her meeting with the Rook, but when Ren eased the kitchen door open, she found her sister curled on the new mattress, breathing softly and evenly in sleep. The needle and fabric fallen from her fingers showed her determination, though, and the fire hadn't yet burned down, so it couldn't have been long since she nodded off.

Ren carefully plucked away the needle before Tess could roll onto it. The mattress took up an inconvenient amount of kitchen floor, but they'd judged that better than heating one of the upstairs bedrooms, especially when they didn't have proper linens. She tugged a blanket over Tess, lit a candle at the hearth, then gathered a few things and went upstairs.

Not to the parlour; that was too much Renata's territory. Instead she went into the unused dining room on the floor above and folded aside the dustcloth on the table, uncovering a corner where she could work.

She exhaled slowly, turning her focus inward, holding the deck in her hands and the Rook in her thoughts: A black-coated whirlwind in Lacewater, his mocking voice demanding her glove as a forfeit. A gleaming blade in the darkness of Mettore's office, and then a warm body behind her in the hidden closet—a reminder of the real person beneath the shadows. An ambush in her kitchen, his fury driving her to breakdown, but then fading to patience and even a touch of kindness. A shawl full of knives and an invitation to assist him.

A thread in the darkness, when everything was lost. A hand reaching down to draw her back from death.

The Rook. A mystery wrapped inside an enigma wrapped inside a coat she dearly wanted to rip off—to lay him open the same way he'd done to her. Not to expose him to others; just to *know*. To restore some kind of balance between them, so she didn't have to rely on his word alone.

Ren's hands began to move. Shuffling the cards, cutting them, lips murmuring the prayers Ivrina had taught her so many years ago. Prayers she hadn't used since her mother's death, except in her nightmare. But the pattern was sacred, and if she wanted the gods and the clan ancestors to grant her their blessings, she owed them respect.

By the light of the candle, she laid out the Rook's pattern, then turned over the lowest row of cards.

Ash had given her thoughts horrific clarity, a twisted version of what some szorsas chased by drugging themselves with aža. This was different. Pattern wasn't a matter of predictability; it was intuition, a sense of the connections between things. In the stillness of her mind, Ren could feel the threads thrumming: spinning for Jump at the Sun, woven for The Laughing Crow, cut for Reeds Unbroken.

She'd hoped the pattern would show her the person beneath the hood, but so far, no—this was for the Rook himself.

There *was* something there, beyond an imbued disguise; the Rook was more than the men and women who had borne that name. Someone had made him, had taken an enormous risk to create the Rook. And succeeded . . . though not without cost. The snapped stalks at the feet of the figure in Reeds Unbroken told Ren that more than a few Rooks had died for the burden they carried. The role was greater than any one person and made the bearers stronger than they would otherwise be; the concealment of the hood was only a small part of what the disguise did for whoever wore it. But it didn't make them invulnerable.

It wasn't accurate to say that no one had ever uncovered the identity of the Rook. There were two birds depicted in The Laughing Crow, and the role had to pass on somehow. But the bearers didn't keep the secret only because they chose to. The Rook himself, whatever he was—ghost, spirit, something unique—pushed them toward silence. And that too carried a toll.

Onward to his present, the good and the ill of it, and that which was—

A spike of pain drilled through her skull as she turned over the middle card, and Ren's vision blurred. She tried to squint, to force her eyes to focus, but she couldn't make out the image or the words, and the pain worsened until finally she slapped the card back facedown and sat there, panting.

Idiot.

Of course something protected the Rook against having his identity uncovered. In her arrogance she'd thought her own gift might be enough to overcome that.

She focused on her breathing, both to dull the throbbing behind her eyes and to regain her clarity, that place of stillness where she could feel the threads of the pattern. Ren eyed the back of the card, wondering if she could identify it by the small marks of wear that had accumulated over the years. *Or I could go through the rest of the deck and see what isn't there.*

No. She'd courted enough danger already. The Rook would keep his secret.

But it was bad luck to abandon a pattern halfway through, and the other two cards in the present line didn't hurt when she looked at them. The ledger discarded by the figure on Ten Coins Sing reminded her of the printing frame she'd found in the drawer. Generosity. The Rook kept his identity hidden, but that didn't mean he never had allies. What he'd done tonight, working alongside her... that was a good thing, even if it didn't last.

On the other side of the facedown card, The Mask of Fools.

That card had occupied the same position in Mettore's pattern.

Like him, the Rook was missing some piece of important information. For Mettore, that had meant Ren herself: a woman conceived on the night of the Great Dream, and whatever he needed her for. That wasn't the case here...but she felt some kind of connection anyway, too faint for her to tease it out. Something dangerous. Something extending past the current Rook to those who had come before, and those who would come after.

If she could have seen the central card, she might have been able to say. As it was, she had no choice but to move on.

The Mask of Worms had always been her least favorite card, long before illness killed her mother. The squirming creatures that made up its shape turned her stomach, haunting her childhood nightmares. Now she felt them squirming through Nadežra, a poison eating away at the city.

Not a new poison, for all that it lay in the future. No, its position in the center of the line—that which was neither good nor ill; sometimes, that which was both—told her something about it was going to change. This had to do with why the Rook existed at all. Everyone knew him as the enemy of the nobility, a doomed-to-fail check against their power, but there was more to it than that. He had a purpose, a mandate. Fighting against this poison, whatever it was. And when it changed...

To its right, The Ember Adamant; to its left, Pearl's Promise. A chance to discharge an obligation, or the risk of laboring without reward. If all went well, the Rook might fulfill his mandate—finally laying to rest whatever had spurred the creation of Nadežra's outlaw.

But if it didn't, then all those generations of Rooks would fail. They'd struggled in the shadows to fight the nobility and the Cinquerat, without people ever knowing their names or what they sacrificed. And all of it would be for nothing.

Ren recited the closing prayer and swept the cards together. She shuffled the deck seven times to thoroughly hide the card fate hadn't wanted her to see. Then she sat with her head in her hands, massaging her temples and feeling like someone had put her brain through a meat grinder.

The pattern hadn't told her what she most wanted to know: who the Rook was.

But it had, in its way, told her what she *needed* to know. So long as she didn't make herself the Rook's enemy, he had no reason to betray her. And given what she'd seen—far beyond what the legends said—she might even manage to help him.

A faint creak alerted her that Tess was awake; a moment later, her sister appeared in the doorway, eyes bleary and curls going every direction. "What are you doing?"

Through the window Ren could see the knife-sharp crescent of Paumillis rising. It was nearly dawn. How long had she spent lost in the intricacies of pattern?

"Getting answers," she said, picking up her cards. "Let's go to the kitchen, and I will tell you what I know."

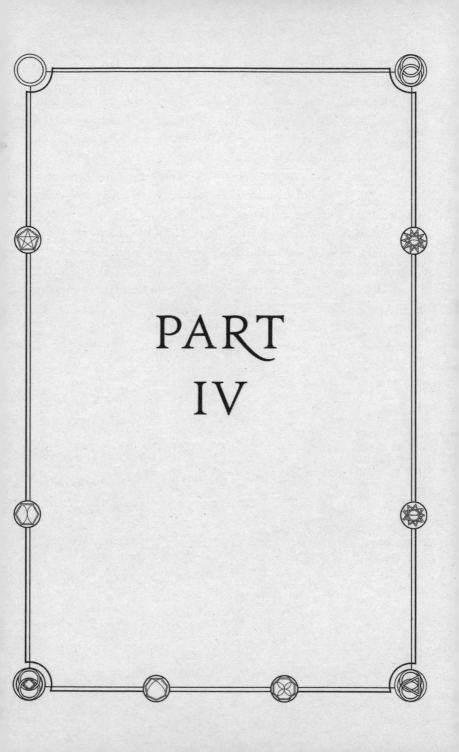

PART

IV

PART

IV

Labyrinth's Heart

Isla Prišta and Isla Traementis: Cyprilun 31

A messenger rang the doorbell at the unholy hour of second sun the next morning, bearing a note from Tanaquis. She believed she'd devised a way to verify Renata's claim of a curse, and wanted to test everyone connected with House Traementis in any capacity to see how far the ill fortune extended. To that end, she'd summoned Renata to Traementis Manor—the last place Ren wanted to set foot.

"What about Giuna?" Tess asked, biting her lip. "Do you think she'll have said anything?"

"Who knows," Ren said grimly. "I suppose I'll find out."

Colbrin at least treated her no differently than usual, except that he guided her and Tess to the ballroom instead of the parlour or study. Luckily, the large numinat Tanaquis had chalked onto the polished floor helped distract Ren from the memories of Leato that haunted the place. The astrologer was busy examining her handiwork, watched by the servants who waited to one side in murmuring rows. As for Giuna...

The girl hesitated at the sight of Renata, then squared her shoulders and approached. "I haven't said anything," she murmured. "Mother doesn't need another shock. Which means you'd best continue calling me Giuna, and I will call you Renata."

A little of Ren's tension vanished. She'd been wondering how to navigate that particular shoal: She didn't want to offend Giuna with her usual familiarity, but she also didn't want Donaia wondering why she'd returned to formal address. Her plan had been to avoid using Giuna's name at all.

"Thank you," she said. "And...thank you for the things you sent."

Color suffused Giuna's cheeks, and of course that was the moment Tanaquis took note of the world around her. "Alta Giuna, are you feeling well?"

Pressing her fingers to her flushed skin, Giuna nodded. "I'm only nervous. I...I won't burn to a cinder if I step in there, will I?"

Her question sank everyone into silence. Less than two weeks had passed since Leato was cremated in the Ninatium.

Renata cleared her throat. "I'll go first. Unless Meda Fienola needs us in a specific order?"

"Hmm? No, that's acceptable. Stand here." Tanaquis tapped the center of a vesica piscis on the sunwise side of the spiral. Then she pulled a small set of scissors from her surcoat pocket. "And I'll need a lock of your hair."

"Here now!" Tess snapped before Tanaquis could bring the shears anywhere near Renata. "I'll be doing that, if you don't mind." Always armed with her own mending kit, Tess carefully unpinned a curl, tied it off with a ribbon, snipped, and handed the cutting to Tanaquis.

Taking part in a numinatrian ritual turned out to be astonishingly boring. All Renata did was stand where Tanaquis had indicated while the astrologer placed the lock of her hair at a different point, then set the focus and closed the circle of the numinat. *At least during a dress fitting I have to turn around and raise my arms occasionally.*

Then she realized a thin curl of smoke was rising from the opposite side of the numinat. As she watched, a flame licked up, and her hair burned away.

Tanaquis made some notes. Then she broke the encircling line. "Thank you, Alta Renata. Alta Giuna, if you'd go next?"

As Tess was cutting Giuna's hair, Donaia arrived. She was far from her usual self; the auburn of her hair was dulled, as though she'd set it with powder rather than washing it, and her surcoat was matted with fur, like she'd been clutching Meatball for comfort.

"You started already? What did I miss?" Then she wrinkled her nose. "And what is that smell?"

Before Renata could answer, Tanaquis set the focus back in place. The stench of burning hair increased as Giuna's lock also went up in flames.

Renata's stomach clenched. Did the hair burning indicate the person was cursed? *But I'm not a member of House Traementis.* She couldn't say that, and despite questions from Donaia and Giuna, Tanaquis provided no answers—only broke the numinat and asked for Donaia next.

Donaia's hair went up in a flash of white flame.

Then Colbrin and the other servants submitted to Tess's shears and Tanaquis's test. Not one lock of hair from them burned. "Fascinating," Tanaquis murmured when they all—even Tess—had taken a turn.

"What. Is. Fascinating?" Donaia asked through gritted teeth.

Looking up from her papers, Tanaquis gestured at the servants. "I don't think they need to be here. Just you, and Altas Giuna and Renata."

"Me?" Renata said, unable to hide the tremor in her voice. "But—I'm not a member of House Traementis. Not by law." *Or by blood.* She might be associated with them . . . but so were the servants.

Tanaquis waited until Colbrin, Tess, and the others had left the room before she shut her book of notes. "Power flows along channels. Sometimes the channel can be a legal connection, sometimes blood, sometimes something else. The numinat I created siphons the power of the curse into the part of the figure that held the hair. If the subject suffers from the curse, the hair burns. If they don't, there's no power to siphon and the lock comes to no harm. I tested it on myself, and nothing happened."

Donaia gripped Renata and Giuna both, hard enough to bruise. "And that means—"

"That Alta Renata's cards were correct. You are cursed—and a powerful curse at that. The power is strongest with you, and about equal between the two altas."

Donaia had to be helped to one of the ballroom chairs before she collapsed. She released Renata to clutch her daughter close, and it was all Ren could do not to visibly reel. Tanaquis's explanation explained nothing; there were no actual connections between her and the Traementis. Not of any sort that could justify her hair burning.

How in the name of all the gods am I cursed?

Maybe because she'd betrayed Ondrakja and her knot. Except that did nothing to explain the Traementis, who certainly had never belonged to a street gang, much less broken their oaths to one. *And Ondrakja isn't even dead*, Ren thought wildly. Not that it erased her betrayal.

Then another thought came to her. Ivrina had never said who Ren's father was. There would be a hideous irony in Ren trying to infiltrate a house she had actual blood connections to.

She didn't believe it for a moment; the coincidence would be far too great. And that wasn't the most pressing question anyway. "Meda Fienola. What do we *do*?"

"That's the interesting part." Tanaquis smiled confidently. "Now we figure out how to block the power and send it back to its source."

"And then?" The question came from Donaia, her arms still wrapped protectively around her daughter. "Will we be safe?"

Tanaquis nodded, smile softening. "I promise, Donaia. I will put an end to this."

Dockwall and Eastbridge: Cyprilun 31

The smell of burning hair lingered in Ren's nostrils with every step she took up the river stairs into Dockwall. *I wanted what they had. I got their curse.*

One of the guards at the perimeter of Vargo's warehouse bowed even before Renata could introduce herself, showing her to a small outbuilding tacked to the side of the warehouse. The door was open to a small office, and through it she spotted the rangy Vraszenian lihosz she'd seen the last time she was here. He was giving Vargo a stern look.

"We'll want to leave as soon as Veiled Waters is over," he said in Vraszenian. "No delays, or behind some Liganti slug train we will be stuck."

Vargo's hand was just visible on his desk, and his fingers drummed an agitated rhythm as he answered in the same language. "My guards will be ready."

The caravan leader saw Renata then. "You have another visitor," he said.

"Renata?" Vargo appeared in the doorway, his surprised smile briefly driving off the air of crime lord and cutthroat merchant. A sniff from the caravan leader summoned it back. "I mean, *alta*."

"My apologies for interrupting," Renata said, wishing she could have eavesdropped for longer.

"It matters not," the caravan leader said in Liganti. "Our business is concluded. Master Vargo."

"Ča Obrašir Dostroske." Vargo watched as the caravan leader left, then gestured Renata into his office.

She kept her expression bland as she sat across from him. "Guards" were not something he could legally provide—but she supposedly didn't speak Vraszenian. "What was that about?" she asked.

"Something I've been meaning to discuss with you." Vargo tucked a sheaf of papers into a leather folder. "I've been granted administration rights to a mercenary charter, from House Coscanum. And I suspect my association with you had something to do with it."

Despite the flattery, the information jolted her. "You're administering another charter?"

"Don't be jealous," Vargo said, amused. "I didn't go through another advocate; there's only you. Eret Coscanum came to me."

Then his playful manner faded. "Are you all right? You look . . . tense."

Apparently, she wasn't hiding it as well as she'd hoped. "Some bad news," Renata said. "A personal matter, concerning House Traementis. Nothing for you to worry about." *Unless the curse takes us all out.*

"If I can help . . ." He left the offer hanging, but frowned as though dissatisfied with it. Toying with the end of the leather cord holding the folder closed, he said, "Would a distraction be useful? Whatever brought you here can be discussed just as easily over a glass of wine. Unless you have engagements this evening."

None except sitting at home and brooding. She'd come here with business in mind; it had occurred to her this morning that she could spend the same coin three times by asking Vargo to find Quientis's "missing" saltpeter. *Get it released for Quientis, help the Stadnem Anduske steal it, then win Quientis's favor again by getting it back.*

But she was so tired of the various burdens she was carrying. The thought of laying them down for a bit of frivolity was enormously tempting. "What did you have in mind?"

He rose and offered her a mock-formal bow. "Care to try your hand against me at cards?"

"That depends," Renata said as he led her out and sent a runner for a sedan chair. "Can your fabric warehouses afford for you to lose?"

The card parlour Vargo took her to was nothing like the one she'd visited with Leato back in Suilun, after the encounter with the Rook. Unlike the Talon and Trick, Breglian's stood on the Upper Bank and served an upscale clientele. Instead of Vraszenian trappings, it boasted a facade of columns, an airy atrium, and a galleried rotunda inside. There were tables for public play, but none of the clamor of betting and carousing that resounded through most nytsa parlours. Most of the alcoves in the second-floor gallery were full, their curtains drawn shut for private play, but after a few quiet words and a bribe passed so subtly Renata almost missed it, they were led up the curving staircase to one that was conveniently—and rapidly—unoccupied.

The host swept a curtain aside for Renata to enter. As she glanced over her shoulder to make sure Vargo was behind her, she saw him falter on the last step, hand going to one of his knees as though to support it.

He made no comment about his stumble, and Renata didn't, either. But she watched out of the corner of her eye as he tugged the curtains partway shut and sat, and saw that he took the majority of his weight on his right leg, sparing the left. As if that knee pained him.

Gossip around the city said the Vigil had chased the Rook out of the Shambles last night, and he'd escaped by leaping—or, according to his detractors, falling—off a rooftop.

Vargo tugged his gloves off and reached for the house deck. "Do you know how to play sixes? Or we could play nytsa instead."

Sixes was a game of lies and risk. Nytsa was gentler, and worked best with two players—and it was a more traditional Vraszenian game. "I know the basics of nytsa. As I'm sure you're quite aware; you're a well-informed man."

He didn't respond to that, but she heard the soft huff of a suppressed laugh as he began to shuffle. Vargo handled the cards like a practiced gambler: no showy flourishes, but the simple dexterity of his scarred hands had its own beauty. Renata blinked away from watching them when he set the deck before her. "Cut?"

She removed her own gloves and did so, thanking the Faces that five months was long enough for her own hands to soften—and that she'd never been Letilia's scullery maid. It wasn't just the gambling that made card-playing a mildly scandalous pastime; it was the fact that shuffling a deck was nearly impossible with silk gloves on, and playing not much easier.

"I'm relieved Iridet agreed to reopen the amphitheatre." The soft slap of cards on the table punctuated Vargo's words. "It would have been a shame for you to miss out on a proper Veiled Waters your first year here."

Renata picked up her cards and fanned them. If there was pattern in them, she couldn't see it. She took Dawn and Dusk from her hand

and matched it to Turtle in Her Shell on the table, claimed them both, then dealt a card from the stockpile to the table. No match, and so it became Vargo's turn. "I thought a proper Veiled Waters only came every seven years."

"That's the Great Dream—which mostly matters if you're Vraszenian."

The man either had damnably good luck, or she should start checking his sleeves for additional cards, because in the second pass he laid down Sleeping Waters. Unaligned cards weren't usually valuable on their own, but this one could form combinations with both The Face of Weaving and The Face of Stars—both of which he'd snagged in the previous pass.

If you're Vraszenian. Did he mean that as a hint?

"Nytsa," he said, and dealt another card to the table. Of course he would call for the hand to continue. She had only four cards in her bank, none of them useful to each other; she was a long way from assembling a combination of her own. She resigned herself to losing this hand.

"Then again," he said, "if the rumblings I'm hearing are true, Veiled Waters might not be at its best this year."

This time her luck was better, matching a card both from her hand and from the draw. If Ir Entrelke saw fit to give her one more unaligned card from the cut thread before Vargo made another combination, she might scrape through after all. There weren't any on the table, though. "What rumblings? Should I be worried?"

Vargo discarded A Spiraling Fire, but she couldn't claim it until he removed his fingers. They slid along the surface of the card, as if he was reconsidering his move. "After the Night of Hells, I think we all have reason to be worried. The Stadnem Anduske—Vraszenian radicals—they're warning people away from the amphitheatre, and there's talk of a protest at the Charterhouse." He withdrew his hand swiftly, glancing down at his own cards rather than meeting her eyes. "So my people tell me. I have them keep an ear out for rumors; you never know what will interfere with business."

She matched Storm Against Stone to the card Vargo had discarded and said, "Close." Her combination was a short thread, worth only one point—doubled to two, since Vargo had called nytsa—but it deprived him of the eight points he would have gotten for his own combinations. Vargo conceded the hand with a philosophical sigh.

"We're sliding back toward business again," he said as she shuffled for the next hand. His expression took on a playful, wicked cast. "And I believe I promised you distraction."

After that, he abandoned all pretense that their game wasn't simply an excuse for flirtation. His kohl-rimmed eyes spent more time on her than on the hand, his voice sank from its usual controlled drawl to a more textured rumble, and when he laid a card down, it was often with a little flourish, or a teasing hesitation before he followed through.

At first she tried to ignore it. Sharps used tricks like that to hide their cheating; she'd done it herself, playing sixes against Leato's friends. But she was playing honestly tonight, if badly, and as near as she could tell, Vargo was doing the same. He was merely giving her something more pleasant to think about than radicals or curses.

And so, bit by bit, she relaxed into it. She began returning his jokes with sallies of her own, his sidelong glances with smiles. They were only playing for tokens, after all, not money. There was no need to keep her guard up. He was manipulating her, yes—but for no more nefarious purpose than the simple, honest pleasure of flirtation. She couldn't remember the last time she'd had a chance to enjoy that.

I'm not sure I ever have.

The realization jolted her. She reached for the deck to shuffle again, and Vargo laid his hand over hers. His calluses were rough against her glove-softened skin. "That's twenty-one points," he said. "Or didn't you notice?"

She knew she'd taken the last hand, but she hadn't calculated the total. "Oh." Then, as Vargo kept his hand on hers, she raised an eyebrow at him. "I half suspect you let me win, as I *know* I wasn't playing very well."

"It seems I've failed to distract you from your problems." He fell silent as he collected the cards and ran his thumb over their smooth-cut edges. "I know you don't want to talk about it—whatever's bothering you—but if you did, I'd listen." He made a face. "Without using it against you." A wince. "Or gossiping." A sigh. "Or judging."

He sounded like a boy being prompted by his mother. It was endearingly awkward. Too blunt, and not at all the way to persuade someone to share a personal secret.

But it was that very bluntness that tempted her.

Here in the semi-private space of the alcove, with the sandalwood and clove scent of his perfume spicing the air, it was easy to forget that the man sitting across from her had issued a veiled threat to Arenza, that he paid Sedge to beat people up, that he ran knots up and down the Lower Bank.

Yes—and you're a knot-breaking murderer. Her past was no cleaner than his. As for their current lives... his was, in its own way, more honest than hers. Everybody knew who and what Vargo was. And if he truly was hiding an identity as the Rook, then he donned his mask for the greater good, which was more than Ren could claim.

"It's..." She hesitated, wishing she still had cards in hand to disguise her nerves. "A spiritual affliction. I don't know what kind. But it's on me, and Giuna, and Donaia."

"You only just learned of this? From whom?" His brow furrowed. In concern, but also that focus he took on when faced with a problem. "Is it some residual effect of your sleeplessness? Why all three of you? Why just you three? What— Ah. I'm talking and not listening, aren't I?"

She couldn't help but laugh. "All very good questions, and ones Meda Fienola is investigating. Along with, I hope, a way to remove it."

"Would you allow me to contact her with an offer of assistance?"

Ren desperately wanted any help she could get. But she'd already taken a risk by sharing this much with him. "While I'd be glad of that... I'm not sure Era Traementis would agree."

"I understand." Setting the deck aside, he covered her hand with his, a gesture of protection rather than flirtation. For once she didn't feel the instinct to pull away, and she let him warm her cold fingers. "The offer remains, or if you just need to talk. I suspect you hate trusting others to take care of you as much as I do."

And to keep my secrets. Ren searched his gaze, and Vargo didn't look away. If he was the Rook, then he knew who lay beneath the masks of Renata and Arenza. And even if he wasn't...

She wanted to tell him. To have someone else she could be honest with. Not family, like Tess and Sedge, but an ally, a partner—a friend.

Before she could do more than absorb the shock of that thought, Vargo's gaze flicked to the gap in the curtains. He pulled his hand away as someone coughed outside. When he twitched the curtain aside, one of Breglian's staff was waiting.

"Deepest apologies, Master Vargo. Alta. I was told you were finished and would be leaving," he said, not sounding particularly apologetic at all. Ghiscolo Acrenix stood two paces away, and behind him Carinci Acrenix was being hoisted up the stairs, chair and all, by two strapping young Vraszenians whose stained aprons suggested they usually worked in the kitchens.

As efficiently as they'd been led to the alcove, Renata found herself and Vargo escorted out of it, receiving a nod from Ghiscolo in passing. She expected Vargo to be all scowls as they walked out the door, but instead he laughed. "That's the nicest boot anybody's ever given me. I apologize for the lackluster end to the evening."

A faint hiss escaped him as they finished descending the stairs, and he leaned against a pedestal holding a statue of some past Cinquerat seat holder—looking casual, but also taking his weight off his knee. "Shall I call you a sedan chair, or offer further distraction in liquid form?"

She couldn't quite tell if that was an invitation back to his house, and she suspected the ambiguity was deliberate. But with the chill, misty air clearing her head, she remembered her original purpose in going to Dockwall. "A sedan chair, I think—but before that, I have a favor to ask of you. It's why I came to your office."

"I'll admit, I was wondering. What favor?"

"A small thing, and it's already been reported to the Vigil—but you have resources they don't. You recall Eret Quientis's shipment of saltpeter? After all my hard work getting it out of Era Destaelio's clutches, someone's gone and stolen it."

He stilled, all traces of playfulness vanishing. "Did you say saltpeter?"

"Yes."

He came off the pedestal like somebody had called him to attention. "An entire shipment?"

"Is that significant?"

His incredulous look broke on a bark of laughter. "Don't you know what saltpeter is used for? Fireworks." All amusement ebbed away. "And other things that explode. *Djek.*"

Black powder. The same material that had burned down the Fiangiolli warehouse and killed Kolya Serrado.

She'd never asked why the Stadnem Anduske wanted the saltpeter—but she should have. *What have I done?*

Vargo pivoted, scanning until he spotted a sedan chair unloading a passenger. "Normally I wouldn't care much about Scaperto Quientis losing something, but—I'll look into it right away. My apologies." With that for a farewell, he set off at a jog, all but knocking a waiting gentleman out of the way to take the chair for himself.

Ren stood outside Breglian's, eyes squeezed shut. The Anduske had put together a printing plate calling for people to gather at the Charterhouse—*after* they'd taken Quientis's saltpeter. She didn't think they were so blinded by their cause that they would murder their own...but use a bombing to incite something? That was all too possible.

I have to tell the Rook. But if she hadn't done that just now, she had no other way of contacting him. And she hadn't told Vargo that it was the Stadnem Anduske who had the saltpeter—because how could Renata Viraudax know that?

She could, however, tell Grey Serrado. He was the one member of the Vigil she could trust with this.

Back in her townhouse, she had just finished scribbling another anonymous message when the bell rang. Tess called her to the door, and a man from Breglian's delivered a small, heavy box. "Your winnings, alta."

Lost for words, she took it. Inside were twenty-one forri: her point total for the game.

She had assumed they were only playing for chips. Apparently Vargo had let her keep that assumption...then turned the tables when it was too late for her to argue.

"Thank you," she said faintly, and shut the door.

Whitesail, Upper Bank: Cyprilun 32

It was a measure of her faith in Vargo's network that Ren hoped to wake up the next morning to the news that he'd found the saltpeter. But no such message awaited her.

Instead a letter came inviting her to visit Tanaquis's townhouse in Whitesail to discuss "spiritual matters." Renata went, puzzled as to why the meeting wasn't happening in Traementis Manor, and discovered it was because Donaia and Giuna hadn't been invited.

"I wanted to talk to you about pattern," Tanaquis said without preamble. "I've spent the past three days questioning szorsas, but they've been...unhelpful."

When Iridet's right-hand woman was interrogating them, Renata wasn't surprised. The Cinquerat's religious seat wasn't known for his tolerance of local "superstition." She said, "I'll tell you what I can, but compared to Vraszenians, I'm quite ignorant."

They hadn't gone to Tanaquis's parlour, but to the top floor of the house, what would ordinarily have been the servants' garret. Someone had knocked out all the interior walls and installed large skylights, creating a bright, open workroom. A star chart enameled in lapis blue and silver covered the largest wall. The polished floorboards at one end held a circle for numinata, and the other end was packed with books. On a platform beneath one of the skylights sat a copper-banded rosewood telescope, with chains connecting the platform to a winch so it could be raised and lowered.

Tanaquis gestured her to a well-cushioned chair. "Your ignorance is less than mine, and at least you won't be foretelling my doom or hard-selling me inferior spotted toadcaps. I apologize for the mess. I rarely have company."

Renata took the offered seat and glanced around again. Other than a bit of chalk dust on Tanaquis's sleeve and a few books stacked on the desk, she saw nothing resembling a mess.

"According to Vraszenians, pattern is linked not only to their cards but to the wellspring, the Great Dream, and the aspect of the Lumen they call Ažerais," Tanaquis said, proffering a glass of wine. "The cards seem to act like the focus of a numinat, but the manner in which they do so is..." She wrinkled her nose. "Unstructured. Illogical. Does that fit with what you know?"

First time in my life I've heard Ažerais called an aspect of the Lumen. "It doesn't seem illogical to me. When I look at the cards...they make sense."

"Yes, but how?" Tanaquis leaned forward, dark eyes bright with curiosity. "Aža allows people to glimpse the realm of mind, and ash lets them physically interact with and sometimes even enter it. As I understand it, pattern offers similar glimpses. Some patterners even use aža to gain greater insight. Clearly there's something to the notion; your reading gave you insight into the Traementis curse. It took me days to come up with a way to reliably verify that. But for you it just...*came.* Without effort. I suspect because you were conceived during Veiled Waters, which brings us back around to the wellspring. And the Vraszenian goddess—well, not a goddess. She lacks a dyadic counterpart. She's merely an ancestor spirit of some sort."

Any Vraszenian would argue that the deities didn't exist in oppositional pairs. They were single entities, with a Face to petition and a Mask to propitiate. Ažerais was special not because she was an ancestor, but because her Face and her Mask were the same.

Clearly the hardest part of this was going to be listening to Tanaquis get Vraszenian religion wrong.

Despite her best efforts, Ren must have given some hint of her irritation, because Tanaquis held up a conciliatory hand. "There *is* power there. But Ažerais falls outside the divine dichotomies, which makes her an odd sort of remainder. Difficult to resolve mathematically, and she has no sigil to let us draw on her power for a numinat, so there hasn't been much study of her. Which is why I wished to speak with you. The pattern you laid out—what cards came up?"

Tanaquis was undeniably brilliant, but it was hard to follow the way her mind jumped from topic to topic. Renata felt a little dizzy as she said, "The Mask of Ashes, The Mask of Night, and The Face of Gold. Why?"

"You don't know the source of power for the Traementis curse—but clearly, *pattern* knows. It showed a connection nobody even suspected, and perhaps offers a path for invocation that lies outside the standard Enthaxn sigils. How fascinating would it be if we could use the conduit of Ažerais's pattern to channel the energy of a numinat!" With her flushed cheeks and sparkling eyes, Tanaquis almost resembled a woman in love. She belatedly tamped down her excitement to add, "And it should break the curse, too."

The only part of that Renata had followed was "break the curse." Cautiously, she said, "That's...good?"

"Yes. Perfect." Tanaquis's enthusiastic nod shook additional wisps of dark hair free of her bun. "It might be possible to use those three cards in a numinat laid out in a tripod configuration to supplement the focus. Essentially, drawing on Ažerais. In theory—but the theory is sound. Would you say that the three cards match somehow to yourself, Donaia, and Giuna?"

Renata blinked. "I...no. It was indicating where the Traementis are now—The Mask of Ashes—what path they will follow, which was The Mask of Night, and where they'll end up, The Face of Gold. I wouldn't call either Era Traementis or Alta Giuna destruction or ill fortune."

The pencil paused. The glow dimmed. "That's too bad. It was ever so tidy that way. Well, we'll work around it." Tanaquis resumed writing. "So, you can bring them?"

"Bring—" Renata pressed her lips together, inhaling through her nose. "Meda Fienola, I'm not an astrologer, nor an inscriptor. What are you talking about?"

Donaia was better at it, but Renata's clipped question still drew Tanaquis's attention back to her visitor. "Your deck is connected to pattern, and thus to Ažerais, the way a focus connects a numinat to a divine aspect of the Lumen. The three cards you drew are connected through pattern to the curse and to its source. Usually, that power flows from the Lumen, through the god's focus, and into the numinat—but I believe I can reverse that flow. I want to scribe a numinat that uses your cards as subsidiary foci in order to draw the power of the curse off you, Donaia, and Giuna, and shunt it back to its source. Does that make more sense?" The furrow of her brow suggested she'd simplified as much as she could.

Motes of chalk dust drifted through the sunlight as Ren sat, wordless. The problem now wasn't that she didn't understand. It was that she *did*.

"The cards..." Her throat was too dry. She swallowed and tried again. "Our hair went up in flames. Please tell me the cards won't do the same."

Tanaquis bit her lip. "That wouldn't be my intent. But I don't know that anyone has tried using cards from a pattern deck as foci. It may not be...stable." Her hand covered Renata's in an unexpected show of compassion. "I know they mean much to you. They must have, for you to defy your mother to protect them. But the alternative is to remain cursed. Donaia and Giuna as well."

In a flash, she remembered the other two decks—the ones she'd bought for street use. "But pattern decks are common here. We could—"

A shake of Tanaquis's head killed that hope. "It should be the cards you used in the reading. They have the strongest, clearest connection."

Of course they did. Tanaquis might not understand pattern, but she understood that much.

But they're my mother's cards. The last remnant she had of Ivrina.

Ren closed her eyes. Risk the cards…or risk all three of them dying.

She knew which one Ivrina would tell her to choose.

"Very well," she said grimly, opening her eyes. "We will try."

Whitesail, Upper Bank: Cyprilun 33

Tanaquis worked fast. Complex numinata often took hours or even days to draw, but the astrologer must have been ready to begin as soon as she had agreement on the cards. The very next evening, Tanaquis summoned all three affected women to her house.

It was cruelty and mercy both. Ren wasn't yet ready to face the possibility of losing part of her mother's deck. But at the same time, the curse now hung over them all like a scythe, and she wouldn't breathe freely until it was gone.

The skylights were open to the moons, Paumillis dark, but Corillis waxing full enough to provide as much light as the stones embedded in the slanted ceiling like stars. The floor that had been bare of all but circle and spiral was now an intricate web of lines and arcs, the chalkwork clean and confident. The tripod Tanaquis had mentioned was a flimsy structure, a small plate hanging from the ceiling, with braided copper threads attached to the floor at three points around the enclosing circle. The circle itself was bordered with a ring of nine triangles within vesicae piscis: three already holding foci, three large enough for a person to sit in the center, and three with an empty, waiting square the size of a pattern card.

"Did you bring them?" Tanaquis asked Renata, holding out a hand dusted with chalk.

Even Ren wasn't a good enough liar to hide her reluctance as she handed the cards over. Only the three she'd drawn for that pattern: The rest of the deck was safe with Tess downstairs, far away from this numinat. Mismatched decks were hardly uncommon, cards getting torn or too badly bent for shuffling, szorsas and gamblers swapping in replacements as needed. She could do the same if she had to.

Ir Entrelke Nedje, she prayed, *don't make me have to.*

"Tanaquis, are you certain this will work?" Donaia asked.

"No," she said, studying each card in turn. "But if it doesn't, we'll try again."

"I mean—" Donaia eyed the numinat warily. "Will it be safe?" She too had to be remembering their hair going up in flames.

Setting a hand on Donaia's shoulder, Tanaquis said, "I won't hurt your family, Donaia. Trust in me."

With anyone else, Renata wasn't sure Donaia would have agreed. But Tanaquis had been a friend to the Traementis, when the curse stripped them of nearly everyone else. Donaia hesitated only a moment more before giving a sharp nod. "What must we do?"

At Tanaquis's direction—and with due care for the precisely chalked lines—each of the three cursed women took up station in one of the larger triangles. "Face outward, turning your backs on the curse. Focus on the tripod thread connecting to your circle," Tanaquis said, placing The Mask of Ashes between Donaia and Giuna, The Mask of Night between Giuna and Renata, and The Face of Gold between Renata and Donaia.

Ren fought the urge to touch each card one last time. *Mama... keep them safe. They're all I have left of you.*

"I'm placing the master focus now. Whatever happens, *do not* leave your position." From behind Ren came the soft clink of a metal disc set down onto the tripod plate. Tanaquis moved past her and out of the numinat. Taking out a piece of chalk, she swiped a bold curve at the open edge, closing the circle.

Unease tightened Ren's gut. Pattern she could interact with—but this was just copper wires, chalk lines on the floor, three pieces of painted paper, and three women praying for salvation.

Her skin began to itch...then crawl...then her whole body

started trembling. The braided thread took on a copper-bright glow, vibrating in time with Ren's body. It resonated with the other two threads she couldn't see, a discordant triple tone that made her teeth ache. A faint ringing noise pierced through it—but she wasn't hearing that with her ears. It reminded her of nothing so much as the ringing in her bones on the Night of Bells, when she'd gotten dizzy and had to leave the plaza to rest.

She couldn't sit still. But Tanaquis had told them not to move.

Ren dug her fingers into her knees, and even so, she felt like she was shifting. No, something *inside* her was shifting—dragging from her one strand at a time, as though fingers were digging under her skin to pull it free.

And she recognized it.

During the nightmare, when she went back to the Charterhouse with that blinded szorsa. She'd felt it then: *two* forces unleashed, represented by Storm Against Stone. One of them was Ažerais. The other...

The other was something else. And it was here, in the circle with them, its power running along the channels of the numinat, draining out of Ren and Giuna and Donaia.

Ren's vision blurred, as if aža were showing her a glimpse into Ažerais's Dream. To her right, The Face of Gold gleamed brightly under the lightstones, transmuted to gold itself. To her left, The Mask of Night darkened to a void, only the two slim crescents of the moons breaking its perfect blackness. She couldn't see The Mask of Ashes behind her, but she smelled it on the air, the dust-dry memory of a fire burned out.

Traementis Manor hadn't burned like her childhood home, but those were the ashes she was tasting: the destruction of the Traementis family, by whatever power she'd felt in the Charterhouse that night. A power that had been around since long before the Night of Hells. It crawled inside her, desperately clinging against the compulsion of the numinat, and her head spun. For an instant she couldn't even remember who she was: a child happy with her mother or weeping for her loss, a Seterin noblewoman fleeing her mother and seeking refuge with the Traementis, a con artist out to take what she wanted from the world, Arenza or Renata or Ren.

With a snap, the threads broke—and it stopped.

The recoil jarred Ren into a slump. She heard Giuna's sharp cry and Donaia's grunt. Then the wet slide of a dampened cloth across wood. Footsteps. A murmured question.

She sat, dazed and aching, until Tanaquis crouched before her, presenting a fan of three cards. "You see. No harm has come to them."

Ren clutched the cards to her with a relieved cry, not giving a damn in that moment if anyone wondered why Renata Viraudax cared so much about a pattern deck.

Whitesail, Upper Bank: Cyprilun 33

Any illusion that Tanaquis had finished with them didn't survive for long. Removing the curse might have been a straightforward affair—though Renata was startled to realize nearly an hour had gone by while they sat in Tanaquis's numinat—but then she had to finish her study of the whole affair.

Starting with asking Renata to lay a new pattern.

She should have seen it coming. Her cards had revealed the curse to begin with; it made sense that Tanaquis would want them to verify its removal. But the thought of laying a pattern with Tanaquis and Donaia and Giuna all watching was nerve-racking—Tanaquis especially. What if the astrologer could somehow see her Vraszenian ancestry at work?

It was a foolish thought, and besides which, Renata didn't have any excuse to refuse. But she only recited the prayers to the ancestors in her mind, not out loud, as she shuffled, cut, and dealt three cards.

The Ember Adamant. Labyrinth's Heart. The Peacock's Web.

"The middle one is pretty," Giuna said, pointing at the woman kneeling in prayer at the center of a labyrinth. "Does that mean it's good?"

Before Renata could answer, Tanaquis said, "My understanding is that even cards that seem good can have negative meanings. Which makes it easier for charlatans to fool the gullible." She frowned at the cards. "These make no sense."

Renata blinked innocently at Tanaquis. "What do you mean?"

With an exasperated huff, Tanaquis pointed at the cards in turn. "That one, The Ember Adamant. I believe it refers to obligations. How is a curse an obligation? The pretty one in the middle makes *some* sense if we assume the curse is lifted. Doesn't it indicate peace? The third is puzzles and riddles, but the only puzzle I see before me is these cards. Lumen give me a good Ninat, saying, 'Yes, this is ended. Well done. Through the gate and on to the next cycle with you.'" She crossed her arms. "Do they say something else to you?"

It was petty to feel satisfaction that Tanaquis couldn't read the cards when she'd just saved all of them from the curse, but listening to a Liganti woman try to explain Ažerais to her had left Ren feeling a touch petty. She had to rein in the desire to speak with utter confidence, even though she had no doubt what the cards meant. "The Ember Adamant is obligations, yes, but... perhaps it would be better to think in terms of burdens? I think it's saying the burden has been lifted. Or that your promise to help us has been fulfilled. Or both."

"Then it worked?" Donaia asked—not Tanaquis, but Renata.

"Yes," she said, and gestured at Labyrinth's Heart. "When the pattern consists of three cards, the second one is the path ahead. This one does indeed mean peace—although..."

She glanced up and saw Donaia and Giuna stiffen at her words. "No, the curse is gone!" she hurried to say. "I was only looking ahead to the last card. Puzzles and riddles—we still don't know *why* we were cursed. And though I'm glad to be free of it, I should like to know where it came from." She shifted her attention to Tanaquis.

"I'm curious myself," the astrologer murmured absently, earning a snort from Donaia and a soft giggle from Giuna. From what Renata knew of Tanaquis, "curious" was an enormous understatement.

But for once, she was in complete agreement with the astrologer. She herself wouldn't be at peace until she knew the answer...

because there was a final piece to the pattern she hadn't mentioned. Labyrinth's Heart was the stillness of the eye of the storm. The Traementis might not be cursed anymore—but the force behind the curse wasn't gone.

Tanaquis clapped her hands briskly. "It's enough for now that it's been dealt with. I need to clean up before this numinat burns my house down." Then she paused, blinking at all three of them. "That's a joke. Inscriptor humor."

She shooed them out of her workroom, leaving them to show themselves out. In the misty street outside, while Tess went to hail three sedan chairs, Donaia stopped Renata with one hand on her arm.

Her brown eyes were weary, but softer than they'd been in weeks. "With everything that's happened, I've been remiss with my gratitude. Thank you. I wish we might have learned of this before—" Her words caught and she swayed, until Giuna steadied her. With a visible effort, Donaia pressed down her grief. "Thank you. Go home and get some rest. In the morning, if you wish to come by, I believe we should discuss something long overdue: inscribing you into the Traementis register."

"Mother!"

"I mean it," Donaia said to Giuna. "We've had enough of endings and loss. Let's mark this turn with good fortune."

Donaia turned her attention to Renata, who kept her face carefully startled. Giuna, out of her mother's view, was staring at her with mute wariness and conflict. Renata might have helped the Traementis, but Giuna hadn't forgotten that she'd also admitted to wanting to feed off their wealth.

This offer was exactly what Ren had set out to get. But if she took it, Giuna would never forgive her.

"Era Traementis...Donaia, if I may." She waited for Donaia's firm nod before she went on. "Your offer means more to me than I can say. But I wouldn't feel at ease in my heart, accepting when Leato's death is still unresolved. Whoever poisoned him in the Charterhouse murdered him—and I intend to see that person answer for what they did."

Donaia protested with half-articulated arguments about her reasons for not offering before, and assurances that Renata need not do anything else to earn her place among them. But Renata stood firm as the first chair arrived, restraining the urge to shove Donaia into the box just to stop her insisting. Fortunately, Giuna helped, getting her mother settled and on her way as a second chair approached.

"Why did you refuse?" Giuna asked then, ignoring the waiting chair. "This is what you wanted."

Ren was tired. Her head ached, and she wanted anything other than to be having this conversation. She knew she ought to be gracious, but she couldn't muster the will. "Because I don't relish living the rest of my life with you hating me. I'll find some other way to make ends meet." A long-term advocacy arrangement with Vargo wouldn't let her sustain the facade of her current life, but she would figure out...something.

Even I can't lie well enough to believe that. There was nothing. She owed too much to House Pattumo, a debt that would come due all too soon. She'd missed her chance to leap to shore, and it was only a matter of time before the bridge beneath her collapsed.

"Oh." Giuna rocked back on her heels, worrying her glove between her fingers. "Well. Thank you. For tonight." She started to retreat, then turned back. "You should come by in the morning anyway. Mother's missed you. And I..."

She caught whatever she'd been about to say, only mumbling, "You should come by."

Giuna probably meant it as kindness. In its own way, it was. It just wasn't a kindness that could save Ren from the trap she'd created, walked into, and slammed shut behind herself.

Westbridge and Seven Knots: Cyprilun 33–34

Tess didn't chide Ren for refusing Donaia's offer. She only hugged her once they were back at the townhouse, then heaved the mattress down from where they propped it against the wall during the daytime. After this many years together, not everything needed words.

Ren dozed fitfully. She'd run from Nadežra once out of fear. The smart thing to do now would be to take her winnings from Breglian's and leave again, this time in less of a panic. Try a smaller version of this con somewhere else. Go south into Vraszan and make her living as a szorsa. Anything other than staying in the tangle she'd created around herself. *Tess would come with me. And Sedge.*

Instead she got up, strung twelve of the forri from her nytsa game on a cord, donned her Vraszenian costume, and went out into the streets.

At ninth earth, the city was as close to silent as it ever got. Drunkards and gamblers had mostly gone to bed; servants hadn't yet risen. Fog wreathed the buildings, swirling around Ren's legs as she walked, thick enough that she suspected Veiled Waters had officially begun. The fog wouldn't lift for seven days: a reliable pattern every year, but not one that began on a set date.

Illogical and unpredictable, just like Tanaquis had said. But also the way of Ažerais.

She headed west, into Seven Knots. The dampness gave her good reason to pull her shawl over her head—the shawl the Rook had sent her, with its hidden throwing knives bumping gently against her shoulders and back. People in Seven Knots might recognize Arenza. She wished, much too late, that she hadn't run from the Kiraly granddaughter. Ren suspected the young woman hadn't meant to frighten her. Maybe she wouldn't even have blamed Ren for the Night of Hells. But deprived of sleep, Ren had been frightened by everything.

Few people, if any, would be at the labyrinth at this hour. She could give thanks for the lifting of the curse and pray for aid, then be gone before the streets filled.

Twelve forri. One for each of the gods of the pattern, the deities that assisted Ažerais's children in the early days of the Vraszenian people. It was a stupid amount of money for someone in Ren's situation to give away, and she still wasn't sure she would follow through.

Her normal purse held enough deciras and centiras to use as offerings instead. But with the depth of trouble she'd gotten herself into, it didn't feel right to pinch mills.

Fog veiled the entrance to the labyrinth when she arrived at the plaza. A swirl of disturbance signaled someone not far ahead, though, and Ren veered sideways, hovering at the edge of a nearby building, waiting for that person to go through the gate first.

Instead they stopped. She—it looked like a woman. Fairer-haired than most Vraszenians; in fact, she looked Liganti. And she held a sack, casting a glance around as she untied it to make sure she wasn't observed. Ren resisted the urge to shrink back into the shadows, knowing the movement might give her away; instead she trusted the fog to keep her hidden.

The woman pulled something from the sack and threw it at the gate of the labyrinth before turning and running.

Ren came forward, apprehension clogging her throat. What the woman had thrown—even in the muffled light of Corillis it gleamed, green and blue and violet, unmoving on the threshold.

It was the corpse of a dreamweaver bird.

A shout came from within the labyrinth. Ren froze, torn, wanting desperately to yank away the desecrated and desecrating body before anyone saw it. But it was too late for that, and maybe too late for anything else.

She bolted. Praying as she went that the person who shouted hadn't seen her face, because Arenza Lenskaya had already been blamed for enough trouble. Through the cramped lanes of Seven Knots, blessing the thin soles of her cheap Vraszenian shoes; it bruised her feet to run in them, but they made no sound.

That eddy in the mist up ahead—yes, it was a person, moving quickly and quietly. Ren followed as closely as she dared, tracking glimpses of that fair Liganti head. The woman's face... She'd seen it before.

The same woman had served the ash-spiked wine to her and Leato in the Charterhouse on the Night of Hells.

Once into Westbridge, the woman's pace slowed. Another

shadow emerged from an adjoining street, swathed in a cloak, and the woman strode to meet him. A brief conversation, too muffled for Ren to hear, then they set off in the direction of the Sunset Bridge.

They walked briskly, but no longer kept to the shadows, nor cast wary glances at every stoop and landing. They had no reason to hide here. When they reached the Sunset Bridge, a third shadow broke from the parapet to meet them. And this one, Ren knew on sight.

Mezzan Indestor.

She made for a river stair, blessing the absurd hour that meant no skiffers were waiting below. It let her creep close enough to overhear them, without being heard.

"Were either of you seen? Followed?" Mezzan asked.

"At this hour? The gnats are all in their nests." That was the woman, and Ren bit down on her tongue. She'd heard that voice once before, from a different hiding spot—in Mettore's office.

"So it's done?" Mezzan again. A pause—Ren guessed the woman was nodding—and then he said, "What about the numinata?"

This time the man answered him. "Yes, altan. They're all in place."

Numinata. Ren remembered that voice and that face from Mezzan's engagement party: Breccone Indestris, the inscriptor from House Simendis, married into Indestor.

"Then head back and tell my father we're ready. I'll take care of the Anduske."

His boots scraped against the ground, but no footsteps sounded; he'd stopped. The woman said, "Altan, is that wise? Who's to say they won't turn against you?"

Mezzan's cocky laugh set Ren's teeth on edge. "That stupid bint eats out of my hand. She won't question anything I tell her. And I'll make certain I'm clear of the Lower Bank before anything starts."

More footsteps, and this time they didn't stop. Ren glanced up the river stair to see Mezzan striding in the direction of Seven Knots. Her hand brushed the edge of her shawl. Once upon a time, she'd been very good at throwing knives.

But that time was five years in the past, and she hadn't practiced. Even if she struck home...murdering the heir to House Indestor wouldn't make anything better. A dreamweaver corpse desecrating the labyrinth could set off a riot.

From the sound of it, that was exactly what Mezzan wanted.

She didn't know why. But at the moment, it didn't matter. As soon as she heard the steps of the other two fading into the distance, she climbed back up to street level and headed for her townhouse.

If she wanted to stop this, she was going to need help.

20

The Mask of Chaos

Horizon Plaza, Westbridge: Cyprilun 34

Shouts rose from the Horizon Plaza in a furious mix of Vraszenian and Liganti, the crowd surging like waves against the line of hawks that barred anyone from passing onto the Sunset Bridge.

"This is getting worse," Grey muttered to Ranieri, low enough that the rest of his squad couldn't hear.

The crowd had been building since dawn, their outrage stoked by stoop-thumpers reminding them of all the wrongs cited in the Stadnem Anduske broadsheets. Word had raced through Seven Knots like a spark through dried tinder: a dead dreamweaver, its body drained of blood, had been thrown against the lintel of the labyrinth during the late earth hours. The Liganti nobility were often accused of eating dreamweavers at their feasts, but desecrating a labyrinth with one's corpse made Grey's own blood beat hot enough that he was tempted to rip off his hexagram pin and lead the charge to the steps of the Charterhouse himself. *If I thought it would do any good . . .*

But it wouldn't. The Vigil's cordon was proof of that. The Cinquerat's response to unrest was always the same: cut off the Lower Bank from the Old Island and the Upper Bank, so the mobs couldn't strike at the heart of their power. There was still the river, of course, and Masks have mercy if the skiffers ever decided to throw their lot in with the Lower Bank...but Fulvet, who licensed the skiffs, was smart enough to keep them on his side.

The Cinquerat was trying to deprive the fire of fuel, but Grey had a sinking certainty it wouldn't work. Not after the Night of Hells. Not with the Stadnem Anduske using this as a rallying point. And not when—according to the warning he'd received—the Anduske had the makings for black powder.

The same contraband that had killed Kolya, leaving Grey to dance the kanina for a burned husk of a body.

The thought of anyone else having to do the same propelled him into motion. Grey cut behind the cordon to where Cercel was standing. "Sir, let me go out there and try to talk them down. Standing here in silence isn't helping."

The hard line of Cercel's mouth said she wasn't any happier with the cordoning tactics than he was, but the look she gave him spoke volumes of doubt. "If I send a hawk out there, Serrado, it's just as likely to be the spark that sets this off as the water that puts it out."

He yanked off his captain's pin. "Then I won't go as a hawk. Let me at least try to stop them from escalating."

That was a risk of a different sort. His uniform made him a target, but authority was also a form of protection. Stripped of that, he might just look like a traitor—a slip-knot whose heart was so Liganti, he didn't care that someone had desecrated their holy ground.

The tendons in Cercel's neck ridged as she fought with herself. Then she took the pin with one curt swipe. "If they turn on you, run. I can't send people out to protect you without making this worse."

Grey's response was to shrug out of his coat and shove it at her, followed by his gloves.

In shirtsleeves and reinforced waistcoat, he vaulted the railing of the bridge and dropped to the shore below, splashing in the ankle-deep water. A nearby river stair brought him up to street level again, and he threaded his way through the restless crowd.

"—take our city, they pave over our wellspring and make us

pay for the privilege of dancing on its grave, they poison our elders with a profane mockery of aža, and now they're desecrating our temples with the bodies of dreamweavers. How are they any different from the Tyrant? How long will we pretend the Accords ever meant anything but a different sort of oppression? How long before it's our faith taken? Our children poisoned? Our blood spilled?"

Rumbles of agreement surrounded Grey. How was he supposed to stop this when he agreed with the stoop-thumper more than he didn't? But mob anger wasn't the way.

"What they did was wrong," he called out, letting his accent shift, searching for an argument that would turn this tide to something productive. "But that is a thing for the ziemetse to address. Whoever did this *wants* us to break from our ways. Giving in only strengthens them and weakens us."

"They *killed* the Kiraly ziemič!" someone roared back in Vraszenian.

I know. I was there for his kanina, too. The protest caught in Grey's throat, the way so many words did. These days he felt like he might burst from all the things he wasn't letting free: anger, grief, fear.

Was he willing to grind his own outrage and pain into dust for the sake of the powers he served?

Before he could answer that, someone slipped through the crowd to his side. "Serrado. I need your help."

His answering curse caught in his teeth at the sight of the pale skin and fine features of Renata Viraudax. But not the elegant Seterin alta as she usually presented herself: She was dressed plainly, in an underdress and loose surcoat that wouldn't have looked out of place on a Lower Bank craftswoman.

She rose onto her toes, speaking close into his ear. "I saw what happened with the bird. I know who's responsible."

For an instant, he thought the angry roar around them was in answer to her words—that despite her caution, the crowd had overheard. But then he saw a train of Liganti-style wagons rumbling into the plaza, forcing the gathered people aside. "What in the

Mask-cursed world do they think they're doing?" Grey snarled. If Cercel let the wagons through to the bridge, the crowd would follow. And then either the unrest would spill onto the Island or the Vigil would break bones stopping it.

"Serrado." She was smart enough not to use his title, but her fingers dug into his wrist. "Help me. We might be able to do something before this gets worse."

Something that didn't involve betraying his own people—or joining them in burning the Lower Bank down.

"Fine. But we need to get clear of this." Grey started pushing his way through the crowd, jerking his chin for her to follow in his wake. Behind him, the roaring grew louder.

Crookleg Alley, the Shambles: Cyprilun 34

Vargo had no intention of letting the city burn today. Especially not the parts of it he owned.

So far, there were only flash points waiting to explode—Horizon Plaza, the Seven Knots labyrinth, parts of Kingfisher—but only a fool waited for the fuse to be lit.

Possibly a literal fuse, depending on the Anduske's plans for that saltpeter.

"Ranislav, put the Roundabout Boys on our businesses, and any place that's under our protection. Keep them safe. I don't want a single report of looters causing trouble." He barely waited for Ranislav's nod before moving onward. "Varuni, pull together as many patrols of fists as you can."

She was already strapping on weighted gloves, her chain whip coiled at her hip. "We work the mobs?"

"Break them up," Vargo clarified. "Bigger they get, more likely they'll turn stupid." His speech was beginning to slip, and he dragged it back with an effort. "Fighting them will only make them angrier. Look for ways to divide them instead."

Varuni looked heartily displeased with the order, but she nod-ded. He could almost hear what she didn't say: *I guess you'll be safe enough if you stay here.*

After she stalked off, Vargo glanced out the window. The morning sun hadn't burned away the river mist, nor would it. The uncanny fog of Veiled Waters had settled over the city, so thick that the far side of the street was little more than a ghostly impression of doors and stoops, windows and eaves. *Doubt we'll get much of a mas-querade this year,* he thought cynically. People wearing masks now would be doing it to hide their faces from the Vigil.

"You need me for something? Or should I just stand behind you and glower?" Sedge asked. If his wrist hadn't been broken in the Depths, it would have been him instead of Varuni leading the fists, and he chafed at standing idle.

"Congratulations, Sedge. You've just volunteered to lead the fire crews."

Sedge groaned and followed Vargo's glance out the window. Fire crew usually meant scanning the roofline for smoke. In this weather... "Fuck me, Vargo. How d'you expect me to—"

"Street by street. I don't care. Figure it out. You can—"

::It's started.::

Vargo stilled, ignoring the curious look Sedge was giving him. *Where?* he asked Alsius.

::Sunset Bridge. Rumor's spreading that House Novrus feasted on dreamweavers last night, and someone threw a rock. Now the Vigil are breaking heads. It's just the plaza, but there's no way this won't get worse.::

"Right. Sedge, focus on Horizon Plaza. Things just broke there."

"How did you—"

::Vargo, there's more.::

Sedge snapped his teeth closed on his question when Vargo held a hand up to silence him. *The saltpeter?*

::No. Numinata. Scattered all through Westbridge and Seven Knots—a lot of earthwise Tuat, Sessat, and Noctat.::

Sunwise numina twisted against their purpose by earthwise

spirals—turning them into curses. Obstruction, breakdown of communication and structures... Somebody *wanted* this to get bad.

"Vargo?" Sedge shifted, glancing around the room uncomfortably.

"Nothing. Go."

Vargo waited for him to leave. Then he said, "Nikory, keep things running here. I'll be back." To Alsius, he said, *I'll get my gear. Where should I start?*

When he stepped out of the townhouse, though, he found Sedge leaning in the doorway across the narrow alley. "Yeah, I heard you," Sedge said. "Sent Canlin to cover fire duty. His eyes are better than mine—and besides, I let you go off alone, Varuni will nail my balls to the Point. Her people have invested too much in you to let you get knifed in a riot."

He wasn't wrong, and Vargo didn't want to waste time arguing. "We're for Thorn Mews in Seven Knots. You know it?"

Sedge shrugged and pushed off the wall. "No, but I'll follow you."

Seven Knots, Lower Bank: Cyprilun 34

I wish I could be two people at once.

That thought dogged Ren as she followed Captain Serrado through Seven Knots. She'd had to be Renata in approaching him; even if he would have believed Arenza's accusation, nobody else in the Vigil would. But now he was taking her among the Vraszenians, where a Seterin alta's word would hold no more water than a leaky sieve.

She hadn't realized what he was doing until they detoured by an ostretta, the Gawping Carp, where Serrado threw a panel coat over his fawn-colored Vigil breeches and a shawl over Renata's surcoat. That was when Ren knew she'd miscalculated, and badly.

He was taking her to see Idusza Polojny.

Ren had planned to find Idusza herself, as Arenza, after she warned Serrado. She had to assume this chaos was part of the Anduske's plan for the saltpeter, and therefore intervening with them would be key to stopping Indestor.

Unfortunately, Serrado also knew about Idusza. And she'd sent him that note about the saltpeter. He wasn't nearly stupid enough to miss the obvious conclusion.

I should have begged out of it. Now it was too late: She was in Seven Knots, with a Vraszenian shawl blurring the line between her two personas, and if she took the time to leave and come back, she might find the place in flames.

Half the people in Seven Knots were closing their doors and shutters, even nailing boards across windows to protect the glass. The other half were congregating on corners and bridges, armed with cobbles and sticks, knives and the tools of their trades. Serrado navigated the district like a skiffer through the shoals, pulling her down narrow passages that avoided the worst of the crowds. It took a few minutes for Ren to realize where he was leading her.

Back to the Seven Knots labyrinth.

The atmosphere wasn't nearly as violent as it had been by the Sunset Bridge, but in other ways it was worse. The crowd stood in hushed fury, pressing close but not jostling, listening to the man speaking from the gate of the labyrinth. The tension was thick enough to pluck like a harp string.

The speaker was cradling the desecrated body of the dream-weaver in his hands. "—what else should we expect from those chalk-faced invaders? They already profaned Ažerais's wellspring. Only fools say on the ziemetse we can depend. They bow to the Cinquerat even when one of their own is killed! And the Vigil is the Cinquerat's tool. Into the mud they stomp us. Our cries for justice go unheard. But the Faces and the Masks hear our prayers..."

Serrado paused at the edge of the crowd, his height giving him an advantage over Renata. Then he led her earthwise around the edge, to where Idusza listened to the speaker with arms crossed and fervor shining in her eyes.

Her head whipped around as they came close, and Serrado put up one hand before she could speak. "I need you to listen to what this woman has to say."

Idusza barely spared Renata a glance; her wariness was all for the hawk. "Wish you to get me killed? Coming up to me like this—"

Tilting his chin at the tense, furious crowd, Serrado said, "I'm more likely to get killed than you, if someone recognizes me. Please—you believed me not before, but this time I have proof."

That got her attention, if not her trust. They drew off to one side, and Renata took a deep breath, trying to calculate what she could use from her previous interactions with Idusza without letting her thoughts slide anywhere near that persona.

At least Idusza showed no sign of recognizing her. "Who are you?"

"My name is Renata Viraudax."

Idusza stiffened. "The Seterin alta who has to the Traementis attached herself. This is your proof?"

That last was delivered to Serrado. He shook his head, frustrated. "Listen to what she says. And *think*."

Renata spoke before Idusza could argue. "I saw how this all began. I live in Westbridge; I was on my way home before dawn this morning when I noticed Mezzan Indestor waiting in Horizon Plaza with Breccone Indestris, their house inscriptor. A woman came up to him—one who works for Eret Indestor; I've seen her before. Mezzan gave her a bag and instructions. I didn't hear it all, but I was suspicious, so I followed her here, to your temple. I saw her throw the dead bird at the gate." It wasn't quite the truth, but she couldn't say she'd been coming to visit the labyrinth.

"You lie," Idusza snapped. "I know the Traementis. You want to drag down Mezzan's family."

"But would I risk my life coming here, at a time like this?"

The speaker had finished his rant. Raising the body of the dreamweaver above his head, he began chanting. "Take the bridge. Take the bridge." Not alone: The crowd joined him, their voices weaving into a single growing roar.

Renata spoke more urgently. "He came to you today, didn't he? And told you about the dead bird—no, that would have been too suspicious, if he were the one to bring the news. But people are saying House Novrus has been eating dreamweavers; that sounds like an Indestor rumor, spread so as to hurt their rivals. Did you hear *that* from Mezzan?"

The thinning of Idusza's lips said her guess had hit the mark. But what would persuade her? Ren didn't dare lean on pattern, not in this persona. *I'll have to come back as Arenza*—

No. Idusza believed in pattern more than she cared to admit, but what she truly trusted were concrete facts—even if Ren had to imbed them in lies. "I heard him say he was going to find you in your rooms in Grednyek Close."

Idusza flinched. "You told her that," she accused Serrado.

"Not me," he said, with genuine surprise.

"I heard it from Mezzan, this morning," Renata insisted. "And the coat he was wearing—it was blue, embroidered with gold bees."

Idusza stepped back, as though Renata's words were a blade. "No...He would not...It is an old coat. You must have seen him wear it some other time, and now you guess." But her eyes glittered with welling tears. She knew.

"Think about it," Serrado said, lapsing into Vraszenian. "Remember what I told you before. What that szorsa read. That injustice you can right—what if this is it?"

Ren could have kissed him for mentioning the szorsa. All her work with the cards, trying to weaken Idusza's faith in Mezzan... She couldn't remind Idusza of that, not in this persona. But Serrado had unwittingly done it for her.

He kept talking, desperation creeping into his voice. "At least let us tell your friends. Let them hear it and decide, before this goes any further. Before you end up playing into Indestor hands."

Idusza cut him off with a single, tense jerk of her head that sent the tears spilling down her cheeks. "Only you. Not her. They will heed her not, and she'll get hurt."

Serrado switched back to Liganti for Renata's sake. "She's taking me to talk to some people who might be able to help, but you can't come. Go into the labyrinth; you'll be safe there. If anyone tries to drag you out, tell them—"

Renata shook her head before he could finish. "I won't be any use hiding. If I go to the Charterhouse, I can persuade someone to make a few concessions to the crowd. It might help calm things down."

Optimistic words, and she knew Serrado knew it. "I can't spare the time to take you out of here."

"Then I'll go on my own. I'll keep my head down and move fast."

Even with the mounting tumult behind them, she could hear his growl of frustration. "If anything happens to you, Leato will never forgive me."

Her smile tasted of bitter regret. "And he'll never forgive *me* if I don't try."

Westbridge, Lower Bank: Cyprilun 34

A bottle smashed into the wall by Sedge's head, close enough for glass shards to strike his cheek and wine to run down it like thin blood. He reflexively flung his arm up to protect his eyes, and clipped a fleeing woman in the tit with his elbow.

Her man took exception to that and answered with fists. A boot to the fellow's knee knocked him off-balance, enough for Sedge to shove him to the wine-stained wall with a forearm across his throat. His bound wrist ached with the pressure, but he kept it up until the man's eyes started to roll white.

"Don't start fights you en't gonna win." It was advice the whole Lower Bank could stand to listen to—not that anybody would. But the fight had gone out of the man. Sedge let the woman shove him aside so she could catch her man's slumping bulk and help him hobble to safety.

Wiping wine from his cheek, Sedge went back to what he'd been doing, which was cursing. He'd lost Vargo.

Not surprising, between the fog and the chaos, but he couldn't shake the notion that Vargo had slipped him on purpose. Ren's suspicions had lodged under his skin, and no logic would shake them loose. Vargo was no hero...but if he had some spirit riding him, who was to say what he might be doing when none of his people were watching?

But he'd left Sedge with no idea of where Thorn Mews was, and dodging a series of rooftop assaults. Most of it was disgusting rather than dangerous—rotted food, pisspot donations, wadded clumps of bird nest and shit. But Vargo hated filth more than most cuffs; the mere fact that he was out here instead of staying safe and sound in Crookleg Alley was odd enough.

No point in chewing on it. Sedge wasn't going to find Vargo, and he wasn't going to find Thorn Mews, neither. Might as well do what he could to break things up—starting with shitlickers who liked to throw things at frightened, fleeing people.

Veiled Waters was a bloody time for this kind of business, people appearing out of the fog without warning and vanishing just as fast. But as Sedge made his way along, through streets as bent as elbows and bridges barely wide enough for two, no longer even sure which district he was in, he spotted a shadow in the mist that he recognized as trouble, just by the sheer size of it.

People on their own might be assholes or afraid. People in small groups might be assholes or clumping together for safety. People in groups that big were looking to fuck something up.

On his own, though, he couldn't do a lot, even if his wrist wasn't busted. Sedge veered left and found himself on a street corner he knew. He was in Westbridge now, and not too far from Ren's townhouse.

Ren. Tess. He might have lost Vargo, but he could at least make sure his sisters were safe.

Before he could take more than three steps, though, he heard voices he recognized. Smuna and Ladnej, two Vraszenians from the

Leek Street Cutters. "Hey," Sedge called out as he approached, so Ladnej wouldn't knife him. "You two on your own?"

"Got separated," Ladnej said, keeping a wary eye around. "We was sent with Varuni."

With Varuni? They could defend themselves, but they weren't fists. Mostly they were good at—

At throwing things.

Sedge's attention went to the sack over Ladnej's shoulder. "You got house bombs in there?" When she nodded, he pivoted and started back in the direction he'd come from. "Follow me."

The mob he'd seen had moved onward, but they weren't hard to find. The sound of shattering windows led Sedge and the two women to Isla Ejče, where the rioters had broken down the door of a moneylender's and dragged out the screaming Liganti proprietor.

Luckily, Sedge's unbroken right arm was his throwing arm. The house bomb Smuna gave him arced neatly overhead and broke against the wall of a draper's, right where the crowd was thickest. Vargo had the house bombs made to drive out vermin before he took a building over. Sedge wasn't convinced they worked, but they sure as hell reeked bad enough to drive out humans. The crowd scattered, retching.

Ladnej laughed and planted a kiss on Smuna's lips. Then all three of them retreated, coughing, as a shift in the breeze brought the stench toward them, the bastard child of rotten eggs and a tanner's yard.

It also brought screams.

"Follow me," Sedge growled.

He knew what he would find even before he got there. This wasn't Sedge's first riot; he could tell the difference between the sound of an angry mob breaking things, and the sound of the Vigil breaking people. Sure enough, a wedge of hawks had caught some of the rioters Sedge had dispersed and were putting them down, hard.

Them, and anyone else who happened to be on the street at the time.

A teenaged boy tried to flee toward Sedge, but the hawks had brought out the dogs. A mastiff weighing more than the boy knocked him to the ground and started tearing into him, while the boy did his best to curl into a protective ball. Sedge snarled and almost lunged out to intervene, but Ladnej grabbed him by the wrist—the bad one—and the spike of pain brought him up short.

"Rule one," she snapped at him. "Don't be stupid." Behind her, Smuna wound up and chucked a house bomb into the plaza.

As the hawks and dogs reared back, Sedge's gaze went past the two women to a stocky, furious shadow emerging from the fog. "Too late for that," he mumbled.

"Sedge." Varuni bit his name off like a threat. "Where's Vargo?"

Charterhouse, Dawngate, Old Island: Cyprilun 34

The boats patrolling the Dežera usually hunted river pirates or examined ships for contraband rather than blocking access to the Upper Bank. But when Renata finally found a skiff willing to carry her east, she had to stand up in the boat and shout at one of the patrols in her Seterin accent before they'd let her past—leveraging Nadežran prejudices that assumed Seterins were automatically more civilized.

The Charterhouse was like a kicked anthill, swarming with hawks and clerks and outraged merchants worried about their warehouses on the Lower Bank, all trying to shout at Prasinet or Caerulet. The offices of Argentet were comparatively empty. At a time like this, nobody was terribly concerned with the city's cultural institutions.

As Renata came down the hallway, she heard Sostira Novrus snarling at some unfortunate minion. "I don't care if you have to swim the bloody river; get down to the Lower Bank, find that press, and *smash it.*"

The Stadnem Anduske. For half an instant, Ren considered it:

She could win a great deal of goodwill from Novrus by telling her about the wainwright's shop in the Shambles. And if that hamstrung Indestor's plan, so much the better.

But there was no plausible reason for Renata to have that information. And the radicals wouldn't have survived this long if they weren't smart enough to move their printing operation after the Rook found it. So she stood aside to let the minion escape, then squared her shoulders and went to do battle.

"Absolutely not!" Sostira's rejection bit off the last of Renata's proposal before she could even give it voice. "I can see you want to end this peacefully, but all you've done is waste your time and mine. I'm not about to reward these gnats for kicking up a swarm—especially not when they're blaming *my* house, with these absurd lies about dead birds. Caerulet just needs a little longer to organize his troops. Then we'll put this nonsense down, hard." She waved a hovering secretary off with an impatient hand. "The Tyrant may have been a glutton and a lecher, but he understood how to deal with the common mob."

"Has it occurred to you that Indestor may be the source of those lies about your house?" Renata snapped, unable to keep her temper fully in check.

Sostira's eyes grew cold. "It has. And Mettore will answer for it in due course. But first we have to deal with the chaos on the Lower Bank, and for that, we need his forces."

"I've seen riots in Seteris, Your Elegance. Answering force with force might end the problem—but *we* will pay the price in destroyed property and further unrest. Whereas a gesture of generosity—a sop to their concerns—"

"Free admission to the Great Amphitheatre for the rest of Veiled Waters is not a sop! Do you have any notion how much money that would cost me?"

She wanted to shake the woman. "Their boycott is already costing you much of that money; these rumors will cost you more. An investment now could undercut Mettore and buy you the goodwill of the entire Vraszenian population."

Sostira snatched up a familiar-looking broadsheet from the papers on her desk. "Vraszenian goodwill isn't worth the paper their treasonous words are printed on." She crushed the sheet in her hand and cast it into an alcove bare of anything other than a numinat, where it flared into a cinder. "That's what their gratitude will be after Veiled Waters has ended. Cinders, smoke, and ash. If I let them in for free this year, next year they'll expect the same, when the whole swarm infests our city."

"I'll pay." The words came out of Renata's mouth before she could stop them.

Sostira's bark of laughter was almost more relief than offense. "If you came from Seteris with that kind of money, no wonder Donaia is panting to get you however she can."

She rounded the desk, her smile like ice. "But I don't think you did. I think you're not much different from your mother. You came here with a beautiful face, a talented seamstress, and enough for a young woman to live on until she could find someone to bear the costs of her comforts. You think that's enough to cover the Veiled Water fees? Forgive me, my dear." One sharp nail traced down Ren's cheek. "But you're not *that* beautiful."

Ren couldn't maintain the pretense of cordiality. Not when she looked at Sostira and saw Ondrakja—the old Ondrakja—her loveliness a weapon and a silk-thin mask for the cruelty beneath.

She felt her own expression harden. "I will get you that money, Your Elegance. Because unlike you, I'm not ready to watch the Lower Bank burn."

Westbridge and Kingfisher, Lower Bank: Cyprilun 34

After Ren went off to find Captain Serrado, there was naught for Tess to do but wait and fret. She knew her sister was smart enough to avoid the worst of the danger, but that didn't make sitting in the kitchen any easier.

When a pounding came at the door, for an instant she thought Ren was back. But no, Ren was currently Renata; she wouldn't come to the kitchen entrance. Tess yanked the door open to find the boy who usually kept watch on tatting days panting on the stoop, wide-eyed and blanch-pale.

"They's coming this way," he said between gulps of air.

"Who?"

"Rioters. Hawks are stopping it up at Horizon Plaza, so it's got nowhere to spill but here."

Tess fumbled blindly for a mill and pressed it into his hand. "Get you gone." He vanished before her words were done.

Leaving Tess alone with her indecision. Stay or go? She paced before the door, willing it to open again and spit Ren into the kitchen. How long since she'd left? How late was it now?

She nearly screamed as crashing glass sounded upstairs, followed by men's voices. Someone had broken into the house. Their rough laughter pressed down on Tess like a smothering blanket.

That decided her. Better to flee Westbridge than wait to get raped.

Snatching her sampler from the wall and stuffing it into the rucksack by the door, Tess ventured out. Smoke tickled her nose the moment she stepped onto the canal walk. The mist of Veiled Waters swirled, thick enough that she couldn't make out the townhouses on the far side of the canal, but down the way she imagined she saw a glow of orange warming the damp grey.

"Raped or burned out," she muttered, pulling her striped woolen over her head and striking off in the opposite direction, through Kingfisher toward Little Alwydd.

She kept as much as she could to the twists and turns of back canals and covered passages, places narrow enough to squeeze the energy out of a rioting crowd—but there was no way to get to Little Alwydd without crossing the Fičaru Canal. And as Tess approached, the press of bodies clogging every street thickened, unnatural as the fog.

A quick scramble onto the back of an abandoned wagon revealed the cause. Armored hawks blocked the way onto the bridge, holding back the crowd with a wall of overlapping shields.

Tess hopped down, trying to think. She didn't know this area as well as she might. Were there any other crossings, and if so, where?

Shouts rose behind her. Before she could duck under the wagon, a mass of laborers armed with cudgels and stinking of zrel surged up around her and swept her into the fray.

She tried to struggle free, and almost went down under their boots. A second attempt got her an elbow to the brow, and her vision burst with stars. After that, she yielded to the press. The rucksack became her shield. When she shoved back against another elbow, she heard her sampler frame crack.

Then the elbower dropped, a crossbow bolt bristling from his neck, and the crowd trampled over him before she could quite understand what had happened. A thin wail began, soon taken up by other voices—

"They're shooting into the crowd!"

The flow broke into a churning morass, battering her on all sides, screams and shouts and shoving first one way, then another. Tess struggled to breathe, to swim to safety, but every head was higher than hers; she couldn't see above the surface to know which way to go.

This must be what drowning feels like, she thought with numb calm. If drowning stank of sweat and fear and voided bowels.

Then a swirl in the crowd spat her out on the shoals of the hawks—not the crossbows, but the shield line keeping the crowd trapped. Tess fell to her knees and writhed between their legs, below the edge of the shields. Behind the line, the air was blessedly clear, but she only managed to suck in two grateful breaths before a hand clamped around her upper arm, hard enough that she feared the bone would snap like her sampler frame.

A hawk dragged her to her feet. "Please, I'm only for Little Alwydd," Tess begged, letting her woolen fall back and hoping her freckles and copper hair spoke louder than her broken whisper.

He had a thin nose and high brow she vaguely recognized—a

face made for sneering, as it did now. "Nobody gets past. Get off the street, unless you'd rather go to the Aerie."

A surge of fury gave her voice strength, and she barely checked the urge to kick the hawk's shin. "I can't get off the street if I've nowhere to go to, you blighted—"

She bit down on the list of things she wanted to call him, but any chance to win his sympathy was gone—if it had ever existed. Grip tightening, he shoved her back toward the shield line, and the screaming chaos and bloodshed beyond it.

"Kaineto!" Another hawk stepped into their path before the first one could throw her to the wolves, cradling instead of grabbing her. "It's all right. I know her. Tess, what are you doing out here? You should be back at the townhouse."

"P-Pavlin?" The elbow must have struck her harder than she realized. The hawk holding her had the face of the prettiest man in Nadežra, even twisted as it was into worry. "What are you doing here? And dressed as a hawk?" Too late, Tess clapped a hand over her mouth. Was this some ruse of his, and she'd just given it away?

The thin-nosed hawk spat and released her. "Get her out of here, Ranieri."

Tess rubbed her aching arm and let Pavlin lead her away. She'd been living the lie with Ren for too long, seeing the same thing everywhere. This wasn't a ruse—at least, not one meant to trick the other hawks. Pavlin pulled her through the lines of men and women in their blue-and-tawnies waiting on the bridge, and they gave way without complaint. Some even nodded at him in recognition.

On the far side of the Fičaru Canal, the streets were deserted, the silence ringing oddly in her ears. Tess pulled back from Pavlin, staring. "You're a hawk."

At least he had the grace to look ashamed, tugging at his hair as though he could drag it down to hide his pretty, lying face. "The captain's off with Alta Renata; they met up in Horizon Plaza and then went somewhere else. But I need to get back before Kaineto makes things worse. Again."

"The captain?" Understanding was blooming—dark and aching as a bruise.

"Serrado." Pavlin squeezed her fingers. "You have somewhere safe to go?"

Tess ripped her hand from his and cradled it to her chest. She couldn't seem to catch her breath, like she'd taken that elbow to the gut instead of the head. "You were spying on me. On us. For him."

How much had Tess given away? Enough to make Donaia question Ren's story? And Sibiliat? She'd almost ruined the whole scheme, flattered into foolishness because someone had noticed her. Had paid attention to her.

Any hope that he might deny her accusation was dashed when he said, "I was. But only at first! I'll explain later. After..." He cast a worried glance back toward the bridge and the chaos beyond.

"Don't trouble yourself, Constable. There's nothing for you to explain," Tess snapped, taking on a poor woman's shadow of the icy tones and rigid posture Ren adopted so easily. "I'll find my own way. You should go back to shooting arrows into crowds of frightened people."

Ren probably would have come up with words a hundred times as cutting, but Tess had to be satisfied with her dull attempt. Nodding curtly, she hitched her rucksack over her shoulder and stormed off toward Little Alwydd.

Seven Knots, Lower Bank: Cyprilun 34

Thorn Mews was bad. The numinat there made the ground unstable, the buildings along the street creaking, swaying, dropping beams like drunkards looking for a fight. The passage by Pozniret Close was worse, a slow-burning numinat that set everything around it to smoldering. Only the dampness of the fogs had prevented fire before Vargo was able to dismantle it and pick off the stamped wax focus. It left an oily residue on his fingers, smelling of juniper. He shoved the broken pieces in his pocket and moved on to the next, and the one after that.

But the seventh, centered on the corner where Uča Obliok spat out into Dmariše Square, baffled Vargo. The snarling mob pulsed with more violence and anger than Vargo had seen anywhere else in Seven Knots, making it hard for him to even get close.

With Alsius's help, he crept his way toward the edge of the outer circle. It had been widened to encompass the entire plaza—and the moment Vargo stepped across that line, his heart began to thud in his chest.

This must be what's riling the crowd, he thought to Alsius. Vargo had never seen a numinat that tried to affect the heart directly. Other body parts, yes; contraceptive numinata worked that way, and he'd seen men stay hard for hours thanks to a Noctat numinat, long after natural desire had faded and all they wanted was to sleep. Affecting the heart was far more dangerous, though.

Where was the numinat itself? He was going to gut the muck-fucking asshole who inscribed these things.

::I think the heart is a side effect,:: Alsius said uneasily as Vargo edged inward. ::The way people are behaving... I think it's affecting their mood directly.::

Vargo stopped dead. "You mean—"

::We've found one.::

Numinatria was the art of channeling energy: heat and cold, light and sound, the life force of the body. It couldn't influence the mind... or so most people thought. Vargo and Alsius knew better—and now it seemed they might have found proof.

Proof, and no time to study it.

"We've got to get to the center of this thing," Vargo said.

Alsius didn't argue. ::There, across that alley. Is there something under the burlap?::

Vargo launched himself forward, only to find his way blocked by a man clearly under the numinat's influence. Vargo ducked his wild punch and jabbed his own fist into the man's throat. Then he went for the neck, digging his thumbs deep into either side. Choking was a slow process; cutting off the blood was a much more efficient way to take down a problem.

But not one Vargo took pleasure in. Usually.

::Vargo! He's out. You can let go.::

Shaking off the red fury that had overtaken him, Vargo stumbled forward until he hit the alley wall. His heart was galloping. He was furious with himself for that lapse of control—and knowing the numinat was feeding that anger didn't help him shake it off. But he had to see how the thing was made, and then take it apart before Dmariše Square was ankle-deep in blood.

A tarp of tattered burlap hung on the wall, but at some point it had been knocked askew, revealing a chalk line. Vargo ripped the whole thing down, uncovering the numinat's focus.

It was blank. A plug of wine-dark glass without a single mark on it.

He stared in disbelief. The whole *point* of a focus was to have something inscribed in it: the name of a god, or whatever was powering the numinat. How the fuck had somebody made a numinat with a blank focus?

::Don't just stand there staring at it, idiot boy,:: Alsius rebuked him. ::Get to work!::

Vargo gritted his teeth, leaning into his anger at himself for getting distracted. Neutralizing a numinat was easy: just swipe a damp cloth across the edge of the containment circle, remove the focus from the center, and have done. Neutralizing one without incinerating yourself or your workspace was a more delicate process. The more complex the numinat and the more skilled the inscriptor, the greater the chance that it had been scribed with multiple Uniats around the interior numinata. Which needed to be erased in a particular order to avoid simply unleashing all the energy within.

Vargo didn't have the faintest clue what would happen if he pulled a blank focus out, because he had no idea how this numinat was working in the first place. All he could do was forge ahead. Wetting his kerchief in a nearby puddle, he got to work.

::Not there, you fool!::

Vargo flinched and barely avoided swiping his cloth into an angle of an octagram. Alsius's chatter was nearly as distracting as the shatter of glass out in the plaza. "You want to take over?" he snarled, moving to the next channel break point.

A frustrated sigh ghosted through Vargo's skull. ::I could do this much faster, if only—::

The driving clang of steel on steel reverberated through the wall. Vargo's glance around the corner revealed what he most dreaded: A flight of hawks was pushing into the plaza, banging the flats of their swords against the bosses of their shields. The threat was usually effective at terrifying troublemakers into compliance. Everyone knew if that didn't work, the hawks would turn their blades against flesh and bone next.

This is going to end badly, he thought grimly to Alsius. Even if he neutralized the numinat, he wasn't certain that would undo its effects. The hawks didn't need magic to incite them to violence, and already several young Vraszenians had formed an arm-linked line to meet the oncoming thunder. Behind them, others were grabbing bottles, wagon whips, wheel spokes—any weapons that came to hand. Fucking idiots were going to get themselves killed.

::Vargo, this isn't right. You're under its influence, too. We both are. You have to get out of here before it's too late.::

I know. But . . .

He glanced at the numinat again, radiating heated fury from every line. A driving need to fight it, to defeat it, had caught him in its grip. Knowing that it was working on him didn't dilute its effect at all.

::Vargo!::

I can change this.

He *wanted* to change it. To prove that he could—that even an impossible numinat wasn't beyond his skill. Shutting out the screaming in his head, Vargo dampened his cloth again and pulled out his chalk. Every lecture Alsius had given him about the dangers of freehanding numinata flew out of his head. Every memory of Alsius saying he could do better spurred Vargo on.

"I have my compass, my edge, my chalk, myself. I need nothing more to know the cosmos."

Pin and string for his compass, the long side of his drafting journal for an edge, he got to work. Never mind making his alterations mimic the original inscriptor's style; if Breccone Indestris had done this, it was on Mettore's orders, and evidence would mean less than piss in the Dežera. Instead Vargo chalked bold lines through the existing numinat, altering it. Passionate sunwise Noctat transformed into a constellation of earthwise Tricat—harmony, community, family. Weren't they all Nadežrans? Wasn't this Veiled Waters, when fog and masks hid their differences and everyone came together to drink from the same wellspring? To counterbalance that on the opposite arm of the golden spiral, he encased the pentagram of Quinat in a hexagon of Sessat: power and domination channeled into fairness, friendship, and cooperation. What the Vigil claimed to represent, and fell obscenely short of.

Behind Vargo, the two sides crashed together, and the tension of the plaza broke into blood. But the mayhem was the barest whisper at the edges of his awareness. Stronger by far was the song of perfection that pulsed through every line he inscribed. It flooded into him; he bled into it. Peace, harmony, order, stability: ideals just out of reach, crumbling like chalk when he reached for them. Ideals he would always fall laughably short of, because of what he was: gutter scum. What he'd been, and would still be, if not for Alsius.

As the numinat changed under his hand, his fury redirected itself. Away from the asshole who'd scribed this thing, and toward his own inadequacy. He *wanted* to be better. That desire drove him. Moving closer and closer, seeking to connect to something bigger than he was and lose himself in it forever.

A sharp prick at the back of his neck broke him out of the trance. His vision danced, and when it cleared, he was staring at an altered numinat he barely recalled inscribing, his muscles and bones aching as though he'd taken a beating. And Alsius was screaming in his head.

::—you blasted idiot! Do you want to end up with your body fallen to dust and your spirit bound into the focus? What gave you the mud-brained notion to imbue a numinat?!::

"Is that what I did?"

::If it weren't for me, you wouldn't be alive for me to yell at you.::

Vargo tried to study the figure on the wall dispassionately, but it nearly dragged him back in; he had to avert his eyes. The lines pulsed with all the idealistic urges that had suffused him, radiating out into the plaza—where, against all logic and history, hawks and Vraszenians were clasping hands, talking softly, even treating injuries across the gulf that had divided them moments before.

Vargo's knees gave out, and he sank to the ground, heedless of the muck.

"Are you sure?"

Alsius's hesitation was too long to be comforting. ::It was a near thing. Now get out of here before someone notices you.::

With Alsius driving him, Vargo managed to stumble to his feet and escape down the Uča Obliok with nobody the wiser. The farther he fled from that pulsing center of peace, the clearer his thoughts became, and the quicker his heart beat. The second time his knees gave out, it was from fear instead of weakness. He caught himself before he took another bath in diseased dirt. "*What did I just do?*"

::That's what I've been asking!::

But they both knew. And his close brush with self-annihilation didn't need to be discussed. It was too real.

::No more numinatria today,:: Alsius said softly.

"Not for us, no." Pulling himself upright again, Vargo continued on as though he weren't trembling from exhaustion. "But let's find Varuni and tell her to start diverting crowds to Dmariše Square."

Sooner or later his improvised changes would break down; he hadn't drawn them accurately enough to last. But until then, he might as well make use of his suicide attempt.

Seven Knots, Lower Bank: Cyprilun 34

The place Idusza led Grey to was near the center of Seven Knots, where the buildings compressed into a single tangled warren. Once they passed the sentry there, they entered a maze of narrow halls half blocked by worn crates and barrels and sackcloth, stairways going up and down again, and once even a window into a neighboring building that no longer gave access to the outside world.

I never would have found this on my own, Grey thought, wondering if he'd be able to find his way out again. He suspected Idusza was deliberately leading him by a long path.

He caught sight of a few faces, pressed like ghosts against cracks in the boards, warily observing their passing. The entire place reeked of bodies, cooked rice, and garlic—familiar scents. He and Kolya had lived in a tangle like this when they first came to Nadežra.

They'd been weaving their way for what felt like hours when he spied the first broadsheet pasted to a wall. Then another, and another—layers of the sedition the Stadnem Anduske had been distributing for years, piling up further and further, marking the way to a heavy door that had once been hinged onto a caravan.

Idusza stopped. "They know you're a hawk. Many of them at the hands of the Vigil have bled, or lost kin. I will do my best to make certain you leave here alive, but expect not that anyone will welcome you."

Grey unbuckled his sword belt and handed the entire kit to her. "To prove my goodwill."

She snorted as she accepted it. "They would have taken it from you inside. But giving it now may help. A little."

Her rhythmic knock on the door was clearly a code, and a narrow slot opened for the watcher inside to examine them both. Idusza murmured at the slot; a brief, low-voiced argument followed; she held up Grey's sword belt for the watcher to see. A clock tower rang ninth sun, the sound muted by the fog and layers of wall, and Grey tried not to tense at how much time was slipping away. If this continued past dusk, there'd be no stopping the fires; darkness was fuel for a riot.

Finally a heavy bolt thunked aside, and the door creaked open.

The room beyond wasn't much different from the other gang hideouts he'd seen in Nadežra. The people crowded inside were well-armed and wary, and the embroidered wall hangings almost certainly hid other entrances and exits. But here everyone's hair was long and braided, and the back of Grey's neck felt naked by comparison.

It wasn't hard to spot which one was Koszar Andrejek, the leader of the Stadnem Anduske. A heavyset man stood at the center of a clump of people, cheeks pitted with old pox scars and wire-coarse hair thick with braids and beads. The people around him looked prepared to throw themselves between their boss and the intruder if Grey so much as blinked wrong. "Ča Andrejek," Grey said, bowing his head and touching his brow.

The man ignored him. "Idusza," he snapped. "You waste our time. This man is the lapdog of the Vigil and the Traementis."

The man spoke in Liganti, a denial of their shared heritage. There was no diplomatic way to answer him. To these people, diplomacy was weakness, and the tool of those who bent the knee to the invaders.

Just as he'd done with Idusza, Grey had to thrust at their weakest point. "So to Mezzan Indestor you will listen, but not someone working to clear our people of blame for the Night of Hells." He spoke in Vraszenian, his accent coated with road dust, unlike the river-slick dialect spoken by those born in Nadežra, and spat on the floor behind him. "Who here is the lapdog?"

"Listen to him," Idusza said, her voice tight. "I wanted more than any of you to believe that Mezzan was with us—but he was so insistent on coming to me early this morning, after he left the gathering at Novrus Manor. And he just *happens* there to have seen a pile of dreamweaver bodies, plucked and half-eaten?"

Several of the seditionists were muttering angrily among themselves. Idusza spoke over them. "Where now is Mezzan? If truly he supports our cause, why defies he not the Cinquerat to stand at our side?"

Arms folded and faces set, Andrejek and his inner circle listened as Grey laid the facts before them: not just what Alta Renata had described, but what he'd come across in his investigations. The street children. Gammer Lindworm. The missing arrest record. Aža twisted into ash.

He made no mention of the stolen saltpeter. They would want to know how he knew, and he needed these people to see him as a friend, not a hawk on the hunt. If he could stop this, perhaps the saltpeter would never be put to use.

"The Night of Hells was an accident—Indestor's own ally turned against him. But he works toward something bigger, and whatever it is, he wants you to take the blame." Grey flexed his fists, wishing he had concrete proof to offer them. "But that succeeds only if you help him. To you our people will listen. You can turn them from this. You can stop Indestor from using you."

Andrejek scoffed. "You want us to . . . what? Stand down? To this blasphemy bend our necks? Indestor, Novrus, they are all the same. If Indestor's doing it was, so much the better that he bleed for it."

Before Grey could point out that Indestor wouldn't bleed nearly as much as the people of Seven Knots would, someone else stepped forward. A younger man, clean-shaven and slight of build. His braids were tied together at the back of his head, and his eyes were lined with kohl. He wasn't quite as tall as Grey, but he came close enough to stare him down, unblinking. The man's tone was mild as he said, "You signed yourself over to the Vigil, slip-knot. Over your own people you chose Caerulet and the Cinquerat. Why should I believe a thing you say?"

A glance at the man Grey had thought was Andrejek showed only surly deference to the one speaking now. He'd been a decoy, ordered to draw Grey out while the real Andrejek watched and judged.

And found Grey wanting, thanks to old choices he couldn't take back. There was no point explaining his reasons for joining the Vigil, the changes he'd hoped to make from within. But even if what Andrejek accused him of was true, he was still Vraszenian by one thread—a thread he would never break. "My brother was Jakoslav Szerado. He died in the Fiangiolli fire. You know of him?"

Andrejek's brow furrowed. "The one the Rook killed."

Anger wouldn't help here, nor would thinking about the Rook.

He met Andrejek's eyes and said in a clear voice, "Mezzan Indestor is not your friend. Mettore Indestor uses your organization to harm our people. If I lie or mislead you, may my brother abandon me. May I never feel him in this life or see him in the next. May those who call him family forget my name, and may his spirit from mine be severed, so I walk alone through Ažerais's Dream."

The collective intake of breath sent the room into a hush.

Andrejek was the only one who didn't react, holding Grey's gaze. Measuring the depth of pain there, making sure it ran all the way to the bone.

"After this is done," Andrejek said softly, "you and I will talk again."

He didn't even wait for a reply, but pivoted to face his people. "Send runners out. Pull our people back, and get them to ground—the hawks will chase them if half a chance they get."

No longer the center of interest, Grey sagged into a chair and placed a hand over his heart—aching, but for the first time since Kolya's death, not empty.

Dawngate, Old Island: Cyprilun 34

Ren walked blindly to the river's edge, trying to come up with a plan. Novrus was right: There was no way Renata herself, or even House Traementis, could pay for people to attend the celebrations in the amphitheatre.

Could Vargo?

He was rich—as rich as some of the noble houses, she suspected. But if he was the Rook, he wouldn't want to pour his wealth into Argentet's coffers. And if he *wasn't* the Rook...then the same was probably true, just for different reasons.

Unless he was willing to do it for her. But for all his warmth the other night, she doubted the tie between them was strong enough for that.

At the Dawngate landing she found Scaperto Quientis, surrounded by skiffers. As she approached, he leaned out to toss something to one of the men down in the water, and almost overbalanced. Renata caught his arm, steadying him. "I thought you were afraid of drowning, Your Grace."

"Drowning?" He blinked at her. "Only in the metaphorical sense. Get moving!" That last was to the skiffers.

Renata watched them descend the river-slicked stairs and start paddling clear. It wasn't just the skiffers; they had others with them, armed with clubs. "You're sending people to fight the rioters?"

"Not to fight. To take people off the Lower Bank—get them clear of the trouble. The innocent shouldn't be caught in this."

She couldn't help staring. Five members of the Cinquerat: five colors of bastard, the common people said. But Quientis actually seemed to be trying to help.

He'd approved the river charter, and not made her pay for it in blood. He'd organized work crews during the winter.

Maybe—just possibly—it was four colors of bastard, and one with an actual heart.

"Your Grace." She stopped herself just short of grabbing his arm again. "You can do better than that. I have an idea, something that will help ease the trouble on the Lower Bank. But I can't do it myself."

He followed her up from the landing to the street and listened as she explained. But even before she finished, he was shaking his head.

"I'm sorry, Alta Renata. Your instincts are noble. But we can't let people get away with this kind of disrespect and violence. I'm doing what I can to protect those who want no part of the trouble, but the rest..." His square face settled into grim, resigned lines. "Caerulet will take care of them."

Renata stood, silent and despairing, as he straightened his coat and began walking back to the Charterhouse. Indestor would take care of it, all right. He would send his hawks and soldiers in to drown the Lower Bank in blood.

She didn't even realize she'd chased after Quientis until she was standing in front of him again, blocking his way. He sighed. "Alta Renata—"

Throwing manners to the wind, she dragged him into the shadow of the Charterhouse steps. "Your Grace. Mettore Indestor *created* this problem. I saw his son meet with the woman who threw the dreamweaver's body at the labyrinth; I saw him *give* her that bird. His pet inscriptor was there, too—probably placing numinata around the Lower Bank to fan the destruction. His own son has taken up with a Vraszenian lover, I think on his orders; he's been pouring poison in the ears of the Stadnem Anduske. They're planning some kind of protest at the Charterhouse the day after tomorrow, and I have no doubt that Indestor intends for it to become a slaughter."

Quientis was staring. She charged on, recklessly. "He planned to drug me on the Night of Hells—it's why the cup I shared with Leato contained a double dose. And the woman who drugged everyone, Gammer Lindworm? He's been working with her. Kidnapping children off the street and using them to make the ash. I don't know what he intends it for... but I know that whatever it is, neither you nor I want to see it come to pass. This riot is part of his plan. We need to end it as peacefully as we can—and as soon as we can."

Quientis's sputters reminded her of those moments in the canal on the Night of Hells. She could see him half starting a thousand questions—*How do you know this? Why would he poison you? Who* are *you?*—but he cast them all aside and cut straight to the one that mattered. "Do you have proof?"

Relief that he hadn't simply laughed in her face washed away under despair. Because what he demanded, she couldn't provide.

Before she could say anything, he turned aside, glare fixing on the plaza. "Of course you don't. Mettore would keep that sort of thing locked away where you can never find it."

All the air went out of her. *He believes me.*

Quientis clamped his hands behind his back. "Sostira will expect immediate payment. Credit won't do. And too much of my own money is currently bound up in a project to stabilize the Lacewater foundations. I have the funds Master Vargo deposited with me to buy materials for the cleansing numinat, but..."

He'll gut me like a fish. Except Vargo owned property up and down the Lower Bank—property that might well burn if she didn't make this leap.

It might burn anyway. But Renata had gotten him that charter by making promises she couldn't keep, and then figuring out how to keep them later; sometimes that was the only way forward.

"Do it," she said. "I'll replace those funds afterward."

Quientis's answering look was cynical. He knew the Traementis situation as well as Novrus did. But he only said, "Sostira's in her office?" At Renata's nod, he tugged his waistcoat down and squared his shoulders. "Right. Let's go see about giving Mettore a bad day."

21

The Mask of Ashes

Horizon Plaza and Westbridge: Cyprilun 34

In the time it took Sostira Novrus and her escort to arrive at the far side of Sunset Bridge, someone had erected a small platform so she could be seen by the entire plaza. The Tuat numinat inscribed on the boards ensured she could be heard as well. The crowds in Horizon Plaza were a stone's throw away from breaking into unrest again, but confusion over the fact that she stood behind a cordon of her personal guards rather than the Vigil was momentarily keeping the aggression at bay.

Sostira's surcoat, a muted apricot stiffened with gold embroidery that caught the blaze of the light staffs, made her a glowing beacon in the twilight mist. With the stage lifting her and the numinat amplifying her voice, Argentet was in her element: She lived for performances like this.

"Citizens of Nadežra. I have heard your complaints, and now I come before you to answer them. But first I must remind you that the violence we have seen today is beneath you. That the harm you cause is to your brothers and sisters. Veiled Waters is a time of renewal; the unrest today is an insult to the gods."

That was a mistake, Renata thought as a low growl answered her last phrase. Most of the time it was easy to forget that Vraszenians and Liganti saw the gods differently. On a day like this, though, with tensions already frayed past the snapping point, the oversight grated.

But Sostira's soft smile and her next words hinted that she'd prepared for that reaction. "When the gods are benevolent, we celebrate them. When they are displeased, we propitiate. I have heard the displeasure of Nadežra's people, whom I serve as a priest serves the gods—and I shall propitiate you.

"I speak now not as Argentet, but as Era Novrus. I have heard it said that I am the source of the insult today—that my house feasts upon the flesh of dreamweaver birds, in blatant disregard for the sacred traditions of the Vraszenian people. I tell you now that this is untrue. And to prove it, I will empty the coffers of House Novrus to personally pay for all who wish to enter the Great Amphitheatre tomorrow. From sunrise to sunset on the day of Andusny, all who would celebrate the Festival of Veiled Waters in that place will do so at my expense."

The noise from the audience turned from angry to astonished. Now Renata was the only one growling. *That wasn't what we agreed to at the Charterhouse.* It wasn't what was going to happen, either. In typical Liganti style, Novrus had demanded a written contract with Quientis before she agreed to make this speech.

Now she was going to take credit for his generosity.

Before Renata could stride toward the platform, though, Scaperto Quientis's hand clamped around her arm. "Let her take credit. I think Sostira will find it's a double-edged blade. She's framing it as largesse, but people resent being given what's rightfully theirs."

He was right: In the long run, it would be Novrus's condescension the Vraszenians remembered, not her charity. Especially the following year, when the price of admission tripled for the Great Dream.

For the moment, though, it was having its desired effect. People expected violence and inflexibility from the Cinquerat and braced themselves to shove back; Novrus bending her knee, however slightly, was like a wrestler giving way so she could pin her opponent to the ground.

But it couldn't drain all the anger away, even as people began to disperse, the wind taken from their sails. Small groups remained in the plaza, muttering among themselves; others trickled off to talk over zrel in the ostrettas. Some would drink themselves up to fury and use the darkness to hide what they did next. The rest, exhausted, would retire for the night.

The real test would come tomorrow. Then Nadežra would see whether the embers had burned out, or whether the morning air would whip them into a blaze again.

Renata thanked Quientis and saw him to a skiff. That done, she sagged against the wall of an ostretta and just breathed for several long minutes. *I hope this helped. Some part of it, at least.*

When she thought her knees might hold her, she pushed upright and began making her way home, keeping a wary eye out as she went. Her shoes crunched on debris: broken glass, shattered cobbles, and the occasional slippery patch of softer refuse. Once she passed a splash of blood on a wall, drying into a dark and sticky spatter.

As she crossed onto the Isla Prišta, she saw Captain Serrado. The panel coat was gone, replaced by his Vigil uniform and hexagram pin, and three constables were with him. He stopped and bowed as she came near.

"You weren't at your townhouse," he said. The words rang like an accusation; Serrado winced as he realized it. "What I mean is, you might want to go to Traementis Manor instead. Some vandals hit Isla Prišta. Most of the houses were damaged."

The muscles that had begun to relax snapped tight. *Tess*—

"Tess is safe," he assured her. "One of my constables found her and helped her get to Little Alwydd."

Ren swayed with relief. In that moment, she didn't care what had happened to the townhouse. Little Alwydd was the Ganllechyn district; Tess would be safe there.

Then she realized she recognized the man Serrado had nodded at. She'd only seen that pretty face twice, too far apart in place and time and context for her to connect them before now. Once on Coster's Walk, right before Serrado ran her off for cold-decking Nikory...and once along the canal behind her house, chatting with Tess as he offered a basket of bread.

Pavlin. The baker's boy.

Is a hawk.

"Thank you for your assistance today," Serrado added. "Idusza helped me convince the Stadnem Anduske. They're talking people down. There wouldn't have been any chance of that without you. I assume you also had something to do with Novrus's concession?"

His voice was a little too loud, his words a little too formal. He'd set Pavlin on her household as a spy, and Ren didn't know what the constable had reported back to him, but Serrado clearly didn't want to have that confrontation right here in the street. For a brief instant she was tempted to force it anyway—to make him answer for the way Pavlin had led Tess on.

But she was too tired, and if the city didn't burn tomorrow, Serrado would be a large part of the reason why.

Besides, Tess needed her.

"Quientis," she said. "He's the one paying for it, though Novrus is taking the credit. I'll owe him for that."

"Quientis—?" Serrado's surprise broke into a grimace of rueful admiration. "Is there anything you can't convince—"

He cut the sentence off, gaze sliding to Pavlin again. "Well then. I won't keep you. Era Traementis knows where I can be found when I'm not at the Aerie."

With a military click of his boots and a signal to his squad, he made his escape.

Ren's gloves stretched tight across her knuckles as she clenched her fists. Pavlin and Serrado were a problem for later. First, she had to take care of Tess.

Little Alwydd and Westbridge, Lower Bank: Cyprilun 34

Little Alwydd was a tiny islet left over from someone's poor planning, shaped into a lopsided triangle by canals cutting at odd angles between larger foundations. But that made it defensible; there were barricades at the two bridges, with torches flaming in the nighttime fog, and people with cudgels and slings ready to repel any trouble that might come toward them.

They didn't try to repel Renata. They just gaped in astonishment that a Seterin alta had come alone, on foot, to retrieve her maid.

The old woman who pecked around Tess like a hen with a chicklet was aged past astonishment. She did, however, have question after question for Renata, until Tess finally snapped that they'd all be withered to cronehood before her curiosity was satisfied. After that, the old woman let them escape with only a huff and one last worried frown for Tess.

And Tess said nothing more until they returned to the townhouse—chilly and damp thanks to the broken parlour window and the fire being out half the day.

"I'll find some coal to build it up." Tess's usual lilt was flattened by exhaustion. She set down the rucksack she'd taken with her and fished out the sampler. It dangled between broken pieces of the frame. Sighing, she tossed it into the cold hearth. "That'll be good as a starter."

"Not on your life." Ren snatched up the damaged sampler before her sister could kindle a flame. It had meant so much to Tess when she made it and hung it in the kitchen. The frame might be broken, and there might be no money to replace it...but Ren would find a way if she had to rob a carpenter's shop to do it.

"As you want." Tess leaned on the table, curls hiding her face. "I'm that glad you came through safe. We heard Sostira Novrus is paying the amphitheatre admissions for everyone. You did that, didn't you?"

She didn't care about the politics. Ren set the sampler down and brushed Tess's hair gently back. There was a cut on her cheek and a bruise swelling up on her forehead, and Tess wouldn't meet her eyes.

"I saw Captain Serrado," Ren said softly. "And...Pavlin."

A hiccup answered that, then another. Tess sank down and wrapped her arms around herself, face buried against her knees.

"I'm so, so sorry," she said. "He was bringing bread, and he seemed harmless, and I just thought he was being nice." Her head rose, cheeks blotchy and shiny with tears, nose dripping snot. "I've thought and thought, and I don't *think* I said anything to make him believe you weren't Letilia's daughter, but then, what do I know. I probably gave the whole thing away, and them all laughing at how easy I was to fool."

Ren knelt at her side, hugging tight around Tess's shoulders. *Just had her heart broken by a lying hawk, and she's worrying about* me *instead.* "Tess, you have nothing to be sorry for. Pavlin it is who should be sorry—him and Serrado, playing with you like this. They hurt you, and I will make them answer for it."

Tess huddled even smaller, curling away from the comfort. "You can't. If they don't suspect now, that'll make them curious for certain—an alta taking vengeance for her maid? And them just doing what they were told to do."

"If Serrado knows not that you are important to me, then the man is blind and deaf and more stupid than a frog. And I care not if they were told to do it. Me they can target all they like, but you are off limits."

Tess swiped at the tears with the back of her hand, doing more to smear them about than clean them away. "It wasn't me they were after. I'm just the weakness in your plan. It was always about you."

She didn't intend the words to cut, but they did, and deeply. Ren almost pulled back out of guilt, but she knew how Tess would read that. Instead she tightened her hug. "Then I am the one who is sorry."

After a moment of stiffness, Tess softened and burrowed into the comfort Ren offered. "Don't be silly," she said, voice muffled by Ren's shoulder. "Then that's the both of us being silly, and the world's falling apart too fast for that. Of course all the attention's on you—*and* all the risk. I wouldn't want that for a seat on the Cinquerat and free run of Vargo's warehouses. But here's me weeping because you're doing what you ought and the plan's working as we intended."

Not at all as they intended. If this con was supposed to win them safety, it had failed beyond comprehension... but Ren understood what she meant. Tess couldn't handle the sort of scrutiny Renata Viraudax attracted. Ren could—as long as she had Tess at her side.

Someone in Little Alwydd had already cleaned up Tess's injuries, but Ren got the fire started, warmed a little water, and washed her sister's face again, wiping away the marks of the tears. They still had some of the imbued ointments Vargo had sent over after the Night of Hells; she daubed those along the cut and over the goose egg on Tess's forehead, with all the delicacy she used to use when picking pockets. There wasn't any food but stale bread, but Ren soaked it in the last of Eret Extaquium's cloying wine and gave it to Tess to eat.

Instead of eating, Tess stared at the bread, fingers curled around it like she was cradling a wounded bird.

Bread. Probably the remains of Pavlin's last basket. Before Ren could snatch away her mistake, Tess whispered, "What do I do if I see him again? I really... I thought..."

And then, quiet enough that it hovered on the edge of sound: "I liked him."

A life full of lies, and Tess thought she'd found a truth she could hold on to. A truth just for herself.

Ren sat on the floor next to her and tipped her head onto Tess's shoulder. "I know."

Upper Bank and Lower Bank: Cyprilun 34

All noble betrothal agreements were posted in the Tuatium in the Pearls until the wedding took place. It took only a brief glance at the Coscanum-Indestor scroll for Vargo to confirm his suspicions, and only a moderately inflated bribe after that to learn where Meda Fienola lived.

"Breccone Indestris," he said without preamble when she came to the door.

"I...I beg your pardon?" She glanced past him, but between the mist and the late hour, there was little to see. "Master Vargo?" Her wrinkled nose was all the mirror Vargo needed to tell him that, despite Alsius's assurances, a quick change and a bucket wash did not in fact leave him looking "perfectly presentable."

Too late to fix that now. He had to convince a cuff to turn against one of her own, on evidence barely more substantial than fog. "Breccone Simendis Indestris is behind the ash production."

At least it made her forget his appearance. "Perhaps we shouldn't have this discussion on my front step," she said, swinging the door wider.

Vargo followed her to a dusty parlour smelling vaguely of damp. The only indication that it ever saw use was the numinat that flared to life when the door closed behind them, bathing the room in steady light.

Fienola didn't offer him a seat or something to drink. Her mind was on other matters. "What makes you think Breccone has anything to do with ash?"

Her use of his unadorned name wasn't encouraging. Breccone might belong to House Indestor now, but he was the grandnephew of Utrinzi Simendis—which was to say Iridet, which was to say Tanaquis's boss. Just because Nadežra's elite tracked kinship through registers and numinatria didn't mean blood lost all meaning for them.

Fishing in his pocket, he drew out the waxy remains of the foci and scattered them across the tea table at his hip. The scent of juniper filled the room.

"You've heard about the riots on the Lower Bank today? They were exacerbated by numinata. I was able to neutralize most of them—I hope. I suspect Altan Breccone intended for them to be destroyed in the chaos, or else he would go back to erase them before anyone could get a good look, but the unrest calmed more quickly than anyone could have guessed." Quickly enough that it took

Vargo by surprise. He'd have to see if Iascat was open to another assignation; the Novrus heir might know what had transformed his aunt into an avatar of Quarat's own generosity.

He added, "That wax carries the same scent as the wax Indestris used for the Coscanum-Indestor betrothal, and the chop used to stamp it is the same style."

Fienola began examining each focus in turn. Her fingers were gloved only in chalk and ink stains, and Vargo's own gloves were lost somewhere in the muck of the Uča Obliok, but she didn't seem to mind.

"These do smell like his," she admitted, picking out some of the larger pieces and fitting them together like a puzzle. "And Breccone does prefer the Muinam style for his chops. Thinks that overwrought complexity equals power."

Vargo snorted reflexively, and Fienola laughed instead of frowning at his disrespect. ::I do like her,:: Alsius said.

Shut up. Her opinions on numinatrian styles wouldn't be worth river mud if she wasn't willing to help them. He played his last card. "There was a seventh numinat. And it was affecting the crowd's emotions."

Fienola's hand flattened on the table, scattering the pieces. "Breccone scribed a numinat that drew on eisar?"

::Marry this girl.::

I'm not your proxy, old man. But Vargo was impressed, too. Only scholars like Alsius knew much about eisar—spirits linked with human emotions—and even then, "much" wasn't very much. "You might ask him about that once he's in custody. Along with how he did it, since the focus was blank." If Vargo could have spared the time, he would have arranged to ambush and interrogate Breccone himself before reporting the man. But with the Lower Bank still smoldering, he didn't dare wait.

"Yes. Of course." Fienola absently flipped the largest piece of wax between her fingers as she thought. "I see your point regarding the riot. But what makes you think this is connected to ash?"

"I've seen the numinat used to make ash. Or the remnants of it, anyway," Vargo said. "And at first I didn't understand what it was used for. I've been studying the traces for a while, trying to reconstruct the figure. I was planning on coming to tell you, but then the riots started, and..." He shrugged.

She accepted the lie. "And Breccone?"

"The linework on the remnants has the same feathering," Vargo said. She was a good enough inscriptor to understand why that was evidence—but it was a long way from understanding his point to doing anything about it. Vargo locked his hands behind his back and waited.

Tanaquis scooped the wax into a decorative bowl, leaving a clean sweep through the dust of the tea table, then stood silent, pondering the bright wood. "These won't prove anything about ash," she finally said. "But they'll be enough to arrest and question Breccone about his involvement in the riots."

Vargo's guess had been right. Fienola's mind went to numinatria first, second, and third; while she wasn't ignorant of politics, those ran a distant fourth to her real concern.

But unlike some of the other Cinquerat seats, Iridet didn't have its own armed force, and Indestor would close ranks to protect Breccone. "If you need help, I can—"

She held up a dusty hand. "I believe Captain Serrado can be trusted to do his duty, and he's seconded to me for the investigation. Good evening, Master Vargo."

He swallowed his protest. Even if he came along, Fienola was hardly going to let him interrogate Indestris mid-arrest. He'd have to arrange something later—through official channels or otherwise.

For now, he accepted her dismissal. Vargo saw himself out and went home to Eastbridge, where he could at least scrub himself properly clean.

When he saw a runner race off as his sedan chair approached the final bridge to Isla Čaprila, he sighed, knowing what awaited him—but to his surprise, although Sedge and Varuni were on his doorstep, neither of them launched into a lecture about him vanishing.

Sedge jerked his chin for Vargo to step aside as Varuni paid the chair bearers.

The fist reeked of filth from the riots, but Vargo held his breath long enough to listen as Sedge told him, "I found your missing saltpeter. It's in a chandler's shop in Grednyek Close, northern part of Seven Knots. Chased one of the agitators in there. Weren't out in the open—they en't that dumb—but after I knocked him out, I saw. Except it en't saltpeter no more."

Vargo didn't need him to say any more. "It's black powder. Let's go."

He paid a skiff to carry them around the Point to the Lower Bank. Despite his best efforts to go on questioning Sedge, he soon ran out of things to ask, and Varuni took full advantage of the remaining river trip to let him know what she thought of assholes who pretended they were going to stay safe and sound and instead ran off the moment her back was turned. Vargo entertained brief visions of having the skiffer assassinated so he couldn't gossip about the conversation with his friends later.

But once they reached the Lower Bank, he had bigger worries. The Vigil was still out in force, patrolling to stop anyone who thought to use the darkness to start more trouble, and clumps of Vraszenians were doing the same. Their trio had to take a circuitous path, hiding more than once, before they got to the shop where Sedge had found the powder.

It was empty.

Not totally cleared out. They'd left behind the bronze mortar and pestle, probably because those were too heavy to move, and the sieves they'd used to corn the powder. But the powder itself was gone.

Sedge let out a stream of curses. "I swear it was here at first earth. Ladnej and Smuna saw it, too—"

"Then maybe you should have left Ladnej and Smuna to keep an eye on it," Vargo snapped.

"We was trying to find you! And to keep the fucking city from burning down! How much more d'you—" Sedge clamped his jaw shut on the rest of it, breathing hard.

"So now instead of burning down, it'll just blow up!"

Vargo might have said more, but a scuff of Varuni's boot on the floorboards stopped him. Truly amazing, how much disapproval that woman could imbue into a blank stare.

Grinding his teeth, Vargo turned to the window, cupping his eyes to the dirty glass pane. An ostretta on the corner seemed closed, but slivers of light glimmered through the boards nailed over its windows. The rest of the square was full of fog and empty of traffic. Intermittent oil lamps failed to provide much illumination, their light a dim nimbus smothered by the mists.

First earth might have seen the lamplighters go through, if they'd been delayed by the unrest.

"Send fists to question the people living around here, anyone who was in that ostretta, and the lamplighters. Someone had to move it. I want to know who. And where."

The Aerie and Eastbridge: Cyprilun 34

Grey didn't even make it to the Aerie steps before Fienola's runner found him. He kept his expression blank as he read her note, and then as he met the curious gazes of his squad.

"Kaineto. Take Levinci and Ecchino and prepare the reports for Commander Cercel. Once that's done, the rest of you are relieved save Ranieri, Tarknias, and Dverli—you're with me."

The constables singled out didn't even try to hide their groans, or the jealous looks they threw at their squadmates, or the death glares aimed at Grey's back. Ranieri matched Grey's stride as they headed toward the Sunrise Bridge.

"Captain, we've been thick in the mud all day," he said, keeping his voice low. With none of the lieutenants there, he was stepping up to do that job, speaking on behalf of his fellow constables. *He'd make a better lieutenant than Kaineto—if only I could promote him.* "We'd been thinking we were finally done, what with everything calming down."

Ranieri must be distracted, not to have considered why Grey might release his three delta gentry headaches and their supporters and keep the constables with no family connections... or to wonder why they would head out again without reporting to Cercel.

"I'm aware, Ranieri. We'll be done soon—after we attend to one thing." He let a grim smile slip through. "I don't think any of you will regret the delay."

They met Meda Fienola at the bridge to the Isla Micchio. She had an Iridet clerk with her, bearing a lantern, and she weighed the Vigil quartet with her gaze as they approached. "This is all you brought?" she asked.

Grey said, "I thought it wiser to move quickly. And not to involve..." He rolled a variety of responses over his tongue. "Unnecessary people."

"Indeed." Fienola led them over the bridge and into the fog-veiled plaza. "Breccone's townhouse is there," she said, gesturing into the murk. Then she frowned, realizing the uselessness of the gesture. "In the back corner, by the Via Trabuso. You should send at least one of your people around to the servants' entrance, in case he takes it into his head to run."

"Any particular danger we should prepare for?" Grey asked. He knew enough about numinatria to be wary of it.

Fienola pondered. "If all goes well, we won't have to enter the house. If it doesn't, then look up, check walls and under rugs. Don't assume the numinat is going to be easily visible." She twisted a loose wisp of hair—a gesture that might have looked flirtatious on a woman not speaking casually about injury and death. "Tossing something flammable ahead of you at intervals is a sensible technique to avoid becoming a cinder."

So comforting. "Ranieri," Grey said. Whatever else Pavlin was struggling with today, he still had the best eye and most sense of any of Grey's people. "We're here to arrest Breccone Simendis Indestris for his part in instigating today's unrest and for reckless use of numinatria. Take Tarknias around the back. If anybody comes out in a hurry, you know what to do."

If he was surprised, Ranieri's face didn't show it; he and Tarknias jogged off. Grey loosened his sword in its sheath. "Lead on, Meda Fienola."

Indestris's butler answered the door in his night-robe, rubbing at his eyes. "What?" he said when Fienola finished delivering her declaration of arrest. "I'm sorry—who did you say you were?"

She repeated herself, by which point the man was more awake, but no more helpful. "Altan Breccone is asleep," he said, as if arrests should only happen during social hours.

"Then wake him," Fienola said with crystalline precision. "Out of respect for his rank, he may have time to dress, but no more."

"I can't wake him!" the butler said, scandalized. "Altan Breccone is very particular. He requires an unbroken night of rest to carry out his work—"

"Meda Fienola, this man is stalling," Grey said, barely able to keep himself from lunging over the threshold. "He knows perfectly well why you're here, and he's trying to buy time—probably for his master to flee."

Fienola tipped her head to one side. "I believe you're correct. Remember my warnings, Captain."

Tacit permission was enough for Grey. He grabbed the butler by the collar before the man could figure out what she meant and shoved him backward into the front hall. *I bet he's flammable.*

Then he realized the butler had more than one reason to stall.

Grey knew enough about ash to know that in the normal way of things, it took the better part of a bell to show its effects. The three men who came charging toward him from a side room were fully in its grip. Someone had tipped off Indestris's household that an arrest party was coming.

Grey dropped the butler and drew his sword to meet their rush.

The world slid both nearer and further away, his senses sharpening to the blade's edge but his mind stepping back. Grey sank into a detached awareness that took in his surroundings without letting the chaos of the moment swallow him whole. It was a kind of imbuing, threading his spirit into his swordsmanship the way crafters did with their wares. It had saved Grey's life in the past, when he'd been jumped by Lower Bank knots or his own fellow hawks.

And it saved him now, as three ash-crazed men tried to tear him apart.

The drug made people strong, not fast. He slipped through the gap between two of the men, though one snagged his arm briefly, and even that fleeting contact was enough to spin Grey around. He ducked and cut low as he went, slashing across the backs of one man's thighs. His target went down in eerie silence: no scream, just an abrupt collapse as his legs wouldn't hold him anymore.

But ash also dulled pain. Crippled and bleeding, the man kept moving, fingernails scraping the marble floor as he clawed toward Fienola.

The other two spun to face Grey. His usual methods wouldn't work here; men on ash had no compunctions about parrying with their hands, trying to wrench his sword from his grip even as it cut their palms open. Behind them, Dverli lost her sword to exactly that tactic. She narrowly avoided being tripped to the floor and grabbed a statue from a niche, smashing it over the head of the hamstrung man.

An instant's evaluation told Grey he couldn't get through to Dverli without exposing his own back to the other two. He had to trust her to keep Fienola safe, and retreated to lure the remaining pair away. For a moment the clarity of his focus wavered: *I hope I'm not backing into some numinat.*

He'd come here hoping to bring as many of Indestris's people in for questioning as possible. With ash flooding them, though, "as many as possible" might be "none." If he kept trying to disable rather than kill, he was going to lose one of his own people in trade.

A clatter of feet on the stairs decided the question for him. Breccone Indestris, fully dressed and clutching a sack, hurtled down into the front hall. He slipped on the blood staining the marble, but kept his feet and rounded the newel post, heading for the back of the house.

Grey put his blade through the throat of one man and then the heart of the other, kicking them away as hard as he could. They dropped—not out, but on their way there—and he leapt past them to pursue Indestris to a half-hidden door and down the servants' stair. Into the kitchen, and the back door wide open—

He was just in time to see Ranieri's fist crash into Indestris's jaw. The man staggered backward, then slumped at Grey's feet.

Ranieri shook his hand out, wincing. The boy was no bare-knuckle brawler; he needed much heavier bones if he wanted to go punching people in the face. But his expression showed no regrets as he said, "That felt good."

"Hold him," Grey said, and flung himself back up the stairs.

He found Fienola binding up what looked like a bite mark on Dverli's hand. The third attacker lay facedown, a knife in his back that was far too delicate to be Vigil issue. "I took care of him," Fienola said when she saw Grey. "This doesn't prove a connection to ash, of course, but it does make our case stronger. Do you have Breccone?"

Grey nodded sharply. "Ranieri stopped him."

"Thank you, Captain. We'll take him to the Sebatium for questioning. Please have your people secure the house until I can make sure Breccone left no traps." She stood, dusting her knees, then turned to the clerk hovering safely on the front step. "Send someone to collect the bodies."

How could she remain so composed? Fire still coursed through Grey, making his heart pound and his muscles twitch. He focused his breathing, forced his calm to match hers. "I'll find something to bind Altan Breccone with," he said, and went to give Ranieri the new orders.

The Aerie was quiet by the time Grey's dragging steps carried him back to file the report. Ranieri had offered to stay at the Sebatium with their prisoner. None of his constables were complaining anymore; Dverli and Tarknias had saluted with enthusiasm when he told them to guard the house. *You're not that much older than them. You've got no excuse to feel this tired.*

But he was—tired enough that he didn't notice the two lumps

huddled in the shadow of the Aerie's steps until they broke free and approached him.

He stopped his hand before it touched his sword. Corillis's light was enough to show him the moon-round face, small features, and dimpled eyes of a dawn child. He'd seen her before, among Arkady's gang. She was old for a street kid, maybe fifteen floods, but the innocence of dawn children all too frequently made them targets for the cruel, so Arkady gave her shelter. Pitjin, that was her name. Behind her was the boy who'd tried to knife Grey when they first ambushed him.

"See, Lupal?" Pitjin said to him. "It's the nice hawk. The one who en't such a fucker."

"Er...yes?" Grey said. Her language rubbed oddly against the sunny grin of a dawn child.

Lupal didn't look nearly as cheerful. "En't no nice ones." He paid more attention to the square than to Grey, keeping watch for threats coming through the fog.

"Shh. He'll help. You'll help, right?"

So much for finding my bed. There was only one reason Arkady's gang would seek him out. "I'll try. Another kid turned up? How long have they been missing?"

"It en't that," Pitjin said, catching his sleeve.

"It's Arkady," Lupal growled. "She's been taken."

Isla Priŝta, Westbridge: Cyprilun 35

Once Ren had the mattress down and Tess tucked snugly in, she meant to sit and think for a while. But the bench wasn't comfortable to sit on, and the parlour was uninhabitable at the moment, so she lay down next to Tess—and passed out like she'd been clubbed.

She woke what seemed like a mere blink later to someone pounding on the kitchen door.

Fear flooded her body. But no one was shouting threats or orders of arrest; it was just an insistent knocking, like someone had been doing it for a while and was on the verge of giving up. Ren almost got up to answer it, then realized her impending mistake and shook Tess instead. "Tess. You must see who is at the door—I can't."

"Mmph. Hurry up and thread the custard," Tess mumbled, dragging her hair over her face like a blanket. A few more shakes got her sitting up and yawning blearily.

Then she heard the knocking and shot to her feet. "Right. Right. I have it. Go hide." She stumbled to the door, waiting until Ren was out of sight.

Ren heard the door open, and conversation too soft for her to make out. Then the door snicked closed again. When she peered into the kitchen, Tess was frowning at a folded note. The lump of candle wax sealing it hadn't been broken. She held it out for Ren to double-check. "From Sedge."

The wax held no seal, of course. Sedge wasn't the kind of person who used seals. "Who brought this?" Ren asked, prying at the lump.

"Corner boy. One of the ones who keeps watch for the tatting circle." Tess sat on the bench, head lolling against the wall. Her teeth snapped closed on another yawn. "I can call him back if you need."

Ren more or less stopped listening after "corner boy," because she had the note open, and was trying to parse the untidy scrawl within. Sedge had mentioned learning to write after he started working for Vargo, but judging by this sample, he'd stopped practicing after the basics.

Found something you need to see. Meet at lodging house. Vargo watching. Use escape window.

Her fingers trembled. *Vargo watching.* What had Sedge found that he needed to hide from his boss?

"Tess," she said, folding the note with careful movements. "Sedge has something for me. You stay here; I'll be back in soon."

"No. I don't want you going off on your own again. Let me just..." Tess looked around blankly, not yet awake enough to hold a thought for more than a few moments. "Shoes?"

Ren wouldn't have taken Tess back to the lodging house if the rest of the city were on fire and that was the only safe building. "No, you stay here. I would not leave the house empty, not until we can board up the parlour windows."

"I could ask…" She saw the moment Tess remembered the previous day's events, in the slump of her shoulders and tremble of her lips. "Never you mind. Go. I'll see to it."

Sedge wouldn't begrudge Ren the moment she took to hug Tess again. Only when Tess pulled back and started gesturing for her to get on with it did she dress herself as Arenza, putting on her makeup in haste and slinging the Rook's shawl of knives around her shoulders. Lacewater was no place for Renata Viraudax, not at this hour.

It wasn't any place for Ren, either. Not with the memories that haunted its narrow lanes. But Sedge had called, and she had to go.

Lacewater, Old Island: Cyprilun 35

Ren had avoided three places in Lacewater since coming back to Nadežra. The first was the Uča Mašno, the street where she'd lived with her mother until the fire destroyed their house and four others. The second was Svajra Square, and the little alley off its southern end, where she'd found her mother's body.

The third was Ondrakja's lodging house.

Every muscle in Ren's body tightened as she approached. The streets hadn't changed; everything was as weathered and as run-down as before, the lanes as cramped, the bridges as rickety.

The building sat on a bend in the Uča Fidou, well-positioned to watch both approaches. Ren crept close in the darkness and fog, studying the exterior. There were no lights in the windows, but that was no surprise; people here didn't waste candles or lamps at this hour. Who had moved in after Ondrakja vanished and the Fingers scattered? She hadn't asked.

But that was probably why Sedge had told her to come in the escape window.

It wasn't a window at all. It was an old coal chute, running from street level down into the cellar, from back when Lacewater was well enough maintained that the river didn't flood its cellars every spring. Knot members weren't supposed to keep secrets from each other, but they'd kept this one from Ondrakja, so they could use it to sneak out without her knowing. The inner and outer doors looked like they'd been nailed shut, but they weren't really, thanks to some unknown predecessor.

Ren eyed the hatch dubiously. Had Sedge really managed to fit down that? Probably not, but for her it would be a quieter way of entering than going through the front door.

At least the countless Fingers who'd slid through the chute had polished away the coal dust. She folded up the Rook's shawl and shoved it inside her shirt for protection, then pried open the hatch and eased herself in, feetfirst.

She landed ankle-deep in water. The cellar around her was pitch dark; she put the shawl back on and tied it securely, then drew one of the knives and palmed it for comfort. She might be out of practice with throwing them, but something was better than nothing. And she could always use the knife to stab.

"Sedge?" she whispered, even though he would have said something if he were down here. The cellar answered with nothing more than the quiet sloshing of the ripples she'd set off. Moving by memory, with her free hand sweeping the air in front of her for obstacles, she made her way to the stair. Its bottom two steps were missing, rotted away by the damp, but when she heaved herself onto the next one its creaking structure held.

The cellar door opened into a pantry and kitchen that hadn't seen a meal cooked since long before Ren was born. Here there was a bit more light to see by, the exterior door hanging half-open and the grey of false dawn brightening the mist outside, but only enough to mold the shadows into shapes—shapes that seemed to loom and creep.

Her fingers tightened painfully on the knife's hilt. How many times had she fallen asleep in this building, clutching a knife for comfort? Comfort and protection both, especially before Sedge came. The Fingers preyed on each other as much as on the cuffs they robbed. Ondrakja encouraged it—up to a point—so they wouldn't band together against her.

Now all that fear returned, like she was a child once again.

An itch crawled up her nose, from the dust-thick air and the earthy smell of long-dried rat droppings. Ren silenced it into her shoulder, three sharp sneezes that made her head throb. Taking a cautious breath afterward, she scented something familiar: a tang as sharp as fear, not quite blanketed by the dust and the droppings.

Zlyzen blood.

Now that she knew to look, she saw its sickly glimmer splashed over the walls, felt its insidious whisper in her bones.

Panic flung her back toward the cellar door, but something was coming up out of the darkness, mold-black and broken-limbed. Ren spun and saw more zlyzen emerging from the shadows, from the empty shell of the pantry and the mist of the street outside. She hurled her knife at one of them and tried to bolt, but they blocked her path, and the only escape was deeper into the lodging house.

Where more of them were waiting. It was like the Fingers themselves had been transformed, all the kids she'd known turned into spindly, charred monsters. But they didn't claw her apart, the way they'd done to Leato. They were only herding her, pushing her back and back—toward the stairs to the second floor.

Ren retreated, throwing a second knife, a third, a fourth. All of them missed. Then she was far enough up the stairs to see a slender chance.

The railing snapped beneath her hand when she put her weight on it, turning her leap into a fall. But she crashed to the ground floor behind the pack of zlyzen and managed to keep her feet, staggering desperately toward the kitchen.

Claws snagged her hair, her skirt, dragging her back. She kicked, pulled out another knife, and slashed with it, felt blood like slime oozing terror over her fingers. The claw tore a hank of hair loose as it let go. One of the other zlyzen hissed.

They're trying not *to hurt me*, Ren realized. And that terrified her more than if they'd been out to kill her.

Her swipes with the knife got wilder. They grabbed her arms in their wrong-jointed claws, twisting them behind her with a strength that could easily have snapped her bones, and the knife fell to the floor. Then they pushed her back toward the stairs, a jostling, flowing crowd, while her breath sobbed in her chest and panic blurred her vision to fog.

She knew where they were taking her.

A croaking tune slithered down the hall, echoed by a smoother voice rising in Ren's memory:

> *"Find them in your pockets,*
> *Find them in your coat;*
> *If you aren't careful,*
> *You'll find them on your throat . . ."*

More frantic struggles only brought more pain, lancing through her shoulder, and all she could see was Sedge on the kitchen floor while Tess levered his joint back in place.

Stop. You need your arms. And your wits. Hard enough to think it, harder still to comply, but Ren forced herself to go limp. The pain eased.

The zlyzen carried her down the hallway and through a curtain of moth-chewed silk, throwing her onto a carpet dank with mold. The same carpet from five years ago; it squelched under her cheek. Through her tangle of hair, she could see the shattered crone that had once been Ondrakja, lounging in a parody of her former grace—as if this parlour were her stronghold again, and the zlyzen her new Fingers.

The big toe of Ondrakja's bare foot loomed before Ren's eyes, the nail fibrous and yellowed with fungus. It hooked her chin and lifted, forcing Ren to look up. Ondrakja took a slow sip from a pristine crystal goblet, something purple-dark and thick as river sludge.

"My little Renyi. You've come home."

"This isn't home," Ren spat. "It never was. You lured me in with the promise of helping me find my mother's koszenie, but it was a lie. Everything you told me and taught me—all lies." Lies she'd clung to. Because the alternative was to have nothing at all.

Ondrakja frowned, rubbery skin twisting over bone so easily the two barely seemed connected. But Ren remembered her frowns well enough to recognize this one. Not anger. Hurt.

"Not a lie. I was going to give it back to you; I was just waiting for the right moment. Once you showed me you'd learned your lesson." Ondrakja's skeletal arms wrapped around herself in a hug. "You would have loved me then."

Ren's mouth turned dry as dust. *I was going to give it back to you.*

Her mama's koszenie. The embroidered shawl every true Vraszenian had, their lineages coded in thread. It had been stolen off Ivrina's body, along with everything else.

"You had it. All along."

Ondrakja cackled with triumph. "Whose Fingers do you think plucked her corpse clean? And you, wandering the streets like a lost duckling, wailing for your mama's shawl... I couldn't give it to you then, of course. You might have left us. I was saving it for when I really needed it, to bind you to me forever. Until you *poisoned* me."

Zlyzen claws dug into Ren's shoulders when she tried to lunge for Ondrakja. "You had it, and you *used* me—"

"All for your own good! My poppet, my little mirror. You couldn't survive on the streets; you would have died with that shawl. But I said I'd take care of you, and I did. I said I'd teach you to use your beauty to get anything you wanted, and look at you now."

She leaned closer, the Acrenix medallion swinging from her withered neck, tangled with other cords, and her face warped into a mockery of a smile. "Alta Renata Viraudax. What mother could be more proud than I?"

Horror gagged Ren. *She knows.* The note from Sedge had been a trick; Ondrakja had sent the messenger. *I should have made sure I knew what his writing looked like.* Should have taken more precautions. Shouldn't have trusted that Ondrakja never knew about the escape window.

Too many "shoulds," going all the way back to the day Ivrina Lenskaya died.

The worst part was, Ondrakja was right. What she'd done as Renata—Ondrakja had taught her that. Her skill at lying, her light fingers, her ability to read people and figure out how to make them dance . . . She'd learned all of that here.

"Call yourself my mother again and I'll cut your tongue out," Ren snarled. "You aren't even Ondrakja anymore. You're a rotted husk full of zlyzen blood. You are Gammer Lindworm."

The glass shattered against the wall, and with it, all pretense of humanity. Gammer Lindworm lunged for Ren, nails digging into her jaw as she forced her head up higher. Breath foul as a river-bloated corpse washed over Ren's face.

"Whose fault is that?" Gammer Lindworm hissed. "You swore the knot oath, and you betrayed it. I died for *days.* Screaming, retching, clawing at my own skin. Until I saw one of them—the beasts—tangled in flood wrack and half-drowned. Tore it apart and drank its blood. I'm a monster now? They kept me alive. *They* are loyal to me—unlike you. And I'm going to feed you to them in pieces."

Sunlight edged through the broken, filthy window behind her. It barely lit the room at all, but an eerie sound filled the air around Ren: an inhuman moan, fear and longing braided together.

It was coming from the zlyzen.

They faded like smoke, into black mist, then nothing at all. Gammer Lindworm let go of Ren's jaw, cursing, yelling at them to come back.

And Ren flung herself backward, clawing her next-to-last knife from the shawl and snapping it directly at the old hag with an underhand throw.

Gammer Lindworm slanted out of the way, impossibly fast. The knife stuck quivering in the age-softened boards of the wall behind.

Ren tried to lurch to her feet, but before she could get them under her, Gammer Lindworm's arms locked around her body and that fetid breath hissed in her ear. "Naughty Renyi. You don't get away that easily. No, you're going to come with me, to start paying for what you've done. And once I've got you safely stowed, I'll collect the other two."

Ren opened her mouth to scream, but the world unraveled around her, just like it had done on the Night of Hells, and the lodging house was gone.

22

Two Roads Cross

Half the night canvassing the Lower Bank, and no sign of the black powder. Up all night, for no good reason, and then for breakfast Sedge got a tirade from Vargo. The man hated it when he couldn't just pull strings and make things happen.

Now it was midmorning, and all Sedge really wanted was sleep. But he didn't know whether Vargo would tell Ren they'd tracked down Quientis's missing saltpeter, given that they'd lost it again right after, and Sedge figured she deserved to know. So he forced his tired feet back toward Westbridge, through streets being swept clean of debris, to Ren's townhouse—

Whose front windows were stove clean in. *Ranislav's gonna bleed for that*, Sedge thought, staring at the splintered frames and shards of glass. He was supposed to make sure none of Vargo's property got damaged.

But to hell with the house. What about Ren and Tess?

He shot down the half stairs to the cellar and pounded on the door, the rhythm that would tell his sisters it was him. The door opened before he could finish the pattern, Tess red-eyed and nest-haired. "It's about ti—Where's Renata?" She shoved him aside, as though Ren might be hiding behind him.

Renata, not *Ren*. The reason became obvious when the door swung wider, revealing a worried-looking Giuna Traementis. He'd heard that she knew about Ren's poverty, but the sight of her in the kitchen—the place that was supposed to be their hidden base, safe from outsiders' eyes—jolted him.

"She en't here?" He felt ill, a thousand times worse than when Vargo had given him the slip.

"Tess said she left to meet you," Giuna said accusingly.

At Sedge's blank look, Tess pulled a crumpled fold of paper from her pocket. "Because of this? The note you sent."

Sedge's heart skipped a beat. "I din't send no note."

A glance at the shaky text was enough for Sedge to know it weren't from Vargo, nor anyone Sedge knew. But it was someone who knew *them*.

Giuna was craning her neck, trying to read the note. Sedge crumpled it again before she could. Lodging house, escape window—it wouldn't mean anything to the alta, but better not to risk questions, especially when he didn't know what Tess had said already.

Who could have sent it? A few other Fingers were still kicking around the Old Island, and Simlin broke bones for one of the Stretsko gangs down in Dockwall when he weren't numbing his own hurts with aža dreams. But nobody had ever returned to the house after Ondrakja's death. Better to sleep rough than return to a nightmare.

And none of the Fingers would have asked a knot-cutting traitor like Ren to meet them at the lodging house, even if they knew she was alive.

Only one person would.

"Ondrakja's got her."

The name slipped out before he could think better of it. He wasn't Ren, always in control of his tongue. Tess clapped both hands to her mouth, a whimper dying in her throat. Fear was something you stayed silent about if you didn't want it to get you. They all carried those lessons with them, in different ways.

Baffled, Giuna said, "Who's Ondrakja?"

Sedge and Tess exchanged helpless looks. What could they say?

A Primordial demon in human form. "Somebody working for Indestor," Sedge offered at last.

Giuna stiffened in fury. "He's kidnapped her? That kinless— Lumen burn him to ash! I'll tell the V—" Her anger stuttered as she realized the Vigil would be no help, but then flared back up. "Captain Serrado. Mother can contact him. He'll know what to do."

"You do that," Sedge said, and Tess echoed him, all but shoving the Traementis alta out the door.

Giuna hesitated on the threshold, looking inexplicably guilty. "I'll get her back," she promised.

Sedge's muscles were knotting tighter with every moment Giuna stayed. He jerked his head in what he hoped looked like acknowledgment. The instant she was out of earshot, he muttered to Tess, "Get back inside. I'll check the lodging house." By the redness of Tess's eyes, it had been hours since Ren left.

"Oh, no. I'm done with being left to wait and worry." Tess tossed her woolen over her shoulders and reached to close the door.

Sedge stopped it with one hand. "What if she's baiting us in? Wants all three of us, and we're just handing ourselves to her?" Ondrakja had used them to hurt each other before.

Digging into a basket by the hearth, Tess drew forth a needle, longer than Sedge's forearm and thick as his little finger. She held it up like a dagger. "Then I poke her full of holes. If everything goes twisted, I can run for help."

En't like she's gonna be safe alone here, with the windows done in and Ondrakja who knows where. He'd rather have Tess where he could protect her. "Let's go," Sedge said.

He hadn't been back to the lodging house since the day Ondrakja did her best to beat him to death, but he could have found his way blindfolded. He didn't bother with the escape window, though; no chance he could fit through it anymore. Instead he kicked the front door in.

And recoiled an instant later. The same pulsing dread that haunted the old burial niches in the Depths waited for him in the dim, crumbling interior. *Fuck!*

If Tess felt it, she didn't let it stop her. She hovered close at his shoulder, knitting needle at the ready. "Ren?" she shouted, loud enough to startle any birds in the rafters.

But the birds had already abandoned the rafters, just like the rats and spiders had abandoned the tunnels in the Depths.

"Tess..." Her name caught in Sedge's throat, weak and airless. She didn't hear.

"Ren, we've come for you. Ondrakja, if you hurt her, I'll make an apron out of your skin. See if I don't!"

Sedge forced his paralyzed limbs to move across the threshold, keeping Tess behind him. As he did so, a glint caught his eye. A small throwing knife on the floor, one edge sticky with the putrid violet of zlyzen blood.

Tess's hand stopped just short of snatching it up. Her face was pale enough to make the freckles look like blood spatters. "It's one of her throwing knives. From the apology shawl."

The one the Rook had sent her. There were more knives scattered about—and more zlyzen blood—in the hall, in the kitchen, near the open door from the cellar. But nothing moved; the house was as silent as death.

Sedge wet his lips. "I'm going upstairs. You wait down here." Where there were open doors and quick escapes, if Tess had to run.

"Like hell I will," Tess muttered, and clung close to his backside as they climbed the stairs together.

A faded door drape lay wadded on the threshold of Ondrakja's parlour. The wreckage inside was mostly timeless—broken furniture, shredded upholstery, a mold-damp carpet. But the zlyzen blood was fresh, as were the remains of a glass shattered against a wall. Embedded in that same wall was another of Ren's knives.

"But where is *she*?" Tess said, voice high. She called out, as though there was any hope left. "Ren?"

Sedge stopped her with one hand on her shoulder. "Ondrakja... she can go into the dream. I think she took Ren with her." There were footprints mashed into the rotting carpet, coming into the room. None going out.

His bones ached with guilt and grief. He'd failed her. Again. The

Night of Hells, when he wasn't there; down in the Depths, when he let Ondrakja toss him around like a rag doll. Now this.

Worse. Ondrakja had used him to lure Ren here. To hurt her.

Again.

A dull pain in his side brought him back to the parlour. Tess poked him a second time with her knitting needle. "Stop it. Whatever you're thinking, it isn't true. And even if it was, it doesn't help now. So Ondrakja's got her. How do we get into the dream? Ash? Do we need ash?"

The thought of Tess on ash was enough to snap him out of his spiral. "Ondrakja had cages down in the Depths, where she kept the kids. Might be she took Ren there. I'll look." How high were the waters now? Hopefully still low enough. He could hold his breath if he had to.

Tess chewed her lip, then shook her head. "I don't like you going, but—I'd only slow you down."

Sedge hugged her. "The house en't safe for you, though. Go to those Traementis cuffs. Make them take you in."

They headed downstairs as he spoke, as though the zlyzen blood was pushing them out of the house. In the street outside, people were reflexively avoiding the building, creating an island of empty space in front of its door. Tess stopped in the middle of that space and faced him. "No. If Ondrakja's coming for us, she'll know to look for me there. Plus, what am I supposed to say to them? 'Protect me, but never you mind about Alta Renata'?" Shaking her head, she tucked her needle through her belt like a dagger. "I've friends in Little Alwydd who won't ask questions. I'll tell the corner boys to keep an eye out for you. Come yourself. No notes."

Taking Sedge's hand, she pressed her wrist to his—scar to scar, blood to blood. "You'll find her. And bring her back safe."

Isla Indestor, the Pearls: Cyprilun 35

Gammer Lindworm dragged Ren through city after city—all of them Nadežra, but different turns in the maze. They slogged through a place of water-paved roads and islets of warehouses, a warren of tunnels carved into the fog. They passed whole blocks of smoked-out ruins, ribs of char cracked red and grey, only for Ren to look back and see nothing but a stained glass landscape of green fields and blue waterways.

She didn't fight. She couldn't. This wasn't the horrors of the Night of Hells—but any relief was short-lived, because zlyzen collected around the two of them like a scurry of rats trailing a grain wagon. A few sniffed at Ren's hair, and Gammer Lindworm shoved them aside. "No, this one isn't for you. Once we're done with her, she's *mine*. Aren't you, Renyi? You don't want me to let the zlyzen feed on your dreams, right?"

She didn't seem to care whether Ren answered or not. All Ondrakja's questions had been rhetorical, until they weren't. That hadn't changed when she became Gammer Lindworm.

Finally they came to a fortress carved from glittering sapphire, whose impenetrable stone melted at Gammer Lindworm's touch. She wormed a passage through, to an empty space at the heart. Wrapping her bony arms around Ren, she heaved...

...and they were in the waking world again, Ren cast onto a luxurious carpet. In a room scented with books and beeswax. Before a monolith of a desk.

And a scowling Mettore Indestor.

"I've brought you a gift," Gammer Lindworm said to him. "Well, not a gift. She's mine. But you can borrow her."

Mettore shot to his feet. "I told you, hag—*not here*. And not without warning. Our agreement doesn't mean you can just show up out of nowhere and drop a filthy gnat on my floor."

Ren knew that carpet, that desk. She'd just never seen them in the light before.

Her limbs were weak and shaking after the trip through Ažerais's Dream, and even if she tried to bolt, Gammer Lindworm would catch her. Instead she opened her mouth and screamed.

A boot crashed into her gut a moment later, driving all the wind from her. A fist to the head followed. Mettore stood over her, swearing.

While Ren retched and tried to suck in breath, he shoved a glove into her mouth and secured it with one of the ties from his curtains.

That might muffle any sounds she made, but it wouldn't stop them entirely. Mettore put one boot across her throat and said, "Go on screaming if you like, gnat. My servants know to ignore minor disturbances."

The pressure increased enough that Ren saw spots. Then it was gone, Indestor sliding across his monstrous desk to crash down on the other side. Papers flew, and weights and pens hit the carpet with muffled thumps.

Gammer Lindworm's bony ankles bracketed Ren's rib cage. She'd thrown Indestor as easily as the wineglass. "I said borrow, not break!" she hissed, sounding like her zlyzen.

"And I said that if you touch me one more time, you'll pay for it," he snarled, climbing to his feet.

She only laughed. "What will you do to me? Chase me into my home? You can't follow me there, and if you try, my friends will tear you apart."

Mettore straightened his coat and answered with the cold smile of a man who never doubted his own power and control. "No—I'll just leave you looking like this. You haven't yet found a physician who can give you back your beauty, have you? No matter how much money or how many monsters you throw at them. If you want the medicine I promised, then you do as I say, hag."

The threat made Gammer Lindworm recoil—but only briefly. The smile she favored Ren with was almost as sickening as Indestor's kick. "You see how stupid men are, my girl? He forgets how useful I am. He doesn't even know I've brought him what he needs."

"I have what I need," Mettore snapped. "That slattern—"

"Is Alta Renata."

A moment passed, measured by the *thip, thip, thip* of spilled ink dripping onto the thick carpet. Then Indestor's footfalls as he came around the desk. Gammer Lindworm backed up, allowing him to catch Ren's chin and lift it, fingers digging into the bruises forming there.

"How the fuck..." His thumb smudged hard across her cheek. Her imbued cosmetics were made to withstand that sort of touch. But the disguise always depended primarily on no one connecting Arenza to Renata; once he knew to look, Mettore could see the truth.

His furious glare shot from her to Gammer Lindworm. "And you brought her here? Dressed like this? Why?"

"This is what she is. Always has been, since before she joined my Fingers. My clever Renyi, making you all dance for her, thinking she's one of you." Gammer Lindworm twirled like a young girl. "Oh, how we'll dance together when I'm better. We'll get Sedge and Tess and my new children, and we'll own you all."

Mettore straightened and began pacing. "You brain-addled crone. You kidnapped a— Wait. No. If she's an imposter, then I'm safe. I'll simply tell everyone the truth: that I discovered her crimes, sentenced her, and sold her as a slave." He stopped, looming over Ren once more. She closed her eyes to block out the sight of his fury transforming to satisfaction. "Pity I bruised her face. But I can't sell her to Sureggio anyway—not under the circumstances—and she'll still fetch a fine price, pretty as she—"

His gloating died on a strangled *urk*. "Don't even *think* of selling what's mine," Gammer Lindworm growled, glaring down the length of her bony arm and tightening her grip around Indestor's throat.

Any hope that the crone might forget her strength and go too far was dashed when she released him. "Now give me my medicine, or I won't help you tonight."

"After we're done," Mettore said, trying and failing to keep the rasp from his voice. "You've proven yourself far too unreliable. I can't trust you not to change the plan again."

Gammer Lindworm's lip peeled back in a snarl, bony shoulders hunching for another attack. But then her mood shifted again, and she knelt beside Ren and petted her hair. "It's all right. I can see what he wants; he'll follow through on his plans. Then I will be beautiful again, and we'll be together."

"But not yet." Mettore was smart enough not to touch Gammer Lindworm. Instead he rang a bell, then grabbed Ren and hauled her roughly to her feet. The Rook's shawl slipped from her shoulders; she caught it in her hands, down by her hips, and felt the weight of the last remaining knife in her palm.

One throwing knife. She palmed it an instant before Mettore yanked the shawl away and threw it in the corner. A heartbeat later the door opened and a woman entered. The same one Ren had seen in Horizon Plaza with Mezzan and Breccone Indestris. The same one who'd poisoned Ren and Leato on the Night of Hells.

"Lock her up with the other one," Mettore said. "It's always better to have a spare."

The Shambles and the Aerie: Cyprilun 35

It took until late afternoon for Grey to track down the truth of what had happened to Arkady. She'd been taken, yes—but not by Gammer Lindworm.

"Yer niece has a mouth on her; that's for certain," said the drunk who admitted he was sleeping it off on a stoop when the commotion woke him up. "And I en't just talking about the cursing and shrieking. Snapping at them all like a damned turtle. Near bit the ear off the one with the wine brow."

Grey's hand fisted around the mill he'd offered the drunk for the story, resenting giving over even that much. "You didn't think to stop them from assaulting a child?"

Watery yellow eyes tried to fix on his face, but kept tracking off center. "What's an old sot like me gonna do against three healthy bucks but get his own self beat?" His broken nails scrabbled at Grey's fingers, and Grey relented, opening his hand and letting the old man take the coin.

At least he had a description—one whose significance didn't require any new hunting. One of the captains under Commander

Nalvoccet had a wine-stain birthmark spanning half his brow; his squad liked to rub it for good luck.

Three hawks out of uniform had taken Arkady Bones. But why? What use was one foul-mouthed street rat to the likes of Mettore Indestor?

Before Grey could escape the Shambles to find out, someone else found *him*.

"Captain Serrado. I've been looking for you," Vargo said, sliding smoothly into his path.

"Congratulations on succeeding." Grey knew Vargo's web spread all through the Lower Bank, but he didn't appreciate finding himself caught in it. "If you have official business for the Vigil, leave a message at the Aerie."

"I'm not entirely certain I'd be welcome at the Aerie. Especially not with this message." Vargo smirked. He was waiting for Grey to take the bait and ask—which only made Grey want to strike his smug face.

But Vargo's Isarnah bodyguard looked like she knew her business, so he refrained. "My condolences that your reputation precedes you. I don't have time to help you. A child has gone missing—"

All manipulation dropped away, leaving the hard edges of the man who'd taken over half the city's underworld. "A pile of black powder has gone missing, too. My guess is that you'll find it somewhere in or around the Charterhouse. Do you have time for *that*?"

Grey's breath left his lungs like a boot had struck him in the gut. Not saltpeter: black powder. "Where was it?"

"Before it walked off? A shop in Grednyek Close. Looks like the Stadnem Anduske had it. I imagine you've heard they're planning a protest at the Charterhouse today. Not likely to be coincidence."

Not coincidence at all. But what exactly was their plan? Possibilities flickered through Grey's mind, like cards in the hands of a streetside entertainer: a strike at the Cinquerat, in retaliation for Indestor's manipulation. Or another part of Indestor's plan, a massacre of Vraszenians for some unknown purpose. Even a massacre planned by the Stadnem Anduske themselves, to provoke a true rebellion—one that might prod the rest of Vraszan into retaking Nadežra at last.

Idusza swore Andrejek wouldn't harm his own people...but the rank and file didn't always know what the leadership was doing. And sometimes radicals decided their goals could only be bought with blood.

Just like in the Fiangiolli warehouse. Somebody deciding their own aims mattered more than the life of a Vraszenian carpenter.

But Grey couldn't do anything if he let the memories of Kolya's death drag him under. "Thank you for bringing this to me." Grey was excellent at being polite to people he disliked. He also knew when he wasn't being told the whole story. "Why don't you walk with me and tell me how you got involved in this business."

"I'd love to, but I've been up all night, and could really use some sleep." Vargo choked up on his cane and flicked it in a mockery of salute. "Good work with Breccone Indestris, by the way." Then he was off down the street, before Grey could ask how Vargo had known about that.

Grey made it as far as the plaza before someone else stopped him. Idusza, worse for the wear since he'd last seen her; her face was bruised, and one eyebrow split.

"Why do I even have an office," he muttered as she jerked her chin for him to follow her.

She didn't lead him far, just to a sheltered stoop out of sight of the Aerie's front steps. "Tell me about the black powder," he growled before Idusza could speak.

"You know about that?"

Grey crossed his arms to keep himself from punching the stone threshold and most likely breaking his hand. "I thought Koszar Andrejek was a man of his word. I guess I was mistaken."

"This isn't us!" Idusza hissed. "We stood down, like we promised. Calmed people as much as we could. And we abandoned our plan...but not everyone agreed."

"So they'll still bomb the Charterhouse."

"What?" Idusza recoiled. Then she laughed—a bitter, wild

laugh. "No. The Charterhouse was meant to *protect* our people. Boycott the amphitheatre and give everyone somewhere else to go. But your Seterin friend ruined it. Now Argentet pays for people to go, so everyone flocks there."

The bottom dropped out of Grey's stomach. *The amphitheatre.* That—not the Charterhouse—was the target.

Blow up the Great Amphitheatre, which Kaius Rex had built in an attempt to destroy the wellspring. The site had been a temple once, a huge open-air labyrinth with the wellspring at its heart, appearing every seven years. The Tyrant paving it over was blasphemy—and Vraszenians had never forgotten.

"You have to stop them."

"We tried." Her eyes were bleak. "Two of our people are dead. Another may join them. And Andrejek is too hurt to stand. The ones who splintered off, they're at the amphitheatre, setting the bombs."

Setting the bombs...and blending in with all the other Vraszenians and Nadežrans taking advantage of Scaperto Quientis's generosity. "They would kill our own people?"

" 'Those who suckle at the teat of the oppressors are no people of ours,' " Idusza quoted hollowly. That line had shown up more than once in the Anduske's broadsheets over the years.

"I'll alert the Aerie," Grey said. "You have to go to the elders. Tell them everything. There still might be a chance to get people out. Thin the crowds, at the very least."

Idusza spread her hands. "And to me the ziemetse will listen? They know I am Stadnem Anduske. I won't get near them."

Grey pinched the bridge of his nose. No, the elders wouldn't listen to her. But Grey had been working with them for weeks. They might listen to him.

But he had to warn Cercel, and a little girl was missing. Even if he split himself in two, it wouldn't be enough.

Something had to give.

I'm sorry, Arkady.

Grey pinned Idusza into place with a glare. "Wait here. I'll rally the Vigil. Then we'll go talk to the elders together."

He barely waited for her nod before he was running across the plaza and hurling himself up the stairs. Inside the Aerie, Cercel wasn't hard to find. She stood at the far end of the front room, one of several commanders snapping orders to captains and lieutenants.

When her gaze lit on him, she came to meet him. "Serrado, good. Era Traementis sent a message. She needs your help—"

Donaia would have to wait. *Everyone* would have to wait. "Commander, your office." Grey didn't wait for her acknowledgment, didn't heed her arched brows or the sudden, shocked silence of the officers around her. He just went upstairs, and Cercel followed.

"You better have a damned good reason for this, Serrado," she said, closing the door behind her.

"The black powder I warned you about—it's not going to be used at the Charterhouse. The target is the Great Amphitheatre. Today."

It stopped her dead. "How do you know this? Another 'anonymous note'?"

Grey hesitated. The splinter group of the Stadnem Anduske could go hang—they were willing to murder innocents for their cause—but he was reluctant to give up Idusza or Andrejek. Or, strangely, Vargo.

"Yes. You need to have the commanders send squads to find the explosives if they can and help evacuate if they can't. I'll talk to the Vraszenian elders. They'll know how to get the word out to their people."

He tried to reach for the door—he had to keep moving; no knowing when the splinter group planned to detonate the bombs— but Cercel caught his arm. "Serrado, I can't. Our orders are to muster at the Charterhouse, no matter what distractions try to pull us away. Every squad that isn't on patrol elsewhere."

"There's no threat to the Charterhouse," he snapped.

"But you told me—"

"I was wrong. Commander, we're deliberately being kept away from the real threat."

Her jaw tensed, and he fought the urge to go on talking. He knew Cercel hated feeling like someone had backed her into a corner; the more he argued, the less she would bend. She was the consummate hawk, dedicated to the Aerie above all. But she'd supported him as a constable, championed his promotion first to lieutenant, then to captain. She wasn't Indestor's tool, any more than Grey was.

Finally she said, "Even if I had the authority to send people up to the Point, a flight of hawks landing would just start the riot all over again."

If the Stadnem Anduske had their way, pretty soon a riot would be the least of their worries. "Fine. If you're going to ignore this, then I won't trouble you any longer." He reached for his captain's pin.

Cercel caught his wrist before he could break the clasp open. "Oh, for—"

She bit off whatever she was going to say. Grey could have pulled free, and in another heartbeat he would have. But then Cercel let go and took his pin off herself. "You've been on duty all night. Your whole squad has—not that it stopped Kaineto from getting his beauty rest. Anyone who went with you to arrest Breccone Indestris is officially released from watch at the Charterhouse, with orders to go home and sleep—orders which I'm sure you wouldn't dream of disobeying. I'll reprimand you for stopping a disaster when this is over."

Stopping a disaster. With only Ranieri, Tarknias, and Dverli instead of the assembled might of the Vigil. Meager as it was, he knew he should thank her, but a wave of exhaustion swept away any gratitude Grey might have felt. He'd wasted enough time here, and could only hope the ziemetse would be more helpful.

Giving Cercel a nod that barely touched the edge of civility, he opened her office door. "You may want to hold on to that pin, Commander. I'm not certain I'll want it back when this is over."

Isla Čaprila, Eastbridge: Cyprilun 35

::Are you going to get that? I would do it myself, but...::

Alsius's voice penetrated the fog of sleep. Vargo stirred, mumbling, "What?"

::The knocking. It's Sedge, and he looks...like he wouldn't be disturbing you without good reason.::

Vargo rolled over, groaning. Now that Alsius mentioned it, he realized the steady banging from downstairs wasn't part of his dreams. One cracked eye showed him misty dimness outside his window, which said nothing useful; during Veiled Waters that could mean dawn, dusk, or any hour between. Only the heaviness of his limbs and head told him he hadn't slept nearly long enough. "What time is it?"

::Ninth sun.::

He'd been asleep less than three bells. Swearing, Vargo levered himself upright and fumbled for a shirt, while the hammering continued without pause. Where the fuck was Varuni?

Right. She'd made Vargo promise to stay put long enough for her to survey her people's holdings, making sure nothing had taken serious damage in the riot. Which meant nobody was around.

As Vargo headed downstairs, Alsius warned him, ::Sedge is covered in river filth. Whatever sent him here, I suspect it's important.::

The warning came a heartbeat before Vargo yanked the door open. The smell assaulted him like Sedge's own fist, made even riper by the damp air. Sedge looked worse than he smelled, mud and streaks of moss slime drying on his rumpled clothes. But his eyes were wide amid the dirt, and his body held the tension of a man who wanted to be running somewhere, if only he knew which direction to run in. "The alta's missing. Renata. Tess says Gammer Lindworm took her. I tried to look for her in the Depths, but I—I—"

Fuck. Vargo held the door wider, jerking one thumb for Sedge to come in, filth and all, and slammed it shut behind him. "Where? How long ago?"

"Last night. But I din't know until today. And I din't know where you were, neither, so I just started looking—"

"Excuses later. You were in the Depths? Were you able to get to the place with the cages?" It was the most likely place for that hag to have taken her.

But Sedge just shook his head, and Vargo cursed. If Gammer

Lindworm could move in and out of the realm of mind, could she take passengers with her?

He buried one hand in his hair, thinking. *Alsius?*

::You might as well cover the basics.::

True. It would be stupid to focus on the impossible and miss the obvious. Vargo nodded at Sedge. "Start waking people up. They complain, tell them I en't sleeping, neither—"

Another knock sounded at the door. "What. Now," Vargo growled, shoving past Sedge to yank it open again.

Tanaquis Fienola stood on his front step, swaying. She grabbed for Vargo's lapel, and caught her balance against the door jamb instead when he evaded her hand. "Master Vargo. You have to help me. I can't do it myself—not now."

One look at her blown pupils was enough to tell Vargo what was wrong. This time when she swayed, he caught her. "Why are there aža-spun inscriptors knocking on my door?" he snapped at nobody in particular.

Fienola sagged in his grip, and he helped her slide to a seat on his front step. "Meda Fienola, now really isn't the time. Alta Renata's missing. I need to concentrate on finding her."

"Renata?" She squirmed around, as if tracking the movement of something through the empty air. "Yes. Breccone said—though he wasn't very clear. For an inscriptor, he had a sadly disorganized mind. Very disappointing."

Tired as he was, Vargo didn't miss her choice of verb. Breccone *had* a disorganized mind.

I should have gone after Breccone myself. Now his chance to question the man was gone.

Before Vargo could vent his fury, Sedge shouldered him out of the way and grabbed Fienola. "What did he say about Alta Renata?"

Her wandering eyes managed to fix on his filth-streaked face. "Not much. He died before he could finish. But that's all right; I put the pieces together myself. Maybe there's something to what Vraszenians say, about aža and dreams and pattern—I'd never really considered it before, but I think I—"

Vargo could put pieces together, too. "Meda Fienola, where is Renata Viraudax?"

"I don't know."

Then she put up both hands, forestalling any reply. "But there's a numinat at the Great Amphitheatre. Enormous thing, astonishingly complex—truly an impressive piece of work. Covers the whole stage floor. It will be a very great pity to destroy it, but I suppose it must be done, before it..." One hand described a vague arc through the air. "Does whatever it's supposed to do. Which I assume will involve Renata."

If Gammer Lindworm took her, then Indestor was probably involved. And if Breccone had created such a numinat, then Indestor was definitely involved. Except— "How the fuck didn't Argentet's people notice a numinat in the middle of the Great Amphitheatre?"

Tanaquis blinked owlishly at him. "Because it isn't in this world, of course. It's in the realm of mind."

I can't do it myself. Not now. That was what she'd said. Because she was on aža...which only let you *see* the realm of mind.

To touch it, you needed ash. And taking ash when you were already spun was asking for death or madness.

Sedge's mind was on the goal, not the road there. "If she's at the amphitheatre, then why en't we heading out already?"

"Shut up," Vargo said softly. The realm of mind was beyond any person's control, but at least when he'd walked it through Fienola's numinat, he'd had control of himself. Ash...would change that.

::I don't like this one bit. Who knows what taking ash will do to us—::

"I said, shut up!"

He caught the glance between Sedge and Fienola, but he couldn't reel the words back in now.

Indestris had inscribed numinata all around Seven Knots to inflame the riot. If that was meant only as a distraction, then Vargo was certain he didn't want to let the main event at the Great Amphitheatre play out unhindered. "I'll need ash," he muttered. Standing, he dried sweating palms on his thighs and extended a hand to help Fienola to her feet. "Can you find your way home?"

Instead of answering or taking his hand, she fumbled in her pockets, of which she had an astonishing number. "Where did I put it? Not there. Not there, either. Damnation—how can anyone think aža is pleasant? Ah, here we go." She drew out a vial of oily purple dust. "That should save you time."

It was Vargo's turn to blink in surprise. "Where did you—"

"Breccone's house. Did you know he was the one supplying ash to the streets? Very profitable trade, apparently." Tanaquis cocked her head at Sedge. "I'm sorry; I only have one. The rest were confiscated. But you don't look like an inscriptor."

"The fuck I'm letting you go alone," Sedge said violently to Vargo. "Varuni will drink coffee out of my skull."

::You did promise to stay here.::

"She knows I'm a shifty bastard," Vargo said to the voices inside and outside his head. "Her mistake if she trusted me."

Leaving them on the front step, he ran upstairs to his study for his kit and a dose of ash left over from his experiments, then threw a waistcoat and coat over his shirt and shoved his feet into boots. By the time he got downstairs again, Sedge had Fienola standing.

Tossing one of the doses to Sedge, he politely shoved Fienola out onto the street. "Go home. We'll take care of it." Vargo popped the cork out of the vial with his thumb and, before he could reconsider, tossed the contents back. Sedge copied him a heartbeat later.

As he headed for the Old Island and the looming shadow of the Point, he heard Sedge mutter behind him, almost too soft to hear. "I hope she's right about you."

The Point, Old Island: Cyprilun 35

Ren couldn't tell how much time had passed.

Mettore's underling had shoved her into a padded box that stank of sweat and fear—proof, if Ren had needed it, that he'd done this sort of thing before. The lid slammed shut over her, a lock clicked into place, and a rattling to either side told her poles were being slid through the brackets so it could be carried. After that there was a long, swaying walk, then the sloshing of water as they journeyed by skiff, then more walking. Ren's best guess was that she'd been taken somewhere on the Point, because toward the end it felt like they were walking uphill. But blind, suffocating, nauseous with terror, she couldn't be sure of anything.

When they finally let her out, it was in a cold, stone-carved room with one other occupant.

"The fuck are you?" the girl snarled as the door clanged shut behind Ren. Her hair was limp with oil, her face streaked with dirt. Newly crusted scabs covered her knuckles, and a bruise blossomed around one of her narrowed eyes. She stood with her back pressed into a corner, brandishing a bit of stone chipped from the wall, baring her teeth like she meant to use those as weapons, too.

"Ren." A sudden, hysterical laugh bubbled up. "So this is what he meant when he said I was the spare."

The stone chip wavered, as did the girl's bravado. Not much; just a subtle curling of her shoulders, a tremor in her voice. "You mean you en't one of them?" She dragged her scowl back into place. "Why're you laughing, then?"

Ren slid to the floor. "Because I'm fucked."

Palming the chip, the girl did the same, wrapping her arms around her knees until she huddled like a sparrow in the cold. "You and me both, Ren. I figure we're for the slave marts in Ommainit. The hawks say anything when they nicked you?"

"Hawks took you?" Ren tipped her head against the stone. "Of course. Indestor."

A gobbet of spit hit the ground between them. "Slug-cock. Drew him nekkid once, and that's a crime to sell me for?"

"No. That is not why he wants us. How old are you—twelve? Born in Equilun?"

"Yeah. Why? You gonna read my stars all Liganti-like? 'Cause I'm betting they'll say, 'Yer fucked, Arkady Bones.'"

Ren couldn't help rolling her eyes at the girl. "Do I look Liganti to you?"

Arkady's chin burrowed farther into her knees. "Guess not," she mumbled before pressing her face to them. Ren thought she might be crying, but when Arkady lifted her head, the tears that had been threatening were blotted away. "So what, then? What's he want with us?"

How could she explain? The familiar terror of slavery had been less frightening to Arkady than the unknown void of what her true fate might be. And Ren had ripped that last shred of comfort away.

"I was conceived on the night of the Great Dream," she said. "I suspect you were, too. How Mettore Indestor found out, I know not, but he needs us—one of us, at least. If I'm right..."

She pushed herself to her feet and began to prowl the edges of the room. Only one barred window for air and light, and it was too high for her to reach. But the walls were chiseled out of solid rock, not built from blocks, and the window also let through the faint echoes of revelry, which suggested her guess was correct. "I think we're up on the Point. One of the chambers around the amphitheatre. He plans something with the wellspring."

"En't it the wrong year for that?"

"Yes," Ren said softly, arranging pieces in her mind. Gammer Lindworm. Zlyzen. Ash. "But in the dream the wellspring is always present—I saw it." In her nightmare it had been an empty pit...but when she climbed out, the waters had been there, at the same time as the empty pit.

Ash made it possible to touch things of dream. Fed to someone conceived on the Great Dream, it sent them there bodily.

Had Mettore known that when he dosed her? Maybe that was what he'd been testing for, on the Night of Hells. He clearly knew that Gammer Lindworm could step in and out at will.

Maybe Mettore didn't need to wait for the Great Dream to do whatever he had planned.

Unfortunately, whoever chose their cell had chosen wisely. The window was too small for Arkady to fit through, even if they could find some way to remove the bars. And when Ren boosted the girl onto her shoulders, all Arkady saw was fog.

When she heard approaching footsteps and jangling keys, she readied herself to fight. She didn't like her odds against a guard, armed with nothing more than a throwing knife and a belligerent twelve-year-old. But it was better than lying down and waiting for the end. At least Arkady might—

"No, you don't." A clawlike hand clamped down on Ren's shoulder. Gammer Lindworm had stepped through from the dream layer—*behind* them. Moist, meat-foul breath caressed Ren's cheek. "You think I don't know every one of your tricks?"

In that moment of distraction, the door opened and light flooded the room. Arkady's howl echoed as she launched herself at the shadows on the threshold, slashing wildly with her chip of stone.

Ren kept her revulsion in check and the knife tight against her wrist. Against Gammer Lindworm's strength, there was no point in using it—not right now. Better to wait for an opening.

The guards knocked Arkady down. Her chip of stone skittered across the floor and was lost. Gammer Lindworm made a disapproving sound. "Disgusting little maggot. Doesn't even have your looks to recommend her. Maybe I'll let the zlyzen have her, after you've served your purpose."

Arkady whimpered and scrambled for the questionable safety of the wall. Ren kept her own voice as steady as she could. "Assuming any of us survive. I know Mettore; he'll never restore your beauty. He will kill you. After he kills me and Arkady."

"No," Gammer Lindworm snarled, arm curling around Ren like a liver-spotted shield. "You're not dying, little Renyi. That wouldn't be adequate punishment for what you did to me. A good mother punishes her daughter."

Ren felt the hard lump of the Acrenix medallion against her back. Tricat, the numen of family. Was that why Gammer Lindworm kept calling Ren her daughter?

You are not my mother. But instead Ren said, "A good mother also teaches her daughter. You're smarter than he. If we work together, we can outwit him."

Gammer Lindworm's claws tangled in her hair. "Smarter than you both, you mean. I'll make him use you instead of that filthy bundle of bones over there. That's your punishment. I'll poison you—it seems only fair, don't you think?—and then we'll use you to poison the wellspring. Once it's destroyed, he'll be satisfied."

Ren barely heard the rest of her words. The roaring in her ears nearly drowned them out. "The wellspring," she whispered, lips numb. "You seek to destroy the wellspring."

"He says the gnats will leave Nadežra if there's no pool to swarm around." She clicked her tongue like an old auntie. "That man is obsessed."

Ren's heart thundered against her ribs. She couldn't even fight as Gammer Lindworm pried open her mouth and poured ash into it. The world spun around her—not quite the chaotic unraveling of the Night of Hells, but she could feel the threads sliding past each other, the weave coming loose. Like she could just...*step through*.

Gammer Lindworm sensed it, an instant after Ren moved. "Wait! Stop!" The claws on her shoulder tightened, but melted through Ren's flesh like knives through fog. "Get back here, you horrid little brat!"

Ren stumbled clear, through and outside the circle of the old hag's arms. The zlyzen were there, sinuous and broken and wrong, but there was more than one Nadežra; she'd seen it when Gammer Lindworm hauled her to Indestor Manor.

And if she was born of Ažerais, then she could move through Ažerais's Dream.

Ren turned her back and fled.

Storm Against Stone

Ažerais's Dream: Cyprilun 35

She ran.

Through the darkened corridors of an amphitheatre, while audiences above shouted in crazed approval of the Tyrant's bloody entertainments. Across the Point of stone bare to the sky. Past the shadows of Vraszenian pilgrims climbing the slope to walk the labyrinth around the wellspring and Liganti soldiers behind defensive fortifications, down into the Old Island, shifting between open ground and suffocating trap and a soulless, well-ordered grid of streets it had never been in the waking world.

Through Nadežra. Through all the dreams of all the Nadežras. And the zlyzen chased her, snarling and snapping, but she outran them. Because she was a river rat, and if there was one thing she knew, it was her city.

On and on, faster than her feet could carry her, streets and canals and bridges flashing by, through districts she recognized to ones she didn't, to the northern edges where the stone foundations of the islets gave way to houses built on stilts in the delta mud, the rich farmland that fed the city, and beyond that, glittering under the light of two ever-changing moons, the sea.

Ren stopped, gasping. Nothing was following her anymore.

But the fear still beat at her, ash's song in her bones. Gammer Lindworm could appear out of nowhere. So could the zlyzen. How far would she have to go to escape them? How far did Ažerais's Dream stretch? Did it stop at the borders of Vraszan, or were there countless dream versions of Ganllech, Seteris, all the cities and nations along the Dawn and Dusk Roads?

Would the dream still be there after the wellspring was destroyed? If the dream ceased to exist... what would happen to Ren?

And not just to her, but to the ancestors. The szekani, the part of the soul that kept watch over that person's kin and descendants, and came forth when called by the kanina.

Ivrina Lenskaya wasn't there. Ren hadn't been able to afford proper rites for her; Ivrina's cremation had been done in the Liganti fashion, with prayers for her spirit to ascend to the Lumen before reincarnating once more. But countless other mothers and fathers were, and grandmothers and grandfathers, aunts and uncles, brothers and sisters and cousins. The threads that bound the Vraszenian people together.

She could see their ghosts around her now, vague shadows working the soil, poling barges, fishing the bounty of the river.

As if pulled by invisible strings, she turned back to see Nadežra.

The City of Dreams. Holy site of Ažerais's wellspring. Held for two hundred years in Liganti hands... but all the more precious because of it.

They were going to poison Arkady with ash, then sacrifice her to destroy the dreams of all Vraszenians, past and present and future.

She couldn't turn her back on that. Couldn't give up on it all.

Ren set her gaze on the stone of the Point, rising impossibly high above the river, and began running again.

Running home.

Old Island: Cyprilun 35

The ash working through Sedge's blood felt like a desecrating mockery of the aža he'd taken for his knot oaths. Nadežra crumbled around him, boards rotting with mold, buildings sinking into mud and silt. It sucked at his boots, threatening to pull them off with every step, until Sedge trudged along stooped over, fists clamped around the straps to keep them at his knees. Like the delta itself was trying to swallow him.

It was one of his oldest nightmares. He'd been just a baby when some clam-digger found him in the sedge by the riverbank, but that bastard Simlin used to tell stories about kids swallowed by river mud. Drowning in dirt.

I en't gonna drown. He was too big for that now. Too big for any of this shit.

Sedge tried to focus on Vargo instead, only to find the man fading in and out of sight as the mist swirled thick around him. "Oi! Don't you fucking take off without me again!" Sedge shouted. And maybe it worked, because Vargo firmed up again, like a guttering candle sheltered from the wind.

"It's not my doing," Vargo said. "It's the realm of mind. We're still in waking Nadežra, but the dream aspects we're seeing aren't the same."

"Then get a rope and tie us together. I en't losing you until we find Ren...ata. The alta, I mean."

Sedge did his best to cover the slip, starting as though he'd seen something in the mist. Then, as if he'd summoned it, there *was* something, drifting through the murk like—

Don't think about that. "En't none of it real," he muttered, clinging to that conviction.

Until that prize bastard Vargo said, "Remember Hraček and Yurdan?"

It was real enough to kill. *Fuck.* "Let's find some rope."

The worst part was that he saw both worlds at once, waking and dreaming. There were people around them—real people, not the foggy ghosts of Ažerais's Dream—but in the fog of Veiled Waters it was hard to tell the two apart, and thanks to the ash, both kinds were solid when Sedge blundered into them. He had to rely on instinct to navigate, the layout of Nadežra mapped onto his bones.

And he had to think in symbols. That thing rising to the left, that must be the Charterhouse: a web of ropes, grey and brown and green and blue and a shimmering rainbow strand—red and white, too, though as soon as he tried to look at those bits they were gone. But it was rope. Sedge grabbed Vargo's arm and pulled him toward it.

They barely made it into the plaza before the way became doubly clogged with living people and faceless ghosts. A line of hawks held the steps, some human, some immovable steel statues, others feathered raptors that towered above the crowd.

Then things more monstrous than humans or hawks came roiling down the stairs—a creeping shadow of spider-thin limbs, the remains of bodies hung and burned and drowned, of gouged eyes, split tongues, severed limbs.

Sedge stumbled back, colliding with Vargo. "The fuck is *that*?"

"It's the price." Vargo—the man who always kept his head, who sometimes let himself show anger but nothing that looked like vulnerability—couldn't stop his voice from trembling. "The price we pay to survive in Nadežra. Fuck the ropes. We have to get out of here."

Sedge let Vargo pull him away. The rope web he'd been heading toward was gone anyway, replaced by a red-soaked tower built from the skeletons of dreamweaver birds.

He lost his bearings, but Vargo seemed to be keeping his head against the ash better than Sedge. A sudden blaze of light and heat turned the fog into a steam bath; they were in Suncross. Huge shadows passing overhead were hawks—actual birds, grown a hundred times their size, like the mythical rocs in the stories of Ptolyev the Wanderer. One of the shadows grew larger and larger, blotting out the sun. "Down!" Sedge barked, tackling Vargo to the ground—

—into the path of a wagon, and whether it was real or dream didn't matter, because they'd be crushed either way. Sedge shoved Vargo aside and just barely rolled clear.

A hush fell over the street in the wake of the wagon. Too quiet. Sedge pushed up to his elbows and realized that was because nothing remained alive to make noise.

Only bodies.

Wagons of them, piles, lone ones slumped in the gutter as though they'd spent their last moments crawling toward safety. Their skin was pocked with pustules, nail beds ghastly blue. The stench of vomit choked him.

Then he spotted Vargo, sprawled on his ass and surrounded by plague-ridden corpses. His complexion had gone pale as the people around him, and almost as waxy. His breathing fluttered like a bird's, high and fast, but otherwise the man was death-still.

Sedge staggered over to him, trying to look at the dream and waking worlds both, ricocheting off somebody who swore at him and shoved him to the ground. But at least he was next to Vargo now. "Come on, boss—gotta keep moving."

Vargo didn't even twitch. Just kept staring at the bodies. Whatever had held him together until now, it wasn't working anymore.

Sedge cursed. Vargo was going to kill him for this later, but— "On your feet," he grunted, sliding one arm around Vargo's chest and hauling. *One good thing about ash, I guess—my wrist en't bothering me.* The pain felt distant, like it was off in the dream without him.

Lifting the man wasn't hard, but Vargo was as much deadweight as the corpses, his legs tangling loosely as Sedge lurched a few steps in the direction of the Point.

Dignity, or effectiveness? Vargo usually prized both, but if it came to one or the other—

Sedge shifted his grip, bending his knees and planting his shoulder. When he straightened, Vargo flopped bonelessly onto his back, ass in the air. But at least he wasn't dragging Sedge off-balance anymore, and Sedge started marching grimly toward the amphitheatre.

They'd passed through two more intersections and fled a pack of Vigil riot dogs that might have been real and might not, when Vargo's rapid breathing broke on a shuddering sigh. He went from limp to board-stiff in a heartbeat, and Sedge didn't need his soft "put me down" to stop and set Vargo on his feet.

Off came his coat. It hit the front window of a shop, buttons rattling against the glass. The waistcoat followed, and Sedge worried that Vargo was going to strip naked in the street to escape his disease-ridden clothing, but he stopped at shirtsleeves and breeches.

His chest rose and fell with several deep, deliberate breaths. Then Vargo shook himself, threw his shoulders back, and retrieved his satchel from the ground. When he faced Sedge, it was as though nothing of note had happened.

"Let's go," he said, and struck off up the slope of the Point.

Sedge knew better than to say anything. Not now, not later.

The slope itself wasn't as bad, maybe because it was too steep and too rocky for anybody to live on it, imprinting it with their fears. But Sedge heard people shouting up ahead, in Liganti and Vraszenian both—something about bombs—and he only realized that it must be happening in the waking world when things failed to start exploding. "Shit," he said involuntarily, breaking his own silence. "The black powder—"

Vargo didn't pause in his march, but he glanced over his shoulder, into the impenetrable mass of fog that had swallowed the rest of the Island. "Not the Charterhouse—the amphitheatre." He shook his head. "Serrado's smarter than I thought."

People were running past—real ones, Sedge thought, and one hawk that was too pretty for his own good yelled at him and Vargo to turn around, go back, it wasn't safe. *We know it en't safe. That's why we're here.* He pushed the pretty one aside and accidentally knocked him down, the ash fucking with his ability to judge his strength.

As they crested the Point, they broke clear of the mist, and the walls of the amphitheatre loomed above them. To the west, a bloody haze marked the setting sun.

The mouth of the main tunnel into the building was a maw that ate Vargo, and Sedge a moment later. In the real world there were lightstones here, but the dream made it pitchy black; when they came out of the tunnel into the stands, he felt disoriented by the dim light.

They were high enough to have a good view of the amphitheatre's stage. And through it, too, the ash revealing not just the stage but the ground beneath, visible only in Ažerais's Dream.

"It's not active yet." Vargo's tone was relieved.

"What en't?" Sedge asked—but then he saw. He'd been expecting the bright lines of chalk that he usually associated with numinatria, but these were so dull they almost blended with the bare stone of the dreamscape.

Plus he'd been looking too small. Fienola hadn't exaggerated: the numinat covered the amphitheatre's entire floor.

"Shit," Sedge breathed. "You sure you can fix it? Or unfix it?"

Planting a hand on the rail that marked the boundary of the commoners' benches, Vargo vaulted down to the nobles' boxes and started weaving through the maze toward the low wall at the edge of the stage. "If it's not active, yes. I just need to figure out how to get below the stage and remove the focus before—"

A faint ringing of city bells marked the shift from the sun hours to the earth hours. Sedge knew it was only his imagination that the fog seemed to dim like the sun was vanishing below the horizon; they were weeks past the spring equinox, and the sun wouldn't set for a while yet.

In the waking world, that was true. But in the dream, the bells and that imagined dimming were answered by a flare of violet blue at the center of the amphitheatre: a deep pool of swirling foam and stars that Sedge had only ever heard described... because he'd never been here on the night of the Great Dream.

The lines arcing across the stage caught the light, flashing through the violet-blue-green shades of a dreamweaver's feathers. No, not caught: flared with a light of their own, bright enough to imprint on the inside of Sedge's eyelids. "You... you can still remove the focus, right? To stop it?" he asked.

Vargo's grip on the railing was knuckle white, his face flickering blue light and shadow with every pulse of the numinat. "The wellspring *is* the focus. This just got... harder."

A hiss from the shadows at the base of the wall seemed to laugh in agreement.

Sedge had only childhood tales and Ren's descriptions to go on, but he knew them the moment he heard the sound. *Zlyzen.*

Vargo was as pale as he'd been in the plague street. "Much harder."

Sedge curled his fingers into fists. His knuckles, beat to hell and gone in years of street fights, cracked like fireworks, and his wrist ached like fury. The pain might be off in the dream—but he'd come to rejoin it. "You do what you gotta do. I'll guard your back."

The Great Amphitheatre, Old Island: Cyprilun 35

Ren felt the moment the dream changed.

Time had been slipping—full sun, full moons, no moons at all—but she heard a distant ringing of bells, and suddenly everything flashed to twilight and stayed that way. The light above the Point surged violet and green and midnight blue, a beacon above a sea of fog.

The wellspring, she thought, and panic climbed into her mouth. *Am I too late?*

But the dream didn't shatter, and the light continued to glow. And she refused to give up.

As she scaled the Point, though, things began to leak through. Not nightmares or dreams of a different Nadežra: the waking world, with shrieking crowds of people streaming down the slope, away from the amphitheatre. For a moment she wondered if they'd been dosed with ash—the Night of Hells all over again—but no. Somehow, the waking world was bleeding across the boundary between the realms.

Ren dodged and wove around the people, not sure if they would be physical to her or she to them. Then, up ahead, she saw an all-too-familiar figure.

Grey Serrado stood at the mouth of the tunnel into the amphitheatre, shouting orders and gesturing people away. To get inside, Ren would have to get past him.

She closed her eyes and tried to will the dream to let her step through. To jump, the way she'd done during the Night of Hells, moving to where she needed to be. But when she opened her eyes again, she was still outside.

She was disguised as Arenza. Would that be enough? He'd only seen her briefly, months ago, and had no reason to make the connection. But it was a risk—

The world shuddered around her, like every thread in the fabric had twanged at once. Ren swore. *What will I do—put my masquerade ahead of this?*

No. But she didn't have to.

She'd changed in the dream once before, from Renata's River Dežera costume to Vraszenian clothes and her own natural appearance. Could she use that to make herself a disguise now? Was she enough in the dream for that to work?

Ren hesitantly wove her fingers through the threads of the dream, tugging gently. A mask—that was what she needed. Like the Rook's hood: something to hide the fear and the fallible human beneath.

Something in the dream answered her call . . . but not the way she expected.

Shadows flowed down her limbs, wrapping them in darkness. Not the Rook's costume, though for a moment she thought it was; instead it was overlapping layers of black silk and leather, like the petals of a rose. Threads stretched across her vision and settled into place, a mask of black lace that was rough against her fingers when she touched it, an instant before gloves twined up over her hands.

What did I just do?

She didn't have time to ponder it. She'd disguised herself; that was all that mattered.

The world was shuddering again, harder this time. She set her black boots against the stone of the Point and hurled herself at Serrado.

She took him by surprise, her hip coming in low and knocking him off-balance. He grabbed at her shoulder, but his hand slipped off the leather, and his startled exclamation faded behind Ren as the tunnel swallowed her. A heartbeat later, she emerged into a burst of light the color of a dying dreamweaver. Someone knelt within the lines of a numinat, visible only as a white shirt radiant against the color, and someone else lurched around him, body-blocking zlyzen and hurling them back.

This was only the sixth year of the cycle; Veiled Waters had come, but not the Great Dream. The wellspring existed only in Ažerais's Dream—and so the numinat had torn apart the veil between realms, collapsing dream into reality.

Within its bounds, the waking world had no substance at all. And like ground eroding at the edge of a hole, the threads of reality's fabric were coming apart, the thinness spreading through the amphitheatre and down the Point. What that would do if it persisted, Ren didn't know—but it would hardly matter soon, if Mettore had his way. The wellspring had been forced into reality, and now it was vulnerable.

It shimmered at the center of the vanished stage, offset from the numinat's center. Ren heard its song in her bones: the melody of Ažerais, a soundless hum. Its light shone pure against the poisonous glow of the numinat.

And beyond that light, movement. Three figures, emerging from behind the low façade that served as a backdrop for performances. Mettore Indestor, Gammer Lindworm, and twisting in Mettore's grip, Arkady.

Ren hurled herself down the stairs, over the railing and the wall at the bottom. The figure kneeling in the numinat moved, reaching out to wipe a break through one of the lines, and she realized with a shock like cold water that it was Vargo, his face pale and set with concentration. And the one defending him—that was Sedge, doing his best to keep the zlyzen back so Vargo could work.

"*Traitor.*" Gammer Lindworm's snarl echoed off the amphitheatre's backdrop, reaching Ren's ears with perfect clarity. "All my generosity, all my kindness—and you don't want it. But I know how to break you, my girl. Break you and remake you, and then you'll be a proper daughter for me."

The swirling mass of zlyzen surged, flowing away from Vargo and toward Ren. Not all of them—but enough and more than enough, and the only weapon she had to hold them back with was a single throwing knife.

She ran toward Mettore and Arkady, praying she could outpace the zlyzen enough to at least pull the girl free. But one sticklike claw caught her ankle, sending her somersaulting forward, and a band of pure lightning burned across her back. Every muscle convulsed, leaving her sprawled on the far side of a glowing numinatrian line. She tried to suck air into her lungs, to get her legs to move, but they wouldn't.

The hiss of the zlyzen surrounded her.

Then a sword flashed through the air, turning aside a sharp-toothed maw just as it would have closed on Ren's arm. Blackness occluded her vision; a moment later she realized it wasn't her sight going, but the long, sweeping skirts of a coat.

The Rook was standing over her.

"And people call me reckless." He reached down a gloved hand. "Can you stand?"

With his aid, she forced her muscles to work again. "They're going to throw Arkady into the wellspring," she panted.

But Arkady was fighting back. Mettore had both arms around her skinny waist and was hoisting her into the air, but her wildly kicking legs unbalanced him enough that one of his heels clipped the edge of a line. Ren watched as the same lightning energy shot through his body. He and Arkady both crashed to the ground.

"Stay off the fucking lines!" Vargo shouted, not looking up from his work.

"And people call me rude," the Rook muttered, blade slashing along a zlyzen's flank.

The Rook. And Vargo.

Unless he could be in two places at once, her suspicions had been wrong. Again.

The Rook cast a quick glance at Arkady, who'd kicked the prone Mettore in the head before sprinting off, several zlyzen on her heels. "Getting to them is going to be hard. Do you have a weapon?"

A breathless laugh burst from her. She held up the throwing knife.

He coughed as though trying *not* to laugh. "An impressive thorn, Lady Rose. But maybe you should let me do the pruning while you deal with the worms." He nodded at Gammer Lindworm, who was stalking after Arkady.

"With pleasure," Ren muttered, and took off—this time staying off the fucking lines.

The Great Amphitheatre, Old Island: Cyprilun 35

Kaius Rex had tried for decades to destroy Ažerais's wellspring. Did Mettore Indestor really think he could succeed where the Tyrant had failed?

Given the glowing numinat before him, Vargo had to take the possibility seriously. He'd wasted several precious moments staring at it—not out of fear, he told himself, but because he needed to understand the blasted thing. Everything about it was wrong, from the off-center decagram surrounding the wellspring; to the other numina, Tuat to Ninat counter-inscribed along the earthwise spiral, folding back into Illi, the one-that-was-all; to the outside enclosure, which wasn't a circle at all, but a decagon.

No wonder Vargo could feel the numinat's influence spilling outward: Breccone Indestris had been mad enough to scribe it without a circle to contain its power. The world was unraveling further with each pulse of the wellspring's light, shredding dream into reality into dream again. It was as though the whole world was on ash.

Not yet—but if that numinat isn't taken down . . .

::I'll guide you,:: Alsius said, his voice the only thing holding Vargo steady against the ash.

Hopefully his aid would be enough. Climbing atop the low wall, Vargo waited for Sedge to crouch beside him. At Vargo's signal, they smashed down on the gathering pack of zlyzen and came up back-to-back, all milling arms and striking knees.

"There en't shit containing that thing, so stay clear of the lines," Vargo warned Sedge as they double-teamed the zlyzen blocking the way to the numinat's edge.

"Lines?" His eyes widened in comprehension as Vargo, bracing himself, stepped over the decagon. Cursing, Sedge heaved a zlyzen into two others and followed.

Sedge was strong, his strength amplified by the ash, and he wouldn't be one of Vargo's fists if he didn't have muscles, brains, and loyalty in equal measure. And yet Vargo hesitated to get to work. To trust someone to defend him against the nightmare-hungry zlyzen, when Vargo knew his mind would be a feast for them.

He hauled your ass out of plague-town. Also, you don't have much of a choice.

Digging in his satchel for a rag and a bottle of turpentine, Vargo traced the pulsing lines to find the last numen on the spiral. Ninat. Of course: To end this working, he would have to begin with the numen of endings.

His first attempt to scrub away one of the points of the nonagram met with a white shock of pain that sent his rag and bottle flying and left Vargo reeling. Sedge, grappling one of the zlyzen, managed to kick his tools back toward him.

::Wait for the pulse to dim?:: Alsius suggested.

Vargo blinked hard in a pointless attempt to banish the black spots in his vision, rolled up his sleeves, and waited for a dimming moment to try again. The line cleaned up too easily, leaving his hands stained red. *This isn't paint.*

::Blood?::

Dreamweaver blood. No wonder the carcass at the labyrinth had been drained. How many birds must have died to create this working? Vargo swallowed against bile rising in his throat and moved along the earthwise spiral to Noctat. Impressive, Tanaquis had called the numinat. He would have said insane.

And he was insane, too, for kneeling here like a housemaid scrubbing the floor clean, instead of running the fuck away like a man with any sense of self-preservation. This wasn't what he'd expected, any of it, when he chose Indestor's downfall as the path to his goals. He could only hope it would pay off in the end.

He scrubbed again as the cycle hit the next dim moment, only for the numinat to unexpectedly surge. His muscles seized painfully, and sheer luck kept him from collapsing across the figure in front of him. While he was still recovering his wits and trying to make his fingers open to drop the rag, the damned thing surged again.

"Stay off the fucking lines!" he snarled at Sedge. Protecting him from the zlyzen wouldn't do any good if Sedge wound up cooking him with numinatria instead.

A stream of curses seemed to be telling him it wasn't Sedge's fault, but Vargo didn't much care. He'd gotten through Ninat, Noctat, Sebat, and Sessat; just four more to go, the light of the wellspring surging brighter every time he took one out, like he was freeing it from chains. But the spiral grew tighter as it arced toward the center, giving him less room to maneuver, and there were more than just zlyzen and Sedge making his life difficult: Other people had joined the fray, surging back and forth across the lines, and Vargo wanted to scream at them all to *stop fucking moving* for one minute and let him work.

Then fire raked down his back. His scream echoed Alsius's in his head. Vargo arched, clawing at whatever was clawing him. *Get it off! Get it off!*

More raking pain. His fear was making it stronger.

"Sedge!" But no help came. Vargo managed to curl forward, twisting so the zlyzen's body fell across the spiral where it passed through broken Quinat. The creature convulsed, its talons digging deeper into his shoulders, but then it released him to writhe away. Vargo's arms trembled with the effort to push himself up. Something fluttered against the searing pain along his back, and he hoped it was just his shirt and not tatters of his skin. "Sedge?"

::He went—Vargo, you have to run. There's more of those things coming.::

Zlyzen. Vargo didn't look—didn't want to look. *Lay a red thread around your bed*... The old song pulsed through his mind in time with the wellspring. Red surrounding him, his blood, dreamweaver blood. It would have to be enough. He'd never had anyone to lay down a thread for him. He'd always been on his own.

::I'm here. Please—Vargo—::

"I can't leave it like this. I'm not done. *We're* not done." His back burned as he reached for the rag he'd dropped and crawled along the spiral to Quarat.

It was an echo of the reckless stupidity that overtook him during the riot, but this time he had only himself to blame. A thousand times in his life he could have given up, but he'd paid in his blood and that of others in order to push through. Because he had a plan. A promise to keep. And he would cut down or cut away anything that held him back.

Quarat. The wellspring surged again. Another zlyzen lunged at him, but Alsius's shout warned him, and Vargo dodged in time to throw it across the lines. Tricat. Its energy pulsed wildly, out of time with the rest, scorching his hand as he scrubbed it away. Tuat—

Cold weight landed on his back, crushing him flat. This time he had no leverage to let him roll. The claws tore in, teeth grinding against the bones of his shoulder, and the lines of Tuat's vesica piscis were out of reach. Vargo screamed, his free hand scrabbling uselessly at the zlyzen's flesh.

Then, blessedly, it stopped.

He felt its claws retract, its mouth pull back—and then it leapt clear, leaving him sprawled on the stone, bleeding and broken.

But not quite done.

Vision blurring, Vargo looked around for his rag. There it was, just beyond his hand. Too far away... until Alsius nudged it forward just far enough for him to snag its edge.

Finish it, a voice said.

He wasn't alone. Fighting the darkness that threatened to overwhelm him, Vargo began to crawl.

It was the Night of Hells all over again: a knife in her hand, the Rook at her side, and a pack of zlyzen snapping and clawing all around.

Except this Rook was the real one, his sword flashing silver in the coruscating light. The wellspring was a radiant pool of rippling waters, not a dry, empty pit. And Ren—

She was still afraid. But this time there was more inside her than simple animal fear.

Gammer Lindworm had Arkady, both arms painfully twisted behind her back and the girl too off-balance to kick. Vargo was working his way inward along the spiral, the wellspring flaring every time he wiped away a line—but to Ren's eye there were still too many figures to go, and she didn't even know if what he was doing would stop this collapse, restoring the boundary between the worlds so the wellspring would be safe. She and Arkady were both dosed with ash; they might stay in the dream, might still pose a threat. If they got too close, it would take only a small shove for Arkady to fall in—or Ren.

She didn't think Mettore recognized her. He only saw someone coming to interfere and lurched to his feet, blood matting the side of his head and streaming into his eye. "I will end all of you fucking gnats. Get the fuck out of my city!"

Beneath the lace of her mask, Ren's lip curled. "It's our city, you chalk-faced bastard."

As Mettore charged, the Rook stepped to meet him. Their blades slid until the guards caught with a dull clang. "Get the girl out of here," the Rook said over his shoulder. "Before the zlyzen—"

He had no time for anything else. Mettore's fist went for his hood. The Rook ducked and thrust him away with a boot to the stomach, and the duel began in earnest.

Leaving Ren to stop Gammer Lindworm. Arkady was writhing with all her ash-enhanced might, but against the old woman's strength, it wasn't nearly enough. Ondrakja had years of experience in controlling children, and she only needed Arkady alive, not unhurt. With a snarl of impatience, she stopped long enough to strike Arkady several times, stunning her into a daze.

Ren leapt across the numinat, trying desperately to avoid the lines. But without the Rook keeping them at bay, the zlyzen rushed forward, and her tiny knife didn't have nearly the reach of his sword. Here in the dream, ash did nothing to shield her from pain; agony ripped through her thigh when one of them raked her with a claw.

Sedge bowled into it from the side, knocking the zlyzen across the ground. They both fell onto the numinat, bodies spasming as the energy poured through them. He'd bought Ren time, but at the cost of leaving Vargo alone; red flowered through the white of Vargo's shirt as one of the creatures raked his back. The Rook was busy with Mettore, Sedge was still convulsing, and Ren was the only thing between Gammer Lindworm and the wellspring.

She felt its energy flowing quietly at her back. It would have been reassuring... except she posed as much danger to it as Arkady did.

And Gammer Lindworm knew it. She dropped the girl's limp body at her feet, stained lips curling in a gap-toothed snarl. "You came back. You always do. Back after you poisoned me, back after I poisoned you, back after you ran away in the Depths, back tonight. Or is this what you came for?" Digging a long-nailed hand under her layers of rags, she pulled out the Acrenix medallion, dangling it like she was luring a cat.

The longer Ren could keep the old hag distracted, the longer the wellspring was safe. Vargo was still moving, reaching out for the pulsing Tricat painted onto the stone. But although Sedge had finally wrenched himself off the numinat, he hadn't gotten up.

I have to keep her talking.

"I came back for the wellspring," Ren said, her voice shaking. "For Ažerais's Dream. For my people."

Gammer Lindworm's cackle shattered the air like a physical thing, ripping across the dream and into reality. "Your people? What people are those? You have no koszenie to record your kin. You have no kin." She drew nearer step by step, dragging Arkady along almost as an afterthought. "Your mother's people cast her out because of you. Your mother died because of you. And now? Now you're letting your friends sacrifice themselves for you." Her gaze flicked past Ren's shoulder to where Sedge lay unmoving. "When we're done, all Nadežra, all *Vraszan* will know you destroyed the wellspring. You'll have *nothing*."

Ren's throat closed up. She wanted to deny it, to say it was all lies...but Gammer Lindworm—Ondrakja—had always known how to hurt the people around her. They'd stayed at her side anyway, bound by the ties of their knot, because they were too young and too vulnerable to know any better.

The old woman still wore her knot charm around her throat, tangled in the chain of the medallion. Stained and filthy, but still recognizably the symbol of the thread that bound her to the Fingers.

Threads.

The wellspring's light surged again as Vargo broke another line. And as it did, Ren saw something flickering in the air, like motes of dust coming visible in sunlight.

Lines: not the geometric precision of the numinat, nor the curving path of the ancient labyrinth, still faintly visible in the stone where the Tyrant had chiseled it away. Lines between people. A strong one from Ren to Sedge; faint ones from Ren to the Rook, and the Rook to Arkady. Something powerful from Vargo himself, even stronger than the one from Ren to Sedge, but she couldn't see where it went; then one from him to Ren. The silver thread he'd spun out when he pulled her spirit from the dream.

And a line from Gammer Lindworm to one of the zlyzen.

All the zlyzen were linked to each other, but the thread from Gammer Lindworm was different. And Ren had been trying so hard not to look at the creatures, she'd missed it: a knotted charm hanging around that zlyzen's neck, the ends of the cord lengthened by a bit of rough string. She hadn't seen that charm in five years—but she still recognized it. She remembered throwing it at Ondrakja's feet.

They're her knot.

The zlyzen wearing the charm pounced on Vargo's back, flattening him to the stone, claws and teeth tearing. The Rook was too far away, locked hilt-to-hilt with Indestor; Arkady and Sedge were both limp. And Ren couldn't fight Gammer Lindworm.

But she could lie.

"You're right." Ren sank to her knees, her voice breaking. "I—I have no one. Not anymore. No knot in this city will take me, not after what I did to you." She laughed, a wild, bitter sound. "Even the Traementis will not have me. I got their son killed. I have no one."

She looked up at Gammer Lindworm. "Ondrakja. Please. Take me back."

Ondrakja halted in her approach, eyes slitted in suspicion. "You know you can't lie to me. I always know when you're lying. I can see what you want," she said—but she took a step closer, keening faintly with each breath.

"Not a lie," Ren whispered. "I will swear the oaths. Already you have given me ash—I am ready."

"This won't save your wellspring," Ondrakja whispered, spittle flying from her lips.

But she held out her hand for Ren to swear upon.

Ren interlaced her fingers with Ondrakja's twisted claw and met the woman's gaze. "All our grudges are washed away. Your secrets are mine, and mine are yours. Between us there will be no debts."

Every word of it nauseated her. But she'd made her choice, years ago: to choose her brother over her knot. And Ren would commit blasphemy again to save Sedge, to save the wellspring—to save everything.

She got a close view of Ondrakja's sharpened teeth and a gust of foul breath as the old woman laughed and pulled Ren to her feet, dragging her close. "Yes. We will be as we were when I—"

The gloating cut short. Gammer Lindworm tried to disentangle their hands, to pull back from the embrace, as she saw too late what Ren intended.

It was true: Ren wanted to rejoin the knot. But only so she could use it.

Her fingers wrapped around the charm's cord and tore it from Gammer Lindworm's neck. The Acrenix medallion clanked to the stone, and Ren twisted in the hag's grip, turning all her attention on the zlyzen tearing Vargo apart.

The zlyzen—and the thread running to it. Ren seized that thread and *pulled.*

The zlyzen's head came up. Like a dog heeling its master, it leapt off Vargo's body and slunk toward Ren. Who tore her arm free of Gammer Lindworm's grip just long enough to fold the charm over the edge of her throwing knife and slice through its stained, filthy cords.

"I cut you out," Ren snarled at Gammer Lindworm. "You are part of this knot no more."

Gammer Lindworm's arm closed down on Ren's throat, a heartbeat too late to silence her. Ren's vision flared white as her air and blood were choked off—but the zlyzen shuddered like waking hounds and turned their skull-dark eyes on Gammer Lindworm with feral intensity. She let go of Ren and reached for them, nails clicking like beetle wings. "My darlings, my children."

The nearest zlyzen snapped at her when her nails brushed its flank. She snatched her hand back. "No. No, that's not what you want. You—you're hungry, yes? I have a child right here..."

Ren staggered clear, gasping for air. It was like watching the Fingers around Ondrakja, trying desperately to figure out how to placate her when she was in one of her rages—but in reverse. Gammer Lindworm kept babbling as the zlyzen gathered, prowling closer, abandoning Vargo and Sedge. The Rook dropped Mettore with a hilt to his temple and started to rush toward Ren, but she stopped him with an outflung hand.

Gammer Lindworm retreated farther, one hand fumbling behind her like she was trying to find Arkady. But instead her heel caught Arkady's outthrust leg, and she fell backward, almost into the wellspring.

It was all the opening the zlyzen needed. Eerie in their silence, they mobbed her: rags and flesh and blood and bone, tearing into her with the cruel abandon of children freed from the trappings of civilization.

Ren looked away, unable to watch—and saw that Vargo wasn't moving.

He was on the far side of the wellspring, past Gammer Lindworm and the zlyzen, just out of reach of the numinat's last element. Desperate, Ren laid her hand on the line that connected them. Pouring herself into that thread, she cried, *Finish it.*

Amid the shattered lines of the numinat, Vargo stirred. Dragged himself the last few inches to the final figure . . . and swiped part of it away.

The poisonous light went out.

Only the wellspring blazed, pure and bright—and then fading, as the veil between the realms began to knit itself back together, restoring the waking world.

Including the stone of the stage, above their heads.

Ren leapt for Arkady, ash-fueled strength helping her throw the girl over one shoulder. Then Sedge, whose solid weight should have been far too much for her to move. The Rook grabbed Vargo's limp and bloody form, and—after a hesitation so brief she almost missed it—Mettore Indestor.

Side by side, they scrambled up to the solid part of the floor, past the borders of the dead numinat. Just before the wellspring faded away entirely, Ren turned and hurled the broken knot charm toward the remains of Gammer Lindworm.

The zlyzen turned to look at Ren—and then they were gone.

24

The Face of Balance

Ren hauled herself over the wall separating the lowest seats from the stage and clung to its top for a moment, wishing she could collapse. But the Rook was lifting Sedge up to her, then Vargo, then Mettore. Finally, he slung a dazed and sniffling Arkady onto his back and climbed over the wall himself.

Ren's gaze went from her throwing knife to the unconscious Mettore. She knew all too well how often money and power kept the guilty safe in Nadežra. The edges of the knife dug into her fingers: the blade was small, but it was enough to cut a throat.

Before she could make up her mind, the Rook was there, one gloved hand coming to rest on hers. "We don't kill," he said softly.

Her jaw tensed beneath the lace of her mask. *You don't.*

She'd killed Ondrakja. She could have pretended the first time didn't count, because the woman had survived. But Ren had murder in her heart then, and again when she smiled and lied and begged to be tied back into the knot. *I'm a murderer and a knot-cutting traitor twice over.*

"I know," she whispered. "But..."

"But how do we make certain he answers for what he's done, and tried to do? I've been struggling with that question for two centuries." His hand curled into a fist and dropped to his side. The Rook's sigh was layered with years of regret. "If you have any suggestions, I'm happy to take them."

Ren stared down at Mettore. She could kill him; to say she didn't have that in herself would be a lie.

But she didn't *want* to go back there. To the cold, empty place where she could commit murder and call it justice.

Justice.

Her gaze came up, searching the shadows beneath the Rook's hood. "Give him to the Vraszenian clan leaders."

In the moment of stillness that followed, she thought he was about to laugh at her suggestion. And he did—but it was tinged with admiration. "You wear the mask of Ažerais's rose, but I think you're more like Clever Natalya. Yes. I'll take him to the elders, and we'll let the Cinquerat try to save him from *their* justice."

Gripping an arm and a leg, the Rook lifted the unconscious Mettore over his shoulder. "I'll also make certain he doesn't share any secrets that need to be kept."

Ren couldn't stop her gaze from flickering to Arkady, now curled into a tight ball in the corner of the nobles' box, watching them with wide eyes. Arkady didn't know Ren was Renata...but she knew Ren had been with her and vanished.

The Rook's hood dipped, following Ren's glance. "I think everyone here knows the value of a secret kept," he said.

Arkady's eyes narrowed in calculation. Ren could almost see her pulling the tattered remnants of her street bravado over the awe of a child in the presence of an old legend...and, judging by the look she gave Ren, a new one.

"Yeah, I know when to yap and when to say nothing," she said, rising to her feet. "En't gonna do me no good if people think I was yowling like a nipper." She scowled in warning at Ren. "Not that I was."

It seemed Arkady Bones had her own secrets. Ren struggled not to laugh. "Of course not," she said.

A smile glimmered in the shadows of the Rook's hood. "Ažerais bless you, Lady Rose. And thank you."

She didn't watch him go, turning to Sedge, who was groaning his way to wakefulness. Vargo was still unconscious, and torn up far worse than Ren had thought. But his pulse held steady, and when noise at the entrance to the amphitheatre heralded the arrival of a few cautious scouts coming to see what had happened, Sedge shoved vaguely at her, saying, "Go."

Ren left the two men in Arkady's care and faded into the shadows.

The ash seemed to be gone from her body—burned out by the numinat, maybe. The world outside was quiet and real. Once she was clear of the Point and down among the buildings of Dusk-gate, she pulled the mask off her face, trying to figure out where she should go and who she should be when she got there—and what to do with the disguise that had apparently come with her.

But when the mask came off, the black clothing faded like mist, leaving her dressed as Arenza once more. The only bit that remained was the lace mask itself, tatted in a pattern of roses.

Nadežra: Cyprilun 36–Fellun 7

The news that Mettore Indestor had intended to destroy the Wellspring of Ažerais and blame it on the Stadnem Anduske's bombing—which would coincidentally bury the evidence of his numinat—nearly sent the Vraszenian population into armed rebellion.

If the Cinquerat had made their usual response, speeches and platitudes for the masses while negotiating a deal with the accused behind the scenes, the city would have burned. But the Cinquerat couldn't negotiate with a man they didn't have. And by the time they knew where he was, Renata Viraudax was very publicly accusing him of every crime under the sun, from kidnapping her to fomenting riot to poisoning the Cinquerat and all the others during the Night of Bells.

It was exhilarating, in a way she hadn't been able to enjoy for weeks. A whirlwind of lies and truth—the lies mostly to cover truths she dared not reveal. Ren couldn't admit she'd been at the amphitheatre, so instead she spun a tale of imprisonment in Indestor Manor. She'd discovered Mettore's plan—a claim Scaperto Quientis was only too happy to back—and so Indestor sent his minion Gammer Lindworm to kidnap her before she could warn anyone else. "The Rook freed me," she told Ghiscolo Acrenix, Sibiliat's father, who'd been appointed by the Cinquerat as a neutral party to investigate the affair. "I know he's an outlaw, but I must say I'm grateful; without him, I might still be trapped."

When Gammer Lindworm's body resurfaced in the amphitheatre, spat out by the dream, Mezzan tried to blame her for everything. To hear him tell it, Ondrakja had been the lead conspirator, controlling his father with her ability to step in and out of the dream. But if Nadežra's elite were reluctant to admit one of their own had engaged in such flagrant crimes, they were even less willing to admit he might have been the pawn of a Lacewater criminal known for running a knot of child thieves. Especially once Tanaquis corroborated Renata's testimony, along with Grey Serrado—and, unexpectedly, someone Ren recognized. The fair-haired woman she'd seen working for Mettore was delivered to the front step of Acrenix Manor, bound and gagged and eager to confess to whatever the authorities wanted. Ren thought at first that was the Rook's doing, but when she mentioned it to Sedge, he simply said, "Vargo."

And that was all he said, beyond assuring her that Vargo would live, when he showed up at the kitchen door with a rucksack and no Fog Spider charm knotted around his wrist.

Almost all. "It's like you said," he muttered, touching the inside of his bare wrist. "Make me choose my sister or my knot, and I'm gonna choose my sister. Every time."

The fresh bruises on his face told Ren there was more to the story. She'd fled after betraying the Fingers, but Sedge had gone back to the Fog Spiders after abandoning Vargo in order to defend Ren at the amphitheatre. They would have punished him before letting him go—and she suspected it was only Sedge's long service that kept it to mere bruises.

But he didn't want to say more, not yet, so she didn't push.

They retrieved Tess from Little Alwydd, and then Ren had to go to Traementis Manor to explain to Donaia and Giuna what had happened—and to be wept over in their relief.

Despite all the testimony against him, when word came that the Vraszenian leaders had executed Mettore, the tension almost erupted into war once again. Ren suspected the only reason the Cinquerat didn't retaliate was because they too had been poisoned on the Night of Hells. Nadežra's leaders might be willing to overlook Mettore's crimes against everyone else, but his conspiracy had made *them* suffer, too. Much easier to make a show of rapport, and turn House Indestor into a very public scapegoat.

When they put their minds to it, the Cinquerat were astonishingly efficient. A bare eight days after the near-destruction of the amphitheatre and the wellspring, they gathered in the Charterhouse to deliver their verdicts.

It was natural irony that this happened in the same audience chamber where they'd held the Ceremony of the Accords. But this time there was no pageant, no Vraszenian presence, no wagon bringing tribute; instead the benches were filled with nearly every noble and delta scion in the city. Renata sat with Donaia and Giuna and Tanaquis, all dressed in their sober finest, to hear how the Cinquerat would address Mettore Indestor's crimes.

The first part surprised no one. By unanimous decision, the Cinquerat posthumously stripped him of the title of Caerulet. They couldn't address crimes of this magnitude without a full set of members. In theory, the seats were supposed to be filled by vote of the current members; in practice, they were almost always hereditary. So when they announced Eret Ghiscolo Acrenix as the new Caerulet in place of Mezzan, it was a harbinger of the fate to come.

From there, each seat addressed Indestor's crimes. Argentet went first, and Sostira Novrus was only too happy to set the tone with vicious aplomb.

"For the crimes of spreading seditious literature and lies that resulted in inciting the populace to riot, and conspiring to destroy two of the city's cultural treasures—the Great Amphitheatre and the Wellspring of Ažerais—Argentet affirms the guilt of Mettore Indestor, Eret Mezzan Indestor, House Indestor, and all those inscribed in that register."

She was performer enough to wait through the astonished murmurs that followed. An individual could commit a crime and not have it touch their house. To condemn an entire register was shocking.

And devastating for the house, as became clear when Sostira continued. "All charters granted to House Indestor by Argentet are revoked; all administration contracts are suspended until those charters can be transferred to other parties. Let this be a lesson to those who threaten the stability of rule in this city: Such treason will not be tolerated." She resumed her seat with a satisfied smile.

Scaperto Quientis had been listening to her verdict with a stoic frown. As he took his place at the podium, that frown deepened. "Argentet's sentence is harsh, but just." His arched brow added *surprisingly so.* "Fulvet concurs. For the crimes of inciting the populace to riot, damaging civic properties and institutions, and endangering the citizenry during the Night of Bells and Veiled Waters, Fulvet affirms the guilt of Mettore Indestor, Eret Mezzan Indestor, House Indestor, and all those inscribed in that register."

His sentence was the same: the loss of all charters. Prasinet, Caerulet, and Iridet delivered their verdicts with less relish, but by the end of the litany, House Indestor had less to call their own than a Lacewater beggar.

With one exception: their charter of ennoblement.

Quientis stood once more, his face grave. "These are extraordinary measures—but so, too, are the crimes of House Indestor. The members of the Cinquerat have conferred, and our agreement is unanimous. By our conjoined authority, we revoke the ennoblement of House Indestor."

The audience chamber erupted into noise, almost drowning out Quientis's words as he went on to say, "The name Indestor is taken from them, and their register will be burned."

Donaia clutched Renata's hand, swaying in her seat. She'd arrived at the Charterhouse with the stony expression of a woman who didn't dare hope for anything better than a slap on the wrist; she knew as well as Ren did what form the Cinquerat's justice often took.

Now that stone cracked into a smile as viciously pleased as Sostira Novrus's, and for a flash, Ren was reminded of the Traementis reputation for vengeance. She'd seen very little of it in Donaia, Giuna, or Leato . . . but traces clearly remained.

Her sheen of tears, though, spoke to something deeper than simple vengeance. "Good," Donaia whispered. "Now you've had justice, my bright boy. Now you can return to the Lumen." Giuna hugged her mother hard.

Era Destaelio took her colleague's place. "Full distribution of the assets formerly belonging to House Indestor must await proper tallying, but—"

"Your Charity." Eret Acrenix interrupted her with a bashfully raised hand. "If I may?"

Confused, she ceded the podium to the new Caerulet.

Unlike the other four, Acrenix wasn't robed in the colors of his seat. But his elevation had clearly come as no surprise; his creamy silk coat was embroidered in tasteful lines of sky blue, a nod to his new role, and his gloves matched perfectly. He curled them around the edges of the podium and spoke.

"With the indulgence of my new colleagues, I wish to raise one matter before we conclude our business here. My first proposal as Caerulet, I suppose. That title . . . will take some getting used to." He smiled, managing to look almost self-deprecating for a man who'd just been elevated to the highest level of power in the city. It broke the tension that had gripped the audience since the verdict, and the chamber echoed with soft laughter.

Renata's skin pricked with unease. She glanced at Quientis, but he looked as baffled as she was. Everything else that day had been coordinated in advance...but not this. Not with him, at least.

Pulling out a set of spectacles and a scroll, Eret Acrenix said, "The Cinquerat punishes with one hand, but it rewards with the other. I propose a reward for an individual who put his life at risk to stop this dreadful plot, and who provided the evidence necessary to prove Indestor's guilt beyond any doubt."

He held up the scroll, letting it unroll enough for the gathering to see the lines of elaborate calligraphy that filled it—and the seal of sapphire-blue wax below. "I have here a charter of ennoblement. I call on the other four members of the Cinquerat to put their seal next to mine and affirm a noble title for Master Derossi Vargo."

The entire chamber gasped. Ennoblement for Vargo...Ren shook her head in shock. She couldn't deny that he'd risked everything to stop Mettore, and nearly died for it.

But he was a Lower Bank crime lord. Raising him to the rank of delta gentry would have been astonishing, but this? And yet Utrinzi Simendis was pressing his seal into the charter, with Cibrial Destaelio just behind him as though the two of them had known what was coming. Sostira Novrus looked like she was drinking river mud while she did it, but she made no objection. Quientis was last, and the look he gave Acrenix echoed Ren's thoughts: *What's going on here?*

"It is done," Acrenix said when the last seal had been affixed. "Bring in Derossi Vargo."

Everyone turned to the opening doors. Renata half expected to see a litter waiting: Vargo would hate the indignity of being carried in, but it was a miracle he'd survived his wounds, and even imbued medicines could only do so much.

And yet he sauntered through the doors as though he'd never suffered an injury in his life. The cane that ticked against the marble floor was an affectation rather than a necessity. He was dressed impeccably as always, in deep blue velvet that echoed the brighter blue of Caerulet's seal, and a spot of color at the edge of his collar said he'd even brought his spider with him.

Ren thought of the scar on his neck, and what Sedge had said the day they went into the Depths. *We all thought he was dead as Ninat, but he's up and walking the next day like he's fucking Kaius Rex.*

Vargo stopped in front of the podium and bowed to the five before him. "I attend at the Cinquerat's pleasure," he said, his voice as smooth as a West Channel eel.

Acrenix held up the charter. "For your services to this city, the Cinquerat of Nadežra elevates you to stand among those dedicated to its protection and improvement. With this charter of ennoblement, you may seek and hold charters, grant their administration as you see fit, bear a sword in defense of your honor and your life, call upon the services of the Vigil, request that any crimes of which you are accused be tried by the Cinquerat, appoint an advocate to speak on your behalf, and keep a register of those protected by your name. What name do you wish your house to be known by?" He held a pen, ready to fill the blank space at the top.

Vargo tucked his cane under his arm. "Just Vargo is fine. No need to get fancy."

That earned a nervous laugh from the assembly. Every noble house took a Seterin-style name; it was part of how they marked themselves apart from the delta gentry and common Nadežrans. But Ghiscolo made no comment; he wrote the name in, sanded it dry, and stepped down from the podium to hand the scroll to Vargo with an avuncular smile. "I realize this must be an overwhelming honor. If you need an inscriptor to start your register—"

Vargo ran a gloved thumb over the five wax seals. "No need, Your Mercy. I can do it myself."

I'm sure you can, Ren thought, dazed. He was certainly inscriptor enough to manage that—a fact many more people were aware of now.

In one great leap, he'd taken himself from the fringes of high society to its very center. She'd known he was ambitious...but not that it went this far.

Vargo retired to the benches, Era Cleoter grudgingly shifting closer to her wife to make space for him. "My apologies, Your

Charity," Acrenix said to Era Destaelio. "But I felt that, as we're about to acknowledge those who contributed to bringing these crimes to light, this should be taken care of first."

"Of course," Destaelio said. The new Caerulet bowed her toward the podium and took his seat once more.

She drew a deep breath, gathering up the scattered threads of her purpose. "As I was saying. Full distribution of the assets formerly belonging to House Indestor must await proper tallying, but the Cinquerat wishes it to be known that they will reward in full those who have served the city in these dangerous times—and those who have suffered as a consequence: Era Sostira Novrus, Eret Scaperto Quientis, Eret Ghiscolo Acrenix, Eret Utrinzi Simendis, Meda Tanaquis Fienola, House Traementis and their cousin by blood Alta Renata Viraudax, and Eret Derossi Vargo. All these people will be compensated and rewarded from the assets of the former House Indestor."

Giuna's head came up from Donaia's shoulder. "What does that mean?" she whispered under the drone of the rote formalities that signaled the end of the Cinquerat's proceedings. "We didn't do anything. Did we?"

"We lost family," Donaia said slowly, her furrowed brow a mirror of Giuna's. "Leato was my heir; that would be enough to bring suit against Indestor's assets. They really are slamming the book closed on this one."

Giuna had avoided Ren's gaze for the past week, but now she met it squarely. "They should have given you an ennoblement charter, too. I'm sorry...cousin. You deserve better than that."

Donaia reached for Renata's hand and gripped it tight. "And you will have it. There's more than one way to join the nobility of Nadežra—and no one can say you haven't fulfilled your promise."

Tears pricked unexpectedly as Ren inhaled. "I...thank you."

They still didn't know the truth about her. But the weight of that truth had changed. And as Leato had told her, just because she wasn't their cousin by blood didn't mean she couldn't earn a place among them—if she tried.

The Charterhouse, Old Island: Fellun 7

Of course that wasn't the end of the matter. With so many earth-shaking decisions handed down, everyone had to spend at least an hour milling about the Charterhouse, gossiping and adjusting to the new balance of power.

Many of them flocked to Ghiscolo, as the new Caerulet. But nearly as many came to the Traementis, full of smiles and congratulations and commiserations on their loss—because now that their chief enemy was gone, and some unknown percentage of his assets would be coming their way, the Traementis were worth paying attention to again. Renata half expected Donaia and Giuna to quit the field rather than stomach such blatant hypocrisy, but Donaia knew how the game was played, and Giuna was learning. They painted smiles on their faces and did their part.

As did she. No one knew the full scope of her involvement, of course. Rumors were circulating about the "Black Rose" who'd been seen at the amphitheatre, and some of those rumors claimed the Rose, not the Rook, was the one who'd delivered Mettore Indestor to the Vraszenians. But Renata Viraudax had spent that eventful night locked in a cellar room at Indestor Manor, doing nothing of significance at all.

Still, her testimony had been a large part of what damned the Indestor, and all the groundwork she'd laid in the months leading up to this moment was paying off. It was at least two bells before she had a breath to turn around and survey the room...whereupon she found Vargo strolling in her direction.

The handle of his cane touched his brow in salute, and his dark, kohl-rimmed eyes glittered with the self-satisfaction of a spider who'd just snared an entire cloud of flies in his web. "Alta Renata. You're looking improved from your ordeal. My apologies for not coming to your rescue, or checking on you afterward. I've been...occupied."

"Busy healing, it seems. Or were the reports of your near-death exaggerated?"

He spread his arms, showing off the fine tailoring and fabrics of his ensemble as much as the health of the body within. "As you can see. Gossip loves a dying man more than one who's only a little scratched. But I'd be happy to accept any sympathies you care to offer."

It was the same flirtatious behavior he'd tempted her with when they played nytsa. It was also a lie. She'd seen him; she'd washed his blood from her hands. Her own thigh still ached where one of the zlyzen had clawed her, and that was nothing next to what he'd suffered.

But she couldn't call him on it. If he wasn't the Rook...then he didn't know the truth about her.

She hoped. Because if he wasn't the Rook, she also had no way to gauge how deep the ruthlessness ran.

"Congratulations on your elevation," she said, trying to keep her tone light. "It's true that 'man nearly dies saving holy site; receives his reward' does have a better ring than 'man gets slightly scratched saving holy site; receives his reward.'"

His smile twisted and he looked away, scanning the gossiping nobility with a shadow of the disdain she'd seen at Mezzan's betrothal party. "Yes, but both are an improvement over 'man happens to save holy site in pursuit of his own interests.' And with this lot, aren't we all one slip away from that sort of shredding?"

People had been approaching him, too. But from what Renata had seen, it was with the same wary fascination that one might study an exotic animal from somewhere along the Dawn Road.

If anyone could shrug that off, though, he could. She said, "Speaking of shredding...I suppose you'll want to tear up our advocacy contract. You don't need me to gain access to charters any longer."

"What makes you think that? Access doesn't mean anyone's going to *give* them to me. Besides—" Laughter warmed his words like brandy. "I've been enjoying our partnership. Haven't you?"

She had. But balanced against that was Sedge's bruised face, and the uncertainty about what Vargo was hiding.

Whatever it was, she stood a better chance of uncovering it if she stayed near him. "Perhaps the contract can remain undamaged, then. You, on the other hand…" She nodded past him to where Carinci Acrenix sat, eyeing Vargo like he was wearing his Night of Bells costume again.

Following Renata's nod, Vargo paled. *Now* he looked like a man who'd nearly been clawed to death by zlyzen. But he shook off his frozen dread with a cleared throat and a straightening of his cuffs. "Yes. Right. Remind me why I agreed to this?"

Without waiting for Renata's answer, he headed toward Carinci, though without his previous swagger.

"Studying the competition? You've proven yourself remarkably skilled at making Nadežra dance to your tune, but that man…"

It was Sostira Novrus. Motioning for her heir, Iascat, to hang back, she glided up to Renata's side, still dressed in the silver and pearl-grey robes of Argentet.

She ought to have looked pleased. Despite Mettore's efforts to make sure House Novrus took as much damage as possible from his schemes, the feud with Indestor had ended decisively in her favor. Her expression, though, was cool and calculating.

"There's no competition here, Your Elegance," Renata said, and began to step away.

But Novrus's next words stopped her. "Do you think any of this was an accident? Ennoblement charters don't fall from the sky—nor are they granted out of simple gratitude. Ghiscolo and *Eret* Vargo have been working together toward this end for some time now." She paused just long enough for Renata to fumble for an answer, then added, "Assuming this is the end."

So much for enjoying the glow of success. "One might almost think you were worried, Your Elegance," Renata said. "Not only about an alliance between Vargo and Acrenix…but Vargo and Traementis. Your attempt to drive a wedge between us is sadly transparent."

Sostira caught her, one hard-fingered hand gripping Renata's wrist so she couldn't escape without making a scene. Ren almost used a river rat trick to break her grip, and never mind the scene; it would have been worth it to see the woman's shock. But she held still as Sostira leaned in and spoke in a low, intense murmur.

"I'm not going to insult your intelligence by assuming you're ignorant of the man's origins, and how he made his fortune. Apparently, it doesn't bother you that he'll kill his enemies without a second thought. Or take someone's money in exchange for planting contraband on a rival's property, and then someone else's money to blow that contraband up. Or use every secret he holds as blackmail—perhaps because he's persuaded you that he'd never do such things to *you*."

Her thin lips bent in a venomous smile. "But he will, my dear. He already has."

Ren knew exactly what reaction Sostira wanted, but she couldn't stop the bottom of her stomach from dropping. "What do you mean?"

Sostira let go of her wrist. The hold wasn't necessary anymore, and they both knew it. "That invitation to the Ceremony of the Accords. It came from him, didn't it? Did you ever stop to wonder where *he* got it from?"

Trade secrets, Vargo had said. A flirtatious echo of her own comment to him—but he'd never answered properly.

"Mettore Indestor gave it to him," Sostira said. "And paid him with administration of a military charter through House Coscanum. All in exchange for making certain *you* would be present at the Charterhouse on the Night of Bells."

Ren stood mute. Every instinct told her to say something, *anything*, to hide that Sostira's knife had found its mark. But she couldn't find any words.

Novrus made a small, pleased sound. "Think about that, my dear." She patted Renata on the cheek and turned away. At a snap of her fingers, Iascat joined her, and together they glided off.

Ren began walking, too. She came to a set of stairs and climbed them, not caring whose offices she was headed toward; the hallways upstairs were mostly silent and deserted, and she needed to be alone so that no one would witness it when her mask shattered.

Vargo. Mettore. The Night of Hells.

Mettore had wanted her for his schemes...and Vargo had *known* it.

I suspect my association with you had something to do with it. Vargo's words when he told her about the military charter with Coscanum. At the time, she'd thought it was flattery.

But he'd sold her out.

That entire night, playing cards at Breglian's. His injured knee—an injury that suddenly ceased to trouble him when she told him about the missing saltpeter, but she'd thought that was because concern over the danger had taken precedence. Now, in hindsight, she saw it for what it was: a performance.

All of it was a performance. The little slips that made it sound like he was covering for something. His pretense of concern for her. He'd figured out that she thought he might be the Rook, and he'd used that to his advantage, luring her into trusting him. Playing the same game she'd played with the Traementis. The whole night had been nothing but manipulation—not honest friendship and flirtation, but a deeper game whose existence she hadn't even suspected.

She'd been so blinded by her own assumptions—by her conviction that she was too good a player to be played, and her desperate wish to have *someone* else she could trust in her life—that she'd never realized he was using her, every step of the way.

Ren staggered to a halt, breath coming too rough and fast; her fingers flexed against the cold surface of a marble column to hold herself up. Only the awareness that someone might come along let her pull herself back together.

When she did, she realized someone *had*.

He stood at a safe distance—safe for her, to run if she felt the need. To know he wasn't a threat. A shadow out of place in the sun-lit marble halls of the Charterhouse.

He put his hands up in a gesture of truce. "So much for my assumption that it would be quiet up here, with everyone occupied downstairs. You do have pattern's own knack for stumbling into my business."

Of course. What better time to break into the Charterhouse than while everyone was distracted?

She had an impulse to lash out with some kind of vicious response. But it wasn't the Rook's fault that she'd let Vargo turn her into his puppet.

Still, her attempt at courtesy came out brittle. "Thank you. For the other night."

"I should be thanking you. You rushed in to save everyone." The hood tilted. He stepped closer, his soft tone laced with concern. "Even I am pleasantly surprised by the thoroughness of the Cinque-rat's verdicts. You're not?"

A hundred different words all stuck in her throat. She couldn't admit the truth to him, not yet. Because she had no idea who was under that hood—who was walking around with full knowledge of her lies. And that was bad enough, without confessing her mistakes to him as well.

"Well, I hope you'll be pleased by this." Digging into his coat, he pulled out a tightly wrapped roll of black, threaded with color-ful embroidery. "I was going to have your corner boy deliver this. I managed to retrieve it before any of Indestor's staff found it."

For half an instant, she thought it was her mother's lost koszenie. But no—that was gone beyond retrieval. What the Rook held was the shawl he'd given her, in apology for that night in the kitchen. As Ren accepted it, he added with a slight laugh, "I'm afraid you're on your own for replacing the knives, though."

The kindness made her vision swim. Ren blinked it away, try-ing to think of something she could do for him in return. Without knowing who he was, how could she know what he wanted?

The Fiangiolli fire.

She clutched the shawl convulsively to her chest. The Rook stiff-ened. "What's wrong?"

"Vargo," she whispered.

Leather creaked as his hand curled into a fist. "What about Vargo?"

The warmth of his tone was gone as if it had never been. Whatever the Rook might have felt about Vargo before, today's events had put him into the ranks of the nobility. The Rook's enemies.

Take someone's money in exchange for planting contraband on a rival's property, and then someone else's money to blow that contraband up. That was what Novrus had said. And Vargo had twice reacted oddly when Ren brought up the fire.

She looked up, into the shadows of the hood, trying to meet the place his eyes would be if she could see them. "I think the note you found was from him. Or about him. He's the one who put the black powder in the Fiangiolli warehouse, then set it off. He's the reason Kolya Serrado died."

The Rook didn't move, not even a breath—yet she felt the shift, the cold radiating from him like a moonless winter night. *We don't kill,* he'd said to her.

For the first time, she questioned it.

"I see," he said, softly enough that she only heard it because the hallway was utterly silent. "It seems I have even more reason to take an interest in Eret Vargo."

Ren straightened her shoulders. "We both do. Perhaps we might assist each other going forward."

"No." The Rook stepped back. "Enough people have been hurt already. I'll take care of this one myself."

The retreat—the rejection—felt like a slap. But before Ren could say anything, laughter came echoing up the stairwell. Without a word of farewell, the Rook moved rapidly across the marble hall, through a door that Ren expected to be locked, and was gone before the trio of clerks crested the landing.

The Charterhouse, Old Island: Fellun 7

The Rook knew the Charterhouse: not only as it was now, but as it had been since the seven clan statues were knocked down and the five faces of the Cinquerat erected. Memories like layers of river silt guided him through forgotten hallways, hidden doors, unused offices covered in dust save for the paths he'd left through them.

Vargo. *Eret* Vargo, now. He'd harbored some dislike for the man, but little interest; the Cinquerat was the Rook's reason for existing. Them, and the corrupted nobility of Nadežra, and the shattered remnants of the Tyrant's power, which poisoned everything it touched.

Up to the attic archives, full of moths and contracts and papers nobody cared about anymore. The window there scraped in its tracks, paint as thick as the Rook's memories making it stick until two quick jerks forced it open. Then he was out, free of the oppressive weight of the building, the proximity to the rot at its core.

With Renata...Arenza...Ren's revelation, he had in his grasp a new thread that might let him drag that rot into the light and eradicate it for good.

The established houses were old, and the source of their power deeply buried. But Vargo's rise had been unnaturally swift. If he owed that to a similar source, it would not be so well-concealed.

Vargo had conspired with Acrenix to gain an ennoblement charter.

Vargo was the enemy.

Levering himself up to the roof of the Charterhouse, the Rook leaned against the curve of the dome, hidden from everyone but the startled pigeons, and tore off his hood.

Grey Serrado fell to his knees, gulping in the cool spring air and biting down on the urge to scream. The murder he'd been blamed for, the murder he blamed *himself* for—Vargo was the one behind it. Vargo planted the black powder that lured Kolya to investigate. Vargo set it off. While Kolya was inside.

We don't kill. It was a cornerstone of the entity that was the Rook. Something Grey had agreed to when he accepted the mantle.

His fingers curled, crumpling the hood under his hand. Slowly, he rose to his feet and slipped it back on. Black silk and leather flowed over his limbs, sheathing him in the armor of his cause.

"We don't kill," the Rook whispered to the oblivious city. "But we can destroy."

The Charterhouse, Old Island: Fellun 7

Ren hid the shawl behind her skirts while the clerks passed. As kind as it was of the Rook to return it, she didn't know what to do with it now: a piece of Ren's life, when she was supposed to be Renata.

In the end she stepped into a narrow, darkened corridor and hiked up her skirts to tie it beneath them, around her hips. The knot made a slight lump, but hopefully no one would notice.

When she was about to step out again, she heard the footfalls of someone approaching. Ren held her breath and remained still. She didn't want anyone asking why she was hiding in the shadows.

Especially not Derossi Vargo.

Her old Finger instincts flared to life as he passed. Ren slipped her shoes off, the marble floor cold against her stockinged feet. She waited until Vargo had turned a corner; then she followed him, silent as a cat.

His path took him to the Caerulet offices, where clerks were already bringing Indestor's furniture and files out. Ghiscolo Acrenix directed them, keeping out of the way as four burly men heaved Mettore's monumental desk through the double doors and down the corridor.

"I see you survived my mother," Ghiscolo said, waving Vargo back down the hallway toward Ren. She retreated swiftly, finding an unlocked office—the Rook's doing?—and slid inside. Leaving the door cracked risked them noticing, so she eased it shut and pressed her ear against the wood.

"Your mother is a formidable woman," Vargo murmured. There was still an edge of deference there, but it was a deference between equals. "I don't believe I let anything slip. I assumed you'd want to inform her yourself."

Ghiscolo snorted. "That's a remarkable bit of discretion, given your recent behavior."

Vargo's cane tapped against the marble floor. "Bringing Mettore down was never going to be discreet. But it was effective—Your Mercy."

Caerulet's title. Ennoblement charters didn't fall from the sky, nor were they given out of simple gratitude...but in exchange for opening up a seat on the Cinquerat? That was all too plausible.

"An effectiveness that I trust has been duly appreciated, *Eret* Vargo."

"Oh, yes." Vargo's voice smooth. "But there's no reason for it to end here. I've been enjoying our partnership. Haven't you?"

Ren flinched. There was no hint of flirtation in his tone...but those were the exact words he'd used with her.

Ghiscolo merely said, "I suppose it depends. Will your association with the Traementis be a problem? Their lovely cousin in particular. You went to some lengths to help her after the Night of Bells, even at risk to yourself."

"The risk was minor, and the gain significant. She's useful as well as attractive, and my investment in the Traementis is paying off even better than I hoped. But if you're worried that it will interfere with anything, you needn't be. I don't get attached to my tools."

Safely hidden behind the door, Ren bit down on her lip. She knew that tone—the cold, careless response of a man who no longer needed to hide behind a mask.

But now she saw his face. And she would never make the mistake of trusting him again.

"Very well," Ghiscolo said. "If I don't bring you into the Illius Praeteri, someone else will anyway; you've made yourself interesting enough to ensure *that*. Now if you'll pardon me, I need to see about getting the Vigil in order. Mettore was far too patient with the rampant nepotism and incompetence. Good day, Eret Vargo."

The steady beat was Ghiscolo walking away. Ren waited, ear pressed to the door, for Vargo to move...but either he was as silent as the Rook, or he was still standing outside.

Like a spider at the center of his web. And Ren could feel its strands around her, snaring her tight.

"Will you be all right?" Vargo's voice broke the silence, causing her to start. Ghiscolo was gone; had someone else approached, without her hearing?

"I've survived worse," a man replied in the crisp, aristocratic tones of Nadežra's Liganti nobility. Ren thought she had met everyone of importance in the city, but she didn't recognize the voice at all. "And it was a necessary step."

"Yes." More tapping, Vargo's cane on the marble. "It's going to get harder from here."

"You mean, you're going to have to be even more ruthless."

Vargo laughed darkly. "Isn't that what I said?"

Sweat broke out on Ren's forehead. Being caught right now—he might kill her. But she had to know whom he was talking to.

With the same steady, feather-light hand she'd once used to pick locks and lift purses, she turned the handle of the door and eased it open the tiniest crack.

Vargo's hands were planted on the sill of a window, his back to her as he looked out over Eastbridge to the shining rooftops of the Pearls.

"Concentrate on winning their trust now. Worry about the rest later."

The words came in that same aristocratic voice—and from the empty air at Vargo's side. He was unmistakably alone...but not.

He talks to himself sometimes, Sedge had said.

Not to himself. To someone else. A spirit, maybe—but not the Rook. Maybe whatever she'd seen him bound to, when she glimpsed the connections in the amphitheatre that night. Maybe whatever kept him alive, when he took wounds that ought to kill him.

Vargo's head turned slightly. Ren froze, fearing he was about to notice her, not daring to swing the door shut because then he *would*. But he stopped, showing only a sliver of his profile—enough to see the cynical smile on his face.

"Trust is the thread that binds us...and the rope that hangs us."

"Hanging is what spiders do best. Let's go home, my boy."

Vargo chuckled. Ren remained utterly still, not even breathing, as he sauntered off down the corridor, cane swinging and clacking against the stone. She waited even after he was gone.

Then one hand slid into her pocket, feeling the roughness there. She'd brought it with her today as a kind of talisman, a prayer for good luck. And maybe, in a twisted fashion, it had worked.

She drew out the black rose mask and spread it in her hands. "Fine, then," she whispered softly. "This is your game? Let's play."

~~Ninat~~

The story continues in...

Book two of the
Rook & Rose trilogy

Acknowledgments

Any story this large and complex is not the work of a single mind—or even two, working together.

First and foremost, we owe a huge debt of gratitude to the players of The Path to Power: Kyle Niedzwiecki, Emily Dare, Wendy Shaffer, and Adrienne Lipoma, who put up with us when a couple of character relationships in the game ran off to become their own little side soap opera, and then encouraged us when that side story grew into a novel trilogy. Particular thanks to Adrienne, who served as our alpha reader, and was very tolerant of us pestering her to live-blog her reactions to each chapter as we finished it. She's also responsible for the lyrics to the creepy Fingers song. We'd also like to acknowledge the players from the original, short-lived incarnation of The Path to Power: Rachel Reader, Beth Dupke, Jesse Decker, and Alec Austin. The last of those is the ancestor of Sedge, by way of a character originally named Thorn, and we thank him for letting us borrow that for this story; Ren wouldn't be the same without her brother.

After that, we have to thank all the people who assisted us in making this book a reality . . . . aining), Carlie St. Clarion West Write-a-Thon, Heather Kalafut, ... ara, Conna Condon, and the Carroll, Blythe Woolston, Georgina Kamsika, and Bob Angell. Additional thanks to Emiko, whose enthusiasm for the idea of crafting Ren's dreamweaver mask was very encouraging to a pair of writers who want to make all the things from this novel.

Special thanks to every person who tried to help us name the pattern cards—a process that literally took almost two years to complete, with us wailing for assistance periodically. They are too many to list individually (and since we wailed for assistance in about eight different places, including ephemeral locations like Twitter, we don't even know who all of them were), but we appreciated all the suggestions, including the ones we didn't end up using; every bit of it helped prod our brains toward phrases we could be happy with. We also thank everyone on Codex who assisted with random research questions along the way, from perfume, to the mathematics of card game probability, to short-term cons, to Slavic-style music for Marie to listen to while writing.

And finally, we have to thank our agents, Eddie Schneider and Paul Stevens, and our editor Priyanka Krishnan for bringing this book into the world.

Dramatis Personae

Ren—aka Renata Viraudax, aka Arenza Lenskaya, a con artist

NOBILITY

House Acrenix

Eret Ghiscolo Acrenix—head of House Acrenix
Carinci Acrenix—his stepmother
Sibiliat Acrenix—his daughter and heir
Fadrin Acrenix—a cousin

House Coscanum

Eret Naldebris Coscanum—head of House Coscanum
Marvisal Coscanum—his grandniece
Bondiro Coscanum—his grandnephew
Faella Coscanum—his sister

House Destaelio

Era Cibrial Destaelio—head of House Destaelio, Prasinet in the Cinquerat

House Extaenius cousin

House Indestor

Eret Mettore Indestor—head of House Indestor, Caerulet in the Cinquerat
Mezzan Indestor—his son and heir
Breccone Simendis Indestris—married in from House Simendis

House Novrus

Era Sostira Novrus—head of House Novrus, Argentet in the Cinquerat
Benvanna Ecchino Novri—her latest wife
Iascat Novrus—her adopted heir

House Quientis

Eret Scaperto Quientis—head of House Quientis, Fulvet in the Cinquerat

House Simendis

Eret Utrinzi Simendis—head of House Simendis, Iridet in the Cinquerat

House Traementis

Era Donaia Traementis—head of House Traementis
Leato Traementis—her son and heir
Giuna Traementis—her daughter
Gianco Traementis—her late husband, former head of House Traementis
Crelitto Traementis—Gianco's father, former Fulvet and head of House Traementis
Letilia Traementis—Gianco's sister, formerly called Lecilla
Colbrin—a servant

DELTA GENTRY

Tanaquis Fienola—an astrologer and inscriptor working for Iridet
Agniet Cercel—a commander in the Vigil
Lu...
Rimbon ...—a lieutenant in the Vigil
Orrucio Amañ... ...cess

VRASZENIANS

Grey Serrado—a captain in the Vig...
Kolya (Jakoslav) Serrado—Grey's brother
Koszar Yureski Andrejek—leader of the Stadne...
Idusza Nadjulskaya Polojny—a radical in the Stadnem...

Dalisva Mladoskaya Korzetsu—granddaughter of the Kiraly clan leader
Mevieny Plemaskaya Straveši—a szorsa
Ivrina Lenskaya—Ren's mother, an outcast

THE STREET

Derossi Vargo—crime lord and enterprising businessman
Nikory—one of Vargo's lieutenants
Pavlin Ranieri—a constable in the Vigil
Arkady Bones—boss of the biggest knot in the Shambles
Dvaran—keeper of the Gawping Carp
Oksana Ryvček—a duelist
Tess—Ren's sister
Sedge—Ren's brother
Ondrakja—former leader of the Fingers

FOREIGNERS

Kaius Sifigno—aka Kaius Rex, aka the Tyrant, conqueror of Nadežra
Varuni—sent to safeguard an investment in Vargo

The Rook—an outlaw

Glossary

advocate: An individual licensed to conduct business within the Charterhouse, usually on behalf of a noble house.

alta/altan: The titles used for nobility who are not the heads of houses.

Argentet: One of the five seats in the Cinquerat, addressed as "Your Elegance." Argentet oversees the cultural affairs of the city, including theatres, festivals, and censorship of written materials.

aža: A drug made from powdered seeds. Although it is commonly spoken of as a hallucinogen, Vraszenians believe that aža allows them to see into Ažerais's Dream.

Ažerais's Dream: This place, called "the realm of mind" by inscriptors, is a many-layered reflection of the waking world, both as it was in the past, and as it may be metaphorically expressed in the present.

Ča: A title used when addressing a Vraszenian.

Caerulet: One of the five seats in the Cinquerat, addressed as "Your Mercy." Caerulet oversees the military affairs of the city, including prisons, fortifications, and the Vigil.

Ceremony of the Accords: A ritual commemorating the signing of the peace agreement that ended the war between the city-states of Vraszan and Nadežra, leaving the latter in the control of its Liga~ nobility. The ceremony involves the ziemetse and the me~ Cinquerat, and takes place each year during the ruling body of

Charterhouse: The seat of Nadežra ~~net, Caerulet, and Iridet.~ seat has its own sphere offices are located ~ed into seven clans: the Anoškin, ~raly, the Meszaros, the Stretsko, and

Cinquerat ~~ N ~

the Varadi. The Ižranyi have been extinct for centuries, following a supernatural calamity. Each clan consists of multiple kretse.

era/eret: The titles used for the heads of noble houses.

Faces and Masks: In Vraszenian religion, the divine duality common to many faiths is seen as being contained within single deities, each of which has a benevolent aspect (the Face) and a malevolent one (the Mask).

Festival of Veiled Waters: A yearly festival occurring during the springtime in Nadežra, when fog covers the city for approximately a week.

Fulvet: One of the five seats in the Cinquerat, addressed as "Your Grace." Fulvet oversees the civic affairs of the city, including land ownership, public works, and the judiciary.

The Great Dream: A sacred event for Vraszenians, during which the Wellspring of Ažerais manifests in the waking world. It occurs once every seven years, during the Festival of Veiled Waters.

Illi: The numen associated with both 0 and 10 in numinatria. It represents beginnings, endings, eternity, the soul, and the inscriptor's self.

imbuing: A form of craft-based magic which has the effect of making objects function more effectively: an imbued blade cuts better and doesn't dull or rust, while an imbued cloak may be warmer, more waterproof, or more concealing. It is also possible, though more difficult, to imbue a performance.

inscriptor: A practitioner of numinatria.

Iridet: One of the five seats in the Cinquerat, addressed as "Your Worship." Iridet oversees the religious affairs of the city, including temples, numinatria, and the pilgrimage of the Great Dream.

Kaius Sifigno/Kaius Rex: See *The Tyrant*.

kanina: The "ancestor dance" of the Vraszenians, used on special occasions such as births, marriages, and deaths. When performed well enough, it has the power to call up the spirits of the dancers' ancestors from Ažerais's Dream.

kn... A term derived from Vraszenian custom for a street gang in Nadežra. ... mark their allegiance with a knotwork charm, though they **koszenie** paternal... d to wear or display it openly.

only for spe... **kretse**: (sing. kut...hawl that records an individual's maternal and third part of a tra... ...ern of its embroidery. It is usually worn vidual belongs to. ... when performing the kanina.

... subdivision of a clan. The ... the kureč an indi-

lihoše: (sing. lihosz) The Vraszenian term for a person born female, but taking on a male role so as to be able to lead his people. Lihoše patronymics end in the plural and gender-neutral "-ske." Their counterparts are the rimaše, born male but taking on a female role so as to become szorsas.

meda/mede: The titles used for members of delta houses.

The Night of Bells: A yearly festival commemorating the death of the Tyrant. It includes the Ceremony of the Accords.

Ninat: The numen associated with 9 in numinatria. It represents death, release, completion, apotheosis, and the boundary between the mundane and the infinite.

Noctat: The numen associated with 8 in numinatria. It represents sensation, sexuality, procreation, honesty, salvation, and repentance.

numina: (sing. numen) The numina are a series of numbers, 0–10, that are used in numinatria to channel magical power. They consist of Illi (which is both 0 and 10), Uniat, Tuat, Tricat, Quarat, Quinat, Sessat, Sebat, Noctat, and Ninat. Each numen has its own particular resonance with concepts such as family or death, as well as associated gods, colors, metals, geometric figures, and so forth.

numinatria: A form of magic based on sacred geometry. A work of numinatria is called a numinat (pl. numinata). Numinatria works by channeling power from the ultimate godhead, the Lumen, which manifests in the numina. In order to function, a numinat must have a focus, through which it draws on the power of the Lumen; most foci feature the name of a god, written in the ancient Enthaxn script.

pattern: In Vraszenian culture, "pattern" is a term for fate and the interconnectedness of things. It is seen as a gift from the ancestral goddess Ažerais, and can be understood through the interpretation of a pattern deck.

pattern deck: A deck currently consisting of

prismatium: An iridescent metal created through the use of numinatria, and associated with Sebat.

Quarat: The numen associated with 4 in numinatria. It represents nature, nourishment, growth, wealth, and luck.

Quinat: The numen associated with 5 in numinatria. It represents power, excellence, leadership, healing, and renewal.

Sebat: The numen associated with 7 in numinatria. It represents craftsmanship, purity, seclusion, transformation, and perfection in imperfection.

Sessat: The numen associated with 6 in numinatria. It represents order, stasis, institutions, simplicity, and friendship.

soul: In Vraszenian cosmology, the soul has three parts: the dlakani or "personal" soul, the szekani or "knotted" soul, and the čekani or "bodily" soul. After death, the dlakani goes to paradise or hell, the szekani lives on in Ažerais's Dream, and the čekani reincarnates. In Liganti cosmology, the soul ascends through the numina to the Lumen, then descends once more to reincarnate.

sun/earth: Contrasting terms used for many purposes in Liganti culture. The sun hours run from 6 a.m. to 6 p.m.; the earth hours run from 6 p.m. to 6 a.m. Sun-handed is right-handed, and earth-handed is left-handed. Sunwise and earthwise mean clockwise and counterclockwise, or when referring to people, a man born female or a woman born male.

szorsa: A reader of a pattern deck.

Tricat: The numen associated with 3 in numinatria. It represents stability, family, community, completion, rigidity, and reconciliation.

Tuat: The numen associated with 2 in numinatria. It represents the other, duality, communication, connection, opposition, and the inscriptor's edge.

Tyrant: Kaius Sifigno, also called Kaius Rex. He was a Liganti com-
furt... Repute... conquered all of Vraszan, but according to legend his
by venereal... The nume... ed by him succumbing to his various desires.
Uniat: The nume... self-awarened... ... was supposedly brought down
body, self-awarened... ... primary for... ... Night of Bells.
tor's chalk. ... primary for... their e... ...sents the
The Vigil: The primary for...
named "hawks" after their e...

army, the Vigil polices the city itself, under the leadership of a high commander who answers to Caerulet. Their headquarters is the Aerie.

Vraszan: The name of the region and loose confederation of city-states of which Nadežra was formerly a part.

Wellspring of Ažerais: The holy site around which the city of Nadežra was founded. The wellspring exists within Ažerais's Dream, and manifests in the waking world only during the Great Dream. Drinking its waters grants a true understanding of pattern.

ziemetse: (sing. ziemič) The leaders of the Vraszenian clans, also referred to as "clan elders." Each has a title taken from the name of their clan: the Anoškinič, Dvornič, Kiralič, Meszarič, Stretskojič, Varadič, and (formerly) Ižranjič.

extras

orbitbooks.net

about the author

M. A. Carrick is the joint pen name of Marie Brennan (author of the *Memoirs of Lady Trent*) and Alyc Helms (author of the *Adventures of Mr. Mystic*). The two met in 2000 on an archaeological dig in Wales and Ireland—including a stint in the town of Carrickmacross—and have built their friendship through two decades of anthropology, writing, and gaming. They live in the San Francisco Bay Area.

Find out more about M. A. Carrick and other Orbit authors by registering for the free monthly newsletter at www.orbitbooks.net.

if you enjoyed

THE MASK OF MIRRORS

look out for

THE OBSIDIAN TOWER

Rooks and Ruins: Book One

by

Melissa Caruso

'*Guard the tower, ward the stone. Find your answers writ in bone. Keep your trust through wits or war – nothing must unseal the door.*'

Deep within Gloamingard Castle lies a black tower. Sealed by magic, it guards a dangerous secret that has been contained for thousands of years.

As Warden, Ryxander knows the warning passed down through generations: nothing must unreal the Door. But one impetuous decision will leave her with blood on her hands – and unleash a threat that could doom the world to fall to darkness.

ONE

There are two kinds of magic.

There is the kind that lifts you up and fills you with wonder, saving you when all is lost or opening doors to new worlds of possibility. And there is the kind that wrecks you, that shatters you, bitter in your mouth and jagged in your hand, breaking everything you touch.

Mine was the second kind.

My father's magic could revive blighted fields, turning them lush and green again, and coax apples from barren boughs in the dead of winter. Grass withered beneath my footsteps. My cousins kept the flocks in their villages healthy and strong, and turned the wolves away to hunt elsewhere; I couldn't enter the stables of my own castle without bringing mortal danger to the horses.

I should have been like the others. Ours was a line of royal vivomancers; life magic flowed in our veins, ancient as the rain that washed down from the hills and nurtured the green valleys of Morgrain. My grandmother was the immortal Witch Lord of Morgrain, the Lady of Owls herself, whose magic coursed so deep through her domain that she could feel the step of every rabbit and the fall of every leaf. And I was Exalted Ryxander, a royal atheling, inheritor of an echo of my grandmother's profound connection to the land and her magical power. Except that I was also Ryx, the family embarrassment, with magic so twisted it was unusably dangerous.

The rest of my family had their place in the cycle, weavers of a great pattern. I'd been born to snarl things up—or more like it, to break the loom and set the tapestry on fire, given my luck.

So I'd made my own place.

At the moment, that place was on the castle roof. One gloved hand clamped onto the delicate bone-carved railing of a nearby balcony for balance, to keep my boots from skidding on the sharply angled shale; the other held the wind-whipped tendrils of dark hair that had escaped my braid back from my face.

"This is a disaster," I muttered.

"I don't see any reason it needs to be, Exalted Warden." Odan, the castle steward—a compact and muscular old man with an extravagant mustache—stood with unruffled dignity on the balcony beside me. I'd clambered over its railing to make room for him, since I couldn't safely share a space that small. "We still have time to prepare guest quarters and make room in the stables."

"That's not the problem. No so-called diplomat arrives a full day early without warning unless they're up to trouble." I glared down at the puffs of dust rising from the northern trade road. Distance obscured the details, but I made out at least thirty riders accompanying the Alevaran envoy's carriage. "And that's too large an escort. They said they were bringing a dozen."

Odan's bristly gray brows descended the broad dome of his forehead. "It's true that I wouldn't expect an ambassador to take so much trouble to be rude."

"They wouldn't. Not if they were planning to negotiate in good faith." And that was what made this a far more serious issue than the mere inconvenience of an early guest. "The Shrike Lord of Alevar is playing games."

Odan blew a breath through his mustache. "Reckless of him, given the fleet of imperial warships sitting off his coast."

"Rather." I hunkered down close to the slate to get under the chill edge that had come into the wind in the past few days, heralding the end of summer. "I worked hard to set up these talks between Alevar and the Serene Empire. What in the Nine Hells is he trying to accomplish?"

The line of riders drew closer along the gray strip of road that wound between bright green farms and swaths of dark forest, approaching the grassy sun-mottled hill that lifted Gloamingard Castle toward a banner-blue sky. The sun winked off the silver-tipped antlers of six proud stags drawing the carriage, a clear announcement that the coach's occupant could bend wildlife to their will—displaying magic in the same way a dignitary of the Serene Empire of Raverra to the south might display wealth, as a sign of status and power.

Another gleam caught my eye, however: the metallic flash of sabers and muskets.

"Pox," I swore. "Those are all soldiers."

Odan scowled down at them. "I'm no diplomat like you, Warden, but it does seem odd to bring an armed platoon to sign a peace treaty."

I almost retorted that I wasn't a diplomat, either. But it was as good a word as any for the role I'd carved out for myself.

Diplomacy wasn't part of a Warden's job. Wardens were mages; it was their duty to use their magic to nurture and sustain life in the area they protected. But my broken magic couldn't nurture. It only destroyed. When my grandmother followed family tradition and named me the Warden of Gloamingard Castle—her own seat of power—on my sixteenth birthday, it had seemed like a cruel joke.

I'd found other ways. If I couldn't increase the bounty of the crops or the health of the flocks with life magic, I could use my Raverran mother's connections to the Serene Empire to enrich our domain with favorable trade agreements. If I couldn't protect Morgrain by rousing the land against bandits or invaders, I could cultivate good relations with Raverra, securing my domain a powerful ally. I'd spent the past five years building that relationship, despite muttering from traditionalists in the family about being too friendly with a nation we'd warred with countless times in centuries past.

I'd done such a good job, in fact, that the Serene Empire had agreed to accept our mediation of an incident with Alevar that threatened to escalate into war.

"I can't let them sabotage these negotiations before they've even started." It wasn't simply a matter of pride; Morgrain lay directly between Alevar and the Serene Empire. If the Shrike Lord wanted to attack the Empire, he'd have to go through us.

The disapproving gaze Odan dropped downhill at the Alevarans could have frozen a lake. "How should we greet them, Warden?"

My gloved fingers dug against the unyielding slate beneath me. "Form an honor guard from some of our nastiest-looking battle chimeras to welcome them. If they're going to make a show of force, we have to answer it." That was Vaskandran politics, all display and spectacle—a stark contrast to the subtle, hidden machinations of Raverrans.

Odan nodded. "Very good, Warden. Anything else?"

The Raverran envoy would arrive tomorrow with a double handful of clerks and advisers, prepared to sit down at a table and speak in a genteel fashion about peace, to find my castle already overrun with a bristling military presence of Alevaran soldiers. That would create a terrible first impression—especially since Alevar and Morgrain were both domains of the great nation of Vaskandar, the Empire's historical enemy. I bit my lip a moment, thinking.

"Quarter no more than a dozen of their escort in the castle," I said at last. "Put the rest in outbuildings or in the town. If the envoy raises a fuss, tell them it's because they arrived so early and increased their party size without warning."

A smile twitched the corners of Odan's mustache. "I like it. And what will you do, Exalted Warden?"

I rose, dusting roof grit from my fine embroidered vestcoat, and tugged my thin leather gloves into place. "I'll prepare to meet this envoy. I want to see if they're deliberately making trouble, or if they're just bad at their job."

Gloamingard was really several castles caught in the act of devouring each other. *Build the castle high and strong*, the Gloaming Lore said, and each successive ruler had taken that as license to impose their own architectural fancies upon the place. The Black Tower reared up stark and ominous at the center, more ancient than the country of Vaskandar itself; an old stone keep surrounded it, buried in fantastical additions woven of living trees and vines. The stark curving ribs of the Bone Palace clawed at the sky on one side, and the perpetual scent of woodsmoke bathed the sharp-peaked roofs of the Great Lodge on the other; my grandmother's predecessor had attempted to build a comfortable wood-paneled manor house smack in the front and center. Each new Witch Lord had run roughshod over the building plans of those who came before them, and the whole place was a glorious mess of hidden doors and dead-end staircases and windows opening onto blank walls.

This made the castle a confusing maze for visitors, but for me, it was perfect. I could navigate through the odd, leftover spaces and closed-off areas, keeping away from the main halls with their deadly risk of bumping into a sprinting page or distracted servant. I haunted my own castle like a ghost.

As I headed toward the Birch Gate to meet the Alevaran envoy, I opened a door in the back of a storage cabinet beneath a little-used stairway, hurried through a dim and dusty space between walls, and came out in a forgotten gallery under a latticework of artistically woven tree roots and stained glass. At the far end, a string of grinning animal faces adorned an arch of twisted wood; an unrolling scroll carved beneath them warned me to *Give No Cunning Voices Heed*. It was a bit of the Gloaming Lore, the old family wisdom passed down through the centuries in verse. Generations of mages had scribed pieces of it into every odd corner of Gloamingard.

I climbed through a window into the dusty old stone keep, which was half fallen to ruin. My grandmother had sealed the main door with thick thorny vines when she became the Witch Lord a hundred and forty years ago; sunbeams fell through holes in the roof onto damp, mossy walls. It still made for a good alternate route across the castle. I hurried down a dim, dust-choked hallway, taking advantage of the lack of people to move a little faster than I normally dared.

Yet I couldn't help slowing almost to a stop when I came to the Door.

It loomed all the way to the ceiling of its deep-set alcove, a flat shining rectangle of polished obsidian. Carved deep into its surface in smooth, precise lines was a circular seal, complex with runes and geometric patterns.

The air around it hung thick with power. The pressure of it made my pulse sound in my ears, a surging dull roar. A thrill of dread trickled down my spine, never mind that I'd passed it countless times.

It was the monster of my childhood stories, the haunt of my

nightmares, the ominous crux of all the Gloaming Lore. Carved through the castle again and again, above windows and under crests, set into floors and wound about pillars, the same words appeared over and over. It was the chorus of the rhyme we learned in the cradle, recited at our adulthood ceremonies, and whispered on our deathbeds: *Nothing must unseal the Door.*

No one knew what lay in the Black Tower, but this was its sole entrance. And every time I walked past it, despite the unsettling aura of power that hung about it like a long bass note too low to hear, despite the warnings drilled into me since birth and scribed all over Gloamingard, curiosity prickled awake in my mind.

I wanted to open it—anyone would. But I wasn't stupid. I kept going, a shiver skimming across my shoulders.

I climbed through another window and came out in the Hall of Chimes, a long corridor hung with swaying strands of white-bleached bones that clattered hollowly in a breeze channeled through cleverly placed windows. The Mantis Lord—my grandmother's grandmother's grandfather—had built the Bone Palace, and he'd apparently had rather morbid taste.

This wasn't some forgotten space entombed by newer construction; I might encounter other people here. I dropped my pace to a brisk walk and kept to the right. On the opposite side of the hall, a slim tendril of leafy vine ran along the floor, dotted irregularly with tiny pale purple flowers. It was a reminder to everyone besides me who lived or worked in the castle to stay to that side, the safe side—life to life. I strained my atheling's sense to its limit, aware of every spider nestled in a dusty corner, ready to slow down the second I detected anyone approaching. Bones clacked overhead as I strode through the hall; I wanted to get to the Birch Gate in time to make certain everything was in place to both welcome and warn the envoy.

I rounded a corner too fast and found myself staring into a pair of widening brown eyes. A dark-haired young woman hurried toward me with a tray of meat buns, nearly in arm's reach, on the wrong side of the corridor.

My side. Death's side.

Too close to stop before I ran into her.

Enter the monthly
Orbit sweepstakes at
www.orbitloot.com

With a different prize every month,
from advance copies of books by
your favourite authors to exclusive
merchandise packs,
**we think you'll find something
you love.**

f facebook.com/OrbitBooksUK

@orbitbooks_uk

@OrbitBooks

www.orbitbooks.net